TANAMERA

'They were golden days, when Singapore was as rich as its climate was steamy, its future as assured as it was busy. And those days were made even better when, as was inevitable, I fell in love with the Chinese beauty of Julie Soong and, against all unwritten canons of Singapore life, we became lovers.'

Teeming with the sights and sounds of Singapore in the 1930s, the opulence of life in the great colonial houses, and the terrors of commando existence in the Japanese-held jungles, TANAMERA pulsates with authentic detail and untamed excitement. Noel Barber's novel is a love story you will never forget.

TANAMERA

TANAMERA

'From the first sentence TANAMERA is a wonderful tale. It has excitement, true detail and the very smell of the East. Noel Barber knows his territory and his people. It's a big story and a *great* read'

Leslie Thomas

'Noel Barber has always done everything in a big way, with style, panache and a dash of adventure. But he has never written a story of such dimensions, such a sense of history and imagination as this first novel ... it is an intensely gripping and convincing story'

Manchester Evening News

'Convincing, exotic, lively, for sheer story-telling it puts other so-called "epics" in the shade'

Standard

Noel Barber first became well known as foreign correspondent of the *Daily Mail*. He was the first Britain to reach the South Pole after Scott, was stabbed five times covering the wars in Morocco, and was shot in the head during the Hungarian uprising. A serious car crash ended his career as a correspondent but enabled him to become a full-time writer. He was the author of several works of non-fiction and in his seventies became a bestselling novelist on the publication of *Tanamera*, his first novel. Noel Barber died in 1988.

NOEL BARBER

TANAMERA

A Novel of Singapore

CORONET BOOKS
Hodder and Stoughton

For Titina, Ben and Simmy

*With love and gratitude for all
the fun you have given me*

Copyright © 1981 Noel Barber

First published in Great Britain 1981 by
Hodder and Stoughton Ltd.
Reprinted five times 1982
Reprinted four times 1983
Reprinted four times 1984
Reprinted once 1985
Reprinted twice 1986
Reprinted once 1987
Reprinted once 1988
Reprinted once 1989
Twenty-first impression 1990

British Library C.I.P.

Barber, Noel
  Tanamera. – (Coronet books)
  I. Title
  823'.914[F]   PR6052.A623

  ISBN 0-340-28262-2

Printed and bound in Great Britain for
Hodder and Stoughton Paperbacks, a
division of Hodder and Stoughton Ltd.,
Mill Road, Dunton Green, Sevenoaks,
Kent TN13 2YA (Editorial Office: 47
Bedford Square, London WC1B 3DP) by
Clays Ltd., St Ives plc.

CONTENTS

SINGAPORE

1 Swimming Club
2 Dexter's Godown
3 New World Dance Hall
4 The Soong Mansion
5 Tanamara
6 Goodwood Park Hotel
7 Tanglin Club
8 The Cadet House
9 Cathay Building
10 YMCA Tennis Club
11 Raffles Hotel
12 Fort Canning
13 Central Fire Station
14 St Andrews Cathedral
15 Adelphi Hotel
16 Singapore Cricket Club
17 Dexter & Co Offices
18 General Hospital
19 Alexandra Hospital
20 Railway Station
21 Raffles Place
22 Robinsons

GLOSSARY

Amah   A woman servant, a nurse.

Attap   An 'attap hut' means one whose roof has been thatched with palm fronds.

Beluka   Secondary jungle.

Canna   Has bright red, yellow or orange flowers and ornamental leaves. A very hardy plant popular in Singapore and Malayan gardens.

Casuarina   A large tree which originated in Australia and South East Asia. Has striking lacy foliage and jointed branches not unlike gigantic horse tails.

Chungkol   A kind of hoe used in gardening, especially when working the ground on rubber estates.

Dhoby   Laundry.

Godown   Originally from the Portuguese, means a warehouse, usually in SE Asia or India.

Gula Malacca   (or Gula Melaka) A dessert of sago, palm sugar and coconut milk, a favourite sweet to cool the mouth after a curry tiffin.

Ikan   Malay word for fish. Thus, *ikan meru* and *ikan kuru* are kinds of fish caught in local waters.

Jagger   A guard who usually sleeps on a trestle bed outside and across a doorway. Frequently the jaggers are Sikhs.

Kumquat   Small orange-like fruit with a sweet rind, can be preserved whole. Like stem ginger.

Lallang   A rough, quickly growing kind of grass that grows on every lawn in Singapore.

Mahmi   Noodles with a spicy sauce, of mixed Malayan and Chinese origin.

Nipa   A palm tree with large feathery leaves – and a sap which can be used to make a highly intoxicating drink.

Padang A large open space, usually a sports ground.

Pandanus A kind of palm tree.

Pomelo A fruit not unlike a grapefruit.

Pulau Ayam (or pulaw ayam) Chicken cooked in Malay style, in which coconut is often used to give it a highly distinctive and delicious flavour.

Songkok A velvet cap often worn by car drivers. It looks rather like an American officer's field cap.

Stengah A very weak whisky with soda water filled to the brim – weak because of the need to quench a thirst in a tropical country.

Sumatra Named after a Dutch island, used in Singapore to denote a sudden brisk wind which sends leaves scurrying and often heralds a short shower.

Syce Originally a Hindu word for groom, now used in Singapore and Malaya for 'chauffeur'.

Thamby A messenger 'boy.' – of any age.

Tiffin Lunch – as in 'a curry tiffin'.

Tuan A Malay form of polite address. 'Sir'.

Tuan bezar The head man of a big commercial or official group, the Malay equivalent of Hong Kong's 'taipan'.

BEFORE

When Grandpa Jack, as he later came to be known to everyone in Singapore, decided to build a great house that he vowed would last for a hundred years, a reporter from the *Straits Times* went to interview him, and in the faded yellow clipping from 1902 it is still possible to decipher what he wrote:

'One of our most illustrious citizens, Mr Jack Dexter of Dexter and Company, has instructed an architect to design a magnificent house with twenty bedrooms, three sitting rooms, a billiards room and a ballroom facing east to west to permit for currents of air, with a platform for Mr Daley's orchestra, and a dance floor large enough to allow two hundred couples to waltz without jostling each other in the heat which is so prevalent in our city.

'Mr Dexter,' he added, 'has stipulated that the walls of the ballroom must be strong enough to last for a hundred years, no mean feat in Singapore where the ants devour everything they can.' And because in those days newspaper reporters spoke their minds, the *Straits Times* added tartly, 'Mr Dexter has refused to divulge the name he intends to bestow on what many might regard as a monstrosity, but some of his business rivals have already christened it "Dexter's Folly".'

The site for the house lay three miles from Raffles Place, on a slight knoll along a dusty road leading to the village of Bukit Timah, three miles further on. The grounds of ten acres were the remains of an earlier plantation in which Grandpa Jack had cleared secondary jungle to grow gambier and pepper. Pepper was always in demand, and tanneries all over the world used gambier. At first the venture was profitable, for the tough gambier shrubs supported the pepper vines, but both crops exhausted the soil. Even worse, the Malays had to fell jungle trees to produce the fires needed to dry the gambier leaves, so the jungle surrounding the plantation began to recede with remarkable speed, and coolies had to go further and further to collect timber for fires. Grandpa Jack closed the plantation down, keeping ten acres on which to build his dream house, and selling off the rest, including the adjacent ten acres, to a successful Chinese called Soong whose ambitions also included building a large mansion as a sign of his social status and success.

By then Grandpa Jack was forty-nine years old, a tall, phenomenally strong, thick-set man with a bushy beard, an 'old man' in a tropical island whose white population was regularly decimated by storm, piracy, beri-beri, malaria, plague, and most of all by the dreaded cholera.

For eight months four hundred Chinese coolies, the men bare-backed, the women in black trousers and jackets and flat straw hats, sweated in temperatures that never dropped below the eighties, laboriously heaving away the red earth, spade by spade, bucket by bucket, as they excavated for the foundations. Only when the rainstorms that tore across the green, lush island made it impossible for one man to see his neighbour did they cease work. Day after day Grandpa Jack visited the site, a figure regarded with awe and fear. Sometimes he arrived in his five-hp, hand-tillered Benz, which he had imported before the turn of the century, and which was known to everyone as the coffee machine, though he only rode in the high-backed newfangled car in fine weather, for if the roads were slippery it had to be pushed uphill. Then he relied on his carriage, pulled by two piebald horses, driven by his Chinese syce★ – the Malay word for groom – called Ah Wok. Most of the syces were Malays, but Ah Wok was an exception, for he was also Grandpa Jack's personal servant and chauffeur.

At a time when every Briton in the stifling heat cocooned himself in heavy broadcloth with a tight-fitting cravat im-
★ There is a glossary on pp. 9–10.

prisoning the air round his neck, Grandpa Jack invariably arrived on the site of 'Dexter's Folly' dressed in white calico pyjamas and a pith helmet, carrying his ash plant in one hand and a fly whisk in the other. Ah Wok followed wherever Grandpa Jack strode or jumped across the red earth, carrying bottles of beer in a felt-wrapped bucket filled with ice. If the beer was warm Grandpa Jack would, without a word, box Ah Wok's ears, then walk silently on, with Ah Wok dancing by his side, twiddling the bottles in the melting ice to make the next beer cooler.

Soon the long straight poles of bamboo scaffolding began to shoot up like plants in a new garden. The framework started to be filled in. Walls appeared, clothing the trellis like a bamboo skeleton. Large verandahs to the east and west – the east verandah to be used for breakfast, the west verandah for the evening drinks – were moulded into recognisable shape.

When it came to building the great ballroom Grandpa Jack, it is said, produced an old tattered picture of Fontainebleau and decided that he wanted a twin staircase sweeping up to the landing from the back of the room. And then he told the architect how to build the walls – the walls that must last for a hundred years – out of a special plaster, which had been used once only before in Singapore, when convict labour built St Andrew's Cathedral in 1860. Grandpa Jack's father had played a part in the construction of the cathedral and he had carefully guarded the secret of its walls, which were guaranteed to withstand all the ravages a tropical climate might inflict on men and material.

He personally supervised the mixing of the plaster, in which lime was used as a foundation; but instead of it being mixed with sand it was stirred with the whites of thousands of eggs, and hundreds of sacks of coarse sugar, the coolies beating it with poles like giant pestles into a paste.

Others filled huge barrels with gallons of water, while yet another group ravaged the island for thousands of coconut husks. The husks were soaked in the water for several days. After that the specially treated water was mixed with the paste to form the plaster. And when the scaffolding was stripped from the white walls, a hundred coolies spent two months rubbing the rough, iron-hard surface with rock crystal until every inch shone and sparkled, and was as smooth to the touch as marble.

Grandpa Jack was a product of his time, like his father before him – like his grandfather too, a Yorkshireman from Hull who had landed in Singapore on the *Indiana* under Captain James Pearl, and carrying that most prestigious of passengers, Thomas Stamford Raffles. The first Dexter had stayed behind to found Dexter and Company after Raffles planted the Union Jack on the rat-infested swampy island in 1819. At first the venture fared badly, but towards the end of the century all had changed, for by then Singapore was on the crest of a great wave of prosperity.

From the moment in 1869 when the Suez Canal opened – two years after Singapore became a Crown Colony – it had become the most profitable emporium in the British Empire, with the steamship opening up boundless possibilities of amassing wealth. Ships queued impatiently in the roads waiting to dock along the three miles of crowded wharves at Tanjong Pagar (of which Grandpa Jack owned a slice of the original shares). There was money for all who had the marrow of adventure in their bones, together with the health to withstand the onslaughts of a tropical climate of hot sun and lashing rain, the lack of sanitation in a country ravaged by malaria, fever, smallpox, a city where the pockmarked streets along which the white men bumped and clattered in their carriages to work were often flanked with gutters in which the stench of nightsoil (as it was politely called) was enough to make you vomit as it flowed to the Singapore River and thence to the sea.

There was every reason in the world why nobody should settle in Singapore. Bugi pirates foraging from the nearby coast of Johore slit your throat for a dollar; tigers still killed an average of one native a day; voracious ants ate their way through a man's library in a week; mildew turned a man's clothes green in a couple of days. Prickly heat tormented some men to the point of madness, the itch accentuated by thick, unhealthy clothes. And yet Singapore was a magnet, drawing to it everyone with red blood in his veins, urged to the island city not only by the quest for riches but also by the challenge of a break from the past, and a glimpse into the unknown realms of the future in a city that had once been called Singapura, the Sanskrit for Lion City.

Until Grandpa Jack decided to build the great house on Bukit Timah Road he lived with his wife in Tanglin, on the outskirts of the city. His wife was a lady about whom little has been recorded, no doubt because in the second half of the nineteenth century Singapore was essentially a male-dominated world; though she did bear him one son in 1880. The contemporary records, which Grandpa Jack carefully preserved in camphor chests, show that he and his wife had a butler who cost eight dollars a month, two underservants, a cook, a tailor, a washerwoman, a syce, gardeners and handymen, all for similarly low wages, and even a Hindu barber who for two dollars a month came regularly to trim his bushy beard.

Grandpa Jack's day started sharp at five a.m. with the boom of the sixty-eight pounder at Fort Canning, the military headquarters, after which he rode or walked 'in the delicious coolness of the morning'. Before breakfast he showered in a bathroom consisting of a brick-tiled floor containing a large 'Shanghai jar' holding fifty gallons of water which had been filled or topped up by the wash boy. He stood on a small wooden grating close to the jar and with a brass pannikin dashed the cold water over his body. Then he breakfasted on fish, curry and rice, sometimes eggs, all washed down with a tumbler or two of claret, before the carriage arrived and he went off to the office behind the jumble of docks, shophouses and godowns.

Most offices were grouped around Raffles Place, the meeting point for all the merchants who bounced along the rutted roads that Raffles had laid out. Once at the office Grandpa Jack, like his father before him, superintended the loading and unloading of anything from tin ore to cases of whisky, sometimes bought and sold on commission, though often the commission was paid by the tin mine of which Dexter and Company was a part owner, and the freight charges were paid to a ship of which Dexter and Company owned a share. As general agents, Dexters dealt in everything from thunderboxes (as the portable toilets were called) to new masts for ships damaged by storm, carriages for the residents, even new-fangled machinery for the growing number of tin mines in up-country Malaya.

Dexters never dabbled in perishable produce; this side of the agency business was left to their friendly rivals, the Soong agency house, whose fortunes had been founded when Soong was awarded a naval contract to supply two British bases in the Christmas Island group.

In his way the head of the Soong agency was as remarkable a character as Grandpa Jack – doubtless one had to be remarkable to survive and prosper in those buccaneering days. Soong was a Baba – his father had come from China and had married a Malay princess; the Babas were much respected by the British who felt they were the perfect product of a union between the Chinese (who were too clever for them) and Malays (who didn't like working).

Like Grandpa Jack, Soong had a passion for the flamboyant. He had built a house on the coast with grounds that boasted hanging gardens and a menagerie. It included an orangutan which enjoyed plentiful supplies of Soong's finest brandy. Because Soong's business consisted mainly of ships' chandling – he supplied vessels with meat, vegetables and bread – and because he was a navy contractor, Soong kept open house for all seafaring officers, naval or merchant marine. He insisted only on one stipulation – formal evening wear, which presented no problem for naval officers, but was not always included in the wardrobes of men in the sailing ships. For them, Soong kept a lavish wardrobe of spare evening clothes.

Soong had opened Singapore's first bakery. He was the first to import ice from America into sweating Singapore, after the Americans early in the nineteenth century started producing blocks of ice from the frozen lakes in winter, and sending them to the Far East insulated in sawdust. Within a few years the Americans were producing ice mechanically in tins holding up to three hundred pounds of water, and Soong promptly built the island's first ice house.

The Dexter fortunes had been amassed in different ways, not all welcome to close scrutiny, though the solid foundations of success had been laid by Grandpa Jack's father who in 1846 put up some of the capital for the new dry dock at Tanjong Pagar which produced regular dividends until it was all but wrecked by a storm in 1865. The shares plummeted – at which moment Dexter bought every share he could lay his hands on. This showed no immediate profit, but old Dexter knew that one day Singapore would become the greatest port in the east, and that those shares would then be worth a fortune.

Grandpa Jack not only had the devil's luck – he made his own, often through his physical courage, as in 1879 when Chinese rioters wrecked a new post office in Singapore which had been opened specially to handle mail between immigrant Chinese and their families in mainland China. Until the post office opened thousands of Singapore Chinese had remitted regular sums home to their families via professional letter-handlers, who more often than not vanished with the cash. Professional letter-writers also flourished, and when a junk was about to sail for China the letter-writers, with their pots of ink, brushes and pads of paper, filled every street near Raffles Place.

They knew their easy pickings would vanish overnight when the post office opened, so they brandished posters denouncing the 'English barbarians' for 'destroying the living of thousands of people'. One even urged, 'If any honest and virtuous man will cut off the heads of post office workers, he will be rewarded.'

This was strong stuff. The police tore down the posters. A mob attacked the post office and tried to wreck it. The police were powerless to stop the rioting from spreading and – as happened regularly – called for volunteers.

Grandpa Jack was, in the words of one of his contemporaries, 'a natural-born volunteer'. He had led tiger hunts, he had fought Bugi pirates, he would volunteer for anything.

'I'm with you,' he cried, and grabbed a wicked-looking parang – a local machete – at police headquarters. With fewer than a dozen volunteers he roared into action.

'Charge! Let the buggers have it!' he shouted, waving the sharp-edged parang. For a moment the crowd faced him defiantly. Then as they wavered Grandpa Jack spotted the ringleader. His shoulder muscles knotted, he swung the parang above his head as the rest of the crowd scattered, and swept it downwards like a meat cleaver, splitting the man's skull, spilling his brains into the dusty street.

'Any more?' he cried. 'Come on, you fucking sons of whores!' Most ran, but one was not quick enough. Again Grandpa Jack swung the parang and the man's head opened like a split coconut.

'Don't mistake me for a man of violence,' he told a friend later. 'No one loves the Chinese and Malays more than I do, but you can only have one boss in a place like this.' His courage was applauded in the *Straits Times*, which had been founded by John Cameron, a ship's captain.

'A special vote of thanks by the community is due to Mr Jack Dexter,' Cameron wrote, 'for quelling the post office riots almost single-handed, despite the failure of the police.' After describing what had happened the article ended, 'Mr Dexter's courage in the cause of the community is deserving of the highest rewards.'

This feat of derring-do led directly to a highly profitable venture in up-country Malaya where the tin mines, operated mostly by Chinese, were booming despite transport problems, for the ore still had to be brought to the coast by bullock cart. It was after the post office riots that Grandpa Jack became involved in the expansion that was taking place.

He was sitting in his office in Robinson Road when a clerk announced that a Mr Masters wanted to see him. In those days Grandpa Jack probably did not have a great deal of work to do and Mr Masters was shown in. He apologised for intruding without a preliminary letter of introduction. He wore white ducks, a blue reefer jacket, a collar and tie of course – that was obligatory when paying a call in Singapore – half hidden by grey mutton-chop whiskers. He carried a trilby with a broad band, and after Grandpa Jack had asked him to sit down, and a thamby had brought some fresh lime juice, Masters came to the point.

'I greatly admired your courage in going for those two Malays sir,' he said in the rather stilted English of the day, 'and as I am shortly leaving for Malaya, and have no knowledge of the local dialects, I need a colleague as a go-between and bodyguard should the need arise.'

Masters explained that he was an engineering consultant. Government officials in Malaya had asked him to assess the possibility of constructing a short railway to carry the tin ore to the coast. 'It would run,' explained Masters, 'from Kuala Lumpur to Klang.'

'Kuala Lumpur?' asked Grandpa Jack.

'The new town,' explained Masters. 'It's little more than a group of thatched huts, but it's the tin centre, and since you speak the lingo, sir, it seemed a good idea to ask you to come along.'

'What's in it for me?' asked Grandpa Jack bluntly.

'Opportunity, sir,' said Masters benignly. 'I'll pay all your transport and all your keep – and you will find more pickings than you ever dreamed of.'

It was typical of Grandpa Jack that he never hesitated. He had a flair for unorthodox ways of making money quickly – as well as the priceless gift of getting on with people of any race and colour, and earning their respect as well as their friendship. And he realised one thing immediately: one day the railway would *have* to come, and if he joined this man Masters he would probably know the proposed route before anyone else.

Long before they set off Grandpa Jack borrowed every cent he could, determined to buy every acre of available land.

A month later the two men, with four bearers, arrived in the shanty town of Kuala Lumpur, footsore, dishevelled and weary, at the very moment in Malaya's history when KL – as Kuala Lumpur soon became known – was an adolescent on the verge of exploding into a grown-up boom city. It was the sweating, humid Oriental counterpart of a Western frontier town, and no exaggeration was too fanciful.

The main street was a muddy stretch leading from the landing stage on the Klang River to the last shanty house before the jungle. An open market, gambling joints, opium dens, brothels, pigsties, slaughter houses jostled cheek by jowl with engineering shops hammering away as they repaired tin-mine machinery. With work for everyone – everyone, that is, who wanted work – Chinese flocked into the city from other parts of Malaya and from China too. When one man was asked why he had come he replied simply, 'In China I knew I would starve to death. Here I might starve – but I might make a fortune.'

Side by side with this influx lived the Malays. To the smallholders whose country this was the expanding population, the new machinery, the clanging noise of the workshops, seemed to make no difference. For they, in their own way, were as rich if not richer than the Chinese interlopers who had come to make money: the Malay families in their kampongs could live on what a bountiful nature provided, from the trees, from the land, from the river, with almost no effort.

Yet by the time Grandpa Jack and Masters arrived the Malays were goggling with amazement at their rulers, the Malay sultans, who suddenly started receiving royalties on all tin mined and spent it on dazzling silken robes, beautiful women and gambling. Many rulers made their first trips to the world outside their own palaces and small villages, for as tin money swept into KL with the speed of a bush fire, the sultans and rajahs became eager participants in a dazzling new life. There were firework displays imported from China, communal feasts, jungle expeditions in style, with champagne carried on the backs of elephants. Grandpa Jack met one Malay ruler who had amassed fifty-thousand Mexican silver dollars and employed a bevy of slaves to keep them polished so he could show them off to visitors. Another ruler regularly rode into KL on an elephant, tossing silver dollars to the crowd who, forewarned of his imminent arrival, lined the muddy streets to scramble for the loot. The sultan thought he was helping the needy to buy food, but once he had returned to his palace the lucky ones made straight for the gambling dens or whorehouses.

Women – some of them very beautiful – became tokens, to be distributed as a rich man's sign of generosity or good will. When Grandpa Jack visited one sultan to acquire land in his area the old man sold Grandpa Jack a parcel at ten cents an acre, and was so tickled when Grandpa Jack paid cash that he insisted on throwing in two girls to seal the bargain. It would have been bad manners to refuse, so Grandpa Jack 'borrowed' the girls until the time came when he returned to Singapore.

'One was fifteen, the other eighteen, and I screwed both of them every night I was in Malaya,' he boasted happily for years afterwards. 'Fancy making a fortune and having a couple of girls thrown in. Best three months of my life!'

It was during this time that Grandpa Jack made the acquaintance of one man whose friendship would be invaluable in later years – Frank Swettenham, an ambitious young officer with a square jaw who had joined the Malayan Civil Service with the firm intention of one day becoming governor of the Straits Settlements. While Grandpa Jack was helping Masters, Swettenham was studying the first attempt to grow a dozen unfamiliar saplings from seeds which had been taken – some say stolen – from trees in Brazil, where they grew wild near the mouth of the Amazon. The seeds had been germinated in Kew Gardens, and some had then been sent to Malaya.

By the time Grandpa Jack saw them, the saplings were fourteen foot high. They were the first rubber trees to grow in Malaya – and nobody was interested in them because it took five or six years before the sticky latex, the basis of rubber, could be extracted from the bark. Coffee was 'the thing' in those days, but Grandpa Jack was a born gambler, fired by Swettenham's excitement. Though he was buying land only to sell he did, on impulse, extract a promise from Swettenham that when more seeds had been germinated he

23

would be given a supply, providing he undertook to start a plantation. Swettenham, who eventually planted a grove of rubber trees at the back of his Residency, admired the young man who wasn't afraid to take a gamble at a time when the Chinese refused to change from coffee planting.

'Come and see me when you've got the land,' said Swettenham.

Acquiring land at a few cents an acre was easy, for Masters quickly discovered that because of swamp and rain forest there was only one possible route for a railway to the coast. Once he knew that, Grandpa Jack bought and bought and bought – quietly, but taking care to acquire legal title deeds from sultans who regarded the jungle land as valueless, and who hailed the mad Englishman – a man *must* be mad to buy jungle! – as an easy sucker. Masters was also buying land, but his purse was limited.

Before he left for Singapore Grandpa Jack returned to KL and reminded Swettenham of his promise to provide free rubber saplings.

'Have you bought the ground?' Swettenham asked him.

Grandpa Jack didn't think it necessary to tell the young government official that he owned land almost all the way to the coast. But he had earmarked one large plot of more than two thousand acres which he had decided to keep. It had one noticeable feature which had fascinated Grandpa Jack. By the dusty track leading to the secondary jungle a huge tree was slowly being strangled by that most sinister of parasites, the ara creeper; the trunk of the creeper – in parts thicker than a man's thigh – had over the years wrapped itself round the parent tree, winding its way upwards forty feet above ground, until it seemed to be suffocating the original tree. By now the roots of the ara hung down from forty feet, some as thin as a bead curtain that Grandpa Jack could brush aside, others as thick as the bars of a jail. These had finally taken root in the earth round the tree, so that by now they imprisoned it. The land was ten miles from KL. Swettenham and Grandpa Jack rode out together on horseback to see the land. Grandpa Jack produced the title deeds, and Swettenham gave him a firm commitment to provide saplings when the time came.

'I'm going to call it the Ara Estate,' said Grandpa Jack. 'Just to get my own back on that sinister creeper.' And that is how Grandpa Jack eventually became owner of one of the first rubber plantations in Malaya.

He had to wait, of course. Long before that the news leaked out that a railway was to be built, and the land which had often cost Grandpa Jack less than ten cents an acre soared in price, especially among speculators anxious to open mines or start coffee plantations. Long before the railway opened in 1886 Grandpa Jack had sold almost all of the land he had bought with borrowed money, sometimes for a hundred dollars an acre. With some of the profit he bought two ships.

Grandpa Jack might have had doubts about growing rubber; but as he told Frank Swettenham, 'Growing coffee is a mug's game. In a few years there won't be a coffee bean in Malaya.' It needed no financial genius to make this prophecy – only a little Yorkshire canniness. For ironically Brazil, from where the original rubber seeds had been taken, would not only be responsible for making Malaya rubber rich, but also killed off Malaya's coffee production. Brazil had over-produced, and when one hundred and seven thousand Negro slaves were freed in 1886, Brazil imported nine hundred thousand Italian peasants to work in the coffee plantations. Production soared from three million sacks a year in 1870 to twelve million before the turn of the century. No one could drink all that coffee. The bottom fell out of the market – and Malayan coffee planters were unable to sell a bean.

It must have been around this time that Grandpa Jack started growing rubber; not only because coffee was not worth planting, not only because Swettenham had promised him free saplings; but also because he had never forgotten a paragraph in the *Straits Times* in 1888 about a Scottish vet who had developed a pneumatic tyre for his bicycle. The man's name was John Boyd Dunlop, and Grandpa Jack forecast at the time, 'Wouldn't be surprised if they don't start putting them on motor cars. One day there won't be enough rubber in all the world to satisfy the demand.'

He planted the Ara Estate with two hundred free saplings to the acre, and here again luck was on his side, for no one had discovered an economical way to extract the juicy white latex from the bark after the trees were six years old. But two years before Grandpa Jack's trees were expected to yield – in 1895 – a British botanist called Henry Ridley developed 'tapping'; he designed a special tool which removed a thin sloping shaving of the outer bark in such a way that the bottom formed a tiny groove down which the latex oozed from the inner bark into a cup which the tappers emptied into a bucket.

Suddenly rubber was 'the thing'. And it was now that Grandpa Jack's 'railway money' and a flourishing agency came in useful. For it was not enough to grow rubber. It needed a capital investment in machinery – tanks for coagulating the latex, smokehouses for drying it out – to make the operation profitable. It needed an agency to sell it, it needed someone to ship it, someone else to insure the cargo. Dexter and Company could handle all these problems – and act as agents and 'secretaries' for small-plantation owners who could handle the plantation yet were too busy to handle the selling and shipping. Dexter and Company acted for ten of the early plantations, in five cases taking a share of the capital in exchange for lending the planters money to buy modern equipment, for which Grandpa Jack had several sole agencies. Everything in the day-to-day running of the estates was left to the local planter – usually British, with Chinese or Indians running the small office and local accounts, and Tamils – coming in increasing numbers to Malaya – doing the actual tapping.

Many rivals were jealous of Grandpa Jack's share of the rubber market, but in fact a small plantation that linked up with Dexters, even if it cost them a percentage of profits, had a distinct advantage over one that preferred to remain aloof. Since Dexters had its own ships and a thriving import and export business and offered credit for machinery, together with insurance, the company could – and did – give the plantation in which it had a financial interest a competitive advantage over the estates that preferred to go it alone. And, after all, Dexters only needed one staff of clerks in Robinson Road to handle every aspect of every shipment from all the different plantations; only one rent was paid for the offices. It was much better for a planter, up-country and cut off from Singapore, to let one agency house handle everything rather than try to save a few cents in the dollar by working with a dozen different firms.

Grandpa Jack dabbled in everything. He even helped to finance a restaurant because he was unable to get a good lunch near his office. In the early days he had driven home each lunchtime, but by the eighties the traffic had become impossible – a phalanx of carriages competing with bullock carts, wheelbarrows and streams of pedestrians who never looked where they were going; it made driving impossible. So when Grandpa Jack failed to persuade the newly-formed Cricket Club to serve lunches he talked to a business friend who not only owned a handsome house facing the waterfront near the cathedral but boasted that his was the finest cook in all Singapore.

Grandpa Jack helped him to launch Singapore's first Tiffin Room, where he had his own table every lunchtime; and the cook *was* so good that within a few weeks it was impossible to get a table unless you telephoned (on the ancient hand-cranked telephone which had been installed in 1878) three days in advance.

Those who preferred could eat in the garden, fanned by sea breezes, against a background of chattering mynah birds with their bright yellow beaks, the tables shaded by scarlet flame trees and slender, pole-straight traveller's palms, which offered a cooling glimpse of the sea through their flat, fan-shaped fronds. The new partners had to give the place a name. But what?

'There's only one choice,' said Grandpa Jack. 'We'll call it Raffles.'

★

Though the Dexter fortunes were flourishing it was not until the turn of the century that Grandpa Jack brought off two major financial coups. He had always had the knack of being in the right place at the right time; and even more exciting, of realising instinctively the moment in which to take instant action. He had done this when buying land in Malaya – and selling it at the right time at the right price. He had also gained a life-long friend in the corridors of power by his enthusiasm for the rubber trees which young Frank Swettenham had shown him in Malaya – when every planter laughed at the idea of growing rubber.

In 1900 Grandpa Jack heard a rumour that consolidated his fortunes for ever. At this time all the tin ore mined up-country was melted into bars at the tin smelting works in Singapore, which were owned by the Straits Trading Company. More than half the world's output of tin was smelted in Singapore and sold by auction on the open market. Grandpa Jack had years previously used some of his railway money to buy into the Straits Trading Company and, as he told the story (repeatedly as he grew older) he heard quite by chance of an astonishing American plot that almost succeeded in closing down the smelting works for ever.

At a formal dinner at Raffles, which Grandpa Jack still considered as his own territory (even though Raffles had long since been bought by three brothers who had turned it into a magnificent hotel) he was seated next to a pleasant young American visiting Singapore who introduced himself as Johnson Holden.

Grandpa Jack never had much time for youngsters other than those in his own family, but Johnson, a cheerful American extrovert, babbled along while Grandpa Jack did his best to stifle his yawns – with copious draughts of champagne – until Johnson mentioned the magic word tin.

Singapore was a city of rumours – both business and private lives thrived and prospered or were torn apart by its silken whispers – and when anyone mentioned a commodity or name that was of interest ears always pricked up.

'Tin?' Grandpa Jack said. 'Are you in tin Mr – may I call you Johnson?'

'Feel free, sir. No, I'm not in tin – but my pa is.'

A man less suspicious than Grandpa Jack – or less percipient – would have murmured a polite, inconsequential remark to the effect that he too was interested in tin. Instead, Grandpa Jack plied Johnson with another drink and asked, 'That's very interesting, m'boy. Is he over here with you?'

'No, sir,' answered Johnson. 'I'm on vacation. My pa will be coming over here when he settles the tin deal.'

Before the end of the evening Johnson Holden was a little worse for wear, but was still insisting that he must see a little of Singapore's night life on his first visit to this exciting new city. Grandpa Jack, who could drink glass for glass with any man in Singapore, still refrained from asking the leading question.

'What sort of night life?' he asked.

'Girls!' said Johnson expansively.

Grandpa Jack, nearing the end of his cigar, had an instinctive feeling that he was on to something. 'Chinese, Indian or Malay?' he asked.

'All three!' cried Johnson. 'And, sir, if I may say so, you're a man after my own heart.'

The couple ended up at one of the most notorious, and one of the best run, bordellos in Macpherson Road, a long, dusty red light area that stretched out beyond the end of Serangoon Road. When Johnson insisted to Grandpa Jack, 'Be my guest, sir,' Grandpa Jack accepted and, it seemed, the two had a thoroughly good time. This was followed by another bottle of champagne, which in turn was followed by the simple but vital information that Johnson's father was a member of a syndicate of rich Americans who were planning to buy tin ore direct from the Malayan mines – and if necessary they would pay higher than the Straits Trading Company in order to corner the market – and then ship it to America to be smelted on the east coast.

Grandpa Jack knew exactly what that would mean. The Americans would pay over the odds to begin with and then, after they had gained a measure of control over Malaya's supplies, they could easily slap a duty on smelted tin entering America as 'a manufactured article'. Without American custom for smelted tin the Singapore works could be closed within months.

Poor Johnson never realised how the casual information would help the Dexter fortunes. Grandpa Jack knew that Frank Swettenham – now Sir Frank and the Governor in Singapore – would be furious if he knew – *when* he knew. He also knew that Swettenham liked him, and remembered how once Swettenham had told him, 'You're a rascal, but I'd trust you in a tight corner.'

Armed with this knowledge, Grandpa Jack did two things, taking care to get his priorities right, for one of his maxims in business was, 'The secret of success lies in doing things in the right order.'

The next morning he secretly bought all the shares he could in the Straits Trading Company. Only then did he ask for an appointment to see Swettenham. Later that day he drove up to Government House in his five-hp Benz, which had cost him all of sixteen pounds.

Sir Frank was by now a fine-looking man, upstanding, with a thick moustache and a good head of hair, who could give anyone he did not like a piercing look from his monocled eye. On the verandah overlooking the park he asked Grandpa Jack what he could do for him. Grandpa Jack told him bluntly what he had learned. The governor was aghast, and Grandpa Jack was ready with advice.

'If you cable Whitehall the Americans will have moved in before you get a decision,' he warned. 'But there's one thing you can do locally to protect our smelting works – put a duty on the export of tin ore; and make it a prohibitive duty. But let smelted tin alone.'

Swettenham did just that. He quickly passed a local enactment without (courageously) informing Whitehall until it had come into force. A prohibitive duty was slapped on the export of tin ore to anywhere outside the Straits or other agreed British possessions.

When local businessmen realised why this apparently

innocuous piece of legislation had been passed the shares of the Straits Trading Company rocketed.

Soon afterwards Grandpa Jack made another killing. His father had been one of the original investors who had put up the money to build the Tanjong Pagar docks. From the very first year the shares had yielded a steady twelve per cent, so that by the turn of the century the original stock, which had cost virtually nothing, was marked up in value at anything from three hundred to four hundred dollars a share. Once again Grandpa Jack latched on to a rumour, this time that the government planned to take over the docks. Although he already held a large parcel of inherited shares, Grandpa Jack bought an extra three thousand at prices up to three hundred and fifty Singapore dollars (about thirty-three pounds) a share. Two days later the government made a monstrous offer of two hundred and fifty dollars a share. All attempts at negotiation failed and for a moment it looked as though Grandpa Jack had lost a small fortune. But finally Whitehall sent out an independent referee, who awarded the dock company eight hundred and eighty dollars a share. Grandpa Jack's profit on the original shares was huge; even on the batch he had just bought before expropriation he netted well over a million dollars' profit. He went straight out and bought two more ships.

By 1903, when he was ready to move from Tanglin to his dream house, Grandpa Jack was a man among men. He was an eccentric. He had, it seems, a prodigious thirst – and he would grow thirstier as the years passed. At times he vanished for days on end, emerging tousled and secretive. He had an equally insatiable appetite for the local ladies, which no doubt contributed to the early death of his long-suffering wife. He was a man born to live life to the full, and so he tolerated no half measures when building the house he was determined would be a visible testimony to the success of Dexter and Company.

The day of the house-warming ball arrived. A drive a quarter of a mile long had been hacked from the jungle and now led from the Bukit Timah Road, the carriages entering through large wrought-iron gates which Grandpa Jack had designed and which had been forged at the local smithy in Bukit Timah village. The rough, coarse lallang – Singapore's own special grass – had been cropped by squatting Malays using short, curved, lethally sharp knives.

In common with all bungalows – every house was called a bungalow in Singapore – the front entrance leading into the ballroom was flanked by a big pillared portico under which guests could alight from their carriages during the heaviest rainstorms.

Even the *Straits Times* forgot all about 'Dexter's Folly' in its description of that splendid evening. 'Singapore has never witnessed a more magnificent social occasion than the christening of Mr Dexter's house,' its correspondent wrote. 'And the gowns of the ladies among the four hundred guests would have done credit in splendour and finery to any of the British or French court balls.'

Grandpa Jack had apparently produced a prodigious repast. It certainly impressed the *Straits Times* reporter. He had continued, 'It bore no resemblance to the light airy meal which one might reasonably have anticipated, bearing in mind the nature of the climate. The supper in the ballroom included soup and fish, roast beef, mutton, turkey and capon, with splendid side dishes of tongue, fowl, cutlets and vegetables; after which curry and rice appeared, garnished with all manner of sambals, native pickles and spices.' The meal was washed down with goblets of champagne, servants attending to the guests' needs. 'The luxuriance of the dessert included pineapples, plantains, ducoos, mangos, rumbutans, pomelos, and mangosteens.'

After the dinner was finished guests were asked to assemble outside for the christening ceremony, while inside the ballroom boys cleared away the tables and prepared the floor for dancing, dusting the newly-laid planks with french chalk.

'Rarely can such a prodigious array of beauty and grace have been assembled in one place,' wrote the *Straits Times*. 'It was warm in the moonlight when Mr Dexter invited the guests to gather in the front of the house where the night was illuminated by flaming torches. As the boys liberally dispensed unlimited quantities of the finest champagne, Mr Dexter asked the military band, which had by gracious permission of the Governor agreed to play, to give him a roll of drums. With a bottle of champagne in one hand, Mr Dexter, dressed not in his pyjama suit but in finely-cut evening clothes, awaited the silence that followed and then bent down and picked up a handful of red earth.'

Letting it fall slowly through his fingers, Grandpa Jack cried, 'The Malay words for red earth are *tana merah* and I deem this to be the perfect name for a house which will, I hope, be home to our family for generations to come.'

It was typical of Grandpa Jack that at this moment he held up his hand for silence, and brought an elderly Chinese into the ring of light from the torches. 'I am particularly pleased,' he said, 'to welcome as a guest my old rival and friend, Mr Soong. Singapore is the greatest place on earth, but if we are to prosper, we must work together, and so I shake hands with you, sir, my neighbour.' Then he beckoned two younger men into the light; one was Soong's son, P.P. Soong; the other was Grandpa Jack's tall, thin son of twenty-three, who would be known later and forever as Papa Jack.

'These are typical of the men who will inherit the goodness of this island,' cried Grandpa Jack. 'And who will always, I trust, remain friends, and never become enemies. For we must never forget that we need each other. Singapore was *their* island, but Britain has made it what it is.' At this the young Chinese and the young Englishman shook hands a little self-consciously and then, to 'oohs' and 'aahs' and squeaks of feminine excitement, Grandpa Jack smashed the bottle of champagne against one of the pillars. The military band struck up 'God Save the King' and the great house of Tanamera was christened, and it was there that I was born on 9 September 1913.

PART ONE

Singapore, 1921–1936

I

There were many times before the winds of war scattered our two families when we were all together; youngsters playing and laughing on the lawns of Tanamera – Natasha my sister, four years older than me, the first-born and named after Mama; Tim, my elder brother; Paul Soong and Julie, his sister; fathers and mothers, and even one grandpa, watching us or drinking their evening stengahs on the west verandah. And later we were all together as teenagers, foxtrotting at Raffles Hotel on Friday nights, or dancing decorously in the huge ballroom when the Dexters entertained in style.

Soon others joined us. There was Miki, the Japanese, who had gained a tennis blue at Cambridge. And Tony Scott, who fell in love with Natasha and who hoped to marry her. Only Natasha was a different kind of girl, hard to tame, especially when she fell in love with Bertrand Bonnard, the mysterious Swiss businessman. There was Vicki who came out from England to Singapore to find a husband; she was young enough to have married me – she wanted that – but in the end married Tony Scott's father.

They were golden days, when Singapore was as rich as its climate was steamy, its future as assured as it was busy. And those days were made even better when, as was inevitable, I fell in love with Julie Soong and, against all the unwritten canons of Singapore life, we became secret lovers.

Even though her body was pale gold and mine was white, even though her father, P.P. Soong, had all the forbidding impassivity of a Chinese millionaire, and even though I would one day be the head of a great trading house in Singapore, with its rigid colour creed, separating white

37

from yellow and brown – dividing them into neat, differently coloured packages of untouchables – nothing on earth could have stopped Julie and me from eventually falling in love.

The lives of the Soongs and the Dexters had always moved together. In business our agencies complemented each other so that we often worked closely for mutual profit. The Soongs were our nearest (though invisible) neighbours, and had been since Grandpa Jack sold P.P. Soong's father the ten acres on which to build a mansion to replace the earlier Soong's crazy folly.

And though there were many occasions when Chinese and British were not permitted to meet under the 'rules' of Singapore – in the clubs, for instance, or at the altar – there was nothing to prevent private friendships, and ours was cemented by one other factor: my mother, Natasha Brown, had been born in America and so had Julie's mother. My father's marriage to an American occasioned no surprise. But for a Chinese – even a millionaire – to marry a white girl was very different. Yet to the astonishment of all Singapore P.P. Soong had gone off on a trip to California returning with a dark-haired vivacious bride called Sonia, a Chinese-American who had no idea of the problems she would face as the white wife of a Chinese. If she was upset at the colour bar in clubs, she didn't show it. She accepted a new and very different life cheerfully, and soon both my mama and Mrs Soong had children; Mrs Soong's son Paul was almost exactly my age, Julie two years younger. We grew up together, playing in each other's gardens, as close as only children can be.

Julie was involved in almost all my early memories of Tanamera, which was home – a sprawling home of thirty rooms filled with gliding, noiseless servants – to three generations of Dexters, all living there together. It was six a.m. on September 9, 1921, when Mama kissed me and whispered, 'Happy birthday Johnnie.' Sitting on the single sheet that covered my bed – all that was needed in Singapore, even in the cool of the morning – she hugged me, her long ash-blonde hair tickling my face, and said,

'Well, young man, how does it feel to be eight?'

Usually I shared a room with Tim, but because of a slight touch of fever I had been sleeping in the Sick Bay, as it had been christened by Grandpa Jack. It was nothing more than another spare bedroom really, but at the slightest sign of a cold, an infection, even a sore from a cut, Mama whisked anyone – from Grandpa Jack to the youngest of the three Dexter children – into 'isolation'.

'You can't take any chances in the tropics,' Mama always insisted; while Grandpa Jack, who terrified me with his horrific tales long before I could understand the details, had once explained in his colourful language, 'It's the maggots, m'boy! In Singapore it's you or the maggots. And there's more maggots than men – they breed faster than dogs on heat.' Grandpa Jack's explanations were so lurid, yet so confusing, that for years I thought maggots were dogs, very hot ones, which would bay and snarl at my heels if I didn't reach the Sick Bay before them.

I loved the little white room, with its rattan blinds against the sun or rain, its lazily turning fan hanging, trembling, from the ceiling, for one reason: normally when Mama woke us in the morning I had to share her with Tim because we slept in the same room. In the Sick Bay I had her to myself for a few minutes, for no children were allowed in on pain of being packed off to bed without supper; so when she woke me I lay back, wallowing in pure happiness, looking at her, most of her hidden in mysterious layers of thin, billowing pink or blue materials, looking up at her large, startlingly blue eyes under a mass of fluffy fair hair.

'You've got my blonde hair, but it needs cutting,' she spoke in her soft American accent as she ruffled it. 'And you're going to be tall like your father – tall and strong. I pronounce your cured,' she said laughingly. 'Sit up now and prepare to receive your presents.'

This was the great moment of all our birthdays. For as long as I can remember it had been the custom in Tanamera that we were each given our presents in bed – early because the day's work started early. The idea had originated with Grandpa Jack, a repository of unusual schemes. Because of his original attitude to life – he saw everything through spectacles, so to speak, which no one else could wear – he was known, even when I was a boy, as Grandpa Jack; Papa Jack was also a living legend, and few people ever called either of them Mr Dexter, though the board above the agency house in Robinson Road proclaimed 'John Dexter and Company'.

At sixty-eight, Grandpa Jack no longer went to the office, so he spent much of his time planning entertainment in the house. Every Christmas the Salvation Army gathered with its shining instruments on the big lawn in front of Tanamera and played hymns; though two conditions were always attached to the large donation they received: Grandpa Jack chose every tune (including 'Rimington' at least three times) and insisted on conducting the band with a long, brass-knobbed poker, surely the only one in Singapore, a city which had never seen a fireplace in a home, but which the first Yorkshire-born Dexter had carried all the way from Hull as a weapon of defence.

At times Grandpa Jack would use the poker in the evenings, inviting in a local choir or the police band for curry and unlimited drinks, after which he conducted the music and singing. All our young lives seemed to be filled with a succession of songs, charades, fancy dress balls and home-made plays, for which we all went to endless trouble; or incredibly fanciful ideas planned by Grandpa Jack.

(Of course there was another side to these high jinks of which I knew nothing until later. Every three months or so Grandpa Jack would leave Tanamera and go on a real bender lasting for days, after which he would be brought back to Tanamera and spend the best part of a week in the Sick Bay. My youth was punctuated by spells when 'poor Grandpa Jack' was ill with 'fever', and all enquiries would receive only evasive parental replies. And since we children were never allowed in the Sick Bay unless ill, the secrets of his regular hangovers were well kept for many years.)

'I can hear them coming,' whispered Mama. 'Sit up!' There was a thunderous knock on the Sick Bay door. It was flung open and in stepped Grandpa Jack, leading a procession. To me he was a hulk of a man with a mop of thick white hair above eyebrows that stood out like spikes, and he had a long white beard. His voice could at times become a fearsome bellow, especially if we spoke at table. 'Let your meat stop your mouth!' he would roar.

Today though, he was in an expansive mood. For each Christmas or birthday Grandpa Jack gave us money, and this time he gave me a hundred dollars. I had no idea of its true worth until he ceremoniously pulled open a string round the neck of a chamois bag, dextrously turned the bag upside down and spilled a stream of silver on the white sheet.

'Thanks, Grandpa!' I shrieked. 'I've never seen so much money – *ever*!'

'Don't spend it all on women,' he advised me mysteriously.

It *was* a fortune (or seemed like one until later in the day, when all but five dollars were taken away by Mama, who explained that she was going to put it in 'the bank', whatever that was).

Papa Jack followed. My father was very straight-backed, over six feet tall, and always dressed in white, freshly starched suits. He always, too, wore a pair of rimless glasses balanced precariously on his nose; a source of amazement to all of us when young, for however hot the sun, however many times he took them off to wipe his face when he was sweating, they never *fell* off.

I jumped up and hugged him and kissed him again and again after I had torn the wrapping off my very first BSA airgun. Mama gave me a cricket bat, Tim a stamp album and Natasha an airtight tin of Parkinson's butterscotch (much prized in Singapore because each golden oblong was separately wrapped in foil paper which didn't stick when unwrapped).

Once the floor was littered with paper – and the bed covered with presents – I had to play my part in another Tanamera custom. Each Christmas and each birthday the staff lined up to wish us well – and when *their* children had birthdays we did the same for them. It was Papa Jack's way of demonstrating that though someone had to be the master of the house each man and woman in Tanamera was a member of the family.

We must have kept at least twenty servants in those days, ranging from old Li, the number one boy or major-domo, down through boys, cooks, amahs to look after us, dhobies to wash our clothes, gardeners to tend our flowers, Sikh jaggers to guard our doors, syces to drive the cars.

They stood, a circle of dark faces and white clothes, on the broad landing outside the Sick Bay, giggling or smiling, happy not only because they took a pride in their work, but because my father had an almost passionate love for the people of Singapore and Malaya. Everyone who worked in Tanamera knew this, everyone knew that no questions were asked if they brought relations to stay in the attap huts behind the main house; everyone knew that if their children were ill Dr Sampson, our doctor, would attend them, and Papa Jack would foot the bill.

As the staff moved away Grandpa Jack, with his usual bull-like bellow, announced, 'Right, young Johnnie! Breakfast in twenty minutes! Just time for a shave, a shower, and a –'

'Grandpa!' Mama warned. I never realised in those days how often she stopped Grandpa Jack in full flood, and it was years before I knew the endings to many of his phrases.

Tim's and my favourite way down to breakfast was to race each other in a slide down the curved banisters. After all, we had one banister each on the ornate staircase leading down to the ballroom. We were too young to realise how the lofty splendour of this room had been sullied with 'formal' furniture which Grandpa Jack, who had little taste, had acquired and obstinately refused to discard.

At one end of the dance floor was a narrow ornamental tiled pool, perhaps eight feet long, with a pretty fountain sprinkling water on a few ferns; the skirting boards round the floor were tiled below the white walls; so were the supports for the carved spindles of the railings on the gallery. On either side of the foot of the stairway large latticed double doors led back into other big rooms; which in turn had more latticed doors leading into still more rooms, giving the appearance, in a curious way, of a church One door led to a formal dining room with two tables; the long one could seat twenty, the round one a dozen guests. They were separated by another tiled pond with lilies in it and more tiled skirting boards.

Behind these, Mama's influence prevailed, as though she had stood in front of Grandpa Jack and cried, 'Thus far but no farther!' For the sitting rooms and library looked as though they belonged to someone else's house. Mama had imported new fabrics from America for covers and curtains, materials rarely seen in Singapore where rattan chairs usually furnished a room. Our living room had a tapestry print of leaves in green and white on the chairs and for the curtains. She had brought a beautiful maplewood chest from America which she used as a small, occasional bar. She had repeated the green and white pattern in the paintwork of chairs and cushions on the two verandahs. In her bedroom, I remember, she covered the bed during the day with one of a dozen patchwork quilts she always seemed to be making, her hands busily cutting small octagonal pieces of coloured cloth as she talked to us.

I never realised in those early days how difficult it must have been for a young American bride to live in the same house as an individualist like Grandpa Jack who had always been accustomed to shouting until he got his way. Nor did I realise the stubborn streak of character with which my mother forced him to let her have *her* way and still remain at peace.

All the rooms were lofty, and even though there was no such thing as air-conditioning in those days most rooms had been designed to catch every whisper of breeze in a climate where the temperature hovered around the eighties or nineties every day of every year; but much of our lives was spent on two verandahs, one facing west for evening drinks, the other – larger than many a good-sized room – facing east so that we could race there for breakfast, wolf down papaya with fresh limes, porridge, toast with Cooper's

43

Oxford marmalade (no other brand was ever allowed at Tanamera) with tea for us and coffee for the grown-ups, all offered to us by gentle brown or yellow hands jutting out from stiff, starched white sleeves.

The verandah overlooked lallang grass dotted with flame trees and beyond it the fringe of jungle, all that remained of the original pepper plantation, a cluster of coconut palms, a hedge of sago, with secondary jungle behind – trees and bushes with thick juicy leaves, fern trees, flame trees, bananas with bright green shiny leaves, and in one corner half a dozen tulip trees. It seemed to us impenetrable and exciting, and the illusion of real jungle was heightened by brightly coloured birds, or monkeys which came ambling towards us, knowing they were safe. No one could overlook us, and apart from the Soongs we hardly knew who our neighbours were.

'Race you to the jungle and back before breakfast,' Tim challenged me, and of course I raced, though I knew that, as always, I would be beaten. Tim was ten years to my eight, he was taller, his legs were longer. I never stood a chance against such advantages, but if I refused he jeered, 'Scary pie! Bad sport!'

In a young, unformulated way I knew there was more to every challenge by Tim than his physical advantage. He would never challenge me at anything unless he *knew* he could win. He could always win at running or swimming, but when I challenged him to games at which I stood a chance of winning – marbles or snap – he always refused to play, jeering 'kids' stuff'.

As we lay panting on the grass near the flame tree by the jungle fringe, I had a sudden feeling, odd at my age, that Tim didn't really like me – but the guilty thought was flushed away; such a thing was impossible. He *had* to like me – he was my brother.

Lying there, waiting for the inevitable challenge to race back, which I knew I would lose, but which I didn't dare to refuse, he *looked* friendly. We didn't resemble each other in the way most brothers do; he was skinnier than I was, not as tall as everyone always said I would one day be; and his hair was dark, which was very different from the blond Dexters.

'Thanks for the stamp album,' I said. 'It must have cost an awful lot.' In fact I was wondering who had bought it for him to give to me.

'That's all right.' He didn't enlighten me.

A girl's voice wafted across the still morning air. 'Breakfast!' The distant gong sounded, and Natasha came walking out to meet us, at twelve very much the young lady, at least in her opinion. 'Come on, you two,' she said. 'Papa's on his way down.'

That was enough to make us hurry. Papa was always furious if we were not waiting at table when he arrived. As we walked towards the east verandah Tim said loftily, 'I won again. I won.'

'You should give Johnnie a start,' said Natasha.

I often called Natasha by a nickname, Natflat, a ridiculous mispronunciation from baby days that had stuck as a kind of symbol between us. She looked just like a sepia photo of Mama taken when she was a girl in America; beautiful (to my eyes, anyway) with the same cornflower blue eyes and fair hair. Because she knew that I worshipped her (or whatever feelings young boys have for elder sisters they love) she responded by being protective to me. And because Tim was often jeering, 'All girls are sissies!' she nearly always took my side.

'You're unfair – you always are,' she said to Tim.

Each day we started breakfast as six-thirty sharp, for the office in Robinson Road opened at seven-thirty. The grown-ups sat at one table, we sat at another. We always dressed for breakfast, Papa Jack in his white suit, white shirt and stiff butterfly collar. Only Mama was allowed to eat breakfast in her negligée. Being a lady she always had a warm bath in a zinc tub, the hot water carried upstairs in relays of buckets. At seven-fifteen precisely an unseen roar announced that the syce was bringing round Papa Jack's four-seater Swift.

'Happy birthday, Johnnie,' he got up to go. 'I'll be back for the party this afternoon.

Mr Soong, who always came to our birthday parties, was austere and thin and vaguely grey, and though he must have been about the same age as Papa he seemed much older, perhaps because his face rarely changed expression, whereas Papa Jack, unless he was cross with us, was usually cheerful and ready for a joke. Mr Soong's face was not exactly melancholy, more mask-like. It was difficult to know whether or not he was really pleased to see us, or even what he was thinking. He was always polite, even to us children, in a curious way treating us like equals, like grown-ups, but sometimes we had the feeling that he was only half aware of what he was saying, that the other half of his mind was somewhere else.

It never occurred to us in those days that though we always called him Mr Soong we always called his wife Aunt Sonia. Of course we saw much more of her than we did of Mr Soong, for there were only a few Americans in Singapore, and though Aunt Sonia was half-Chinese she and Mama were close friends. Aunt Sonia always seemed to be popping in for tea, arriving in a large Chevrolet driven by a syce who, in spite of the fact that all other drivers in Singapore invariably wore white, was dressed in a dark blue uniform with brass buttons, and in place of the traditional velvet *songkok* worn by every driver – even the governor's – had a round blue hat with a shiny peak, like an officer's.

Aunt Sonia was always up and down, bursting with energy, smothering us with kisses, always saying, 'Let's go!', always ready to join in our games, anything from hide and seek to musical chairs or postman's knock. She had a mass of dark curly hair, and once I said to Natflat, 'She's very pretty – almost as beautiful as Mama.' In my eyes there could be no higher praise. Yet even as children we were sometimes aware of hidden tensions behind her sense of fun. We could not tell, then, that her brightness was sometimes flawed, or why. Natasha told me that she walked into Mama's sitting room one evening and Aunt Sonia was crying. 'Another time I saw her getting out of the car, and her eyes were all puffy and she looked furious.' But we were brought up never to ask awkward questions and

46

we never did. Besides, that aspect only appeared occasionally.

Usually – as now, on my birthday – she radiated excitement as we waited under the portico. She jumped out before anyone else – almost before the car stopped, before Mr Soong, Paul and Julie. Hugging me before she entered the house she whispered, 'Happy birthday! Let's say hullo to your mother and then we'll open the presents.'

She swept aside, the others following.

'You spoil them,' Mama protested, for as usual Aunt Sonia insisted on bringing one joint present that graced each of our birthdays, always the same, a large flat box of bars of chocolate that we never saw anywhere else, each slim bar wrapped in shiny purple paper on which was written in bold, silver letters the word HERSHEY. This year Aunt Sonia gave me an extra special present – two American tennis racquets, each one labelled Junior Champion.

Dressed in a white skirt and blouse and wearing a floppy hat which miraculously stayed in position, she took me on the tennis court behind Tanamera and gave me my very first lesson in the game which was to become one of the passions of my life.

'Let me show you how to hold it,' she said. She put her soft pink hand on mine and made me grip the racquet the proper way. Then she lobbed a ball to me – which I missed at first, but soon, after I had got the hang of it, managed to return. 'Gee – you're a born tennis player,' she cried. 'You'll end up at Forest Hills, you mark my words!' She shouted to Paul, 'Come on, come and have a game with Johnnie.'

Paul was always beautifully dressed – even as a boy he seemed to enjoy the feeling of wearing good clothes; despite the wet heat his shirt was always neatly tucked into this trouser tops, mine was always untidily hanging out. He didn't look American, or Chinese; halfway between, I suppose, for he had Aunt Sonia's big eyes, but a touch of his father's pale gold skin. I thought him very handsome, but Tim didn't like him, perhaps because he didn't really like the Chinese.

47

Julie had the same big staring eyes as Paul, and despite the long, glossy black hair and the pale gold skin she looked in a curious way like her mama. You could see that she wasn't a white girl, but I thought she was beautiful. She had a slow smile, and her dark eyes seemed to tease you.

'Would you like to borrow my racquet?' I asked her politely, but she shook her head. 'Would you like to swim?' I asked, equally politely, and this time Julie nodded eagerly.

For at Tanamera we had a rarity in those days – a pool. Some years ago Grandpa Jack had dug a hole in the ground and constructed a rough swimming pool, the first one ever at a private house in Singapore. There were no tiles in those days – not to be wasted on pools, anyway – but he had lined the hole with plaster painted pale blue; there was no modern filtration, so the pool was only filled at weekends, after which the water was drained away and the pool refilled the following Saturday. No one was ever allowed to swim until after five p.m. because of the heat of the sun.

But what Grandpa Jack called the 'water rule' was broken on our birthdays. Whatever the day of the week, the pool was cleaned out by gardeners during the night and filled so that, for as long as any one of us could remember, each birthday party ended with a swim.

'Julie wants to go swimming,' I cried to Papa, knowing that if I used her name we might be able to start swimming a little earlier than usual.

But this day there was no swimming. Old Li came in and whispered to Papa Jack, and I could see something was wrong by the way he was wringing his hands. Nothing was *ever* supposed to go wrong at Tanamera.

'I'm sorry children – no water,' said Papa finally. 'It's no one's fault. There's no pressure at the mains. Don't know why.'

'Well,' I cried without thinking, 'let's all go to Tanglin.' Singapore's most prestigious club had a beautiful pool, and members were allowed to take children at certain hours.

The Dexters and the Soongs exchanged swift glances before Mama said gently, 'I think it's a little bit late, darling.'

'It's my birthday!' I shouted, 'And I want to take Julie swimming.'

'We'll take a rain check on the swimming,' said Aunt Sonia a little too brightly. 'Let's play tennis instead.'

Children have an instinct which tells them when something is wrong, when parents are conspiring to hide something. Actually I preferred tennis to swimming, yet because I knew something was being hidden from me I screamed, 'It's my birthday! I want to go to Tanglin!'

'Stop shouting,' Papa Jack shook my shoulders roughly, 'Or I'll give you a good spanking and send you to bed – birthday or no birthday.'

The threat worked instantly – and in a few moments all was forgotten. Mrs Soong was on one side of the tennis net while I was partnered by Paul on the other.

Only when the party was over, only when the Soongs had left around six o'clock and Paul and Julie had each said a polite 'Thank you' to Mama, did I remember the swimming. We were sitting on the west verandah in that brief magical half hour before dark falls swiftly in the tropics. A breeze ruffled the palm trees and the casuarinas on the edge of the jungle, and in the same distance I could see a flurry of leaves dancing on the lallang – the sure herald of a sumatra, the local name for the brief showers that were always welcomed gratefully as they cooled the air.

Grandpa Jack and Papa Jack were drinking their first stengahs, which Li always served unbidden promptly at six, and I was lolling back in a deckchair examining one of my new racquets and drinking my way steadily through my fourth fresh lime juice. Mama was reading some magazines that had arrived on the last ship.

'That's the last one, Johnnie,' she looked up. 'You don't want to spoil your birthday by having tummy-ache.'

Spoil my birthday! Without thinking, yet in a sense with a childish instinct that was trying to force someone to admit what I knew, I asked petulantly, 'Why couldn't I take Julie to the Tanglin?'

Grandpa and Papa Jack were talking, and with a smile Mama almost whispered, 'Not now, darling.'

Tim, who had been sitting with the insufferable superior air of one who is two years older, suddenly jeered, 'Johnnie loves Julie! Johnnie loves Julie!'

'No, I don't.' I felt myself going red. 'No, I don't!' I shouted almost in tears. 'Mama – I only wanted to know –'

'Be quiet, boys,' said Papa Jack, but not before Tim shouted 'She's a Chink! That's why she can't go to the Tanglin Club.'

I had known it, of course; we had been brought up from our earliest days to live with a colour bar. But some devil inside me had made me want to hear someone tell me, and when Tim sneered the truth I suddenly choked with rage and tears and with an instant reflex threw my new tennis racquet at him. With a scream he tried to duck. His chair gave way, and as he fell, he grabbed at the drinks table and pulled it over with him. The racquet hit him a glancing blow on the forehead and the jug of lime juice spilled all over him, while the glasses fell, some smashed, on the ground.

Tim's reactions were instinctive and predictable – they always were. He hurled himself at me, toppling my chair over, and I felt the scratches on my face as he clawed at me with one hand, and with the other started pulling at my hair. I clawed back, but he was bigger. He was kicking me too, screaming with fury as I heard a bull-like roar from Grandpa Jack, 'Stop it you little buggers!' And almost like an echo, Mama's faintly protesting, 'Language, please!'

And then two huge hands – Grandpa Jack's hands – banged our two heads together and he hauled us up by the collars of our sodden shirts, flecked with blood, and roared, 'I heard you! No man in Tanamera ever calls a Chinese a Chink. You want your bloody arse beaten black and blue.' This was to Tim. To me he snarled, 'And you're just as bad. If you want to fight anyone use your fists.'

My scratches were not very deep but when it was time for bed Mama insisted on putting me in the Sick Bay for the night and cleaning up my face.

'You're very naughty, Johnnie,' she sighed as she dabbed my face gently. 'Keep still, darling. You can't go around throwing things at people. You wouldn't like it if Papa threw something at me would you?'

'I'd fight him.'

'I'm sure you would, but that's not the point. Papa would never throw anything at me, so why should you throw anything at Tim?'

'He called Julie a Chink.'

'That was very naughty, but I'm sure he didn't really mean it. There! Now your face is beautiful again.'

'He did mean it, he *did*, Mama.' I could feel tears smarting behind my eyelids. 'He hates Julie because she's my friend, and Tim hasn't got any friends.'

With a sigh – almost as though she sadly agreed – Mama leant over, kissed me, and walked quietly from the room.

After Mama had gone I heard talking on the west verandah below and I scuttled across the corridor to Natasha's room to fetch her. Because so much time in Tanamera was spent in the open air, listening to grown-ups was one of our favourite games – though often we didn't have the faintest idea what they were talking about.

It never entered our heads that we were doing wrong. 'Listening' was just another game – like hunt the slipper or musical chairs. By the door to the Sick Bay a small staircase led down to the west side of the house, often used by the amahs carrying linen to the bedrooms. It had a kind of balcony almost immediately above the west verandah where Grandpa Jack and my father always sat before dinner.

Natasha loved 'the game'. Fingers to lips, looking very pretty in her pink nightie, she led me, tiptoeing carefully to the balcony. Grandpa Jack was talking – and you could usually hear him without any difficulty.

'Well,' he growled, 'Young master Tim makes it clear that he doesn't like the Chinese. You can see it in the way he treats 'em. Like dirt. Bad thing.'

'He's only ten,' said my father.

'Young habits die hard. And I suppose Tim will be *tuan bezar* when you retire. Won't help much if he doesn't get on with the locals. You're going to have trouble with him, you watch out.'

'I know,' said Papa slowly, 'but I'm much more worried about his sense of – I can't explain it, but it's funny how kids often see to the heart of things. Johnnie said something that made me think – he senses that Tim's going to be a loner. And that worries me much more.'

'Johnnie sees a lot,' said Grandpa Jack. 'Did you see him drooling over little Miss Julie? *She's* going to be a handful, that girl. I know her sort – they always get what they want. She'll be hot stuff. And so will little Miss Dexter! She's got a naughty twinkle in her eyes.'

Natasha could hardly suppress a giggle as she nudged me, pointing proudly to her chest. I had no idea what a twinkle was, but I did realise it was naughty.

'We'll marry her off in good time,' Papa laughed.

'Better get Johnnie married off too,' growled Grandpa Jack, 'or if he takes after his mother you'll have trouble between him and Julie Soong in another ten years.'

2

Grandpa Jack was only three years out in his calculations, for it was in the summer of 1934, and I was nearly twenty-one, when I started meeting Julie secretly. There was no loving yet, only a swiftly mounting infatuation. Of course we had met regularly at parties over the years, and I often used to imagine what it would be like to be in love with her, to love her, but they were passing thoughts because we never met alone.

We danced at parties, we met for curry tiffin with Paul and Natflat and Tim and sometimes our parents; and of course there was always a sense of attraction when I was close to her; but then someone would join us and so we never seemed to get to know each other. Perhaps because we had been brought up together as kids, because I knew the shibboleths that dominated Singapore, I never really imagined for long what it would be like to be in bed with her. Or perhaps it was because I was only twenty and already had a girlfriend of sorts who I didn't love but liked.

Then it all changed. It was after a game of tennis. Normally I played at the Cricket Club – Europeans only, of course – but by 1934 there were only half a dozen of us who could give each other a good hard game of singles – the sort of game that made my heart pound like a sledgehammer – and unless I arranged a match days in advance I would sometimes find myself without a game.

In those days I wanted to play singles every day, leaving the office about four and serving the last ball just before half past six when dusk started to shroud the immaculate courts, their positions changed and new lines marked daily so that in Singapore we never suffered from worn patches along the base lines.

Tennis soon came to mean as much to me as work and so, to make sure I could always get a game, I also joined the YMCA, which had some very good Chinese and Malay players and one Japanese, Jiroh Miki, in his late twenties, who had been junior champion of Japan. He and I played at least once a week opposite the main YMCA building near the junction of Stamford and Orchard roads.

I could almost hold my own with Miki – who worked for his father's construction business – until the day when I kept looking at the next court where four players were giggling their way through a mixed doubles. To Miki's surprise he rattled off four games in a row.

It was Julie, of course. I had recognised her immediately – a pair of long pale-gold legs below white shorts, the effect of gold accentuated by the shorts and the setting sun, and the long black hair.

After the game she sat with her friends on the verandah of the rather tatty one-storey wooden pavilion, and I was dying for a cold drink, but the refrigerator had broken down. As it was the YMCA there was no beer on sale

53

anyway, only bottled fruit juices by Fraser and Neave. But Miki sent a messenger to buy a cold Tiger beer from a street stall, and as I sipped it Julie came over, sat down on a rattan chair, smiled and said, 'I didn't know you were a member. You nearly won.'

I hadn't seen Julie for a month or so and, sitting there looking at her, I couldn't help thinking how she would have graced the Cricket Club, how well she compared with the healthy pink European girls who never sweated, only perspired. It wasn't only her generous mouth – always it seemed in those days laughing – her eyes laughed too, gave her a vaguely naughty look as though she would be prepared to search for excitement whatever the cost – if the chance ever came in her strict Chinese household.

Yes, it was the eyes really that betrayed her real self. Her polite and decorous manners were the result of rigid discipline in the home. But neither her Chinese father nor her American mother could do anything about the eyes, which hinted that one day, if she wanted something, if she thought it worth while, she would fight to the end for it.

How silly it was really that this long-legged, well-educated, eighteen-year-old daughter of a millionaire could only play tennis in a run-down club where you couldn't even get a cold drink.

'Can I give you a lift home?' I asked her.

'Paul's coming to fetch me,' she shook her head, adding with the slight smile of someone who, even at eighteen, could see the ironic side of life, 'My tennis is strictly chaperoned. Father only lets me play if Paul can collect me – and not later than half past six.'

'In that case,' I looked at my watch, 'I'll wait and say hullo to Paul. We've got twenty minutes. Do they have to be chaperoned too?'

At the Cricket Club players stayed after they had showered, drinking, playing bridge, or snooker, but as there were no drinks at the YMCA (and no games either) the place was soon deserted. Only one small group lingered as dusk fell with the swiftness of a theatre curtain cutting off the stage from reality. One minute you could play, the next

Stamford Road was a river of car lights twinkling and dancing behind the filigree of the casuarina trees separating the courts from the street.

That was how it began, innocently, devoid of drama, no confrontations, no declarations of love, no thoughts of lovemaking. But that was the day, really – if one has to pinpoint one exact moment in one's life when all changes – when we ceased to be the casual acquaintances who met with our families or friends but became instead conspirators, only quite safe from detection because there was nothing to detect. At first I would play a couple of sets with Miki then spend an hour on the verandah with Julie until Paul came to collect her. But then came the day when I had a twinge of tennis elbow. It was impossible to play, but knowing Julie would expect me I went to the YMCA.

'I thought I'd watch you,' I explained. She didn't say a word, but went into the ladies' changing room and returned a few minutes later, saying with that half-secret smile of hers,

'I got out of my four.'

Even when she was young Julie had a fascinating quality of making flat statements without explanation, as though I would know why she had taken a decision without having to be told. It produced a reaction of excitement so that, suddenly reckless, I said, 'Let's go to Raffles.'

Raffles was not a hideaway where we might be discovered in circumstances giving rise to suspicion. If we were seen once – but only once – in the huge dance room, it would be obvious to anyone that we were there for a perfectly normal reason, for if we had anything to hide we would never go there; and anyway nobody went to Raffles in the afternoons – 'nobody' meaning people we knew; and even if they did – well, I did have tennis elbow, and Julie, an old family friend, *did* have to wait for Paul. Why should we hang around in a dreary tennis pavilion when it took five minutes to drive down Bras Basah Road, turn left into Beach Road and draw my low-slung Morgan up with a flourish in front of the traveller's palms?

Singh, the turbanned jagger, saluted us into the marbleflagged hall leading to the barn-like lounge. A couple of planters and some up-country tin miners propped up the Long Bar at the end of the room, banging for drinks and arguing cheerfully. A few tourists – there were not many in those days – strolled along the arcade that ran behind the length of the room, leading from the gardens and separated from the dance floor by a colonnade. Overhead, a dozen fans whirred on quivering, agitated stems, as though they would never last out the day.

Opposite the Long Bar Dan Hopkins' band played decorous music for the daily *thé dansant*, as it was proudly advertised. Somehow they managed to transform the popular 'You're Driving me Crazy' into a slow foxtrot, no doubt in order to prevent excessive sweating. Two couples revolved on the large floor, lost in space.

After Julie's first sip of fresh lime juice and my first gulp of Tiger, I said, but only after a split second of hesitation, 'Let's dance, shall we?'

'Should we?' Was she scared? Or did she – like me – harbour a vague feeling that dancing in the afternoons was unseemly?

'Just this once.'

The band had switched to 'Just a Song in my Heart'. The melody was gentle, lilting, slow, and as we danced and I held her closer than I would ever dare to at a Tanamera party, smelling her blue-black hair as it brushed against my cheek, feeling her body mould against mine, I whispered, 'This is better than tennis! Nervous?'

'A bit. Father would have a fit!'

'So would mine. Still' – cheerfully – 'they don't know, do they?'

After that we danced to almost every tune, holding each other more tightly each time we took the floor. I was nervous too; I kept looking round the room for faces I might recognise.

'You *are* scared,' she laughed softly.

'Not really. But it's the sort of place Tim comes to occasionally. And he's – well –' I broke off awkwardly.

'You mean he wouldn't approve? You don't have to feel

56

embarrassed, Johnnie.' I felt the preassure of her arm on my shoulder increase slightly, and responded.

'We'd better start thinking about going,' I said and walked her to the table.

She sat quietly while I signalled the boy to bring me a chit, so quietly, as though she were far away, that I put my hand on hers on the table and asked, 'A penny for them?'

'If they're worth it. I was thinking of my trip to San Francisco last year with Mummy, and all the boys taking me dancing at the Mark Hopkins, and no – well, none of this – you know what I mean.'

'This is Singapore,' I sighed, and almost thankfully I saw the street lamps in Beach Road had been lit. 'My God!' I cried. 'It's nearly dark.'

I signed the chit and we raced back to the YMCA in the Morgan, she holding her long hair to stop it blowing all over the place. I drew up with a screech outside the tatty entrance.

'Let's dance again soon,' I whispered and then, without thinking, as though it was the most natural thing in the world, I leaned over and kissed her on the mouth, feeling her lips open slightly. Five minutes later, when we were seated demurely on the pavilion verandah, Paul arrived.

Before long Julie and I were dancing at Raffles every Thursday afternoon.

I hadn't spent my late teens behaving like a monk, all desires stifled by tennis and cold baths. Paul and I had experimented with the local girls in Macpherson Road, and one weekend we had even gone to Bangkok together – and no holds were barred in the Siamese capital.

Quite a few of the secretary girls at the Swimming Club were as bored – and as curious – as we were, but none equalled the girl I met a few weeks before Julie and I started dancing at Raffles. Her name was Vicki, and we first met at a party.

Vicki had arrived in Singapore from England to become a top secretary – more than a secretary really, a personal assistant – and Paul introduced her to me after a whispered,

'She's really come out to find a husband, and the rumour is that old man Scott has gone gaga about her, but she's squeezing as much out of life as she can before she names the date.'

'Scott! That old man; he's –'

'I know. And she's younger than Scott's son Tony.'

That gave the situation a bizarre twist. For Tony Scott still had an understanding with Natasha. What a lark if Natflat married Tony – as everyone presumed they would – and found that old Scott, her father-in-law, was getting married to a girl younger than Natasha or Tony.

Vicki was a honey, a bit brassy perhaps, not the soft blonde hair of Mama, maybe a touch of peroxide, but she was fun. She was very pretty, and had a generous mouth that did not belie her good nature and generous disposition. I knew that Paul had been to bed with her, and since we were all of the same age group I considered it quite natural that I should try to get on her list.

That had been some weeks before the dancing started and Vicki and I hit it off like a bomb. She made no secret of the fact that she wanted to get married – and that she would ditch Scott like a shot if I proposed to her. But she knew we weren't in love, never would be. So she settled for the next best thing – as much fun as she could snatch before she settled down. And to us, with our prudish ways, she was an exciting newcomer – from England (or as the Tamils said, 'UK returned') – and in England they were already talking of sexual freedom among girls in a way that would have horrified the mamas of Singapore.

'You and bed were made for each other,' I teased her the first time we made love. In fact, despite her liberated attitude to sex, Vicki was a 'nice' girl, healthily English, reminding me of one of those slightly bronzed ladies, scantily clad in Grecian robes, caught in the act of loping along a deserted beach advertising perfume or chocolates.

By now I had spent two years becoming a part of the family business – learning every aspect thoroughly because of an unexpected family bombshell. Tim, who would have normally succeeded Papa Jack, announced soon after he left Raffles College that he wanted to go to England to make the army a career.

'Fucking treachery!' cried Grandpa Jack (fortunately out of Mama's hearing). Grandpa felt that *no one* had the right to refuse to join Dexters, especially an eldest son. It was more than a tradition for father to succeed son; it was a way of life. But in fact – and I found this curious – my father didn't rant and rave like Grandpa Jack did. Though the family hierarchy had never been broken since the first Dexter stepped ashore with Raffles, my father made no attempt to persuade Tim to stay. And when I asked Tim why he was going, he just said, 'Why don't you mind your own bloody business?'

I suddenly realised that perhaps Tim did not have the vocation for the army which my father cited as the reason for his departure. There was something more sinister, as though he were being hustled out of Singapore as quickly as possible. One or two strange men came to Tanamera and spent some time closeted with my father. There were endless cables between Singapore and London before my father was able to announce – not so much with triumph but more with a sigh of relief – that Tim had been accepted for a commission in the King's Own Yorkshire Light Infantry, the KOYLIs for short. I could not find out the truth – not for many, many years – but I sensed that something fishy was going on, when I learned that he planned to sail for England early in 1935. So I automatically started training to become the next *tuan bezar*. Not that Papa Jack was near retirement – far from it – but there had always been a father and son working in harness at Dexters. That was how it was.

I didn't mind. I actually enjoyed the work. The office opened at eight each morning now instead of seven-thirty and I left around four, which gave me plenty of time for tennis (or secret dancing on Thursdays). I not only enjoyed the work, I loved Singapore. I loved it more than any other place I knew.

The offices of Dexter and Company in Robinson Road, a

jumble of ancient buildings facing the Telok Ayer Basin, had hardly changed in the last fifty years. The ground floor consisted of godowns or warehouses, where incoming or outgoing cargos might be stored for a day or two until they were collected or shipped. At times the godowns resembled a gigantic junk shop, cluttered with newly painted machinery for planters or tin miners, a consignment of toilets, washbasins and baths in another corner; cases of whisky and gin, bales of cloth; crates of crockery for Robinson's, the big store in Raffles Place; a shipment of beauty aids for Maynard's, the chemists in Battery Road; ten cases of assorted books for Kelly and Walsh. The only product that we shipped all the time but never stored in Robinson Road was rubber.

The latex stank to high heaven. You could never get rid of the smell of it, so the rubber was stored in separate go-downs, one at the far end of Anson Road, the rest in our main rubber godown, a huge building on the bank of the sluggish, dirty Kallang River near the village of Geylang, in the opposite direction, four miles east of Singapore. The Kallang wasn't much of a river – it wasn't even as wide as the Singapore River – but it was big enough for our lighters, which could load directly from the godown and take the bales out to the vessels in the roads.

This meant an enormous saving. Trucks in Anson Road could only carry five tons of latex sheets at a time; a lighter carried up to a hundred tons – straight to the waiting ship.

I spent my first three months in Kallang godown learning the tricks of the rubber trade. It was huge, measuring eight thousand square feet, the air saturated with the stink of rubber, much of it from Ara, our own estate. The thin sheets were packed into two-hundred-and-fifty-pound bales, each bale wrapped in other sheets of smoked rubber still so tacky that, in order to stop the bales sticking to each other, women coolies 'painted' each one with a solution of old rubber scraps dissolved in turpentine and thickened with talcum powder. They slapped the mixture on to bales with thick wide brushes, and though the talcum prevented sticking everything and everyone in the godown was always coated in white dust.

Yet someone had to watch every moment, and Papa believed that the more I knew about the fiddling in rubber shipping the easier my work would be later. Sometimes the bales would be miscounted – deliberately. At others, they would be rejected as damaged – and the damaged goods spirited away and sold. Some arrived short in weight – with coolies bribed to give the bales three extra coats of talcum paint so that they would tip the red scales at the right weight. These scales stood at either side of the foreman's desk, and someone had to see that the talcum had not been applied too thickly.

At one end of the godown steps led to an office on a high gallery. Curtained windows overlooked the foreman's desk with his weighing machines, while others looked down on the loading bay where the coolies, handling the bales with wicked-looking pointed iron hooks, pulled them off their trollies on to primitive conveyor belts of rollers close to each other, along which a woman could easily push a bale straight on to the lighter.

Three months of that was enough, and then I went to head office – the only office, really. Stone steps from the unimposing front entrance led to the first floor, where the large main office was studded with tables for typists and several old, Dickensian-type desks with brass rails for the Chinese and Eurasian book-keepers. Those desks must have arrived in Singapore with the first cargo of furniture.

My father occupied the largest private office, inherited from Grandpa Jack, and I used my father's old room. Two other offices, little more than cubicles, housed the only two European assistants, Ball and Rawlings, who had in fact taught me everything I knew about the business. Ball was short and fussy and liked a drop of Scotch at lunchtime, after which he leaned close to me and became very confidential. Rawlings was younger and suffered from such poor eyesight that he had to wear pebble glasses. Both had originally been recruited in London, living at first as bachelors in the Cadet House, an old bungalow in Nassim Hill, near the end of Orchard Road, where they were housed and fed until they or Papa Jack decided whether they would stay in Singapore or return to work in the London office. By the time I joined the firm they were both married and both firmly anchored in Singapore.

What made life so exciting was not only Julie, innocent conspiracy, work, play, but the fact that I felt an integral part of Singapore, part of the city in which every street I explored seemed to lead to the sea, to ships shimmering on the fiery horizon, to a glimpse of passenger liners in the outer roads surrounded by a flurry of sampans, or battered rusting freighters that might have figured in stories by Conrad or Maugham, for the Singapore of my youth was still the Singapore of Somerset Maugham.

I grew up with the smell of the Singapore River – the smell of the tropics, compounded of drains, swamp, dried fish, of a score of sweet spices waiting to be unloaded from boats arriving from Bali, Java or the Celebes. Visitors held their noses in disgust, but it was not unpleasant, and once smelled was never forgotten, for it was the smell of Singapore itself, the trademark of an exciting, polyglot, opulent city built on swamp, where the heat and humidity pressed down day after day like a blanket on half a million Malays, Chinese, Indians and a handful of Europeans, as the whites were called.

It made work more exciting to be part of this, not an interloper, to be able to talk in Cantonese or Malay to Chinese families pecking at lunch with chopsticks on the roadside, or Malays offering fruit of every taste and colour from mounds spilling into the road.

Julie's brother Paul and I often went to tiny Chinese or Malay restaurants which he knew, tucked away in hidden corners, and offering exotic dishes you never found in larger restaurants, dishes like clay pots filled with huge prawns cooked in coconut milk.

Paul had grown into a very elegant young man with a wardrobe I envied. He always looked spick and span. He never seemed to sweat as I did. Even in his teens and twenties he was more worldly-wise than I was because, while I was being educated at Raffles Institution, he had been to school in California. Aunt Sonia had insisted on an American education for her only son, and he had returned with a polish unknown at Raffles. Nor had he any desire to work.

'Mum would really like me to live in America,' he said, 'but I'm going to stay here for the time being. The girls in America are terrible,' he said, adding loftily, 'haven't a clue how to work up a man. Much more willing here.'

'Won't you *have* to work in the office?' I asked one day.

'No. I'm lucky. Your old man thinks it's a sort of status symbol for you to be a hard worker. My father thinks that if I work it's lowering the family dignity. Why should I try to change his mind?'

I said I knew why Paul didn't have to work. P.P. Soong had returned from a trip to mainland China with a young man called Soong Kai-shek – no blood relative; his divorced mother had married a Soong and the boy had taken the name of Soong.

'That's about right,' Paul agreed. 'Father's going to train him to run the business. He's an ugly piece of work – nasty temper too – but, knowing my father, I wouldn't be surprised if he doesn't plan to marry Kai-shek off to Julie.'

'He can't do that!' I blurted out.

'Well, *you* can't marry her,' laughed Paul. As my mouth dropped open he added, 'Come off it, Johnnie. I wasn't born yesterday. I know all about your cuddling and canoodling in the YMCA.'

I couldn't say a word until he added, 'Don't worry. He can't force Julie to marry anyone. I don't know how, but Mum's got some sort of hold over my father. I think she's got proof that he's keeping a couple of concubines on the side.'

'You can't be serious? *Two!*'

'It's perfectly normal among Chinese. You know, you get bored with the same wife, you try a bit of a change – only Mum doesn't see it that way. Can't blame her. They have the most hellish rows. Boy – can my mother yell when she's mad. She's threatened to walk out more than once, and Dad doesn't want that. He'd lose an awful lot of face among his friends. So she forced him to set up trust funds for both of us, Julie and yours truly. I know – I had to sign one. So we'll be okay.'

I had heard about the rows in the Soong household before. Grandpa Jack had hinted at undercurrents between the two, but I had until now tended to dismiss them as the embroidered fancies of an old man who enjoyed retailing gossip, usually comparing it with his own murky – and apparently energetic – past.

'Can't think why Sonia ever married P.P.,' he had said once as I poured out his nightly Scotch. With the years his drink had been rationed, and his evening allowance of whisky was such an event that when I returned from the club after tennis he liked me to pour it out personally for him in a special glass with an intricate design, which he called 'the pretty', and which reached a third of the way up from the base.

He watched greedily as I poured, with the suspicion of old age, afraid I was going to cheat him. 'Make sure it's up to the top of the pretty,' he growled every evening.

He was eighty-one and still very much a man, with a strong voice and equally strong beliefs. He shuffled rather than walked now, slept downstairs, and used a heavy Malacca cane with a rubber tip, especially when he walked in the grounds. He still had his mop of white hair and his bushy, patriarchal beard was untouched by a single strand of dirty grey.

'Don't misunderstand me.' He was thinking again about P.P. 'Great respect for him, great worker, shrewd as hell. But Chinese are all the same. Work like devils in the office, but once they close the door behind them – bang! they think of nothing but their cocks. Bet he's led your Aunt Sonia a dance!' With a sly look he added, 'Never get entangled with a Chinese, m'boy.'

All these revelations – and we weren't the only people who gossiped about the Soongs – must have made our friends feel that by comparison life at Tanamera and at our office was a dull affair. It wasn't, of course – not for me, anyway. Even work seemed to be a pleasure, to be intermingled with my life, even with my tennis, for I made a valuable new contact through Miki, who mentioned after one game at the YMCA that a Swiss friend of his was anxious to meet me with a view to doing some business.

I agreed immediately, for Miki was shrewd. He bore no resemblance to the stock caricature of a Japanese. True, he wore glasses and his teeth were very white, but he didn't have too many. Put like that, I realise now how condescending, even racialist, that summing-up sounds. But in those days the white man's superiority over all other races was so drummed into us that we all thought in terms like that. It was even natural that I should say to Natasha, 'But he can't be a bad chap. He got a Blue for tennis at Cambridge.'

His friend's name was Bertrand Bonnard, and I arranged to meet him at the Cricket Club, driving into 'white' Singapore, the narrow streets of Chinatown replaced by wide avenues lined with cropped grass verges and flame-of-the-forest or frangipani trees, with policemen at every corner directing the traffic with basketwork wings strapped across their backs to save them the effort of waving their arms in the heat. All they needed to do when halting traffic was turn their feet.

With the orderliness of a colonial city, the slim spire of the cathedral looked down from its island of carefully tended green lawn not far from the dome of the Supreme Court and the gentlemanly government offices, separated from the waterfront by a padang of the Cricket Club where I parked my car.

Monsieur Bonnard turned out to be an elegant French-speaking Swiss with a wife who disliked the Far East (without apparently having ever visited it), and who remained in Geneva near the head office of her husband's business, though he operated mostly in Asia. He was about thirty, I suppose, but when Mama later asked what Bonnard looked like I found it difficult to describe his actual appearance because it was so very normal. He was as slim as I was, not quite so tall – I had now topped six feet – and he wore his hair a little on the long side. His face was pleasant, long rather than round, with strong white teeth and intelligent, adventurous eyes.

He did have something else – a touch of French arrogance, not marked, but enough to emphasise that it was perfectly natural for a European to be more in tune with life than an English colonial. I had noticed in many Frenchmen an irritating sense of superiority, though God knows what it was founded on, except good food and wine. But still, Bonnard wasn't French; so I didn't think much of it.

He certainly did look like a man of the world used to meeting beautiful women and ordering expensive meals, and returning bottles of wine he found corked. And I probably gaped when he told me that he not only kept a flat in Singapore but another in Tokyo, a third in Shanghai. 'Hotels are so *dreary*,' he said. We, the Dexters, could easily have maintained flats wherever we liked, but we were 'Yorkshire' and didn't go in for that kind of showy life. Secretly, though, I envied him being able to walk into his own flat several thousand miles away at a moment's notice.

'One day, *mon cher ami*, I will be asking you to help me,' he said, which was a very courteous way of saying that he would put some business our way. Bonnard and I met fairly often after that; I put him up for the club, bypassing the waiting list, and took him to Tanamera to meet the family, where he was an immediate success, arriving the first time with an enormous bunch of flowers for Mama.

On the third or fourth visit, Bertrand – it was Bertrand by then – brought *two* bunches of very expensive roses (they had to be expensive: they were grown in the cool of Fraser's Hill up-country, and sent down on the overnight train). The largest was for Mama, the other for Natasha; after which Mama could hardly refuse his request to take Natasha out dancing one evening.

At twenty-five Natflat had developed into a stunner, her hair even more ash-blonde than Mama's, her eyes an even more startling blue. And she had something Mama didn't have – at least no longer – what Grandpa Jack once called naughty eyes. No doubt this was why the family had been gently pushing her into an unofficial understanding with Tony Scott. I wondered if Bonnard knew about Tony.

'None of your business,' said Natasha when I taxed her. 'Bertrand is the most divine dancer in the world and Tony dances like a carthorse. That's all there is to it.'

'That's what you say.'

'Well, anyway, he's married,' she said, as though to her that ended all discussion. 'His wife lives in Switzerland.'

'Makes no difference to a frog.' I said. 'All the frogs are hot stuff.'

'He's not a frog. He's a Swiss.'

'He behaves like a frog. Has he given you a French kiss yet?'

'Beast! You're disgusting.' She pretended to beat my chest with her fists.

'You didn't answer the question. You know what I mean – come on, Natflat, no secrets,' I put out the tip of my tongue and waggled it. 'It's bloody exciting!'

She went suddenly quite still, standing there in a pink dress, and then her face flamed scarlet and she ran into the house.

'Crafty bugger,' I said to myself. 'And a married man too.' But it was not my business, I wasn't my sister's keeper, and anyway Bonnard was edging towards a deal with Dexters: in fact within three months he arranged with me to supply a firm he ran with Miki's father in Japan with a huge order for earth-moving equipment. It was worth two million Straits dollars – a lot of money in those days. I checked with Papa Jack about the advisability of trading with Japan, for there had been vague Chinese rumblings earlier in the year when the Russians sold off the Chinese Eastern Railway in Manchuria not to China but to Japan, and I wanted to be sure there would be no repercussions among our rich Chinese clients.

'Carry on,' said my father. 'Of course, get a written guarantee from this Swiss chap that the machinery won't be sent to Manchuria. There could be trouble there one day.'

Bonnard was horrified. '*Mai jamais, mon ami.*' He wrote

the letter immediately. 'This is to prepare sites in southern Japan for camps for earthquake victims.'

So the deal went through, the biggest I had ever handled. I arranged credits to buy equipment from European Bulldozers Ltd., the largest firm of its kind in Europe. They, too, wanted assurances about the ultimate destination and use, but the fact that the equipment was being bought through Dexters, one of the most reputable firms in Asia, for shipment to a Swiss firm with a branch in southern Japan allayed any niggling doubts. And I could hardly believe my eyes when Bonnard gave Dexters a cheque for twenty-five per cent of the deal to seal the bargain.

But what made it even more worthwhile was the smile of pleasure on Papa Jack's face when I handed him the cheque. It wasn't the money – it didn't matter that much – it was the tangible proof (or so he hoped) that I was shaping up to be the next *tuan bezar*. I knew he had been disappointed when Tim – who was expected to leave in a few months for England – refused to join the family business; and I wanted to show my father that I was doing well. I *wanted* to please him; I liked to see the crinkle of appreciation on his face when I did something of which he approved.

3

When I teased Natasha about French kisses I was speaking from practical experience with Vicki, who almost took my breath away each time she locked her mouth on to mine. No, it wasn't Julie. Of course it wasn't. Though I was soon looking forward to Thursday afternoons more than any other day in the week it never entered my head to try to do anything other than dance and kiss and cuddle a bit – and 'English' kisses at that.

I just didn't want to spoil Thursdays by starting some-

68

thing I knew could lead nowhere. I knew it, she knew it, so if I was tempted to talk about 'love' Julie usually headed me off.

'After dancing close to you like this' – we hadn't missed one dance on this particular day at Raffles – 'don't you feel like – well, like I do?'

'What do *you* think? You're the first man who's ever danced close to me like this. Of course it makes me feel – well, excited.'

'Perhaps we should dance like our parents,' I laughed and held her away from me, twirling sedately, head in air.

'Ass!' That was a great term of endearment in those days. 'I may be a bit scared sometimes – of myself – but I enjoy the way we dance. I like the excitement of our meetings and' – a little shyly – 'the way you hold me, pressing close to me. Life at home – mother is sweet, but nothing ever happens except rows, and I feel that with you' – without thinking she pressed herself closer to me than she had ever done before – 'I'm pinching a bit of someone else's excitement that I'm not supposed to enjoy. I'm too young.'

'Some people are *married* at your age, Julie. But come on – let's go back to the pavilion and wait there till Paul comes. You remember, he's going to be an hour late today.'

'Won't it be closed?'

I shook my head.

'Why not?'

Paul had warned me he would not be picking Julie up until half past seven, so I had bribed the head groundsman at the YMCA to let us stay on after the club closed. He would return to lock up just before Paul was due to arrive.

In the dusk of the tatty pavilion I held her in my arms, smothering her with kisses, she responding, clutching each other as we lay on a rattan sofa. When I stroked her long, slim brown legs I felt I never wanted to let go.

'I've longed for this moment – only, be careful! Don't make it harder for me.'

'Harder?' I asked.

'To say no. Don't you think I feel like you do? Oh, darling' – holding me so tightly I thought I would choke –

'we both know our parents – don't tempt me – I might give in.'

'Don't worry.' I could hardly talk, I was stroking her breasts, her legs above the knee, and yet I knew I couldn't do anything more. I don't know what emotion kept acting as a brake, stopping me. I was tortured with desire, burning inside, feeling the need to thrust, and I knew she would gasp out a willing 'yes'.

But the thirties *were* different – in Singapore anyway. Some part of me knew – or was it just a lesson learned by rote as a child? – that it was wrong to make love to a girl I had known as a child, to a 'good' girl. Girls, I had been told so often when young (I was forgetting that at twenty-one I was still young), didn't feel the way men did – not nice girls – unless they were tempted to respond, and that could only be the fault of a man. So a little kissing and cuddling, that was fine up to a point, but never go too far. What hypocritical nonsense! And yet it was there. All I wanted at that moment was to tear off Julie's clothes and make love to her. It was the most natural desire in the world between two people who loved each other, or even *believed* they were in love. But I had been told otherwise. We all had – since parents were invented, as Paul once said.

'You're sure it's not because you're like Mark Twain's Mister Wilson,' she teased, and when I looked puzzled (for to me Mark Twain meant Tom Sawyer) she semi-quoted, 'Adam didn't want the apple for the apple's sake, but only because it was forbidden.'

'You can't believe that.'

'No, I don't. You'd like Mark Twain, he wrote some beautiful poetry. I spend all my money buying poetry books – but all the love stories end so unhappily, specially when they're forbidden – like ours.'

'I'll buy a book tomorrow. Who by?'

'You will? Promise? There's a new edition of Housman in at Kelly and Walsh. Our first keepsake!'

'Promise, I'll go round tomorrow.'

'Then I'll read some of it to you – if you ever stop kissing me long enough.'

I still wonder whether we might not have 'gone the whole hog' – another of Paul's phrases – if we had been granted another quarter of an hour of temptation, but there was a sudden discreet knock on the front door of the pavilion and the lilting voice of a Tamil groundsman saying, 'Very sorry, tuan, but must be starting to close up now.'

'One day we'll make love,' I promised her as she smoothed down her white dress. 'I want to so much, Julie – I feel so awful. But I'm glad I didn't – half glad. You understand? If I didn't love you so much I would have done. One day, I'm sure – but not like this,' I looked round the dusty pavilion with its cheap rattan furniture.

'When you say, Johnnie,' she answered gravely. 'I'll always be yours if you want me.' And then, as we stood together outside the front entrance, Paul's car came swinging round the corner from Bras Basah Road, and the next minute she was gone.

The physical problem – the ache in my loins as I stood there – was more than my body could stand. I was still bursting with desire, and for a moment I thought of driving to Macpherson Road and finding a girl there. But I couldn't; it seemed too sordid for words. Wouldn't it be much better, much 'cleaner', more sensible, to go to Vicki, who knew I didn't love her, than to go to a tart who probably had a dose of clap?

That was the answer! I phoned, and she was in. She was free.

Vicki and I had a quick bite at the Adelphi and then I rushed her back to her tiny flat behind Orchard Road and I made love in a way I had never done before. I never really saw Vicki's blonde hair, never noticed her legs, beautiful legs really, I never saw her, never thought of her, never felt her. All I could see, all I could feel, was Julie, black hair like a pool of ink on the white pillows, grave eyes staring into mine. I can't remember anything about that half hour, how I did it, what I did. It was just Julie there.

The first moment I did remember was when she lit a cigarette, looked at me for a long time, breathed deeply and exhaled bluish smoke in a long stream before sighing happily, 'My God, Johnnie. If I make love every night until I die it can never be as good again.'

I wondered what her thoughts would have been had I told her it was all 'pretending'; that I had been thinking of someone else. And I wondered too what she would say when I told her – as I realised I had to, now, before I left the cosy flat – that there must never be another time – not for us. The after-sensation of sex, the sharpened emotions, brought back my guilt. I was thinking how mad I would have been had Julie done the same thing. The thoughts were incoherent, not even very intelligent, but the central thought was clear – lay off Vicki. She made some coffee and then I told her. I can't remember what I said, though I didn't mention Julie by name.

When I finished I drew a deep breath – not only of relief, but of apprehension. Vicki wasn't exactly pleased.

'You certainly choose your moment to tell a girl,' she lit another cigarette. 'I think you might have told me before you used me as a – a sort of sexual punchbag.'

'I'm sorry,' I mumbled.

'I suppose it's my fault as much as yours,' she sighed. 'Only please don't come here again if you're feeling' – with a touch of sarcasm – 'overwrought.'

I don't remember exactly when the family began to notice that I was behaving differently. But in the office one morning Papa Jack took off his rimless glasses, leaving the bright red mark on the bridge of his nose, and said with a conspiratorial, half-embarrassed air, 'You're looking very pleased with yourself these days, Johnnie. Everything all right? Feeling your oats? Been going down to Macpherson Road?'

In Tanamera the word sex was hardly mentioned except by Grandpa Jack. Papa and Mama regarded it as a word you just avoided, a *subject* to avoid too. I wondered what my father really thought about sex as I watched him, looking as he always did in the office – white ducks, white shirt with stiff collar, sleeves rolled up once he arrived, white jacket carefully hung up on a hanger by a thamby, on the same peg it had hung on for years. As he spoke, I realised how he must have rehearsed the words, the effort it must have cost him to start an embarrassing conversation. I wondered for a moment if Mama had asked him too.

Papa still looked fit and young for his fifty-four years. He had a good head of hair, the same straight-backed figure I had known from my earliest days, and he always walked with a spring in his step. But in the view of Natflat and myself he hadn't moved with the times, with (what we then thought of as) the swinging thirties. Sex was a part of life, but Papa didn't talk about it unless necessary, at least not with the young. I'm sure my father didn't disapprove of sex; he just didn't know how to pronounce it, so to speak. I was rather touched by his sudden remark, by his determination to be 'modern' with me. It must have cost him an effort.

'Not Macpherson Road,' I almost laughed at the memory of my first attempts to learn the facts of life in that dreary thoroughfare. I had gone with Paul, but what a flop the first evening had been. It put me off that sort of place for life.

'But girl trouble?'

'Well – I do meet a few,' I smiled.

'Hope so. But don't do anything that'd upset your mother. You know how touchy women are, specially mothers.' He was being conspiratorial, 'we men' together. 'Specially with any of the local girls. And don't get entangled. Don't get married too soon. Fatal.'

'I won't, I promise you.'

'Can't stop young blood.' He fixed his rimless glasses on his nose. The conversation was obviously over, and as I made for the door he added, 'Hope you're using something. There's a lot of clap around. If anything goes wrong, for God's sake come and tell me. Every day counts.'

Mama was more subtle. I often think that Mama was, in a way, a little resigned to life in Singapore. She never complained, she was certainly not unhappy, but I fancy that just as Aunt Sonia missed California Mama missed New York, or at least America; and I always had the feeling that, given the opportunity, she might have found it hard to resist the advances of any handsome man who declared his love for her. Of course, being her son (with the attitudes of those days), it never entered my head that my own mother would ever *permit* any such advances, would ever do anything but resist, yet she might have had a small, very small, twinge of regret in resisting.

We were all having breakfast on the east verandah on one of those cool mornings when the lallang glistened as though it had rained. I had been for a ten-minute walk before my shower, across to the edge of the jungle with its glimpses of kampongs, attap huts, wisps of blue smoke, tiny worlds sheltered and all but hidden tall palms and the shorter, thick-leaved clumps of bananas, and everywhere the wet smell of a tropical morning.

I was ravenous and Li, the son of old Li and now second boy, helped to serve me with papaya. Our breakfasts were very old-fashioned. A long table, running along the back wall of the verandah, was laid out each morning with chafing dishes warmed by spirit lamps. No continental breakfasts for the Dexters. Even though Grandpa Jack now had his breakfast in bed, he sometimes roared for a steak, while we would choose from scrambled eggs, kidneys, kippers bought at the Cold Storage in Orchard Road and sausages (tinned, safer that way). For my part, I ate everything I could.

'I've noticed,' said Mama slyly, 'that Johnnie always eats a huge breakfast on Fridays. Has anybody else noticed?' She turned to Natasha and I felt myself going pink.

'Must be in love,' said Natasha cheerfully.

'That's more than you are,' I retorted. '*Walking* out with Tony Scott and *dancing* out with Monsieur Bonnard,' I emphasised the word monsieur.

'It's not my fault if Tony can't dance,' Natasha giggled.

'That was very nasty of you,' Mama turned to me. 'You apologise.' And after I did so – with a huge secret wink to Natasha – Mama continued coolly, 'I expect it's your Thursday tennis match with Mr – I forget his name, your Japanese friend.'

'Miki.'

'Of course.' Then she made me gulp my hot coffee, 'I

74

think I'll come and watch you one Thursday. I've never been to the YMCA.'

'It's a pretty dreadful place,' I said – hopefully; wondering whether my mother was telling me that she knew more than she was saying. Oblique hints were always being dropped in Tanamera, casual sayings with hidden or double meanings. It wasn't done in an unpleasant way; I think the habit had grown because Mama and Papa had to be so careful through all their married life of anything they said in front of Grandpa Jack. I never realised when I was young the hidden strains that come when whole families share a house, however big. As she got up, breakfast over, Mama smiled and said, 'Don't worry, darling – I won't pry into your secrets.'

As Mama walked into the house, Natflat, Tim and I sat at the table waiting for Papa to set off for the office, but as Natasha said 'I'm going to pick some flowers,' she added, with a devilish look in her eyes, 'think she knows about *that*?' and put out the tip of her tongue and waggled it.

Tim had been silent but as I threw a piece of bread at Natflat's retreating figure he said darkly, 'I know it's not tennis,' and for no particular reason added, 'I saw you at the Adelphi not long ago with Vicki. I hear she's going to marry Tony Scott's father.' I nodded. 'Well, if she's going to *marry* him, I don't understand. I'll bet you've been to bed with her.'

'You've won your bet!' I said cheerfully. 'Now you know why I've got such a good appetite.'

'But what about Scott? Don't you feel a shit?'

'Look, Tim, Scott is a rich middle-aged man, and every Thursday he goes to the Rubber Association meeting. For the rest of the week he keeps the poor kid on a pretty tight rein. Once or twice I've given her a break, that's all – though it's all over now.'

'You *are* a shit,' His voice held real venom. 'I'll be glad when I sail for England next week.'

'If you don't like it here, piss off,' I said. 'Nobody's going to miss you.'

What *was* the matter with him? He walked away filled

75

with hate and rage. What business was it of his if I screwed everyone in Singapore? As he stalked off I was thinking for the hundredth time, how is it possible to live for twenty-one years with your own brother, share boyhood secrets, sleep for years in the same room, grow up together, and yet have the feeling that you don't really know him? Sometimes I had a sense of relief that he *was* going to England.

Papa still hadn't brought the car round – it was not yet a quarter to eight – and I called out to Natasha by the bed of cannas, 'What's eating him? Why is he always so bloody nasty to me?'

'He's jealous of you,' she returned to the lake. 'Envious. He'd love to do the things you do, but he can't.' As I looked puzzled, she added, 'No, not physically, you ass. Up here!' She tapped her head. 'He can't bring himself to try anything.'

'Maybe when he's in the army – away from us all. Tanamera *does* sometimes have a stifling effect, doesn't it?'

'And how!' Natflat was always picking up American-isms, not so much from Mama as from the films. 'But Tim'll never change. Strange how different he is from us – you and me. Thank God for you. We like the same things, don't we?' And with another giggle she put out the tiniest tip of pink, pointed tongue. 'I'll bet poor Tim has never done *that*! I know *you* have, I can tell. I'm going to call it "Johnnie's special" – then we can talk about French kissing in front of other people. Don't ever tell Mama – she'd have a fit – but I *love* it.'

'With Bertrand?'

'Well,' with a sigh, 'he *is* a bit more dashing than your Cricket Club crowd. A girl has a right to lead someone a bit of a dance before she settles down.'

'With Tony?'

'I guess so. Papa and Mama are always hinting about "naming the day". I'm in no hurry, but –' The sound of the Buick's klaxon cut into the end of the sentence, and I prepared to set off with my father for the office.

★

Three weeks later Natasha and Tony told the family they wanted to make their engagement official. There was to be no public announcement yet, but Grandpa Jack's immediate reaction was that we should hold a dance to honour the occasion. There were no dissenters.

Poor Natflat! Despite her beauty, she couldn't bring herself to look like the classical radiant bride-to-be, and I sympathised, for I knew why. Bonnard was returning to Europe for a few weeks by Imperial Airways flying boat to be with his wife, who was having a baby. To be fair to Bonnard, he had not kept his wife's condition a secret. But Natasha must have had a live-for-today crush on him that hurt more deeply than I realised.

Tony was likeable enough, but as Paul Soong put it, 'He's not a mental heavyweight.' In fact, with his curly hair, apple cheeks and tough physique, he resembled an overgrown schoolboy, even though he was two years older than me. He had a passion for rugger. He liked to spend Sunday mornings at the Swimming Club drinking pints – and dragging Natasha along. He was partial to harmless but irritating escapades. He once jumped into the Tanglin pool fully dressed – for a five-dollar bet. But he was universally popular, and he would make Natasha a loyal, faithful, adoring husband – and no doubt a safer one than a man like Bonnard. The trouble was – I didn't really know what Natasha was really after.

The day Grandpa Jack suggested holding a ball at Tanamera was also the day that Mama cornered me and said sweetly, 'I saw Mrs Dillon of Boustead's yesterday. She said she'd seen you.'

'Me?' I asked without a trace of anxiety.

'Yes, darling. At Raffles. Last Thursday. Dancing, she said.'

Thank God it had rained last Thursday! I stumbled mentally and verbally for a couple of seconds before saying, as steadily as I could, 'The game was rained off, Mama. I took one of the girls out for tea.'

Mama knew perfectly well that no European girls were

members of the YMCA – or none that we counted as friends – but she didn't ask who the girl was. I could only hope she didn't know.

'Don't do anything silly,' she said. 'You know how upset your father gets at any gossip. I didn't mention this to him because I didn't think it was important . . .' Mama had a habit of leaving sentences unfinished, wrapped in flimsy but suggestive meanings, endings that always reminded me of her vague pink and blue dressing gowns that had fascinated me as a boy.

As I waited for her next words, I was thinking: mustn't go to Raffles next Thursday. Where else, where instead, what can I do, how can I warn Julie, how can I see her, what plans can I make? I *had* to see Julie. Maybe Paul could help. Yes, Paul . . . I hardly heard Mama's voice cut into my thoughts, 'Once in a while doesn't matter Johnnie, but don't make a habit of it.'

'Of course not,' I lied. 'It *was* raining.'

'I understand. But bad habits have a habit of,' she laughed at her mixed-up words, 'how many habits! Of becoming permanent.' She hesitated, then said, 'We don't talk about other people's affairs, Johnnie, but look how terribly unhappy poor Aunt Sonia is.' It was the first time she had ever mentioned the Soong marriage.

'I know,' I said. 'Paul sort of hinted to me –'

'Poor Paul. And just imagine how – yes, tragic isn't too strong a word – how tragic it would be if Paul married a European in Singapore. Or, for that matter' – did I imagine that she was pausing for dramatic effect, in order to rub in a lesson, or was it only imagination? – 'if poor Julie married a European.'

'But she *is* almost European – and she's an American citizen.'

'Of course, darling. America's different. But I'm talking about people who have to live in Singapore, whose work is here, who are tied to Singapore.' Was she talking about me, the perfect example of a man whose whole future was bound up with Singapore? Could my mother really be so devious in her warnings?

'Julie is so beautiful,' she sighed, 'so vulnerable, with all the trouble at home. She must ache to escape – everything. But any European who raised any false hopes – who let her think they might remain in love forever – he would ruin her life.'

Mama didn't wait for an answer, but added brightly, 'All this gossip about nothing! I mustn't waste the next *tuan bezar*'s time.' Then she put her arms on my shoulders, kissed me lightly and said, 'You're just like your father when he was young. All the girls were after him. And now that Tim is already on his way to England, your father's very proud of the way you've settled down in the business. And he needs you.'

A few days later Vicki rang me up at the office and announced that she was going to marry Ian Scott. I wished her luck, meaning it. 'When's the happy day?'

'Not for a few months,' she explained, 'but then it would be at St Andrew's Cathedral.

'Naturally. He's a *tuan*.'

'I only hope I'm doing the right thing.' She sounded sad.

'Maybe you should announce your engagement officially, have a party, the same day as Natasha and Tony. A sort of double event. Just think of it, Vick.'

'What a super idea.' She was half laughing. 'Only *don't* call me Vick. It makes me sound like a cough mixture.'

That is just what happened. What I had suggested to Vicki almost as a joke was hailed at Tanamera as a brilliant idea. Vicki's husband-to-be, Ian Scott, was not only an old family friend but a valued business acquaintance, and after all, when his son married Natasha, old Scott would be her father-in-law. Such a double announcement would be an historic event – and what better way to celebrate it than with a great ball at Tanamera?

4

Despite his great age, Grandpa Jack welcomed every opportunity to hold a party at Tanamera, and he liked to think that he was still very much in command. 'After all,' I heard him roar once, 'it's my bloody house. I built it.'

Behind the scenes, though, Mama ruled Tanamera with the softest velvet gloves ever encasing an iron fist. Hiding the tensions involved when young and old live together year in, year out, she knew exactly what she wanted, yet would seek Grandpa's advice until finally he was convinced he had conceived the original idea.

It was Mama who wanted the drive for the ball to be lit with a double line of flaming torches. It was (somehow) Grandpa Jack who suggested it, adding for good measure, 'Let's have fireworks too.'

We spent evening after evening discussing the plans and guest list, usually over drinks before dinner, sometimes on the west verandah or, if it was raining, in the 'study' – which was no more a study than a small spare bedroom was a Sick Bay. Many rooms in Tanamera had their own names, probably dating from the days when Grandpa Jack, leafing through old copies of the *Illustrated London News*, read that the stately homes of England were often called The Blue Room or The West Room.

He had liked the idea, and so one room became the study, though it contained virtually no books, for they would have become mildewed in a matter of days. Nobody ever *studied* in Tanamera. We worked in the office – that was what an office was for – and we played away from it – that was what leisure was for. But the study was one of the most comfortable rooms in the house, furnished by Mama, a relaxing room with two large sofas and half a dozen deep armchairs, loosely covered in bright chintzes which were changed weekly.

Sooner or later every discussion would be interrupted with a roar, 'Where's my bloody barley water?' For now that Grandpa Jack was limited to one whisky a day, and the occasional bottle of Tiger (after his last alcoholic bout Dr Sampson warned him he would be dead in a year unless he stopped drinking) my grandfather drank quarts of Robinson's barley water flavoured with fresh limes.

'Can't stop the habit of raising my right arm,' he growled. Old Li, the number one boy (for Ah Wok had long since died) had become Grandpa Jack's personal boy in the evening, and followed him around with a light, small, square bamboo table, its top decorated with a heavily varnished picture of flowers on a dark-stained background. On this rested his jug of barley water, the top covered with muslin, weighted round the edges with blue glass beads.

Grandpa Jack still had a bull-like voice, and if that flimsy table was not by his side when he wanted a drink his voice bellowed, no matter who was speaking, 'Where's my bloody barley water?' Poor Li! He was the modern counter-part of Ah Wok, who had trodden the ground where we now sat a thousand times, following Grandpa Jack around with beer while Tanamera was being built. It seemed hard sometimes to realise that Grandpa Jack was the same man. To me he confided, 'This stuff tastes like weasel pee, but at my age you're a gonner if you don't keep the waterworks operating.'

Sitting there in the study, bushy white beard almost hiding his flowing black tie, he reminded me of an old Victorian photograph, an upstanding patriarch pictured against an oval sepia background, the rest of the print left white in an old oak frame.

The effect was heightened because he had his own specially made high-backed cane chair; it resembled a throne, for it was not only wide but so high that it had a built-in footrest above the claw feet. This was a cunning device. By pulling a lever at the back old Li could lower four small hidden wheels when Grandpa Jack was too tired to walk. On each arm of the chair slats of wood swivelled outwards, like the extensions for legs on a long chair. The right one contained a hole specially cut to fit Grandpa Jack's glass with the 'pretty'. The other slat had a hollow depression which old Li kept filled with salted nuts, which Grandpa Jack liked to nibble – ceaselessly, though one at a time.

When the doctor said he must sleep on the ground floor – which had enough space for a dozen bedrooms – my father had suggested installing a lift, which would have been quite easy. Grandpa Jack had thundered, 'What the hell do you think I am? A bloody invalid?' Though the answer was yes, nobody dared to say so, for Grandpa Jack was not going to be robbed of the last years of his life hidden in the Sick Bay.

The ball was planned for the spring of 1935 and most of the guest list sorted itself out. We had standard lists for all occasions. So had everyone else. They were interchangeable, but I had wondered if my tennis friend Miki might be invited. He had taken me several times to the Japanese Club to play, and since I couldn't ask him back to the Cricket Club I was beginning to feel a little embarrassed. I waited until an evening when Grandpa Jack was not present, and broached the subject. However, Papa Jack shook his head decisively.

'Oh no, Johnnie – not a Japanese.'

'He *did* put us in touch with Bonnard, the Swiss – and we made a tidy profit on the deal.'

'I know we did,' my father agreed. 'But we can't have any Japanese if we invite the Soongs – as we must – and other Chinese guests. Feelings are running very high between the two countries. You've only got to read the *Straits Times*.' He didn't need to say any more, for the newspapers had been full of Japanese activity in Manchuria.

'There's going to be a lot of trouble on the Chinese mainland.'

I had half expected as much, but I must have looked disappointed, for Papa Jack added, 'Nothing personal, it's just that –' he shrugged his shoulders, 'Singapore's a very touchy place these days.'

'Is there anybody else you want?' Mama asked.

Before I could say anything Natasha interrupted, 'Why don't you ask Bertrand? He's back, isn't he – without a wife?'

'Yes, he is.' I had only seen Bonnard a couple of times, but couldn't help adding nastily, 'He's a proud father now.'

'What difference does that make?' asked Natasha.

'He seemed very pleasant when he used to come here,' said Mama, adding practically, 'and extra men are always welcome at a dance.'

'He's all right,' agreed Papa Jack. 'Got a good head on his shoulders. Ask him.'

I cornered Natasha later. 'It's your *engagement* ball,' I said. 'You can't ask Bertrand.'

'Why not? What's wrong? We've been dancing a bit, but Tony knows. There was nothing underhand –'

'Sure?'

'Don't be stupid. And anyway, Father's asked him – or he's going to.'

'I still think it's wrong.'

'Don't be so stuffy.' And then suddenly I saw the beginning of a tear in the corner of her eye.

'I know I'm silly,' she dabbed with a handkerchief. 'We had a bit of a walk-out. It's all over, I'm getting married, but I'd like to see him, just in a crowd.'

'You swear there was nothing between you. Except –' with a grin 'a – Johnnie's special.'

'You and your specials! It was just a feeling,' and then she added, 'how would *you* like it, Johnnie, if Julie wasn't invited to the ball?'

I felt suddenly guilty and ashamed.

'Sorry, Natflat, I didn't understand,' and I really did feel sorry for her, sorry I had been so stupid, sorry I hadn't realised that marriage and love aren't necessarily synonymous, that she might love Tony in the accepted wifely term of the word but that she was deliberately deciding on a course of action, skilfully aided and abetted by our parents with what they considered to be a move in her best interests. And I felt guilty too at the thought of Julie. Who was I to lecture a sister four years older than me when I had been desiring one girl for months and sleeping with another girl whose engagement was about to be announced? 'Forgive me,' I said again, too young to realise that there is no easier way of minimising guilt than by apology.

As the first guests' cars appeared in the drive, which was ablaze with flaming, gusting torches, Grandpa Jack took up his position in the ballroom to greet them. I often wondered what newcomers thought as they approached this ancient living legend for the first time; people like Bertrand Bonnard, sophisticated world travellers, who were expected to make a modern kow-tow to Grandpa Jack, sitting on his 'throne' and proudly surveying 'his' room; I stood with him, as I so often did, for the first half hour because I knew that he felt (rightly or wrongly) that in me he could see a reflection of his own youth, which had been a tough, bawdy, no-holds-barred struggle, trampling on anyone who stood in his way; an image far removed from my own life. No, perhaps it was not that, not quite. He had in me someone to whom he could unburden the past which, as he touched the edge of senility, seemed to consist more and more of an unending series of sexual adventures. He came to me because he was a little afraid of Papa Jack. Papa was no prude, but Grandpa could never unbend with him. Nor had he ever been able to confide in Tim before he left Singapore, for he despised Tim, and had always regarded him as prissy. 'Looks as though he lives on skimmed milk,' he growled to me once. With age Grandpa's voice had deepened into a threatening growl and this, together with the heavy black horn-rimmed glasses which he used for reading, and his habit of banging his stick, holding it by the knob, gave newcomers an impression of ferocity – which he loved.

'A high-stepping floosie, this girl who's going to marry Ian Scott,' he gave what I imagine he thought a leer. 'Good catch for her – but he must be daft, for she's as young as his own son.'

He was silent for a moment, and I could see that he was trying to work something out. Finally he asked with a chuckle, 'Is it illegal for a man's son to go to bed with his stepmother?'

When I pretended to be shocked, he chuckled again, 'Care to bet? Ten dollars Singapore? Propinquity, my lad, propinquity.'

He rolled the word round his tongue, 'Propinquity – that's what leads to the horizontal position.'

Grandpa looked round approvingly. He loved the huge, vulgar ballroom, never more than when it was filled up, as now, with women in long dresses and men in white bum-freezers or sharkskin dinner jackets, sipping champagne or whisky, lolling against the Italian-style gilded tables which in truth clashed horribly with French furniture quite out of place in Tanamera, yet all the rage when Grandpa built the house. Mama had tried in vain to modernise the ballroom, but this was Grandpa's territory and he was obdurate. And in a way it didn't matter. Years of living there had dulled us to its tastelessness, and it was hidden from us too by the love we all had for Tanamera, for the good times we had had there. Though this was not a lived-in room, it had been the scene of magnificent celebrations – birthdays, engagements, weddings, any excuse for a party. Once again, watching the band arrive, I wondered what guests like Bonnard made of it, the ornate staircase parting in the middle, the high ceiling beamed and white, the two incongruous chandeliers hanging between the fans, the walls draped with any old pictures that unscrupulous dealers had been able to foist on Grandpa Jack when he built the house and which, with the passing years, he had come to believe were family heirlooms.

(I once saw him buttonhole his favourite kind of prey, a visitor passing through Singapore, and point out to him three large portraits of three demure girls which had been hanging there as long as I can remember, each in an old gilded oval frame. As the visitor politely admired them, Grandpa Jack confided, with the complete conviction that he was telling the truth, 'My three beautiful daughters born

85

out of wedlock.' Adding defiantly, 'But I always looked after 'em, y'know, even after I married them off!')

I saw Paul Soong in a corner and beckoned to him. As usual he was immaculately dressed; a beautifully cut shark-skin jacket draped his slim, tall figure. At twenty-one he was far more sophisticated than me, so that at times I was touched with a shaft of envy, perhaps because he was also good-looking. With his mixed blood he looked like an Italian, an effect heightened by his languid manner and the slow, easy, educated mid-Atlantic drawl picked up at school in San Francisco, or during holidays at Carmel or Yosemite. His slow smile helped, always half mocking, as though life was too big a joke to be taken seriously.

Paul could do little wrong in my eyes, but the man he brought along with him was a horror – the only word to describe Soong Kai-shek, the 'cousin' who had come from mainland China to live with the Soongs a year ago.

As a member of the family he was automatically invited to all parties which the Soongs attended. Fortunately he didn't often accept.

Kai-shek, who preferred the correct Chinese procedure of placing the family name first, was in his late twenties, dark and wiry, his face so thin that the taut skin seemed to have been stretched in order to reach across the high cheek-bones; and this produced the illusion of deep, sunken, staring eyes. I had disliked him not only on sight, but because he made no secret of his hatred for the British. And though I was reasonably polite, I made my feelings obvious. I had noticed too that now and again when I was talking to Julie at parties he was watching us, face glowering.

Bonnard had joined us as we stood near Grandpa Jack, who was sitting comfortably on his throne. Grandpa Jack took a swig of barley water and asked Kai-shek, 'What's the latest news of the Japanese?'

There had been more rumours of sporadic fighting in Manchuria.

'Bad,' replied Kai-shek shortly. 'They are the enemies of China. They always have been. They always will be until they are destroyed.'

86

'Tall order, m'boy,' Grandpa Jack chuckled.

'Do you think so, Monsieur Bonnard?' Kai-shek turned to Bertrand.

'We neutral Swiss –'

Bertrand tried to laugh off the question – unfortunately for him. For like a flash Kai-shek almost snarled, 'Not neutral enough to send the Japanese heavy machinery – with the help of a British firm.' He glared at me now.

Paul tried to interrupt, but Bonnard was far too clever to get angry, and was more than a match for Kai-shek.

'They were for Red Cross work in case of earthquakes – and earthquakes, I think, are neutral,' he said. 'China also has natural catastrophes – floods and famines – only you don't seem to bother about people who suffer.'

'We are too big. China cannot –'

'I understand, of course,' said Bonnard. 'But the next time the Yellow River overflows and a million peasants face starvation, do get in touch with me. I'm sure the Swiss can arrange excellent credit facilities. Only if nobody *bothers* – if nobody *asks*, how can we know?' He gave a slight, almost French inclination of the head towards Grandpa Jack.

'One in the eye for you, young Soong,' Grandpa Jack slapped a thigh in sheer delight. But Kai-shek, eyes black with anger, had already turned away.

'He's a little aggressive,' murmured Bonnard.

'He's going to ruin our family,' said Paul, 'and I don't mind who hears me say so.' And as Bonnard moved away to talk to Natasha, who had waved to him, Paul said to me, 'I wish he had never come to Singapore. He spies – I'm sure he does. He's quietly worming his way into my father's confidence and will end up by ruining him.'

'I don't think your father's that dumb,' I said, and anxious to change the conversation, asked, 'Where's Aunt Sonia? And Julie?'

'Mother's on her way to America,' he said shortly. 'She left in rather a rush.' His voice – specially for one so gentle-mannered and polite as Paul – was abrupt. It didn't invite further questions.

'That's terrible. We always rely on her to make our

parties go. It's not the same without her.' And I couldn't refrain from asking, 'Nothing the matter, is there?'

Paul himself had told me about the rows. He must have known that the situation in the Soong house was common gossip, but it is impossible to tell what the Chinese are thinking. Ask a European an embarrassing question and if he doesn't want to reply he will produce an evasive answer. The Chinese have a disconcerting habit of simply ignoring such questions.

'Julie's somewhere around – she's worried about your tennis. Or' – with a sardonic grin – 'your pseudo-tennis.'

'Where is she?' I asked. 'I'll have to do *something* about Thursdays. But I'm scared of your father.'

'Don't wonder! Here's Dad now. With Julie.'

I looked towards the entrance, where she stood with her father. To me it was a very simple scene. When the double doors opened the most beautiful girl in the world looked at me and smiled. I walked up to her, paid my respects to P.P., as everyone called Soong, and asked her to dance.

She was wearing a low-backed white dress, very simple, with a thin gold belt and gold sandals, and a strip of gold holding her hair away from her eyes, so that it fell back over her neck. As we started dancing, I said, 'I'm sorry about the tennis. But we've got to be careful. Paul told you we'd been spotted at Raffles?'

It may seem stupid for me to have been so worried. After all I was twenty-one now, I had done nothing wrong. But even though there would have been an appalling row in *my* family if my parents thought I was getting mixed up with Julie, that didn't frighten me. Well, not much.

What really scared me was the certain knowledge that if P.P. Soong suspected he would never let me see Julie again. Julie would be put on the next boat sailing to God knows where. And that prospect terrified me – because there would be no way I could fight back.

There were no exceptions to the rigid set of rules that separated the different races. We could be friends with families like the Soongs, yes; and for that matter they could be our friends too, for the colour bar wasn't entirely one-sided; the Chinese didn't like to become too close to the white men. There was nothing wrong in Paul Soong and me being close friends. It was equally proper that I should have regarded Li's son as my closest playmate when I was very young; to have a son of your number one boy as a 'baby friend' was a good example of British democracy in action, and to Papa Jack men like Li were members of the family. But girls were different. 'If you want to split the black oak,' as Grandpa Jack put it graphically, 'then you'll find it's great – down Macpherson Road or among the taxi dancers at the Great World.'

Mixed marriages were out – there were no exceptions, no alibis, no discussions. It made no difference if you fell in love with the daughter of a Chinese or Eurasian millionaire – the girls we met and greeted politely at our mixed parties, in their houses or ours, were not available, and never could be. A liaison with one of them not only spelt social ruin for either the girl or boy (for what that stigma was worth); it was unfair to the girl because nothing could ever come of it, even if she had a child, for then her father would kick her out. Girls didn't do that sort of thing before marriage – not well brought up Chinese girls, anyway. 'The richer the girl, the poorer the bastard,' was another of Grandpa Jack's maxims, to which he added, 'when Kipling wrote that stuff about east and west and never the twain shall meet, he didn't mean they shouldn't *meet*. What he did mean was that they should never meet at the altar.'

Of course, looking back to the pre-war days, from the vantage point of a *tuan bezar* in a multiracial state, I some-times feel a sense of real shame at the way we all behaved, even *thought*. How absurd they were, the shibboleths, the snobbery, the spurious dignity that divided the British and other 'Europeans' from the people whose country this really was.

Papa was always telling us how wonderful the 'natives' were, but his was a lone voice. We were all guilty, I suppose. The code of conduct had been devised when the British had first opened up India. It had never been revised. The world was changing, *had* changed, but not the attitudes of white men to those whose skins were darker. In fact, the more the world *did* change the more apprehensive the white colonial governors became, and so they fought harder than ever to divide and rule.

Many of us did stupid things, for it was bred into the system; and though Paul and I were unknowingly proving the system wasn't necessary the rules cut too deeply into our lives for anyone else to notice.

The room was already crowded as we started to dance. Bonnard was squiring Mama, who looked beautiful and relaxed. She was obviously delighted with the attentions of this charming foreigner. As they sidled past us, Bonnard said to me, making sure Mama could hear, '*Elle est ravissante, votre Mama!*' Natasha and Tony bumped into us and her comment was more down to earth, a cheerful sisterly, 'Mind those big feet of yours!'

Yet though I grinned and smiled dutifully at each face, and bowed slightly when I saw P.P. talking to old Scott, I hardly noticed anybody, for I had been seized with a kind of rage at the way life was treating Julie and me. I was thinking, not for the first time, how stupid it was that Julie and I couldn't kiss, make love, announce *our* engagement. Often, at times like this, my mind raced with wild ideas. What *would* happen if we ran away? Why shouldn't we bolt? What right had parents – yellow or white or any damn colour – to tell us how to live our lives?

With mounting anger I held her tight and close to me – that was one advantage of a slow foxtrot – and I could feel myself pushing her hard – until *she* could feel it. I knew because she squeezed my hand and then arched her back slightly, as though to encourage me. She whispered, 'I love you to do that, Johnnie. Nobody can see.'

'I'm going to blow up,' I groaned and turned, smiling, 'Lovely to see you, Mrs Dickinson,' before whispering again, 'If only we could go somewhere. Would you?'

'Yes. Anywhere.'

'You have to be sure, Julie,' I smiled at Mama floating past, until I remembered her warning that anyone – and I'm sure she meant me – leading Julie on would 'ruin her life'. I stubbed Julie's toe as I missed a step and said, 'It's a terrible thing I'm asking you. It's wicked of me.'

'It isn't. I don't care. I'm old enough – and I love you.' It was her turn to smile at someone dancing past before she almost hissed, 'But this way – you're being cruel. We're torturing each other.'

At that moment Papa Jack banged on the big dinner gong at the foot of the stairs and everyone stopped dancing as the band drummed a chord. The chattering ceased abruptly, as though a radio had been turned off. Only the boys slid between people, white ghosts balancing trays loaded with champagne, sometimes above their heads. Even Grandpa Jack was silent, for he always had a sense of occasion.

Though my father was splendidly attired in a new white dinner jacket I thought he looked a little tired. Perhaps it was only age. His face was beginning to sag a little, the jowls were filling out. But he still had a mind that was razor-sharp, combined with an agreeable old-fashioned attitude – not an aggressive one like Grandpa Jack's, but a pleasant one. You could sum it up by the way he always agreed that the new horn-rimmed spectacles were undoubtedly an excellent innovation, but it made no difference to him; he would still wear his rimless glasses, balancing them on his nose. And each morning he still looked at the heels of his shoes before inspecting the toecaps to make sure the back as well as the front had been properly shined.

The evening was of course in honour of the two engaged couples, yet in a way it was Papa Jack's evening too, because though he would never have *forced* Natasha to marry Tony Scott he had thrown his weight behind the idea, and I knew he was delighted it had turned out as it had. I had no doubt that this was one of the main reasons why we were also celebrating the engagement of Ian Scott and Vicki. Scott handled a great deal of rubber, as managing director of Consolidated Latex. He and Papa Jack often worked together, and by bringing young Tony into the family, strong bonds were inevitably forged, commercial knots quietly tied. Papa always had an eye for business. He made a speech, brief, a few anecdotes, just enough to raise dutiful chuckles.

Natasha and Tony walked to the second step of the staircase from where they could look down on us as we raised our glasses. They kissed, and I must say looked very handsome. Mama kissed her son-in-law-to-be. Papa Jack adjusted his rimless glasses and started again, 'And now, like son, like father!' Then up came Vicki, looking much more demure than I had usually seen her, and Ian, proud, the beginnings of a middle-aged spread, the satisfied look of a widower who had made a good bargain – as he had.

I can't remember what Papa said, there was such a crush of people, all facing the same way, but suddenly as we stood there, without knowing what was happening, I felt Julie's hand in mine, and without looking at her I whispered, 'If only it was us!'

'So three cheers for the brides to be,' cried my father. 'Supper is now being served in the garden.'

Outside, with the torches blazing and gusting all the way along the drive, the thick, springy lallang was dotted with tables and chairs. No one was ever asked to stand up and balance plates and glasses at a Tanamera buffet. ('God preserve the world from fork suppers,' Grandpa Jack had once growled.) Each table had an electric lamp, each hot bulb buzzed with moths. Christmas-tree fairylights were looped between the tables; new tree lights, specially ordered from England by Papa the previous year, lit the trees from underneath and behind, soaring up in hidden beams of light, searching out and resting on the clumps of fat leaves or feathery fronds. White-clad boys waited to serve turkeys, saddle of mutton, ribs of beef, a dozen salads. There were fillets of *ikan meru* on chafing dishes, and plates of Johore crabs for those industrious enough to tangle with the messy but tasty shellfish caught just beyond the causeway.

Nearby, cooks behind a dozen braziers prepared *satay* – chicken or beef or pork threaded on thin ribs of wood, cooked swiftly on charcoal, and then dipped and twisted round in a thick, dripping, khaki-coloured sauce before the perilous journey (specially for those with white dresses) from dip to lip.

Half a dozen other young people had joined us for supper, including Tony and Natasha, her new ring sparkling on her finger, and Bertrand. A waiter offered us plates and as Julie took hers I led her to one of the long tables laden with food and then, away from the others, I gasped, 'I can't eat. I must see you alone. Follow me.'

'Of course,' was all she said.

My heart was pounding. 'Put a bit of stuff on your plate.' I held mine out to a waiter. 'Nobody'll miss us during supper. We've half an hour. You drift away to the summer house.' I had no need to tell her where it was: we had played in the summer house by the tennis court dozens of times. 'I'll watch – if nobody sees you go, I'll follow.'

She nodded.

'Darling Julie, you are sure?' I asked. 'You know what it means?'

She said nothing, just touched her lips with a finger and left. A minute later, sure I had not been seen, I slipped into the darkness beyond the trees and ran towards the summer house, reaching it just as she did, and then I was kissing her and running my hands through her hair, stroking her, squeezing her against me so that I could feel her breasts yield, as I led her inside.

There was no door to the big open verandah, while inside was a divan and some long chairs.

'Here, darling,' I whispered above the sound of crickets and bullfrogs. We undressed, I don't know how, everything pulled off in a rush, and yet we had to be careful: we had to return to the dance. Suddenly she was naked and so was I.

'It's going to be over so quickly,' I said. 'Come into the garden first. I just want to look at you in the moonlight – for the first time.'

She stood there, so did I, almost embarrassed by my size; I could feel myself throbbing as I looked at her, stroked her long legs and then the beautiful silky secret hair, damp with excitement. I touched her there, just touched her with my left hand as I kissed her – this time with my chest held hard against her – and she trembled as I touched her again, trembled as I carried her inside and laid her on the bed. I felt as though I had waited for this moment all my life.

There was no need for any guidance, for any help. I just lay on her in the warm starry night, heads buried in kisses, hardly noticing her gasping and then, almost without moving, it was all over, a beautiful agony, the climax of months of longing.

For a few moments she lay nestling in the crook of my shoulder, black hair all over my face, toes touching mine, pressing against them. I knew I had not satisfied her, could feel her still straining against me.

'This next time is yours,' I whispered, and touched her between her legs until, as she started moving, I took my hand away. 'Don't!' she cried. 'Don't leave me!' I fumbled with her right hand and guided it to where my hand had been. I had the feeling that she might be ashamed or morti-fied if she did anything in front of me that worried her, but on this first night I was telling her without a word not to be bashful – that she had the same rights to ecstasy as I.

I had no idea how long we had been there before I heard the sound of music, bursts of laughter in the distance. I recognised 'Love in Bloom', the hit of the moment in Singapore. Supper must have ended, the dancing had started. 'Darling Julie, we must go. But I promise you – I'll find somewhere we can be alone together.' As we fumbled to find our clothes, I said awkwardly, 'I've never said this before, Julie but – I love you. Don't ever think – you know, this was just –'

'I'll never love anyone else but you,' she said, and kissed me again.

'Two minutes then we *must* go. My God!' The tension had been released. I could almost laugh. 'If they only knew what we're doing – what they've been missing!'

She was struggling to fasten her bra and as I helped her I had a sudden thought. 'You're not afraid? Nothing's going to happen?'

'Don't worry,' she reassured me. 'I've started doing two mornings a week voluntary work at the Alexandra Hospital. I knew – I hoped – this was going to happen some day — I dreamed about it — so I got —' a little shyly — 'well, some advice from one of the older nurses. I didn't want to spoil anything by being scared.'

She was fumbling in her bag, searching for a comb for her hair when I suddenly realised that something was wrong — nothing to do with us, but something dreadful.

'Listen.' I held her hand.

'I can't hear anything.'

'Neither can I. Something's happened.'

Every fragment of noise had ceased. The background talk, the music, the clink of glasses, the shouts of 'Boy!' — suddenly everything was stilled. One minute I could hear the beat of the drum, like the heartbeat of the party, voices outside, the faint notes of the tune; the next was frozen into the kind of trembling, death-like silence that heralds an earthquake.

And then, as I strained to hear, holding her, the silence was split by a terrible shriek, a wind of shouting without laughter, a kind of wail. I ran to the verandah and peered out. Under the floodlight of some illuminated trees one boy, balancing a pile of plates, came into my sight. He dropped the load. Just dropped them, let them fall and put his hands to his head and let out a cry of grief.

'My God, something terrible's happened.' All the beauty and passion slid away and I could sense Julie's fear. 'Go back the way you came.' I rushed out, leaving her, tumbling on to the lallang, mopping the sweat from my face. My hand-kerchief was a rag. As I ran past the west verandah, trying to straighten my bow tie, to straighten the creases on my thin white jacket, one of the boys tried to stop me, crying, '*Tuan* — sir!' I brushed him aside.

The moment I walked into the great ballroom, in that first split second, I was suddenly whisked back to the time when as a schoolboy my father had taken us to London for a family holiday, and we had visited Madame Tussaud's wax-works. The huge, foolish chandeliers blazed down on what looked like a tableau of dummies, frozen into silence and — so it seemed — stillness. Natasha sat on the bottom step of the wide staircase, dabbing her face. I caught hazy glimpses of faces I knew – Vicki with Scott; P.P. Soong, hands clasped, head bowed, a grey Chinese celadon statue. At the far end of the long room, hushed and hot despite the fans, the once-mighty body of Grandpa Jack sprawled like a sack on the floor near his throne of a chair. Two boys were sweeping broken glass away – Grandpa must have knocked over his barley water as he fell. My father and two other men were grouped round the body, trying to open the collar, take off the tie.

'Is he dead?' someone whispered.

'No, it's a stroke,' said someone else. Grandpa Jack's head was lolling to one side, with what looked like a foolish, lop-sided grin. His eyes were open, staring. As I reached his ridiculous high chair I realised he did not seem to be breathing. But what terrified me more was that his face – the stern outline replaced by the foolish grin, like a pumpkin on Hallowe'en – was the colour of beetroot. Perhaps he had bruised it in falling.

'Undo the studs!' someone – perhaps my father – said.

The stillness – the effect of a tableau – lasted only seconds, replaced as I pushed towards the chair by whispers – almost guilty whispers, as though people knew that illness demanded silence as a mark of respect, yet the healthy demanded noise if decisions were to be made. I heard someone mutter, 'I think we ought to be going home.' But no one seemed to move.

Mama crossed the room towards the band. The guests fell back, opening up a corridor with a kind of deference that greets royalty at a garden party; as though a crisis had suddenly elevated Mama's right to respect – or perhaps it was instinctive embarrassment. As I reached her she squeezed my hand and whispered, 'Go and help your father, darling.' The musicians started to pack their saxophones and trumpets.

Ian Scott and my father were struggling to lift Grandpa Jack. Two boys held his feet off the platform at the bottom of his chair.

'Let me help.' I pushed one of the boys aside. I could think of nothing else to say as I looked at my father's face, strained and tearless.

'I looked for you, where were you? Here, hold up this shoulder,' was all he said as we tried to lift Grandpa Jack.

'I was in the garden.'

Vicki was standing near Ian. She gave me the kind of conspiratorial look that only ex-lovers can exchange, saying without words, 'I know what you were up to out there.'

Dr Sampson, who had been invited as a guest – after all, he had brought Natasha into the world – had sent two boys to bring an old door to use as a stretcher. Somehow we managed to get the huge bulk of Grandpa Jack on to it, and we carried him through the double latticed doors by the side of the stairs.

'How bad is it?' I asked the doctor. He shook his head and said, 'Pretty bad. I've given him an injection but now –' he stopped, as if to say that we must wait and see – and not hope too much. But then he added, 'You never know. He's as tough as old boots. There's always a chance, even at that age.'

My father behaved as though Grandpa Jack was already dead, and in a sense all the life had been wrenched out of the old man in that flash of a sudden disabling twist or rupture of some hair-thin nerve end, or whatever it was that led to the brain. I didn't feel any real shock. Unable to take it in, I suppose; or perhaps a little overwhelmed by the sense of drama, the people around me.

'Sampson says he's still breathing.' My father was panting from the exertion of laying the makeshift stretcher on Grandpa's bed. 'I've arranged with the hospital to send round an ambulance to take him to the General. What do you think, Doctor?'

'I'll stay here until it comes,' said Sampson. 'He's in a coma now. We have to wait and see.'

It was awful, that night. Some illnesses, however grave, can be taken more easily than others. Broken limbs, burns, accidents, they are all illnesses capable of being healed; but a stroke – it has a sinister connotation, it lends itself to images of men lingering on for years, more dead than alive, unable to do anything except stare, and I could sense this thought in the minds of some of the guests, who stood around in small knots, the men looking longingly into empty glasses, but afraid to ask for a drink in case they were thought lacking in respect.

'Don't give up hope.' Paul was the first to comfort me. 'He'll pull through, you wait and see.'

Mr Soong and Julie were with Paul. I didn't dare look at her, to meet her eyes. To be in the act of making love at the very moment when someone nearby was writhing in a stroke seemed somehow terribly wrong – though it wasn't, of course, but I kept on having those odd thoughts. P.P. put a hand on my shoulder and said, 'In China we have a saying that it takes three deaths to kill a man of iron. And he is a man of iron, Grandpa Jack.' Julie still didn't look at me.

My father crossed the room and started whispering earnestly to Mama. Another unworthy thought crept into my mind. Looking at him, I wondered if worry for the guests – what to do with them – had crowded out grief, or even if in his heart my father might not be relieved if Grandpa Jack died quickly and peacefully instead of lingering on, an embarrassment to everyone. I tried to banish the thought, but I couldn't; it persisted, in the way that sometimes in church, as the parson droned on, I would mentally undress the woman in the next pew, and ashamed of such 'blasphemy' would try to erase the picture, but couldn't.

At that moment Papa Jack banged the gong and stood at the foot of the stairs, arm upraised for silence.

'My friends,' he said in a steady voice, 'as you know Grandpa Jack has suffered a stroke. We can only hope and pray. I know how you all feel, and want to say how sorry I am that this party for Natasha and Vicki has been spoiled – but,' he braced himself, 'of one thing I am certain. Friends who love Grandpa Jack know he would be horrified if his son didn't behave in the tradition of Tanamera and offer you some refreshment while you wait for your cars. Boys! Champagne and stengahs!'

A collective sigh of relief flooded the room. Perhaps there

was no more noise really, just the rustle and movement of long dresses, as Papa Jack stepped down. But the tension snapped, and, as though by pre-arrangement, a swarm of boys brought in trays of drinks. More than one man downed his first stengah in a couple of gulps and reached for a second glass before the boy moved to the next group.

Mama caught hold of my arm. 'Tell everyone there's a bar on the verandah,' she whispered. 'Poor Grandpa Jack. It's so awful, Johnnie. Still, I think some men might like to help themselves to an extra drink or two.'

'Are you all right?' I was whispering like everyone else.

'It happened so quickly.'

There was nothing to do but wait for the cars to arrive, but then at midnight, when the guests had thinned out, the night was split by the rat-a-tat of sudden explosions at the edge of the jungle fringe. I grabbed Mama as her hand flew to her mouth.

The noise stopped, to be replaced by a sudden swooshing sound. Everyone rushed outside – just in time to see the night filled with a cascade of multi-coloured stars, the swish of rockets bursting far up and ahead – green, blue, scarlet, white – hanging like flowers in the sky, hanging, suddenly vanishing, to be replaced with others. Everyone had forgotten the fireworks which had been timed to start at midnight near the jungle trees by the boys who had been camping out there. They doubtless had no idea of what had happened.

I thought of running across the lallang, almost started to go. Paul stopped me. 'You'll never get there in time.' And in a way it didn't matter as more rockets swished and swooshed into the sky, filling it, competing, however briefly, with the Milky Way.

'When Grandpa Jack learns about this,' Paul tried to cheer me up, 'he'll think it's the greatest lark of his life.'

If. There didn't seem much 'if' left.

5

For nearly three weeks Grandpa Jack lay in a coma, his body
stiff as a board. Eyes closed, he breathed heavily but without movement, immune to every sense of touch. When I
visited him in hospital the day nurse would chat him up
with the irritating kind of baby talk they so often use,
'Come along, now. Be a good patient and move those
twinkle toes.' She would tickle the soles of his feet, hoping
for a twitch of life, but none came.

Worst of all was the colour of his mask-like face. It was
blood-red all over, but with a strange translucence to the
skin, like a great bloated bladder. At home in Tanamera the
servants moved as if on silent oiled wheels, even though
Grandpa Jack was miles away. They talked in whispers, as if
afraid to waken him.

There was little I could do, except make regular visits and
appear a dutiful and suitably anxious grandson. I tried to
sympathise with my father, but he didn't really want to be
embarrassed and put a hand on my shoulder with a smile of
thanks. And I noticed that when a letter arrived from Tim in
England, in answer to Papa's telegram, my father read it,
handed it over to Mama at the breakfast table, and thought
no more of it, almost as though he had decided to put
Grandpa Jack's illness out of his mind (or was it Tim he
wanted to forget?). My father was shocked of course, but as
Paul said, not unkindly, 'The old man has had a super life
and your father must know that.'

My father's worry couldn't compare, for example, with
the anguish of someone we knew whose son had lost a leg to
a shark when swimming for a dare outside the protective
nets that we always erected in water off the beach to stop big

fish coming in close. When sometimes I wondered if inconvenience wasn't as much a problem as any deeper emotions Mama was practical. 'Go and play more tennis,' she insisted. 'There's nothing *anyone* can do. Anyway, I'm going to a ladies' patchwork lunch today.'

Papa Jack and I went to the office, though one of us always kept near a telephone. Ball, the head clerk (dignified with the title of assistant manager), at first proffered fussy condolences, even more confidential after one of his whisky lunches, but my father cut him short, saying sharply, 'Don't be so morbid, Ball. My father isn't dead yet.'

He wasn't. But all the same, the *Straits Times* telephoned Tanamera at ten o'clock each evening, not necessarily to print anything, but to make sure they would be in a position to announce the funeral arrangements the following morning, in order to give friends of the family the only notice they were likely to receive of when to pay their last respects. In Singapore, when someone you knew was critically ill, people turned to the obituary columns, with their details of funeral arrangements, before they looked at the weather forecast. The weather never changed anyway.

Those twenty days were hell. Poor Grandpa Jack was, I hoped, better off than we were, with no knowledge of what it was like waiting to die. At times his face, very thin now, looked almost beatific, for the lopsided mouth had straightened itself out.

It was a moody time, and for me made worse by my inability to see Julie. I had never before been involved in this kind of lingering limbo, in which every attempt by the family to act normally seemed a vague affront to the patient. It wasn't of course, but it was hard to ignore instinct.

Natasha made herself scarce. She could escape to the friendly territory of the Scotts' bungalow in Tanglin. And perhaps my mother and father could escape into their joined lives. They had each other, not only to provide consolation, but to voice thoughts they didn't want to utter before me. But I had none of this. I couldn't have gone to see Vicki, even had I wanted to – and I certainly didn't – and I couldn't at first see Julie, the only single person I wanted to see after what had happened. We had spent in each other's arms the most important moments in our young lives – and now I couldn't even find a *reason* to call on Soong. I was torn and desperate until finally I told Paul I had to see her. I didn't say what had happened between us at the Tanamera ball, but I didn't care what he might suspect from the urgency in my voice. He nodded, smiled, and the next day Julie and I met in the tatty tennis pavilion of the YMCA.

There was nothing we could do that first time except plan to meet again and kiss, pressing each other in the dim narrow corridor leading to the dressing rooms. Before she arrived I was tortured by the thought that as I hadn't seen her for a week she might believe I didn't want her any more. But one look, the light in her eyes as she rushed to meet me, and I knew nothing had changed, that nothing ever would. And though I had done nothing to make it possible for us to meet, Julie had. I was astounded when she told me that her father had agreed to let her do one evening shift – from six to nine-thirty a week – at the Alexandra Hospital, where she had now become a qualified volunteer, in order to learn the procedures used by the sisters when starting night duties. It showed a new dimension to Julie's character, a determination to get what she wanted.

'I love you, Johnnie,' she said. 'I've loved you since we were children together. I'll do anything in the world I can to be with you. Until the dance at Tanamera, I couldn't tell you. I didn't dare. I knew that you – well, you fancied me. But I honestly thought that as I was Chinese – well, we both know the rules.'

'Damn the rules,' I said.

'You can't. Only secretly.' And then she said what I had so often thought. 'If Daddy ever finds out he'll pack me off to America on the next boat. So, darling Johnnie, my first boyfriend, do be careful.'

I was still staggered by her skill in manoeuvre; she told me how she had become friendly with one of the sisters, and hinted to her that she had a boyfriend. The sister had told her to volunteer for the night shift.

'That way I knew I could see you once a week.'

'But your father?'

'The sister is a sweetie – and *she's* got a boyfriend, so she's sympathetic. She came round to our house and told Daddy that China might soon be at war with Japan and every Chinese girl ought to learn to be useful and – oh, she went on for hours. Daddy agreed so long as Paul fetched me every Thursday, and you know Paul – he's always ready to help.' And then, with the half-secret smile I was beginning to know well, she added, 'The sister's a real chum. She knows I'll not be there.'

As the YMCA groundsmen prepared to close down – warning us with hostile stares and glances at wristwatches – she said simply, 'Perhaps it's just love for you, Johnnie – perhaps it's because it was the first time – but I can hardly wait for Thursday. You'll be able to find a place, won't you?' It was more than a question, it was a plea from the heart.

But – where? I had two days in which to find somewhere. I knew that neither of us would settle for snatched moments in the back of a car, yet where could we go? I had the money to book a room in a seedy hotel, but I didn't dare to, for in Singapore every shuttered window had a pair of peering eyes behind it, every street corner was peopled with shuffling or slinking figures. The Dexters were household names, and no plant needed as much water as the Chinese grapevine needed gossip. It was like one of those flowers that open up, catch insects, then devour them. Someone always knew a face in the dark; someone always knew the number of a car. Even if I booked a room in secret, every hotel, every boarding house, had its boys who never seemed to sleep, so that the moment you arrived, even in the dead of night, they cheerfully switched on fans, turned down beds, checked on bathroom towels – and took a good look at your face. Sooner or later the Chinese grapevine would whisper to your boy or amah or syce, to your best friend or worst enemy.

I racked my brains to make plans. I even toyed with the idea of asking Vicki if I could borrow her flat – but the thought of making love to Julie on Vicki's bed, going to

Vicki's bathroom afterwards, with Vicki's Chinese kimono hanging on the door – no, I couldn't do that.

Finally, I did the only thing possible. I had never done it before, but there was only one place to go – the office. I picked Julie up at the Alexandra at six o'clock after Paul had dropped her, then drove her to Robinson Road. Dexter and Company always closed sharp at five, but I made sure, by casual enquiry, that Ball and Rawlings would not by some mischance be working late – though I knew they never did, because of the time difference with London. The only problem was the Sikh jagger, planted firmly all night on his trestle bed astride the front entrance by the foot of the stone steps.

With the jagger I had to brazen it out. His main duty was to guard the godowns on the ground floor, which at times were crammed with goods in transit that did not belong to us; but in fact he couldn't have stopped a petty thief. He was a 'sign', visible evidence, which any insurance company demanded for the all-in policy which covered temporary cargos in the godowns. He was only there courtesy of tradition. He would hardly realise (or care) if I arrived after normal office hours and muttered something about having to work late with my secretary. He certainly could not have the faintest idea of Julie's identity. For that matter he didn't know one secretary from another, for he only appeared in the upstairs office each Friday to collect his wages from Ball.

So to hell with it! Even if he *were* suspicious he could only imagine I had picked up a girl, and if the young *tuan* wanted to indulge himself it was none of his business. As I thought of all the possibilities of discovery I knew that he could never whisper the name Soong in his wildest gossip; so even if my father did hear any whispers, if he did confront me, I could brazen it out, and the most he could do was to be angry because I had involved the staff in tittle-tattle.

All my fears were unfounded. The jagger hardly noticed Julie as he saluted. I unlocked the front door, switched on the lights, led the way up the stairs, pushed open the door to my small office and the next moment we were in each other's arms.

★

On the twentieth day after the party — it was a Tuesday — I went straight to the hospital after tennis at the Cricket Club for what had now become a duty without hope; my regular visit to Grandpa Jack. He lay motionless, the top of a sarcophagus. As though waiting for a signal, the nurse greeted my arrival with her usual baby talk, and began to tickle his foot.

As I shouted — the sound came out of my throat before I could control it — the nurse dropped the sheet, eyes staring, mouth dropping open — I yelled, 'He moved! I saw his foot move!'

The nurse was intelligent. As her hand grabbed his pulse, she shouted to the sister to phone Dr Sampson. For a moment I looked at the thin, tired face above a beard no longer full and rich but like the rag-tag ends of a fly whisk. As though Grandpa Jack had heard my first cry — though this was obviously an illusion — two bleary, watery eyes opened for a split second, looked at me before the heavy eyelids fell back like one of those built-in covers that roll over to keep a dish warm.

I dashed to the waiting room to phone Papa Jack, shouting, 'He's alive! He's alive!' Nurses came running — I hadn't seen any of them actually run before, and soon my father swept into the bedroom.

It was a miracle. Within a week dear old Grandpa Jack was opening his eyes for a few seconds two or three times a day. Within two weeks a few slurred words were dribbling out of his mouth, unintelligible, but still — *sounds*!

'It's nothing short of astounding,' confessed Dr Sampson, 'to come out of a coma at his age. It *is* a miracle — but now, with time, he will recover enough to live a reasonable life.' Then — almost with a sigh of envy — 'They made them tough in those days.'

It took many months before Grandpa Jack recovered — as much as he ever would. Progress was painfully slow, and he needed constant attention, but his physique was so tough that he did show progress — visible progress — week by week. You could almost see him growing stronger. Because his left leg was partly paralysed he was never able to walk properly again. His left arm was not much good either but, though he could not lift a fork to his mouth, he could hold one in his left hand, hold it on the plate when using his right hand; so when he returned to Tanamera, after four months, he was able to sit at the table in his wheelchair and have a Sunday curry tiffin with us – the easiest of meals because all good Singaporeans ate it with a spoon in their right hand.

After eight months he was even able to shuffle a few steps with the aid of old Li or the nurses. This meant that, provided someone was there to help, he could at least walk to the loo or even from time to time manage to get into a car to be taken for a drive. 'That's where money comes in useful,' said Papa. 'We've got four nurses in relays – and they're worth every penny.' But Grandpa Jack didn't go in the car very often. He preferred to go for 'walks' in the grounds, with Li pushing the wheelchair.

All this treatment and recovery took up most of that happy, peaceful, wonderful year of 1935; wonderful because long before the end of the year Julie and I had not only found a place of our own – well, not really, but we liked to pretend it was – but the early excitement and curiosity or whatever one likes to call it had become something deeper, more emotional; it sounds silly for someone who had only become twenty-one in September to talk about passions and feelings more usually ascribed to adults, to men and women who have yardsticks of comparison. I had nothing with which I could compare our love, because I had never felt in the same way for anyone else. I was mad about her, besotted, the desperation increased because she on her part made no attempt to disguise her need for me – not only having me next to her, but my physical lovemaking. It was extraordinary; at parties she seemed normal, quiet, a beautiful girl; but underneath that calm exterior she was on fire. I would never have believed it, not at first when I suppose a natural shyness inhibited her, but later, when she came to know me, I realised that she was that rarity – a one-man girl, a girl who would be faithful as long as she loved you, but a girl who, if the genes had been arranged differently, might easily have become a nymphomaniac, just out of frustration, out of physical need.

'It isn't wrong, is it, to show that you want a man?'

'Not if it's me.'

'It'll always be you. But will it always be me? I've been told that if a woman is too forward she loses her man in the end.'

'Nonsense. Just imagine what would happen if you were frigid? *That's* the easy way to lose a man.'

'Well, if I were frigid we'd never have started,' she said. 'Don't you realise that I started all this?'

'Are you trying to accuse me of being backward in coming forward?'

'Well, when did it start? Which actual moment?' She ruffled my hair, 'I love that blond hair. It started, my beloved Johnnie, at the ball.'

'Right. When I begged you to come with me.'

'No. Before that. When I *made* you beg me. When you were dancing too close to me, and I leaned backwards, so that you knew I was feeling you – and *that* made you ask me.'

She was right, of course.

It was Bonnard of all people who found the flat for us, or rather made one available. I knew that we had been taking risks, going sometimes to the office, at other times to bachelor flats lent for a couple of hours by friends at the Cricket Club, but I didn't know who *had* spotted us until one evening, without preamble, Bonnard peered into his whisky glass and said, almost casually, 'You were seen last week, Johnnie, with a well-known young lady – leaving a flat in Cluny Road.'

My hands tightened round my glass. I wasn t angry – only terrified. Couldn't *anyone* keep a secret in this bloody city? Before I could speak Bonnard said easily, 'Not to worry – one of my associates told me.' I was too horrified to wonder who the associate was, or why he should be interested in us.

Bonnard ordered a couple more stengahs. 'I hope we're good friends enough – I feel we are – for me to be able to say openly that perhaps I can help you.'

'Me? I don't see how. And –' – feeling slightly annoyed instead of grateful – 'this *is* rather private.'

'Of course, I understand. Only –' he hesitated. 'I'm married, and even though my wife lives in Geneva, I don't like to bring girls back to my flat in the Cathay. So – I have another flat – one room –'

'As well as those in Hong Kong and Tokyo!' I couldn't help laughing. 'Business must be good.'

'It is. But this place – well, it was my bachelor pad, and when I got married I just kept it – on the quiet. You can borrow it whenever you like.'

Before I could say anything he held up his hand and added, 'A few friends use it from time to time.' He told me where the place was and I knew it by sight. Abingdon Mansions, up Scotts Road beyond the Goodwood Park Hotel, a square, four-storey block of studio-type flats.

'And it has one great advantage,' Bonnard explained. 'There are four entrances, and two lifts at the back. So people can go into the building by one of four different ways. Even a taxi or rickshaw dropping a passenger at the side or front entrance can never see who's going in at the back. I've had to make strict rules. Two people never arrive or leave at the same time.'

He produced a key and gave it to me. 'That means you've got to be there first, ready to open the door when someone you're expecting knocks. There's another rule. Please never go without checking with me – just in case. Often the place isn't used for days on end, but you can't be too careful.'

That is how I came to be a member of what Bonnard facetiously called *Le Club d'amour* – the Love Club. The flat consisted of a kitchenette with a refrigerator, a bathroom with cold tap only, and one square white room with a large bed and rather too many mirrors. All the flats were cleaned each morning, and the sheets changed daily, as was usual in Singapore. I bought – and kept replenished – a modest stock of gin and beer. I noticed that other people also contributed from time to time to the stocks.

Often Julie and I were able to meet at lunchtime; for old man Soong had agreed that Julie should not only continue as a volunteer at the Alexandra Hospital but had also enrolled her in a Chinese academy which trained well-brought-up girls in secretarial duties. Fortunately the fees were so stiff that Madame Chang, the owner, hated the prospect of losing a pupil, so rarely complained if Julie was (in theory) late from the hospital after lunch. Nor did the hospital complain if she had to leave early (in theory) for her secretarial college. We were very careful. I would arrive first — often with a parcel of sandwiches for lunch — and it was easy for Julie to pick up one of the little Ford Eight taxis that had just become popular in Singapore, and make her way to the back entrance of Abingdon Mansions.

It was the start of a never-to-be-forgotten interlude, each day spiced with the excitement of conspiracy. When you are young and healthy and in love, you don't really need to demonstrate your emotions except to the one you love. Of course I would have enjoyed taking Julie dancing, showing her off, lunching, dining, but when you know something is impossible it is easier to settle for an alternative. Each day when the time came for Julie to return to college and for me to return to the office she left the Love Club a quarter of an hour before I did.

From a window in the studio I could watch the road leading from the back entrance into Scotts Road, and after a few minutes — the time it took the lift to descend — I could see her, long legs striding out towards the taxi rank, black hair over her shoulders, sometimes happily swinging her handbag. Even from the way she walked away, face hidden, she somehow looked happy — carefree — and satisfied. Then I washed up the plates and glasses and left to take my place again in the outside world, the custodian of a bewildering, illegal, secret life of which I could never breathe a word to a living soul, like someone who has stolen a rare old master painting and can never show it.

When the Dexters and the Soongs met at parties, which

was fairly often, I saw Julie almost as a different person; we talked politely, danced decorously, both uplifted by the silky intoxication of our secret. Perhaps earlier that very day, while our parents had been dressing for the party, we had been tearing our clothes off for a few moments of smuggled love, far more wonderful than anyone else at the party could possibly experience. This was life – to be grabbed, savoured – every second of it – lying entwined, fighting for predominance, gasping with passion, praying for the strength to make it last. That and the knowledge that, if we were discovered, nothing could ever be so wonderful again, that the old Jewish proverb which Grandpa Jack had often quoted to me was true: 'What comes after is worse.'

Sometimes I would feel a surge of pity for those around me. Ian Scott was now married to Vicki, and though *he* seemed happy, what did he know of the things we did? Poor Vicki – for her there were only memories, and not as full as mine would one day be. Natflat was not yet married. She and Tony were expecting the date to be fixed for early 1936 – and I knew that she was in no hurry. Poor Natflat! I could see the light in her eyes every time she danced with Bonnard. I wondered what *she* would think if she knew about Abingdon Mansions.

I even found myself feeling sorry one evening for Papa and Mama as I watched them decorously having a duty dance together, feeling sad that I couldn't tell them everything, that I couldn't unburden my soul to them, recount the excitement which I felt sure they had never known. How sad for them that they had never made love in the back of a car, or on the sofa of a borrowed flat. Never having seen them as young and carefree it never entered my head that they had once been young, that they might have done the things I was doing.

6

The first months of 1936, a year of snatched secret meetings, wonderful each separate time, were also ones of increased pressures at the office; and in a way this contributed to the excitement of a dual life. The daily chores at Dexters increased because Papa Jack pushed more and more work my way, whether because he was tired or whether because he was quietly training me to take over I didn't know: probably a combination of both.

But there was more to it than that. Singapore itself was passing through a difficult phase – one that meant long hours, business dinners and lunches at short notice at home. The city seemed to be reflecting the economic danger signals in Europe and America, and Dexters were involved in all of them. The wealth of Singapore as an entrepôt port had always depended on the state of other nations, and as a leading agency house we depended on the state of Singapore and Malaya.

Our biggest headache was rubber – and the bureaucratic forms we had to complete day after day for the privilege of *not* being allowed to produce the rubber we knew we could produce. By 1936 rubber was under eight pence a pound, and almost every estate was sacking its European assistants, leaving only a manager in charge. To avoid a glut, quotas had been set by the International Rubber Regulation Committee – and that meant we were even forbidden to plant new trees.

Early attempts to control the supply of rubber in order to keep the price up had failed. The Stevenson Scheme, which existed from 1922 to 1928, had been the worst failure of all, partly because of the depression, but mainly because the Dutch East Indies, a major producer, stayed out. Now we had a new scheme which regulated ninety-eight per cent of the world's rubber exports; but the real trouble was that nothing could force people who didn't want rubber to buy it except at cut rates, and those rates – as we knew on the Ara Estate – meant that we couldn't pay the estate wages out of income.

'And to think,' Papa Jack groaned one day in the office, 'that in 1910 we were selling all the rubber we could produce at over eight *shillings* a pound. Now it's not even eight *pence*. Remember the estates owned by the Linggi Plantation? That was a public company and in 1910 they paid their shareholders a dividend of two hundred and thirty-seven per cent.'

Those days were gone – forever, perhaps. Though we could absorb the losses on the estate, we felt the pinch in other ways. Imports which we had shipped for decades started to fall, and in order to keep the holds of our ships filled we had to go out and more or less tout for extra and different business.

In those days – in my early twenties – I knew little about high finance or international politics, but I had been brought up in an agency business, and I knew how it worked. And I could see around me that the low price of rubber made very little difference to the way of life of our friends. It was the big businessmen in London – firms owning several estates – who were in trouble, for their pessimism was a reflection of the unease gripping the world. We could see it in the headlines of the *Straits Times* and the *Malaya Tribune* day after day.

Germany had already – a few months previously – repudiated the Versailles Treaty, and Hitler's swastika had become the official flag of Germany.

'And they've also outlawed Jews,' said Papa Jack. 'This chap Hitler must be crazy. He'll never be allowed to get away with it.' But he *had* got away with it – by occupying the Rhineland to a few ineffective bleats of protest from French and British politicians.

'The world's gone mad,' said Papa Jack. 'Look at this man Mussolini calmly invading Abyssinia.'

On the other hand Papa Jack was a shrewd enough busi-nessman to know that every ill wind blew some good – in this case to us, for European disquiet finally forced Britain to increase work on a major defence project, the Singapore Naval Base. The base had first been mooted in 1925, but successive governments had, for financial or political reasons, stopped work, then restarted, only to stop again. Now they seemed to be building in earnest, and even more important the RAF early in 1936 decided to build a series of airfields in Malaya – and they needed raw materials and housing.

When our rivals the Soong Agency were awarded a big contract to provide food and drink we got the shipping contract to import building materials and steel, and to supply out latest gimmick – prefabricated barrack huts.

I was secretly proud that I was the one who had first seen the potential of what Papa Jack called ready-to-wear houses. We had big interests in timber, both in central Malaya and a share in a firm in Burma, and I persuaded Papa Jack that it was more profitable to turn the timber into finished products than just to sell planks of wood. Our semi-prefabricated houses were not really finished products; that would have been pointless in a country with such cheap labour; instead we devised ready-made components – corner posts, roofing slats, window frames, doors, wall planks – all the timber treated for ants, with everything cut into a standardised size so that a house or a barracks or a labour office could be built to any size with the same basic materials. You just added on another section. The frame-work of a building could be constructed even in the jungle without the need to bring in mechanical saws and other heavy equipment, with local labour able to thatch the walls and roofs with attap or pandanus.

The kits were variable. They could not only be extended to any reasonable size, they could include accessories for plumbing, with small pumps and pipes which could bring a supply of non-drinking water from a nearby river, lake or spring. They were ideal for coolie housing, and cheap for short-term projects. What is more, they were an instant success. In fact we saved the British Navy, Army and RAF hundreds of thousands of pounds when they needed temporary buildings for construction gangs of coolies building airfields and the naval base.

'At least we're helping Britain to show the flag in Malaya,' said my father. 'If only to scare the Japs. I don't like the way they're behaving.'

Nor did anyone else in the Far East – for early in 1936 a group of Japanese officers murdered several of their ministers and high-ranking politicians and formed a cabinet that read like a list of the High Command.

'Bullying is catching,' said George Hammonds, the assistant editor of the *Malaya Tribune*, a man I liked enormously and met regularly at the Cricket Club where we were deadly rivals at volunteer snooker. George Hammonds was a few years older than me, a mine of information, a man who often knew things he was never permitted to publish. Tall, but not gangling, eyes serious behind his spectacles, for ever clutching a round 'fifty tin' of Players Cigarettes, George was one of those characters every polyglot city produces, a man known to everyone, a man who could always find you a room in a hotel that was booked up, a seat on a plane that was filled.

'The Japs have seen what Hitler and Mussolini have got away with in Europe and they're doing the same in Asia,' he said.

Hammonds had come to Tanamera for a drink, and Mama, sitting back in her favourite sitting room, asked him, 'Do you think it'll mean war, George?'

'I hope not.' He shook another cigarette from his round tin. 'But they're not like us, they don't think in the same way we do. The Japs are always liable to go bonkers.'

'Everyone knows that war is futile.' With age Papa tended to utter trite remarks as though he had just thought of them. 'Even the winner loses. The last war proved that. Still – it's not a bad idea to show the flag. *And* in the form of a few airfields and a naval base.' He added with a chuckle, 'And Dexter buildings.'

'I think they *will* attack China,' said P.P. Soong, who was also having a drink with us, adding in his slightly stilted English, 'My compatriots inform me they are gravely worried.'

'Well – I doubt it,' Papa Jack did his best to disguise the fact that he didn't consider *that* a war, any more than the Italian invasion of Abyssinia. To the old die-hards of Singapore a war was only a war if it involved Britain. Everything else was a local skirmish.

'The real war is going on now,' George nodded when Li offered him another stengah, adding, 'but don't worry – it's between the RAF and the army.' And when everyone looked puzzled he explained, 'The army's furious. The top brass won't even speak to the RAF top brass. It seems the RAF decided on their own, without any consultation, where they were going to build the airstrips up in Malaya – using your huts. The army says some of them are so isolated they'll never be able to defend them.'

'Since there's never going to be a war here,' my father shrugged, 'does it really matter?'

It was nearly half past seven. Soong had left, but George Hammonds had just cheerfully agreed to stay for dinner when Natasha came in, flushed and pink and, as always these days, in a terrible rush.

'Have a drink, darling,' said Mama. 'One of your new ones.' Natasha had just 'discovered' vodka. 'George is going to take pot luck with us.'

George almost grinned. Mama was always vaguely apologising for pot luck – though she knew as well as everyone who stayed unexpectedly for a meal that there was no such thing at Tanamera. Every meal was as good as the last, better than any meal served in most Singapore restaurants.

'Sorry, darlings,' Natasha took a sip of my drink. 'Oooh! Scotch! Horrible. Just rushed in for a bath and a change. Then I must dash.'

'Who with?' Sometimes Papa Jack forgot she was twenty-seven.

'Just the usual crowd. There's a dance at the Swimming Club.'

'Might pop in after dinner for a look,' murmured Hammonds.

'Super. Only' – a little defensively – 'there's going to be a terrible crush. Don't blame me if you can't find me.'

George Hammonds was talking rubber to Papa Jack, and Mama beckoned me over, patting the green and white cushion next to her on her favourite sofa.

'Don't you find Natasha is behaving a bit oddly?' she asked in an undertone. 'You know – a bit *fast*.' She pronounced the word with the distaste usually reserved for other more popular four-letter words. 'I have to take her side when your father starts getting annoyed, but –'

Sons and daughters rarely dare to say what is really on their minds. I personally had a feeling that my own parents didn't *want* to hear unpleasant truths; they asked questions and expected answers of which they could approve. I decided not to answer at all. Instead I laughed and said, 'I often wonder, darling Mama, what you think of us? Me?' I had expected some noncommittal reply and was staggered when she said, 'I think it's a great shame that you never realise that once – not long ago, you know – your father and I were behaving just like you.'

Well, I thought, not *quite*. I had visions of Julie getting undressed in Abingdon Mansions, so desperate she could hardly wait.

'You all think it's a different world,' Mama was half laughing, 'but nothing *really* changes, Johnnie. Except that as you get a bit older it gets a bit more tiring.'

'What gets tiring?'

'All this dashing around' – she was laughing at me, enjoying a private joke. 'What else could you possibly think I meant? Unless you have a secret life.'

It was my turn to laugh, though uneasily. 'Did you have secrets, Mama?'

'Well, we had trouble. My father flatly forbade me to marry your father – "this English colonialist", he called him.'

'But that's wonderful! I always thought – you know,

your parents more or less brought you together – like Natasha and Tony.'

'All sons and daughters think like that. You mustn't think you're the only man in the world who has a secret life – or had?' She looked at me, still laughing quietly.

Did she suspect something? Was she, yet again, warning me? She rarely made flat statements; just dropped hints, like clues in a crossword puzzle, leaving you to fill in the blank spaces.

Papa Jack interrupted, 'Did I hear you talking about Natasha? Time she stopped this gadding about. After all, it's only – how long to the wedding?'

'Six weeks. Easter. And don't fuss, dear. If Tony doesn't like being dragged out dancing –' she let her sentence trail away. 'And when they're married she'll settle down.'

'After they're married I'm hoping young Tony Scott will take charge of Ara,' Papa Jack confided to Hammonds, who knew all about our estate near Kuala Lumpur. 'Ian wants him to learn rubber from the bottom for a year or two. It's a fine estate – just the place for Natasha to bring up her first baby.'

'Dear, they're not even married yet,' protested Mama.

'Wish I had the chance,' George sighed. 'Not to have a baby! But I've always thought life on an estate must be perfect.'

'You'd hate to be anything but a journalist,' I said.

'Now, perhaps. But for a young man – it must be a great life. Cities complicate life so much. Even here. Singapore's changing every day. It's getting to the stage where you can't even park a car.'

'My syce has no trouble,' said Papa Jack with all the authority of one who hadn't driven a car in the city for years, and who was blindly oblivious to the fact that if his syce couldn't find a place to park he just drove the Buick round and round the block for hours.

'Johnnie and I drive ourselves,' George laughed. 'Not even the Dexters can cope with modern rush. I saw Natasha the other day – and even she was struggling to find a place in Scotts Road.'

'Well – that's because the Tanglin Club –'

'That I understand – specially on Sundays. But,' said George without thinking, and I was hardly paying attention, 'it was further up. Ye Gods! Ten years ago you never saw a single car parked there – that's before they built Abingdon Mansions. Don't worry – trust the Dexters, she found a place.'

I thought my heart had stopped. My father made some inconsequential remark. George answered – I heard the words in a kind of haze – 'Well, it *is* the biggest complex of apartments in Asia. Outside Shanghai, of course.'

I almost had to struggle to catch my breath as Mama looked at her watch, waiting for dinner. Abingdon Mansions! I knew why *she* had parked there. There was only one reason to park in a residential area. My God! Both of us. My beautiful sister. And it could be only one man. Beautiful Natflat was being screwed by Bonnard.

My mind raced. How long had it been going on? How often? On the same bloody bed that we used! And all this time Natflat had been hiding it from me, secretly smiling as she lied to me. Well, she couldn't openly tell me – I had to be sensible. Your own sister could hardly tell you with a laugh, 'I'm being screwed by a married man –' or whatever. But still – it was awful. And that bugger Bonnard, knowing about Julie and me, and yet taking my own sister to the same bed, perhaps half an hour after we had warmed it for her, then greeting me with a smile maybe an hour or two later.

Maybe it wasn't true. Maybe she had just been visiting friends. We must know *somebody* in that big rectangular white building which held hidden in its bowels one small mirrored room dedicated to love, real or counterfeit. Yes, it might be a coincidence. And yet I knew it couldn't be. I thought for a moment of a confrontation – not with Natasha, but with Bonnard. A showdown – an indignant brother defending the honour of his seduced sister. But I knew I never would, because I knew instinctively that there was no real honour to defend, only Tony's 'honour' – and that was his problem. I could see Bonnard's reaction if I confronted him. The slow, slightly mocking smile, some Frenchifield remark, 'I'm not raping her, you know. She *is* twenty-seven and she enjoys it.' Or even, 'Perhaps we Europeans are more skilled than you locals. I'm not doing her any harm, you know.' Or perhaps a nastier reply, 'Tell me, *mon cher ami*, when are you planning to marry Miss Soong — when you've finished with my bed, of course?'

I knew he would never say things like that. Bonnard had such good manners that he would never descend to vulgar abuse or brawling. But I would have loved to hit that slightly supercilious face – the look so many Frenchmen have, the pitying look they bestow on other races. But I couldn't. And, oddly, there was another, quite different reason why. I couldn't have a row with Bonnard at this particular moment because we were on the point of signing a deal that was far, far bigger than the original one for bulldozers and tractors. And if that fell through because I had given Bonnard a bloody nose . . .

What about Natasha? How could I stop her? Well, what right did I have to try? And anyway, I couldn't. If I told her I knew what went on in Abingdon Mansions it could only be because I was doing the same thing. And Natasha would know it was Julie, and so I would be betraying Julie.

Still, the next morning I tackled her after breakfast, which we still all ate together, Mama in her dressing gown, on the east verandah. It was my favourite meal and nothing spoiled my appetite. I wolfed down everything I could find, with Mama still saying, though mechanically now, like a record stuck in a groove, 'Don't eat so fast, Johnnie.'

Natasha and I were usually last to leave the table, after our parents had gone to prepare for Papa Jack's trip to the office with me. And I had sensed all through the meal that Natflat was depressed. I suddenly felt terribly sorry for her, and even understood the reason for what she had been doing. With the wedding only six weeks away, I realised for the first time how much she was dreading it.

'Why don't you pack it in?' I asked her. 'You wouldn't be the first girl to change her mind at the altar.'

'If I hated Tony it would be easy – but I don't hate him,'

she sighed. 'I rather like him. He's a nice teddy bear – it's rather like marrying a cuddly toy.'

'What a formula for wedded bliss!'

'Is it so bad? Tony's –' she searched for the right words, 'so *dependable*. And I *am* twenty-seven now. I'll be an old maid if I'm not careful.'

She was joking, of course. I knew half a dozen men would have been glad to marry her. But I knew the trouble. It had to be Bonnard.

'It *is* Bonnard, isn't it?'

'No, no, no!' she lied. 'Why do you always have to bring him into it? What business is it of yours anyway?'

'I'm only trying to help. And he has been "in" it, as you put it, for a long time.'

'Not really,' she lied again. 'It's not only Bertrand, though he's great fun – it's what he represents.'

I obviously looked puzzled, for she went on, 'Fun out of life, Europe, travel, dancing, hotels – everything I want out of life – everything I can never get in this dreary hole. *That's* what gets me down, really. What I'm missing – and even worse what I'm *going* to miss by settling down. I'll end up like – like Papa and Mama. They're sweet – but could there be a more awful, dreary life to look forward to? I know *they* are happy, but life was different when they were young.'

'Poor parents. But they're happy – in their way.'

'I don't *want* to be happy,' she cried. 'I've been happy all my life. When I marry Tony I'll be happy – for want of a better word – I'll be happy for the rest of my life. I want something else.'

'In between? Like a sandwich. But you can't just go out and order one.'

'You can grab one if it's there, can't you?'

'Natflat,' I almost pleaded. 'Be careful. You can't marry Bonnard – even if *he* wanted to – and he doesn't. Catholics never divorce. And anyway, don't you feel' – I was trying to be careful – 'that to him – well, it's not as serious as it is to you. You know what I mean.'

'Let's forget the whole thing, Johnnie. You don't understand. It's not a question of marriage – or even love. Just don't talk about it.'

'I won't. Sorry, darling. But I won't – not even to Bonnard when I see him next week.'

'Bertrand – you're going to see him? Why?' her voice was almost harsh.

'Business. After all, if it hadn't been for business you'd never have met him.'

'I didn't know you had business deals still. He never told me.'

'Neither did I.'

'You won't –'

'All is forgotten.' I gave her a brotherly kiss. 'And don't insult me by not trusting me. Just remember what Grandpa Jack used to say – if you can't be good, be careful.'

The reason I was seeing Bonnard was ironically due to Papa Jack's conviction that the Japanese would never dare to challenge the might of the British Empire. It had led us to start negotiations for a huge order with Japan – for the same kind of construction units we were supplying to the British forces in Malaya. Only in Japan they would be used to help save thousands of people who had been made homeless in still another earthquake.

Despite the fighting in Manchuria there was no violent anti-Japanese feeling in Singapore in those days, though the Chinese were wary of making social friends with them. Most of the Japanese were fishermen – and much more efficient and hard-working than the Malays who were content to lay traps, then sit back and hope for the best. But there was also a colony of shrewd Japanese businessmen like Jiroh Miki; and it was after a game of tennis with Miki at the Japanese Club that he told me his father's company had been delegated to build a refugee camp for Japanese earthquake victims. Would we be interested? Our prefabricated huts sounded exactly what they wanted. I was a little chary of repercussions from our Chinese clients, but I wasn't going to turn away business sight unseen.

Miki saw my flicker of doubt instantly. 'This is an inter-national effort, *hai*!' he smiled, using the Japanese equivalent of 'okay'. 'Our joint friend, Monsieur Bonnard, he is handling Swiss financial side. Very humane!'

That altered things; but I still decided to mention the matter to my father.

'I think he's all right, but you see him, Johnnie,' said Papa Jack. 'And be careful. After what P.P. said the other night it's perhaps just as well if I don't get mixed up with any Japs until the military cabinet business in Tokyo blows over – or,' with a Yorkshire afterthought, 'unless it's a really big deal with cash down.'

A big deal it certainly was. 'We are asking five thousand buildings, very quick,' said Miki. 'For a big camp on island of Yakushima.'

'Five thousand!' I echoed. 'That's a hell of a lot of buildings.'

'Ah so! Government and Swiss contract!' Miki gave the slightest hint of a polite hiss.

'And where's this place? –'

'Yakushima. Small island south of Kyushu. Government plan send hundred thousand people from earthquake areas to build new life.'

'But the government's been changed – it's different – it's a military gang.'

'This project okay.' Miki flourished a cable at me. 'I receive last night. Please – we meet soon with Monsieur Bonnard. You like Japanese sukiyaki?'

Miki, Bonnard and I dined in a private room – made private by the skilful use of tatami mats – in the Tokyo Restaurant off Dunearn Road. I can't say I had been looking forward to the meeting since I learned about Natasha; still, I couldn't get out of it. It was supposed to be strictly business – but that wasn't easy with someone who was a frequent visitor to your home, lent you a bed and borrowed your sister. So I found it hard to disguise my hostility – though really what had happened was none of my business, and I knew it.

Bertrand noticed it, for when Miki went to fetch some blueprints from his car, he asked, 'Anything the matter, Johnnie?'

'Nothing,' I shook my head. 'Why do you ask?'

'I have a sixth sense. You seem on edge. I hope,' he searched for the right phrase, 'all's well at Abingdon Mansions?'

'Thanks. Fine.'

'Good. But be careful. Don't relax your guard.'

'And you? Doesn't that apply to you too?'

'To all of us.' He was determined to be cheerful. 'Even neutrals.'

Miki returned; and as we plunged into the technicalities I forgot my irritation, for I had to hand it to Bonnard, he had a brain as sharp as a razor, while Miki showed an astonishing grasp of the technical details. It was common knowledge that our ready-to-wear houses were flexible, so I had expected a lot of preliminary hoo-ha to be followed at a later date by a meeting with technicians – if, that is, the deal went through, for it was a big deal, and I presumed they would have to tender with other firms.

'We won't tender,' said Bonnard. 'Because you make the best, and in fact the only ones in Asia of the kind we need.'

'When are we going to decide on sizes?'

'Already decided,' Miki hissed politely and produced his blueprints. 'Each section of your hut is fifty-five feet, I think, *hai*? Can join three together for each building we require.'

That sounded feasible, though I was surprised they had done so much homework. 'Far brighter than our British customers,' I laughed. 'We'll have to discuss water, lighting and so on.'

'Plenty water,' Miki produced a large-scale map of the island with the unpronounceable name. 'Our planners estimate nine hundred yards number three plumbing piping for each hut, leading to central water supply. They join every fifty yards, yes?'

'You seem to be very well informed,' I said almost dryly. I was in fact thinking of the logistical problems. Our prefabrication company was centred up-country where the slopes of Malaya's central mountain range spilled into Pahang, producing almost unlimited cheap timber.

Normally it was trucked to rubber plantations or tin mines – and now to the airfield sites – but in this case we would have to take the treated prefabricated sections to the east coast port of Kuantan and load it on to one of our ships. There didn't seem to be any problems.

'Miki *has* done his homework,' Bonnard laughed with the familiarity of one who shares secrets. 'But he's showing off really. In fact, the size of the barrack houses is exactly the same as those you're building for the RAF up-country in Malaya.'

I gaped. The RAF plan was supposed to be confidential. Dexters had certainly been warned to keep silent.

'You know,' Bonnard added easily. 'The ones at places like Malim Nawar and just outside Sungei Siput.'

'But they're *secret*,' I blurted out. I couldn't believe a Swiss would have even *heard* of a place like Malim Nawar. 'How the hell did you know about them – and the others, I suppose?'

'They may be secret in theory,' Bonnard laughed again, 'but we're not spies, I can assure you. Miki told me.'

'Pictures in *Malaya Tribune*,' Miki fished a newspaper clipping from his briefcase. 'And full description too.'

It was incredible, but there it was. The RAF had let newspaper reporters take photos of the proposed sites. I had a faint tingle of apprehension. If the military could be as stupid as that I hoped, for the sake of Malaya, that Papa Jack was right in laughing off any thought of Japan making warlike noises.

'It's not possible to keep this sort of thing secret,' said Bonnard, 'once you start recruiting local labour.'

'Well, let's hope that private individuals can keep their affairs secret better then governments.' I couldn't help saying it – and looking at him right between the eyes as I spoke.

There remained one question, but it was never asked. Miki forestalled me. 'This joint Swiss and government contract,' he said politely. 'So M Bonnard authorised pay twenty-five per cent on signature, twenty-five per cent when deliveries start, final balance when last shipment reaches Japanese shore. This satisfactory?'

No man could have asked for more. We agreed that I should talk to Papa Jack, and then Ball and Rawlings would thrash out details such as costing and delivery dates, then prepare the final contract.

We had long since made a routine check on the financial background of Bonnard – even before we signed the first contract for bulldozers – and there were no problems with his firm, the Agence de Construction Oriental S.A. which was registered in Vaduz, the capital of Lichtenstein, with the operating office in the rue de la Corraterie in Geneva. All the same, the nagging doubts about Japan still persisted and so, to be on the safe side, I took the whole thing up with the government in Singapore.

After exhaustive enquiries and diplomatic discussions, they approved enthusiastically of our 'humane' deal to help the unfortunate victims of an earthquake which, since it was an act of God, was automatically apart from and above such mundane matters as warmongering Japanese generals who had virtually seized control of the country and were baying for blood – as far as I could see, anyone's blood.

'Bad show in Japan, I agree,' drawled a senior officer from Government House, 'but since they'd never dare to attack us, not really our affair. Is it, old chap?'

7

Most lovers fondly imagine they can keep a secret. Even after learning about Natasha, Julie and I had no real qualms. We always arrived separately. Because my Morgan was distinctive, I parked it at the Cricket Club and took a taxi, asking the driver to drop me fifty yards from Abingdon Mansions. I used different entrances each time. In all our visits I never saw a soul I recognised.

So I still didn't have the faintest idea that *anyone* knew when Julie phoned me at the office. On mornings when we planned to meet she phoned (without giving her name) to check that nothing had turned up to put off our arrangements. But this morning she whispered hurriedly that it was she who couldn't make it. We never discussed reasons on the phone. All I said was, 'On Thursday?' and all she said was, 'Of course.'

I was on the point of ringing Paul to see if we could lunch at Raffles when Vicki – now Mrs Ian Scott – phoned me. Her voice sounded urgent.

'Can you pop into our bungalow for a couple of minutes? As soon as you can?'

'Do you think I ought to?' I was being facetious.

'This isn't a joking matter, Johnnie. Someone wants to see you – badly.'

In the way that a jagged flash of electricity bounds between two separate wires, suddenly I knew that both phone calls were connected. I almost shouted, 'It's not? –' but Vicki spoke first.

'Don't worry. It isn't your beloved Julie. Though she *will* be there.'

The phone clicked as she rang off. I was stunned. How much did Vicki know? Or, for that matter, what exactly was going on?

I set off, never imagining who wanted to see me. Skirting the Cricket Club, then swerving right past the Supreme Court, I raced along the side of the padang, into Stamford Road, Orchard Road, then swung the Morgan right at Keok Road, squealing to a stop in front of the Scott bungalow in its green grounds near the junction of Clemenceau Avenue.

Vicki reached the door almost as the boy opened it. She said, 'Don't panic, Johnnie, but it's your sister.'

'Natasha!'

'She wants to see you. Insisted.'

'Where is she?'

I strode into the living room, noticing subconsciously that Vicki had thrown out all Ian's old, dark Victorian furniture, bought presumably by his first wife. She had replaced it with new chairs, sofas, modern furniture, and in one corner low, white-painted bookshelves had been built round a divan. On the divan lay my sister. Julie was pressing something on her head, too busy to look up.

My first thought was Accident. But it couldn't be that; she'd have been taken to hospital. Natasha was dressed, but deathly pale and in obvious pain.

'Where's Ian?' I asked as I walked towards her.

'Up in KL for the night.'

'Tony?'

Vicki shook her head warningly, put a finger to her lips.

'I'm sorry, Johnnie.' Natasha held out a hand. It was cold and clammy. I touched her forehead. The sweat was cold. 'Nothing to worry about, but I had to see you – to ask you –'

'You're cold as ice,' I said.

'Don't worry' – it was Julie speaking – 'It's the normal symptom, shock.'

'But *Julie* – why is *she* here? What's happened?'

'Relax,' said Vicki, 'Nobody's going to die.'

'Well,' I exploded, 'will one of you girls explain, for God's sake?'

'I had to go to a doctor,' Natasha's face had a blank look and occasionally she shuddered. 'Then I felt worse, and I –'

'She rang me up,' Vicki finished the sentence for her, 'and asked if she could rest for a bit. And then – well, she started bleeding, I got frightened –'

'But where the hell's Dr Sampson?'

'I knew Julie goes to the Alexandra – I phoned her and she came.' Vicki drew me aside. 'Natasha can't see Sampson.'

'Johnnie, come and sit by me,' Natasha patted the divan into a place. 'I want to stay here tonight. Can you fix it with Papa? Say anything you like to him, but just –'

I nodded. 'Of course. But shouldn't I fetch Tony?'

'God, no! If he knew I'd had an abortion –'

It was the first time the word had been used. Julie, who had been silent, took my arm, smiled and kissed me and said, 'She was at her wits' end – she went to some Chinese butcher – but she'll be all right after a night's rest.'

'But Tony?'

127

'Better if no one knows,' Natasha sighed. 'Least of all Tony. Promise you'll fix it with Papa?'

'Who was it?' I asked Vicki.

'First – I don't know. And second – don't ask questions. It's none of your business. You just make sure your father doesn't find out. Julie's been wonderful. As good as your Dr Sampson.'

'I just gave her half a grain of chloral hydrate. I pinched it from the hospital. She's agitated and upset, but the bleeding's stopped. This will knock her out for a few hours.'

'She's an angel,' Natasha looked up. 'You don't know how lucky you are. Johnnie, I envy you so much.'

'Let her sleep,' Julie suggested. 'That's what she needs more than anything. She's lost a lot of blood.' Then without realising the incongruity of her next words, she said, 'I must go now or I'll be late for school. But I'll come tomorrow lunchtime if that's all right, Johnnie?'

I kissed her as she left, suddenly realising that it was the first time in my life I had kissed her properly in front of other people. I held her in my arms, hugged her, kissed her. But as the door closed behind her and I went back into the room, I was thinking, if only I could shoot that bastard Bonnard.

'Be careful,' Vicki warned me as I prepared to leave. 'I'm not the only one who knows.'

'How did you find out?'

'I honestly can't tell you. From Natasha, I suppose – I just sort of knew.'

'Anyone else know?'

'Paul, I imagine – he's no fool. But I'm not sure.'

'Anyone else?'

'I've the feeling that the other Soong boy – Kai-shek, the one you dislike, knows. I'm not sure, but Natasha told me he's been ferreting around, checking on Julie at the hospital. You know that he's hoping to marry her – with her father's blessing.'

'I'd kill him first.'

'You may have to. I wouldn't mind. Cruel-looking bastard. Now, off you go, Johnnie. I'll look after Natasha, you make sure her father doesn't find out. look after the family end, and,' with a peck on the cheek, 'my replacement.'

Natasha came home the next evening and went straight to the Sick Bay. The old rules that prevented us as children from visiting each other had long since been forgotten and I popped in to see her the moment I got back from the office.

'Sorry to involve you.' She was in bed, but her colour had returned and she looked almost normal, 'But when Julie came – and I'd had an idea about you two for months –'

I didn't say I knew about *her*. All I said was, 'Bonnard, I suppose?'

She nodded.

'Mama have any suspicions?'

'God, no. I told her I'd got the curse badly. I wish to God I had.'

'What about Tony? Any idea?'

She shook her head. 'He never will have. Is it wrong – for us to get married? Now you and the others know what happened?'

'Don't ask me. Everybody seems to be doing it these days! Wouldn't help if you told him. Though it would hurt like hell if he ever found out afterwards.'

'He won't. Never. And the crazy thing is that one half of me wants to get married. Forget what I said to you not long ago – it's a sort of scared feeling I have.'

'You don't look scared.' And she didn't.

'I am, though. Of everything – myself. Tony's solid – and in a way I might love him longer for that than if it was just – well, making love.'

'You can't be *afraid* of Bonnard?'

She pulled the sheet up round her neck, straightening it with her long fingers. 'Not really. But he – I find it very hard to say no to him. I'm not a nymphomaniac. Nor am I like your beautiful Julie.'

Instinctively I looked to be sure the door was closed.

'Julie,' she was thinking aloud, 'radiates a sort of suppressed desire – you can feel it, specially when she's looking at you. Don't get me wrong. I didn't say *she's* a nympho –

129

but Julie's physical. My problem is more mental. I enjoy it – but to be honest I do it more for kicks – even to please a man – more than because I need it.'

'I'll watch both of you at the Koo party next week,' I said dryly. 'And compare you both.'

'Do that, darling brother – if I'm there. I'm not sure I will be. But don't stare too much at Julie. Other eyes are watching you. Specially Kai-shek.'

Once a year the Koo brothers, who owned four of Singapore's nightclubs, and were already opening others in Hong Kong, invited 'all' Singapore to a tiffin party at their home in Tanglin. They already fancied themselves as the future oriental moguls they were hoping to become, and had established for themselves a lifestyle based on Hollywood magazines to which they had added none-too-subtle Chinese overtones. Because the houses of the stars in Hollywood always seemed (in magazines anyway) ablaze with flowers, the Koo brothers insisted on potted plants everywhere. But for some inexplicable reason the orchids were always ranged in rows on the floors against the walls – hundreds of them – so that as you made your way inside the entrance hall to the gardens it was like walking through a funeral parlour.

The two unmarried brothers shared their ornate white stone house overlooking the Tanglin golf course, and their pride was a large garden in which they had erected rows of palladian-type columns, topped with white trellis from which vines and flowering creepers trailed in profusion; each man-made alley led to contrived corners occupied for the party by eager Chinese servants pressing food and drink on the guests, for the annual Koo buffet lunch was so famous that Singaporeans hastened to cancel any previous engagement if they were clever enough to wangle a last-minute invitation.

In one corner, under a small dome of striped tenting, chefs cooked *saté* with its sweet smell of peanut butter sauce. In another carvers dextrously dissected turkeys and chickens – dozens of them. Near the Koos' famous rose arbour, with its hedges of Frensham roses which they had imported from England, half a dozen different Singapore curries cooked in huge pans over spirit stoves, the pale brown juice flat and still, except for the occasional bubble; like some volcanic lake in outer space. Sydney rock oysters had been flown in from Australia; fresh strawberries had been sent down from Fraser's Hill during the night.

We went every year. So did the Soongs, so did men like Ian Scott, so did George Hammonds. This year Papa Jack was up in KL hoping to fix a contract to handle the Elphil and Kitson rubber estates near Sungei Siput, and Mama rarely attended non-European parties without Papa Jack, but I went suitably dressed – jacket, collar and tie despite the stifling heat – together with Tony Scott and Natasha, fully recovered and – apparently – full of beans. We had arranged to meet old man Scott and Vicki at the party.

I hadn't seen Ian Scott for some time and he looked a different man. It was not for me to compliment an older man on the fact that he had obviously lost a great deal of weight, but Vicki must have noticed my surprise for she said brightly, 'Ian's been on a diet. Don't you think it agrees with him?'

'You look fine, sir,' said Paul Soong (in the thirties young men tended to call anyone over forty sir).

'It's not only the diet,' said Scott indulgently, 'it's marriage. Splendid innovation. I can highly recommend it.'

I always liked old Scott, even when I was 'friendly' with Vicki, and I knew he would make a very good, if dull, husband. But she had changed him entirely. He had the sleek contented look of a cat that is happily brushed for hours each day. He was positively shining with health and satisfaction.

'And you, Julie?' he turned to her. 'Your turn next? Let's see – you must be? –'

Julie smiled. 'I think I'll wait a bit. At least until I've learned my shorthand and typing and nursing.' She told him about her secretarial college, and her shifts as a hospital nurse.

George Hammonds joined us, clutching his usual round

tin of Players. 'I hear Papa Jack's gone up to Sungei Siput,' he said.

'That's right,' I nodded, watching Scott carefully as I added cheerfully, 'There's no secret about it, he's trying to do a deal with two big estates up there. We could handle the sales and transport for them. America's suddenly started crying out for more rubber.'

I was really teasing Scott because he hated to be beaten in a deal, and though his son Tony was engaged to Natasha he wasn't yet one of the clan, and business was business. Scott had plenty of work for his agency but he always had an eye for more, and the Elphil and Kitson estates would be a wonderful account. I could see his mind ticking over, wondering what was happening.

'What *is* happening,' I whispered to George Hammonds, as Scott moved away, 'is that when Papa Jack hears of a chance he doesn't send one of his underlings up – not even me – he goes north himself on the first train. Scott writes a letter and hopes for the best.'

'There's enough cake for everyone,' said George, and indeed there was. Work on the naval base had meant thousands of coolies earning good – comparatively good – money shifting millions of cubic feet of earth, deflecting a river, erecting oil tanks to hold millions of gallons of fuel, building dry docks, graving docks, giant cranes, underground munition dumps – and erecting Dexter houses. 'Someone in the navy told me that when the floating dock's finished, sixty thousand men will be able to stand on its bottom,' said Paul.

'For what?' asked Tony Scott contemptuously.

'For *war*.' I turned round. P.P. Soong, quiet as usual, carefully balancing a glass of champagne, had been listening to us and stood there with a slightly faded smile, looking less grey than usual in the dappled sunlight that drove relentlessly in bands through the creepers on the trellis above us.

'But who's going to fight who, Mr Soong?' asked Tony.

'Who knows?' Soong shrugged his shoulders. 'All I know is what history tells: that in our kind of world, big nations don't suddenly start cornering supplies of vital raw materials unless — well, unless they're afraid. America alone is buying half our rubber and over half our tin. It can't all be for tyres and corned beef. They are stockpiling.'

It was the sort of vague war-or-no-war talk that often took place on social occasions like this. George Hammonds interrupted.

'We've had lots of strikes and labour troubles and anti-British riots lately, Mr Soong — they're growing. *Do* you think honestly — but off the record — there's any danger of serious disruption here?'

Soong shook his head and answered carefully, 'Not yet. But one day it will come. Here in Singapore we have four hundred thousand Chinese, nearly a hundred thousand Malays and Indians — and eight thousand Europeans "ruling the roost" as you call it. It's,' he searched for a polite phrase, 'rather unbalanced, isn't it?'

'What about the Communist threat?' asked George.

'Depends, Mr Hammonds, on the circumstances,' Soong was noncommital. 'Communists strike better when their enemy is already reeling. They're the jackals who move in for the kill.'

I could sense that George was not posing idle questions. Suddenly he asked, very quietly, very deliberately, 'Will Loi Tek make any difference?'

For a split second Soong stood stock still. 'Where did you hear that name?' he asked at last.

'Oh, I read in some confidential document that he's come to Singapore to ginger up the Malayan Communist Party,' George answered airily.

'But if it's confidential,' Soong's voice held a note of asperity, 'surely it means what it says — that it shouldn't be talked about?'

'Not at all, Mr Soong. The notice asking us not to mention the name is stuck up in the Tribune office for all the staff to read.' Then he added bitterly, 'When a government department says something's confidential it usually means that anyone can talk about the subject but you can't print what everyone's talking about.'

'Loi Tek is a brilliant man, and very dangerous,' said Soong quietly. 'He's not Chinese, by the way. He's an Annamite, and he's been sent down by the Third International to put some force into the Communist party here. I believe that he'll be the leader of the party before very long.'★

As Soong moved to another group Bonnard joined us and, turning to Paul, asked, 'Do men like your father – men of influence – ever talk about independence for Malaya?'

Paul shrugged his shoulders, 'Chinese fathers rarely confide in Chinese sons. Personally, I think that if we had independence, the Malays and the Chinese would start fighting each other right away. Much better to let the British run the show – they keep the peace, they let the Chinese make fortunes out of British tin, and let the Malay sultans spend fortunes out of the British royalties. Suits everyone.'

The lunch dragged on, and I was almost ready to leave when I saw P.P. Soong coming my way. Out of the corner of my eye I saw Soong beckon Paul and start talking to him earnestly. Then P.P. came over to me and asked in his precise English, 'Something needs attention immediately and I want Paul to come with me for a few minutes. Would you do me a favour and take Julie home when you leave?'

'Of course.' I tried not to betray my elation at the prospect of taking Julie for a drive – legally.

'There is no hurry. We only have a short call to make and we may even arrive at our home before you do. Julie,' he called to her. 'Johnnie is to take you home.'

'Yes, father,' she said.

I watched Soong and Paul depart and then, never anticipating what was about to happen – something so impossible and frightening that no one could have imagined

★Years later, Professor Anthony Short in his book *The Communist Insurrection in Malaya* (Frederick Muller 1975) described Loi Tak (the spelling varies): 'He arrived in Singapore in the early 1930s with a dazzling reputation . . . He had studied Communism in Russia and France; had assisted the Vietnamese Communist Party in its early struggles; and had served on the Shanghai Town Committee of the China Communist Party. He also spoke French as well as English.'

it — I whispered to Julie, 'Let's go, darling. We've got time to take a drive — just a few minutes alone.'

We walked demurely out to the street where dozens of cars were parked along the shady side of the road, some with syces waiting, some like my little Morgan, with the hood up but unfastened so the seats wouldn't get hot. I pulled the hood down and we drove out along the coast road, holding hands, stroking legs, just happy to be alone until we reached the open country with white, foam-lapped beaches framed in bending palms and occasional stretches of tangled mangrove swamp, the tortuous, evil-looking roots of the trees trailing into the sea, catching driftwood and anything the water had to offer as though trapping them in a spider's web.

Just before we reached the Swimming Club we started to head for home, following the creek by Lavender Street — the dirty smelly creek where Raffles had found a pile of skulls left by pirates — until it crossed Jalan Besar and then we were making for the Bukit Timah Road and heading for Julie's home, the house invisible from the road in the last compound before Tanamera.

No one could miss the entrance, which was marked by twelve-foot twin pillars of grey stone, on each of which was mounted a hideous grey dragon, tongue darting out, one front paw stretching downwards, so cunningly devised that it seemed to be killing one of the writhing wrought-iron serpents which formed the pattern of each huge gate.

'Gives me the willies,' I grinned as I slammed the Morgan into third and drove up the drive without the vaguest premonition that in the next few minutes I would be more terrified than I had ever been in my life.

Soong's gardens were famous throughout Asia — the Singapore equivalent of the gardens of famous houses in England, photographs of which appeared regularly in the glossy magazines. Every visitor tried to get an invitation to see Soong's prized dwarf bamboos, his shrubs cut into the shapes of animals, or the aviary with peacocks which were let out on to the lawn during parties. In the centre of the lawn was a huge circular pond whose still, black waters were studded with magnificent lotus blossoms.

The house was a very different matter. Even when we used to go to parties there as children we had found it bleak and friendless, a house for stiff conversation, not a home for laughter.

Julie pushed open the heavy studded front door, and led me into the heart of the house, a huge circular room with a domed roof, so that when you entered and went under an arch into it there were no straight lines except the floor and two glass doors at the back. The room must have measured fifty feet across. The walls were of grey stone, pierced with large, glassless windows; a split-level floor increased the effect of height and space.

Papa Jack might laughingly tell friends that Tanamera was the ancestral home of the Dexters, but the Soong mansion was an Ancestral Home with capital letters. It was, for instance, a repository for precious Chinese pieces, and the long narrow Ming table underneath one window must have been priceless. So were the carpets and the scrolls – silk on paper – hanging on the walls. In the centre of the room was another long table surrounded by chairs, stiff and uncomfortable, and obviously to be used on formal occasions, all echoes of a rich Chinese life. At each end of the central table old Shanghai jars – originally used in bathrooms to hold cold water – had been filled with dried branches and leaves.

'Hang on a couple of minutes,' said Julie. 'I'm just popping upstairs.'

I sat down in a more comfortable corner, half-hidden by a tall, six-panelled screen in black, dark and light blues, a conversation corner in which all the chairs were deep, comfortable and with oatmeal-coloured covers obviously chosen by Aunt Sonia. Apart from the ashtrays – flat, with brass designs on pewter – the only item of Chinese furniture in this part of the room was a large square lacquered table, its top depicting a story in brilliant gold leaf. It was so heavily lacquered that it repelled any spilled alcohol, and it had fascinated me ever since I first visited the Soong house as a boy, particularly the crisscross bars linking the four legs, for in fact the table could be dismantled. The top lifted off, the legs folded, and a Chinese nobleman in the old days would have taken it, strapped to a camel, with him as a picnic table when travelling. Years before – long before Julie – Soong had shown me how it worked, and seeing my fascination had promised me that when he died he would leave the table to me.

As I picked up a magazine I heard quick footsteps and Soong Kai-shek came in through the glass doors that led to a patio and pool. His hair was an untidy shock, his pockmarked skin was sallow, and as usual he *looked* aggressive, which was understandable for his mother was a Hakka, and Kai-shek had inherited all the arrogance which has stamped Hakkas since they originated in the tough climate of northern China.

Still, though I disliked him, I said politely, 'Hullo! We missed you at the Koo party.'

His reply, totally unexpected, was like a bucket of iced water thrown in my face.

'Stand up when you speak to me, white monkey!' he screamed. From a Chinese, who will even kill you with a special brand of courtesy, the words were so shattering that instinctively I *did* stand up. I had no conscious thoughts of slapping his face, of shouting back at him. I just said, astonished, 'Hey! Who the hell do you think –'

As I stepped forward he screamed, 'Stay where you are!'

He shouted an order in Chinese. That was when my heart almost stopped. An enormous Alsatian bounded into the room. All Chinese love big dogs, but never before had I seen a bigger, more ferocious Alsatian than this. Kai-shek shouted a second command. The dog stopped barking and stood growling, ears pricked, waiting only for the order to pounce. I realised I was trembling with fear. I didn't mind the insults – Kai-shek might be off his rocker for all I knew – but I realised that if he gave just one word of command that dog would tear me to pieces. I didn't know what to do, but I must have instinctively looked round the huge room, wondering if there were any chance of escape.

'Scared, eh? You would like to run away, wouldn't you?

No chance, frightened white monkey,' sneered Kai-shek.

'Why *me* –?'

'Why me? Why me, flightened white monkey!' he mimicked my English accent, losing control of his rs. 'Don't be flightened. You stand still. I won't hurt you. But you make one move –' he spoke to the dog, which, as though stalking its prey, bared its teeth, and advanced slowly towards me. Kai-shek shouted another command. It crouched, belly on floor, perhaps ten feet away.

· At that moment I heard footsteps in the hall outside behind the arch. The Alsatian pricked up its ears again and looked towards the stairs. Julie was coming down without the faintest idea of what she would find. I had no time to warn her. As she walked in she screamed, 'Kai-shek!' After that I don't know what they shouted to each other in Chinese. I started to take a step forward, but the dog rose snarling.

Kai-shek shouted, 'I won't hurt the white monkey – but *you* - you get out, whore. Get out.'

Julie looked at me helplessly, burst into tears and ran out of the room – for help, because a few minutes later two boys in white came running into the room.

'Get out!' Kai-shek shouted in Malay. As they hesitated, irresolute, he ordered the dog to advance towards them. Before I had a chance to move they ran, shrieking. The dog turned round to face me – this time standing, as big as a small pony, its teeth bared, a touch of white foam flecking a panting mouth. Julie had vanished.

All this had taken only a few moments – though it seemed hours since I had first walked into the cold, grey room. I had been riveted to one spot. All I could do was change the weight from one leg to another. If I moved even a couple of inches the dog advanced. And yet, though I was still scared, the first terror was ebbing, and jumbled alternatives were racing through my mind. Kai-shek had shouted that I was not going to be harmed. So what the hell was happening? Maybe he was a looney – but I didn't dare speak. Maybe he was drugged? Or just anti-British? I caught sight of an amah's terrified brown face, framing white eyes, peering round the arch. The Alsatian picked up her scent and turned its head. As the woman started to say something Kai-shek shouted in Malay and the face vanished with the speed of a puppet jerked out of sight by an unseen, manipulating hand. Feet scuttled away.

'Don't worry, white monkey,' Kai-shek was quieter now. 'I've been waiting to catch you alone to see how you look when you're frightened.'

'But *why*?'

'Because, white monkey,' he sneered, 'I know everything. You have violated the honour of the Soongs. Don't deny it.'

'I *do* deny it,' I lied. 'You must be mad. Stark raving mad.'

'How about your brothel in Abingdon Mansions?'

This was the instant when shock replaced fear, driving it away completely. I suddenly thought that Vicki had been right – he must have had Julie followed.

'Don't worry, I'm not going to prison for attacking white trash like you. Not yet. But one day! I'll be there to see you pay.'

Future threats, indefinite. I realised that he never *would* dare attack me. White Singapore would crucify a Chinese who had the temerity to molest an Englishman.

But he knew – that was the terrible thought flashing through my mind. He *knew* – and Julie – it was all over, it had to be. He was crazy, capable of doing anything. The Soongs were powerful – big enough to seek the aid of the tongs, hired killers. I was frightened for Julie – if old Soong found out. If. They wouldn't harm Julie physically – like Kai-shek would like to harm me – but they could send her away within days; and if she refused to go . . . as my mind raced through different agonies, I suddenly thought – if only Julie's mother were here to help her now. But Aunt Sonia was in America – and rumours said she wasn't returning.

'Listen,' I tried pleading, though my voice was shaking. 'This is absurd. Take that dog away and let's talk.' The words sounded as though they had been spoken by someone else.

'You move an inch before I tell you to and the dog *will*

tear you to bits,' he said again. 'And if that happens – you are an intruder – this dog is trained to attack intruders.'

My legs felt as though they didn't belong to me any more than my voice did. I had the curious feeling I wasn't really there – that all this was happening to someone else, that I was looking on. And again the thought of Julie – what would happen to her? Did Kai-shek really know what he was talking about, or were these wild, improbable guesses?

Almost as though the Chinese had been reading my mind he cried, 'You have soiled her honour. But the Chinese do not wash their dirty linen in public – specially when it has been dirtied by a white monkey. You will never again see Julie as long as you live. The Soongs will see to that.'

'You can't stop me –'

'I can stop you *now* – without the dog,' he shouted. 'I use the dog because I don't wish to dirty my hands with a white monkey. But look at these –' he held out his hands. I was too far away to see them, but I knew about Kai-shek's fingers, broken a dozen times as he learned to become a karate Black Belt. There was even a rumour that he had killed one sparring partner. 'No, I don't need a dog,' he sneered.

I don't know what would have happened, but suddenly I heard Julie's voice shouting, 'In there!' and the sound of hurrying footsteps.

I saw the hazy outline of Julie – hazy because a film of fear made it impossible to focus, blotted out every hard outline. She held something in her hands. The dog rose, the growl deepened, became more threatening. Kai-shek screamed, 'Get out, you whore! Get out before I set the dog on your monkey lover.'

'You mad bastard,' I shouted. 'Leave her out of this. Go, Julie!' I moved forward – just one step, that was all. An instinctive step, simply because I couldn't stand there like a bloody dummy while he spat at Julie. Without even a split second's hesitation, the spring uncoiled inside those brown haunches, the dog was at my legs and sinking its teeth into my shoes.

Kai-shek shouted. The dog snarled, backed away, perhaps five feet. Out of the corner of my eye I saw Julie step forward, still carrying something. Kai-shek screamed, 'Don't be a fool!'

The great, grey circular room exploded with noise. At the same moment acrid smoke filled my lungs and I started coughing my guts out as one noise superseded another. In place of the crack of the shot, I heard a whimper.

For a moment I thought Julie had shot Kai-shek, but he was still there, standing. In front of him, at his feet, the Alsatian lay in its death throes. Julie was standing over it, holding the revolver as though it was glued to her hands, as though she would never be able to drop it. It was still pointing at the twitching, bleeding dog.

Kai-shek gave a cry of anguish and I thought he was going down on to his knees, to try to bring the dog back to life. But he changed his mind. Fury supplanted grief as he leapt at Julie.

That was the moment the jelly vanished from my trembling legs, the moment I came back to life. As he leapt forward, so did I. Just as he reached her, hands clawing, I hit him between the eyes so hard I heard the nose bone crack. It tore the skin from my knuckles, and I knew I wouldn't be able to use that bruised left hand for a long time.

His glasses splintered as his nose broke, as he fell I knew this was no time for Queensberry rules. Apart from the fact that I wanted to kill him, apart from the fact that I already knew Julie and I were on the edge of the biggest crisis of our lives, Kai-shek *was* a Black Belt, he *was* a killer by instinct; and now with all the technique of a killer's art he would kill me if I let him.

Thank God he had broken his glasses. As he stumbled, groping, unable to focus, I brought my right knee up with all the strength left in me. It went straight into his groin. He flopped down screaming.

'Julie,' I cried as he fell, 'are you all right?'

'I knew where we kept the gun – we've always kept it since we were burgled,' her voice was steady but her hands were shaking. 'If only I had had the courage to kill *him*.'

At that moment I heard the front door slam, and in walked Julie's father and brother.

Paul rushed forward, but old P.P. Soong just stood there, taking in every detail of the scene – Julie still holding the gun, the dog a dead mass of bloodstained fur at her feet, Kai-shek trying to get up off the floor.

'He has defiled our sister,' Kai-shek, still on his knees, pointed a finger at me. 'This man is her lover. I saw them come back together – openly –'

Without a word Soong stepped up and slapped Kai-shek on both sides of his face. I felt my entire body droop, go slack. I managed to cry, 'It's not true, Mr Soong –'

'There have been other times – they have a flat –'

'Silence!' roared Soong. 'You have insulted the son of an honoured friend. To set a dog on an honoured friend is unpardonable. You will apologise.'

'Never!' cried Kai-shek.

'It doesn't matter,' I mumbled. 'It's all forgotten –' though I knew it never would be. Two boys came rushing in, followed by the terrified amah wringing her hands. There was a lot of cross-talk I didn't understand.

I tried to say something but my legs had gone weak again and I felt I was going to pass out. Julie saw it, and stepped towards me.

'Go to your room my daughter,' said Soong, but though his voice was stern it was not harsh, and even as I stumbled on to the couch I realised that it was immeasurably sad. He had been bitterly and deeply hurt and his grey face showed it. I must have passed out. When I came round the room was empty except for Paul.

'You'd better go,' he said quietly. 'I'll try to get in touch. You can't drive – our syce will take you home in your car. He can walk back.'

8

'You're not only a damn fool. A man can live with a fool – but what you've done – to the daughter of one of our oldest friends – and a decent girl, who was –' he spluttered to avoid the word virgin – 'untouched. That is despicable.'

I had never seen my father so angry. 'Well, don't stand there,' he shouted, 'Can't you at least show some signs of remorse – aren't you even sorry for what you've done?'

'Of course I'm sorry,' I began.

'That's a lie – and you know it.' His lip curled as though he despised me. 'You're not sorry. It takes someone with a bit of decency to be sorry. You're only sorry because you've been found out.'

I didn't deny it. We were standing in the study. How he had learned about Julie and me I didn't know; presumably he and Soong had met and talked after that nightmarish scene following the Koo party. The story would be all over Singapore by now.

'You don't understand,' I tried again to speak, but if this was a slanging match it was one-sided – so far. I not only had the feeling I was the central figure in someone else's nightmare, that I wasn't there standing in the room, but I was also physically in agony. My left hand was a swollen blue-green mess and the pain constantly shot up my arm.

'Be quiet,' my father shouted. 'How dare you interrupt me?'

'You asked me –'

'Twenty-two! A man! *Supposed* to be a man,' he said bitterly. 'What a fiasco – the next *tuan bezar*! A likely prospect. Where's your sense of responsibility? Your honour? What about the pack of lies you've been telling your mother and me?'

'If you'd let me just *say* something –'

'More lies? More damned lies to your own father in his own house? Say something? Can you tell me it's all untrue, that you've never touched Julie Soong?'

I said nothing.

'Of course not,' he said contemptuously. 'Unless you can deny everything, what the hell *is* there to say?'

Standing there, half my mind tortured with anxiety for Julie, I was trying (a relic of upbringing, of Mama's influence on us as children) to exercise patience, to wait until my father ran out of steam; then, I hoped, I might be able to explain, make him see that in no way was I shit, a seducer. I don't suppose in a way it mattered *what* my father thought, yet I hoped that he might understand because I knew I had hurt him deeply. His face had the resigned grey mask I had glimpsed when looking at Soong. But my father would only allow himself to believe the worst about me. I think he believed I had been to bed with Julie for the fun of it, that I had been secretly chortling over just another conquest. In the thirties parents did feel like that, they did believe there were two kinds of girls; they did believe in honour among sons — this despite the hypocrisy of the Victorian age, to say nothing of the hypocrisy of their own youth. But one thing they *didn't* believe in was young love. I respected my father — respect for parents had been instilled in me from the earliest days — and I *was* upset that I had upset *him*, even though I knew his anger had been magnified because of the slur to his honour. The sons of Singapore *tuans* didn't take virgins from the great Chinese families to bed. It was not only a stain on the honour of the Soongs, it was a stain on our family honour too. That was what really hurt him.

Standing there, listening to him shout, his lip curled with something very close to hatred, I suddenly thought of Julie lying naked in bed at Abingdon Mansions and giggling, 'What a row there'd be if our parents ever found out. But if they do, well, it's our lives, not theirs. They don't own our lives, do they?'

It was our lives that were at stake. Ours — to do what we liked with — within reason. They didn't belong to our fathers. What right had my father to stand there treating me like an outcast? Suddenly I found myself saying in a loud voice, 'Can I speak? Can I *speak*?'

'When I've finished.'

'Okay. I'm off.' I turned towards the lattice door.

'Stay here!' my father shouted. 'Where the hell do you think you're going?'

'Out. What do you care?'

'I haven't finished.'

'Well, I have. I'm sorry, Father, but I'm off. I'm not going to stand here while you foam at the mouth.'

He walked towards the door. I had a sudden awful feeling that he might have a heart attack. His face was bright red.

'You stay here,' he said savagely.

'I'll stay if I can talk. *You* talk about *me*! What's fair about shouting for an hour, telling me I've behaved like a shit, without letting me defend myself? I'm not a schoolkid. I'm off. I can get a job. For the first time in my life I'm beginning to realise that Tim was bright.'

I had never spoken to my father like that before, and as he looked at me I couldn't tell from his face whether anger was mounting at my 'insolence' or whether it registered stupefaction. He stood back a pace and pressed the spring on the thin gold bridge of his rimless glasses, took them off, leaving his naked eyes pale and watery and looking very different. He wiped his glasses, put them back on his nose and said harshly, 'Well, I'm listening.'

I swallowed hard and muttered as defiantly as I could, 'Julie and I love each other. We always have.'

He didn't shout. He didn't argue. He did something worse. He laughed. 'I knew it was coming! I could almost have written the title of your romance – *Romeo and Julie!* You insufferable prig – ruining the friendship of two families, shaming your parents, all for a bit of dick disguised as love. What the hell do *you* know about love, at your age? It's just an excuse for –'

'I don't have to listen to this. It's never been like that. Never.'

I had known what his reaction would be. In fact I had almost been afraid to use the word love – because in a way I could understand the feelings of older people in Singapore. In those days white youngsters were, I realise now, basically immature in Singapore, cocooned in relationships with parents that made them ill-equipped to stand up against fathers and mothers. And of course I knew what was coming next.

'And where is this great love affair going to end? Marriage? To a Chinese girl in Singapore? You must be mad.'

'Well,' I muttered, very unsure of myself, 'if I could get a job in America – it's different there.'

'You forget one thing.' My father was now adopting the air of a teacher trying to explain a simple problem to a backward child. 'My God, you *are* a stupid fool. You can go to Timbuctoo and stay there for all I care, but *Julie's father is a Chinese*. Even if I agreed that you could marry, do you think he would? A Chinese – a respected businessman, a leader of the community whose family honour had been shamed by a white man. You can be certain of only one thing, young man – you'll never see your precious Julie again.'

'I'm off!' I shouted. 'If you're *determined* to think the worst of me – I'm off, and please get away from that door. I love you, Father, I really do, but if you try to stop me I'm going to push you away.'

His face seemed to sag. I *did* love him; I loved and respected him, though he was too old to understand my feelings. And it was because I felt like this that I put out an arm towards him.

'Don't touch me,' he muttered as he let me pass.

It was just before noon when I dashed out of the house and round to the attap-roofed shelter that served as garage for all our cars. I wasn't doing anything dramatic, but I had to get out of the house for a while, and I ended up at the Cricket Club. Armed with a gin pahit, I made my way to the verandah, sat down, lit a cigarette and stared across the padang at the traffic bowling along behind the line of flame trees; little taxis, sleek cars, rickshaw pullers. I was thinking – with all the tragic thoughts of youth – What the hell can I do? Julie might have been right in theory when she said that our lives were our own, but in practice our lives were not our own – certainly hers wasn't. She was not only a minor, she was subject to the rigid discipline of a Chinese family bound by autocratic rules impossible to violate, subject to the will of a father whose authority, by Chinese custom, was absolute. She didn't even have Aunt Sonia near her to cushion the terrible cold fury that I could imagine surrounded her. What could we do? Could we run away –

bolt for it? Certainly I had a few thousand pounds in London from a trust fund that had matured on my twenty-first birthday, but what good was money if it couldn't buy Julie her freedom? She couldn't escape, and I couldn't kidnap her, though even that crazy thought flashed through my head.

If I couldn't see Julie, talk to her, then I must talk to Paul, find out what was happening. But how? I shouted for the boy to bring me another gin just as George Hammonds arrived. He knew. George knew everything that went on in Singapore — specially news of any misdemeanours by the sons of *tuans*. And though I was a few years younger than George, he always treated me as an equal in age if not in grey matter. Also — and this was typical of George — he didn't make any stupid references to what had happened. All he said, in his slightly hesitant voice, was, 'You don't look in the mood for volunteer snooker.'

'You're right. I'm not, but you could do me a favour.'

He did. As though telephoning on a *Malaya Tribune* enquiry, he spoke to Paul and arranged for him to meet me at Raffles in half an hour. By the time I arrived, he was propping up the long bar.

'Not a hope,' he said bluntly when I asked if I could see Julie secretly. 'No good my kidding you. She's not allowed out of the house — and you'd have to be a cat burglar to get in.'

'I'll wait at the hospital — at the secretarial college.'

'All cancelled by my father.' He signalled to the barman.

'But this is 1936,' I said desperately. 'You can't keep a girl a prisoner —'

'It may be 1936 here — it's 1836 in our house. Just at the moment it's a chunk of feudal China ten thousand miles from Singapore.' He held his glass up to the light. 'I know how you feel, Johnnie. Believe me, I do. But what you've both done — both of you, not you alone — is as heinous a crime as you can commit in a Chinese family. My father can't cut your balls off, but he would if he could get away with it, and if you don't watch out one day Kai-shek will.'

'But Paul — we're in love.'

'Love is a secondary emotion in China. Look at my

147

father – and mother. He was delighted to marry her – but what he really enjoys are the times he spends with the other girls. Marriage and love – they don't mix for sophisticated Chinese.'

'Well, we were – are – in love,' I insisted stubbornly.

'I believe you, but you're both a bit, well, *too* romantic. You know – hearts and flowers stuff, mooning around. Don't take offence, I respect you for it. If I didn't, do you think I'd have let you carry on when I realised what was happening? I was educated in California. My father wasn't. My Western feelings run deep. He only has a veneer of Western thought. I let you go on for two reasons. First, you were making Julie happy – happier than she may ever be again in her life, and she deserves that. And secondly, I knew you wouldn't let her down.'

'But I have.'

'You haven't. Kai-shek fucked it all up. But at least Julie – and she is only twenty – both of you have something super to look back on.'

'Christ, Paul! I want to look *forward*. I want to marry Julie. Maybe we could go to America. That's what I've been thinking. What the hell do you mean, looking *back*? And what's going to happen when we meet at parties – we're bound to –'

Paul led the way to a corner table at the far end of the room, away from the palm court music of Dan Hopkins and his orchestra. 'There *is* no future, Johnnie.' He pointed to a chair. 'You take that one. I'll sit here – and put your glass on the table. I don't want you to drop it.'

'I'm not tight, if that's what you mean.'

'You might as well know – In two days Julie's leaving.'

I did knock the glass over. 'You can't mean it.'

'Sorry, old chum, but I do, and there's no point in trying to soften the blow. Julie's been – for want of a better word – banished. She's sailing for San Francisco on the *Pacific Princess*. Father wangled a berth, mother wangled a place at Berkeley.'

Paul fished in the pocket of his lightweight jacket and produced a small piece of paper.

'She gave me this note for you,' he said. 'She didn't have time to write, but you know how she is — always messing around with poetry, and she scribbled it.' Paul didn't ask me what she had written. It was a snatch of poetry by a man I had never heard of. Julie just wrote 'With love from J and Humbert Wolfe.' Underneath it she had written,

If it must be so, let's not weep nor complain
If I have failed, or you, or life turned sullen.
We have had these things, they do not come again,
But the flag still flies, and the city has not fallen.

I read it through with the dull feeling of a man receiving a farewell note before being sent to prison — for life.

'They can't keep her away forever, in America I mean?'

'I don't suppose they will,' said Paul. 'But certainly until all this has blown over.'

'It'll *never* blow over,' I vowed. 'Never.'

'It will, Johnnie. For all our sakes I hope it will. And for Julie more than anyone.' Seeing my anger mounting he added, 'And don't lose your temper. You've both had a wonderful love affair together and you'll never forget it. But if you were allowed to defy the rules of Singapore — come on Johnnie, take a look at those who have. What a bloody mess they've made of it. You would end up hating each other.'

'I'd take the chance.'

'That's what they all say. I know you would. So would Julie. But sorry, chum, I'm glad she won't be allowed to. Isn't there some feeble joke about the wrongs and rights when Wongs marry whites? As mother used to say when she felt lonesome for California, "You can't buck the system."'

The knowledge that Julie was leaving knocked all the stuffing out of me, but on the other hand there was a finality about the news that pulled me up and made me think a little more coherently. Because Paul and I were such close friends, I felt that a lot of what he said at Raffles did make sense. At twenty-two I might feel like hell – even like suicide, with life hardly worth living – but the Grandpa Jack in me whispered that Paul was right – pain does have a habit of becoming less acute, however intense it is at first. I knew I would never love anyone else; but I had to go on breathing.

Driving home after lunch I was thinking – always in pictures, snapshots of Abingdon Mansions and other places – that we had always known it would end like this, that however much we pretended, there was no way we would ever have been able to marry. In a curious way this un-discussed but shared knowledge had not only sharpened our emotions but given us an added tenderness, as though each knew that, like invalids, our lives hung on a thread; and because of this we had to be kind and understanding to each other, leaving no room for the violent emotions of jealousy and envy. It was that which had made everything so won-derful.

But now – now she was being banished without even a goodbye kiss. As I swung into the drive of Tanamera – the warm family home transformed into a cold, inhospitable white shell – I was thinking of the bleak future mapped out for Julie and me. Surely to God, I thought, whatever the crime this was a time when a son and daughter needed sympathy and help; when a father should try to comfort me, to try to understand, at least *believe* me. If I had been arrested on a murder charge Papa Jack would have spent every last cent on lawyers to get an acquittal, whether he thought me innocent or guilty. Yet for loving a girl who loved me he was treating me as a criminal undeserving of sympathy.

The fact that I had become entangled with the well-brought-up daughter of a close Chinese friend – that was what made them so angry and unforgiving, for it was an entanglement that could not be ignored. Had I become involved with some unknown floosie – of any colour, any creed – she would have been paid off if necessary, and everything would have been brushed under the carpet, the affair soon forgotten. I might even have earned a fatherly chuckle, 'Young fellows *will* get into trouble.' But this was different. Our feelings didn't count.

I couldn't be bothered to back the Morgan into the attap shed, but parked it outside the portico. As I pulled the hood loosely over the seats to shield them from the sun, Grandpa Jack, wheeled by old Li, waved towards me. He was an old man now, the face lined and thinner, the beard straggly, the eyes magnified by new and stronger glasses that gave him a curious piercing look which was hardly matched by his voice, no longer coarse and gruff, but high-pitched, sometimes almost a cackle. But even so he had made an astonishing recovery. Despite a slight slur occasionally, his words still made sense, and that part of his brain unaffected by the stroke was sharp and tough. I knew that I was his favourite; I knew that he and Li often waited outside in the garden deliberately hoping to trap me into some pseudo-confidential talk. Why not? I could always find time to spare for Grandpa Jack; perhaps because each of us saw in the other some kind of reflection.

Old Li put the brake on the wheelchair and beamed. His wrinkled parchment of a face looked as creased as a crumpled bag. Grandpa Jack came right to the point, 'You're in the shit, eh?' It was a statement more than a query, so I just nodded.

'Sorry,' he said. 'Happened to me dozens of times. My old man took a belt to me once – buckle end on my arse. Hurt like hell, but I went straight out and laid her again. Indian.' He loved to recount adventures I had heard a dozen times, but which with the forgetfulness of age he was convinced he had just remembered for the first time in years. 'Don't blame you. Admire your taste. If you've got to do that sort of thing, choose the best.' He was thinking deeply, and I didn't like the way the conversation was heading. Knowing him, the next thing would be a question on what it was like.

'Forget it, Grandpa Jack,' I said. 'All over now.'

It switched him to a new train of thought. 'Bet your father was hopping mad.' Then, mysteriously, 'People in glass houses – he was young once.'

I smiled. One of the pleasant things about talking to old men is that you don't need to use words. They don't expect you to reply, only to nod and agree or register surprise. 'Put it down to experience,' he said.

'You know they're sending Julie to America?'

'Aye, that hurts. But it's for the best, m'boy. And don't be too hard on your father.'

'On my *father*!' My astonishment must have shown.

'Yes. He's probably been hurt more than you.'

Grandpa Jack was ruminating, moving his mouth as he rehearsed words silently before he said something I never forgot. 'You started a few years too soon,' he grunted, 'or you might have got away with it. World's changing. If there's a war in Europe it'll come over here, you remember what I say. And then everything – even Singapore – will change. Wouldn't be a bit surprised to see whites marrying nig-nogs in Africa or Chinese in Asia.'

'I must go,' I said, taking hold of his good hand – the right one – and giving it a squeeze. Two minutes was as long as half an hour to Grandpa Jack, and I knew it was time to go when he started talking nonsense about the future. Whites marrying nig-nogs! My God, what next?

With an old man's stubbornness, Grandpa Jack clung to the vulgarity that had marked his long, lecherous and liquid life, and with a metaphorical dig in the ribs he said, 'Don't give up hope, m'boy! You may have to wait years, but who knows. At the moment the Gods are pissing on you from a great height. But put up your brolly and keep on walking!'

That night we made it up. Papa Jack was out playing golf when I walked into the house, thinking of what Grandpa Jack had just said, and when I found Mama in the sitting room I'm not ashamed to say that I put my head on her shoulder and let her put an arm round me.

'I'll apologise to Father,' I said, 'and I'll mean it. I am sorry if I hurt him – really sorry.'

'So is he, Johnnie. About what he said. You get so worked up, you Dexters. I've never seen him so upset.' She stroked my hair and said absently, 'it's still a beautiful blond colour, your hair.'

'The sun,' I laughed.

'We'll have a lovely dinner together this evening. Natasha and Tony are coming. I'll tell the boy to put some champagne on ice.'

'Papa might not feel like it. And I couldn't drink it – knowing that Julie's leaving.'

'He loves you, Johnnie. And he needs you. He'll be so pleased and happy, you see.'

As I got up, she added, 'And don't ever think *my* heart isn't breaking to see you suffering like this. To me Julie is the loveliest and sweetest girl in the world. I would *love* her as a daughter – if it wasn't impossible.'

'I don't see why it can't be possible. But Mama, if only you promise that *you* understand – it wasn't just a bit of fun.'

'I know, darling. For months I saw you falling in love. It happened the night of Grandpa Jack's stroke, didn't it?'

I was flabbergasted. 'How on earth did you know?'

'Your eyes. They were shining. You couldn't disguise it. I saw that shining look only once before in my life – the look of conquest no man can hide – in eyes just like yours, in a face just like yours. Nine months before Natasha was born.'

When Papa Jack returned from golf I stopped him in the ballroom as soon as the boy had gone. I put my arms round him, we both muttered 'Sorry,' and everything was understood. He put an arm on my shoulder and led the way to a ceremonial stengah on the west verandah.

As he sat there, his white ducks half hidden under the table, his shirt open-necked (allowed for sports but not otherwise) his jacket thrown over the next chair, I realised how tired and grey he looked. He said, 'Now that Tim's in the army, I'm depending on you, Johnnie. I'm getting on for sixty.'

Was *that* why father looked so resigned? Was it because of Tim? Tim was a loss, an amputation, for while I took after

Grandpa Jack (and so was forgiven the occasional wild escapade) Tim was the elder son, the one whom a father always hopes will step into his shoes and fulfil the dream of every father – to produce a son in his image.

Was that it? And yet I wasn't sure. So when I said, 'I wish Tim was here,' I wasn't surprised when my father answered, 'That's not the problem. I always knew he would never run the business. He's – well, he's different from you, Johnnie. You cause me a lot of trouble, but you *are* a businessman. And you do love Singapore.'

He only mentioned 'the Julie problem' once and briefly. 'I don't want you to think I had anything to do with P.P.'s plan to send Julie to America. He's very Chinese, and maybe it's for the best. And I've been thinking a lot about you, Johnnie – a change might do *you* good. We've got your Japanese contract moving into action – no problems, all the snags ironed out – so why don't you go to the London office for a year or so? Assistant manager. You should know how the London end ticks before I retire.'

I didn't really want to go – not at first. But one thing made me decide. Ghosts. It was the prospect of seeing the ghost of Julie everywhere I went – each time I played tennis with Miki at the YMCA, each time I danced with some other girl at a Raffles party, each time I turned the car into Scotts Road. I knew that in a way I was being banished too. But anything to get away.

Only the best champagne – vintage Taittinger – was served at dinner that night, and we couldn't even finish the last bottle, despite the fact that I drank it down solidly. For a while I felt miserable. Natflat looked adorable, Tony looked dependable, Mama looked misty-eyed, Papa looked proud, and even proposed a toast, 'To our new assistant manager in London. Johnnie!'

Three weeks later – two days after Natasha and Tony were married – I took a last look round Tanamera, shook hands with young Li, and sailed for England on the *Blantyre Castle*.

PART TWO

London, 1936–1937

9

When I landed in London in the late spring of 1936, on a blustery rain-lashed day, I felt like a convicted man starting a prison sentence. As a family we had visited London regularly – in Singapore in those days most people took six months leave every three years – but this was very different. Hearts of twenty-three-year-olds may not break as easily in fact as they do in fiction, but all the same they bruise, and bruising hurts for a long time. A dream life had been shattered and my head was filled with crazy, half-formed schemes to pick up the pieces and stick the dream together again. Most of them revolved round plans for spiriting Julie out of America and starting a new life in some distant country where we could live unmolested. I had a little money, and felt that would tide us over until I could find a job. But how to contact Julie except through her mother? In my heart I knew nothing could be done. I was indulging in the usual daydreams of the thwarted lover, a form of masochistic enjoyment which perhaps has the virtue of covering the real pain with a patina of false hope.

The office where I was now doomed to work was at the corner of Swallow Street and Piccadilly. The modest brass plate 'Dexter and Company, Singapore and London' led to an equally modest suite of five offices on the second floor of the corner building. Two dark rooms overlooked a courtyard on Vine Street, but the three main rooms faced Piccadilly, the corner room right in front of Wren's church, with its single magnolia tree in the courtyard.

Behind the desk, in the room with the best view, sat the London manager, Mr Cowley, a stout, important-looking man in his fifties, very conscious of his position, and who seemed to my youthful eyes to be far too imposing ever to have been burdened with a Christian name. I remembered him from the time when he had lived as a bachelor in Cadet House in Singapore. But though he had been adept at learning the business there had been rumours of an entanglement – ah! that word: it was used, even then – with an Indian girl who had been discovered in bed in the sacrosanct Cadet House, an unforgivable sin.

Mr Cowley had been sent back to London 'for his own good' – just like me – and now, having lived down the scandal, had risen to become our London manager. He was also married with children and a house in Highgate and wore a black jacket, pepper and salt trousers, and a gold chain across his stomach.

As I went into the office on the first morning and he got up to greet me, touching his trousers to ensure they were well creased, I thought irreverently of the night he must have spent taking them down in front of his Indian girlfriend, and then had the even more irreverent picture of him taking them down to pleasure Mrs Cowley at the end of a day's work at the office. It seemed impossible that old pompous people could find the same beauty as Julie and I had done in secret exercises. How sad for them, I thought.

'Ah! Welcome to London, Mr Dexter. And how is the young *tuan*?' His voice was indulgent, the tone of a trusted senior employee who, I suspected, had received a private note from Papa Jack to keep an eye on me. He had, he explained, arranged for me to use the small office next to his, a room traditionally kept for Papa Jack, or in the old days for Grandpa Jack.

'Some coffee is coming.' He beckoned me to the old leather couch which had a Japanese coffee table in front of it. When a secretary brought in the tray, he introduced me, 'This is Gwen.' She was a pert, pretty girl in her early twenties. 'She has only been with us a year, but she is already invaluable.'

'I hope you enjoy it here, Gwen,' I said rather fatuously.

'Ever so, thanks.' She smiled – invitingly. However I was in no mood to initiate or reciprocate any advances. I was too miserable.

Mr Cowley was at great pains to show his gratitude for my arrival. Rubber and tin were booming, and there was too much work for the small staff of five. 'And too much responsibility,' he added. 'You know as well as I do, Johnnie – I may call you Johnnie? – that one false move under pressure – if you buy or sell ahead at the wrong price – and you can lose a fortune. Or' – indulgently – 'make one. I'm afraid we tend to get out of touch with the *feeling* in Singapore, and I'm sure that you'll be able to help us.'

We sat talking most of the morning. As he explained, the International Rubber Regulation Scheme – which had been introduced in 1934 – was certainly controlling world rubber exports. 'But,' he sighed, 'it's fraught – yes, *fraught* with problems!'

Under the scheme, each country was allocated a basic export quota roughly equal to its production capacity. 'But the trouble is, each country is left to its own devices to control its exports, so the unscrupulous are cheating. As you know, each estate in Malaya is issued with export coupons giving it the right to export rubber up to the face value of the coupons. But the Chinese! They are forging coupons like confetti. It makes a mockery of honest British toil.'

The pert Gwen came in to take away the tray – at the very moment when I was saying to Mr Cowley, 'I'm fascinated. Perhaps we could lunch together – what about a cut off the joint at Stone's Chop House?'

'Well,' he sounded doubtful, 'it's a *little* difficult – I do have a previous lunch engagement, but –'

As he hesitated I intercepted the look that flashed between Cowley and Gwen. Poor Mr Cowley, his Indian girlfriend long forgotten, was serving not only a master but a mistress.

I did manage to find myself a flat, a kind of studio on the Fulham Road backing on to Stamford Bridge football ground. An Italian sculptor called Mario Manenti – a cheerful, rubicund individual with a large floppy hat which somehow gave him the appearance of an old-fashioned Italian painting – had bought two ugly, square white houses, together with their large gardens behind. The houses were unchanged, but behind them Manenti had transformed the gardens into patios linked by narrow plant-lined paths flanking thirty or forty studios which he had designed himself. Each one was different, and charming. Mine – Studio Z – had a lawn the size of a handkerchief in front, with one large pear tree in the centre. Its one room, lit by a large skylight, was furnished with a divan in the corner and bookshelves round it. It was large enough for an old grand piano, chairs, and had a Victorian circular cast-iron staircase leading up to a gallery running the length of the room under the sloping roof. The gallery in turn led to a bedroom which had been built over a bathroom and a tiny kitchen below.

I took it on the spot for six pounds a week furnished – thinking what a wonderful retreat it would have made had Julie been with me. I had brought with me one photograph of Julie, so I bought a second-hand silver frame from the antique dealer near the bridge on the Fulham Road and stood the photograph on the piano. Apart from a few books it was my only personal item of furniture.

Manenti was the sort of man who was always anxious to see that his tenants were happy. He used to ask me in for drinks and talk to me about Italian art. He found a Mrs Fisher for me, who came in for an hour or so every morning to clean up after I had left for the office. He took me across the Fulham Road and introduced me to Mr Davis, the newsagent, who delivered the papers; and Mr Strang who kept the equivalent of a village store, for he sold just about everything from tinned salmon to fresh vegetables and his assistant always wore a green baize apron when delivering anything that I or Mrs Fisher ordered.

The only way I could let off steam to combat frustration and self-pity was in playing tennis, but even that was not satis-factory. I made few friends, even when I joined Queen's Club. It was easy to get to Queen's – the tube from Piccadilly took me directly to Barons Court, an ancient station with green tiles flanking the ticket office, and the name of each platform proudly displayed on blue tiles that would last a hundred years. Getting there was one thing. Finding opponents was more difficult. I soon discovered that the only chance of a regular game lay in engaging the pro, a taciturn individual called Jenkins. No one else was even remotely interested in a stranger from the colonies. And since Jenkins was adept after years of practice at playing a customer's game it wasn't much fun, even on the covered courts which sheltered us from the foul weather.

I had been in London a few weeks when I walked into my office one morning and there on the desk was a pale blue envelope with two American stamps on it. My heart leapt. Dexters did receive correspondence from American clients but the letters usually went to Cowley. This one, however, was not only addressed to me but was marked personal. I *knew* this must be from her.

For a few moments I let it lie there, savouring the joys of anticipation, studying the postmark, looking at the up-and-down writing, girlish in one way (a Singapore education) yet with strong strokes and a powerful, dashed-off line under the word England. I imagined her in the moment of writing, what she had been wearing, where she had been sitting. Finally I slit the envelope open.

The letter read:
Darling Johnnie,
   I never thought I could miss anyone so much, and though Mummy is trying to be kind I hate San Francisco and I think of you, and in my heart hope that perhaps you hate London just as much! Mummy has ordered me not to write you — she says it will only make life more diffi-cult — but I had to. Oh, Johnnie, how I miss you! Some-times when I see the American girls in our class I think of the Love Club and the fact that we have in a way been 'married' and it makes me feel so superior.
   But I would change it and change everything to be with

you, even for a day, an hour. I wonder what will have happened to both of us when we meet again, if we ever do. This is the very first love letter I have ever written and it's funny, I find it hard to write down what I always found so easy to tell you, that I love you, and how much, and that, whatever happens, I always will. We are studying American philosophy and literature and I came across this poem which Robert Frost might have written for us,

> Two roads diverged in a wood, and I –
> I took the one less travelled by.

She had given me an address at Berkeley to which she said I could safely write, and her letter sounded so lonely and sad that I sat down that same day and poured out my heart in a long, rambling, passionate reply.

Two months passed before I received the next letter – there was no regular airmail then – but though the postmark was San Francisco the writing this time was different, more formed. It had the mature look of someone whose feet were firmly planted on the ground.

It was from Aunt Sonia, and I only had to read the first lines to imagine the anger that had prompted her to write. We had always thought of her as *Aunt* Sonia, the good sport, the fun aunt who joined in all our games. Even at parties in the Soong mansion she had never seemed to play the role of mother. But she did now, very much the mother determined to protect a wronged daughter.

The letter started, 'It was very wicked of you to write to Julie with all those foolish promises which you know perfectly well you can never keep.' She did not say how she had come across the letter, but added, 'I blame Julie too because she gave me her word not to write to you and obviously yours was a reply to one written by her. Julie *is* unhappy, and if you write to her in secret you will be deliberately torturing her and prolonging that unhappiness. The only way to give Julie a chance is for you to leave her alone, so that it will be easier to put what has happened in the past.

162

'You know as well as I do that marriage between you is impossible. In America things are different, but your whole life is bound up with Singapore and, as I have found out to my cost, mixed marriages do not work out there. I am *determined*' – underlined three times – 'that Julie shall not suffer as I have done.'

Towards the end of the letter, which covered seven pages, she tried to make me understand that she didn't *altogether* blame me, at least not for falling in love. She wrote: 'In a place like Singapore it was unforgivable of you to seduce Julie. Yet I do forgive you, even understand, because I cannot see how anyone could resist Julie and I know that your intentions were, in a way, honourable. And we parents are also to blame for throwing you so much together. Because I hope you are still the nice and honest Johnnie I knew as a child I know you will promise me not to write again to Julie. You will have to live the rest of your life in Singapore; and the sooner you marry a nice English (American?) girl the better for both of you.'

Underneath her flowing signature was a PS: 'Don't stay in London too long. There's going to be a war, but England will have a good friend now that Roosevelt is certain to be re-elected in the fall.'

What could I do? Is there any more wicked parental weapon than an appeal to their children's honesty, loyalty or pity? What hypocrisy lies hidden behind every muttered remark about a boy or girl's 'better nature'. What honesty had Aunt Sonia and her husband displayed to each other, whoever was to blame? Who had thought of Paul and Julie when they fought and shouted in that huge grey house that was not a home? What rights had they to appeal? My father had also appealed to my 'better nature' – not only to my 'duty' as an 'honourable' son, but (in some undefined way) even citing my future as a *tuan*; as though I would supervise the books better or get more business if I 'behaved myself' – behaviour being measured not by Christian ethics but by home-made Singapore shibboleths. Why, I thought as I reread Aunt Sonia's letter, Grandpa Jack was the only honest parent in both our families. He had cheerfully screwed his way through the spectrum of local coloured ladies and enjoyed every minute of it. And he had been drunk. And he had made a fortune.

Aunt Sonia's appeal to my better nature was all the worse because she was right. Her appeal I could not ignore because, above all, I did not want to hurt Julie, or to prolong any hurt. Yet I hesitated at first to obey. After all, Julie had given her mother her word not to write me and had then promptly broken it. Why shouldn't I do the same thing? But then she had been discovered. What had happened between mother and daughter in San Francisco? Had there been a tough, angry showdown with mother threatening daughter? Knowing Julie's rebellious nature and her love of adventure, I hardly thought so. More likely Aunt Sonia had put forward to Julie the same arguments (but with different premises) that she had written to me, appealing to Julie not to ruin the life of a young Englishman. A true and despicable argument. Certainly something had prevented Julie from writing a second letter.

I didn't decide what to do in an hour, a week, a month. But I did realise that Aunt Sonia's appeal to me was based on the fact that she *knew* I loved Julie. In the end I decided to wait and see what happened; if nothing happened I would do nothing. I had written last and now I waited. If Julie didn't reply to my letter, it meant she was being 'wise' – and then I would have to try to help her by not writing.

That is what happened. The letters ceased. I dreamed of Julie – always with love, and often – but as the months of 1936 sped by, with plenty of work to occupy me, the thought of Julie ceased to torment me. The love was there, but the instant desire, the anguish of want, grew less with each month.

London had been in a turmoil even since I arrived, with King Edward, who had become monarch at the beginning of the year, vaccillating between love for an American divorcée and duty to the British throne. Even I began to be seized with the excitement, which was heightened by the lack of official information, for at first British newspapers agreed not to mention the crisis despite its being headlined day after day in every American paper. Everybody knew, of course. People passed foreign newspapers around, and the excitement mounted as it became more evident that the man so popular as Prince of Wales was actually considering abdication.

I saw the poor king's dilemma as a reflection of my own: he was the victim of forces stronger than himself which were fighting to deny him the right to marry someone *they* considered unsuitable, just as similar forces had sought to stop me marrying a girl *they* thought unsuitable. When finally, in December, he *did* abdicate, I envied him the courage he displayed in making a life of his own; a courage I seemed to lack, as I sat at my desk overlooking Piccadilly, telephoning rubber or tin brokers or arranging shipments of plantation or mining equipment to Malaya.

I made only a few friends that winter, and we went together on the occasional pub crawl or to the cinema. Tim, by now a second lieutenant, was stationed near Richmond in Yorkshire and came down to London for a couple of weekend leaves. Each time we did a theatre together, but the evenings, though agreeable, were not memorable. But in the spring of 1937 a new life suddenly opened for me. The man who brought about this transformation – which led to many new friendships and much more than that – was none other than Jiroh Miki.

'I don't believe it!' I cried when, shortly after arriving at the office one morning, a sibilant voice on the phone asked, 'You like game tennis?'

'Miki!' I said. 'What the hell are you doing here?'

'I came on flyboat for three months work.'

'It must be a very big deal.'

'Ah so!'

'What are you up to – what's the deal?' I asked without thinking.

'Top secret.' I could visualise him beaming as he almost hissed, 'I stay at Savoy Hotel. Very good place.'

Miki had joined Queen's when he got his tennis Blue at

Cambridge, and had made dozens of friends there. He had kept in touch, and we started playing regularly. Soon his friends became mine.

The Japanese were coming under increasing criticism because of their warlike noises in China, but it was still a vague condemnation rarely directed at individuals; in much the same way that one disapproved of the Italians murdering Abbysinians, but still kept Italian friends; or despised Hitler as a bully but didn't refuse to speak to a German friend.

The ordinary British people knew nothing really about the Japanese; and Miki, who was not only very pleasant but a fine tennis player, even gained some sympathy. As one member put it: 'If a big country like Germany demands *lebensraum* and gets away with it – well, poor Japan has *no* room, and there's plenty to spare in China.' No doubt this argument was advanced by many members of Queen's who vaguely assumed that since both races were yellow and had slant eyes there was no more difference between 'the Chinks and the Japs' than between the people of Yorkshire and Lancashire.

Suddenly, after my form had been established – that of a player who might not be able to beat Miki but could be relied upon to give him a reasonable game – I was inundated with people who swiftly readjusted their values, no longer regarding me as someone from some colonial outpost. My popularity (such as it was) was further enhanced when it was discovered that I was able to escape from the office to play tennis at times when most opponents were at work.

Miki also seemed able to play during working hours and, though I did not see him more than a couple of times a week, I was intrigued by the mysterious construction contract which could justify a stay of three months at the Savoy. Sometimes he vanished with a polite, 'Going up north', or 'west', but he never gave any details, and turned away my teasing questions with a polite, barely audible indrawn breath, a display of beautiful white teeth, and a smiling, 'Very important'.

The spring of 1937 turned into early summer. It became much more fun to feel the springy, yielding, close-cropped grass courts under our feet again, and though I missed the Tamil ball-boys without whose help we would never have dreamed of playing tennis in Singapore, it was pleasant after a tough game on a sunny day to sit on the broad terrace of the pavilion, gulping down pints of shandy, watching the other players in white, sweating and grunting on the Number One court. When the sun was shining it was not a bad substitute for the Singapore Cricket Club. But, alas, it would never be a substitute for the tennis courts at the Singapore YMCA.

It was Miki who asked me one day in May, 'You like play garden party tennis Sunday?'

'Good God no, I can't think of anything worse.'

'Ah so. Pity.' His teeth flashed in a sardonic smile, 'Best courts in London – everyone international player or Blue except you. And I have a motorcar.'

Of course I went.

The Bradshaws, as befitted a famous tennis-playing family, lived in a large double-fronted house on Parkside, facing Wimbledon Common. In the drive stood a sleek, unusual and expensive Isotta Fraschini. The front door was open and we made our way into the hall. It was very English – hunting prints on the walls, an ornate wrought-iron umbrella stand, a polished table for hats and coats, silver plates, a broad carpeted staircase with gleaming white banisters.

'Very nice house,' Miki beamed. 'Very good tennis too.' The hall cut straight through the house from front to back, giving out on to a large garden with two immaculate courts flanked by carefully nurtured herbaceous borders. The scene reminded me of a picture from *Homes and Gardens*.

'Though I say it as shouldn't,' said Sir Keith, who had once played at Wimbledon and was a member of the All England, 'my courts are almost as good as the centre courts. Should be! Same groundsman, y'know. Comes in once a week to titivate them.'

Chairs for those who weren't playing had been arranged on a bank well above the two courts. A discreet butler in a white jacket made certain the trestle tables were fully laden with iced drinks. During an interval for tea there were not only strawberries and cream but whisky cake from Fortnum's and thin, damp cucumber sandwiches which Lady Bradshaw, who wore a floppy hat that any painter would have chosen to match the scene, offered to me with a charming if vague question. 'You come from Singapore, Mr Dexter? How exciting. Tell me, how *can* you play tennis in that awful Indian heat?'

'Mummy, you really *are* silly. Singapore is not in India.'

'This is my daughter, Irene.' With a languid wave I was introduced to a tall, leggy girl with a laughing smile and blonde hair tumbling over her shoulders. She fitted into the picture garden as perfectly as her mother; a typically well-mannered English girl, not beautiful, but attractive, fun-loving, and with a slight suggestion – perhaps the large mouth – that, given the right man at the right moment, she would be anything but passive.

'You're not playing?' I asked her.

'Never – my legs are my best feature,' she laughed. 'I'm not going to ruin them. I've never played *any* games – even when I was at Roedean.'

She had none of the vagueness of her mother, who probably thought I spent my time in Singapore thrashing the natives; and she must have read my thoughts for she laughed again and said, 'I'm Daddy's daughter – apart from not playing tennis.'

Daddy, I could see, was a no-nonsense man. Even the way in which he arranged the games or called the man-servant was brisk and decisive. His vague job of 'something in the City' consisted, I learned later, mainly of boardroom lunches and bridge at White's: not only to spend some of his obvious wealth but to give him an excuse to get out of the house.

They seemed a very agreeable English family. They had two sons in their twenties who both knew Miki and who had both earned half Blues at Cambridge. But Miki had told me before we arrived that Bill, the older one, was a tennis bum; he refused to work, he lived at home for nothing, played tennis at every tournament he could enter and was, it seemed, something of a trial to the family.

Still, I knew nothing of this, and when the sons included 'Pater' in a doubles it was very pleasant to see the way they never sent him a punishing ball, even at vital points, yet equally never gave him an obviously easy lob. It took a lot of skill to play such a cleverly-disguised customer's game – far more subtlety than Jenkins had displayed against me at Queen's.

I loved that afternoon – and yet I felt more homesick than ever before. Sitting on the lawn, waiting for my turn to play, I suddenly realised how desperately I missed Singapore, and Tanamera – not only Julie, but everything. What a cruel punishment – to dump me ten thousand miles from home, cut off from everything I loved – the hot, wet, smell of Singapore itself, the crazy traffic darting round Raffles Place, Li on the east verandah in the early misty morning serving me papaya before eggs and toast and coffee, and most of all Julie, pale gold, black-haired Julie. I thought of the Love Club, of the moments after she left, when I would peep out of the window and watch her walking away, swinging her handbag, black hair falling over shoulders, long legs striding out.

Perhaps it was because the family life of the Bradshaws so reminded me of Tanamera that I started going regularly to Wimbledon on Sunday afternoons. There was always a good game of tennis – and there was always pleasant company. And as the habit grew I usually stayed to a huge and typically English Sunday cold supper – pink beef, ham with Major Grey chutney, slices of tongue, a pie, and afterwards strawberries or a trifle and Stilton, everything passed cheerfully and unceremoniously round the polished mahogany D-ended dining-room table. I went even more often after Miki had returned to Singapore, his three months up, perhaps partly because I was lonely, but also I had lost a link with Singapore, and missed him.

'He seemed a decent enough feller, your Japanese friend,' said Sir Keith as he cut off the end of what looked like a very expensive cigar. 'Can't say I like what the Japs are doing in China though. You see they've taken Peking? And they're threatening Shanghai.'

'He's not really a friend of mine,' I found myself apologising. 'We just played tennis together in Singapore.'

'Does your father every worry about the Japanese? War, y'know – like we worry about this feller Hitler? Living space? Japanese breed like rabbits.'

'Keith!' said Lady Bradshaw.

'Well,' he replied defensively. 'No good hiding basic facts.'

'They may *do* it,' said Lady Bradshaw. 'But is that a suitable reason for talking about it during supper?'

'Quite right, m'dear.' He wiped his lips vigorously with a napkin so starched it could have stood up on end.

'We're not worried about the *Japanese*,' I tried to explain. 'My father says it's the Americans who are afraid of them, and he's afraid of what the Americans will do.'

'Americans? Don't get it. What can they do?'

'They've always felt China is their special sphere of influence, and they're scared of Japanese expansion there. The *Japanese* are being pretty tough.'

'Maybe. But the Americans can't go to war –'

'I don't think it's a question of war, Sir Keith. But there's talk of America trying to persuade its allies to limit Japanese supplies of oil and other raw materials. To slow down her war machine.'

'The Americans tend to panic,' Sir Keith said, echoing a prevalent British assessment of their character. 'Hope they don't go too far. Push people into a corner they have to fight their way out.'

'I don't think that'll happen.'

'Well – hope not. Bloody stupid, wars. Everybody loses in the end.'

'That's enough about stuffy politics,' said Irene firmly. 'Johnnie and I are going to play some records in the nursery.'

As the Bradshaw children grew up, the old nursery facing the garden at the back of the house had slowly changed. 'Into what the Americans call a rumpus room,' Irene explained. It still bore traces of the nursery – faded pink walls, old pictures on them, books that no one would ever read again – but they seemed to melt into the warm sunny room with its sagging old sofa and badly fitting loose covers, obviously an item of furniture relegated to the children after it had been replaced in the living room.

Irene had a black portable HMV and a stack of records – everything that Noel Coward had ever sung, and dozens of dance tunes played by Ambrose, Jack Hylton or Carroll Gibbons. The room was uncarpeted and we fitted perfectly, as we danced to Jack Hylton batting out 'Oh! Give me Something to Remember You By'. And there was no one (except me) to notice the way Irene arched her shoulders back so that she pushed against me where I felt it most – and where she could tell I was feeling it most.

I didn't really want to go to bed with her – well, perhaps it was a Vicki situation, but I didn't *really* want to. I could more or less manage to control my desires by liberal doses of tennis and cold showers – but not if provoked; not if a pretty girl stuck her tummy against mine and intimated, as we danced, that she had now completely got over an unhappy love affair 'with a married man'.

And there was something very appealing about her. Though not beautiful, she was attractive in a cheerful, healthy, clean, blonde way. She looked as though life was meant to be enjoyed, and to hell with the consequences. She reminded me a lot of Natflat though she was less pretty. No doubt being the daughter of a rich family made hers an easy philosophy, but she never so much as hinted that she had a crush on me; she just wanted a friend, with no holds.

The point of no return came when I realised that to repay the hospitality lavished upon me by the Bradshaws I must at least take Irene out. I couldn't entertain the entire family in my Fulham Road studio, but I had to do *something*.

'What about the Aldwych?' I asked her. Tom Walls,

Robertson Hare and Ralph Lynn were making London chuckle in the latest Ben Travers farce.

'You're an angel! I'm dying to see it.'

Getting her home presented a problem as I had no car.

'It's no problem. I'll stay with Jane.' She mentioned an old school friend, now married, who occasionally turned up with her husband at Wimbledon on Sunday. 'I'll give her a ring as soon as you've got the tickets. I always stay with her when I'm doing a theatre.'

It was a beautiful warm July evening and London was still sparkling with post-coronation revels – the abdication was already history and George VI had been crowned with hysterical fervour less than a month ago. As we walked round the curve of the Aldwych and into the Strand the streets were lined with flags and banners to welcome the delegates to the Imperial Conference.

We had a late supper at the Savoy and danced to Carroll Gibbons, but soon – and rather to my surprise – Irene whispered, 'Let's go, shall we?'

'Already? Of course, if you want to.' I paid the bill and said, 'I'll get a taxi.' And then, without thinking – or rather thinking that she must be either tired or bored – added, 'Then I can drop you off at Jane's flat.'

'Jane's flat? You *are* funny, Johnnie.'

'What's funny?'

'I'm not going to Jane's. What on earth gave you that idea? Jane is my alibi, she always is and always has been. I want to see this famous studio of yours.'

Well, *that* was clear – what she expected. As I fumbled for the studio key in the corridor I had a sudden, almost sick, feeling that I was on the edge of a precipice; that I ought to run away, quickly, bolt, kick her out, never speak to her again, go back to Singapore. I visualised Julie, alone in San Francisco six thousand miles away. A year had passed since her one and only letter arrived; anything could have happened to her, even – a stab of jealousy – falling in love with someone else. But still – wasn't I a bastard even to think of taking Irene into my flat, knowing exactly what was expected of me?

I switched on the light and let her go in first, then got out a bottle of Scotch.

'It's beautiful!' she said. 'Heavenly. I'm so glad I came.'

After I had poured her a drink she looked at me and said, 'You're in love, aren't you?'

I nodded.

'Are you going to marry her?' And when I shook my head, she said, 'Poor Johnnie. And yet – I don't *want* to get married, I don't *want* to fall in love. If I ever do get married it won't be for love.'

'You can't really mean that.'

'I do. I hate getting involved. I want someone like you around.'

'Oh!' I pretended dismay, yet felt a sudden surge of relief. Getting deeply involved, having someone fall in love with me – that *was* being unfaithful to Julie. But if this was another Vicki – fun, and no regrets or scenes – then to my way of thinking I would be no more immoral or unfaithful than the engaged Frenchman who respected the virginity of his fiancée by visiting the local brothel.

'You know what I mean. You're a *friend*, Johnnie. And why shouldn't friends be able to – well, make each other happy?'

'Why not?' She even talked like Vicki – though Irene was two years older than me.

'In a way, isn't it even better? Without all the misery? The hell and the problems?'

I knew it wasn't. I had tried it both ways, and I knew that nothing could touch the magic of making love to someone you couldn't bear to live without.

'Well, it has its points,' I laughed. 'And I'm sure it's better for your legs than tennis.'

'Wretch!' she kissed me. Almost a sisterly kiss.

I had left the dim bed light on in the tiny, sharply-eaved bedroom, and later, as she lay in my arms, she said, twisting my blond hair, 'You have funny moments when you don't talk much. You really *are* in love – badly, I mean.'

I nodded. There didn't seem anything to say.

'We're good for each other,' she decided. 'No strings, but

I'm very glad we met – and all this. Let's keep it this way. What's the phrase they use in newspapers – just good friends.'

'Very intimate.' I laughed.

'Intimate – and *hungry*! What time is it? Two o'clock!' And with animal energy she jumped out of bed, long straight legs, slipped on my Chinese kimono and cried, 'The bathroom's downstairs, isn't it? As soon as I've washed I'll cook some bacon and eggs. I'll call you when they're ready.'

I lay back smoking – something I rarely did in bed – as the smell and sound of bacon sizzling drifted up from the kitchen below. Bacon and eggs in the middle of the night after a wonderful time in bed. What a life! Even though I knew I would never be in love with anyone but Julie.

10

In mid-August Tim phoned me that he was coming to London on leave again.

'Any chance of a party – nothing fancy?' he asked. 'It seems years since I was in London, but could you rustle up a couple of girls – I mean just to do a theatre or maybe for a spot of dinner?'

'I'll try,' I promised, and when the dates had been arranged I telephoned Irene. The Bradshaw house always seemed to be alive with laughing, healthy girls. 'Just pick one out of a hat,' I suggested to Irene. 'Anyone will do. He's a bit stodgy, I'm afraid.'

Tim had arranged to stay with a fellow officer whose parents lived off the King's Road, but during the day he popped into the office. I hadn't seen him for some months, and now he looked even thinner, more austere, and in a curious way slightly forbidding – nothing sinister, just that he never had oozed an excess of brotherly love. He was dressed in flannels and blazer.

'It's not really done to wear uniform when you're out of camp,' he said, a trifle superciliously. As soon as Mr Cowley heard that Tim was in my office he hurried in, beaming managerial pomposity. He, too, looked nonplussed at the sight of Tim's Oxford bags.

'Welcome to our office, Lieutenant,' he said.

'Still the same – the place and the people.' Tim always had a slight touch of condescension; not unpleasant, just a matter of being the *tuan bezar*'s eldest son, and I had always noticed that it went down well with the employees of Dexters in Singapore. They *expected* the boss's son to behave like that.

'We miss you, Lieutenant,' said Mr Cowley sonorously, 'but we admire you for putting your country first. We need to plan for the defence of –' his voice tailed off, though for a moment I thought he was going to discuss the defence of the Dexter empire.

'Balls!' I said – but under my breath. Tim took Cowley's words as a perfectly normal compliment. 'The army's a vocation,' he explained.

I didn't see him again until we met the girls, and I must say that he looked smart in a dinner jacket – they were still being worn in London.

'And it still fits,' I grinned as I looked at him. 'Good old Ah Chum.' Ah Chum, the Chinese tailor at the bottom of Orchard Road, had clothed the male Dexters for as long as anyone could remember.

'Who? Of course, yes – I'd forgotten the name,' he murmured. How could he? He had been to Ah Chum's a hundred times. Yet anyone would have thought Tim had only spent one weekend in Singapore. It was the army, I told myself. And perhaps (this was only a passing thought) a defence mechanism on the part of a man like Tim who had arrived in an army camp, the only 'foreigner' among a batch of young men who had been born and bred in Yorkshire, the Oxford and Cambridge sons of squires, proud of their heritage and apt to look upon interlopers in the KOYLIs with the same kind of superiority that Tim used to Dexter employees.

The girls had arranged to meet us at Studio Z for drinks before going to dine and dance to Ambrose at the Mayfair. Irene had invited Jill, another Sunday tennis-playing visitor whom I had met but whose surname I had never been able to decipher from mumbled and typically vague English introductions. She had apparently been chosen partly because she could provide transport with her bullet-nosed Morris.

The evening was a huge success – mainly because Tim was obviously smitten, not with Jill, but with Irene.

'She's an absolute corker!' he said to me after the girls had left the table to undertake feminine repairs. 'How on earth did you meet?' He made the question sound as if I had somehow stepped out of line – had aimed, as the Victorians used to say, above my station.

'Tennis,' I said, and when I saw his face fall, laughed, 'No – she never plays. She says it would spoil her legs.'

'She's quite right not to play,' Tim exclaimed. 'She's not your – er, well, steady? . . .'

'Good Lord, no!' I laughed. 'I do take her out occasionally – really to repay the Bradshaws' hospitality – and I must say she's great fun.'

I think Tim was going to ask me the same question he had asked me – so long ago, it seemed – about Vicki. Had I been to bed with Irene? If only he had! But at that moment, just as Ambrose struck up 'Love Is the Sweetest Thing', the girls came back to the table, and Tim was on his feet asking Irene, 'This is a wonderful tune –'

At that age none of us ever missed a dance, and as both girls danced well it didn't matter to me who was my partner. But I caught myself wishing the girls had not returned at the very moment they did. Had Tim asked me, I would have told him the truth. It might have changed a great many things later on.

The next morning both Tim and Irene phoned me at the office; Tim to say he had asked Irene out that evening, in a tone that enquired, without asking, if I minded. Irene phoned to tell me, almost with a giggle, that Tim had invited her out. But she *did* ask, 'You don't mind, Johnnie?'

'Of course not. We're just good friends, remember.'

'Beast,' she laughed. 'You don't even care.'

Tim and Irene not only went out that evening, they went out every single evening until the end of his leave. I was surprised, if only because Tim had never seemed interested in girls. And then on the day before he was due to return to Richmond Tim rang and invited himself round to Studio Z for a drink. 'I've got something to tell you.' His voice sounded mysterious.

He arrived about seven, and after I had poured out two gin and tonics he blurted out, 'We're engaged!'

I was so shattered I dropped the glass, caught it in midair but only after all the contents had drenched my trousers. Swearing heavily, I tried to wipe away the sticky tonic.

'Well – aren't you going to congratulate me?'

I shook hands – stickily.

'That's wonderful, Tim. I'm delighted. Are you sure?'

'I was sure the moment we met,' he spoke with his particular brand of infuriating authority, as though to indicate that if *he* was sure then there could be no possibility of error.

'She's a great girl,' I said. 'And I'm delighted for her as well as for you. The Bradshaws are a wonderful family.'

'Yes, I know. Of course I had to go and ask Sir Keith's permission.'

'Of course.' He failed to realise I was being ironic.

'No hard feelings, old boy?' He gave me another of those infuriating looks – this time to say that all's fair in love and war and may the best man win – and that the best man *had* won.

'When's the wedding?'

'Not yet. Irene and I have bought the ring at Cartier's. I cabled Papa Jack. He offered us the ring as a sort of pre-marriage present. Damn sporting.'

'Well, I'll have to go and buy you a toast-rack,' I grinned. My first thought was that Tim must never know what had happened between us, a point stressed urgently by Irene who came to lunch with me at Veeraswamy's near the office, the day after Tim had gone north.

'I don't *really* want to get married at all.' She sounded almost desperate, just like Natasha had done. 'But I'm twenty-five – and Daddy's on at me all the time – and I know *you* don't want to get married – and Tim – well, Daddy and Mummy are rather excited at the idea of an army officer – and oh! I don't know – I'm fed up living at home – I just want to get away from home.'

'Of course I understand, Irene darling. Well no, I *don't*,' I laughed. 'You have such a happy home – such a close family –'

'It might seem happy on Sundays,' she said bitterly. 'But I can't take it any more. Daddy and Mummy are always fighting. It's always about one thing – my damn brother Bill. He's a bum, Johnnie. He won't work, he won't help. Daddy gets furious and threatens to chuck him out and Mummy protects him.'

'He seemed okay to me.'

'Oh, he's loving all right – so long as he doesn't have to sacrifice anything. No, I'll be glad to get out.'

'I'm going to miss you,' I said. 'It's an extraordinary thing – but I seem to spend my life saying goodbye to pretty girls who –' I was thinking of Vicki.

'Perhaps they want to get married and you don't.'

'Well, anyway, Irene, what's happened between us has never really happened, but you and I will always be friends.'

'That's just what I knew you'd say.'

I was intrigued by one thing – Tim's sudden infatuation. He had never struck me as a ladies' man, in fact the reverse. I had noticed often at Tanamera that he shrank from physical contact with a woman, even Mama; he didn't do or say anything you could explain easily, but he would back away. And I never saw him kiss Natasha. Maybe the fact that I always seemed involved with girls added to his basic dislike of me; or perhaps it just made me a little too sensitive, imagining things. But I did wonder how he had performed with Irene.

'Tell me,' I asked her almost enviously, 'is Tim as good in bed as I am?'

'What a horror you are, Johnnie!' she giggled conspiratorially. 'Tim's never done anything like *that*. He's got a very strong moral sense. He told me he believes that if you love someone you should wait for the wedding night.'

'Well – you'll have to wait too! I may be a horror – but even I can't continue an affair with the fiancée of my own brother. For that's what you are now.'

'Of course you can't. Neither could I. I'm always faithful to the man in my life. And I know you understand that. We must stop seeing each other. It's only fair, isn't it?'

And that, I thought, was the end of a pleasant and enjoyable friendship, a Vicki-style attachment that had lasted for several happy and trouble-free weeks.

II

By the autumn of 1937 Britain was slowly realising that war in Europe was a possibility. I could sense a new reaction to events in Europe – and to a lesser degree in the Far East, where the Japanese, after taking Peking, had marched into Shanghai leaving the city's International Settlement a white island in a turbulent yellow sea.

Letters from Papa Jack showed clearly that Singapore was reacting ever more sharply to Japanese aggression. I had one urgent cable from the office asking an extraordinary question: How long had Miki spent in England? When I cabled, I received a reply, 'Await urgent airmail letter'.

This explained that Bonnard and Miki were proposing to place another huge order for our off-the-peg barrack huts. My father wanted to know if Miki had mentioned the matter to me, and if he had been sounding out British firms for similar orders. Would I also enquire in the City and

Whitehall if there was a serious anti-Japanese lobby.

'It's a big order and I like Bonnard,' wrote Papa Jack, 'but the Singapore Chinese Association is talking about a total boycott of Japanese trade, and I can't say I blame them. And I certainly don't want to upset our Chinese friends. The long-term situation has to be considered.'

I was able to write back that, though there was a definite anti-Japanese *feeling* in England – almost official in Whitehall – there was not the slightest apprehension about the Japanese escalating their war in China.

In fact, now that I was a part of London's daily life, I could see why the British never gave the Japanese more than a passing thought. They were becoming more and more frightened of war in Europe. Earlier in the year income tax had been raised from four and ninepence to five shillings to manufacture arms, and Baldwin, a man thoroughly disliked for the role he played in the Mrs Simpson affair, had resigned in May. Most people felt that Neville Chamberlain was no better.

The fear of war was very real. Not of losing a war – it always astounded me that the British never considered the possibility of *losing* – but more of the devastation that would ruin big cities and decimate populations if the Germans ever attacked from the air. German planes had shown in Spain – particularly in the bombing of Guernica earlier in the year – the terrible effects of high explosives dropped on innocent civilians.

An ARP warden service was set up; the government assumed (projecting from the scanty data of the Great War) that every ton of high explosives dropped would cause fifty casualties, killed or wounded. They also assumed that if war broke out Germany would be able to send such a huge armada of bombers against British cities that more than half a million could be killed and twice that number injured – which meant that one in twenty-five Britons could be a casualty.

Ironically, this meant for Dexters more work, more trade and increased demand, for ARP helmets, gas masks and armoured cars needed either rubber or tin. Malaya and

Brunei had more than three million acres of planted rubber – and plans were almost ready to raise the ban on new planting; so that when rubber rose from less than tenpence a pound in 1935 to nearly one and twopence a pound, it made a huge difference to all of us. It was the same with tin. Rearmament plans soon started the rush of speculative buying, at one time pushing the price to more than two hundred and thirty-three pounds a ton. Everything was booming, even freight rates had doubled by 1937.

One curious fact was that though everyone I met was aware of the threat of war it seemed to make no difference to their everyday lives. In a strange way Britain was flaunting an aloof unconcern for the future, as though closing a collective eye to the dangers ahead, determined instead to enjoy the last pleasures of yesterday before the doom of tomorrow.

They were much more excited when Amelia Earhart perished flying alone across the Pacific; when the Zeppelin *Hindenburg* burned itself out while landing in America; when the *Normandie* crossed the Atlantic in less than four days.

No one seemed worried, least of all me – until three weeks after I had said goodbye to Irene, and she rang me. Her voice sounded very frightened. 'I must see you right away.' Even on the phone I could sense the urgency.

'But we agreed not to meet –'

'I know – but I must – everything's changed.'

'Tim back out?'

'No, no. Don't be silly. Can I come round this evening?'

When she arrived at Studio Z I hadn't the faintest idea of the shock about to engulf me. There was no preamble, no warning, no time to catch my breath.

'A drink?' I asked.

'I'm late,' she announced in a dull, flat, final voice. 'Five weeks.'

My immediate thought was: if only strait-laced Tim had gone to bed with her.

'It's mine?'

She nodded. 'We've always been friends, Johnnie, and I'd

never do the dirty on you. I like you too much.' She laughed wryly. 'The fact is – I like you better than Tim. And the other thing is – I *am* a one-man girl. While it lasted you were the only one.'

I knew that – and said so, if only to comfort her.

One thought struck me. 'I thought that – after the first time – you'd taken some sort of precautions?'

'I did. Jane gave me the name of some powders and the place where you can buy them. I put one sachet in water each time I washed after making love – but they don't seem to have worked, and now I'm desperate.'

She sat down on the edge of the divan in the corner. 'And terrified. I *will* have that drink, Johnnie.'

I went to the kitchen for some ice, and when I returned she said in a helpless kind of way, 'I just don't know what to do. I daren't tell Daddy. He'll blow his top, and so will Tim.'

'They're rather a pair, aren't they – Tim and Daddy?'

'You're right. I don't know who scares me most.'

I made the drink strong – half gin, half tonic – and she took a long pull at it. 'I've read about abortions and things – but I haven't got a clue how to go about that sort of thing.'

'Take it easy.' I sat down beside her. 'We'll think of a way.'

'I'm scared, Johnnie. I'll do anything, but I'm afraid of back-street places.'

So was I, specially when I thought of the day I rushed round to Vicki's flat, and there was Natasha, lying on the sofa, looking as though she was going to faint, and Julie saying, 'She's been to a butcher.'

I was not only afraid. I, too, hadn't the faintest idea what to do. In 1937 abortion was a dirty word. I know that some old-fashioned friendly family doctors did, from time to time, help, in unorthodox ways, patients they could trust; but the Dexters had no old-fashioned friendly doctors in England.

'What'll Tim say?' Her voice was almost a whisper.

'God knows. But it won't be very pleasant.'

'Who's going to tell him?'

'And who's going to tell your father?'

'Oh Johnnie, I'm so sorry about all this mess. You don't think Tim —?'

I shook my head. 'Not with a baby on the way. Not on your life – specially if he finds out it's mine. You know, I shouldn't really say this, but in an odd sort of way Tim hates my guts.'

'I don't believe that —'

'I do.'

'But why?'

'I think he hates me because I get the most out of life. It's envy that's turned to a kind of bitterness. It's not really hate, of course. I may not always be happy, but I do have a lot of fun. But he's moody, he doesn't get anything out of life – or didn't until he met you. He's a queer fish. Imagine falling for a super girl like you and not dragging you by your hair into bed!'

'If only he *had* dragged me to bed,' she echoed my earlier thoughts, 'there'd be no problem.'

'Well, at least we'd never know whose it was, would we?'

'You are a rotter, Johnnie,' she said, but she was laughing.

She was a little calmer when she left. I wouldn't let her stay the night, and the next day I set about trying to find a solution. I might as well have tried to fly to the moon. Among my small band of friends none had the faintest knowledge of illegal abortions. The idea of 'doing something' about a 'nice' girl in trouble was unthinkable. 'You just take your medicine, old chap, like most of us,' chuckled one man in the bar at Queen's.

'Medicine?' I hadn't the faintest idea what he meant.

'My dear fellow,' he explained, 'Half our friends wouldn't be married if they hadn't put a girl in the family way.'

'Oh, I see.' The penny dropped.

'Marry the girl!' and with a roar of laughter as he ordered two pints he added, 'After a couple of years of married strife you won't know the difference.'

I suppose it was this conversation at Queen's that first

planted the idea in my head that really for a 'gentleman' (even from Singapore) the only right thing to do was to marry. I didn't love Irene, but since I would never be able to marry Julie — that by now seemed certain — I felt at the back of my mind that I might even be better off marrying a girl I didn't love, but one who would make an eminently suitable wife of a future *tuan bezar*, who would be a good mother for the younger Dexter and fit in at Tanamera. (The thought that, once married, we would live in any other house than Tanamera never entered my head.) And our cosy relationship might in the long run make for a more stable future than one based on passion that might be hard to replace once spent.

Since I couldn't marry Julie I didn't really *want* to get married to anyone. I preferred my bachelor life. But when eventually the time came for me to return to Singapore (with added responsibilities) there would be no Vickis or Julies available.

And I thought, too, of Aunt Sonia's letter. She was right. When Julie returned to live in Singapore life would be less difficult for all of us if I had married a nice English girl. Apart from anything else, the Soongs and the Dexters had to live next to each other, meet frequently, and if I were married it would wipe out any prospects of embarrassment when Julie and I met, as we were bound to do. That in itself was not enough reason to marry, but I also hoped that if I settled down I would be able to meet Julie without the ache I once had to hug and kiss her. It all seemed to fit in, to make a neat package out of a life that I was messing up. Even Papa Jack would be delighted, specially as Irene was just the right kind of girl for a *tuan bezar*'s wife.

I rang her up three days later.

'Have you arranged anything?' she asked anxiously.

'There's no chance of anyone listening?'

'No, Johnnie. Tell me — any news?'

'Can we have dinner tomorrow? And maybe spend the night at Jane's — you know what I mean.'

'You mean at your place? No.'

'I thought we'd have dinner at home – you cook something – then we'd go to bed together until it's time for you to cook breakfast.' I was teasing her.

'You know it's ridiculous to suggest –' she kept her voice light, yet there was a tremor in it.

'Miss Bradshaw,' I said sternly, 'I'm not old-fashioned like my brother Tim. I believe that if I'm going to marry a girl we should both try each other out first. It's only right and proper.'

I heard a gasp on the other end of the line, then a sigh. Happiness? Relief? Doubt? Then, 'Johnnie – you can't really mean it?'

'We're both in the potage,' I said. 'This is the simplest way out of a hell of a mess. And' – with a laugh – 'it might even be fun.'

'It won't be my fault if it isn't,' she had a catch in her voice.

The following evening she came to Studio Z.

'Only one thing worries me,' she said. 'Are you still in love with someone else?'

'It's a lost cause.'

'The girl on the piano?'

I nodded. 'It's all finished.'

'Tell me about her. No, it's not just womanly curiosity. I want to play fair, Johnnie. I know you don't *really* want to get married – we both agreed on that so, you know, darling, it's a big step we're being forced to take – *you're* being forced to take. And so this girl – is it over?' She picked up the photo of Julie in its silver frame. 'She's beautiful, Johnnie. You never told me her name.'

'Julie.'

'You say you can never marry. But why? Is she married?'

I shook my head. 'I don't want any secrets either. It's a lousy way to start a marriage. Julie and I were lovers for a long, long time.'

'What happened?'

'You've heard the saying, "I'm free, white and twenty-one"? Well, Julie's free and she's twenty-one now. But she isn't white. Her mother's Chinese-American, and her father's Chinese.'

'But surely?' Irene didn't need to finish the question.

'Never. All hell broke loose when we were found out. Julie's father is not only a Chinese millionaire, he's the leader of the Chinese community. For his virgin daughter to be seduced — and by a red–haired barbarian — that's the old Chinese name for Europeans — was a loss of face he couldn't stand. He banished her. He shipped Julie to her mother who lives in America. She's separated from her husband. And I was banished here.'

'But couldn't you fight?'

I lit a cigarette and looked at the photo. 'It's too big to fight. I tried. We had the most terrible family rows. But you can't beat the system, Irene — not in Singapore. Even if I *had* persuaded my father to let us marry, Julie would never have been allowed to.'

'But now — you're older. Can't you fight back *now*? I shouldn't be putting ideas into your head,' she smiled a little sadly, 'talking you out of marrying me.'

'You won't do that. I'd racked my brain for ages long before we met. There's nothing to be done. You see, I'll be the boss of Dexters one day. It's one of the biggest firms in the Far East. And the rules of the game in Singapore are more rigid than at the MCC or Wimbledon. There's no place for mixed marriages.'

'You mean for business reasons?'

'No. Social reasons. People wouldn't stop trading with Dexters just because I had a Chinese wife — who, as you can see from the photo, looks more American than Chinese anyway. That's not the problem. We'd just be quietly — well, dropped.'

'Would that matter?'

'A man can take it. But Julie comes from one of the oldest and greatest Singapore families. If she was ostracised — and if I was looked down on — for her it would be terrible, simply because she *is* a Soong. I'm not a social bloke, Irene, but you've no idea how tough it can be if you've been used to the best. And Julie has been — and for that matter, so have

I. It's not only being invited to parties. To hell with them. We wouldn't even be able to get a decent table at Raffles. We couldn't join the same clubs – I couldn't join hers, she couldn't join mine. In the end our only friends would be other mixed married couples – mostly second raters.'

'Poor Johnnie. I'm sorry. And I'm glad you told me. But you're certain that if we got married – you'd never want to run off?'

'You don't have to worry. In fact, you'll help.'

'I hope so. I don't want you *ever* to throw it in my face – that I stopped you –'

'I'll never do that,' I promised.

'I'll do everything to make up,' she promised, and I knew she would.

The prospect of telling the Bradshaws that Irene was pregnant was a major problem – until I realised there was no need to tell *anyone* she was expecting a baby. 'It's the baby that's going to upset Tim – and Daddy,' she said. We were eating an omelette and chips with a bottle of cheap wine.

'Why tell them?' I suddenly asked her. 'They don't suspect anything – why should they know anything?'

'Could we?'

'Why not? If Tim knew I'd been going to bed with his fiancée his pride would be shattered. It *is* a blow – it would be to anyone. I tried to tell him, you know, before he became involved – that night at the Mayfair.'

'I thought you'd been talking about me. I could sense it.'

'It's a pity you didn't wait a couple of minutes longer –'

'Is it? Perhaps it won't be.'

'I didn't mean it in a nasty way.'

'We needn't tell Daddy either – about the baby, I mean?'

'Why should we? You're just a flighty girl who keeps changing her mind.'

'Only,' she patted her tummy, 'we can't wait very long, can we?'

I had it all planned. Both of us would write to Tim – difficult letters, but they had to be written. I would go to see

Sir Keith. I also drafted, that evening, a long cable to Papa Jack. It read:

> THIS A SHOCK BUT IRENE MARRYING ME IN-
> STEAD OF TIM WITH HER PARENTS FULL
> APPROVAL STOP PLANNING MARRY MID-
> OCTOBER STOP BRADSHAWS PLANNING BIG
> WEDDING SO PLEASE FLY OVER STOP
> WOULD LIKE RETURN SINGAPORE IMMEDI-
> ATELY AFTER WEDDING USING BOAT TRIP AS
> HONEYMOON STOP THIS EXTREMELY
> IMPORTANT PLEASE SAY YOU AGREE AND
> THAT YOU AND MAMA ARE COMING STOP
> LOVE JOHNNIE

Three days later I received a cable:

> BAFFLED BUT DELIGHTED BOTH FLYING
> OVER FOR WEDDING STOP GOOD IDEA YOU
> RETURN SINGAPORE LEAVE YOU BOOK
> PASSAGE PAPA MAMA

'By the time we've had the sea trip and are back in Singapore,' I told Irene, 'nobody will be able to count the months any more. And anyway – seven-month babies are all the rage.'

'What are we going to call it?'

'Bengy,' I never hesitated. 'You remember in the Bible – the afterthought.'

'It might be a girl.'

'It won't,' I promised her.

I wrote to Tim – and it wasn't easy since I couldn't tell the truth. I didn't expect a reply and I didn't get one. But my interview with the Bradshaws took on all the overtones of a musical comedy.

'Bit stunning, the whole thing,' said Sir Keith. 'Can't tell with girls these days, can you? Frankly, though, I'm rather glad. Always thought this summer you'd be a damned useful tennis addition to the family – thought you'd never come to the boil – nearly pipped at the post, eh?'

Lady Bradshaw didn't seem to realise there was any difference between Tim and me. 'I'm sure she'd be very happy with either of you,' she said vaguely. 'The only pity is, living so far away in India.'

Mr Cowley was deeply impressed – particularly that I was marrying the daughter of a knight.

'A baronet,' I corrected him.

'The real aristocracy, not one of your jumped-up new titles. I congratulate you, my dear Johnnie.' Almost dreamily he added, as though thinking aloud, 'It's such a pity we don't follow the Spanish custom. There, a man who marries into the nobility inherits his wife's title. So sensible.'

'But even if I were Spanish,' I pointed out mildly, 'my fiancée does have two brothers who would take preference over me.'

'Oh! Ah! Yes, of course, I was thinking generally. By the way, there's a cable for you. It's on your desk.'

I tore open the envelope casually. It read:

CONGRATULATIONS YOUR ENGAGEMENT STOP ARRIVING FROM NEW YORK BY BERENGARIA ARRIVING SAVOY EVENING OCTOBER FOURTEEN STOP STAYING LONDON ONE WEEK THEN ESCORTING HER TO FINISHING SCHOOL IN FRANCE HOPE SEE YOU PAUL

I knew who 'her' was. And I also knew by now that October the fifteenth was the date on which Irene and I were to be married.

For a few minutes I sat back in the tilting desk chair in my office overlooking Piccadilly, my mind racing with thoughts as I stared out of the window. People were hurrying past the lovely old Wren church, on their way to Simpson's, Hatchard's, 'F and M' or the Burlington Arcade, others dawdling, everyone a stranger, never to be spoken to by me, never to be seen again. And here, inside this bloody, mouldering office, my hand was trembling as I read and reread the scrap of flimsy paper.

She was coming. Julie. What would I feel like, meeting her after all these months? And what would *she* feel like? Our young, growing-up life, our learning life, had been detonated by a secret, tempestuous love affair, one in which we were not only learning about one another each time we made love but about love itself, and finally about life itself. What were we going to feel like, or say, when we met again, almost two years later?

What had happened to Julie in the time between? Experience? Another love – perhaps with an older man, more talented and knowledgable in the arts of making love than I had been when we lay together in Abingdon Mansions? Would she regard with a touch of tolerance our wonderful, bemused gropings? I had suffered the loneliness of the damned for the first months. Had she?

For a moment, staring at the cable, I all but panicked. Maybe it would be better if I found out when the *Berengaria* sailed and cabled the ship that I wouldn't be in London when they arrived. If only the wedding had been advanced a couple of days! I wouldn't have been tortured into making a decision. But – I wanted to see Julie, just to see her. And I knew that, whatever had happened to her in San Francisco, she must have been the one who asked Paul to arrange a meeting.

There was no harm in it. Or was there? What would Irene think – do – if I told her? She wouldn't like it. A month before the wedding perhaps, a week before, but you couldn't go and see the love of your life on the day of the actual ceremony. Yet that was the only morning we *could* meet. And that meant that if I did see Julie I mustn't tell Irene. And *that* produced an uneasy feeling of guilt which I could not suppress. It was hardly the way to start married life.

But then – or so I argued as I tried to square my conscience – didn't I owe something to Julie? I had started a train of events that day at the YMCA which, whatever the pleasure I gave her, had broken up her family life, had shamed her father whom I respected. And anyway, if Julie wanted to meet me to say a kind of goodbye, then I must.

I was grown up now (or so I thought) and so there was no danger. If I were really selfish, headstrong or stupid, then I would beg her to run away with me, ditch Irene and set off with Julie for Gretna Green and marry her over the anvil, defying everyone in the course of 'true love'. But I knew I would never do that. I was just going to say goodbye.

Suddenly I couldn't stand the office any more. I knocked on Mr Cowley's door and muttered an excuse about a headache, not feeling very well, and before he had time to say anything I was rushing past the lift door, running down the stone stairs and into Swallow Street. I hailed a taxi and went straight home. And there, though it was only early afternoon, I poured out what Li would have called a triple stengah, and then a second, and then a third, wondering in my self-pity why life was so complicated, so overbearing, always pressing down on me, always forcing me to take decisions.

I fell asleep and it was dark when I woke, with a foul taste in my mouth and a splitting head, and I only woke then because of an insistent, heavy banging on the front door which led from the corridor straight into the studio. I stumbled to my feet, groped for the switch which turned on the standard lamp by the fireplace and shouted 'Coming!'

I reeled towards the door, shielding my eyes from the light. As I twisted the Yale knob the door was burst open with such ferocity that it knocked me straight over.

'Christ! Be careful!' I cried. It was a burglar, I was certain. I shouted 'Police! Help!' I tried to get to my feet. A figure loomed over me. What seemed like a blow from a hammer hit me straight in the crutch, right between my legs. I doubled up, falling back to the floor. Like a shadow I saw a boot start the arc of another kick, this time towards my face. Instinctively I brought my hands up to protect myself. The boot flashed past them on to my cheek. I felt the blood spurt even before the pain hit me.

'I've just come off an assault course and that's the way we

treat bastards like you,' snarled Tim. 'Get up. Get up before I kick you again.'

I tried to shout. No words came. It's funny how, in moments of terror, the inconsequential takes over. As the blood poured from my cheek I was overwhelmed with one thought – what would Manenti, the landlord, say if I ruined his carpet?

I made a wild grab for Tim's legs and pulled. He came hurtling down on top of me, gasping as he hit the corner of an armchair. But he wasn't really hurt. Arms flailing, he hit me where he could – everywhere, it seemed. I was bleeding like a pig – but that wasn't what hurt. It was the agony between my legs. I still couldn't get up. Then I saw the arc of his boot again and rolled away behind a chair. I tried to use the chair as a shield. Almost contemptuously he thrust it away and lunged towards me. Somehow I managed to croak, 'Stop it, you bloody idiot.' The boot came in again, this time straight into the chest. I could hear – I could actually hear – my ribs crack.

'That'll teach you to mess around with someone else's girl,' he shouted.

'You stupid bugger,' I managed to scream as I clawed at his legs and brought him down again. His arms were coming at me, but now I was really scared – frightened he would kill me. And that fear gave me an added strength. Even on the floor he was trying to kick, grunting, 'Swine! Bastard!' Somehow I reached the base of the standard lamp. I had no strength, I had no skill, I had no hatred even. Only self-protection fired my adrenalin. I grasped the bottom of the tall slender brass lamp with one blood-soaked hand, swung it round – or rather let it swing itself with me guiding it – and then as the shade toppled off, and with no idea what I was doing, I hurled the lamp towards him.

Luckily it didn't miss. The hot bulb hit him between the eyes and seemed to stay there, glued to his face. I smelled flesh burning. Clawing, he tried to tear the bulb away, grabbing the bulb with both hands, screaming as it shattered, slicing open his face and hands, and then I knew I was safe. And once safety was assured, the tiny hidden reserve of strength left me. I passed out.

Mario Manenti must have come to the rescue, attracted by the noise, perhaps brought in by neighbours, I never really found out. An Italian doctor friend of his lived opposite on the other side of the Fulham Road, and he patched us both up. He put eleven stitches in my right cheek and bandaged up three broken ribs. I don't even know if Tim was there while the doctor treated me because I vaguely remember feeling the jab of a needle and passing out again. Only later did I learn that Tim was badly burned on the face and hands and had to be treated in hospital. But his eyes were unharmed. It was lucky, for otherwise the police would have had to be called in.

We were lucky too because Manenti, like most Italians, was frightened of the police – specially as Italians in London were being denounced in Trafalgar Square for their savagery in Abyssinia. So when he was sure that neither of us was permanently injured the family quarrel was quietly forgotten.

12

Papa Jack and Mama arrived and, in the tradition long since laid down by Grandpa Jack, installed themselves in a suite at the Hyde Park Hotel. They never stayed anywhere else. Grandpa Jack had always been a firm believer in suites – on ships, in hotels. And the Hyde Park Hotel was a way of life for the Dexters – and their servants in the days of Grandpa Jack, who believed in style. Ah Wok, and later Li and sometimes an amah had always travelled with the family.

The Dexters liked the Hyde Park because it was the perfect Yorkshire compromise; not too flashy or spectacular like staying at Claridges, which would have been showing off; but solid, with immaculate service, particularly in times of stress; Grandpa Jack had vowed never to stay at any other hotel in London since the time he had a bad recurrence of malaria, and the willing staff had scurried round changing sheets four times in one night as he sweated out the fever.

Of course I was longing to see my parents — though not without misgivings. The stitches had been taken out of my face, but it was still disfigured by three ugly strips of plaster. And I couldn't button up my jacket because of the bulge round my ribs. Even worse, I could only walk upright with an effort, though the pain in my groin was fading. I had told Irene the truth, though to everyone else I put my injuries down to a tough game of rugger. But I knew I had an awful lot of explaining to do.

My mother wailed as she tried to kiss me and I had gently to hold her away as she squeezed my cracked ribs. 'It's nothing, Mama darling. I've just got a sore chest — and face. It's wonderful to see you. All ready for the wedding?'

'What have you been *doing*, Johnnie?'

'Nothing,' I lied. 'I got into a tough game of rugger. I'll be better in a few days.'

'You never used to play rugger.'

'I won't any more — promise. Let me look at you. Beautiful Mama!'

She looked stunning. Mama was always a little vague about her age, but I remember my father once telling me — with a touch of pride — that she was about ten years younger than he was and he must have been fifty-seven by now. If she was in her mid-forties she was a marvel.

'Isn't your father looking well?' she asked. He was. The years had dropped off him. His colour was better, the lines seemed to have been ironed out.

'I've discovered vitamin pills,' he said. 'See you in the bar in ten minutes after I've got your mother settled in our suite.'

This was the confrontation I had been dreading. I might be able to fool Mama, but my father was a very different matter.

'You've never played a game of rugger since you left school,' he said. 'What the hell's been happening?'

'I got into a bit of a fight.'

He looked at me for a moment, and then said, 'Couldn't have anything to do with the bride changing her mind?'

I said nothing. There was nothing to say.

'So I was right. It was Tim? Is he all right?'

'Yes. He's back at camp now.'

'Was it over Irene?'

There was only one way forward – tell my father everything. He had to know *why* Irene had ditched Tim for me – and only I could tell him that she was expecting a baby.

'Her father know?'

I shook my head. 'No one knows except you. No one will. That's why I cabled asking you if we could go back to Singapore. Sort of confuse people with dates.'

'You're a sore trial sometimes,' my father sighed. 'Can't you *ever* keep your hands off girls? Don't you ever think of anything but – well, you know?'

'Of course I do. Irene is the only one since I came to London. And she's a great girl. You'll love her.'

'At least if you had to make a bloody fool of yourself again thank God it wasn't the Soong girl. But really – I just can't understand you. You're a good-looker, you're a great catch, London must be full of pretty girls – why the hell do you have to go and pinch your own brother's girl?'

'I *didn't* pinch her. I met her long before Tim. We never thought of getting married – and then Tim asked her to marry him. And she didn't know until after she'd said yes that she was on the way.'

'Tim know about the baby? The reason why?'

'No one knows but you,' I said again.

'Tim'll never forgive you – not only for taking his girl, but for making him look a fool. I'm going to see him at Catterick' – that was the name of the big army camp near Richmond – 'after you leave for Singapore. I gather he's refused to come to the wedding.'

I nodded.

'Can't say I blame him,' Papa Jack sighed again.

'And Natasha couldn't come?'

'She wanted to — but *she's* expecting a baby, so I wouldn't let her. These flying boat trips are pretty rugged. She sent her love. You know that Tony has taken over Ara and is running it?'

'Yes.' Natflat had written me that she was living there, and apparently enjoying it.

'Well, you certainly do live a mixed-up life.' My father ordered more drinks. 'Young people make life so much more difficult than it need be. That's what I can't understand. But all's well that ends well — at least I hope so,' he went on. 'This Irene sounds a very agreeable girl. And marriage might,' with a dry note — 'help to tame you a bit. At least it means you've got Julie Soong out of your blood.'

It was on the tip of my tongue to say that I hoped to see her. It was also on the tip of my tongue to say that because you get a girl into trouble you don't have to love her — or forget a different, lost love.

'Perhaps you'll settle down now. With Tim in the army you'll be the *tuan* soon — and things are changing — you'll have a very different world to deal with, Johnnie.'

'Thanks a million for letting us go back to Singapore. I'm looking forward to working there again. But what do you mean — changing?'

'It's hard to say — but there's a *feeling* of change. The local people want a bigger say in things. I'm all for it. There's nothing dramatic about it — just something you can sense. I'm not one of those socialists who want to give the Empire away, but the time's coming when we'll have to work out some sort of partnership.' He added a trifle dryly, 'With us the senior partners of course. But if we *don't* do something there's always the danger we'll get overtaken by events.'

'I don't think Mr Cowley would think like that — or my new father-in-law. He's all for the British Raj.'

'Perhaps I exaggerate a bit. But I do hope this means you're settling down, Johnnie — and *if* there are any changes, I think you might find it easier to adapt than Tim would have done.'

Long before my wedding day dawned the last strappings had been torn off my chest. I looked fairly normal when at ten o'clock on the morning of 15 October I walked down the Strand and into the Savoy. I had arranged to meet Paul in the lobby. The wedding at Wimbledon was timed for two-thirty that afternoon.

Paul looked as immaculate as ever, his skin a little more olive against the pinks that surrounded him, and I was so accustomed to seeing him in tropical white that his neatly pressed blue suit and polished shoes looked slightly out of place in London. But the smile of welcome was wonderful. Had we been alone instead of surrounded by potted palms and people we would have fallen into each other's arms. I had wondered whether, after so many months apart, and after the trauma of the discovery, our meeting might also have been awkward; but it was as though we had said goodbye only the previous day.

'For God's sake come back to Singapore soon.' His slow, infectious smile was unchanged. 'I miss you. Bloody bored without you, in fact. You've lost weight.'

'Tennis.'

'And fornicating? Or is that all over now?' He was laughing.

'Tell me about Singapore. How's George Hammonds? And Bonnard? He's the one you should ask about screwing!' I wanted to hear everything about Singapore, and peppered him with questions.

'Hey! Take it easy,' he laughed. 'It's two months since I was there. I went across the Pacific to pick up Julie, and then across the Atlantic. For the free trip. I'm going to dump her at Tours, where she'll be staying six months, and then I'm hot-footing it back to Singapore.'

'And Julie?' That was the one question above all I had been aching to ask.

'She's upstairs waiting for you. She's a bit sad about you getting married, but she's changed a lot – grown up –

and she knows you can't beat the system. And I think she realises it's for the best. Only I have to say – not to be quoted, for God's sake – that she's still carrying a torch for you.'

I felt like echoing 'Me too!'

Instead I said, 'God, I missed you, Paul. If you don't waste too much time with those French girls you'll be back in Singapore almost as soon as I am.'

'Yeah – only you'll be a married man, remember? No more bachelor sprees. When I saw the announcement in the *Straits Times* I knew I'd have to start looking round for a new friend.'

'Wait a minute while I wipe away the tears! Come on, I came to see Julie.' I paused. 'One thing about her going to America: got her away from that shit Kai-shek.'

'What a creep! More than a creep; he's been worming his way into the old man's business – everything.'

'Did your father forgive him – for what happened that afternoon, after the Koo party?'

'He'll never really forgive him for the way he acted. You know how the Chinese value manners. But my father needs him. That was a hell of an afternoon – and it changed all our lives. Strange, isn't it, to think that if you'd left the Koo party before my father spoke to you everything might have been different. My father never got over the loss of face. He's tired. So Kai-shek is taking over more and more responsibility. And he *is* bright. I've got to hand that to him.'

'Is he going to marry Julie?'

'No – that's definite.'

It seems incredible, but though this was my wedding day I felt a sudden leap of happiness. I wasn't jealous of Kai-shek – or rather that wasn't the basic reason – I was happy for Julie's sake. The thought of her married to Kai-shek had haunted me. Now at least that nightmare had ended.

'She's upstairs waiting for you,' said Paul. 'And my congratulations, Johnnie – I mean that. It's the best thing. You'd never have been able to marry Julie – and this way at least the break's final.'

He told me the number of their suite and I made for the lift, heart thumping. Outside 505-6-7 I hesitated, then knocked.

'Come in, Johnnie,' said Julie's voice, and I pushed the door open. She walked towards me, quickened her step, and we fell into each other's arms, smothering each other with kisses, squeezing the breath out of each other, half crying, half laughing.

At last I pushed her away from me, held her at arm's length and looked at her. She had her own special half-sad smile, and with a rush all the past came back to us.

'Do you remember? –' I began.

'Not now, Johnnie.' She looked at me steadily.

'It all seems so long ago – everything before you went to America.'

'If only we lived there. It's so wonderful. I wanted to love it so much, but every time I began to enjoy life you came up and stopped me. Not deliberately, I know,' she smiled. 'Perhaps because I wanted you to.'

Paul was right. The two years had etched subtle changes in her appearance. Her hair had been cut in a different style. 'But I'm glad you didn't cut it off – you know, shorten it,' I said. In a way she was even more beautiful than I remembered – memory having been crystallised into one photograph – for now the girl I had known had acquired assurance. Her eyes still sparkled but – was it my imagination? – the look of mischief, what I used to call the naughty look, was missing. Perhaps not. Perhaps women's eyes adjusted to the occasion. And of course the real truth was Julie had just grown up. She was a woman.

'Your hair is darker,' she said.

'No sun.'

'And your face – what's that faint scar on your cheek?'

'Someone kicked me.'

She obviously thought I was joking, for she simply went on, 'And you're thinner.'

'Unrequited love. I don't want to sound maudlin, but in those first months in London all I wanted to do was die.'

'I felt the same. And when mother found your letter to

me – I've never seen her so angry. But she was right to stop it all.'

'Was she? I wonder.'

'I think she was. She said that everyone gets over a love affair like ours in time – but only if the other one helps.'

'Do they?' I knew as I spoke that it was a silly thing to say.

'Well – you seem to have.'

I didn't want to get on dangerous ground. I had come to the Savoy to see her, because I *had* to see her. But I had to say, 'That's not true Julie.'

'You're getting married,' she said sadly.

'You yourself said that *we* could never marry. But that doesn't mean that I don't think of you the way I've always done. And when you get married you'll feel the same about me.'

'I'll always love you,' she said quietly. 'Even if we never meet again. And as for marriage – perhaps one day – but it won't be the same.'

'It isn't the same for me either.' I had made up my mind not to tell her I was getting married on this very day, and when we sat down I tried to keep away from the subject of Irene. I just wanted us to be together in what we both knew might well be the last time we would ever be alone together. Neither of us wanted to spoil it, yet inevitably the conversation drifted back to Irene.

'Things aren't always what they seem,' I said. 'You're not angry with me, are you?'

'I can never be cross with you. In a way I'm even happy – for my sake as well as yours. You getting married sort of ties everything up neatly. No rough edges showing – and that's going to mean that it'll be easier for all of us when I return to Singapore.'

She couldn't resist the most female of all questions, 'Do you really still love me?'

'Julie – you *know* I do. I always will. Forever.'

'More than –? I've forgotten her name.'

'Much more. It's not a very nice thing to say but – Irene's a great girl, yet I will never love her the way I love you.'

I didn't want a tearful parting, so I had deliberately asked Paul to ring the suite after half an hour – all, in fact, that I could spare on this eventful day of my life. And as the phone stuttered and she announced that Paul was on his way up, I said, 'I want to go before he comes. I want to see you alone – like this – with no one else. And Julie – we'll meet again. It's fate. We will.'

Standing by the door, as I had my hand on the knob, she said, 'I know we could never have married, Johnnie. But – did you *have* to?'

'Can't you guess, Julie? It's a shotgun wedding. She's going to have a baby.'

'I wondered.' Two tears welled at the corner of those big dark eyes. 'Isn't it bad luck? If only I'd been the one who was going to have a baby.'

She closed the door behind me. I couldn't bear the thought of meeting Paul with tears in my eyes, so I stumbled through the emergency exit and down the stairs to the floor below. There I took the lift, walked through the Savoy's swing doors and crossed the Strand towards Moss Brothers to collect my hired morning suit for the ceremony.

The wedding was a great success and that evening we took the boat train to Southampton to catch the *Orient Princess*. She was a fine ship and I had sailed on her before, though never with a wife. And, whatever my feelings, at least they were bound to recede a little at the excitement of setting off on a sea voyage. The *Princess* oozed the allure of the sea, with its long, mahogany-lined corridors, the central staircase leading to the ship's lounge, the wall decorated with a huge fanciful mural of Father Neptune. Some early arrivals were already examining the books in the ship's library; a few others propped up the bar. There was a general air of bustle and preparation.

'It's so exciting, darling,' Irene squeezed my arm. 'I've never been on a long voyage. Just think of it – three weeks! No regrets?'

'Silly girl. Do I look regretful?'

One of the purser's staff led us to our cabin, very posh,

with real beds instead of bunks, a small bathroom and a cupboard in which to put our trunks.

'Let's unpack tomorrow,' said Irene. 'I want to go up on deck and watch.'

When the last of the luggage had been swung aboard, and the big empty net on the crane hung limply over the dockside, a loudspeaker blared, 'All visitors ashore, please!' Only a few sightseers waited and watched on the quayside as the gangplank was lashed into place. The siren hooted a warning for the last time, the thick hawsers were cast off, and slowly we backed away from the dockside.

This, I knew, was the final break. I had to put Julie behind me – now and for ever. And I could, I was sure of it. I had to look forward, to the future, to a life with a pretty wife, the hopes of a son while I was young enough to enjoy him, and if there was a dull ache at the thought of Julie at least I knew that the pain would fade.

The only thought that never entered my head was that my smiling, happy bride, leaning excitedly over the deck rail, looking down on the dark water below, watching the dockside recede, would hate Singapore almost from the moment she set foot on the island.

PART THREE

Singapore, 1937–1941

God, it was good to be home! As we approached the roads outside the harbour in the early morning the sea haze lifted and there, in dancing, almost liquid heat, lay Singapore – an unromantic line of shining circular petrol tanks on the left, and on the right a fringe of coconut palms; a flurry of sampans, a forest of junk masts, and all round were tiny off-shore islands, some little more than rocks in the sea. Above everything else rose the sun. As I guided Irene down the gangplank of the *Orient Princess* a blast of hot air hit me in the face; the sweet smell of the river clogged my nostrils; the clamour and the chant of coolies, the strident voices of Chinese overseers, the cries of hawkers, hit my ears. It added a spring to my step. When I breathed in deeply it was not just a biological process enabling me to stay alive; I was breathing in the joy of living. This was my home, the city I loved more than any other I knew, and I was too young to be plagued by the lassitude, the enervation, the cynicism that gripped older men. Not for me a stifled longing for England, for snow, for fog; *this* was my home, so that arriving in Singapore was like breaking free from a jail in a cold and inhospitable climate.

I don't know what Irene had expected, though I had done my best on the voyage out to give her some idea of what Singapore was like. But of course it is a big change in a woman's life to leave home, the tranquillity of Wimbledon (and even allowing for family rows, it was a lovely home) and travel ten thousand miles to a dot of an island less than a hundred miles from the equator, hiding a secret pregnancy, and facing an entirely new set of friends, in-laws, servants, customs, climate and then – heat. It was a daunting challenge, though of course she wasn't the first bride who had eagerly accepted it. I knew I could help to a certain extent, cushion her; but in her mind, in her own thoughts, it was essentially her problem.

She didn't say much as we got into the car, but then anyone would be fully occupied absorbing the colour and movement of the streets as we drove to Tanamera. It was so new to her, so different – and doubtless so unexpected – that at first I thought she hardly spoke because she was so busy looking.

There was, however, a different reason: she was gasping from the heat. It was something I had never thought about, for I had been born in it. Despite its inconvenience, despite the overpowering humidity, it was the heat I missed when I lived in London more than any other Singapore element. It had been a part of all my life. Now I remembered that even at Port Said Irene had been fanning herself and complaining, even though the dry desert heat during our brief stop there was nothing compared to the wet heat of Singapore, from which no one could escape.

She did her best to cope, sitting bolt upright in the car because the back of her white dress was wet through. She fanned herself with one of those small giveaway rattan fans and said, 'Sorry, darling. It started the moment the ship dropped anchor. Tell me, when does the hot season end?'

I hadn't the heart to tell her that the thermometer hardly varied from one month to another.

It was a little cooler when we turned into Bukit Timah Road, and as we passed through the gates and the drive curved, giving a frontal view of the white walls, I told the syce to stop the car.

'Jump out and take a look.' I helped her from the car. 'There you are – Tanamera! Our new home, darling.'

For a moment or two she stood there, squinting in the bright sun, and then with a laugh asked, 'All of it? It's beautiful, Johnnie – but it's big enough for a museum.'

The arrival of the first new *memsahib* at Tanamera since my father brought my mother to the house was an historic event – especially to the domestic staff, for everyone knew they were meeting the *mem* who would one day be their mistress. They lined up on either side of the portico, while mother and father, who had deliberately driven home ahead of us while we fussed our way through customs, were waiting to give Irene an official welcome. And there, too, in his wheelchair, was the patriarch of the family, a little older than when I last saw him, a little more subdued. Twenty years ago he would have welcomed Irene with a brass band and conducted it with his poker. Those days were gone.

It was typical of Irene that she knew just what to do to win the hearts of everyone standing there, and she did it without a moment's hesitation. She walked straight up to the wheel-chair, smiled and cried, 'Hullo, Grandpa Jack!' Before he could reply, she planted a firm kiss on his bushy bearded cheek, and with a laugh said, 'I've heard more about you than anyone else in Singapore.'

I am not sure how Irene really felt about kissing an old man of eighty-four whom she had never seen before; but Grandpa Jack was delighted and muttered something no one could understand. But my father was even more pleased. It was the ultimate compliment to him, to the family, to the house.

I had already told Irene in London that, unless she had any violent objection, we would as a matter of course live in Tanamera. In fact it had never entered my head to live anywhere else; but that was because *I* would not be the one living with new in-laws. I wouldn't be asked to share the Bradshaw home in Wimbledon. Would I have thought that a good idea? I remembered how in the past, whenever Paul and I joked about the dire dangers of marriage, we always regarded the stage mother-in-law as the ultimate disaster. And I had often thought what an awful burden is imposed on newlyweds, already faced with the traumas of the first months of marriage, to have to accept as a matter of course relations they hardly know or care about. But to live with them! Irene might well have refused if she hadn't met my mother before we married. They got on from the first moment, with Mama going out of her way to explain that really Tanamera was like a hotel in which we would have our own rooms.

Our arrival was made doubly exciting because of an unexpected wedding present. Papa Jack had given us the traditional cheque and had paid our passages on the *Orient Princess*. But in London he had hinted at an extra present.

'You'll have to wait until you get home,' he had told Irene. 'We'll unveil it when we welcome you to Tanamera.'

Papa Jack had taken an immediate fancy to Irene, and it was reciprocated; they had a kind of affinity that made me feel that if Irene and I ever quarrelled my father would automatically take her side. In fact he said to me once, 'She's my idea of the perfect daughter-in-law.'

When he had hinted about the present in London Irene had teased him, 'Come on, Papa Jack' – she used the name from the first day they met – 'do tell.'

'No, no. Well,' relenting with a chuckle, 'I'll just say that it does include a very comfortable – and very strong – double bed.'

'Honestly,' Irene laughed, 'you Yorkshire boys only think of one thing.' And now, when the formalities were over, Irene asked, 'Now, Papa Jack – where's this present?'

'Follow me.' he brushed aside Mama's faint protest that Irene might like a cup of tea, and led us all up the double stairway at the back of the ballroom. Just behind the gallery, he opened a door with a flourish – a door that I remembered vaguely led to an unused room – and cried, 'There!'

He and Mama had transformed five rooms into a self-contained flat, which was instantly christened the married quarters. It included a big sitting room with a verandah, a dressing room, a tiny kitchenette with a fridge for drinks and a stove on which we could make tea or coffee or toast if we wanted to be alone; and, most exciting of all, an air-conditioned bedroom. Even as 1937 turned into 1938 this was the height of luxury in Singapore. Machines used in private homes were so underpowered they would only cool the air efficiently if all the windows were boarded up, so the room was fairly small. Still, I knew how wonderful it would be to arrive back from the office, mix a couple of stengahs in the kitchenette, and take them into the bedroom and cool off over a long drink. And it was equally wonderful to sleep under a couple of blankets at night.

Everyone adored Irene – and she seemed to be happy, if a little tired, which was understandable. Natasha came down from Ara now and again to visit us once her baby could be safely left with the amah – under Tony's watchful eyes; he was mad about Victoria. He liked running the estate too, but Natflat got bored. She and Irene were much of an age, and it was Natasha who persuaded Irene to go out a bit more, took her shopping, forced me to take them to dinner at Raffles. Vicki was always coming round too. She had blossomed since her marriage to Ian Scott, softened in a way hard to explain; it had taken some of the brassiness out of her. I could see that she was determined to make a go of her marriage to an older man. All the old gang were there. We saw a lot of Bonnard – no longer a threat now that Natasha was a young mother; and of course it was easier to invite Paul to Tanamera because his sister – who was still in Tours – was no threat now that I was about to be a father. In fact most of us were settling down. Only Paul – and I suppose Bonnard, since his wife was so far away in Switzerland – were spare men.

It was amazing how quickly London faded into (for me) a bad dream; and if I thought of Julie sometimes it was with the tenderness of a love that was over and could therefore never be spoiled. I was busy too. The business was booming and demanded more and more of my time. And I discovered that they had actually missed me on the courts of the Cricket Club. Occasionally Irene and I went out alone to dine at Raffles or the Tanglin, but with the baby on the way it wasn't easy, and anyway we always seemed to be involved in business dinners.

Mama was wonderful in her ethereal, rather vague kind of way, for behind her vagueness she had the superb knack of never being in the way of a newly-married couple, but of being there at the moments when Irene needed her. It was almost uncanny, for in those moments she knew exactly what to say, what to do. And Mama also sensed danger signals.

'Don't you think you're a bit selfish with Irene?' she said to me one day. I gave a gasp of surprise.

'That's the one thing I'm not!' I said.

'Perhaps you should take her out a little more?'

'But Mama,' I protested, 'she's having a baby – and we're working like hell at the office.' Which was true, for with anxiety about a war in Europe mounting the boom in rubber and tin was taking off, and that meant long, difficult hours at the office. 'I come home fagged out.'

'Of course you're working hard, darling,' she said. 'And your father is very proud of the way you've settled down, but,' with the faintest smile, 'perhaps you'd be less tired if you didn't go straight from the office to play tennis nearly every day.'

'But I've always done that.'

'I know,' she was almost laughing, 'but you weren't always married.'

'But,' I felt slightly aggrieved, 'Irene comes from a tennis family. They're all mad about tennis. That's how I met her.'

'She never plays, does she? But forget it, Johnnie, it's not the end of the world. I just think that she's a little lonely – she needs a bit of special attention. She's very sweet, you know.'

Of course it wasn't only tennis and selfishness. I could see that, apart from the younger set – Vicki, Natasha, Bonnard, our friends – most of the old business acquaintances of the Dexters bored Irene. She never showed it – she was a nice girl, and really tried to make a go of it – but I could tell. The trouble was that the success of Dexters as a company had always rested on intimate contact with 'friends' so close that if ever they faced a business choice they turned to us almost instinctively. These 'friendships' were cemented by an unending stream of dinners at Tanamera, and since I was next in line to become *tuan bezar* my presence was obligatory. And though I often found them boring I had been brought up playing a part in this rigmarole; to me Dexters was a way of life that had to be protected. Dinner parties were merely an extension of office hours.

Nor could Irene ask to be excused – not until she could plead her advanced pregnancy – for all our business acquaintances, who usually came with their wives, were dying to meet the new and pretty wife of the next *tuan bezar*. And they not only came to see her – they insisted that she should come to see *them*, for they were all charmed by her; she was attractive, she had good manners, she was skilfully demure at the dinner table of her mother-in-law; in fact Bonnard described her as 'the perfect *jeune fille de la maison*'. She possessed a delightful knack of making any man to whom she was talking – or rather listening to – feel that what he had to say fascinated her. I had noticed that at Wimbledon, and later in the studio at Fulham. In fact I am sure that this is what had attracted Tim

'Lucky young man!' Ian Scott, who had spruced up amazingly since he married Vicki, gave me a metaphorical dig in the ribs and a conspiratorial wink

'I can't be luckier than you, sir ' I answered respectfully – and, of course, knowingly.

Even P.P. Soong tended to unbend to mellow a little from his grey stiffness, though any smile always looked as though it was the result of an inner struggle barely won. I am sure P.P. wanted to be friendly and warm; it was not in his nature to be anything but sphinx-like, but there was perhaps another reason. Aunt Sonia had written from San Francisco that she wasn't returning: the break was final. And according to Paul, Soong was very upset at losing his wife. On the other hand he no doubt felt easier in his mind now that I had been married off. I knew Soong would never forgive me, but he had to accept me because the Soongs and the Dexters were now working more closely together than ever before. And I could hardly be left out of the negotiations.

Dexters dealt mainly in rubber, tin, timber, insurance and shipping; and our prefabricated construction company was booming. Soongs operated differently. Since the day the first Soong won a navy contract to supply a depot in a

Christmas Island group they had concentrated on building up a huge import business supplying day-to-day necessities. For the best part of a century Soongs had held a Chritmas Island contract, managing it with such honesty (and content with such a small profit margin) that successive British Government officials had never considered any change in the status quo. They were quite right – they could never have struck a better bargain, or dealt with a more astute trader. The Soongs had ploughed profits back into the business, building a network of depots all over Malaya, from which they could distribute the same kinds of goods they sent to the Indian Ocean. Just as an early Soong had monopolised the ice supply, and opened the first bakery, his successors had exclusive contracts to import and distribute tinned food, household goods, refrigerators – in fact everything from a gas burner to ice cream. Their goods came from all over the world – corned beef from Argentina, tinned sausages from England, bottled beer from Germany and tinned fruit and vegetables from Australia and America which, despite the wonderful fruits and vegetables in Malaya, were always popular.

When Soongs' goods reached Singapore they were sent up-country by rail, though Dexters took a modest share in the transaction, for we handled the insurance; our coolies also helped with unloading and, if necessary, we sometimes stored their consignments in our godowns. When supplying Christmas Island, the Soongs relied on us to ship the goods in our fleet of tramps, each one three or four thousand tons, christened nostalgically by Grandpa Jack with the names of villages near Hull that his father had talked about – the *Anlaby*, the *Ferriby*, the *Willerby*, the *Brough*.

Of course anyone could use any cargo space on any of our vessels, provided they paid. But suddenly in early 1938, with Irene seven months pregnant, Soong asked for every available cubic foot in our holds. And though he did not – could not – offer more than the going rate, he offered us another major incentive.

Papa Jack came into my small cubbyhole of an office on that morning and – rather unlike him – didn't ask if I were free, but said briskly, 'I want you to drop everything and come for lunch with me. P.P. and his general manager have taken a private room at Raffles. He wants shipping space. I haven't the faintest idea what's in the wind – but it must be big for Soong to arrange a private lunch for today at' – he looked at his old-fashioned pocket watch – 'eleven o'clock.'

Papa Jack shouted for Ball, who came in quickly, short and fussy and glowing with importance. Papa Jack asked him, 'Would you and Bill Rawlings prepare an analysis for all our free shipping space over the next three months?'

'When for?' asked Ball.

'Tomorrow morning. Can you?'

'Will do.' Ball loved to use crisp, 'smart', short sentences – before lunch. He spoke at greater length after his lunch-time session.

Soong was not the sort of man to keep people in suspense – and Papa Jack was not the sort of man to be kept in suspense. Each knew and respected the other, and P.P. had arranged for a cold buffet on a side table in a private room over the original tiffin room which Grandpa Jack had helped to create when Raffles first opened. In the cream-painted room, with its trembling fans and open windows overlooking the lawns below, it didn't take much imagination to see Grandpa Jack arriving in his trap drawn by piebald horses, and settling down to a huge curry tiffin.

Soong waved a hand to a bar of drinks, ice, water in one corner. Next to it was the table loaded with cold meats and salads. Soong explained to my father, 'I thought if we had a cold buffet we wouldn't be disturbed by waiters.'

Papa Jack poured out a pink gin; I mixed myself a gimlet. Soong had some freshly squeezed papaya juice and his manager, T. L. Tan, a short, squat, black-haired man with bags under his eyes, the power behind the Soong empire and vice-president of the Chinese Chamber of Commerce, poured out a Tiger beer. I was glad to see that Kai-shek was not present.

'What I have to say is confidential until the official an-nouncement next Monday,' Soong began, 'but I don't have to impress that on the Dexters.' He smiled faintly, as though it cost him an effort, and raised his glass of papaya juice in a toast. 'It's very simple. The British navy is going to build a training base on Pulau Tenara near Christmas Island.'

'Pulau Tenara?' I cried. 'That dead-alive hole! Even the convicts couldn't stand it.' The island of Pulau Tenara – once used as a penal settlement – was a quirk of nature, for it was so tiny – barely ten miles long – that normally it would have hardly merited a place in a gazetteer of the world, yet ironically was firmly marked on even the smallest atlas. The reason was simple. Though the island was small it lay protected from even the heaviest storms behind an encircling coral reef fifty miles in circumference, which was such a hazard to shipping that despite the unimportance of the island itself Pulau Tenara had to be marked on every chart. In fact it is to the Indian Ocean what the equally small but equally dangerous atoll of Suvarov is to the Pacific.

Papa Jack's reaction was different. 'A training base?' he whistled. 'That looks ominous.'

'I doubt if it is,' said P.P. in his precise voice. 'As you know, my family has' – he coughed politely – 'looked after some of the Christmas Island group for a long time. This gave me the occasion once to visit Pulau Tenara, and it bears no resemblance to the other islands in the area. It's rocky, sandy, and of course uninhabited, though there is plenty of water. I have been told in confidence that the army plans to use it for training men in – they called it desert warfare.'

'Even if there is a war we don't have any deserts in Europe,' Papa Jack laughed.

'I think the British believe,' Mr Tan spoke for the first time, 'that if war does break out in Europe the Italians might side with Hitler, and that could mean fighting in North Africa.'

'All this is supposition.' P.P. helped himself to some cold turkey and salad. 'But the decision has been made – I think it's stupid – and because of our links with Christmas Island the government approached me first. Army engineers will build all the installations, but they've asked me if we could land the supplies there, food, clothing, stores and so on, together with timber and building materials.'

'And can you, P.P.?' asked Papa Jack.

'I said yes immediately, but' – with a faint smile – 'I don't really know. It depends on you. I can supply the stores. That's no problem. But before the momentum's reached, before everything is running smoothly, when we would only require normal shipping, we will need a lot of cargo space. And,' he added thoughtfully, 'timber, roofing, machinery, plumbing installations – and I feel that it would be the natural gesture for me to offer this business to my oldest friend.'

The inference was obvious. We could have the highly profitable business – and it would range from supplying tractors and buildings to nuts and bolts – if we could make a firm offer to put most of our shipping at Soong's disposal, so that he could get his initial stocks to the island. There was nothing sinister in the inference. It was just good business. And it would make a great deal of money for all of us.

I usually kept tabs on our shipping movements, and though Ball was working out the details Papa Jack turned to me with a few questions. Then he asked Soong, 'What would the starting date be?'

'Probably three months from now. The army construction teams will have to be assembled. They will erect your huts, radio stations, generators and so on. But they'll want all the heavy equipment there – and waiting – before they arrive on the scene.'

'The *Anlaby* is in Kuching and the *Willerby* is down in Cheribon,' I told Papa Jack. 'I see no real problems – though what about unloading facilities? What's the harbour like? None of us except you, Mr Soong, has seen this place.'

No serious problems, Soong assured us. At the time the island had been a penal settlement a deep water jetty had been built inside the lagoon, shielded by its huge circle of coral, to accommodate ships bringing in stores for warders and convicts.

'The government says there's an excellent passage through the reef, wide enough to admit a fair-sized vessel –

certainly one of yours,' said P.P. The roughly-built jetty, stretching like a finger into deep water, was still serviceable. 'We'll have to plan how to get the unloading equipment ashore first,' Soong conceded, 'but I see no difficulties ahead.'

We finished lunch. The financial wallahs would start to work out the cost plus figures and sort out the details. But that was when the really hard work – for me – began, because a few days later, when Papa Jack and I had sat down to breakfast before the others, and Li was serving papaya, Papa Jack turned to me and said, with a touch of regret, 'I'm getting on for sixty, Johnnie, and I don't really want to get too involved in the Pulau Tenara business, so I'd like you to handle it all with Soong's men, with the shipping and the construction company – and just keep me in the general picture.'

I must have hesitated because he asked, 'Think you can do it? Too much on your plate?'

'I don't mind the work. But sometimes I get a bit worried about Irene. I was thinking that I might take her up to Cameron Highlands for some cool air.'

'You could do that anyway. Is she a bit' – he searched for the right word – 'depressed?'

'It's a strong word,' I confessed. 'But, you know, I don't think she really *likes* Singapore. It's an awful thing to say, but after London I suppose it seems provincial and dull. I've never asked you, Papa, but how did Mama like Singapore after living in New York?'

'She hated it. Every minute of it, and you know, you and I, we're different, we *love* it here, but I can understand Irene – young and pretty, dumped in – well, I'm very fond of Irene, and I can understand how she feels.'

'Mama got over it,' I laughed.

He hesitated for a moment, as though considering how much a father should confide in a son, specially about a wife and mother. Finally, with a kind of wry smile he said, 'Its old history now, Johnnie, but it was touch and go.'

I couldn't believe it. *My parents!* 'You mean – divorce or whatever?'

'That was never discussed. I don't think it existed in Singapore when we were your age.' He laughed at that, before adding, 'But she was in such a bad way after Natasha was born that I did suggest sending her away for a bit. And she went. It was never a split, Johnnie, so don't get any wild ideas. But I packed her off to New York for a few months – and she was the one who asked to come back. She was a different girl.'

I didn't know what to say, so said nothing. And Papa was perhaps embarrassed at this sudden confidence after all these years, for he said almost too cheerfully, 'So I wouldn't worry too much about Irene. She's homesick. After the baby, let her have a holiday in England. Maybe you could go too. Fly – it's the coming way to travel. And now back to business. Think you can handle it?'

'Of course,' I was playing for a little time while I recovered from his words. 'There's a lot of money involved.'

'The more money at stake the easier the problem,' my father replied cheerfully. 'It gives you a margin for error – it's when you're scratching for a cash flow that the problems arise. And don't imagine that this isn't a useful break for us,' he added. 'We're in a very tricky situation. There's a sudden glut in rubber and the price is falling every day.'

It was a fantastic paradox. In 1937 the International Rubber Regulation Committee, aware of the American demand for rubber, had raised the output quota to ninety per cent of what we were capable of producing. Everyone was overjoyed. New labour was engaged. With the price at nearly one and twopence at the time – and with everyone clamouring for rubber – it seemed as though fortunes were waiting to be made. And then came disaster. By March 1938 stocks were so huge the price had slid down to fivepence a pound.

'So now we're handling more rubber than ever,' said Papa Jack, 'and practically losing money. This new business in Christmas Island will give our ships just the kind of tonnage they need.'

We helped ourselves to some more bacon and scrambled eggs from the chafing dish at the back of the east verandah.

'And anyway, Johnnie,' he added, 'it's all mad money. We might as well take it – if we don't someone else will. But fancy a British government wasting money on a crazy idea like this. A desert war! There'll be no war in Europe, let alone in Africa. Chamberlain and Hitler – they'll do a deal, you mark my words.'

'Who's going to pay for it?' I asked.

'The taxpayer,' said Papa Jack. 'The poor bloody British taxpayer. You saw that Sir John Simon pushed income tax in the UK up to five and six in the last budget. That's the way they're getting the money to pay for Pulau Tenara.'

'The money's a fleabite anyway to the enormous cost of rearming – specially the naval base in Singapore,' I said.

'The base is different,' said Papa Jack. 'Britain does need a major naval base in the Pacific – just to show everyone we do still have the most powerful navy in the world. It's the best way of showing the flag. I don't *trust* the Japs, though I don't think they'll fight – specially if we boast a bit. By the way,' he asked as an afterthought, 'see much of our Japanese friend Miki? The man in the construction business – the chap who introduced you to Irene?'

I shook my head. 'It's damn silly, really. We used to play tennis together but they won't let him play at the YMCA any more.'

By now an increasing anti-Japanese feeling was becoming noticeable in Singapore. The relatively small Japanese community was still allowed to continue – its fishing boats were always active – but the Japanese were no longer accepted socially, certainly not by the Chinese. I did play one game of tennis with Miki – to me a harmless pawn caught up in suspicions that did not concern him. And it was Paul Soong who had warned me that I ought not to see him.

'Nothing to do with me' – we were having a drink at Raffles – 'but I'd hate you to get a knife in your back. Or,' with a grin, 'those beautiful ears of yours chopped off.'

'All this war talk, Paul,' I said. 'There'll *never* be a war here. Not out here. Not with the naval base and those beautiful fifteen-inch guns of ours.'

Paul's voice when he wanted to make a point had its own

gentle, almost languid intonation. 'But the war's already started between *us* – between China and Japan. And Hitler has recognised Japan as the ruler of Manchuria. That's why the Chinese tongs have given the order – any Chinese found dealing with the Japanese has his ears cut off. There were twelve cases last week. Six lots of ears were posted back to the owners. We're not worried about the Japanese coming *here* – perhaps they won't, but if they ever *did* that'd be a British problem. On the other hand, the Japanese already occupy a hell of a lot of China.'

'And it's your war – even if you're a British citizen living in Singapore?' I left the rest of the sentence unanswered.

'Yes. You and I are both Singaporeans, Johnnie – both born here, both live here. But how would you feel if the Germans started bombing London?'

'Furious!' I laughed.

'And I'll bet you'd kick all German members out of the Cricket Club the next morning.'

'Well, yes,' I laughed again, 'I suppose we would.' And then because we were close enough friends I switched the subject to ask, 'Any news of Julie?'

'Dutiful letters to her father,' Paul shrugged his elegant shoulders. 'I imagine our Mom – that's what they call them in America, you know – filled her with anti-Chinese propaganda before she left America for France.'

I could feel my heart hammering.

'She'll be back in Singapore by the end of this year or early in 1939.' Almost with a grin, Paul added, 'Not that you'll be interested, of course, because you're a staid old married man!'

I gave him a playful dig in the ribs. Paul knew damn well that if I married a dozen times my heart would still leap every time I caught sight of Julie. What a wonderful friend Paul was! In Singapore I knew dozens of people with mixed Asian and Western blood – Eurasians we called them in those days – and almost every one seemed to have a chip on his shoulder. I could understand why. It made my blood boil to see how some British treated them shamefully as inferior beings. But Paul came into a different category.

Possibly it was his American blood. Or perhaps his family's wealth shielded him from the inferiority complexes that haunted thousands of lowly-paid clerks whose only aspirations were to find steady jobs in the government services, and who always referred to England, the country they would never see, as home.

Paul could have become a mortal enemy of the white man who had — to use his mother's words — seduced his sister; instead he understood, for he had a great capacity for understanding. I think it was because Singapore was his country, and I was one of the few Englishmen who also felt that this was my country, so that we shared it and thought alike. Most Europeans in Singapore lived like exiles in an alien land, as they strived to make their fortunes or waited patiently for their pensions to mature. For the most part they skimmed over the surface of what they politely called native life without ever seeing, without even noticing, the placid happiness of the Malays, the beautiful, languid rhythm of the riverine kampong life; nor could they really see the energy of the Chinese throngs busily pursuing their life, which to the uninterested white men was so remote they might have been inhabiting a different planet.

In a way this was one of the biggest problems facing Irene. No one could expect her, after only a few weeks in Singapore, to become part of it in the way Paul and I were. That difference would take years to bridge.

On the other hand, when I said to Papa Jack that I was worried about Irene I hadn't meant she was so depressed that we were always having rows. It was nothing like that. On the numberless occasions when we held our social-cum-business dinners she charmed everyone. And she could be very sweet to me, and understanding. But having a baby in the climate of Singapore was not much fun anyway, though Dr Sampson said she was bearing up very well. Irritations tended to become magnified. She had always enjoyed cooking — and it frustrated her not to be allowed in the kitchen. It was too hot for her to go shopping. And so everything that went wrong became invested with a spurious significance.

Oddly enough Grandpa Jack more than anyone else could light up her face with a smile. When she first arrived at Tanamera I was worried that the proximity of this old man in a wheelchair would irritate her; in fact she adored him and spent more time with him than other members of the family. I *did* try to give him some of my time, but now I had a wife and a great deal of work to claim my attention.

Grandpa Jack was amazing. It was years since that dreadful night when he had had a stroke, and though we had despaired of his life, here he was, the voice a little slurred towards sundown, the movements a little feebler, but still a man amongst men.

'I like that girl,' he said one evening when we were alone. 'But she hates it here. You agree?'

I nodded. There was nothing to say.

'Send her to London for a trip when the baby arrives. That's what your father did with your mother when she got a fit of the blues. Taking a chance – she might never come back. But,' with a conspiratorial chuckle, 'your mother did – if only just.'

I ignored that one and just said, 'Surely the danger of war in Europe is increasing. And if there's a war, Grandpa Jack, she'd be better here – safer, too, with our child.'

'Might be more *dangerous* in London,' he growled. 'But more *miserable* here. Which would you choose for your wife?'

Poor Miki, who I hardly saw now, provided a typical reason for Irene's frustration. 'It's ages since I saw him,' she said one day, 'and, after all, he did introduce us. Could we have him up for a drink?'

I had to tell her that it was unwise.

She wasn't cross, but flabbergasted. 'You really mean you're frightened to ask him because your father would disapprove?'

'It's not that. There's a terrific anti-Japanese feeling at the moment.'

'I thought he was a friend of yours.' Her voice was harsh.

'He was a tennis partner, darling.'

'Well – if it hadn't been for him we wouldn't be married. Honestly, Singapore is more hidebound than Wimbledon. It's so – what's the word? – so *parochial*.'

We were sitting in the study waiting, in fact, for Bertrand Bonnard who had been spending several weeks in Tokyo, and when he arrived a few minutes later he took Irene's side.

'As a Swiss I suppose we regard everyone as – well, the same. I can understand the Chinese not liking the Japanese – I wouldn't invite Jiroh here with Mr Soong. But I find the Japanese very pleasant.' And he added to Irene, 'If you want to see Jiroh, and if Johnnie doesn't mind, I'll fix a dinner in my flat.'

'Wonderful!' she cried. 'Anything to get away from this suburban atmosphere. And' – to me – 'did you know Natasha's coming down for a week while Tony goes on some course, or something? Could she come along, Bertrand?'

'Of course,' he smiled. 'She's a charming married lady.'

Bengy was born on 8 May 1938; a lusty seven pounds eleven ounces, and he was born in the air-conditioned bedroom of the married quarters on the advice of Dr Sampson who, weighing the advantages of hospital against home, said, 'Let her have the baby at Tanamera. Irene suffers badly from the heat, and she'll be less nervous, less depressed in her own room.' There was no air conditioning in any hospital wards, only in one or two operating theatres.

To me all newborn babies look much the same (not that I had seen many) but I had to agree with Irene that the new son and heir was wonderful.

'You'll see.' She lay in bed, very tired. 'He'll make all the problems we faced worthwhile for you. For me too, darling, but specially for you.'

'You've made everything worthwhile. And soon we'll have you up and about again.'

But we didn't – though not because of illness. We had her up but not about, for though Irene had had a comparatively easy time when Bengy was born, the month leading up to the birth had been trying – not only for her, but for all of us.

I realised she had felt cut off from her own family, from the beautiful house and garden in Wimbledon. I had suggested that her mother should come out – Papa Jack delicately offered to pay the fare – but in 1938 taking a plane journey was regarded by many people as taking an unnecessary risk, and the suggestion came to nothing.

It was not only the narrow, hidebound world of Singapore that wore Irene down. She disliked it, but that dislike was compounded by the unrelenting heat that drove her to spend long hours in our air-conditioned bedroom – which meant that she never really gave herself a chance to become used to the heat. For the heat and humidity of Singapore was there as a trial of strength, a challenge, to every white man or woman. It was a fight you had to win if you wanted to survive happily. And you could only win it by meeting it head on; by going out into the heat, gasping for air, drenched with sweat, until the miraculous day arrived when you hardly noticed it any more. Irene never really gave herself a chance to win that battle.

I hoped that when she got over the birth Irene would forget that month of lonely waiting, but she didn't. She had got into a habit and she refused to give it up. She was always with the family when expected to be. As she put it with a laugh, 'I'm always on parade,' and there was no outward evidence at dinner parties that anything was amiss. Nor were there any signs of illness – for the very good reason that she wasn't ill. She recovered from the pregnancy very quickly. And I don't doubt that if by some miracle we had been able to air-condition the rooms downstairs – an impossibility in those days – she would have been downstairs more often. She *liked* us all – and we liked her. She loved Bengy – and so did we. But she disliked the heat. And since she was too much of a lady to spend her time complaining she took to staying in her room with 'headaches'. Once or twice I entered the married quarters unexpectedly and found her playing with Bengy, laughing and giggling. And if I said I would stay with her any suggestions of illness vanished immediately.

But the result was that she not only developed a phobia

about the heat – which wasn't as bad as all that in the evenings – but also about the other irritations of life in the tropics. They seemed to drive her to desperation. At times it was the buzz of mosquitos, at others the incessant croaking of bullfrogs from the jungle at the edge of the compound, booming towards the western verandah for hours on end. The moths plagued the lights dangling on the ceiling. Once she shrieked in terror at the sight of a snake lying curled on the grass – and nearly vomited when one of the gardeners crept up and chopped it in pieces with his parang. Another time she arrived for dinner to find two monkeys, so used to us they were almost tame, sitting, tails down, hooting at us from the thickest branch of a flame tree that almost over-hung the verandah. After that it was a week before she would come down again for an evening drink.

14

Oddly enough I met Miki by chance at the Adelphi not long after we had dinner with him at Bonnard's flat.

'Sorry I haven't been able to fix up a game of tennis,' I apologised. 'But you know how it is. Any international bust-up and everyone has to work twice as hard for half the money.'

'I too am very occupied.' Miki probably knew perfectly well that I was playing tennis four times a week. Sitting in the basketwork chairs of the Adelphi lounge, the fans whirring overhead, I said, 'You Japanese are going it a bit in China, aren't you?' I smiled to rob the words of any offence. Miki gave the Japanese version of a sigh, an indrawn hiss of annoyance. 'Too many stupid men in Japan. They make the rest of world very angry.'

'They're certainly making the Singapore Chinese angry.'

'China, Japan, ancient enemies. Not important. But our stupid leaders also very frightened – *that* important.'

I asked him to explain – briefly: for though I did like Miki, I still had an uncomfortable feeling that really I shouldn't be seen with him. The first rumours of bestial conduct by Japanese troops had reached Singapore, and I didn't want to be involved in a scene if the Chinese waiters refused to serve him.

'Because we need oil, Japanese make silly threats to United States. But America very strong. Ah so! I see my friend.' – an Indian was coming towards us. As Miki got up he said, 'If we play tennis at Japanese Club okay, yes? Give my best regards to Irene. I hear from Sir Keith last week.'

'Bradshaw!' I was really surprised.

'Maybe I go to England for business trip and Britain immigration like visitors from Japan to bear a letter of guarantee. Irene's father help me.'

We not only faced problems over the Sino-Japanese war; by the autumn of 1938 the fear of war in Europe seemed very real. We could even sense it in Singapore.

It wasn't only Hitler and Mussolini. The background was so depressing. By 1938 two million people in Britain were out of work and one-third of the population was existing on or near the poverty line.

'Look at this.' Papa Jack tossed across a copy of a British magazine called *Picture Post* which had just been launched. It showed pictures of a London man with a wife and four children. He couldn't get a job, so they were living on bread, margarine and tea – all they could afford out of the man's dole and benefits which came to two pounds, seven and six. Special government food supplies were now being hoarded in case of war; in September the navy had been mobilised; gas masks were issued to everyone.

'And it isn't only England that's in trouble,' said Papa Jack. 'Look at America. More than twenty-three million people on relief – one in six. I read earlier this year there were eleven million out of work in America.'

To us in Singapore, so far away from Europe and America, the Munich crisis in September had flashed across our newsreels with the unreality of a fictional war film, even

225

though plans to evacuate London had been published. All these headlines now reached us via KLM only three or four days after publication.

Even while Chamberlain, Hitler and Mussolini were meeting in Munich the ARP in London was being mobilised, and we saw the first photographs of barrage balloons hanging like grey sausages over London's rooftops. Squads of bare-chested men grinned as they thrust their spades into the grass of Hyde Park digging trenches or erecting shelters. Roosevelt had cabled Hitler asking him to behave.

And there, on Movietone News, was Chamberlain crying, 'How incredible it is that we should be digging trenches and trying on gas masks here because of a quarrel in a far-away country between people of whom we know nothing.'

Then – within a couple of days it seemed, as if history were being telescoped – the crisis was over, and there was Chamberlain again, with his umbrella, but this time waving a bit of paper as he stepped off the plane; and the next day on the radio he was proclaiming, 'I believe it is peace for our time.'

'I wonder what poor Tim's doing,' Mama said one evening.

'Thoroughly enjoying himself,' I replied.

'You're very heartless.'

'Mama darling – Tim will love it. Bossing private soldiers who can't answer back! Far more fun than buying or selling rubber.'

Paul had come round for a drink as he often did. 'I'd love to be in the army, but they'd never have me,' he said languidly. 'Don't trust us.'

'How's your mother?' asked Mama hastily – she always shied away from embarrassments.

'She sent her love to you all in her last letter. And Julie will be coming back before long. The family agrees for once – that it's silly to let her stay in France with all this war talk. But she says she'll only come if she's allowed to take a job.'

'Doing what, Paul?' asked Mama.

'Apparently she took her nursing certificate in America

and wants to come back to look after us all. The lady with the lamp.'

I wondered what Julie would look like – what we would say to each other when we met, as we inevitably would. After all this time, how would we behave – the married man and father and 'the girl on the piano'? I longed just to look at her.

As for the war in Europe – it was even harder to take the prospect seriously now that Chamberlain had 'guaranteed' peace and after reading how the *Queen Mary* had regained the Atlantic Blue Ribband; nor did it seem warlike to launch an even bigger passenger liner, the *Queen Elizabeth*, in September. A New York radio broadcast about an invasion by Martians – a spoof by a young actor and writer called Orson Welles – seemed more martial than the posturings of the European dictators. The Japanese on the rampage in China presented a much closer threat to us, because, even if it wasn't our fight – and it certainly wasn't – the Chinese were a powerful influence in Singapore business circles. The Chinese had, so it was said, lost a million dead. The Japanese had followed their earlier successes by taking Hankow, and Chiang Kai-shek had retreated to Chungking.

All this posed difficult problems for the agency house, and more than once Papa Jack had said, '*If* there's a war in Europe, I ought to go back and run the London office. There'll be such a scramble for war material we won't know what's hit us.'

'Couldn't Mr Cowley cope?' I had a sudden flashback to those days in London when I met Irene.

'Not a hope. He would never be up to it – specially with the end of the International Regulations Scheme. There could be one hell of a free-for-all.'

I had the feeling that Papa Jack, unlike Grandpa Jack, was *anxious* to go. Surely he couldn't be homesick for an England he only knew as a visitor? But he was fifty-eight – and though he was very fit the heat and humidity did sap people's strength.

'But if there isn't a war – and *you* don't think it's likely – why go to England? And if there *is* – well, I suppose I'd have to join up; and then you'd be needed here.'

'*You* join up! I never heard such nonsense,' my father retorted sharply. 'Tim'll do his share for the family if there's a war – and I never said there would be – but your job would be to keep the vital supplies moving and take over the firm.'

I was so surprised – shocked almost – by the sudden feeling that Papa Jack was tired of Singapore – tired of everything? – that a few days later when I found Mama alone I asked her if anything was the matter with him.

'Old age, that's all, Johnnie,' she smiled. 'Your father needs to relax – to take things easy –'

'But Grandpa Jack is in his eighties!'

'Really? Nobody's said your father's going to die.' Mama was half laughing, but I suddenly realised that though she was several years younger than Papa everyone was growing older – and that included her. The telltale signs were there: brown spots on the hands, a few lines round the throat.

'I didn't mean that, Mama.'

'Things are so different nowadays. Grandpa Jack only had to fight the climate and his rivals. He could beat them both. Now – well, *you* know how it is in the office – your father keeps telling me about it – red tape or whatever you call it –'

'But I could look after all the bumf.'

'What extraordinary words you pick up, Johnnie.' Then she added, 'It's the way the old order is changing. That's what's getting your father down.'

'But it's changing in England.'

'That's not the same – what happens there doesn't matter to your father, because he's never been part of the old order in England. So he wouldn't have any old standards as a comparison. Here he *has* – and he hates what's happening.' She sighed as she cut little octagonal pieces of coloured material for her latest patchwork quilt. 'Your father's had a blazing row with the governor.'

I must have looked flabbergasted.

'Don't worry,' she laughed. 'He's not going to jail.'

'Shenton Thomas? That jumped-up little –'

'Careful!' Mama really did hate bad language – perhaps because she had had to tolerate so much from Grandpa Jack.

She told me briefly what had happened. The Sultan of Johore had invited a cabaret dancer from London to replace the wife he had recently divorced.

'Lydia Hill?'

'Oh. You know about her?' Mama seemed surprised.

'She's a corker.'

'Is she?' With a smile she asked, 'Doesn't she remind you of Vicki?'

'Vicki? Why should she? And tell me – why shouldn't the sultan invite a pretty face to stay with him?'

Mama explained what had happened. Shenton Thomas was so incensed at the way Lydia Hill was paraded as a new mistress that when the sultan held his annual party in the Istana in Johore Bahru the governor ordered the government service to boycott it. Though he couldn't forbid the business community to attend he told the president of the Chamber of Commerce to warn members that he also expected business leaders to boycott the sultan's party – adding grimly, 'And the names of those who do attend will be noted.' The inference was sinister – coming from a government which could, without giving a reason, withhold a trading licence or refuse to issue one of a dozen other permits that might be necessary. The Chamber of Commerce duly passed a resolution advising its members not to attend.

'I don't think I have ever seen your father so furious,' said Mama. 'He demanded to see Shenton Thomas – and he did. But you know, that rather ordinary little man just looked up at your father and told him coldly, "The choice is yours – and the advice is mine".'

What really angered my father was the fact that people like the Dexters – and the Soongs and many others – had made Singapore what it was, had built it, fought for it to become the greatest city in Asia. The government should have been allies of the business community.

Papa, who knew that it would be his turn as president of the Chamber of Commerce next year, was determined to go to the party – and he did. Apart from a couple of news-paper reporters and a few Americans, his was the only white face at the party. Within a week an embarrassed, deeply-upset leader of the business community told Papa Jack privately that his name would not be put forward when the Chamber of Commerce elections were discussed. Perhaps next year, when things had blown over.

It was preposterous. Why, every Dexter had *automatically* been elected for a stint as president since the Chamber of Commerce was formed.

Papa Jack was not the only one to suffer at the hands of the governor. The DSO – Defence Security Officer – in Singapore at the time was Hayley Bell, a man of vast experience in the Orient, who against all odds made contact with a spy anxious to sell information to the British.

The man was half Swiss, half Japanese, and Hayley Bell met him in the Botanical Gardens facing Napier Road. He told Bell the Japanese were already training an army to invade Malaya. It seemed preposterous, but the man gave sufficient details to convince Bell there was some truth in his revelations. But the spy wanted to sell the complete dossier of secrets, which included photographs taken at an island in south Japan, for a large sum of money. Bell went to see Shenton Thomas.

The governor listened in silence and then retorted, 'No one but a fool, Bell, would suggest that the Japanese want to attack Singapore.'*

The Hayley Bell incident left me with a queasy feeling in my stomach. The spy had not said *where* the Japanese army was training, but not for the first time I wondered just how bonafide were the earthquake victims living on the island of Yakushima.

I didn't tell my father about my vague suspicions, which were soon forgotten anyway, but not long after the Hayley Bell and Chamber of Commerce incidents Papa Jack and I

* Bell told the details of this encounter to his daughter Mary Hayley Bell, the playwright who married actor John Mills. She described the incident in her autobiography, *What Shall We Do Tomorrow?*

were lunching together at the Tanglin Club (every second Thursday Mama had a ladies' lunch and we never went near Tanamera) and Papa said, 'I've been wondering about your mother – I think she ought to go home to America for a spell –'

'You don't really think there's going to be a war?' I attacked my *pulau ayam* – a Malayan chicken dish not unlike a curry – which was served at Tanglin every Thursday.

'I hope not. But even without a war here it could be hell if the Chinese start anti-Japanese riots or demand sanctions – and anyway your mother needs a holiday.'

'What about you?'

'I suppose Cowley can manage in London for the time being.'

'Well, he's got a very good secretary called Gwen. I'm sure she does everything she's asked to.'

Missing the point, Papa said, 'War or not, things are going to be difficult here. I'm not sure about the London Office – I'll think it over. Boy!' My father waved his hand with a motion showing he was ready to sign the bill.

He did not have to make any difficult decision himself – a decision I felt he was shirking. Unexpected events forced the issue for all of us.

Irene 'attended' all Mama's lunches – sometimes with older guests but at other times with Natasha, who came to Tanamera for a break more often these days, leaving Tony on the Ara estate; he didn't seem to mind. He had a full-time job managing the estate, and the planters were a friendly lot when they met at the club each evening.

On ladies' lunch days I never hurried home. Sometimes the ladies lingered on until four in the afternoon, and their departure was followed by a siesta. If I could have joined Irene in our little air-conditioned bedroom I would have hurried home, but like many women Irene's attitude to sex changed after marriage. It was gradual, but obvious.

Having babies – before and after the actual event – hardly helps women to enjoy sex, but the change in Irene was more fundamental. Rightly or wrongly I came to the conclusion that her premarital romps had been experimental – an attempt to discover what it was all about, and had finally led her to believe that it was in fact rather a bore.

She didn't flatly refuse me, nor did we row, but gradually it was clear that what had (apparently) been a pleasure in Fulham had become more of a duty in Singapore. Now, though she still said yes more often than no, it was often a one-sided arrangement in order that I should enjoy myself, but in which she gently stopped my attempts to arouse her. She was kind and, outwardly, we were happily married; she had just gone off sex, which presumably to her had been more fun when she was not supposed to indulge in it.

Of course Bengy took up a lot of our time. My feeling of pride had been a bit vague when he was just a squalling infant, but it was amazing how quickly he became a human being. By the time he was a year old and we held his first birthday party – in May 1939 – he had developed not only a will of his own but a charm, a way of getting what he wanted from either of us. If anybody had told me a couple of years previously that I could become potty about a boy aged one year I would have thought them crazy. But Bengy was something special. Mama adored him. Papa played with him. Even Grandpa Jack, on one of the rare occasions when he was wheeled in to see what Mama called the infant prodigy, took a long look at the boy and said, 'He's a better boy than Tim'll ever have. If he ever has one.' Luckily Mama wasn't there.

So during the time when Irene and I were both apparently a normal married couple – perhaps we were; perhaps I didn't realise how normal frustration in marriage can be – Bengy did take up a lot of our time. Even so, Irene faced none of the problems of most wives. I could understand that when a couple are kept awake by a screaming child in the same room with no one to help, even to give them an hour or two of sleep, the last activity a hard-pressed wife wants is sex; specially in an age where each time you make love you risk the chance of having another screaming brat nine months later. But Irene was cushioned from all this. The amah looked after Bengy with as much devotion as a mother. The irreplaceable Li attended to our every whim. Servants we never saw cooked our meals, surreptitiously bundled our laundry away; others waited on us at meal-times.

It seemed an ideal life for a young bride who had recently become a mother. Yet as her diplomatic headaches became more frequent I found it increasingly difficult to ask, because even the most carefully masked hint of a rebuff left me more despondent than before.

We even got to the stage of talking it over.

'I know something's wrong, darling,' I said, 'and I only wish there was something I could do. If the bloody war situation didn't look so dangerous I'd suggest you go to Wimbledon for a break. But –'

'Don't worry, Johnnie, of course I can't go. I wouldn't risk taking Bengy. No, it's not your fault. It's the way things go. I know I *should* be happy here. I have everything I need. It's something I can't understand, even to myself.'

'And as for jig–a–jig . . .' Ruefully I used our own word for sex.

'It isn't that I don't love you. As much as you love me, that is. Everything seems such an effort. Perhaps this is what marriage is like: a question of illusion.'

Oddly enough it was Vicki – alias Mrs Ian Scott – who finally dispelled my illusions. We met on a summer's evening at a black tie party given by the Rubber Association, at the Sea View Hotel on the East Coast Road past the Swimming Club. The surrounds of the big rectangular ballroom, open to the sea along most of one side, had been crowded with small tables, each holding four people, leaving a square in the middle for dancing. The tables would be pushed back after the meal was over. An alphabetical list at the entrance showed each guest the number of his or her table – husbands and wives of course were never placed next to each other in Singapore – and when I reached mine I was delighted to find myself next to Vicki. What a long time ago it seemed since she had hoped to marry me, since she had been my surrogate partner in bed before Julie and I became lovers! After dinner I had a duty dance with Irene and then I was able to drink in gratefully the sight of this pretty girl dressed in a long white sharkskin dress, devoid of the frills and flounces so beloved by Singapore matrons. She hardly looked a day older.

'You're better off than if you'd married me,' I teased her when the other two people at the table were dancing and we were alone.

'I'm sure I am,' she retorted cheerfully.

'Eh? Steady on! You don't have to sound so convincing about it. Show a *bit* of doubt.'

'Well, you would have been fun,' she confessed. 'But only while it lasted.'

'I'm insulted.'

'I didn't really mean it. You're wonderful, and I still adore you. But I think you make a better boyfriend than a husband.'

'Nonsense. You've only tried me as a boyfriend.'

'You're not exactly selfish – but you Dexters are tough. You always want things done your way – and you make sure they are. Ian says you're a ruthless bunch – that's why the firm is so prosperous, of course.'

'We're not ruthless.' I was laughing, but I was astounded at her words. 'We're just an old-fashioned firm.'

'You give that impression to the world. Maybe you even think you are. But you're tough.' She hesitated. 'It's none of my business really, but – well, look at the way you treat Irene.'

'Irene? But she has a wonderful time.'

'Does she? She's bored to death. And, darling Johnnie, what do you do about it?'

'What can I do?'

'For a start – why not catch the next boat to Hong Kong – just for a change? Or Bali. I made Ian take me there. It's super.'

'But we're working all day. I can't just walk out of the office like that. And anyway, it's not all my fault. She gets very stroppy, you know. Depressed. Headaches – and always at the time when I feel amorous.'

'I know – we married couples. I'm sure it's not all your

fault. But don't get too tough, Johnnie, and spoil yourself.'

'Well, I'm glad I'm not too tough yet.' Out of the corner of my eye I saw the other couple who shared our table returning and whispered hastily, 'Shall we dance? I want to hear more.'

The band had started a medley from *Snow White and the Seven Dwarfs*, the Disney film which was a smash hit at the Capitol. As we danced she suddenly smiled and said, 'It must be hard for you. Everyone knows you're the all-time stud of Singapore.'

'Just because we used to do it twice a night.'

'Ssh!' she pretended to be horrified. 'Remember, I'm a respectable married woman.'

'Well,' I said a trifle enviously, 'I bet your husband doesn't do it twice a night.'

'Thank God.' She really meant it, especially when she added with a trace of a giggle, 'He's lucky if he can do it twice a week.'

'But that's terrible for a girl in her twenties!' I steered her to the edge of the floor, and beckoned the boy for more drinks. 'Let's have a drink on the balcony,' I told him. 'Twice a week – but you of all girls, Vicki . . .' I didn't need to say any more.

After the boy had handed us a couple of stengahs she studied the soda water bubbles in her glass thoughtfully, and said, 'It's a funny thing, Johnnie, how we change. Twice a week's enough.'

'But you used to eat men for breakfast.'

'Well, now it's papaya and the *Straits Times*.' She laughed again. 'It's odd, but marriage *does* change you. Ian's great – generous, considerate –'

'Any good in bed?' I asked brutally.

'Not bad. But after a couple of years of marriage everything changes. Making love becomes a very pleasant kind of exercise. It's great fun, it's enjoyable – don't get me wrong – but the passion that started it all off is bound to fade. It's a good thing – it only leads to trouble.'

The band started to play 'Love in Bloom' and I had a sudden memory of a newspaper item I had read years ago and never forgotten, about a man accused of beating his wife and when she forgave him and saved him from jail the judge asked her whether their sex life was satisfactory. 'Oh yes, Your Honour,' she had replied. 'He's very considerate and doesn't trouble me very much.' Was I 'troubling' Irene too much? Was Vicki lucky because she wasn't 'troubled' too often?

'But you must feel sexy sometimes?' I felt a surge inside me.

'Of course,' she said frankly. 'But that's different. Every married woman secretly dreams of being raped – by a friend, of course.'

'Not by the husband?'

'Husbands don't rape you.' She was laughing again. 'And it depends on the circumstances. You meet someone – it's safe – and so long as you don't harm anyone what the hell, what difference does it make to anyone else?'

'Think I would be a good rapist?' My voice was thickening.

'You ought to set up a business as "Your friendly neighbourhood rapist!" Much more fun than running Dexters.'

'I'll think about it.' I was afraid to go too far.

'Don't think too long. For a woman it must be at the very moment when it arrives or never – before she has a chance to realise she shouldn't.'

'Fine in theory – but where?' I was still only half serious.

She looked me straight in the eyes. 'Isn't the beach good enough?' And then in a voice that was almost harsh she added, '*Now!*'

The Sea View almost lapped the beach, and if you walked down a few wooden steps and turned left you came upon a row of private striped beach tents on the narrow strip of sand fronting the water. Everyone used to go and see their friends there on a Sunday morning. Without a word we moved towards them. Hidden by the pillars, we stepped on to the soft sand.

'This one – *any one*!' She tore open the flap of the first tent and we fell together on to a rubber mattress. I never discovered whose tent it was – I didn't care – I just dropped into her arms, pulling my trousers half down as she pulled her dress up, my mouth locked on hers.

'Be quick, darling,' she gasped. And I was. It was all over in a few minutes. Somehow I managed to hold off until she was ready, and we both reached a climax at the same split second; there was nothing false about it. I knew she had been liberated. And so had I, though in a different way, for as I thrust myself into her, making her gasp with the first feel of me, I forgot all about Vicki, I forgot all about Irene, I forgot all about everything, I was inside Julie, making love to her, desperate to hold out so that we could both come together, and then it was over.

For a few moments I lay there, heart pounding like a sledge-hammer. I had forgotten what it was like, the threshing, the undulating waves, the nails tearing at the back of my jacket, all ending in ecstasy. Did all married women behave like this? Had Irene, who had made love this way in Studio Z, ever tried to tear the skin off the back of a lover in a snatched coupling in someone else's tent or bedroom?

Vicki lay still for a moment, then said from the heart – or from some other part of her body – 'God! That was good.'

I was terrified someone would find us, or that Irene would wonder where I was. Perhaps the owner of the tent might saunter down on to the beach (though probably he wasn't even at the dinner). But I was so nervous that I instinctively started to get ready to go, until, no passion left, she leaned across, kissed me gently, stroked my hair and said, almost sadly, 'I guess I wasn't really there, was I? You must love Julie very much.'

'It's all over – Julie, I mean. But thanks, Vicki, you're – the only word I can think of is stupendous.'

She giggled, with a sudden change of mood. 'That was *wicked* of us – but, Johnnie, that's what I mean about un-married love.'

With a typical womanly sense of the practical she offered me some tissues from her bag before I buttoned up my trousers, tucked some into herself, pulled her panties tight to keep them in place, and then suggested, 'I'll go straight to Irene's table and tell her you were suddenly feeling sick.'

'Irene!'

'Well, darling – you can't go back with your shirt and bum freezer crumpled up unless you've got a good excuse.' She would return up the steps the way she had come. I would go to the hotel loo and stay there a few minutes.

Just before we parted – with no kisses, no embraces – she said, 'And Johnnie, don't think you have to try and phone when Ian's out of the house to make any arrangements. We don't have to do this once a week. That's not my style at all. Basically I'm a very faithful woman. Just forget it happened, and then at another party – we'll know when we both want it again.'

Before I could answer she was walking briskly up the steps, as though nothing was troubling her in the world.

By the time I reappeared people had changed tables, sitting with their own families and friends, pulling tables together so that large groups were forming on the edge of the dance floor. Irene was with Papa Jack and Mama and Ian and Vicki, Natasha and Bertrand Bonnard: real family gathering. I never cease to be amazed by the matter-of-fact way women behave after a traumatic experience. A few minutes ago Vicki had been lying on her back, skirt pulled up to her neck, not even making love, for that implied *love*, but *fucking* on the first empty space she could find – and now here she was, almost one of the family, looking as though butter wouldn't melt in her mouth.

As I reached the table, suitably apologetic, Vicki was whispering a giggled secret to Irene as though these bosom friends had never left each other's side all evening, with Vicki showing no trace of what had happened – or for that matter the slight discomfort she must have been experiencing underneath that beautiful white sharkskin dress.

'You look terrible, darling.' Irene was really concerned. 'What happened?'

'Haven't the faintest idea,' I muttered. 'I just suddenly felt –'

'I told him to take it easy,' Vicki said innocently to Papa Jack.

'Want to go home?' said Papa Jack looking at me, but I shook my head.

'Probably a bit of bad ikan,' Ian Scott always blamed fish when people were sick.

'I'm fine now,' I said, because I knew that by tradition the Dexter sons always asked Mama for one dance when we were out together. She always said, 'Just to be *asked* to dance makes me feel young.'

Mama got up as I reached her chair and said, 'Shall we —?' In flimsy, billowing pale blue chiffon that showed off her blue eyes and ash-blonde hair, she still danced well, but my thoughts must have been straying — to someone's tent on the beach, perhaps? — for she said gently, without faltering in the step of the slow fox trot, 'You remind me of the time when I caught you coming out of the kitchen hiding a cake which cookie had given you.'

'Mama! That's the most extraordinary thing to say in the middle of a dance. What *do* you mean?'

'Darling Johnnie,' she said serenely. 'You have the same guilty look.'

15

In August 1939, barely a month before England declared war against Germany, Julie returned to Singapore. I couldn't help thinking she had been foolish not to go from France to California, for the Americans were vociferous in their determination not to let Europe trick them into sending American troops to Europe if a war did break out.

Irene didn't mention her return at first, though she must have known that Julie was the girl on the piano. Perhaps she dismissed it as forgotten calf love. Mama, though, did mention it — in no uncertain terms. She actually trapped me into having a long talk alone with her in the study.

'You've always been wild, Johnnie, but now you're

nearly twenty-six – and I've grown *very* fond of Irene. She's a real daughter to me – a wonderful girl, so I want no – what's the word? – hanky-panky, now Julie's back.'

As I groped for some vague promise of good conduct – which I certainly intended to keep – she staggered me by saying in an almost assumed casual tone, 'I trust you.'

'Thank you, Mama.'

'You see' – her voice took on a sterner edge – 'when you're married it must be a point of honour not to let your wife down. I don't approve of modern married life – getting carried away' – her smile was positively mischievous – 'on a convenient beach at a dance. But I can *understand*, even if I don't condone. But Julie – who is so adorable – that would be different. Unfair and selfish. And *that's* when honour comes in. I don't think I could ever feel the same about you if you let Irene – and us – down in that way.'

'Don't worry, Mama. It's all over – for ever.'

'Good. Now be an angel and fetch me my patchwork.'

I met Julie at a party soon after my talk with Mama – or rather her talk to me – and I was astonished how easy it was to stand next to her and our friends and talk about nothing in particular. Of course the sight of her prompted immediate stirrings; it would never be otherwise as long as I lived. I was glad that Irene had said she would be arriving late at the party. It gave me a chance to watch Julie. Not for the first time – before marriage, after marriage – I thought what a fool I had been not to grab her, defy everyone, and marry her. Too late now, I knew, remembering the night in the pavilion, the lunchtimes in Abingdon Mansions. Everything about her seemed perfect – the long neck framed in a white silk blouse that was rather like a man's shirt and invisibly shouted 'made in Paris'; the black hair, black as night, yet shining; the slim legs, tiny wrists, long fingers, nails which I noticed for the first time were varnished red. That was Paris too.

But there was more to her than that. Without warning she turned her head and saw me watching her. She smiled and with it I could feel her physical magnetism, a warmth that communicated itself to me instantly, as though she were talking to me without using words. It was not a question of urgent desire; in a way I felt thankful just to be looking at her, more grown up after what Paul called 'the American experience'. Though I could see through that silk blouse without using my eyes, I was looking with grateful memories of yesterday rather than with hopes of to-morrow.

I walked across, didn't kiss, but said, 'Wonderful to see you.'

She asked shyly, 'How's your son?'

We both made noncommittal remarks for a few moments, and she asked, 'Is your wife here? I'd love to meet her.'

Finally I said, 'It sounds so silly, you and I talking like this, Julie. It can't be wrong, just because I'm a married man, to say that I've missed you terribly. Nor for – well, you know what I mean, but just having you *around* – even just looking at you. I'm a respectable married man now, but God! You'd tempt a saint.'

'Don't worry. That's one thing I'm not – a temptress. Of course it's wonderful for me to see you too. But we're both changed. I always knew it would never last. And it's a relief in a way that you're happily married.'

'I know.' I glanced at the others to see if anyone who knew about our past might be watching us, but nobody seemed concerned. 'Sometimes I *do* think of you in – well, the old way. I dreamed not long ago that Irene had left me and you were just coming into the room when – dammit! I woke up.'

'I'm not a snatcher,' she laughed. 'But if you were on your own – really on your own, I don't mean for a day or a week or a month – well, I wonder? I still adore you. I don't think I could resist coming to get you.'

'Would you?'

'I suppose not. But I might.' She suddenly laughed. 'If only to stop someone else grabbing you. That would be *too* much.'

'It's not likely to happen, but I'll remember.' I too laughed.

She was looking round the room and suddenly asked, 'Is that your wife over there?'

Irene was standing in the corner and I beckoned to her. They had to meet sooner or later, so best get the confrontation over as quickly as possible. But any doubts I entertained about womanly dislike were groundless. They couldn't have been more charming to each other – not a snide double meaning in their conversation; due without doubt to the fact that Irene had a good heart, and knew how to behave. She took one look at Julie and said gently, 'I feel I know so much about you. Johnnie told me how much you meant to him, how you grew up together, and I just have to like anyone who helped make him so happy.'

The small talk continued. Invitations were exchanged (without dates) discussions centred on Paris dresses and American lipsticks. They might have been bosom friends for years, and only late that night, in the cool air-conditioned bedroom of the married quarters, did Irene say anything. She was rubbing the make-up off her face with cold cream from a big pink jar, and she just said, 'It makes it so much easier – being Mrs Dexter, I mean – now that I've met Julie.'

'She's a sweet kid,' I said unthinkingly, trying to be nonchalant.

'A sweet kid? *Well!* I'm not sure, but I hope so for all our sakes, including Ben's. Because one thing's certain – she's still in love with you, Johnnie, so watch your step.'

At first the war in Europe made little difference to life in Singapore – except that many men in rubber and tin became richer. But the distance, the remoteness, made it difficult to take seriously a ranting tyrant who shouted but at first seemed unwilling to act. Newspapers arriving from England showed pictures of cheery British troops in France singing 'We're gonna hang out the washing on the Siegfried Line'. A headline across page one of the *Daily Express* ran, 'Come on Hitler! Dares Ironside.' Underneath General Ironside, then Chief of the Imperial General Staff, declared, 'Frankly we would welcome an attack. We are sure of ourselves.' On the same day in April 1940 Chamberlain announced, 'Whatever may be the reason – whether it is that Hitler thought he could get away without fighting for it, this is certain – he has missed the bus.'

To us, nearly ten thousand miles from Europe, it was like a game at which we were unwilling spectators – until everything changed, when Germany launched the greatest attack in history, almost as though Hitler had been infuriated by Chamberlain's derisive taunt.

People who had insisted the French army was the best in the world now saw that army running away, abject and demoralised, while French politicians vacillated. But not until France fell, and Britain was on its own, was there a different reaction in Malaya. More planters joined the FMSVR – the Federated Malay States Volunteer Reserve, our equivalent to the British Territorial Army. Most planters were proud to enrol as privates, regarding it as some kind of all-male club. A number of faces disappeared – men who had left for home to join up, the bachelors impelled by the twin spurs of patriotism and adventure, or the husbands who were embroiled in dull, frustrated marriages, grabbing a heaven-sent opportunity to escape.

Some women started knitting comforts for the troops. Others joined semi-military volunteer units. Vicki Scott took a secretarial job at military headquarters in Fort Canning. I was astounded one day to meet Julie at a party and find her dressed in nurse's uniform. She had, she explained, come straight from the Alexandra Hospital where she had enrolled as a full-time volunteer nurse.

Then came the Battle of Britain and the Blitz, all of it shown daily on Pathé News in the local cinemas. Now, for the first time, the people in Britain became identifiable, a part of us. Unreality was replaced with pride.

In one case the word brother was literally true, for Irene's brother Bill Bradshaw – the one-time tennis bum – had become something of a hero as a Spitfire pilot. I could understand why – he had just the right mixture of dash and *élan* needed – and he had by now been decorated with the DFC and bar and had been personally presented to King

George during a tour of airfields 'somewhere in England'. We even saw his picture on the newsreels. I was delighted for Irene – I knew he was living dangerously, but it did give her something to boast about! Her other brother was training pilots in Canada, and old Sir Keith had managed to wangle for himself a red-tabbed brigadier's desk job.

The only reaction Irene felt was an increasing desire to go to England – to see her mother and father. 'I know the bombing must be hell,' she said, 'but that's not the important thing. I hate the idea of them alone, lonely, probably no servants by now, Mummy working mornings in some volunteer canteen. I feel so awful living the way we do here.'

There wasn't really anything we could do. It was unthinkable to allow Bengy to go to England; and it was out of the question for Irene to go to England for a limited period, for a visit, so to speak. 'I know,' she sighed. 'But I still feel homesick – and guilty.'

We heard little news of Tim, for though he wrote regularly each letter was so carefully worded with an eye to censorship that it might just as well have been one of our standard forms in Chinese or Tamil which planters issued to illiterates, each letter containing a series of printed phrases, 'I am well' or 'I am not well' or 'We now have two/three/four/five children'. A friend who could read and write would strike out words that did not apply. At first I thought that Tim, with his regard for rules and regulations, was taking care not to divulge his whereabouts. All letters bore English postmarks and we could only presume he was in England. But then Tim made a tiny slip – and it could have been done deliberately. It was a simple sentence, 'Ran into Jimmy Cartright who wants to be remembered to the family.'

'Old Cartright!' cried Papa Jack. 'I had a letter from him the other day. He's in Cairo, working at the university.'

Cartright was one of the world's most erudite Arabists and an old friend; and as a civilian in Egypt he had been able to write to us without any question of hiding his whereabouts, as happened in the forces.

'That means Tim is in North Africa,' I explained to Mama, while my father added a more practical comment, 'It seems as though the British were right to start a desert warfare training programme near Christmas Island.'

'Don't you think I might join up?' I asked for the hundredth time.

'Not even the Volunteers,' replied Papa Jack firmly. 'We've been told a hundred times that anyone who's a rubber expert is more important in civilian clothes than in uniform.' And that was that.

Soon after the monsoon, in the summer of 1941, Irene, Bengy and I went for our annual holiday. It wasn't much of a holiday really, but our once-yearly trip to stay with Natasha and Tony, who for more than three years had been running the Ara Estate eleven miles outside Kuala Lumpur. Tony's appointment had pleased and suited everyone. His father had started out as a lonely planter at nineteen; Consolidated Latex, Ian Scott's rubber business, was flourishing, but nobody could buy and sell a difficult commodity without a detailed knowledge of rubber, and what better way to learn than by working on an estate? So Ian was delighted that his son was not only consolidating the Dexter-Scott alliance but was learning the business in the field. Papa Jack was delighted to have a planter he could control if anything went wrong. Mama was pleased because Natasha was near her and came home to Singapore regularly. We were pleased because it was fun to visit Ara where I had once worked for six months, learning what I could about rubber. Natasha was pleased because she seemed to enjoy the life of a planter's wife with trips to Singapore. Their baby daughter Victoria was nearly four and of course Bengy, now a lusty three-year-old, loved playing with her. It seemed a perfect arrangement.

We planned to spend two weeks at Ara, and arrived there in the family Buick during the first week in June, driving past the original tree at the gate, still standing, the sinister creeper nearly – but never quite – suffocating the host tree.

It had stood there, surrounded by the tall, straight, cathedral-like trees of the jungle since the day Grandpa Jack first bought the land and went to his friend Swettenham to cadge some free saplings.

We drove along the red laterite road to the bungalow which was built on a slope in the heart of the estate. Though hemmed in by rubber it had more space round it than most bungalows, for a nearby block of old rubber trees had been replaced with seedlings. In front of the bungalow Tony had built a small paddling pool for his daughter, with a summer house, and Natasha, who had taken up gardening as an antidote to boredom, had planted beds of vivid yellow cannas and hibiscus. In the corner stood two beautiful old flame trees. Apart from that, and the lines where the work force lived, the two thousand or so acres were covered with the cavernous aisles of the rubber, thousands and thousands of trees, uniform in height, in leaves, in colour, where by eleven each morning the full force of the sun pressed down without a breath of air on the sweating faces of the tappers.

Natasha was at the front door to welcome us. 'I heard you tooting as you drove up.' She hugged me, kissed Irene and gave Bengy a big squeeze as we walked into the hall with its Victorian hat stand and locked gun case and on into the living room. Natasha had inherited Mama's flair for colour, warmth and comfort. The usual standardised planter's furniture, which often made it hard to tell whose bungalow you were in, had been thrown out and replaced with comfortable chairs covered with cheerful chintzes. But the heart of the home was the spacious verandah, with its rattan chairs and room for a dozen people to sit and look out, the vegetable garden beyond shielded by banana leaves and papaya trees, the heavy fruit hanging on impossibly thin branches.

The peace was so complete, so beautiful, that the war in Europe seemed a distant dream – until Natasha switched on the radio and the BBC came through. As always, the news was terrible. The *Bismarck* had sunk HMS *Hood*, the Germans had taken Kiev and were poised at the gates of Leningrad. Only from North Africa was there a glint of hope. We were chasing the Italians across the desert, and I could almost visualise the relish in brother Tim's eyes as he led the attack. Then there came news from London. It could now be revealed, said the announcer, that in a recent German bombing raid on London enemy aircraft had virtually destroyed the House of Commons.

'Switch it off, *please*!' Irene begged. 'I feel so awful, with Mummy and Daddy being bombed and here we are, calmly taking a holiday. Oh Johnnie, I wish I could go back to be with them.'

I tried to reassure her. 'Wimbledon's a long way from Whitehall. Please don't worry. And you wouldn't like Ben to be there, would you?'

'You're a Londoner and your family's there,' Natasha had turned off the radio. 'Of course it makes it worse. It's different for us – even though I know it shouldn't be. But you can't help it when you're Singaporeans and your family is here. In a part of the world where there'll never be a war.'

'Where's Tony?' I asked.

'Still out on his rounds,' said Natasha. 'There's been a bit of labour trouble, so he might be late. Help yourself to a drink.'

I thought she looked a little tense, or perhaps just tired, and Irene must have sensed it too, for when the boy had placed small wooden bowls of coconut chips and nuts on the tables she said, 'I read in the *Malaya Tribune* about the labour troubles you mentioned. Are they very bad?'

'Not *bad*, but stupid. They're behaving like a lot of kids,' said Natasha cheerfully. 'Tony's convinced paid agitators are behind it.'

'That explains it,' said Irene. 'You need a break.'

'You're right.' To Irene, Natasha's quick acceptance of the reason for her tiredness seemed normal, but brothers and sisters have extrasensory bonds of communication, and I knew that Natasha had agreed a little too eagerly, grabbed at Irene's words because she was glad that we – having spotted that she *was* off-colour – should have made an assumption which was incorrect, but which she was grateful to accept to avoid further questions.

As I watched her I wondered if Tony had been doing a Vicki on her (thinking irrationally that it was all right if I did such a thing, but that no man should behave like that to my sister). Who knows, Tony might have had a girlfriend on the side, and Natasha had found out. . . ? At least, so my imagination ran on.

I thought I might try to find out if Tony was up to anything, and the chance was made easier when he asked if I would like to do the rounds with him next morning. I had undertaken that morning drill scores of times at Ara, and still loved the early morning in up-country Malaya, with the earth fresh and green and not yet battered by heat. Often in the past I had gone down to the river bank before breakfast, just to be alone, with the sluggish river in front framed by long-leaf nipah palms and sinister mangroves, the jungle on the other bank, the tall straight trees towering up two hundred feet, some as straight as pillars.

The boy woke me at five-thirty with bed tea – there was no breakfast for a few hours – and I walked down to the lines. Ara had a labour force of about three hundred men and women who together with their children were fed by the estate. Already the rows of huts, on stilts and arranged round three sides of a rectangular 'parade ground', were alive. Each hut was divided into small compartments in which a family lived. Below, on the ground, I could hear the swish of water from hidden standpipes. Thin spires of blue smoke drifted from cooking fires tended by squatting women or their children before the latter went off to the small estate school or crêche.

Tony arrived just as the Indian conductor – the labour force supervisor – was allotting the day's work. Most of it was routine, for the tappers normally worked the same block of trees, tapping each tree on alternate days from six-thirty to ten-thirty a.m., after which the latex tended to dry up. Others, however, had to be ordered to different jobs – weeding, maintaining drains, spraying against pest and disease and so on.

Tony had filled out since the day when his engagement to Natasha had been announced. His brown wiry hair never needed a comb and he had kept his figure trim by playing every sport available in the local club or the Spotted Dog in KL. He was ideal planter material – popular with the other planters, a good shot and a good sport; a volunteer in the local FMSVR. He drank enough but not too much; he played a crafty game of poker but not for stakes high enough to ruin him.

He was thirty now, three years older than me, but younger than Natasha, and he enjoyed the life of a planter. He was good at it. I could tell by the way he watched the tappers working, making spot checks as the men skilfully cut downward into the outer bark of the tree, so quickly yet so carefully that in a month the total depth of the fifteen cuts he made would always measure less than an inch from top to bottom.

'This is a good bloke' – Tony, I noticed, knew many tappers by name, but interfered as little as possible. 'See his dots? First-class.' Down the side of the tree was a perpendicular row of tiny black dots, each one painted by the tapper at the end of each month, each dot never more than three quarters of an inch above the one below, representing a month of shaving – fifteen cuts. 'This chap taps three hundred trees a day.' Tony turned to him and said in Tamil, 'Well done, Singh. No trouble with strikers?'

'Not yet, *tuan*,' the man lilted. 'But they try to stop us working. They cry, "What for you work for no more money?"'

'It's spreading,' said Tony. 'I wouldn't be surprised if it reaches us in the next day or so. No, no,' he went on in answer to my questioning look. 'There's no *danger* – but with the present demand for rubber, paid agitators are asking for more money. Our trees are in super condition. We're getting up to six pounds of latex a year from each tree, and with two hundred trees to the acre and over two thousand acres – well, you work it out. The agitators know damned well we've got a wonderful yield, as good as any in Malaya – over a hundred pounds of dry rubber an acre.'

There certainly seemed no shortage of liquid in the aluminium factory tanks, where after breakfast we watched the tappers carry their buckets of sticky liquid.

'We've put in two new tanks,' Tony said as he watched the factory workers pour the latex into four of the six tanks.

As we walked up to the bungalow I asked him, 'You really love it here, don't you, Tony?'

He nodded, adding cheerfully, 'I don't mind telling you I'm dreading the moment when the old man yanks me back to the big city.'

'Well, it has its advantages — company, good food again and' — after a moment's hesitation — 'girls! It must be rather boring just seeing the same people all the time.'

'There are a few English girls around in KL — but it's not worth it, Johnnie.' Tony grinned. 'I've seen a few of the married blokes start messing around — it always gets messier. Besides' — the grin grew wider — 'don't forget, Natasha's a Dexter. I've no complaints. She's not only the best looker in this district, she's still willing and eager.' And then he asked suddenly, 'How's it with you? I hear Julie's back. Boy! I'll never forget when that bomb exploded. You could hear the shouting from Singapore to San Francisco.'

'It's all over,' I sighed. 'No way out.'

'I guess it has to be. But you must have had something pretty strong running between you. And it's hard to forget — especially when the original bobby-dazzler is back again at the same parties.'

'You can't *forget*, Tony. I never will, not really. You've just got to carry on regardless, as they say. Thank God for Ben. He's made all the difference.'

'It's a great life if you don't weaken.'

We showered, put on clean shirts and shorts and started in on the pink gin and then Natasha presided as we ate a huge curry tiffin washed down with Tiger beer and cooled off with *gula malacca*.

'This is the life for me,' I said, stretching.

'This and a siesta,' said Irene who had been giggling secrets with Natasha through lunch and who seemed to be in a wonderful mood.

'Me too,' said Tony. 'I'm whacked. All agreed that we go to the club tonight? There's the monthly dance.'

The children were safely resting with the amah and Irene and I went to the spare room – pretty, with pale, yellow-painted walls and a large bed with a carefully maintained mosquito net – always the sign of a good planter.

'Lovely to be here in Ara, isn't it?' I was stretched out on my back, and so was Irene.

'Heavenly.' And then, almost with a chuckle, she asked, using an almost forgotten code, 'Does the lord and master feel like a Fulham Road?'

Used by Irene, who normally had a curious reluctance to ask me to make love to her – to *satisfy* her – a Fulham Road meant not a favour to *me* but a need for *her*.

She didn't ask often because if she sensed that I wanted her – or rather just wanted to make love – and she felt kindly, she would look at me and smile, rather like an elder sister, and ask, 'Would you like to make love, darling?' She rarely dared to admit that *she* needed *me*. That had to be disguised, by reference to our premarital days in London when she was less inhibited. A Fulham Road meant that I would serve just the same purpose I had served with Vicki – but simpler, because I was her husband. And, I loved a Fulham Road.

When I woke half an hour later I saw that Irene was lying on her back, eyes open. I always had to be careful what I said after the rare occasions when Irene let herself go.

'You remember we both noticed that Natasha looked a bit off colour,' I said, 'well, I don't think it's a family row – I mean, no girl trouble with Tony.'

'I could have told you that.' She lit a cigarette and smiled. 'You men always think that if a wife's worried it must be because of a man.'

'Isn't it?'

'In a way – yes. But in another – no.'

'Riddles!'

'Darling Johnnie, you're so naive. Can't you really guess what's the matter with your beloved sister?'

'Well – tell.'

'She's suffering from the same complaint that I hope to be suffering from after this afternoon in bed with you.'

'*You?*' I nearly jumped out of bed. 'She can't be – Tony – '

Irene sat up, the sheet drawn circumspectly over her breasts and gave me her tolerant and amused 'mother's smile'. 'She ought to know. And, by the way, she hasn't told Tony yet.'

'What did you mean about *you*?'

She inhaled, then said almost shyly, 'Let's just say that I didn't do anything before we made love.'

'Why?'

'It's time Ben had a brother or sister. I think it would be a good thing. I know you feel marriage is dreary – but it isn't, you know. It's different, that's all. But you haven't really grown up. I suppose I'm *not* as good in bed as – well, we won't mention names from the past. But you can't change my nature. Or yours. You're sweet – and generous – but I know that you don't really love me –'

'That sounds a damn funny reason for deciding to have a baby.'

'It's the best reason. Maybe another baby would help.'

16

We set off in high jinks for the club, Tony driving the estate wagon, the girls in the back. It was only eleven miles along the Bentong Road and Tony explained, 'Usually we don't serve food at the club but once a month on dance nights we have bangers and mash.'

The club was already filling up when we arrived – black ties, long dresses, all slightly incongruous against the tatty atmosphere, for the low building consisted mainly of one long room with a bar and a piano against the far wall, and another room partitioned to accommodate a billiards table at one end and a card room with three worn bridge tables at the other. The dancing – which would take place in the main room – hadn't started, and several women were sitting in basketwork chairs under the rows of fans; they listlessly leafed through old copies of the *Tatler*, the *Illustrated London News* or the *Daily Telegraph*.

I walked to the verandah and peered into the night. A half moon lit the rugby posts and tennis nets on the padang between the clubhouse and the river. The ochre-tinted water had been transformed into silver silk by the pale light. Not far from the bank stood a group of arekas, tall white trunks, the palms from which the Malays and Tamils harvest betel nuts, their favourite chew, which stains the pavements blood-red when they spit it out. A group of shrubs sparkled with fireflies against the black shadows of the jungle on the far side of the river; only the Milky Way showed where the massive trees ended and the sky began.

Below the balcony the night was alive with the chatter of cicadas, vaguely irritating, as monotonous as a drizzle of rain, broken occasionally by the click-click of billiard balls behind me. I loved the night. I could stand for hours, looking, listening, dreaming, and I almost jumped out of my skin when a hand touched my shoulder and Natasha's voice whispered, 'I love it too.'

We sat for a few minutes and then unexpectedly she asked, 'Do you ever see Julie?'

'What an odd question.'

'I was thinking of her the other day, you and her. She was adorable, so lovely. I haven't seen her for ages. She is back, isn't she? Do you run into her often?'

'At parties.'

'What's it feel like – banging into the past?' And without waiting for an answer she asked, 'Do you still love her, Johnnie?'

'That's an unfair question. Why do you ask? Any hidden motives?'

She shook her head with a laugh – but an uneasy laugh.

'Love her?' I said. 'Yes, I'm sorry to say I still do. But long for her? I'm thankful to say, not so much.'

'No need to apologise for loving someone.'

'Not even when you're married to someone else? Remember you're an old married woman, Mrs Scott.'

'Come off it – you of all people, you with your Johnnie specials!'

'That's not *love*. They're professional skill.'

She looked out over the padang and sighed, 'You can't stop loving people or things, you know that. You can't just block things out of your life. Is Julie still beautiful?'

'More than ever.'

'That's a pity – well, in a way. I thought America might have changed her. American girls seem so – not exactly tough, but – is worldly the right word?'

'It did change her, but for the better.' Seeking to change the conversation, I asked, 'Where are the others?'

'Irene and Tony have been pressured into a bridge four – there's always bridge before dancing, and they're always short of a fourth. Yes,' in answer to my unasked question, 'I *will* have a drink, Johnnie.'

I banged the palm of my hand on the old-fashioned circular brass bell and ordered two stengahs. She signed for them – I couldn't as a guest. 'Kept by my elder sister!' I joked deliberately, for I had a premonition that she wanted to confide in me. 'How does it feel to be over thirty?' I asked.

'How does it feel to be a juvenile delinquent at twenty-eight?' she teased back, as we always had done. Then she added, 'Seriously, though – Julie and you – it was such a big thing. I remember I used to think how wonderful it must be, to be in love like that.'

'Well, it was wonderful. *Was*.'

'But worth it?'

I nodded.

'But when you see her with others at a party,' she asked, 'don't you ever feel – I mean? –'

'Randy?'

'Well – yes.' She laughed. 'Do you remember when you first explained what randy meant?'

I had forgotten. Long before Julie – I must have been

254

about thirteen – we had been indulging in our favourite pastime of eavesdropping and we heard Grandpa Jack pronounce to my father (a propos of what we never discovered), 'Remember: a randy cock knows no conscience.' I had tried to explain what it meant – and how it was possible for the mysterious male organ to change size at the sight of a pretty girl with no clothes on. At first Natasha refused to believe it, but then whispered, 'If I took my knickers off and you looked at me would you get randy?' We tried and I did and Natasha had been fascinated.

'All that sort of thing – it wasn't wrong, was it?' she asked. 'Most brothers and sisters learn from each other, don't they?'

'Sure – it's part of growing up – and it's fun.'

'Is it fun? When it becomes serious? Was it *really* fun – you and Julie? It made you so unhappy afterwards. Can it have been worth it?'

'Of *course* it was. Every second of it.' And then, 'Tell me, darling sister – is something worrying you?' Knowing as I did about the baby it was a loaded question, but I sensed that the conversation was not as casual as she pretended. 'Anything I can do?'

She said nothing for what seemed a long time. Then without warning she took a deep breath, clutched my hand as she used to do when we were children and, almost in tears, cried, 'I'm so bloody unhappy! I'm in such a damned mess.'

I put an arm round her shoulder and asked gently, 'Natflat darling – what's the trouble? Tell me.'

She dabbed her eyes. Without looking at me, she said, 'I've got to get away, Johnnie. Do you think you could persuade Papa Jack to let me go to England?'

'England? And be bombed to bits!'

'I don't care. Anything.'

'Is it Tony?'

'No. Poor Tony – if only it was as easy as that. No, Johnnie. You know I'm going to have a baby?'

'Yes.' There was no point in denying that Irene had told me. Natasha, after all, was married and she knew perfectly well that all wives tell their husbands every secret – unless it is about themselves.

'Well.' She took another deep breath and gripped my arm tightly. 'I'm in love with someone – and the baby isn't Tony's.'

My first reaction was almost a groan. 'Natflat darling – not again!' My mind raced back to the day in Vicki's flat. This was the second time she had gone off the rails. Yet she, more than any other girl I knew, gave the outward impression of a contented wife in her early thirties, without apparently a care in the world.

'I'm so bloody stupid. Tony hasn't the faintest idea. But he's bound to find out. And he'll know it isn't his.'

I didn't like to ask why. He wouldn't be the first parent of a child he hadn't fathered.

'It happened on one of my visits to Tanamera – the month Tony flew to Batavia for the meeting of the Rubber Regulation Committee.'

'Do I know him?' And with an awful foreboding I almost groaned out the two-word question to which I was convinced I knew the answer, '*Not Bonnard?*'

She said nothing, just nodded. In the background, against the clink of glasses in the clubhouse a gong sounded – the time-honoured signal for members to order drinks as dinner would be served in fifteen minutes.

'Darling Natflat, how *could* you? I thought it was all over years and years ago.'

'Like you and Julie?' she said almost bitterly. 'It wasn't easy for you. You were parted. I wasn't. All right, I came here to Ara, but I'm often in Singapore. And Johnnie, I'm in love with him. I always have been.'

'Tony – does he know, suspect?'

'No. I'm certain. Tony is always going off to meetings or something, and when he does I always go to Tanamera.'

'But a *baby*.' I couldn't really take it in. 'Couldn't you be more careful? I mean, take precautions. I thought every girl did.'

Then my beloved sister really staggered me. Almost

defiantly she said, 'I decided I *wanted* to have Bertrand's baby. It was deliberate, the whole thing.'

'And doesn't he mind? He agrees? After all, he's married too. And he's Catholic.'

'Good God, Bertrand doesn't know. He'd have a fit. It's my baby, mine to keep. He will never know. I just felt — I know you will say I'm silly, but I felt that if I couldn't marry him I would have something of his.'

'And is this trifling plan for a keepsake going to fit in with your married life?' I could hardly keep the sarcasm out of my voice. 'Are you going to pass it off as Tony's?'

'That's why I want to get away.'

'But that doesn't answer my question. And you've got to face up to it.'

'I did. At first I thought that I could — well, like you said. No one would know but me. And then' — ruefully — 'I got to thinking again. And I knew I couldn't, not to poor Tony. If I hated him I could, but I don't. In a funny sort of way — habit, I suppose — I love him. Only I'm not in love with him. I never was.'

'Then why marry him?'

'Everyone was on to me — you know how the family goes on —'

'But nobody forced you, Natflat.'

'It isn't forcing, as you call it. It's what they expect you to do — and it seemed okay at the time —'

I thought to myself, shades of Irene! Two girls brought up ten thousand miles apart, each with loving and tender parents, yet each desperate to break out of the kindness that can suffocate.

'I thought — after the abortion —'

'I've tried to break it off. I've tried and tried. I can't. But I thought, seeing you tonight, perhaps *you* found out the secret of breaking something off — *you* got Julie out of your system by being ten thousand miles apart.'

I could see that she was thinking and so I said nothing. After the boy had brought us two more stengahs, she said, 'I know I shouldn't have the baby and pretend — it's wrong, morally, it's a wicked thing to do to Tony. But it would also

257

be wicked to hurt him. I want to think things out, Johnnie. And I can't do that unless I can get away, not see Bertrand – make it impossible for him to see me. That's why I want to go to England – if I could get there. He *couldn't*. But I ought to be able to go home. I *am* British.'

'I'm not sure you could. But if you can't go to England, what about America?'

'Maybe. Oh hell! What a bloody mess I've made of my life. Thanks for the shoulder, Johnnie. I always thought you were the crazy one. But you've been smarter than I've been, damn you!' The second gong sounded – five minutes to dinner.

'Come on,' she said. 'We'd better go in or people will wonder what's happened to us. Let me dab my face first.'

'Women have an enormous advantage in Malaya,' I tried to cheer her up. 'If your face looks the worse for wear you can always blame the heat.'

I was on the point of going to look for Irene when without warning a dozen sounds split the air and seemed to roll into one – a single rifle shot piercing the night, the crashing of shattered window glass, the screams of panic.

It came from a small conservatory behind the bridge room. I dropped my glass of whisky, and screamed 'Irene!' – screaming without thinking, just because I knew she was playing bridge behind the rattan screen that split the two main rooms. 'I'm coming!' I shouted uselessly and barged towards the screen. As I reached it, smelling cordite, I was hit by a dozen women like a tide as they rushed from the other side of the screen. The room was filled with shouting: 'It's a striker!' 'Bloody Communists!' and 'Let's go after the bugger!' and 'Watch out – keep away from glass. He might fire again.'

But he didn't – and as suddenly as the frightening scene had erupted calm returned. For after all the screams had been involuntary. There was no panic. There were barely fifty people in the club, and nobody was going to be trampled to death.

'I'm fine,' Irene was a little breathless as she came out. 'But I won't say no to a double Scotch.'

Nobody, it soon transpired, had been injured, and soon the club was filled with more shouts of 'Bloody strikers!' and 'Put the buggers in jail, everyone of 'em.' Someone cried, 'Bill! Let's go after 'em.' Another, 'Boy! A double brandy and quick, damn your eyes.' The club secretary – a cheerful roly-poly ex-planter – banged on the bar with the butt end of a revolver and shouted, 'Just a moment, please!'

Silence cut off the chatter like a curtain. 'Nothing to worry about, but don't go out on the verandah, anyone. It was just one crazy fool – but he might still be out there.'

A dozen lusty voices urged, 'Let's go after him,' 'Are you sure it's only one man, Jim?' and 'Come on, chaps, who's for a spot of big game shooting?'

'Shut up everyone.' The secretary was maintaining a very creditable good humour. 'The police are on their way from KL – and cookie says the bangers and mash are ready.'

A spirited cheer filled the room. The very fact that sausages and mashed potatoes had a plebeian touch to it added an extra chumminess to the already friendly evenings in which everyone, anyway, knew everyone else. They were 'slumming' – but only among friends. The club rules insisted that everyone had to sit in the vacant seat to the left of one already occupied on the two long trestle tables. This in itself caused a great deal of hilarity. Some dashed in when they saw who would be next to them for supper – others hung back with cries of mock despair, 'You go first, Bill. I'm damned if I'm going to sit next to the mem on my night off.' One man pushed another man forward, 'Sit next to Jill – but get a move on before Derek gets there – no woman's safe with him – he keeps his hands under the table all through dinner.'

'They're like schoolkids,' Natasha smiled – with, I felt, the tolerance and slightly superior air that a secret love gives you. 'It's like sausage-and-mash musical chairs.'

I waited until Natasha grabbed my arm and cried, 'Quick! There're two seats next to Molly Saunders. You sit between us – she's sweet.' Tony was sitting with Irene who was looking very pretty – relaxed, I thought to myself, after the afternoon. It was odd, really – even though Irene hated Singapore she always seemed to enjoy Ara. Nobody could say the company and surroundings bubbled – it was a long way even from the weekly parties in Wimbledon – but she was obviously having more fun than at the stodgy parties at Tanamera.

Long before the remains of the tinned sausages were cleared away, the secretary banged a chord on the piano and announced, 'Ladies and gentlemen. Fellow sausage mashers. The police have caught our man!' There was a cheer before he added, 'Mr. Langworthy, the CPO, wants a word with you.'

H. B. Langworthy, Chief Police Officer, held up his hand for silence. In his thirties, ex-navy, he was drssed in khaki drill and looked very spick and span. Everyone knew H.B. – an old hand whose devotion to his police force was a byword throughout Malaya.

'No cause for alarm ' he announced. 'So don't panic at what I'm going to say It looks as though the gunman was planted outside the club as a diversion to bring the police here. There's a spot of labour trouble brewing at several estates.' Amid a collective gasp of surprise or fear, he said calmly, 'Nothing's happened except that a few stones have been thrown. But it would be a good idea for everyone to go back to their bungalows.'

Irene leant across the long table, its white cloth stained with the rings of overflowing beer glasses. 'Let's go, Johnnie – Bengy and Victoria – I'm scared.'

'Of course.' I got up, ready to be first out of the car park with Tony in case the roads were jammed.

'One more thing,' cried Langworthy. 'All members of the Volunteers – report in uniform at HQ tomorrow before four ack emma.'

'Christ, it must be bloody serious,' cried Tony. 'Let's beat it back to the estate.'

As we reached the car a white police officer saluted Tony, who introduced him to me. 'Sergeant Corrie.'

'I'll ride back with you if I may. There's a bit of a hoo-ha at Ara.' Then as Natasha interrupted, 'Nothing to worry about, Mrs Scott. We've had a policeman at your bungalow since we first got the alarm.'

'Shouldn't we phone first?' asked Natasha.

Corrie hesitated. 'I'm afraid the line has been cut at Ara,' he said in a flat voice. 'Lots of phones are down.'

Tony broke every local speed record as we tore back, headlights scything the narrow jungle-lined road, brakes screaming at every corner. 'What's it all about?' I leant forward and shouted above the din.

Apparently – as I pieced the story together before returning to Singapore – several estates had been bedevilled with a few short-lived strikes by Indian labourers. Most were settled on the spot. But the previous week police had arrested an Indian named Nathan on charges of offences against the State. Agitators used the arrest – and the vague nature of the charges – to intimidate the gullible. A couple of days later three hundred Indians marched in protest to the office of the Controller of Labour in KL. Most Indians hardly knew what was happening – most didn't really want to strike – but intimidation was a very real threat. If only one tapper was beaten up in the lines the rest of the workforce – their wives and children mostly unprotected – cringed with terror.

We tore round the final bend off the main Bentong–KL road and half a mile later Tony slammed on the brakes as we approached the entrance to Ara. Just inside the estate two dancing bonfires lit the dark, throwing into shadow shouting, gesticulating figures, black like a frieze, film extras performing grotesque dances. Behind them, towering into the sky, the tall, straight monument of the ara overshadowed everything else, like a totem pole.

Almost before the car stopped Tony wrenched the door open and clambered out crying, 'What the hell do these bloody zombies think they're doing on my estate?'

I really believe that if Tony had been armed he would have fired – if only into the air. But the police officer was quicker than he was. In one smooth coordinated movement Corrie seemed to push open the left-hand front door, unwind his long legs and be out in front of the car before Tony.

As I jumped out of the back he put an arm on Tony's shoulder and I heard him say – curiously he didn't seem to raise his voice, yet I heard the words clearly above the din – 'Leave it to me, sir, just for a moment please.'

The shouting, catcalling, dancing figures were enough to scare anyone – they certainly scared me – as they surged forward, seemed to stop, then started to move on again, waves ebbing and flowing. There must have been a couple of hundred, some armed with sticks, some with parangs, caught like moving pictures in the car's headlights. Most were in sarongs and there were a few women, even a clutch of wide-eyed kids, some naked, others in their shirt tails.

Corrie had a revolver in a holster on his belt, but as he walked forward deliberately, step by step, never faltering, eyes straight ahead, he made no attempt even to undo the strap of the holster. It was as though he was telling the crowd they were not important enough to warrant the use of firearms. The shouting changed to a mutter; Corrie never hesitated, never changed the length of his stride by an inch. No one moved. He raised a hand. The muttering dwindled into a murmur.

Then, very politely, he said, 'Mr and Mrs Scott have had a very tiring day and they're anxious to see their daughter and go to bed. Will you please return to the lines and let them pass.'

For one moment the crowd stood irresolute, on the verge of dispersing. I could see one or two figures take faltering backward steps, impressed by Corrie's matter-of-fact attitude. Then one Indian jumped up, screamed abuse. At first I couldn't hear what he said, but as Tony and I raced forward, Corrie, patting the air, palm downwards in a 'play it cool' gesture to us, I heard the Indian scream, 'What of people treated as slaves! What of chappatis for infants?'

Tony was behind the police officer and said in English, 'He's not on my workforce. I know 'em all. He's an outside agitator.'

With the barest inclination of the head to show he had heard, Corrie turned to the man. The crowd silently watched the impending battle between two men. Corrie asked, his voice a little harsher now, 'You! Which section of the estate do you work on?'

'I ask you,' shouted the Indian, 'What of payment rates, what of bonuses?'

'When you work here you may ask those questions.'

'Questions must be answered now. It is owners v. workers, not coppers v. workers. This time management will toe the line. I am doing no wrong.'

'Oh yes you are,' Corrie said almost cheerfully. 'This is private property. You are trespassing. Get off the Ara estate, please.'

'What of freedom of speech? You have no right to threaten me. I am of innocence!'

'Can't I?' said Corrie. 'If you're not off this private property in thirty seconds I shall arrest you for trespass and you'll go straight to the cells.'

It was uncanny to watch the crowd, and to listen – the indrawn breath, like communal gasps, the ohs!, the children aware that something was wrong and hiding their faces in their mothers' sarongs. It took no imagination to realise that the workers, stimulated not only by agitators but with betel nut, or the fermented palm tree sap sold in the estate toddy shop, were only really playing the game half-heartedly. Now the bonfires were dying, so even the back-drop to the scene had lost its violent impact.

The Indian agitator must have known he was losing, otherwise he would never had done what he did. With one final arrogant gesture, he shouted, 'Imperialist police! Where is honesty and justice?' And that wouldn't have mattered, but he could not stop spitting, a full mouthful of blood-red betel nut juice. I am sure he did not deliberately spit at Corrie – but one blob of red landed on the police-man's boot.

Never in my life have I seen any man change in character, in attitude, in everything – physically, mentally – as swiftly as Sergeant Corrie. One moment he was smiling almost paternalistically at wayward children. But after the filthy blob landed on his boot the quiet policeman moved forward quicker than the eye could see, and with all his power slapped the Indian twice across the face – a backhander, so quick, so effortlessly, that even before I heard the long drawn-out 'Aah!' from the crowd the Indian was on the ground, his hand wiping blood or betel juice from a split lip, and Corrie was standing over him, all the politeness gone, snarling, 'Get up, you bastard. Assaulting a police officer is a criminal offence and can be punished by deportation. I'm taking you straight into KL – and if I have anything to do with it, back to India.'

Deportation was the one punishment most feared by any Chinese or Indians in Malaya – because they knew this country of ours was ten times better, a hundred times better, than the hovels from which they had emigrated.

Corrie knew this. To the crowd he shouted, 'Do you want to go back to India? Return to the lines now,' and waving to the Indian to get up, said, 'One word out of you and you'll be shot resisting arrest.'

He turned back to Tony. 'No problems now,' he said. 'Sorry about losing the old temper – but I love the FMS police and I'm not going to have any buggers spitting on its uniform.'

The bungalow was quiet, the lights on. The women rushed up to see their babies, both blissfully asleep, the amah snoring on a trestle bed in the corridor separating the two bedrooms. Nothing had happened, the boy was waiting with iced water (in old gin bottles as usual) ready to see if we wanted any food. No one in the bungalow except the Malay policeman, in khaki shorts and blue puttees, even knew about the scene at the gate. A whisper can travel miles along some open ground, but rubber can smother the most terrifying screams of anguish.

I drank a stengah – gratefully, I needed one – while Tony made a quick check of the bungalow and changed before joining his unit.

'There's no danger tonight,' he said. 'But this business is going to get worse before it gets better.'

It did get worse. Within two days seven thousand labourers were on strike on nearly twenty estates, including Ara.

The strange part was that our bungalow itself was not at first threatened, nor were most other estate bungalows. Quite apart from the fact that we had police protection, the lines were so far away down the hill that the bungalow belonged to another world, not to be disturbed. And it was clear that intimidators were not spoiling for a fight, but trying to stop production by terrifying workers.

Tony came home once or twice a day, rattling up the dusty red road in his armoured car, accompanied by one or two Volunteer chums, all of them thirsty, all of them enjoying every minute of their 'active service'.

'There's no danger to the bungalow,' he said. 'Unless you provoke them. They're too busy slashing the tappers' bicycle tyres and intimidating them.'

Even so, by the next day sixteen thousand labourers were striking, nearly four thousand of them around Kuala Lumpur. And that was the signal for Kidd, the Resident, to declare a State of Emergency in Selangor, and call in a military presence. By dawn a battalion of Indian troops arrived.

There had to be a bloodletting – and, unluckily for us, chance chose the Ara estate as a battlefield.

17

The battle for Ara, as the *Malaya Tribune* graphically described it, came about purely by accident. On the day the trouble erupted everything seemed to go wrong. At eight that morning Tony phoned to say he was being ordered to Klang to mop up rioters and wouldn't be back until late that night. Then around ten o'clock a blue Ford saloon came roaring up the red drive, leaving a cloud of dust behind it. Most estate cars were known to neighbouring planters, and Natasha screwed up her face and cried, 'It's Rickie Sando.

Probably his cook's gone on strike and he wants a free breakfast.'

'You don't sound too pleased.'

'Oh, he's all right. Just a bit too tough for me. Okay in a crowd, but – well, I'm glad you're here.'

He came bouncing in, so angry that at first he could hardly splutter out what had happened. 'Sando estate is surrounded,' he cried. 'Must have been a couple of hundred of the buggers baying for my blood. Tried to force me out, would you believe it.'

Sando had inherited one of the few small privately-owned estates in the area from his father and he was aggressive – tough, opinionated, and known in the area as a harsh boss. There was a cold glint in his eyes, and though he said now, 'I was damned scared, I can tell you,' fear was the one emotion absent from his tanned face. Standing there sipping an early morning beer – brought by the boy without being asked, I was intrigued to notice – he was a typical planter, in khaki shorts, stockings up to his knees and an open-necked blue shirt. I suppose he was in his late thirties; and not the kind of man to tolerate any nonsense. Though we had met occasionally it had always been at long intervals and I hardly knew him.

'Not to worry, Rickie,' said Natasha, and I noticed, not for the first time, how she tended to treat all the planters with the amused tolerance of a mother. Or was it a secret knowledge, a secret life that gave her a feeling of being superior to them?

'Old boy around?' asked Sando.

'Won't be back until late tonight.'

'Shit! Sorry, Mrs Dexter. Slipped out.'

'He's gone to Klang,' I said.

Rickie Sando smacked his lips, hesitated for a moment then said, 'I'm not really *worried* – but they *were* raving mad back at Sando. I had to bolt by the back door. I hope they don't come here.'

So did I. We were guarded by one unarmed policeman and five Indian soldiers. And I knew that if tempers were rising they might come. Sando estate was perhaps eight

266

miles by road from Ara, but the distance was much less as the crow flies – or rather as the tapper walks.

Irene spoke for the first time. 'Don't you think you should phone the police?'

I nodded. 'But let me take a quick peep out towards the lines first,' I said. From the verandah everything seemed calm and peaceful and beautiful. The children, in their tiny woollen bathing shorts, were playing in the paddling pool, their bodies shaded from the sun by a large attap roof standing on four posts (and looking rather like a rural bus stop). The amah was half dozing nearby. Below, beyond the estate office, I could see the lines, smoke drifting above them. All seemed quiet.

Fortunately Sergeant Corrie was on duty when I asked for him at Kuala Lumpur police headquarters. And he was very crisp and businesslike when I told him that Sando had taken refuge with us.

'Then you can expect trouble – serious trouble,' he said. 'Mr Sando probably doesn't know it, but the mob rushed his bungalow when they saw him drive off and they've set fire to it. It's burning like hell at this very moment, and the Indians are thirsting for his blood. I'll send a platoon to Ara right away, by armoured truck. If you see *anything* suspicious get on the buzzer right away. I don't want to scare you, but keep the children upstairs at the back. They want Mr Sando.'

'Just what has he done, Sergeant?'

'He got mad the other day and beat up a troublemaker. Nor for the first time. It's always leading to trouble. *We* can beat people up, but not civilians.'

I dashed out to the verandah again to see what was happening. Far below, at the bottom of the rise near the lines, a throng of men had appeared. They had not been there before. And the children were still in the garden.

Shouting to the women to be careful, I sprinted down to the paddling pool. The amah looked up with a lazy smile.

'*Lekaslah!*' I shouted.

The babies looked up, knowing enough Malay to understand. 'Come along.' I used the English phrase to them instead of speaking Malay, and tried to soften my voice. 'Time to get out of the sun.'

There were squeals of protest. I shouted again to the girls to come and help. I could now see, as Irene arrived, that a huge crowd was gathering: it looked to me as though it might be forming up to march towards us.

'My God,' whispered Irene. 'What'll we do with the babies?'

'Into the back bedroom,' I said. 'Come on, kids. And tell Natasha to load the twelve-bores in the hall.'

While there was still time I wanted to turn our cars round in the area behind the bungalow where they were parked in the shade, so they would be ready, facing the right way, if we had to make a dash for it.

As I looked at Sando, I was thinking, what a bloody fool! Men like him – and there were dozens – caused more racial friction than any segregation laws. I had been brought up by Papa Jack to believe that the Chinese and Malays were as good as we were, that they had the right to human dignity, even when doing menial tasks. We treated our boys at Tanamera as members of the family, always had done, and our work force at Ara too. We didn't stand any *nonsense*: someone had to be the boss, and as Grandpa Jack used to say, 'Don't you forget, young feller-me-lad, the British are God's chosen people.' But ruling millions of lives gave you a responsibility. You couldn't run an empire, a work force, even a friendship, by beating up people.

The crowd – shouting and gesticulating – had passed the estate office and was marching towards the green lawns and Natflat's precious beds of cannas in front of the bungalow. Thankfully I noticed that no one seemed to be going round to the back of the bungalow – and that indicated a confrontation rather than a siege. But it was an ugly crowd. There must have been at least three hundred, armed with parangs and six-foot poles to which they had fastened murderous-looking hooks; others wielded rakes or chungkols.

There was a great deal of shouting – much of it abuse,

threats or unintelligible screams – but now and again I heard one name roared out: 'Sando!'

'They seem to want you,' I said to him.

'They'll have to get me,' he shouted back.

'It's not you I'm worried about,' I couldn't stop the anger mounting. 'It's the children – thanks to you.'

He seemed unabashed – and, I must say, brave. 'Sorry about that,' he gave a crooked grin. 'But don't worry. They're all cowards.'

I had to do *something*. I looked round. Irene had gone upstairs to be near the babies, so I said to Natasha, 'I'm going to talk to them.'

'No. Let me go,' she suggested. 'They know me.'

'I don't think they do,' I said. 'Because they're not your work force. Corrie told me they're marching from Sando.'

This seemed to quieten her, so I made my way out on to the verandah, held up a hand, and shouted, 'Let me talk please!' Catcalls, jeers and shouts of 'Sando' drowned my voice. I saw Sando edge to the front of the room behind me, the room leading to the verandah.

'Get out of sight, for Chrissake,' I said savagely. He backed into the room.

The sole policeman, armed only with a stave, stood stolidly by the front porch, with the crowd perhaps a hundred yards away, though so far there was no direct threat. I couldn't understand what the rioters were shouting, and the mob was completely disorganised. They seemed to have no spokesman. In a way this made it more dangerous, specially as they were not on the rampage because of intimidation (though that of course had started the whole business) but consisted of men in whom I could sense an undercurrent of hate, a thirst to revenge insults suffered at the hands of Sando.

Then they started to march towards us.

The crowd was still fifty yards away when I heard the rumble of traffic coming up the drive, but out of sight. Long before I could see the platoon I saw the welcome haze of dust hanging in the air round the corners of the twisting road. I knew then that we would be able to hang on, contain the trouble, for I saw some of the crowd halt and shout, then look back.

At that moment Sando came out on to the verandah brandishing one of the shotguns. I tried to wrest it from him as the sullen crowd regrouped and surged. Before I could do anything the gun went off – harmlessly. But it was as though Sando had beaten up a dozen more workers. There was a roar, a charge – and then two more shots, obviously from the soldiers.

'Put that fucking gun down, you stupid oaf,' I shouted, and he did. I must admit that he had never intended to fire it, but that didn't stop the mob's anger spreading. The next moment a short, steel-bladed parang – which could split a man's skull or slice off an arm, came whistling past my head and stuck in the door behind me. More shots split the air.

Then I saw the first man in the mob fall – almost at the same moment I heard a fourth or fifth shot. The Indian was barely thirty yards away. His head seemed to explode in a bright red gush. Half the crowd turned and ran, pushing into those behind. But those behind didn't realise what had happened and started to surge forward. At that moment, as the first armoured vehicle arrived at the rear, a fusillade of knives, bricks, even poles thrown like javelins, came hurtling towards me. I ducked behind some furniture.

'That's the way!' Sando shouted almost gleefully, as twenty Indian soldiers, with fixed bayonets, lined up by the side of the bungalow.

I dashed to the stairs again and shouted to Irene. 'Okay, darling, the reinforcements have arrived.' As I ran back I heard the command, 'Fire – Advance!' There was a burst of rifle fire, spattered unconnected shots, screams from the mob – but this time screams of a different kind, of pain, anguish. I reached the verandah. The crowd began to tear back down the slope. Only a few diehards stayed on. Some started throwing their chungkols at the soldiers, others shouted abuse. One of the soldiers fell, wounded. The other soldiers marched forward with the inexorable, studied movements of robots. Almost all the other Indians fled.

Only a hard core – perhaps thirty – remained. I heard another command from the army vehicle, 'Prepare to charge!' That meant the bayonet, and that was what happened. As the file of soldiers advanced most rioters fled, but some still refused to move; stood there, almost like the sack dummies I had seen in newsreel shots of soldiers training. I wanted to shout out 'Stop!' but I couldn't. Sando, his shirt scarlet, cried, 'Give it to the buggers!'

I couldn't believe at first that the Indian troops would still move forward. The knot of rioters – now perhaps twenty in all, though it was hard to see anything clearly – stood shouting defiantly, waving their weapons. The soldiers marched on, rifles pointed out in front of them, bayonets glinting. It was the seemingly nonchalant way they advanced, I think, that made the hard core of rioters believe it was all play-acting. But then the rioters didn't understand the significance of military orders. The last one had been 'Prepare to charge!' Now the final order blared through the megaphone, 'Charge!' And in an instant the lackadaisical, upright position of the Indian soldiers changed into an animal crouch. The walk became a run – bayonets well forward, heads well down against any attack.

The rioters tried to flee. Most did, and got away. But a lesson had to be taught, a lesson had to be learned. 'You can't threaten the white man.' I saw the first soldier charge, thrust his bayonet deep into the stomach of one man, pinning his flapping shirt tail to his belly as he screamed with fear. The soldier pulled the bayonet out, and charged again. I turned away, almost vomiting, praying the girls upstairs had remained in the back room.

It was all over then, the battle for Ara.

When the last of the rioters had run for it, all the heart dragged out of them, five bodies lay staining the green lallang in front of the bungalow. Three had been shot, two bayoneted. A sixth man was writhing from his wounds, and later died in hospital. One soldier was badly wounded but recovered. As the girls came down – leaving the kids upstairs with the amah – the two army vehicles tore across the lawn and down the rise towards the lines where they overtook the remnants and arrested nearly two hundred men. None came from Ara.

News of the fight was soon being broadcast on the radio. Because of the casualties, the government issued an official communiqué giving the bare details. Tony was on the phone first because he heard the news on the army radio circuit.

I couldn't say much to Sando. It takes all sorts to make a multiracial world, and I couldn't blame him for seeking refuge in the nearest bungalow. 'Sorry about all this,' he said to Natasha. 'But who knows? One day I might be able to help you out.' The prophetic remark passed unnoticed in the rush.

Papa Jack rang up that night. By then exaggerated accounts of the battle had been given full coverage on the radio. When he was sure we were all right he had *his* news to impart. He wanted me to get back to Singapore for several reasons. First we had been asked to attend a top-level conference called by the military at Fort Canning. 'It seems the Japs have been making nasty noises about Southeast Asia,' he said.

'Heard that one before,' I laughed.

'Well, George Hammonds says there's some sort of proof of Japanese invasion preparations. But that's not the worst. I've got bad news from London.'

He had indeed. Poor Cowley had been killed in the Blitz. 'Got a cable this morning. I suppose now I'll *have* to go to London.'

I agreed to drive back the following day, thinking as I replaced the phone, 'Maybe this will give Natflat a good excuse to get out of Ara for a bit.' For if Papa went to London Mama would surely go too. So why not Irene, homesick for her own family? And if they went, why not Natasha? Of course she would never go unless she took her beloved Victoria – and that was the moment, turning thoughts around in my head, when I realised that if Irene went Bengy would have to go too.

The next morning the State of Emergency was lifted, and

by the time I was back in Singapore Tony had put his Volunteer's uniform back in mothballs.

18

Even I was astounded at the news of Japanese duplicity which greeted dozens of leading businessmen who had been summoned to Fort Canning for the off the record military conference. It seemed incredible to be sitting in the conference hall, our obligatory ties imprisoning the heat, and listening to an officer calmly warning us that the long-drawn-out Japanese-American negotiations in Washington were on the verge of a breakdown because America refused to change her stance and allow oil supplies to the Japanese. The gravity of the situation was underlined because during this summer of 1941 the Japanese had taken over Indo-China, 'and that gives them a jumping-off ground a thousand miles nearer Malaya,' said the officer. 'But worst of all,' he added, 'the British High Command has information that Japan has formulated plans for a possible invasion of Southeast Asia, and we cannot rule out the possibility that this area would include Malaya.' We were well defended, of course; our new airfields were ready, there was no *real* danger, the government assured us. But one thing the military spokesman did stress: 'When financially possible, wives and children should be sent to some safer country.'

It was, however, the news behind the conference that left me with a sick feeling. George Hammonds had been at Fort Canning and afterwards, over a drink, he said bitterly, 'These bloody government wallahs will *never* learn. People want to know the *truth*. Not soft soap.'

'But wasn't the report pretty tough?'

'Not tough enough. They don't *trust* people. They only

273

told us half the story. They still don't realise that people *respond* to truth.'

'But what's the truth? Is it secret? Can you trust *me*?'

'Sure.' He called for another round. 'The fact is the Japs aren't *formulating* plans as that red-tabbed idiot put it – they're ready. Military intelligence has got photos – actual photos – of Japanese troops in training.' George paused for a moment then added, 'You remember telling me about Hayley Bell and the way the governor bawled him out? Poor Hayley Bell was right all along. It was typical of Shenton Thomas. I've *seen* the details of the report – it clearly confirms the information the spy tried to flog to Bell and which Shenton Thomas dismissed.'

The queasy feeling in my stomach increased, but I had to ask, 'Does it name this Japanese training ground? Where is it?'

'Sure. It's a small island called Yakushima.'

I had felt it, of course, vague stirrings, though I had refused to believe the awful truth – that the highly respected firm of Dexter and Company had supplied a possible – no, probable – enemy with five thousand barrack huts to train a force of crack troops to attack us.

'Not a word to anyone,' George warned me. 'I'll be for the chop if this is ever leaked.'

'Of course not,' I replied absently, for my mind was racing ahead. The deal was over and done with – there was nothing I could do about that. And I was not worried about the firm. We were in the clear – we had even obtained government approval. I wasn't even thinking of the moral balls-up. I knew the Japs would have trained their force with or without our help. My mind was occupied instead with thoughts of those who had lured us into this trap.

Miki – the man who had introduced me to Irene, the man who had been so secretive about his trips to London, the man who had even asked Irene's father to guarantee his last visit to England – was he to be trusted? Even if I *wanted* to trust him, he was a Japanese, and he must have deliberately tricked us.

What about Bonnard? That was far more serious.

Bonnard was a respectable, married, neutral Swiss whose background had been thoroughly investigated and found impeccable. But Bonnard was also the man who had been going to bed with my beautiful sister for years, who wouldn't leave her alone, who was all but ruining her life. Was he a spy?

I thought back to the Love Club, to his first invitation to me to use it. He had told me that a friend of his had seen Julie and me together, a contact he called him. I had wondered at the time what he meant. Had we been followed deliberately? Had I been offered the use of the Love Club as a lure so that if I didn't respond to the deals offered by Miki – if I became suspicious – Julie and I could be blackmailed? It seemed far-fetched, yet everything was crazy. For, if it came to that, why would an astute businessman like Bonnard keep an *extra* flat when he lived in luxury, a virtual bachelor with a wife who had never visited Singapore in her life? (If he had a wife, I wondered suddenly.)

What should I do? At first I thought of seeking out some officer at Fort Canning, but it didn't make sense. There was no war – there probably wouldn't ever be one. Our deal had been done with government approval, even encouragement. Bonnard might not even be a spy. He, too, could be a dupe of Miki's. Christ! If he ever learned that I was accusing him of being a spy – talk about an action for slander! I decided to leave Bonnard alone, but for the moment watch him as carefully as I could when we met.

Miki was different. I liked Miki. But I had to warn someone. Not Fort Canning. After all, Miki was a civilian. He had done nothing wrong – except, if the reports were true, fool a young and not very bright businessman. But I could unburden my soul – or part of it – to Dickie Dickinson, Chief Inspector of Police, and an old family friend. Dickie was known to his friends as the gentle policeman because of his unfailing courtesy, even to criminals. I went to see him in his office in South Bridge Road. Almost with a sigh of relief he told me, after getting someone to look through the files, that Miki had returned to Japan.

*

All this was by the way – a personal problem of my own – for we now realised that arrangements had to be made urgently for Papa Jack to leave for London. I had already seen the cable announcing Cowley's death. Papa Jack had told me on the phone that another member of the staff had been killed but the cable didn't give a name, and I wondered who it was – until the airmail letter arrived a few days later.

'There's something I don't quite understand,' Papa Jack reread the flimsy blue sheet, 'Cowley wasn't at home or in the office when he was killed. He was in a building in Soho. Why should someone else from the office be there?'

'Does it give the name?' I asked.

'A Miss Rankin – killed instantly. Do you know her, Johnnie?'

The name meant nothing to me until I asked, 'Did she have a first name?'

'Only an initial – G.'

'Gwen!' I cried. 'She's his secretary. Good old Cowley. Screwing to the last.'

'You mean our manager – and – a *secretary*? I can't believe it.'

'Come on, Papa Jack,' I said. 'Everybody does it, you know.'

Papa Jack had to get to London quickly. Even the government and the military authorities – each begging for rubber and tin – realised the importance of staffing the London office as soon as possible. But several snags quickly developed. Britain by now really was an embattled island, and each ship ploughing the Atlantic had to fight every inch of the way before it could land its precious cargo of good or war material, all so desperately needed. German U-boats were sinking so much merchant shipping that – quite apart from personal dangers involved – unnecessary human beings were unwelcome. There wasn't a cubic foot of space to spare; all was needed for more valuable cargoes.

After the first flurry of cables between Singapore and Whitehall, my father was told he could fly to England, via Ceylon, South Africa, up the west coast to Lisbon in several hops. From there the last plane would take him from neutral Portugal to England.

'But what about me?' asked Mama. It was the first time for years I had seen her so angry. 'How dare they separate husband and wife!'

'But there's a war on,' replied my father almost plaintively.

It was comical really, Mama's inability (real or professed) to understand the logistics involved in a war where our illusions, fostered by distance, made it almost impossible to grasp reality. One person didn't make that much difference. But if one went, then a thousand would demand to go. She was used to priorities for the Dexters.

'Really! Just one extra person. I've never heard such nonsense. Anyway, war or no war, I'm not letting you go alone.'

'Oh yes, you are,' laughed my father.

'Isn't it dangerous? Flying, I mean. Couldn't you go by sea?' asked Irene.

In fact the last stages of the sea voyage might well be more dangerous than the air trip, but the question didn't arise because there were no more ships leaving Singapore for Britain. Papa Jack could have travelled part of the way by sea, it was true, but as he pointed out his presence was urgently needed, and if he got to West Africa by sea he might have to spend weeks, even months, waiting for an empty troopship returning to Britain. And through dangerous waters. It was certainly quicker and probably safer to fly from Lisbon, despite the risk of air attacks from German fighters based in France.

'Then I shall stay here with Johnnie,' my mother insisted firmly.

'No you won't, my dear.' My father was almost enjoying his authority, the more so since the options hadn't been made by him, so he couldn't be blamed for the fact that nobody liked them. 'There's an American passenger vessel leaving before the end of July for the West Coast. I'll have gone, but Johnnie will see you on board. Then you can make your way to New York.'

'But what about me?' It was Irene's turn to be angry. 'They can't keep a daughter from going to see her own father and mother.'

'They can do *anything*, my dear, during a war,' answered my father.

'But – it's *family*!'

'I did put the question to the shipping authorities,' said Papa Jack. 'They weren't very complimentary. They said that evacuation to a *safe area* – that's the official phrase – was one thing. But if you feel equal to facing the dangers of war they suggested that your first priority was with your husband rather than your parents. After all, Johnnie's the one who's going to be left alone. For him it's like – well, being in the army without the glamour. He's not staying for fun. His job is damned important.'

'Of course I'll stay here,' said Irene, turning to me. 'Only it was you who said it might be dangerous.'

'Don't worry.' I patted her hand. 'We'll get you to England.'

'You're all treating me like an invalid,' Irene was half joking. 'I'm not Grandpa Jack, you know.'

'Are we going to America?' asked Bengy who had come into the room. 'Grandpa too?'

'Of course.' My father turned to the amah. 'Take my grandson to the nursery.'

'I'll come and see you in a minute,' I kissed him.

'Grandpa Jack *could* go to South Africa or Australia if he wanted to,' explained my father, 'but we couldn't do that to him. And the doctors are better in America. He's getting weaker; he'll need medical help soon.'

'And Natasha?'

'America too. I phoned her the other day at Ara. Tony's all for it. He wants her evacuated. And it has to be America. If you went anywhere else – South Africa, say – then you'd never be able to get to England. You'd be stuck there for the duration. But once you're in New York I'll be able to pull strings. I might find it impossible to get a seat on a plane, but ships are larger. Lots of them are crossing the Atlantic on convoy. I don't see any trouble.'

That was not the story I had heard, but not until we were alone in the office the following day did my father confide in me. 'You don't think I'm going to let that wonderful grandson of mine go to London, do you?' he smiled. 'My god! It'd be murder. I *have* to go – just like you have to stay – but thousands of kids have been evacuated *from* England to North America. There won't be a hope in hell of Bengy being allowed to go. I'll see to that. I can pull strings both ways. Same with Natasha and Victoria. Don't worry, Johnnie. Your mother is different. We're better together. I've got a job to do, and I need her. It might be a bit selfish, but in fact it'll make your mother happier even if she is uncomfortable.'

So that was how it was planned. Papa Jack prepared to fly, the others to travel by sea. The family was booked on the *Pacific Rover*, a good, solid neutral American passenger vessel of fifteen thousand tons, run on a peacetime basis, still with the suites of luxury cabins so beloved by the Dexters. We had no trouble getting accommodation. Not many women could afford the luxury of being evacuated to America. Most had chosen Australia.

But if Papa Jack had planned everything, he faced one rebellion he could not overcome. It came from Grandpa Jack.

I suppose we had all in a way over the years almost taken this old man in his wheelchair too much for granted, someone who was in no position to disobey, threaten, even argue. After all, he had been sitting in that wheelchair for over six years, he was in his eighties: what could he say or do?

'I'll tell you what I can say' – he gave a very passable imitation of his old bull-like roar. 'I can say – NO! No, bloody no!' He was sitting in his chair on the west verandah. 'I'm not bloody well going and that's the end of it.'

'You have to,' said my father mildly.

'I don't have to do *anything*. I built Tanamera, damn everyone. I'm not going to be driven out of my own bungalow because you're scared of some bloody Japanese a thousand miles away.' For a moment the unexpected outburst tired him, and his breath came in short gasps, but he still managed to wag his good right arm.

'You!' He pointed to my father. 'That's different. You're going into the war – because you have to. The women,' he snorted, 'that's all right. But *me*? America! You think I'll run away from one lot of savages to live with another lot of savages?'

'I think they've changed, Grandpa Jack,' said Mama, defending the country of her birth.

'Mebbe they have. But I'm staying put. You and I, Johnnie, eh? We'll see the bloody Japs off if they get fresh.'

The family tried everything to persuade the old man. They argued, they cajoled, the women resorted to tears. And then suddenly I felt terribly sorry for the way they were badgering Grandpa Jack – for his own good, they thought. But was it? I had always been closer to Grandpa Jack than anyone else, we two each seeing in the other traces of ourselves, and I suddenly realised my grandfather was waiting for death; not morbidly, but he was expecting it, perhaps at last ready to welcome it. We had never thought – all of us so busy with our own little lives – of the misery that could beset a once-active man chained for years to a wheelchair. Grandpa Jack was not the complaining type, yet now I realised – knew – he was waiting for death.

Then suddenly, in the midst of his resigned anticipation, a new and fierce element had torn its way into his thoughts, striking terror into his fragile life; so much so that it had given him extra strength to cry out in protest. It was not the terror of death. It was the fear that his own family would rob him of his final pleasure in life, the right to meet death on his home ground – in his beloved Tanamera. It came in a flash, the realisation that I must help him.

We were in the study that night and Papa Jack was due to fly in two days. Everyone was exhausted with the wrangling and last-minute pleas – everyone except Grandpa Jack. He did, it is true, slide off into small snatches of semi-sleep now and again, but each time he woke it was as though his feeble batteries had been recharged. He woke up now and cried, 'What are you saying?'

I cleared my throat, hoping for quiet. When it came, I said clearly in a very loud voice, 'I think Grandpa Jack should stay in Singapore. I'm sure I'll be needing his advice.'

A stupefied silence greeted my words. I went over to Grandpa Jack's chair and grasped his good right arm, thin and veined now, the hand covered with brown stains. 'I'll look after you,' I said. And in case he hadn't heard, I added, 'I'll be needing you.'

'You see,' growled the old man to my father. 'He needs me.'

In effect that ended all discussion. It went on in desultory fashion for a day longer, but only as a matter of family pride. There were muttered references to the fact that the decision might hasten his death, but I could sense that all of them were secretly grateful to be relieved of the responsibility. He would have been a burden, he would have fretted, and this after all was the only home he had known since the day when he christened Tanamera.

For Mama the break with Singapore — and with my father, though that would only be short — was tempered by the fact that she had cousins and even a sister living at Brewster in New York State. But for Irene it was different, a torture because New York would still be a long way from her home in London. 'The idea of skulking in America,' she said to me. 'It's awful. Like a coward.'

I tried to tell her that there was really no difference between living in Singapore and New York. Both places were helping a Britain at war, but neither would ever be the scene of any fighting. And at least New York *would* be nearer to London.

I didn't tell her the truth — that the Japanese were getting ready for war and that I did feel Bengy ought to be evacuated. The Japanese could never invade Malaya, of course, but if there was any trouble in nearby countries like Siam I wanted to be sure that Ben and Irene would be spared the complications of tropical life when things go wrong — water shortages, disease, the hissing rains when the roof caves in, the hot sun when shelter has vanished. On the other hand, I did not want him to face bombings in London.

'Don't worry about that,' Irene promised me. 'I feel awful leaving you, darling – but – and it is a big but – for two years now Mother and Father have been through hell. They're old. I want to see them. But if I do – if I can wangle a trip – then I give you my word I'll leave Bengy in New York with Natasha and Victoria. They're staying anyway. Do you think I'd harm Ben?'

Papa Jack left in mid-July on a military aircraft – a Sunderland, I was told later – but I could not see him off from the guarded RAF building. We had a farewell drinks party at the office, with Ball, Rawlings and the typists all guzzling free drinks in his honour. Before he went he confided to me, 'Don't worry about Irene. I'll keep her in New York until the bombing is over.'

'Don't do that,' I asked him. 'She's really homesick. Now that she's promised to leave Ben with Natasha, let her try. If she fails, then there's nothing she can do. But give her a chance to see the Bradshaws again.'

When Mama had almost finished her packing, Li came to the verandah and said, 'The mem asks if you could be kind enough to go to her room, tuan.'

I went upstairs, wondering if there was to be a tearful farewell.

'It won't last forever,' I said as she patted down some blouses folded in tissue paper.

'I hope not,' she sighed. 'But I hate leaving you alone darling. It seems so unfair. Yet your father is right. In a way you're fighting just like Tim. It seems funny being separated from my two boys – and they're separated from each other too. But I'll write. There'll be no censor in America, will there? So I'll write *everything* before I set off to London.'

I felt that she was much more unhappy at leaving me alone than she showed. Perhaps worried, I didn't know. 'Papa is so proud of you,' she smiled, her mother smile, 'You really have made good. You're the *tuan bezar* now. Don't – well, don't spoil it. Papa has put you on a pedestal.

Don't tarnish the image, darling. With Julie Soong, I mean.'

'Don't worry, Mama.' I let her into the secret. 'Irene's hoping we've clicked. And' – lightheartedly – 'I've always been told that a *tuan* never chases the girls when the mem's preggers!'

All Irene said about Julie was, 'I won't ask you to make any promises, darling. Apart from anything else, I don't think you'd be able to keep them if this bloody war drags on. And it looks like lasting for years. But when you are tempted – and we all know who by – think that you might be a father all over again before the war's over.'

I had rather dreaded the goodbye scenes, Mama's tears, Irene's doubts, Ben's puzzled looks. I knew they all had a guilty feeling at leaving their all-in-one husband, son, father, in Singapore. Luckily I was spared the long embarrassing farewells, stretched over days, for the sailing date was kept secret until the last moment and passengers were only given twenty-four hours to board her.

The *Pacific Rover* still managed to have a traditional farewell party, always a feature of Singapore in the days when the average man and his family took one long leave every three or four years – and each leave was a signal for a party. Ben hardly realised what was happening – not, anyway, from the moment when Victoria arrived and he had someone to play with. The rest – well, the steward was busy passing round drinks, there were other families we knew who hailed us. Promises were extracted from me to behave. Natflat handed me a tiny note, saying conspiratorially, 'Thanks, darling, for all your help', there were kisses all round for everyone from me and of course from Tony who had come down from Ara three days previously.

A hooter blared. An impersonal megaphone voice cried, 'All visitors ashore please!' As I waved for the last time from the dockside it seemed only yesterday that I had listened to the same cry when Irene and I prepared to sail on the *Orient Princess*. It passed through my mind that she had been pregnant then.

As I drove back with Tony I wondered if any of them

would ever return. Or if they did, when. For what on earth was going to happen – either in Britain or Singapore? I suddenly felt lonely, and a little afraid – not of war, but of the future, the responsibility. For as Mama said, now I was the *tuan bezar*.

I hardly realised my new status until I swung my Morris Minor, which had replaced my beloved Morgan, through the ornate gates which Grandpa Jack had ordered from the local smithy so long ago. As I drove slowly down the drive, with Tony by my side, the beautiful white house, walls shining like silk, stood there in front of me and I realised that – for the time being anyway – I was lord of all I surveyed.

I drew up under the portico. The syce, who had returned earlier in the family car, came to take the Morris away and clean it. Young Li – one-time playmate, now my personal boy – stood at the door, upright, white-clad, face crinkled with pleasure and, with a sense of drama befitting the occasion asked, with special emphasis on the very last word of the sentence, 'Shall I bring stengahs to west verandah, *tuan bezar*?'

Wiping the sweat of Singapore from my face, I nodded.

'Come on, Tony,' I cried, throwing my jacket over a chair. 'I think we both deserve a drink.'

'Here,' he stooped. 'This dropped out of your pocket.'

Idly I read it, not knowing until I spread out the creased paper what it was. It was a note. It read, 'Darling brother Johnnie, please tell you-know-who *casually* that I've gone, but don't tell him anything else. Kisses – Natflat.'

'It's nothing.' I raised my glass to Natasha's husband. 'Here's to a murky future!'

PART FOUR

Singapore, 1941–1942

19

By November 1941 it had become obvious that Japan was preparing to attack *somewhere* in Southeast Asia. We all expected increased fighting in Indo-China and perhaps an assault on Siam, but no one believed Japan would attack Malaya; even so, if the war with China escalated, who could tell what might happen?

Once I had received a series of cables from the family, telling me they had arrived safely, I felt almost relieved to be on my own – freer, and less worried at what might happen, simply because I had shed all my responsibilities, a wife, a child, a mother, a father, a sister. Only the office – and Grandpa Jack – remained.

Papa Jack's cable was the first to arrive. He was installed in his beloved Hyde Park Hotel. Soon afterwards news reached me that Mama and the wives and children had arrived in San Francisco. A letter followed from Irene telling me nothing, but that Ben missed me and sent a big kiss. Once there, they set off for New York where – to my surprise – Mama had little difficulty in getting passage to 'somewhere in England'. It had, I learned later, been fixed by father. Knowing the urgent need of his presence in London he had in effect blackmailed the authorities, and Mama was given top priority. Within three weeks I received a cable saying, simply, 'Papa and I send all love Mama.' So she was in London. It was a weight off my mind; I knew the trip was dangerous.

Tony spent a few days with me before returning to Ara, and then only Grandpa Jack and I remained in Tanamera. I saw him very little, mostly in the grounds when I returned from the office, old Li pushing him or occasionally helping him to stagger around on his feet. One thing was certain: the decision to let him stay in Tanamera had stripped years from him. He couldn't walk much, but he looked healthier – and happier.

In normal times the departure of the memsahib on home leave was a signal for any husband left behind to fill his bungalow with old cronies for those few months when he could relive the role of bachelor. But it was different now. The cronies were too busy, many of them had disappeared, and Tanamera had the air of a hotel to which I had travelled in the expectation of having a good time, only to find all the amenities closed.

I didn't want cronies anyway, and sometimes, on the rare occasions when Li prepared dinner at home, I thought of the one person I *really* wanted to see at Tanamera. I did see Julie from time to time – no threats of war were going to interrupt the round of parties in Singapore – but I never saw her alone, and I knew it had to be that way. Indeed, I was politely warned one evening – by none other than Vicki.

Several times I dined with the Scotts, and on this occasion, when Ian had been called to the phone, Vicki looked at me as she twiddled her balloon brandy glass, and just said, 'Don't do it, Johnnie. Never open old wounds. I know you're on your own, but I love you both so much I don't want either of you to get hurt.'

Vicki was right. And thank God I was busy, really busy. It stopped me thinking about her – and the fact that I wasn't in uniform. Singapore was bursting with troops and I envied them – though I did realise that keeping the supplies of tin and rubber moving out of Singapore was certainly more valuable, if less spectacular, than wielding a gun. At the ripe old age of twenty-eight I was the *tuan bezar* of one of Singapore's most prestigious agency houses, and with Britain and America clamouring for more raw materials, firms like ours faced increasing problems as the coolies raced to fill the holds of vessels lining the quays of Keppel Harbour.

The war against Germany was more than two years old by now, yet despite the evidence that it might spread to the

Pacific it was almost impossible to whip up any warlike feeling in a city thriving in a boom. When I dined one night at the Cathay I could hardly believe the variety of the menu. Sydney Rock oysters and smoked salmon had been flown in from Australia. Strawberries packed in ice had been sent from the up-country hill station of Cameron Highlands. It was the same at the Cold Storage in Orchard Road. The shelves were stocked with French bread freshly baked each morning and with row after row of tinned goods evoking thoughts of the next trip home to England – sausages, baked beans, Irish stew, ice cream, all of which had the supreme quality of being safe. In Battery Road, the narrow street leading from the waterfront to Raffles Place, Maynard's the chemists displayed a card in the window warning lady customers there was a waiting list of three weeks for an Elizabeth Arden facial. Around the corner, Robinson's store, an institution whose big new building dominated Raffles Place, had never been so busy. Robinson's would sell you anything – a bottle of aspirin over the counter to a casual customer or a motor lawn mower which they would deliver to a lonely plantation near the Siamese border.

The pace of work also gave me an uncomfortable feeling. Working hard is a relative term. Nobody could hurry in a country where the temperature hovered in the upper eighties or nineties every day of the year and where work finished around five. We prepared for the worst – it eased our consciences, for we were after all a limb of Britain fighting for its life. There were practice brown-outs, sessions of bandage rolling; I even joined the ARP – though the duties were not very clearly defined. We volunteered for blood transfusions. But despite the fact that my parents were now being bombed in London, I found the war in Europe hard to *believe*. And even more, the prospect of war in Asia.

By now thousands of troops crowded the streets. The officers donned their best blues to dine at Raffles – there were red tabs everywhere – while the other ranks queued in Change Alley to buy souvenirs or have their photos taken (by a Japanese photographer behind Raffles Hotel) for their mums, wives or sweethearts back home. If I ever had doubts they were always blown away by politicians and military leaders reiterating almost daily – and with the same persuasion displayed by Chamberlain after Munich – that there would be no war. And with rubber to be tapped, tin to be mined, ships to be loaded, money to be made, it was all too easy to want to believe them.

One worry still niggled me: Bonnard. It was bad enough that he and Natasha had been secret lovers all these years, specially when he professed to be a family friend. But on top of that he had – unwittingly, I still hoped – been instrumental in letting Dexters actually help to train the armed forces of a potential enemy.

I had to see him. I had to confront him with my information about the Japanese – and I didn't relish the prospect, knowing about Natasha. Luckily I saw him at the Koos, together with Paul and Julie.

Julie was now working five days a week as a volunteer nurse at the Alexandra, but though we still met at parties like this I was determined that our past should lie quietly undisturbed. Yet my heart still pounded each time I saw her. America and France had not only polished her – given her a dress sense, for one thing – they had subtly given her more confidence. She aired opinions she would never have expressed in the past, simply because in the old days Chinese girls never spoke unless spoken to. I suppose, too, watching her talk to someone, laughing as we all drank champagne in the preposterous Koo gardens, that I forget she was now a woman – twenty-five or twenty-six. I suddenly realised that when Mama was twenty-six Natasha had been seven years old.

Paul was talking to Bertrand, and as I looked at the Swiss his charm seemed more oily, more smooth than before. Imagination? It is one thing to see the good points in a lady-killer when he's just a friend; it's different when the lady he's killing is your sister; and married; and when you know but can't accuse. Not that I had any right to accuse.

Natasha's married life was much the same as mine – happy or at least not unhappy enough to make it impossible to share a double bed. But nothing could stop the bile rising as I touched Bonnard's shoulder and led him away from Paul. (Curiously, I started thinking of him as Bonnard more often than Bertrand.)

'Ah, *mon cher*, it is always nice to see my friend.'

'And screw my sister,' I thought savagely, then with an effort switched my thoughts and asked him, 'Heard from Miki lately?'

'*Mais non*. Things are tricky in Japan, eh? I think he is keeping quiet.' After a moment he asked, 'Any special reason you want to see him?'

'Yes, there is,' I said. 'You know our humanitarian project to help Japanese earthquake victims? Well, it was about as humanitarian as Hitler's bombs.' I watched his expression carefully. 'The Japs have filled our huts with a crack invasion force.'

'*C'est pas possible!* You are wrong, Johnnie. Miki would never do this to us – to me.'

'You're certain? And surely *you* must have had *some* idea. You – you or Miki or both – have dropped us right in the shit.'

'I don't believe what you tell me. Why would neutral Switzerland give you such vast sums?'

'Did the financing actually come from the Swiss government?'

'Of course.'

'A government cheque?'

'Not exactly. Government funds are always channelled into different paying accounts. An account is opened for a big project like ours and closed when the deal is paid for and over with. As a matter of fact I handled it. With government approval, of course.'

On the spur of the moment I invented something – just to make him think. 'Well maybe,' I said. 'Maybe – I remember my sister Natasha saying – you know her, I believe?'

'*Mais oui*. We used to dance together.'

'Yes, and fuck together,' I thought.

'She said what?' he asked.

'She said something to the effect that not every Swiss is what he seems to be.'

'Nobody is,' he laughed easily. 'Let me find out, Johnnie, what has happened. I will cable Switzerland – and I'll also look up Miki. With the present war scare it is less embarrassing for me than for you. I will let you know.'

'Do you trust Miki?'

'I think so. Yes. You know what I think. We made this deal a long time ago, in good faith. But things have changed. What is to stop Japanese from turning a peaceful project into a warlike one?'

'I hope you're right.' I declined an offer of dinner that night, and we joined the others.

On an impulse I told part of the story to Grandpa Jack the following evening. He might be feeble and his brain no longer as keen, but he still retained traces of what Ian Scott had once grudgingly called 'the Dexter nose'. I had noticed it often in the casual, almost throwaway asides he made when listening to Papa Jack's business discussions with me.

Once, when we were in the early stages of developing my 'ready-to-wear' prefabricated huts, my father and I talked at length after dinner, hardly noticing Grandpa Jack's presence, and as we got up to join the ladies he grunted, 'Don't make 'em too easy to assemble.'

'But that's the whole object,' I retorted.

'I didn't say "Don't make 'em difficult". But leave a man *something* to do, to think out. Give a man who can't think the chance to believe he *is* thinking, and he'll end up sure he's getting value for money.'

Now, when I explained a little of what had happened, his first question was, 'Get paid in full?' And when I nodded, he said, 'Don't worry – for two good reasons.'

I asked him to elaborate.

'Every Jap in Singapore is a spy. Dickie Dickinson told me that weeks ago. So you're not the only sucker. Second, they'd have got what they wanted if you had refused. They'd have gone somewhere else.'

'And Bonnard?'

'Watch him, Johnnie. No businessman dealing with Japan can be so damned stupid.'

It was about this time that I received another long letter from Irene. Uncensored, of course. The postmark was New York State. 'I can't see a hope in hell of getting to England,' she wrote. 'I've pulled every string, but the shipping people won't even give me any idea of how long I'll have to wait. We are all living at Brewster in your mother's old family home, such a pretty American town, a couple of hours from New York by car – sorry, I should say automobile. We miss your mother, but the house is lovely and Americans are so hospitable, especially with two young wives – Natasha and yours truly – who are pregnant. Yes, it's sure. After I missed again I went to the local doctor. Cost a fortune just to tell me I was expecting. Ben is wonderful and I can tell he misses you. Oh dear! What a misery this war is. I do hope it will be over before he forgets what you look like.'

So the autumn passed into December, and the first festive decorations started sprouting in Singapore's shop windows. Placards exhorted us to post early for Christmas. Newspapers started advertising hotel rooms in the up-country stations of Fraser's Hill and Cameron Highlands, tempting the sweating with slogans, 'Why not have a *real* Christmas – where you need two blankets on your bed?'

Everyone tried to make everyone else (and themselves?) ignore the increasingly bad news from Japan. 'Don't let rumour ruin your Christmas!' announced one newspaper early in December. A deluded, gullible people, deliberately lied to by wicked government and military leaders, steadfastly ignored the threat of war until it was upon us.

Then I met Julie Soong again. It was on December 7th, that beautiful Sunday, the last day of peace.

*

Sunday morning was Sea View morning, a weekly occasion for meeting and drinking at the Sea View Hotel, by now invested with overtones of sentimentality and nostalgia, the Singapore equivalent of Sunday morning drinks at the local pub back home in England.

The weather was perfect. In the heat-laden water beyond the hotel beach the lacy, spidery lines of Malay fishing traps broke the view of hot, green islands out to sea. At the far end of the hotel's pillared terrace, with its dome in the centre, flowers in tubs lined a platform on which an orchestra, with violins predominating, churned out palm court music.

By the time I arrived the terrace was packed with men in their Sunday uniform of open-necked shirts and shorts, but still sweating as they signalled the Chinese boys for a gimlet or a Tiger beer. Many of the women wore shorts, fanning themselves as they gasped for air, dabbing the beads of moisture on their foreheads with minute handkerchiefs. I had arranged to meet George Hammonds of the *Tribune* to hear the latest news – George could still not publish everything he knew. I spied him almost at once, among the crowded tables where he had kept a place for me.

The news was serious. The *Tribune*'s main headline was '27 Japanese Transports Sighted', and the story said they were steaming towards the east coast of Malaya. The front page contained other stories equally ominous – a government warning to people not to travel, another one urging those on vacation to return home.

'The balloon's gone up,' said George. 'Nothing can stop war now.' He had produced a gimlet for me just before the orchestra struck up a resounding chord for which the drinkers had been waiting. The starling-like chatter ceased abruptly and everyone picked up small rectangular cards which were placed on the tables each Sunday. They bore the verses and chorus of 'There'll always be an England'. This pre-lunch Sunday singsong had become a ritual since the start of the war in Europe, and another chord gave us our final cue. By the time the chorus was reached every man and woman was lustily singing the cheap sentimental words:

There'll always be an England,
And England will be free,
If England means as much to you
As England means to me.

It was as if the throaty, out-of-tune voices united everyone briefly in a burst of shared loneliness; not only the
civilians but the soldiers, all of us thousands of miles away
from the last raid on London, the fighting in North Africa,
the Russians defending the gates of Moscow. It seemed to
bridge for a few moments the distance which made a far-off
war almost incomprehensible.

Soon after the last chorus the tables thinned. The first to
depart were the parents of fretful children who had been left
with their amahs at the Swimming Club. Then suddenly I
saw Paul Soong, immaculate in white sharkskin trousers
and silk shirt. Julie was with him, and they were standing at
the rim of the table area. I waved to them to join us for a
drink.

'Do you sing patriotic songs?' I teased Paul. Then I turned
to Julie. Not with any awkwardness; yet I had to fight to
stop the catch in my throat as she stood there, tall, graceful,
enormous soft pools of dark eyes framed in high cheek-
bones and pale skin, blue-black hair tumbling over her
shoulders, her smile as she asked for an orange juice grave,
yet really looking as though she was pleased to see me.

'How's the nursing?' I asked.

'I'm a fully fledged nurse now. Night shifts as well as day
duty.'

'And father's furious,' Paul grinned. 'He thinks it's highly
improper for his daughter to look at men who haven't got
any clothes on.'

'I'm in the women's ward.' Julie laughed before asking
me, 'And you, Johnnie? Heard any news of Bengy?'

'The family's trapped near New York,' I said. 'Not a bad
place these days.'

George Hammonds rose to go. 'To another bloody military briefing where they'll tell us everything but the truth.'
He picked up his tin of cigarettes and made for the car park.

'See you, George.' I waved him goodbye and turned to Paul. 'I'm on my own. Maybe we could all lunch together – here?'

Paul, it appeared, had a lunch date but almost slyly he suggested, 'Why don't you invite Julie for lunch? You'd have much more fun without me.'

I had visions of their father finding out.

'Don't worry about that,' said Paul, guessing my thoughts. 'Julie has to do an extra session at the Alexandra – in theory, anyway.' He added with a grin, 'That's her story and I'm sticking to it.'

'Would you like to?' I felt almost shy.

'I can't think of anything in the world I'd rather do,' she said.

'That's settled,' said Paul. 'Now that I've managed to dump my kid sister I can live a life of my own.'

'Only for lunch,' I laughed.

'Lunches can stretch,' he said airily. 'Bye now.'

As Paul left I ordered two gimlets – the Sea View made the best in Singapore, ice cold and always served in champagne glasses – and told the boy to keep us a table for lunch in the restaurant; it was too hot to eat outside.

'Feels a bit strange,' I began. 'Alone like this, after so many years. Nervous?'

'Not really. But I do feel as though everyone's looking at us.'

'They're not, you know. People have other things to talk about – war, separations – all hell's going to be let loose soon.'

'I know. It's just a silly feeling I have – remember how in the old days I was always scared somebody might spot us together?'

'Still frightened?' I leaned forward and touched her hand and stroked her wrist. The pale gold was like silk.

'You mustn't stroke my arm in public – people might talk,' she almost giggled, she *was* nervous. 'Do you remember, you used to say I must be made of gold leaf.'

'I remember everything.'

'So do I.'

I looked round the crowded tables. 'Damn all the people! I wish there was some place I could take you where we could be alone, but I daren't take you home – next door.'

'You're sure you don't want me alone because' – she was teasing, not bitter – 'because I'm not white?'

'Come on, Julie. What balls.'

She laughed. 'That's more like my old Johnnie.'

'Everything's changing,' I said. 'You're behind the times.'

'Do you really think there'll be a war? Here, I mean?'

'It's madness, but I don't see how anyone can stop it.'

'It'll change everything, Johnnie. It's awful. You might not see your family for years.'

'I've thought of that.'

'And if they start bombing us I might never see *you* again.'

'Darling Julie, don't be so morbid.'

'I'm not. But when I think back – those beautiful days – and now, if war comes, doesn't it change everything?'

'If you mean that in war you've got to grab what you can – it's live for today because you could be killed to-morrow – yes, of course.'

'Are you sure?'

'Yes.' I looked at her steadily. 'And there *is* going to be a war. And a lot of people *are* going to be killed.'

She finished her gimlet, asked for another, and asked very quietly, 'Are you really hungry?'

'No – not now, not really.'

'I see you've changed your Morgan for a baby Morris. You've got it here?' It was more of a statement than a question, and as I nodded she leaned forward, not too obviously, and this time it was Julie who stroked *my* arm.

'Let's forget lunch,' she said a little unsteadily. 'Drive me to Tasek Layang at Changi. It's empty. The servants have been doing war work for weeks. We'll have a swim, then I'll cook you some *mahmi*.'

Tasek Layang was the Soongs' weekend beach bunga-low. Now my heart really started to thump against my ribs. Desire or fear? Or maybe a bit of each? No, looking at Julie her eyes steady, desire came first. She sat there, very grave, but full lips smiling, soft black hair slightly blown by the sea breeze. It seemed only yesterday that we had been secret lovers, and then I had a sudden vision of Irene and Bengy. Just a swift incoherent (guilty?) thought, so that I blurted out with a laugh, 'Are you propositioning a married man?'

'If you hadn't laughed, I might have got up and walked out. It *is* rather crude, the way you put it.'

'Julie darling, I didn't mean it that way.'

'I know. I'll have another gimlet.'

'Your third!'

'I'm plucking up courage.'

I wanted her with almost unbearable physical ache, even though I was niggled by shafts of guilt – not so much for Irene, but for a *pregnant* Irene. I didn't speak as the boy put the gimlet on the white table and I signed the chit.

'Don't think of me as – what's the phrase they use in novels? – as a brazen hussy, tempting you. But I've been thinking so much, so hard. I don't quite know how to start – it sounds so tough, but I found in America that people do talk more openly than here.'

'You a hussy!'

'Will you answer me a question?' And when I nodded, she asked: 'Are you *sure* there is going to be a war – soon? What did George Hammonds say? He knows everything.'

'There's going to be a war – and damn soon. It's only a matter of hours. Then, to quote George, the balloon's going up.'

'It seems incredible that people can do this – it's going to be terrible.'

'Well, not physically for us, not here. I mean, the Japs can't do much against the British empire – the naval base, the big guns – but it will mean a world war, a hell of a lot of hardships in Asia. And God knows when it'll end.'

'Does it make you very miserable, darling?'

The way she said the word darling – casually, as she used to say it when we were lovers! That one word – and the years rolled back and there might have been no other life between then and now. I tried to say as calmly as possible,

'I'm not overjoyed. It's Papa Jack and Mother I think about most, bombed and half starving in England.'

'And your wife – and Ben?'

'They're all right, thank God. So is Natasha. New York is okay. Safe, lots of lights and food – no real shortages. Just like Singapore.'

I was thinking, it *is* war. It *is* going to be a fight that will separate us for years. And surely in the scheme of things, that must make a difference. A war that tore families from each other's arms, that killed indiscriminately, surely *must* alter the value of words like infidelity. When I thought of Bengy, sturdy, starting to chatter, picking up flowers and giving them to me, now far away – doing what? – I thought, NO! War is just an excuse, an easy way out for men who can't resist temptation. But when I looked at Julie, sitting opposite, her face troubled, war no longer seemed a phoney excuse to be unfaithful but a valid reason. I had *tried* to be a good husband and father. But four months had slipped by since Irene left – four whole months in which I had never looked twice at the girl whom I felt I would love all my life, a girl whose body was no secret for me, and who was now living next door again.

Now, though, war was a certainty – which had to mean a total rearrangement of everyone's lives. Didn't that make a difference? If men, governments, politicians, generals, could flout moral standards by deliberately killing their neighbours, did they have the right to break one commandment yet prevent Julie and me from breaking another?

I hardly realised Julie was speaking until she said, 'Remember what I said at the party when I returned from America? *You* said we could never return to the past, and I said you were right – unless you were left alone. Then I would come and get you before anyone else stepped in.'

'I remember.' I must have looked a bit depressed, for she touched my arm again and said, 'Don't look so sad, Johnnie. Do you think I would ever have loved you if it wasn't because you're decent and nice – and loyal, because you don't want to hurt people. That's *why* I love you and always will – because I respect you. But now – everything *is* different. A war starts – and until it ends we're all in a kind of vacuum. Suspended animation. What happens during that time between a man and a woman has no more moral significance than a man shooting an enemy to death. We're all acting in circumstances we didn't ask to be placed in.' She lightened the tension by adding with a laugh, 'You have to remember, I *did* major in philosophy at Berkeley.'

'You don't have to convince me, Julie. I know what you're trying to tell me – that we are both in love – and we're alone together through no fault of our own, perhaps for years. I know.'

She sipped the last of her gimlet and said simply, 'I love you, Johnnie, and I always will. It may sound selfish to say this, but it's as though the whole world is going to hell. Just to give us a second chance.'

'Of heaven?'

'Yes. A temporary heaven. I'm not the sort of woman who goes around breaking up marriages. I told you that. I've been back a year – and both of us have behaved perfectly. But I feel that because you are who you are, you feel guilty. Just a twinge?'

'Aren't you?'

'The last year I knew I could never have you again. I never dreamed of even having a drink with you – even if I knew we could get away with it. I'm not that sort. But we're different people now – everything about us has changed except our names – we're suddenly being plunged into a sort of self-contained world in which we might all be killed next week. And my God, I'm not ashamed to say it, but I couldn't bear to die if I missed the chance of having that week with you.'

I was thinking once again of Mama's advice – the dishonour – that was the word – of becoming involved with Julie. But Julie was right. She wasn't talking with desperation, but with a quiet intensity, and oddly she brought the word honour into her very next sentence.

'You see darling, you have behaved very honourably with Irene. Don't forget that. Even before you married her.

You *are* a very honourable man. But who knows who will ever see who again? Don't you think – in these special circumstances – you've paid your debt of honour?'

'I didn't want to make you suffer again but you're right.' I said. 'How ridiculous that we should be sitting here *discussing* being in love! We *are* in love. We always have been. I've no moral scruples. I've wanted you every moment of my life since the last time we made love. If morals came into it, I'd be divorced by now – because of the number of times I've made love to Irene and pretended it was you. Its not that. I'm afraid.'

'Not of Kai-shek?'

'God no, that little bugger!'

'Then what?'

'The future.'

'But there *is* no future. Not until the war ends. And that could be months – no, even years. When it does come we'll think again.'

'You've changed, Julie. America altered you.'

She laughed.

'Aren't you afraid – just a little? Your father? Rumours?'

She shook her head. 'I would have been, but everything's changed. I'm a nurse now. I can arrange to be 'ordered' to live in the Alexandra – an emergency measure. So I'll have the opportunities. If or when war comes no one will have any time to worry about us.'

'My beautiful Julie, I'm just trying to be a "gentleman" to warn you,' I said. 'I want to go to bed with you more than anything else in the world. I'll go to Tasek Layang *now* – this minute – but no false pretences. If we go we're burning every boat. We'll be discreet, we'll be careful, but we'll never really be able to go back.'

She looked out to the islands in the haze beyond the fish traps. 'I just had this awful longing to see you again. Who knows? We may never see each other again. I've never been to the Sea View alone in my life – Papa would have a fit! – but he's in Malacca. What frightens me is that we're on the edge of a terrible war. And because we had such a beautiful time together – and in case there's no future –'

'Don't say any more, darling.' I signed for the drinks, cancelled the table, and we left.

As Julie climbed into the left-hand seat of the Morris I knew that we were embarking on yet another stage of my life and that after it was ended life could never go back. The Sea View was on the coast road leading to Changi, where the Soongs had their weekend bungalow by the sea, and as I revved up the starter, she said, 'I'll slide down out of sight until we get a bit further out of town.'

The fresh air tasted and smelled heavenly. The wind that rushed past us was warm and kind and scented, sometimes with the sea, sometimes with the sudden smell of food as we passed a fruit market or a group of café stalls. Half-clad Chinese sat eating rice voraciously from bowls held up to their mouths, sometimes, if the café was a hole in the wall, under pools of light from hissing pressure lamps.

After we had passed the Swimming Club Julie sat up and I drove with one hand, the other arm round her. Then suddenly I stopped the car with a jerk and kissed her open mouth, and then roared away in a flurry of dust and passion, my left hand on her leg, stroking her thigh as I had done in the summer house at Tanamera. Traffic flashed past. I missed a barrow by a miracle. Then I took my hand away and held hers and steered it towards me, but she held back. 'Wait,' she whispered.

Changi was surprisingly alive, very hot, scores of soldiers, the pavements crowded, the Indian men walking in couples, holding each other's hands as they often do. Julie slid out of sight again, giving me instructions as I drove up the main street, with its lines of flame trees shading the pavement shops. We turned right at the end of the street and into a dusty red road – little more than a lane, really, winding through some local plantations of rubber and banana patches and the occasional kampong. It was very silent. We reached the edge of the bungalow which had an iron gate. I jumped out and opened it. Julie got out too.

'We'll leave the car here,' she said. 'The main gate is locked.'

Tasek Layang was secluded, in the way that only the

Chinese can manage to arrange for their privacy, the stretch of garden leading to the beach in front shaded with high rattan fences, and the sea netted against sharks so that the swimming area resembled a flimsily constructed pool in the sea.

The big square verandah was cluttered with furniture, shabby, tatty, the most lived-in part of the bungalow, with cane long chairs, a big divan in the corner, tables, newspaper racks, a great deal of what looked like inherited furniture. Tied up above the green posts separating the verandah from the grass leading to the sea were rattan curtains which could be unrolled when it rained.

Then she was in my arms and we were kissing wildly, frantically, as though we had only two minutes left together before eternal separation. I had forgotten Julie's impetuousness. With her there was never any nonsense about wiping away lipstick or worrying about ruined make-up. Everything she did was ruled by instinct – instinct or desire. And to me, back in the arms of someone I had known secretly before I was married, it was a kind of loving I had forgotten existed. Without thinking, I said, 'Let's go outside, in the warm air. No one can see us.'

She walked out on to the lallang and without a word put one hand behind her in the way that only women seem able to twist their arms, and unzipped her skirt, then took off her blouse. As it fell to the ground her arms were behind her back again and – all in one movement, it seemed – she undid her bra and then pulled off her blue panties and stood there, pale gold, black hair over her shoulders, a triangle of black hair just as luxurious , just as thick, at the join of her legs. I almost groaned with desire as, pressing her to me, I felt her breasts crush against my chest.

'Let me undress you,' she whispered. 'I remember how it used to excite you.' She undid my shirt buttons, pulled the shirt off, undid the belt of my white trousers, the buttons on the front of my trousers. They slid down and I stood there in my underpants. Carefully she pulled them off, then knelt and stroked and kissed me.

'It's unfair, Julie! I can't wait.'

'I don't want you to wait,' she stood up now, kissing me on the lips; long, exploringly, lovingly, gently, her left arm round my neck stroking the back of my hair, her right hand still stroking me between the legs.

In the hot afternoon the silence was broken only by the whispering casuarina trees and the murmur of the flat sea breaking gently on the beach. The sky, stretching away in front of the bungalow like a huge burnished steel bowl, was suddenly filled with extra light, the diffused flash of silent, blazing sheet lightning, as though an electric torch had been switched on. The distant rumble of thunder followed, and for a split second, standing there naked in the heat, I imagined it was the growl of gunfire. I had an equally sudden thought that this was the last day on earth — but that it didn't matter; that Irene, the children, Papa Jack, Mama, Soong — none of them mattered. If this *was* the last day on earth, so be it. I could never ask anything more out of life.

I heard Julie whisper, 'Don't wait, darling. Don't think about me. This is my present to you. I've dreamed for years of doing just this — taking your clothes off — this is for you. The next time — after lunch — you can do it all over again for me.'

As we lay afterwards in the garden I had an unwanted picture of life at home, of sex at home, of waiting until we were both in bed, of preparations, of cold cream, of doors being locked, of handkerchiefs ready ('Be careful of the sheets, darling!'), of the time it took. The sudden memory didn't spoil anything, it enhanced the moment, it made me realise what I had missed all these years, what I suppose one always misses eventually in long relationships, the urge that can't be controlled, the desperate desire to make the beautiful moment last just those few seconds longer.

We were lying on an old blanket spread out on the ground in the hidden garden. I caught her looking pensive and asked what she was thinking about.

'An old poem, a Russian one I think, but I've adapted it to suit us when we make love in the garden.

For you will be counting the lallang,
And I will be counting the stars.

304

We'll remember that when we make love tonight.'

She brushed aside the black cloud of her hair. 'That's the poetry of love,' she whispered. 'But what I said still holds – I'm not a homebreaker, and when this is all over I'll fade away. But meantime – this is the sort of day I hope will never end.'

20

That night – or rather, in the early hours of the morning – war came to Malaya. It was the explosion of bombs that woke us, locked in each other's arms, for we had decided to spend the night at Tasek Layang. There seemed no danger. P.P. Soong was in Malacca and anyway, as Julie assured me, she had often stayed overnight at the Alexandra.

'But when I have to stay I always phone,' she had said during the afternoon. 'I'd better contact Paul now with an alibi.'

There was no phone in the bungalow. So before dark, after a lazy afternoon swimming and making love, we drove down to Changi village a couple of miles away. In the background stood the sinister grey walls of the jail. First Julie phoned home, then we went shopping for food. The once-lazy village was thriving, British troops were everywhere, some of them with frangipani blossoms stuck in their berets, all of them cheerful, grinning, freckled, fingering the 'bargains' in Da Sanda's, the Singalese souvenir shop, or asking the prices at Only For Men, the Indian tailor who guaranteed, with the aid of one ancient Singer sewing machine outside his shop (and a lot of friends inside) to make you a tropical suit in six hours. But despite their cheery temper, the troops had one grouse.

'We've been bloody conned in coming out 'ere,' said one sergeant bitterly. 'I've been nine years in the Argylls –

we've been trained to fight, not for garrison duty in a place where there'll never be a bloody war.'

We went from shop to shop buying the few provisions we needed – some plantains, those exquisite tiny speckled bananas, eggs, noodles and vegetables to make a mahmi, milk powder, bottled water, ice and Tiger beer. I managed to find a bottle of Scotch. We only needed to buy enough for supper and breakfast, but even this simple exercise gave me a sense of excitement, physical as well as mental. We were playing one of the classic roles of lovers, shopping together in secret for a forbidden feast, and it was completely out of character with my normal married life.

Irene and I had hardly walked into a food shop together since we were married – not only because everyone in Tanamera regarded marketing as the cookie's job, but because with my limited spare time (from tennis, I admit, as well as work) the prospect of slow, indecisive shopping appalled me. It was a chore I couldn't stand, the apparent pleasure women seemed to get in spending hours in shops, sometimes not even buying anything. Yet here I was actually enjoying shopping.

Why? Why hadn't I let Julie drive the car into Changi while I took a shower? Was even shopping for groceries coated with an added excitement just because it was forbidden? Or was it more simple, more exciting, simply because it was new – new in a way – the time limited by a moving clock so that every second counted; that and the fierce feeling of possession and intimate knowledge of showing Julie off – something I had never been able to do – so that I had a feeling of superiority each time a soldier gave a wolf-whistle as he undressed Julie's long, slender figure with his eyes.

I smiled back at each whistler, a knowing smile, almost a shared smirk, telling him without a word, 'She's a bit of all right, eh? But you should see her as I did this afternoon – without a stitch on!' At times, after a whistle, I wanted to shout my thoughts aloud, not that there was any need to. They could see, the sex-starved wolf-whistlers. See, imagine, envy.

That was the afternoon. In the evening, just before dark, we swam naked in the warm, salty sea. The early passion had been replaced with an extra tenderness. We tried to make love in the water but it ended in giggles, for there was nothing to hold on to and we kept falling over. We lay down instead on the cooling, wet sand where the water lapped over us, Julie lying with me inside her, hardly moving but always stirring, arms round each other until Julie shrieked, 'A snake!'

It was tiny and harmless, but after that I carried her on to the divan on the verandah. And later she fried some eggs and then we took our pleasure with the contentment and easy tenderness of long friends, fading into sleep in each other's arms, tired with the joy of loving. I don't think I can ever remember a happier day in my life.

Then came the night. The noise – blurred by distance, yet with undertones of evil because these were no echoes of the afternoon thunder – woke us instantly from deep sleep. One crump followed another.

'Christ! Those are bombs. It's started.' I rubbed the sleep from my eyes and tried to see the time on my watch. A quarter past four. I rushed out on to the lallang, Julie following. I don't know what I expected to see miles away. Searchlights, I suppose, silhouettes of planes perhaps. I waited for more noise – gunfire from the dozens of anti-aircraft batteries sited all over the island. The noise never came: only an uncanny silence.

'Are you sure you didn't imagine it?' Julie clutched my hand.

Standing there, naked in the warm moonlight, I wondered too. There had been an unreal sound, perhaps transformed by distance. It had all happened too quickly, had ended too swiftly. I had never been in an air raid, but the London newspapers always gave the impression of a cacophonous hell that lasted for hours.

'Maybe you're right,' I agreed. 'And yet – I'm not sure.' Then, without thinking, as I put my arm round her, I joked, 'Don't you think it's very rude standing here without any clothes on?' I scratched the small of her back gently as I felt excitement mounting. 'Perhaps I made a mistake. Let's go back to bed.'

She was about to turn – I could feel her sense of excitement matching mine – when she pointed in the direction of the city.

'Oh God!' she whispered. 'Look at that.' The distant sky, always faintly glowing, had subtly changed. The metallic haze that comes from thousands of street lamps had given way to a faintly sinister sheen, a hazy, rosy cloud.

'Those are fires.' I hustled her inside. 'God knows what's been happening in Singapore.'

We dressed quickly and set off for the city, shivering a little with apprehension. I had no idea then that three hours earlier the Japanese had landed at Kota Bahru on the east coast; that General Percival had telephoned the governor with the news; that Shenton Thomas had replied with a sentence so fatuous it would go down as a classic of its kind. 'Well,' Thomas had said. 'I suppose you'll have to shove the little men off.'

Driving to the city as fast as we could, we held a shouted conference, deciding that I would drop Julie at the Alexandra Hospital. It would not only provide an alibi if her father in Malacca phoned; I was also afraid to draw up with her in the car either outside Tanamera or the Soong house. People would surely be out watching, gossiping.

Grating the gears of the Morris, I approached the outskirts of Singapore. To reach the Alexandra meant crossing the city, and I was baffled by what I saw. Everything pointed to an air raid, yet Singapore was blazing with lights. Even military headquarters at Fort Canning were bathed in floodlights. As we drove past the Cricket Club padang, arc lamps picked out the new law courts and the municipal buildings. The illuminated clock tower of the Victoria Memorial Hall shone like a torch. From time to time a burst of AA gunfire split the air. The waterfront – on the other side of the padang – was crowded with people watching the free 'show'.

'This is no bloody game.' I banged the gears of the Morris into low as we approached the Anderson bridge, and looked at Julie, hunched in the low seat, almost shivering – not with fear, I knew, but with disbelief. 'Are you all right darling?'

'It's like a nightmare. I keep on thinking I'm going to wake up in Tasek Layang.'

'It *is* a nightmare, but it's coming true.' We crossed the bridge and approached Fullerton Building. An ambulance clanged noisily into Battery Road. Someone shouted that Robinson's had received a direct hit, but I drove past the post office and straight along Collyer Quay as a fire engine chased the red embers of a blaze. Then I turned right and made for the Alexandra.

Our farewells were snatched. 'I must rush.' She kissed me. 'There may be wounded.'

'Only if you promise to phone me tomorrow – sorry, today – at the office. Promise? I must see you again – I don't know how, I'll manage something.'

Then she was gone. Dawn was not far off, and I drove to Tanamera, suddenly panicking at the thought of Grandpa Jack alone except for the servants. An air raid was just the kind of shock that could kill a man who had suffered a major stroke.

I drove silently, wondering what Irene would be thinking. But perhaps she didn't know yet. It would be the day before, all those miles away. Or the day after? I never could master the International Date Line. So perhaps she was blissfully unaware that Singapore had been bombed, and equally unaware how her husband had spent the last night of peace, that I had transferred my love – such as I had to offer – to someone else, the night passing without a single thought of her or any of the family.

Now, driving towards Bukit Timah Road, I did think of them, specially Bengy. But there was nothing I could do except indulge in the luxury of feeling guilty. Suddenly I shouted above the wind rushing past the open car, to no one in particular, 'But there's a war! Nothing counts any more.'

There would be a tally, that I knew – but on a date long into the future, and who knows, I thought – I hoped – there might by then be some counting to be done on the other side of the balance sheet. My English master at Raffles, despairing of the way I over-egged my essays with the liberal use of adjectives, used to say of them and the way I diminished their value, 'One plus one equals half.' Could guilt be halved if it was shared by two people?

But God, I felt good! I swept up the drive towards Tanamera, and Li saw the arc of the headlights and was waiting for me as I braked under the portico.

'Don't worry,' I said. 'It'll take more than a few bloody Japs to kill me off.'

'*Tuan* right.' He opened the car door. 'Japs no bloody good, *tuan*.'

'Is my grandfather all right?'

'*Tuan* Glanpajack vellee happy,' Li grinned even more broadly.

It seemed an odd word to choose – but it was the right word. 'Bloody fine show!' grunted Grandpa Jack when I went to see him. 'Wouldn't have missed it for anything. That'll show these little yellow sods.'

His mind wasn't exactly wandering, but it certainly didn't seem to occur to him that 'these yellow little sods' were showing *us*.

'You've been out all night?' he asked suddenly. 'On the tiles? Lucky bugger!'

'That's right,' I agreed cheerfully. 'Luckier than I ever dreamed I'd be.'

I took the stairs two at a time to the Married Quarters to have a shower. I suddenly realised I was ravenously hungry. Nothing like a night of love – and a war! – to stimulate the appetite. I shouted to Li, 'Breakfast in ten minutes! And tell Cookie I want the works – bacon and sausages, toast and marmalade, and make sure we've got some fresh limes.'

It was a private joke. We grew our own limes at the back of the compound, but throughout my youth Cookie had insisted on serving wedges of lemon with papaya. Year after year he insisted, 'Limes vellee common fluit, only for Chinese.' All this, of course, because the limes were free, growing on the property, while the lemons had to be bought, and Cookie no doubt got a rake-off. When I was younger — and afraid of Cookie or any authority — Li and I had played a game. Cookie served lemons, Li picked limes, and when I ate my papaya, he secretly exchanged limes for lemons. I never did discover what happened to the limes after I had squeezed them, but over the years the lime joke had become a symbol that I was in a good humour, and that all was well with the world — my world.

And all *was* well with my world. On this one morning of all mornings, when I should have been filled with foreboding at the start of a war that might last for months, I felt deliriously happy. As I sluiced myself with cold water, letting the shower prick me with its force, soaping what my amah used to call 'your middle bit', I felt wonderful.

I could not remember a night like it, passionate yet never sordid; beautiful, filled with tenderness, on and on until finally I couldn't even try to make love again, and we fell asleep without saying goodnight.

How long since I had lived through a night like that, with every slightest touch tempting me to try again, afraid *not* to try, even if I could do nothing, even if it only lasted for a minute or two before I stopped exhausted, and fell into a semi-sleep, an exquisite failure.

I dried myself, pushed open the slatted door into the cold bedroom which Irene and I had shared since I first brought her to Singapore. Photos of her and Ben in tortoiseshell frames (silver frames became black in two days) stared at me, together with some of the feminine knick-knacks Irene had left behind — a big glass jar filled with coloured wool from America, a Thermos for the iced water she needed when taking her sodium amytal each night; a book she had never finished — *Gone with the Wind*. Surely, I thought inconsequentially, she must be the only woman in the world who had started but never finished it.

I should have felt guilty, an interloper in a room where we had made love, and even in a neutral kind of way been happy — but I didn't. For as I slipped on a clean shirt and newly-starched white ducks I was busy thinking not of war, not of devastation, but of the ways and means by which the war and misfortune would enable me to see more of Julie. I was in the ARP – and that meant nights when I could pretend to be on duty and disappear. As Li brought my bacon and sausages I was thinking that perhaps after all Julie might be able to pretend to live in at the hospital. Where would we meet? That was for the future.

As I speared the last morsel of tinned sausage the one thought that never entered my head was that the Japanese would ever reach Singapore. Those fifteen-inch guns facing the sea made the prospect of a seaborne invasion little more than a ludicrous joke; while the impenetrable mountain and jungle down the length of Malaya would deter any Japanese from attacking Singapore from the north, via Johore. The idea was preposterous.

I switched on the portable radio on the verandah breakfast table. The latest bulletin announced, 'A small body of Japanese who landed at Kota Bahru has been repelled, and only a few bombs were dropped on an airfield outside the town without causing casualties . . .' The communiqué ended, 'All Japanese surface craft are retiring at high speed and the few troops left on the beach are being heavily machine-gunned.'

That was more like it. The *Malaya Tribune* arrived. It was more cautious, but pointed out that even if the Japanese *did* retain a foothold on the east coast with its silvery beaches, four-fifths of Malaya was covered with impassable rain forests, with only the poorest roads across the backbone of granite mountains, rising to seven thousand feet, which formed a spinal column down most of the four hundred miles between the Siamese border and the Straits of Johore. To me – and to all of us – it seemed inconceivable that this puny Japanese force should not only be defeated, but thrashed for its temerity.

At this moment the normal broadcast was interrupted by a solemn voice. I turned up the volume. Would everybody stand by for an important news announcement. I had no idea what to expect – certainly not the shattering news that emerged from the impersonal black box of tricks: Japanese aircraft had bombed Pearl Harbor. There was great loss of American life. The voice – as unconcerned as though reciting the weather forecast – droned on, 'It is understood that the Japanese scored several direct hits on a number of US capital ships. More details will be given at regular intervals during the day.'

America? The Japanese must be mad! How on earth *dared* they attack the two mightiest naval powers in the world? Mad, the whole lot of them. An entire nation was committing hari-kiri.

Julie telephoned me at the office later in the day, but we did not meet until towards the end of the week, for Singapore was in a chaotic state. The first reaction of supercilious bewilderment – almost bordering on amusement – began to be torn with doubts. The Japanese had also invaded Hong Kong and the Philippines. They had struck at the heart of the American navy. They had killed sixty-one people in Singapore and injured another hundred in their first raid on the city.

The raid itself left many unanswered questions: why no warning sirens, why no black-out? As Julie and I had seen it was a bright moonlit night, but where were the British night fighters? When I met George Hammonds at the Cricket Club he told me that pilots were actually seated in their aircraft, their engines warmed up for take-off, when they were suddenly refused permission to fly.

'Why on earth?'

'You'll find it hard to believe,' said George. 'But the top brass of the RAF – not the pilots, of course – were scared. Not of the Japs, but of the British AA gunners. Thought that because they were inexperienced they might shoot down our planes by mistake.'

The Cricket Club was crowded with noisy drinkers, all asking questions, all offering dozens of rumours in answer. 'The raid was a freak success,' said someone. It could never be repeated because the Japs were myopic and couldn't see in the dark.

'The truth is,' said George Hammonds, 'we've got nothing to match their Zero planes. It's also true that at one ARP lecture an officer did say the Japs can't fly at night.

Incredible, isn't it?' On land the Japanese had been driven off, said someone – until another voice shouted that they had also landed at Kuantan on the east coast – and that was a long way south of the original landing at Kota Bahru.

Everyone aired his point of view – between calling for drinks. Yet amid all the hullabaloo of differing opinions, theories, arguments, one suggestion was never broached: that we might be in serious trouble. Sure, the drinkers admitted, there could be more raids, maybe shelling from the sea, but the idea that Singapore, with its mighty naval base, plus nearly a hundred thousand crack troops up-country, would ever be in peril – it was too ridiculous to think about. 'Any man who even suggests it as a joke ought to be clapped in jail,' said one peppery British officer, a temporary member. 'Just for spreading defeatist talk.'

'I hope he's right,' George said as he ordered another round. 'But it's not going to be plain sailing all the way.'

'You say that, George, but be honest: it's clear from the communiqué that everything's under control.'

'It was a mass of bloody lies,' said George angrily. 'Come over here.' We found a couple of rattan chairs in a corner of the verandah. To our left, the municipal buildings shone a vivid white in the sun so glaring it hurt the eyes. In front of us Tamil boys were marking out the tennis courts next to the bowling green, cropped and free of weeds, and as beautiful as a bolt of green silk.

'For Christ's sake don't repeat what I'm going to tell you,' he began. 'I'm not an alarmist, but do you want to know what *really* happened at Kota Bahru?'

According to Hammonds, who had been to an off-the-record briefing at Fort Canning, the Japanese had landed on the beaches in bright moonlight. The British were out-numbered but fought well, though the Japanese captured two vital strongpoints just before dawn. Even so, this first crucial battle was by no means lost until everything was changed by a sudden disaster. British troops were still holding the airfield outside the town when a rumour swept the line that the Japanese had broken through and were at the perimeter.

'It was all balls,' said Hammonds. 'Not a word of truth in it. But right away someone in authority – and we'll never be told *his* name – gave instructions to evacuate the airfield. Everyone bolted – in any vehicle they could grab. Bombs, gasoline, runways were left in perfect order – a present to the Japanese.'

'But the communiqué talked about Japanese surface craft retiring at high speed – I think those were the actual words,' I said.

'Of course they were bolting. They'd done their job, they'd landed the troops, why the hell should they hang around?'

'It's terrible – it gave *me* the impression of a few poor Japs left to be sacrificed on the beaches while their pals in the navy ran away.'

'That's what you were meant to believe,' agreed George bitterly. 'That's what's known as keeping up civilian morale.' He added with a grin, 'Just think how cheerful you were until you met me.'

'I suppose they've rounded up the Japs in Singapore?' I asked.

'Sure. The police are a damned sight more efficient than the army. I heard earlier today what happened. One bomb shook police headquarters where Dickie Dickinson was supervising the seizure of forty-five Japanese fishing vessels, and rounding up about twelve hundred Japs who've been interned.'

'I wonder if Miki was among them.'

'Oh, they didn't get *him*,' George almost chuckled. 'He left some time ago. It turns out that your tennis-playing chum Miki was a full-blown colonel in the Japanese army. Intelligence.'

On the Thursday evening I picked up Julie at the Alexandra. She looked adorable – she took on a new dimension in her nurse's uniform. Red and white and golden.

'My father's back,' she said. 'You shouldn't really be seen with me.'

I had planned everything – even down to an old groundsheet in the car. Once away from the front door of the hospital I made her slide halfway down the seat and covered her. 'You'll sweat like hell,' I said cheerfully, 'but I'll give you a bath of sorts later.' Then – without telling her where I was going – I drove her back to Tanamera, parked the Morris round the back, and took her to the summer house. I had told Li the previous day to fill the pool. Some ridiculous moral sense prevented me from taking her into the house itself.

I knew that Li must have known about Julie in the old days. Chinese boys know *everything*. But I wasn't going to let him confront Julie, perhaps with a conniving smile, so I had told him to put a Thermos of cold water and some Scotch and vodka and sandwiches in the summer house. What he *thought* didn't matter.

It all seemed wonderful in anticipation. Reality, though, was a desperate disappointment. I knew Julie found hiding – deception – furtive and sordid. The first time in the summer house, when she was young, the sense of adventure, of desperate need, outweighed every other emotion, but that was years ago; now she was a woman, and though she gave herself to me with love and tenderness, I knew she wasn't happy.

'We'll never do this again,' I promised. 'I don't like it any more than you, this hole-in-the-corner business, but I had to see you.'

'What about the Love Club?'

'I haven't seen Bonnard since before the war.' How odd it sounded, that phrase, 'before the war'! I added, 'I'll find a place somehow.'

I had one other worry on my mind, but this I didn't tell her. My talk at the club with George Hammonds had made me decide to join up. I had never, until now, thought that troops – more troops – would be needed. We had thousands of them sent from home, every one of them grumbling until now because they believed the Japanese would never attack. And even now, as the colonel at the club had spluttered, it was unthinkable that British boys, with British guts and cold steel, could not wipe the floor with a bunch of yellow zombies. And yet – what was it that Papa Jack had said in London before I married? 'Times are changing, and if we don't play our part events may engulf us.' I could see him warning me in the Hyde Park Hotel, hoping I would understand, hoping with fatherly love that his wayward son would be man enough to recognise the moment of change if or when it came, and also be man enough to play a role in it.

Was this the moment of change? Since it was inconceivable that a small country like Japan could ever hope to defeat the combined might of the British Empire and the United States, was it something other than lust for conquest that had prompted this global suicide attack across the length and breadth of the Pacific? Was it a demonstration on behalf of all Asian races to give notice that the white man was no longer invincible? Was that why Japan had launched these savage, dispersed attacks – as a warning, or even more as an act of revenge for insults borne in silence at the hands of the white man? An act in which the symbolic gesture was almost as important as victory; just as in the old days on the negro plantations manacled slaves attacked their masters without caring about the terrible retribution they knew would follow.

I had no desire to go overseas – not now, not with Julie so close – but I just felt, in some bewildered way, that I must do *something*. I was under no illusion that the Japanese would ever reach Singapore itself – the very thought was ridiculous. But perhaps every soldier *did* count in wartime; and, I argued, since I was young and healthy and had a smattering of Chinese and spoke fluent Malay, there must be something I could do to help the war effort.

But despite the horrific news and the sense of urgency, volunteering to join the forces proved extremely difficult, even when using the pull of a *tuan* which enabled me to get an introduction to a recruiting major who had installed himself in a suite at the Adelphi Hotel.

'Appreciate your patriotism,' said the languid, rather precious Colonel Chalfont. 'Damn sporting of you – but I

317

see you're the only Dexter left in the family business. Rubber and tin and shipping eh? Damned important job, yours.'

'Bullshit, Colonel. I've got two bloody good clerks – Ball and Rawlings – who can carry the business on. We only do what the government or army tells us to, anyway.'

'I see you're in the ARP?' He studied the form I had filled in.

'That's for *older* men,' I said patiently. 'And what about my languages? I speak Malay better than I speak English – and Cantonese – surely –?'

'Damn difficult,' he murmured.

'But don't you *want* any soldiers, Colonel?'

'Actual fact, old boy, we don't. Rubber, yes. Cannon fodder, no. Sorry about all that. At the moment you're a reserved occupation. Absolutely vital to the cause. Naturally things change. I'll file your docks away in case.'

I stamped out of the Adelphi into the hot sun, raging as I strode past the Memorial Theatre. 'Bloody fairy,' I muttered to myself. In the bar of the Cricket Club I met Hammonds.

'Christ, George,' I said furiously, 'if that's the sort of second-rater they're sending out – God help Malaya. What's the matter with these bloody men? I'm fit and healthy – don't they want soldiers?'

Good old George. He put his round tin of Players on the bar, polished his glasses, replaced them, looked at me over the rim of his glass and said, 'Perhaps they think there won't be enough time to train you.'

Looking back, I realise that I was wrong about many of the army men as they were about the 'whisky-swilling planters'. But in those days no one thought rationally. All I said was, 'Well, I've done my best.' I mopped my brow. It was a hot, sultry day, and I ordered another stengah for George and a Tiger for me. The sweat came oozing out of my shirt the second I swallowed the first long, frothy mouthful. 'He did say he'd file my particulars,' I said sarcastically. 'But I bet I'll never see that ineffectual little bugger boy again.'

It cannot be easy for those who were not in Singapore at the time to appreciate the bewilderment of that first week of the war. The disasters that hit us like sledgehammer blows, one after the other, were bad enough, but the real agony cut in more deeply, for it had nothing to do with fear or the possibility of defeat, but was compounded of a sense of guilt that we, the inhabitants of a great and noble city, had been found wanting and unprepared, and a bitterness with the government and the military for misleading us, for deliberately concealing the truth. Of course we felt guilty because the civilian preparations – shelters, dugouts, blackouts, hospitals and so on – were pitifully inadequate. We all knew that, not only in Singapore but across Malaya.

But how can you go out and dig a trench when the government says you would be helping to breed mosquitos? How can you learn to roll bandages when everyone in authority laughs at you and promises you that your island fortress is impregnable, impossible to attack from the land, and with guns heavy enough to repulse any sea-borne invasion? Why, the thought of disaster was absurd. The government said so.

And what could you think of your military commanders, some old-fashioned to the point of madness, some just plain stupid? I know I was not the only man who felt a sense of complete helplessness at their antics. I might still have retained a few delusions, had I not, by an extraordinary chance, been summoned to attend a meeting of the War Council as an observer, to answer, if necessary, questions on rubber and tin deliveries and shipping problems.

The War Council met daily, and apparently co-opted civilians with expert knowledge. I found it the most depressing experience of my life. I would never have believed that men in responsible positions could behave as they did. Though Shenton Thomas was the governor, Churchill had sent Duff Cooper to Singapore with Whitehall cabinet rank, a kind of overlord. The commander-in-chief of all forces was Air Chief Marshal Sir Robert Brooke-Popham, and at first I almost burst out laughing, for as Thomas and Duff Cooper sparred verbally, Brooke-Popham had fallen asleep. (I learned later that he often fell asleep on the slightest pretext, and the habit enraged Duff Cooper who had an alert, uncompromising brain.) Suddenly Brooke-Popham woke up and listened to a discussion about who should give and who should take orders. Politely, but firmly, Brooke-Popham said that he took his orders from the chiefs of staff in Whitehall and certainly not from Duff Cooper. 'And I don't propose to change,' he added.

Almost spluttering with rage, Duff Cooper retorted, 'You've produced the worst example of the old school tie I have ever met.'

Brooke-Popham merely smiled quietly and drawled, 'That's not fair.'

Shenton Thomas, I could see, supported Brooke-Popham – which meant that the governor and Duff Cooper were sworn enemies from then on. (In fact Thomas told a friend later, 'From the time of his arrival to the time of his appointment as chairman of the War Council, he was as pleasant as could be; thereafter he was exactly the reverse.')

I left the wrangling in high places with a sense of dismay, made all the worse because I had signed a chit binding me to secrecy and could not even tell friends like George Hammonds what I had learned. Blinded by the sun, sweating from the sudden heat, I made for the car park and drove to the Cricket Club. Perhaps it was as well that my anger had time to cool, that I had a breathing spell, before I learned that at the very time our politicians and officers were quarrelling on this first Wednesday we were about to receive two mortal blows from which civilian morale would never have a chance to recover.

The war was only three days old. And then came the first blow: Japanese forces had attacked the island of Penang – off the *west* coast of Malaya, far from the first Japanese landing on the *east* coast. The streets of George Town, the capital of that beautiful, lazy island four hundred miles or so north of Singapore, were plastered with a boldly printed Order of the Day proclaiming, 'We are ready; our preparations have been made and tested; our defences are strong and our weapons efficient'.

Lies, bloody lies! When the Japanese bombed the island the only defence consisted of two six-pounders. There was not a British fighter in the sky, and more than a thousand people died – believing until the moment of death in British assurances of authority. And when (a week later) the British residents bolted by night – on military orders, abandoning the Asians – they left Penang Radio Station in working order, an oil refinery, oil and petrol warehouses and scores of boats, all gifts to the Japanese.

In a way Penang appalled us more than the next catastrophe, which followed later the same day. I had reached the Cricket Club and was on the verandah sitting in a long chair, my legs resting on its swivelling extensions, when I realised that the radio music had stopped, that a voice was speaking. The Cricket Club was always noisy – but suddenly there was an uncanny silence, the room behind me utterly still except for one voice announcing that Britain's two great ships, the battleship *Prince of Wales* and the battle-cruiser *Repulse* had been sunk by Japanese aircraft.

The silence continued for perhaps thirty seconds – until an elderly member dropped his glass. Like a starting pistol the sudden shattering noise began a pandemonium of bewildered conversation. Someone I had never seen, one of dozens of honorary members, walked near me and stood leaning on the green railings looking over the padang. He turned to me, nodded, but he was really not speaking to me, he was voicing thoughts he could no longer keep to himself. 'Within a few days the Japs have bombed Singapore,' he muttered, 'captured a strategic airfield, taken Penang and sunk two of our biggest warships. Christ! There must be something bloody wrong somewhere.'

I met Julie again on the Friday evening, thanks to Paul. I was sure he knew what had happened on that last Sunday of peace, for he certainly knew about the past, and since he himself was no slouch with the girls he must have guessed that we didn't spend Sunday afternoon looking at the ocean in front of the Sea View. But all he said was, 'Julie's been working round the clock, but she's got Friday night off and needs cheering up. Let's all three dine at Raffles.'

They arrived together, Julie wearing a long white dress that accentuated her pale gold skin and dark hair. Her only jewellery was a thick flat gold necklace. Since it was Friday, Paul and I both wore mess jackets and black ties. I didn't kiss her, even on the cheek, for this was Raffles Hotel, the island's greatest outpost of gossip. We ordered stengahs and settled down to enjoy an evening in the rambling, ornate hotel which had been a part of our lives since we first learned to dance and was now doing its best to live up to the motto of 'business as usual'.

The square tables were grouped round the large dance floor, and in one corner several had been placed together for a party of about thirty noisy people. As we arrived, the band struck up 'Happy Birthday!' and the party raised their glasses as a Chinese waiter brought in a white cake, alive with a ring of small, flickering candles. At the Long Bar at the far end of the room a couple of men were arguing loudly; they had the tanned look, the easy slouch, of planters. Near them a party of officers in best blues, together with their ladies, regarded them with distaste, but the planters never noticed through the haze of their alcoholic fumes.

It was obviously a point of honour with the management not to let the Japanese interfere with anyone's evening of pleasure. Fresh orchids decorated every table in the vast roofed-over verandah. Behind the room lay the cropped lawns, with their line of tall, fan-like traveller's palms. Before the war the gardens had always been illuminated, and the front of the dance room had been open to the sea. Now it was blacked out – after a fashion – and despite the whirring of a dozen fans I was soon sweating. Paul of course looked as though he had just come out of a bandbox. He never looked hot, his clothes never seemed to crease, he was always cool and calm, with that slightly sardonic look.

'Did you suggest this evening?' I asked her when we ambled through a slow fox-trot played by Dan Hopkins and his band on the platform opposite the Long Bar.

'Of course,' she whispered. 'I had to see you – even like

this, surrounded by other people.'

'I've tried to find a place, but no luck. Are you still living at home?'

She nodded. 'But the Alexandra has said that if I want to live in I can – because of transport difficulties.'

'Would your father mind?'

'He's resigned to the emancipation of women in wartime.'

'But,' – I was thinking aloud – 'supposing I *could* find a place – a flat or something. Tell me – could you pretend to the family that you had to live in at the Alexandra – and then – if I could find a place?'

'Live with you – a married man?' There was nothing in the world more wonderful than Julie's directness, her enthusiasm, born really of a sense of honesty. 'Yes, I could – and I would,' she answered simply and added with an almost mischievous grin, 'and I'm sure I could arrange to be always on duty and available if anyone was nosey enough to phone the hospital.' She hesitated then added, 'The only thing is – it's one thing to spend a night at Tasek Layang. It's carrying everything a stage further if we *live* together. Quite apart from the fact that it's hard to keep a secret, it *is* involving everyone – including you and Irene.'

I was silent for a moment and then, as we danced slowly round the room, I said, 'I wish you hadn't said that. I just want to forget – *everything*. You know that corny old phrase, live for today.'

Very slightly, not to be noticed by other couples, I felt the pressure of her arm on my shoulder tighten. 'This *is* life for today, Johnnie. And' – she smiled over my shoulder to someone she knew, and kept looking as though we were discussing the weather – 'don't be afraid. When the war's over, that'll be it.'

'Maybe I won't feel like that. Perhaps I will refuse to end it.'

'You'll have to, darling. You can get away with murder in wartime but not afterwards.'

'But everything's *changing*. Don't you realise that? Even when we've won, when the troops have gone, Singapore will be different, even if it's still British. It'll never be the same again.'

'We'll see,' she smiled fondly. 'I have a new name for you. You're not the demon Dexter, you're the dreamer Dexter. I like men who dream.'

I took her back to our table. It never *had* entered my head to break up my marriage, to split the family. I had always loved Julie, but abandoning Bengy – and one more child? – well, it was a big step. Yet, though I realised the dangers, I wanted to see Julie more than just occasionally; I wanted to wake up in her arms each morning and have breakfast together.

In the past I had wanted to marry her – all dreams, impossible to realise. But now, with the trick that war had played on all our lives, couldn't we *play* at being husband and wife for a little while?

'All right,' I whispered during the next dance, 'I'll settle for now – for the time being. And pray that now lasts forever.'

'That's a terrible thing to say.'

'It's how I feel. But what I have to do now is find a place for you. I want everything with you to be clean and – you know – no underhand back street hotels. Something will sort itself out.'

In fact everything was 'sorted out' later that night – and by the Japanese. We were all struggling through the evening, which in spite of Julie's presence tended to drag, but which I could not bear to end. The indifferent blackout arrangements meant that we could hardly see each other. A few couples danced round the floor and there was a certain amount of forced banter as they bumped into each other, with cries of 'I *knew* it would be you with those big feet!' Most of us carried pencil torches so we could distinguish which chits to sign. But I couldn't really dance with Julie too often and leave Paul sitting alone in the semi-dark.

The evening ended abruptly – with the wail of the sirens. Every waiter bolted. I saw one man at the birthday table gulp a swig from the whisky bottle standing near the cake. Then he took another long gulp before making for the doors. Almost immediately I heard the swoosh of bombs, though some distance away. All the lights went out.

'Let's go, Paul,' Julie turned to her brother instinctively. 'I'm always scared when we leave Father alone.'

'Me too,' I yelled. 'Grandpa Jack's all alone in Tanamera.'

We had both parked our cars in Beach Road between Raffles and the sea.

'You take Julie,' shouted Paul thoughtfully. 'We'll meet by our front gate.' As I turned right at the corner and drove up Bras Basah Road, we could hear more bombs dropping.

'I'm not *afraid* for Father,' Julie held my arm. 'I just don't like him to be alone, that's all. You feel the same about Grandpa Jack, don't you?'

Nodding, I watched the dark road carefully. Most street lamps were out and the moon was on the wane. The brightness of that first night of bombs had dimmed, and I had to concentrate. As I was about to cross the corner at North Bridge Road, I slowed down and nearly jumped out of the car when a clap of anti-aircraft fire blasted my ears.

'Guns in the Cathedral grounds,' I yelled. 'Enough to wake the dead!'

In the hot night air, with suddenly a whiff of the Singapore River outsmelling cordite, noise hit us everywhere. Guns, shouts, screams, everything was mixed as though the death throes of squealing pigs were mingling with the machinery of a Chicago meat packer. From time to time a different, more menacing sound, a sinister whistle descending the chromatic scale, dampened every other sound; the short, heart-pounding wait – each moment an eternity – for the crump of the bomb, wondering where it would land – how near, how distant, with untold thousands (liars if they denied it) uttering unspoken prayers, 'Oh God! Let it not hit me.' With the noise was anguished movement, figures running blindly, screaming, whimpering, uncanny, eerie movements, ghosts darting across darkened streets.

As we crossed Victoria Street an ancient fire engine showing no lights, the clang of bells hardly sounding above the general noise, raced across our path, almost hitting us. I couldn't see Paul's car – not that it really mattered; we would meet at the gates. There was no cause for fear, for the bombs were obviously dropping some distance from us. I wondered if perhaps the Japanese were aiming for the McRitchie reservoir.

At Bencoolen Street a soldier waved a torch to stop us. He displayed a military police armband.

'What the bloody hell are you doing out in this?' he shouted. 'Take shelter! Nobody's allowed out in the street.'

'And nobody's allowed to shine a torch,' I shouted back rashly. 'You trying to tell the Japs where we are?'

He shone the torch in my face, saw my mess jacket and black tie, sneered, 'Mr Clever, eh? It's monkeys like you in monkey jackets who are going to give the Japs a present of Singapore. Get out of the bloody car.'

I felt Julie's hand pressing my knee, warning me not to lose my temper – especially in a situation I could never win.

'I'm just taking this lady home, sergeant.' I tried to be polite. 'She lives up the road.' He swivelled the beam of light towards the left-hand seat, picking out Julie's face. In the reflected light I could see his leer. 'Ah! Like that is it? A bit of chocolate? Well, bugger off,' and then to me he added, 'I hope you get a dose. Serve you fucking well right.'

At that moment – just when I could stand it no longer – a bomb fell. It must have been in Jalan Besar or Serangoon Road. The stationary Morris lurched, half left the ground. As the soldier leaning over the open door window stumbled, I jammed the car into gear and shot off. 'How *dare* he say that,' I was almost sobbing, 'my lovely Julie!'

Even as I drove she leaned over, kissing me gently, soothing me, whispering, 'It means nothing.'

I planned to bear right into Selegie Road, but three ambulances blocked the junction of the corner of Orchard Road. I could see a fire raging ahead at the junction with Bukit Timah Road. Another ambulance raced past, bells clanging. A man with an ARP helmet – one of the few helmets issued to volunteers – came up as I stopped.

'Bad?' I asked.

'A big one.' He was polite and I recognised him in a vague sort of way. 'Better get home as fast as you can.' There was nothing for it but to turn off Orchard Road. We skirted the grounds of Government House, and went straight up Clemenceau Avenue until it joined Bukit Timah Road.

'We'll be home –' I started to speak then stopped. Straight ahead, to the left of Bukit Timah Road, flames seared the night. For no reason I thought for a split second of a Guy Fawkes party in the English countryside when I was a boy, and the outsized fire on the village green. Bukit Timah Road was dotted with lavish bungalows, well separated by their compounds, and at the moment we turned in from Clemenceau Avenue it was impossible to see where the blaze was coming from because the houses were set back from the road.

'Hurry, darling,' Julie begged me – until I jammed the brakes as my front wheels lurched into a tangled skein of hoses and pipes from the fire engine. Standing out starkly against the red sky behind was yet another engine, blocking our path.

'It's our house!' cried Julie.

'Don't worry – it's not yours,' I said. 'But we'll have to walk.' And then as we clambered out of the car I realised, 'My God! It's Tanamera. Grandpa Jack!'

Tanamera, with its large grounds, stood much farther back from the road than any of its neighbours, so that any blaze was hidden by trees between the house and the road. Only the glow in the sky, like the sunset fade-out in one of the FitzPatrick travelogues (shown regularly in those days) glowing above the black, jagged silhouette of the trees warned me.

The gates of the Soong house were three hundred yards or so before Tanamera, and Paul was waiting for us.

'I haven't been to see,' he said, 'but a fireman told me the house hasn't been hit. A bomb hit the outbuildings at the back, the servants' quarters, but you'd better rush, Johnnie. I'll take Julie home.'

'Hear anything about Grandpa Jack?'

He shook his head.

'See you,' I kissed Julie briefly, forgetting Paul was there. No, not forgetting: not worrying.

Outside the gates Li stood in shorts and singlet, forlorn, weeping, a white phantom against the dying red backdrop, arms outstretched as though beseeching help, crying, '*Tuan! Tuan!* They take *tuan* Glanpa Jack away.'

'What the hell do you mean,' I tried to rush past him.

'He very okay,' cried Li, 'No worry.'

'But – take him *away*? My grandfather? What happened? Why?'

'Bomb hit near house. Glanpa Jack very excited, he laugh, he think very nice. He keep on laughing, but firemen say not good leave old man alone.'

My heart settled. I had for a moment felt the shock might have killed him. But as I gave a huge sigh of relief I realised that what Li said made sense. I cursed myself for ever having left a man in a wheelchair all alone. But that was unfair to me – I had to leave him for hours during the day. 'You okay, Li? And the others? Nobody hurt?'

'Very okay, *tuan*. House okay too. Back buildings die of fire.'

'Die?' I thought he meant some of the staff.

'No. We all okay. Only buildings die. Tanamera okay.'

Where had Grandpa Jack gone? I wondered. He would be mad with rage at being treated like an invalid! I had to find out where he was. I realised I was still standing at the gates amid mud from leaking hoses. Firemen had broken the fence and trampled down the screen of shrubs in order to get their engines and ladders to the rear of the house, and I could see the ruts which the engines had churned in the lawns and beds of cannas which had always been Papa's pride. I found myself muttering, 'My God! Papa Jack'll play hell if he ever sees this.' As I started to run down the gravel drive I almost bumped into a man with a short white beard.

'Wilf,' I cried. 'How bad is it?'

Wilf Broadbent was a professional fire chief who had been seconded to head the Auxiliary Fire Service, a mainly volunteer force formed in case the war which nobody expected did break out. Already he had done a fine job. Wilf was a real professional; we had known him for years.

'Where's Grandpa Jack?' I asked.

'General hospital. Was he mad! But we couldn't leave him here.'

'I'll go and see him right away.'

'I wouldn't bother, Johnnie. The ambulance men gave him a pill. He needs rest. It's a shattering shock, you know, for an old man. He won't wake up till morning.'

'The building?'

'No real damage – and by a miracle no one was in the outbuildings behind, or they'd all have been killed. The house wasn't hit, but I wouldn't sleep there until it's been properly checked for structural weaknesses. It's an old house, you know.'

The next morning, after a wretched night in which I disregarded Wilf's advice and tried to sleep in the Married Quarters, I made straight for the General Infirmary to see Grandpa Jack. I was dreading telling him he couldn't return to Tanamera, but to my surprise he took the news more calmly than I had expected.

'A few yards nearer,' he chuckled, 'and you wouldn't be saying good morning to me. But I'll be back as soon as I feel a bit stronger.'

I didn't know quite what to do with him. He couldn't be left alone any more, with raids increasing in violence and frequency.

'I hate to say this,' I told him, 'but for the moment – for a little while – you will be able to get better attention here.' I didn't dare to tell him that the private room to which he had been taken might not be private much longer. Julie had told me horrific tales of wounded being forced to sleep on corridor floors. But we would meet that problem later.

'I'll come and see you every day,' I told him, and quite meekly he said, 'That's great, young feller-me-lad.' Not until I had left the hospital did it occur to me that Grandpa Jack had really suffered a traumatic shock. The bomb at the back might only have been a small one, but it was close — and he knew it. It had calmed down the old tiger for the first time in years.

I had several things to do. I had to cable Papa Jack. The news wasn't that bad, Tanamera had not actually been hit, but I would have to let him know and that his own father was being comfortably treated in the General. And I had to let him know that I wasn't in fact staying — for the time being anyway — at Tanamera; if only because Tanamera was a famous landmark in Singapore and if by chance it was bombed again — and destroyed — well, it was the sort of news item that might be published in the London newspapers. (That was the way my mind reasoned. I didn't know that newspapers in Britain were only two or four sheets, with no room to spare for that kind of news, even if it passed the censor.) I had to let Irene know. They were minor problems, but they had to be done.

More serious was the question of where I could sleep, for Wilf had been right. Part of the first-floor landing had given way when I walked on it. A banister on the double staircase leading from the ballroom came away in my hands. The magnificent white walls of Tanamera still stood — nothing would shake *them*, I thought — but it was obvious that Tanamera was not safe structurally. Meanwhile, where would I sleep?

I set off for the office in Robinson Road, mentally preparing myself to break the news to the staff that Tanamera had had a near miss, and was no longer habitable — for the time being anyway. But they knew all about it long before I arrived, even that its structure had to be examined. At the top of the stone steps I shouted for someone to make coffee, and I had no sooner sat down in my small office — small because we had recently installed air conditioning — before Ball and Rawlings tapped on the plate glass of the door. They wore the smug looks that so often appear on the faces of people offering sympathy. I should have known the efficiency of the Singapore grapevine. I cut short their commiseration with a curt, 'There's a war on, remember.' Ten minutes later Rawlings came back and asked if he could have a word with me.

Though as a *tuan* I was treated with the dignity the position warranted, Ball and Rawlings always exercised a little familiarity. They had helped to train me, and in the early days when I was learning the business I had often turned to them for help since they were more polite in giving advice than my father would have been.

'I wondered if you've decided where you're going to live now?' Rawlings peered at me through pebble glasses that always gave him a slightly worried look.

'Sit down.' I poured him some coffee from the Thermos, adding, 'I haven't the foggiest idea.'

'I just thought,' he said tentatively, 'what about the Cadet House?'

I must have looked astonished. 'But the army's in it,' I said.

The Cadet House on the edge of the Tanglin area had been bought by the firm long before I was born and transformed into a block of old-fashioned service flatlets – a kind of mess – for the young cadets we recruited in London as trainees for the business in the old days, most of them to return to London after a year or so of training in Singapore. Both Ball and Rawlings had lived there as bachelor trainees before marrying and settling in Singapore, instead of returning to London, as Cowley had been forced to do after his 'Indian adventure'.

'The army didn't want it,' said Rawlings. 'Too small, they said. I didn't worry you about the details.'

'Any of the rooms empty?'

'The whole building's empty. It's furnished, of course – pretty rough, but –'

'Servants?'

He shook his head. 'No one had lived there for three months.'

'Got the keys? You have? Go and fetch them, there's a good chap. I'll drive up and see what it looks like. Send a syce with the office car to collect Li at Tanamera and tell him

331

to drive Li straight to the Cadet House and wait for me if he gets there first.'

The Cadet House! It was years since I had visited this institution in our firm, the sort of place that elderly directors in London, like the late Mr Cowley, looked back on with the envy of age for youth, remembering their first fling in a tropical country. Just past the end of Orchard Road I branched left towards Tanglin instead of taking the right-hand fork up Orange Grove Road. Here Orchard Road became Nassim Road and within three minutes I saw the sign on the right, Nassim Hill. It was hardly a hill, not even a road, but little more than a lane with a slight incline, and at the end a sign, Cadet House, in front of the big white building, with its dark roof and mock-Tudor beams; a sweep of gravel led round the left-hand side to the front door.

I switched off the engine under the portico. The entrance was on my right. On my left lawns sloped away to clumps of bamboo at the bottom of the large garden.

My heart was pounding, my mouth suddenly dry – not with recollections of the past, but because of the wild idea that had come to me the second Rawlings told me this place was empty – an idea that had been spinning round my brain for every second of the drive along Orchard Road.

Why not? If ever man had built a perfect hiding place, this was it. Secluded, few neighbours, empty for three months, it might have been built for the two of us.

But would Julie come? Would she dare? Until this wretched war started – this blessed war, I thought for one wicked, selfish moment – the idea would have been laughable, but now she was needed away from home and the Alexandra provided a perfect alibi. With a war raging, with bombs falling, even the strictest father could not stop her doing war work; and it would obviously be impossible to telephone her easily; indeed, she had already told me that colleagues would help her if she was supposed to be in the hospital and wasn't. She could in theory live in at the hospital; in practice she could stay at the Cadet House. Of course she would agree! She was Julie!

The front door was unlocked, but though the bungalow

was not occupied neither was it empty. I heard a cry of surprise. Two Chinese women emerged, bowing and grinning. They spoke Cantonese and explained that as part of a routine office arrangement they came twice a week to clean up, to keep down the ants and mice and make sure the place had not been burgled.

I remembered a communal dining room on the ground floor, and opened the door to the right. The room was still furnished with a heavy old table and six solid chairs round it. In the hall a staircase led to the so-called flats – nothing more, really, than comfortable bedrooms – each with a cold shower, and a balcony large enough to rank as a private room for those who didn't want to mingle in the 'mess'. In the centre of the first floor, near the bedrooms, was a large square 'outdoor room', built over the roof of the portico, and furnished mostly with teak and rattan. I lingered at the far end, leaning on the rails, looking over the garden, beautiful, green, still fairly well kept. In days gone by there had been a tennis court on the lower of two terraces, the top garden separated from the bottom half by a sharp slope with half a dozen steps cut into the grassy bank so spectators could watch the tennis. I had a sudden memory of Sunday afternoons at Wimbledon. At the far end thick bamboo not only hid the sight of busy Napier Road, but most of the sounds as well.

It was still only ten o'clock when Li arrived, and I felt a stab of guilt as the office car crunched to a halt on the drive. It was one thing for a man to make love to a girl while his wife was away (and could never find out) but wasn't this a fearful further step for the father of a fine son to take? I would be setting up house – for the duration of the war. And not doing this in some remote place where I had been posted, but in Singapore, the city I would one day have to share again with Irene and Ben.

As Li got out of the car I said, 'This is our new home. Keep the office car all day. Just go backwards and forwards and get enough clothes or anything else you can carry from Tanamera. If you need anything you can't find there, buy it.'

I gave him some money, adding, 'Better leave Cookie at Tanamera. He would be upset moving.' That was true, but that was not the only reason I wanted to leave him there. Cookie had served us for a long, long time, and his loyalties might lie with Mama more than with me. Better not to have a spy. And any structural defects in Tanamera wouldn't worry him. They would rebuild the shacks in the kampong behind in a matter of days.

'Can you find a new cookie?' I asked Li.

'Can do.' His face beamed with delight of adventure, and he added, 'My father at General with *tuan* Glandpa Jack.'

For a moment I thought old Li had been taken ill. He must have been nearly as old as Grandpa Jack – not really, but he looked as old. 'No, no, he velly well,' Li reassured me. 'He want be next to *tuan* Glanpa, so arrangements made he sleep in corridor.'

I could feel the pleasure bursting inside Li – the wonderful pride that makes the Chinese so devoted – and my heart, too, was bursting with excitement at the thought of what I would soon be telling Julie. I decided to take Li into my confidence. I couldn't keep the secret from my own servant so it was better to tell him the truth right from the start. Anyway, he knew about the past.

'You have been with me a long time, Li, I trust you, so be careful with your words.' At my severe appearance he looked horrified at the prospect of being thought anything but discreet. I added, 'Missee coming to stay with me here.'

For a second he seemed not to understand, then beamed, 'Memsahib come back?'

I shook my head. He beamed again, even more happily, as he realised who was coming.

The phone wasn't working, but I knew the office could pull strings to get it reconnected. I drove to the Goodwood Park Hotel, in those days small and cosy with its two red tennis courts by the side of the road. A boy brought me a Tiger beer and I took it to the phone in the corner of the modest reception area and asked the clerk to get me the Alexandra Hospital.

'Darling, wonderful Julie, I've found it – our place, our

first home together,' I said, and started blurting out a torrent of details.

'Wait a minute,' she laughed, 'What's this all about?'

I explained to her and then – tortured by a sudden doubt – I asked, 'You will come, won't you?'

'Of course. You know that.'

I had already planned what to do. 'Go home after your shift at the hospital,' I suggested, 'and just tell your father you've been ordered to live in at the Alexandra. You've got tomorrow morning off, I believe? Then I'll meet you outside Robinson's at noon for coffee.'

'Robinson's? Isn't that risky?'

'Just this once, to arrange things. We can always say we bumped into each other if someone sees us.'

So we agreed to meet the next morning, and that is what I meant when I said that the Japanese arranged everything for us.

21

Early in the morning a curtain of rain blotted out Singapore. I had dossed down in the Cadet House, and at six Li slid into the room with a tea tray on which no spoons, cups or saucers had ever been known to clatter. I was awakened with a time-honoured ritual. Carefully opening the door, he began to murmur a soft, indistinguishable tune, almost like a prayer chant. Every morning he sang it, and years ago I had asked him what he was singing, and he answered simply, 'Nothing, *tuan*.' 'Then why sing?' 'So *tuan* not wake up too sudden and frightened,' he beamed. I had been sung awake ever since.

As I sipped my tea, the rain lashed down across the roof, slanting diagonally away from the verandah, a sheet of water so fierce I could not even see the bamboo clumps at the bottom of the garden. It was the kind of tropical rain that made it necessary for every bungalow to have a large portico, so that after breakfast and a shower I was able to jump into my Morris without wearing a raincoat which would have drenched me in sweat.

As I turned into Orchard Road the rain belted down so hard that for a few moments I had to stop the car. The wipers simply could not make an impression on the sheets of water and I could see nothing ahead. After a few minutes I started to drive slowly towards the civic centre. The concrete ditches edging the pavements were a swilling, swirling mass of tumbling water. And then, as I reached Stamford Road, near the YMCA, I drove out of the rain. One moment it was beating down mercilessly, the next, Stamford Road was as dry as a bone. It hadn't rained at all, the dry roadway was separated from the rainy one by a demarcation line as straight as if someone had used a ruler.

After checking the office post I walked along Robinson Road to Raffles Place. Julie arrived at Robinson's on the dot of noon, looking cool in a short-sleeved white blouse and a lime green skirt. She never attempted to cover any embarrassment she might have felt with feeble, forced humour. There was no mock-cheerful, 'Well, here I am, the die is cast,' small talk. Not even a squeeze on the arm to mark the fact that we were entering a new kind of relationship; for on this day the era of snatched nights of love was about to end; she was coming to live with me. Secretly, we hoped – but who could be sure of that? Looking at her I thought rashly, 'Who gives a damn, anyway?'

I was very proud of her that morning, for to Julie this must have been a momentous decision; and though she had made it instantly she must have known that if the secret were ever discovered – that she had become the mistress of a married man – her father would disown her without hesitation. Chinese etiquette enforced stricter penalties than any in the West. She would never be allowed to enter her father's home again.

How extraordinary – and how wonderful – women are in their attitude to the great decisions they have taken, the manner in which, once the decision *has* been taken, sentiment and romance give way almost immediately to a sense of the practical.

At this moment, ordering coffee in Robinson's, she had left home, lied to her father, and (as she told me later) arranged a kind of cover-up at the Alexandra Hospital. To me, sitting there, looking at her, I was still struggling with the emotions that her actions had aroused in me – thinking how much she must love me to do such a thing, to take such a risk, when she asked me, 'What about the black-out?'

'The *what*?' I was so startled I had no idea what she was talking about.

'At *home*, darling.' We might have been a married couple discussing the house in which we had lived for years. 'The windows in the Cadet House.'

'I've never given the matter a moment's thought. All I've been thinking about is the romantic notion of carrying you across the threshold when we get there.'

We were drinking coffee in the basement, where Robinson's had installed a makeshift café after their much-publicised air-conditioned restaurant was bombed in the first raid.

'I know that, but we must have some curtains or something, so we might as well buy them while we're here. If anyone sees us together I can say we met by chance and I'm helping you.'

It took us nearly an hour to get near the counter selling bolts of cloth. Almost in a panic, frenzied women begged for material to black out their windows and open doorways. Luckily there was plenty for sale. The trouble was lack of assistants. Some were cleaning up a carpet of broken glass, others were removing damaged furniture. There was an uneasy despair about the way people moved, not worried by the prospect of being involved in any actual fighting but beginning to realise the inconvenience that would follow the battles far to the north. We managed to buy several yards of material, not enough for a complete black-out – that was impossible in the sweltering heat of Singapore anyway – but for a compromise brown-out that we

337

planned, so that just enough light from the inside rooms would filter out on to the balcony where, like most Europeans in Singapore, we expected to spend the evenings, ready to switch off the lights when the sirens sounded.

Apart from the ground floor, which had always been used as common rooms, the Cadet House had five bedrooms with showers, and I had picked the largest, a corner room with a wide verandah running round two sides and overlooking the garden. It was furnished with a rattan sofa, three or four chairs and a table large enough to serve breakfast on. The big bedroom was painted white, with a touch of green on the woodwork. In the centre of the ceiling an ancient four-bladed fan made frightening, clanking noises. Originally, as in all the rooms in the Cadet House, there had been only one bed. Li, aided by friends – house-boys of neighbouring houses always helped each other out for a small consideration which, presumably, was added to the grocery bill – brought in an identical bed from another room, and another night table. I had no fancy to spend this idyllic 'honeymoon' with the girl I loved in a single bed, so I decided to buy a double mattress to cover both beds. However, when I started to throw my weight around, it got me nowhere. Didn't I know there was a war on? Finally Li and I laid two mattresses cross-ways across both beds. Some of the rooms were interlinked – after all, this had originally been built as a private house – and Li turned the room next to our bedroom into a dressing room, not so much because I wanted to dress alone, but in order to store my clothes and give Julie more room for hers.

Out of nowhere Li had rounded up his relations – an amah to wash, another to cook (there was by now a scarcity of cook boys) and a small, shy Indian boy who cleaned my Morris, for I had decided that Papa Jack's *syce*, in his white suit with velvet *songkok* on his head, should be attached to the office, to transport staff in difficult times and generally run errands. I could use him if necessary, but I had never had a driver of my own.

Julie had a small car too. She had learned to drive in

America, though at first when she started working full time at the Alexandra her father had insisted on sending her to the hospital with a driver; but soon, with Paul's help, she had persuaded him that there was nothing immoral in a girl driving.

The radio begged us daily to build shelters, but as so often happens with official advice in times of stress it wasn't as easy as the announcer made it sound; however, Li and his colleagues took several mattresses from other beds and put them on top of the dining room table downstairs, then stacked chairs and other furniture to make a wall round it. It would never resist a direct hit, but it might save us from splinters. And at least we had virtually no glass round us – few windows, and only one or two mirrors. Though we blacked out our bedroom with the material we had bought at Robinson's we had nothing to dim the lights downstairs – in the hall for example, until Li on one of his foraging trips to Tanamera returned triumphantly bearing two large parcels. They held brocaded Indian shawls and some lengths of silk which Irene had planned to take home as presents until at the last moment she was warned to restrict the amount of luggage.

At first Li tried to pin them together to cover our windows, but he wasn't very successful, and of course we didn't have the trained staff from Tanamera.

'Here, give it to me,' said Julie, and out of nowhere produced an old-fashioned brocaded sewing box.

'You don't *sew*!'

'Why not? I'm a home girl at heart. Mummy taught me all the arts.' It gave me a turn of happiness to watch her sewing the shawls together, holding the needle up to the light as she tried to thread it, and then, the job done, examining the sewn-up pieces to see if they would hold, and finally biting off the end of the cotton and sticking the needle into a pincushion.

Almost sadly, I said, 'You should be married, a mother.'

'If only I could be,' she sighed. 'But the one thing above all that we have to remember is – discretion. This is our secret life. Don't forget, I'm a quarter Malay, and the

Moslems have a saying, "A sin concealed is two parts forgiven."'

Despite the shattering reverses up-country, despite the extra work entailed by ARP duty, the last two weeks in December were the happiest in all my life. Because the raids were less frequent, the tension slackened. And though there was no immediate danger the sensation of unease, of an evil snake creeping nearer each day, gave a zest to life and love, a feeling that every moment was too precious not to be savoured to the full. When most husbands in Singapore embarked on love affairs while their wives were in England the in-built knowledge that the *mem* would return at a given date added a kind of piquancy to an affair; but with us the excitement was intensified because our life in the Cadet House would not end with the arrival of a ship and its passengers on a given date for which we could prepare; but by the fortunes of war over which we had no control.

'Even though we're surrounded by people,' said Julie, lying next to me on the bed one morning, 'it's like living on a desert island. Of course we know it'll have to end – but we don't know when or how.' Another morning she asked me, 'Do you ever feel any pangs of guilt?'

'About ruining the reputation of a beautiful girl?' I tried to skirt round her real question.

'You haven't ruined me, darling,' she sounded almost sad for a moment. 'There's an old Chinese saying that everyone lives a hundred lives, but only one of them is a life to remember. This is *my* life to remember. I shall never ask for any more favours, because nothing can be as beautiful as this.'

'Well, I don't feel guilty,' I said. 'I dare say I would if after making love to you, I had to go back to a wife and children and tell lies, but I don't have to do that. For the moment – for the duration, as they call it – you are my wife. I know that's not fair to Irene, but that's the way I feel.'

'Sometimes I *do* feel wicked about what we're doing,' Julie went on. 'Isn't it awful that people have to steal from other people in order to be happy? Sometimes I feel I ought to go home – and then *you* arrive – late, tired out, and then you touch me, and I think, how much longer? One day? One hour? One minute? Don't we have the right to live it since we *are* here? We *are* breathing an air that kills. That's it – *kills*. Where did I read those words?'

She went to the small desk where she kept her books of poetry and riffled through the pages. It always amazed me that Julie could somehow remember just where she had read something; the book, the page even. This was another of her anthologies.

'I like dipping into them when I'm on night duty and things are quiet,' she had once explained. 'Ah! Here it is, "the air that kills". It makes me shudder with fear. Listen – it's by Housman: 'Into my heart an air that kills From yon far country blows.' Doesn't that sum up everything the Japs are doing to us?' she asked.

It *was* like being on a desert island (except when I was at the office). I had no real idea where anyone was; the only member of the family I could even picture was Papa Jack. I could see him in Cowley's office at the corner of Swallow Street, and I could visualise him in the Hyde Park Hotel where he was living. But the existences of the others were blurred by lack of knowledge.

I had no idea where Tony Scott was until one morning he telephoned me.

'Thank God' – the line was quite clear – 'I'm in KL, but it's taken three days to get through to you. Where's Natasha?'

'You haven't heard?'

'Not a word. I was told to report to the Volunteers on the Sunday – and I've never been back to Ara. Not for a second. I got into an armoured car and the next thing we were heading for Sungei Siput. I just had to go. I didn't even have a spare handkerchief. It's been bloody hell ever since – we've been pushed back every hour of every day.'

I was able to tell him that Natflat and Victoria were in New York with Irene.

'Thank God for that.' I could hear the sigh of relief on the phone. Like every soldier I spoke to, his attitude changed immediately he knew his family was safe.

'I can't write from here,' said Tony. 'There's nothing – not pen or ink. I can't even get a piece of paper for a shit! But I've got to let her know I'm all right.'

I thought for a few minutes. I wondered if he knew about the baby on the way, if Natasha had told him at the last minute. I hadn't the faintest idea.

'Posting letters is pretty hopeless here too,' I said, 'but I know – I'll send a subtle cable to Papa Jack asking him to forward information to our New York office.'

'That's great. You heard anything?'

'A couple of letters from Irene, one written before the Pearl Harbor bust-up.'

'I bet you miss her, Johnnie. But thank God the girls aren't here. I tell you, these Japs are buggers for handing out punishment. I'll –' then the crackling went dead. The line had been cut.

Talking to Tony had been wonderful – and yet only increased my sense of anger and frustration at still being a civilian. An air that kills: how right Julie was! In the midst of all my happiness I felt more and more guilty not to be in uniform, not be doing *something* to help save not only ourselves but the city. I had tried to enlist, only to be turned down by that ridiculous Colonel Chalfont. But it made no difference, so that I began to imagine that army officers were treating with contempt all civilians whose cushy, easy life they had been ordered to safeguard. In the Tanglin Club, where senior officers automatically became honorary members, some of them did refuse to talk to civilians, to join them for drinks.

Relations had become even more strained over a series of incidents which had shown up civilians in an appalling light. When the army wanted to cut down some trees in one of the golf club grounds in order to site some AA guns, the secretary had primly told them they couldn't possibly do such a thing until after the next committee meeting. The army had been exasperated in all sorts of ways – by the sloppy, conflicting attitudes of the civilian government, by the lack of shelters, the inadequate fire precautions in China-town where the wooden buildings invited a blaze, cried out to be set on fire. And even though at times I was annoyed by the gibes, I could see why the army didn't think much of us.

In the Cricket Club, though, it was different. The officers were younger, everything was a great adventure to them, they were thirsting for 'a scrap'. But it was obvious that even they didn't think much of the Volunteers or the Malay Regiment. Paul had been turned down again for the Malay Regiment because he was officially classed as Chinese. I had been turned down by Chalfont on the grounds that I was organising the supply of vitally needed war materials. It was true — but God! I was too young and too fit to be doing that sort of job. And in a curious way it was the very happiness with Julie that made me feel it must be paid for.

22

Just before Christmas I was trying to sort out a shipment of rubber that we had to get away after the vessel which should have taken it was bombed in the harbour, and I had been battling all day with some naval commander unable to grasp the fact that in order to ship the rubber for which Britain and America were clamouring we had to have a ship.

The trouble was that when dealing with the military you couldn't act like a *tuan*. You couldn't lose your temper. From the time of Grandpa Jack — even before, I suppose — any hitch in arrangements had caused an apoplectic outburst that was followed miraculously by instant action. But the first time I had lost my temper on the phone with a particularly obtuse colonel who refused to let a load of tin ore through, he had said frostily, 'Listen, you cocky little bastard. The next time you speak to me like that I'll have you arrested.' Then he had banged the receiver down and it took us ten days to get the ore, which was barely half a mile away, but which nobody could release without his signed order.

I was facing a similar problem now, and I had been trying most of the morning to keep my temper with this navy man. So I wasn't in a particularly receptive mood when the phone on my desk tinkled and a languid voice asked, 'John Dexter?'

Where had I heard that voice before? I knew it vaguely, though I was unable to place it. 'Yes,' I said irritably, 'I'm very busy, I'm afraid. Who's that?'

'Terribly sorry to interrupt you old boy,' the familiar voice apologised. 'Robin Chalfont here.'

The name meant nothing to me. 'You're on the wrong line,' I said, 'Hang on – I'll get you put through to the general office.' Before he could say anything I had put the old-fashioned earpiece on my desk and shouted, 'Rawlings! Get this call transferred. I don't know who he wants.'

I heard the click as the call was taken off my line. Two minutes later Rawlings knocked on the door and peered round, pebble glasses like a pair of binoculars.

'It *is* for you – it's a Colonel Chalfont.'

Christ! It was the fairy who didn't want me to become a soldier. Maybe he's changed his mind, I thought.

I picked up the phone, hoping, praying. 'I'm terribly sorry Colonel. Very rude of me.'

'Not at all, old boy. Very understandable. Must be worked to the bone, eh?'

Was he being sarcastic, I wondered? I asked him, 'Any luck? Any developments?'

'That's what I wanted to talk to you about, old chap. But for the moment it's rather hush-hush.'

'Would you like me to come round to the Adelphi?'

He hesitated – just perceptibly. 'Could you make it around six this evening?'

'Of course,' I said.

'At the YMCA?'

'The ARP headquarters!' My voice must have betrayed my astonishment. Bill Jackson, one of the chief wardens, had told me the YMCA had been taken over by the ARP, and indeed, every time I drove along Stamford Road I could see evidence of bustle and activity – Nissen huts sprouting on those beautiful green courts where I had spent so much time with Julie and played so many games with Miki.

'Well, old boy, you *are* in the ARP aren't you?'

'I'm trying to get out,' I said a trifle frostily. 'I thought you knew that.'

'Jolly good,' he chuckled. 'Six o'clock, then? And, oh. Come dressed for the part, will you? I mean your armband, helmet, mask and all that nonsense. Look the part, old boy.'

I don't quite know what I expected when I parked the Morris outside the grubby front door of the YMCA clubhouse. An ARP warden I had never seen asked my name. Usually the word Dexter meant something in Singapore, but he didn't seem impressed, and ran his finger down a list of names before finally looking up and asking, 'John Dexter?'

'That's it.'

'You're expected, sir,' he said. I almost said that I could have told him that myself, but I was stopped by a sudden realisation that the man wasn't a Singaporean, that there was something odd about the whole business. It was even slightly sinister that I should be asked to meet an army officer in a civilian ARP post.

'This way, sir,' the warden said civilly, and I walked through the door into the old clubhouse. At first I didn't recognise the man in baggy flannels, with a helmet and armband, who was waiting by the old reception desk where I used to check in to find which court had been reserved for me.

'Good of you to come,' said Colonel Chalfont. 'Sorry to drag you out all this way.'

I must have looked bemused. The last time I had seen Chalfont he had been decked out in red tabs with a Sam Browne as polished as a looking glass.

'Bit of a shock finding a fellow warden, eh?' he laughed. 'Come and have a drink.'

The YMCA lounge had been completely refurnished. A

bar ran along one side, staffed by two burly-looking Europeans in white jackets. Europeans! White barmen were rarely seen in Singapore, where Chinese dispensed all the drinks. New armchairs, sofas, coffee tables filled the room. In a flash, perhaps as I watched the two Britons pouring our stengahs, I realised that this must be an army camp. But it must be a secret one – otherwise, why all the ARP disguise? And why were the other men, lolling in the chairs sipping drinks, all dressed as civilians? And why was Colonel Chalfont dressed up like a warden when he hadn't a clue what to do in a bombing raid?

After one drink he took me into a bare, cream-painted room and motioned me to a chair on one side of a long table. Opposite me sat three officers in uniform. Chalfont introduced me. 'This is Dexter, sir.' I was never told any of the officers' names, though I could see that one was a brigadier. He was a nondescript man with grey hair and pale unblinking blue eyes. I put him as being in his late forties, and he opened the conversation, 'Good evening, Dexter. I understand you wish to volunteer for His Majesty's Army?'

I nodded.

'Right.' He had a deceptive, even more nondescript accent. I hadn't the faintest idea which part of Britain he came from. 'At the end of this interview you can walk out and forget everything if you wish to remain a civilian. But while you're here you will be, so to speak, under army discipline. Understand? You will now sign this Official Secrets form.' He pushed it towards me. 'It's binding – and if you sign it, and then start talking about our conversation –' he shrugged. 'But of course, if you want you can leave the room now.'

I signed. Colonel Chalfont briefly outlined my career. I was astounded how much he knew about me. He seemed to know everything – not only about the business, the turnover, but about Papa Jack and Irene, even the names of Bengy and Natasha – and where they were.

'Normally it's quite impossible to accept volunteers from reserved occupations.' The brigadier read some notes in front of him and toyed with a yellow pencil. 'But we do have special powers for special people – specially those who speak languages we require – Malay, Chinese, Japanese.'

For a moment I had a horrible premonition that he wanted me to become an interpreter. Then he began firing questions at me, everything from, 'Why do you want to volunteer?' to 'What's your assessment of the military situation at the present time?'

So far neither of the other officers had spoken. Suddenly one started asking questions in Malay, then the third officer talked in Cantonese. I answered them fairly well.

Finally the Brigadier got up and started pacing up and down behind the bare table and then shot a question at me: 'Ever considered the possibility that we're going to lose? Going to be kicked out of Malaya, then Singapore?'

'No, sir.' I felt the blood rushing to my head at such defeatist talk. 'Never! It's impossible.'

'Glad you think so,' he said dryly. 'But just supposing – well, if we did lose, what would you do?'

'Win it back.'

'How?'

'I – I don't know, sir.'

'At least you're honest,' he hesitated, then sat down and faced me squarely. 'Dexter – we still hope we may be able to beat the Japanese, but we have to prepare ourselves for every eventuality – including the possibility of defeat – and defeat means planning *before* we lose for eventual recapture afterwards.'

'Sir, it's not possible –'

'Please refrain from interrupting me,' he said testily. I realised that he was unused to interruptions. 'Ever heard of Colonel Spencer Chapman?'

'No, sir.'

'You will – not if we win, but if we lose. He's one of the leaders of a new unit to be known as Force 136. It will operate from Colombo.'

'Colombo? Ceylon!' I almost shouted. 'I don't want any bloody desk job thousands of miles away. If I join up I want to fight *here* to help to save Singapore –'

Suddenly he said, in a cold tight voice, as though he was

being serious for the first time, 'It's rather late to save Singapore. Nothing can save it.'

My heart almost missed a beat – and then the incredible words he had used made me more angry than I can remember. 'Talk about defeatism! Christ! The army's always telling us that we out here are soft – but to hear a soldier –'

'Kindly refrain from interrupting. I am in the process of telling you a few facts. The truth is that though Churchill is talking about turning Singapore into a second Stalingrad – after all, he was responsible for sending two battleships here without a carrier – he's given up Singapore now, and you – *all of you*. I'm not saying he's wrong, mark you. It's a damn sight more important to hold Burma and India. But you're expendable, make no mistake of that.'

'I just don't believe you.'

'There's nothing anybody can do about it. If nothing else beats you, the lack of water will force you to surrender in the end, as Hong Kong did in less than three weeks. There's nothing any of you can do about it, however much you try.'

I didn't say anything for a minute, I was so horrified. I couldn't really believe it – and yet he was sitting there, his tone so matter of fact, so casual, I felt suddenly that he might be telling the truth. All I could think of saying was, 'I still don't want to go to Colombo.'

'Nobody said anything about leaving,' he said to me gently. '*Somebody* will have to fight to get Singapore back from the Japanese.' And as I digested those words he added, almost indulgently, 'The Japs might win the battle of Singapore – but they're not going to win the war.'

'I find everything you tell me impossible to believe, sir,' I said slowly. 'I *can't* believe it. Surely it's our job to fight like hell and kill as many Japs as possible – and even hope for a miracle.'

'Of course. The troops are doing that. I'm all in favour of fighting. But I'm only telling you what Churchill and Roosevelt believe. Surely it's sensible to think of the future as well?' He hesitated before adding, 'We are recruiting specialists for one of the most dangerous jobs in the war – to be trained as stay-behind parties if Singapore falls.'

I felt my heart miss a beat, then start thumping. What was a stay-behind party?

'We hope these trained men will never be needed. But if they are – if Singapore falls – anyone who has the guts to join our outfit will only have one chance in three of not being killed.' Then he added thoughtfully, 'After torture.'

'But sir' – I couldn't help myself – 'if I stay behind, as you call it – every Japanese would see I was British.'

The Brigadier turned to Chalfont and said wearily, 'Explain exactly what happens to recruits who are accepted will you, Colonel? And then give Dexter a guided tour.' And to me he added, a little more kindly, 'Go and have a drink with the Colonel. Report back here in an hour.'

It was over a stengah that Chalfont explained. Spencer Chapman was apparently a brilliant, unorthodox exponent of jungle warfare. Those who were accepted to work with Force 136 would be dropped behind the Japanese lines or landed by submarine up-country off the coast of Malaya if surrender became inevitable. They would work with Chinese who had already been recruited and were at this very moment being trained in secret. Supplies – arms, food, PE (plastic explosives) – would be dropped to jungle hide-outs from headquarters in Ceylon.

'Can I ask where I come into this?' I accepted another drink.

'The Chinese are already being trained in jungle warfare. Many of them are toughs but though they're all dedicated to one thing – slitting Japanese throats – many are dedicated to something else – Communism.'

It was essential for these Chinese guerilla units to be controlled firmly by British officers operating behind enemy lines. 'That's politically vital,' he explained. 'We don't want a bunch of Chinese telling us they won the war for us.'

I asked, in all innocence, who my fellow officers would be if – and only if – I joined what seemed like a crazy scheme.

'That'd be telling, wouldn't it?' he laughed. 'I dare say you'll find the odd chum up there. But no one asks any questions in Force 136. Better that way, old boy. What you don't know you can't betray, eh?' And as a chilly afterthought he added, 'The Japs are dab hands at torture. We found one poor bugger up at Muar wandering around. The Japs had poked both his eyes out, and cut off both arms and cauterised the stumps in the old-fashioned way with tar. He took a long time to die.' He added thoughtfully, 'That's why secrecy is so essential. We keep tabs on everyone who joins us – and if anyone blabs, he's out. I should tell you that we've already lost three Europeans who talked too much.'

'Where do you come into this, Colonel?'

'Oh, I'm a sort of recruiting wallah,' he laughed.

'What did the brigadier mean about a guided tour?' I asked.

'Come on, I'll show you.'

It was the tour that really decided me. As I went from one Nissen hut to another, more open-mouthed at each new experience, I suddenly realised that some people were determined that if Singapore *did* fall they would not give in completely.

'The first hut is fairly orthodox,' explained Chalfont. 'We call it the acclimatisation hut. But be careful. Everything's booby-trapped.' He pushed the door open and I might have been in the heart of the jungle – except that it seemed twice as hot. Chalfont explained that the heat was deliberately intensified so that once men were in the real jungle they would find conditions almost a relief. 'In other huts you'll learn all sorts of different things – karate, how to kill silently – but of course you've got to be able to stand the jungle first.'

The huge floor area was covered with dense undergrowth, thick matted, tangled vines, lallang, even trees rising up to twenty feet.

'How on earth –' I began. 'It's like a Hollywood movie.'

'Watch your step!' As Chalfont shouted, a python slithered towards me. It must have been thirty feet long. I leapt for my life – grabbing a branch of the nearest tree and hauling myself up.

'Shoot it before it climbs the tree!' I shouted.

'Good reaction on your part, old boy,' cried Chalfont – just as the branch snapped and I fell straight on to the slimy, fleshy, writhing snake.

'Never trust trees,' said Chalfont. 'You'll soon learn to spot the dead ones.'

I scrambled up, cursing – yet astonished that I had fallen on a python without being bitten.

'Defanged,' explained the colonel languidly. 'We do a lot of jungle hazard work. Here, let me show you the next hut.'

I walked through the door, Chalfont always behind me, and fell straight into a pit, carefully disguised with undergrowth. Fortunately – deliberately – the bottom had been filled with four thick mattresses, so I came to no harm. But the pit had been lined with sharply pointed stakes, hanging downwards, and hidden by the undergrowth. When the weight of the vegetation was removed – after I fell through it – the spiked pieces of wood opened up and were now hanging down above me, just a few inches from my face, pointing downwards and inwards. I could never have got out. A sergeant who was walking two steps behind Chalfont must have pulled a hidden lever, for the spikes were suddenly flattened against the side of the pit and a rope ladder appeared. I scrambled out.

'We call it the Jap trap,' explained Chalfont, almost conversationally. 'You just can't get out of it. Trouble is, the Japs don't kill you. Too easy. The Japs want to terrorise the locals. So they pour a bit of petrol over you and then chuck a match in. Not enough to burn you to death, just char you up a bit. It's a great deterrent, I can tell you.'

Every hut had something astonishing and new. One had been transformed into a huge pool, with rope bridges, guide lines and so on. The floor of another was a sea of swampy mud. 'Bloody hard to get out of – and even harder to clean yourself up afterwards.' In another was an old rusting bicycle on a stand.

'Funny thing, human reaction,' Chalfont pointed to the bicycle. 'Twice a week everyone has to do a two-hour non-stop spell on the bike. And everyone hates it more than anything else – even the mud bath.'

I patted my flat stomach. 'Well, I don't think I need to lose weight,' I said almost facetiously.

'Not *weight*, old boy. In the jungle you'll have to peddle a bicycle like mad for up to four hours at a time to produce power for your radio transmitter. We call it the treadmill. Bloody hard work. Now then: seen enough?'

We returned to the small bare room.

'Before you say anything,' said the brigadier when we were all seated, 'I want to make one thing clear. And you're not going to like it, Dexter. If you join us not a soul must know. No one. The success of Force 136 depends on secrecy. Once people know who's going into the jungle, the chain will snap and every man could die. You'll find some friends of yours in the jungle – if you ever go there. They'll be just as surprised as you are when you meet. Not a *soul* must know – understand?'

I nodded. He examined a piece of paper in front of him. 'Your wife's in America – that's good. You won't tell her, of course?'

'I understand, sir,' I said.

And then he leaned forward, his pale blue, unwavering eyes looking straight into mine, 'And you won't breathe a word to your Chinese mistress, will you?'

'Look here, sir!' I shouted as I stood up.

Almost despairingly the brigadier turned to Chalfont and said peevishly, 'Why does this man keep on interrupting me?'

'I'm sorry, sir,' said Chalfont.

'I'm sorry too, sir,' I echoed.

'You see, Dexter, we've done our homework. And frankly, at first we considered you a bad security risk. No, *no*! Don't interrupt again *please*. Not *you* – the girl.'

'May I ask what you mean?'

'Ever heard of Loi Tek?' he asked.

'The head of the Malayan Communist Party?' I asked him. 'I don't know him, sir, but I have heard of him.'

'Special Branch are keeping an eye on him,' said the Brigadier. 'And amongst his occasional visitors is Mr Soong.'

'I can't believe it, sir! Mr Soong a Communist?'

'I didn't say he was. But I didn't say he wasn't. I just said that he visits Communist headquarters. Right, Colonel' – he turned briskly to Chalfont – 'if Mr Dexter still wants to volunteer' – it was the first time he had called me 'Mister' – 'then have him gazetted as a captain.'

'You knew I was going to say yes?' I asked him.

'Of course. It's the Colonel's job to find the men. It's my job to weigh them up.' Then, almost as an afterthought, he added, 'Colonel Chalfont will explain the drill. There is just one thing I'd like to make absolutely clear before you sign. You'll remain in the ARP, and you'll report here daily and train for four hours. No specific times. You come when you want to come, so that no one suspects anything. The training staff is on duty twenty-four hours a day. You'll be gazetted, but the news won't be published. You'll come here as an ARP warden, you'll be issued with fatigue clothes each time you report for training. Miss one session without a satisfactory explanation and you're out. You won't get a uniform unless Singapore falls, and even then it'll only be jungle greens. Then you'll be told what to do. Until then' – once again he looked at me not unkindly – 'you'll be just another civilian waiting for the army to rescue you. And believe me, young man, that is going to be the hardest test of your character. Don't let me down.'

As he and his silent partners stalked out I looked at Chalfont almost despairingly. 'Cheerful cove, isn't he?'

'He knows his job,' said Chalfont. 'I hope *you* realise the tough time you're in for.'

'It might never come. Singapore might never fall.'

'Not *that*. Most men find a little bit extra when they face someone who's going to kill them.'

'What did you mean, then, by a tough time?'

Chalfont led the way to the bar and ordered a final drink. 'Before the fall,' he said. 'That's the toughest role you'll ever play, believe me – the part of a young and healthy civilian over six feet tall, surrounded by troops who've been sent here to save your skin and your way of life. *That's* what I mean.'

There was no answer to that — especially from me, who had already felt ashamed at not joining up. More than anything — certainly at this stage, more than the prospect of living in the jungle — I suddenly felt sick at the thought of the charade. I had dreamed of joining up — and now I had succeeded. But I couldn't tell anyone. Not even Julie.

'If Singapore falls,' I asked, '*if*, mark you, what about my parents and my wife?'

'If you cop it next-of-kin will be informed of the gallant Captain Dexter's death,' he replied cheerfully. 'Before that? Well, we're trying to work out a system which won't give any details, but will let your people know you're safe.'

'This brigadier who's been grilling me,' I asked, 'does he really know what he's talking about?'

Chalfont nodded. 'Most certainly. He was a professor of psychology at Oxford before the war.'

'Ah!' I exclaimed. 'That explains a lot. And this jungle business — how can he know anything about working behind enemy lines?'

'Well,' admitted Chalfont, 'he only arrived here after the first Japanese attack, so he can't know anything about the jungle.'

As I started another knowledgeable 'Ah!' Chalfont added sweetly, 'He was seconded to the Far East after being dropped in occupied France three times.'

My respect for Chalfont increased.

23

Much of what happened in late December passed me by in a kind of daze because my life had been detonated by a new daily regime: training — that, and the need to carry on as usual in the office, and — the most difficult of all — keep my secret from Julie. At times I arrived home so exhausted I could hardly eat, let alone make love, and in excuse could only offer a mumbled, 'We had a tough ARP exercise today.' Luckily security demanded that I train my daily four hours without apparent dislocation to my normal life. And since the office on the whole ran smoothly — we now had to do what we were told by authorities — it was simple for me to tell Ball or Rawlings that I was detailed for ARP duties — and to arrange the duties to coincide with Julie's rosters at the Alexandra. In fact sometimes I drove straight from 'ARP' at the YMCA to collect her at the hospital.

From the first day after I had been accepted as a trainee officer in Force 136 I had been drawn into a kind of zombie existence, an agony sandwiched into my normal life, a four-hour-a-day world, ruled by men in jungle greens, most of them burly Scots, who ended each command to the fledgeling captain they were training with cries of, 'Now, sorrr!' 'Try agin, sorrr!' Under their watchful eyes I climbed trees skilfully planted in Nissen huts, I wallowed in artificial swamp and rolled in jungle mud — after which I had to wash my uniform in the way I would have to if I were living in the jungle. I rode the bloody, unmoving bicycle until my legs felt as though they would drop off. And all this had to be done with virtually no liquid intake. Every request for a glass of water was met with a cheerful refusal. 'No, sorrr,' said the sergeant. 'We dinna want you to rely on water you'll na be able to find.'

Over the weeks I began to learn something of the work for which I was being trained, the duties that awaited proven officers of the elite Force 136. The main objective would be to establish raiding parties, subversive squads in the jungles of Malaya if or when the Japanese took Singapore. In many ways we were the Asian counterpart of the French maquis. Like them we would — if present plans matured — be supplied with weapons from air drops, be in touch with headquarters by radio. Everything we did would point to undermining and dislocating Japanese authority. 'Your job will be to make life hell for them day and night,' said Chalfont on one occasion.

We did differ in one respect from the French underground. They could pass themselves off as Frenchmen even if they were Britishers who had been dropped in France. With our white faces we would have to plan, but usually rely on our Chinese allies, working with us, to carry out a sabotage attack.

And that in turn led to political considerations in Force 136 which were of paramount importance. We would have to maintain the strictest discipline – with the gun if necessary – among the Chinese, many of whom were dedicated Communists. We would have to make certain that we were in charge, that we gave the orders, or the Chinese would pose as victors over the Japanese when the war ended.

'At the same time,' Chalfont observed, 'don't think you won't be involved in actual fighting. You will – and you'll have to make decisions a Chinese will never be called on to make. Above all, you have to learn to kill unhesitatingly, and if necessary sacrifice a colleague in the process. The objective is all that counts. I would never hesitate to sacrifice any men who had to be liquidated, and if you and I were fighting together I would expect you to sacrifice me if you had to.'

They were grim words and always emphasised before the one session I dreaded: it sounds brutal written down, but it was only another lesson – on how to cut a man's throat. Not just dig a knife into it, or hack him, but how to do it professionally before he had a chance to make more than one stifled gurgle when the blood spurted out of his neck. The killing knife was a wicked, razor-sharp blade with a hilt that seemed built to fit into my fingers. It had been specially designed by Force 136 boffins for *offensive* killing – not *defensive* measures such as stabbing a man who was rushing you. No, this was to be used when you crept up silently behind a man who was going to die before he knew what had happened, but who would live an eternity in the seconds when he saw you, felt you, felt the knife, yet could not cry out.

'Anyone can stab a fellow in the chest,' said Chalfont on one of his rare meetings with me in the YMCA bar. 'But it takes a very special kind of nerve to cut a man's throat.

Damned tricky business – and you never have a second chance.'

Over and over instructors and I stimulated 'creep-up' attacks, but as Chalfont said, 'The pity is that we can never give you a chance to practise on the real thing.'

'Thank God,' I said.

'They do in Russia,' he said. 'They use prisoners condemned to death. When you're expert, it's a quicker death than hanging, I can tell you. But it all depends on speed. Could you do it in cold blood?'

'I hope so. I wonder sometimes –'

'Don't wonder too much!'

I knew the drill by heart, and recited it off parrot-fashion. 'Silent attack from the rear, jerk head back to cause choking and consequent silence, plunge knife into left-hand side of throat then draw weapon across to right ear. Scheduled time, eighteen seconds.'

'Word perfect,' Chalfont almost grinned. 'There's just one thing to remember if you ever have to make this split-second decision. The truest old saying on earth is the one about he who hesitates is lost.'

Usually the training sessions slowed down towards the end, so that I did not cause suspicion by tottering into the outside world exhausted. So we started off with an enormous expenditure of physical energy, gradually tapering off as I reached the final hour, when I could recover my breath (and the use of my limbs) by more relaxed training – assembling Bren guns, sabotage techniques, the use of plastic high explosives, incendiary devices, and a daily lesson in the art of coding and decoding messages.

Everything was shrouded in secrecy. Though I was regularly taught by the same instructors, I hardly saw another recruit – certainly never one I knew. Occasionally I caught a glimpse of someone covered in mud leaving the swamp hut as I was about to enter, but it was almost as though, in the interests of security, we were juggled about so that no two men were ever trained at the same time in the same hut.

My secret was sometimes almost revealed. When Christmas came Julie felt that she must spend the night of

Christmas Eve, and Christmas Day, with her father. I naturally agreed. I had long since been forgiven by Soong (if a Chinese can ever forgive) for our boy-and-girl love, and he invited me for Christmas lunch. But I also knew that Julie had told her father she must rush off to the Alexandra after lunch, when in fact she was not on duty until seven p.m. Of course she planned to return to the Cadet House and I would follow. But *that* meant I would have to put in a stint of training *before* lunch on Christmas Day. Which I did – leaving Julie mystified when she phoned the Cadet House during the morning and Li told her I had gone to ARP training.

'On Christmas morning?' she teased me afterwards. 'You're very secretive these days. Are you sure there isn't another girl somewhere?' She was joking, but she was puzzled – and I had to watch every step.

Once or twice I almost told Julie – but then, at a meeting with Colonel Chalfont, he said something that chilled my blood.

'Don't forget the need for security,' he warned me. 'Did I ever tell you about three chaps who *did* talk? They were all bumped off, you know.' He added, almost cheerfully, 'and not by the enemy. We can't afford to take any risks with blokes we can't trust.'

Since Julie was spending Christmas Eve at the Soong house I joined the rowdy crowd of lonely males celebrating at the Cricket Club where turkey was being served on Christmas Eve as well as on Christmas Day for the benefit of volunteers in the ARP and other services on shift work.

Even their attitudes had changed with war. Since time immemorial nine out of ten healthy young husbands in Singapore would start giving their chums sly winks and nudges when the *mem* and the children went on leave to England. There were whispered references to the illicit delights in the small hotels along Macpherson Road, the Happy World and its taxi dancers, while the really knowing ones ('I've done all this before, old boy') would mention by name girls like Anita, half Philippino, a quarter Japanese, a quarter Indian, known as the most remarkable hermaphrodite in the Orient, and a supposed favourite of the Sultan of Johore.

Most grass-widowers had originally married not for love but because they were lonely. Singapore was full of happy couples who had never really loved each other, and never really would – bachelors made randy by the heat, daughters of planters or box wallahs, together with a few aventurous girls (known as the fishing fleet) who had deliberately come to Singapore knowing girls were in short supply and that they would soon find a husband. They married. They copulated cheerfully – in the heat it was much less trouble when it was legal – and they were vaguely happy, though aware that something was missing, no doubt because in those days the average white girl in Singapore was untutored sexually, and most would have been appalled if a husband told them to wiggle a bit in bed instead of just lying flat on their backs. And they would have been even more disgusted if a husband had suggested encouraging themselves as they had furtively done at boarding school. So husbands and wives were left with the niggling sense that they had lost out on 'real love'. But all changed when husbands were left on their own for a few months. The local girls *did* wriggle and twist and gasp – much of it simulated, no doubt – and they even offered to do all the work, for this was the 'mysterious Orient' where the women were 'past masters in the art of pleasing men'. It wasn't altogether true; but enthusiasm covers a multitude of shortcomings.

The air of festivity in the Cricket Club was not simulated, however, for Christmas had always meant a great deal in Singapore. No doubt because of a subconscious yearning for home, the Europeans went to extravagant lengths to make Christmas the biggest celebration of the year, though the Chinese waited a couple of weeks before celebrating their New Year in January. Despite the war the club was festooned with long lines of expanding coloured paper decorations, the sort one buys in a flat pack and which when pulled stretch across the room. Balloons hung from the fans, writhing with each turn of the four blades. The Christmas tree was decked so liberally with tinsel it was almost impossible to see the green branches of sharp fir.

The young officers who had become temporary members were mostly lieutenants, mostly conscripted, and anxious, it seemed, to enjoy every evening away from the majors and colonels who frequented the Tanglin. Often the senior officers were professionals whose extra pips and crowns intimidated the lieutenants, all of them anxious to meet the locals like myself. They never talked about the war – of which they were probably as ignorant as we were – but about us, the city, rubber and tins, girls, their chatter almost always tinged with envy. 'I'll bet you're looking forward to getting back to normal. This must be a great place to live.' 'I applied to be a planter once but they turned me down.' 'I wanted to be a tea planter – but they don't grow tea here, do they?' And inevitably, as the drinks flowed, 'Sometimes I envy the other ranks. We can't go for the local girls, of course; sets a bad example.'

None of these pink young officers seemed to think it wrong that I was not in uniform. In fact I was the one who felt embarrassed; the more so since I *was* a soldier, but could never admit the fact. I was often afraid that if some disparaging officer sneered at my civilian status I might lose my temper. But none did. Instead, they enquired what I did for a living, and when I murmured the vague words rubber and tin, they nodded as though that explained everything. One man did ask me outright, 'Don't you feel you'd like to be in the forces at a time like this?' As I offered the other magic words, 'Reserved occupation,' he added hastily, 'I know that, but it must be *hell* being a civilian at times like this. We chaps have much more fun. We're looked after – all that sort of thing.'

Maybe they were, but I felt sorry for them because they had to think twice before spending an extra cent of their miserable pay. I stood several rounds and thought how awful it must be to have to set an example by leaving the girls alone in a beautiful city like ours, when you might soon be buried, unknown, in a little corner of a remote country painted red on the map by other youngsters who had also been taught to set an example.

There followed toast after toast to absent friends and in a slightly maudlin state I wondered how Irene was spending Christmas in New York, what kind of presents she had been able to buy for Bengy. I had tried to send something from Singapore, only to be told primly that it was unpatriotic to take up even one cubic foot of valuable cargo space. Irene wrote regularly, each letter composed with care, telling nothing to which a censor could take exception. Mama wrote too, saying that Papa was working too hard. I found it difficult to write to them; every letter had to be a lie, and I wasn't a good liar. It was much easier to write to Papa Jack, for I was allowed to talk guardedly about the business – indeed I had to, though I could not reveal details of shipments. These I passed to the government, which cabled details to London in code.

At midnight we all wished each other a merry Christmas, linked arms and sang 'Auld Lang Syne', and I rolled into a lonely bed at three in the morning.

With a tingle of apprehension – for Soong might forgive, but would never forget – I arrived at twelve-thirty on Christmas Day, exhausted after my ARP session, and waited in the salon – the only word to describe the huge circular room with its domed roof and priceless Chinese furniture. I was looking at the lacquered table which Soong had promised to leave to me when he died when he came in and said in his grave voice, 'Admiring your table, Johnnie?'

He looked tired, as though the war had already aged him. He had always been tall for a Chinese, very thin, and now everything about him seemed swathed in an aura of grey. His hair was grey, his face had an unhealthy greyish pallor, his tie, his suit, his socks – all were grey. Even the rims of his glasses were vaguely grey. Every movement he made was deliberate, as though he couldn't make up his mind if it were worthwhile. When he asked me if I would like a drink, even the half-smile seemed an effort – not painful, he placed his hand on my shoulder and was genuinely upset when asking about the bomb damage to Tanamera; but his smile never blossomed. He wanted to smile, he started to smile, but was unable to maintain it.

It was not only war that had aged him; he had also suffered loss of face among the Chinese community when his wife had walked out on him. Paul and Julie never talked about the break-up, and P. P. behaved with strict decorum. No unmarried ladies ever visited his house; though it was rumoured that he kept two Chinese women each in her own apartment. Whatever the truth he looked an unhappy man.

He led me to the 'comfortable' corner of the room and mixed me a gin pahit. In order to house his bottles, Soong had installed priceless Chinese carved shelving against the wall, lacy red and gold lacquer that looked like a gigantic piece of fretwork. He had obviously acquired it from a temple; it had no long straight shelves but irregular short ones, so that two bottles were perched here, two bottles there, together with an ice bucket. Another shelf held the impedimenta of a bar, crown cork openers, corkscrews, an ice hammer. In front of this really beautiful shelving Soong had placed an ugly modern bar, a fitted affair with a rail for one's feet and tall stools. The top was covered with an assortment of hotel labels collected from all over the world, stuck on the wood and protected by a sheet of glass. On one corner stood a large Malay basket filled with other trophies of travel – in the form of book matches.

Paul and Julie came in as I sipped my pink gin. I badly needed it. Demurely Julie asked for tomato juice; obviously her father disapproved of alcohol for his only daughter, and she was humouring him.

I heard the old-fashioned doorbell peal, and Paul turned to me. 'Father's asked Ian and Vicki Scott along.' With a whispered aside he added, 'Help to cheer things up.'

Because of my unexpected elevation in the family business, the disparity in ages seemed to have shrunk, and once I had shaken hands I asked Ian if he had heard from Tony lately.

'I spoke to him two days ago,' said Ian. 'He *says* he hopes to get a spot of leave soon, but I doubt it.'

Beckoning me aside he asked rather pompously, in the

voice of one *tuan* to another, 'I find the army very difficult, don't you? I've got a contract to supply rubber, and I can't get enough. They won't let me have it.'

'We've got too much,' I sighed, 'and the bloody authorities won't provide the ships. Care to trade?'

'It makes no difference,' Scott shrugged his shoulders. 'We're all in the same boat.'

The girls were talking in one corner so I asked him, 'Are you thinking of getting Vicki away? Evacuate her, I mean?'

'Good Lord, no.' He seemed astounded. 'Why on earth should I?'

I pointed out that hundreds of women *had* been evacuated, the war news was getting worse, and it might give him peace of mind if he knew his wife was safe. 'Just as I sent Irene to America,' I added brightly.

He gave me an odd look, and then said, 'Irene is rather different. After all, no offence Johnnie, she's not a *real* Singaporean.'

'Like Vicki?' I joked.

'She's a great help at Fort Canning,' he said shortly.

Paul chipped in, 'I tried to get Bertrand Bonnard for lunch – thought he might be lonesome on his own – but he seems to have vanished into thin air.'

'I haven't seen him for ages,' I said. 'Maybe he's left. After all, he is a neutral.'

'*Could* he leave the island?' asked Ian. 'Don't you need an exit permit now?'

'But he would get one, surely,' said P.P. Soong. 'As a Swiss citizen, I mean.'

'There aren't really many ships leaving now,' said Paul.

It was certainly odd. One day Bonnard had been part of our crowd, the next he was no longer to be seen. Thinking of Bonnard set me wondering what had happened to Natasha – whether the baby was on the way. She never mentioned the matter (or Bonnard) in her rare letters.

Even with Vicki there, lunch was dull, and the presence of Soong Kai-shek, glowering and silent, hardly helped provide a Christmas spirit. It was kind of Soong to take pity on someone whose family was at the other end of the world, but in truth I would much rather have lunched at the Swimming Club, watching the water polo before tucking into a curry tiffin. But of course Julie had to be with her father – and she wouldn't have been allowed into the Swimming Club, anyway. As I waited patiently for the meal to end – and for me to make my excuses – Soong asked a question the significance of which I didn't realise at the time.

Wiping his lips fastidiously on his starched, monogrammed napkin, he said, as though to make casual conversation, 'Why don't the British use the Communists? They would make wonderful jungle trackers –'

'Are there enough?' asked Paul.

'And don't the Communists hate the British?' asked Scott. 'Why should they help even if they were asked to?'

'I understand' – Soong spoke in his usual slow careful tone – 'that up-country the Japanese often fight in vests and shorts, and the British troops can't always tell them from Malays until it's too late. Wouldn't it help to have trained men helping?'

'But surely local Malays and Chinese could help just as easily?' I asked.

'They're too scared,' Soong shook his head. 'They know they'll be executed if the Japs find out they've helped the British. The Communists aren't scared. They wouldn't be Communists if they were.'

'You sound as though –' Paul began jokingly.

'Not at all. I'm only concerned with helping to save Malaya and Singapore.'

Kai-shek broke in, 'Since most Communists have been jailed, why should they leave the safety of prison just to be killed?'

That was *my* thought, but Soong insisted. 'That is no argument. The Japanese will slaughter every Communist they can. And they'll be easier to catch in a locked prison if the British are forced to withdraw. In fact, my suggestion gives the Communists their only chance to stay alive.'

'They wouldn't be in prison without any trial if it wasn't for the British,' said Kai-shek.

'There *is* a war on.' Ian Scott's voice was sharp and angry.

'Yes – and the British are finding out that the white men aren't as superior as they thought.'

'That's enough,' it was Soong's turn to speak sharply.

'I meant nothing personal,' muttered Kai-shek, 'and I hate the Japanese as much as everyone here. But you can't ignore the fact that Asians are showing up the weakness of the white man everywhere – from Honolulu to Singapore. I wonder if white men will ever again be able to lord it over Asians.'

'If I had my way I'd shoot all the Communists,' Scott proclaimed. 'You mark my words, they're going to cause a lot of trouble after the war. This man Roosevelt has been taken in by Stalin. You remember what I'm saying. There's no such thing as a good Communist.'

Soon afterwards Julie announced that she had to leave for the hospital. I knew she was going back to the Cadet House to spend the afternoon in bed with me. With just the correct degree of formal politeness I said goodbye to her along with the others, and prepared to stay a little longer for the sake of appearances before announcing that I had to go on ARP duty.

When the coffee was served – a concession to Western guests – Paul and I and Vicki sat once again in the 'comfortable corner', talking about nothing in particular until Soong called in his precise voice, 'Paul, can you spare me a moment?'

Almost before Paul moved away Vicki was looking at me with the excited eyes of – what was it, a predatory female? An echo of the night at the Sea View? I thought she was going to remind me, to hint, but I was wrong. In the hurried whisper of a conspirator, she said, 'She's grown really beautiful.'

'Beautiful?'

'Julie! You know perfectly well who I mean. Everyone in Singapore knows you're potty about her.'

The words gave me a nasty jar – and yet, I would have been a fool if they had surprised me. War – and its duties at unusual hours – was a wonderful camouflage, but of course we must have been seen together. Still, even as I was answering Vicki, I was thinking, gossip is one thing, so long as no one discovers we are actually living together.

'I'm glad for your sake,' Vicki whispered. 'But be careful. Ian said someone at the Singapore Club told him. So watch out.'

When Paul returned I realised I had only said one single word. Now I added unsteadily, 'Afraid I must go. Duty calls.' By the time I reached Nassim Hill Julie was already in bed, undressed and waiting. I decided to say nothing. I didn't want to spoil an evening surprise I had arranged for her.

After dusk I set off in the Morris to take Julie to the hospital. They were very busy at the Alexandra, with every bed occupied with wounded, either from raids or from the trains bringing half-dead soldiers from Malaya. As she settled into the left-hand seat next to me, I said, 'Don't you think I'm a pretty mean sort of man, not giving my girl-friend a Christmas present?'

'I didn't buy *you* one,' she answered. 'Somehow there's no Christmas spirit this year. We didn't give any to each other at home. We just lunched together because it was Christmas Day. It means nothing to us except what we've been taught by you.'

'Well, I *have* bought you one.'

She clapped her hands. 'Where is it?'

'Not here. We're going to pick it up on the way to the hospital.'

'But what is it? At least tell me.'

I shook my head. 'Come on.' I kissed her casually, happily, filled with love for her. 'Time to go and start washing your boyfriends' bottoms. Do you think it gives your patients a thrill?'

'What is it?' She put her arms round me. 'Come on – tell.'

'Patience!' I drove to the end of Orchard Road, into Stamford Road, and then bore right towards High Street. I braked the Morris outside da Silva's, the oldest jewellers in Singapore, just behind the City Hall. The Dexter family had patronised da Silva's since he first came from Ceylon to

Singapore. My father and my father's father had both bought their engagement and wedding rings from the old man and his family.

'Not jewellery?' Like any woman her eyes sparkled as we jumped out in front of the double windows, shrouded in the semi-darkness of the black-out. We pushed the door open, and blinked as we walked into bright lights reflecting the dazzling display of stones and brooches and rings on the glass-topped counters arranged round three sides of the room.

'I am keeping specially open for you, *tuan*,' lilted da Silva, snapping his fingers at an assistant to bring bottled lime juice and a beer and some straws.

'So it's not a spur-of-the-moment present?' asked Julie, and I could see she was pleased.

I shall never forget Julie's gasp of delight. For a moment the war was forgotten, and nothing mattered except da Silva, his slightly pockmarked face looking grave as befitted the moment when he produced on a black velvet tray a triple eternity ring – one circle of rubies, one of emeralds, the third of sapphires, joined together in gold trimmed with tiny diamonds.

'Look, here's the inscription.' I showed her the inside of the ring. 'To J from J with love.'

For a moment I thought she was going to cry. Her wide dark eyes looked at mine and one tear did trickle out. I wiped it away with my handkerchief, and there was a catch in her voice as she said, 'It's the happiest Christmas I've ever spent – not only for this.' She put it on, twirling her hand so that the stones caught the light and sent patterns dancing across the ceiling. 'Because of what's written inside, because you *planned* it. Whatever happens, darling, I'll always wear it.'

Afterwards she snuggled up to me in the Morris, squeezed me, and then said, 'I just want you to touch my heart. Go on! I know it's just another heart, but feel it – it's banging like this just for you.'

There were still tears of happiness in her eyes as she got out of the car at the Alexandra. 'I'll be home tomorrow

367

morning.' She kissed me, and then repeated the word lovingly, '*home* darling!'

24

December slid into January 1942, in chaos and confusion, with appalling military reverses up-country disguised as 'strategic withdrawals' in fatuous communiqués. One newspaper, commenting on a particularly bad rout of allied troops, insisted that since the Japanese had attempted to fight a face-to-face battle, and the allies had withdrawn, the Japanese had failed in their plans and thus we had gained a strategic victory. Meanwhile the stories of wrangling that seeped out of the War Council were equally appalling. Shenton Thomas and Duff Cooper hardly exchanged civilities, for Thomas knew the country and its people but was unable to handle a crisis, while Duff Cooper might have been a good politician in London but was pitifully ignorant of our country and its people. The navy was at loggerheads with the RAF; the RAF still incurred the undying hatred of the army after constructing up-country airfields without consulting army engineers. Brooke-Popham was an old dodderer who continued to fall asleep during high-level conferences, until mercifully he was sent back to London.

Yet though the news from Malaya was more and more depressing, the implications were so carefully masked that most of us lived in a dream world. Up-country Malaya was as remote from Singapore as France must have been from England in 1940. We were in the war raging up-country but not part of it, and so, gasping with heat, drenched with the heavy monsoon rains that had now started, we drifted from day to day on a diet of false information supplemented with rumours.

Most real news of events in Malaya was censored, but it

was not difficult to discover something of the truth. Because Dexters had dealt with planters and miners – and their banks – all over Malaya for generations I could easily trace the Japanese advances on a map simply by reading the advertisements of the Chartered Bank or the Hong Kong and Shanghai Bank, which gave a daily list of branches that had been closed 'until further notice'.

Yet it was hard to believe that, out of sight, out of real knowledge, hard-pressed troops were falling back on one ill-prepared position after another, worn out, hungry, drenched in the hissing rains of the jungle; that, while the troops starved, supplies in Singapore were plentiful. Though many foods were rationed Li could still buy two tins of fruit a day for each of us. Our butter and meat rations were three times as large as in England. The Cold Storage vans still delivered milk and cream to the Cadet House. Eating out presented no problems, for though hotels scrupulously observed the rule of two meatless days a week it made hardly any difference, as poultry and game didn't count and Malay fishermen were 'carrying on as usual'. There was plenty of petrol, for though it was rationed almost everyone drew an extra allowance allotted to civil defence workers, and since most families had at least two cars it was a simple matter to leave the big one in the garage and use all the petrol in small cars like my Morris.

We rarely used the big car now, but kept it – together with a ten-hundredweight truck – in a godown below the office in Robinson Road, where my father's syce, who had once worked for Grandpa Jack, polished the Buick daily.

I personally kept a close watch on the petrol, for we needed all our rations. There were trips to ARP training – well, that was how I still thought of them – and longer trips which I had to make regularly to check on rubber stocks at our huge godown on the river near Geylang. Then at times I had to pick up Julie at the Alexandra. And there were my daily visits to Grandpa Jack.

I was a little puzzled about him. He seemed so – not resigned by defeat, but content with acceptance. It was not in his nature to surrender anything. But though he now had to share a ward with twenty other patients he actually seemed content. He had plenty of visitors, cronies from the Singapore Club, or men like Ball from the office, and of course old Li was always on hand. Even the elderly syce took time off from polishing the unused car to visit his one-time boss.

In a way he was enjoying himself, relaxing in his bed or in his wheelchair, with a lift to take him to the ground level so that he could be wheeled through the grounds in fine weather. He liked the nurses – I am sure he found them more friendly than any of the women in Tanamera, because he could make jokes based on what he thought was subtle innuendo and be sure that a nurse would reply, with well-simulated archness, 'Really, Grandpa Jack. You ought to be ashamed of yourself!' He wore a faint look of cunning, I thought, but perhaps I was mistaken. I felt in my heart that whatever happened to Singapore Grandpa Jack would never leave the General Hospital. Happily for all of us, he didn't seem to mind. Or that was what I thought.

My visits to him had to be limited because at work we faced red tape in the docks that made us despair. Our godowns were filled to the roofs with stocks of rubber for which Britain was clamouring. It was our job to load them on board the ships in the harbour – and at times there were scores of cargo vessels waiting. But we couldn't, because the incoming ships could not always be unloaded. Coolies refused work because they could earn more money elsewhere. The military could not give them extra danger pay, which God knows they deserved, because Whitehall refused to sanction an increase of two cents an hour, even when ships were bringing in equipment desperately needed by our retreating troops.

Rawlings came into the office one day explaining, 'There's a ten-thousand tonner, the *Sandringham* out in the roads. We've got all the papers ready to load her up. She's to take all the rubber in godowns six and seven. But nobody will unload her.'

'What's she carrying?' I asked.

He checked on the papers. 'Army stores.'

'What about our usual coolies? Can't you persuade them?'

'I've tried — they can get two cents an hour more working on a non-government ship.'

I made a quick decision. 'Just keep it quiet, Rawlings, but go and offer them two cents an hour more to unload for us. We'll stand the extra cost. We've got to get the bloody rubber moving. There's more rubber arriving every day, and we just haven't got any space in the godowns.'

Rawlings was delighted. And so was I — for twenty-four hours. I knew it would only take two days to unload the *Sandringham*. At least we were doing something practical for the war effort. Or so I thought.

The next morning the glass door of my office burst open and a red-faced officer stood before me. He seemed surprised to see a young man behind the desk.

'I want to see Mr Dexter, the man in charge,' he barked.

'Do you ever knock before opening doors?'

'Somebody's unloading my ship.'

'I am.' Then I shouted, 'Rawlings!'

Nervously Rawlings edged past the officer — I saw the man was a full colonel. I said as quietly as I could, 'Show the colonel the way out.'

'Just a moment — are *you* Mr Dexter?'

I nodded.

'What the hell do you mean by unloading government property without authorisation?'

'I'll tell you, Colonel. I'm making sure Britain gets the rubber before the Japanese.'

'I know nothing about that,' he snapped. 'Those are army stores — government stores — on the *Sandringham*. It's our job to arrange the unloading. You civilians make me sick. This war would be a damn sight easier to win if you bloody planters stopped interfering.' Then he snorted. 'Two cents an hour more, I suppose?'

I was speechless. I just couldn't be angry at such stupidity. Here was I trying to help, spending good Dexter cash so the army could get its stores and Britain get its rubber.

'I'm not a planter,' I said finally, adding quickly, 'and I'm just trying to help you, Colonel. We're standing the cost.'

'And what are the rest of the coolies going to do when they hear what you've done?'

I hadn't thought of that. 'Well,' I said a little lamely, 'it's too late now anyway.'

'We'll see about that!' As the colonel turned to the door he looked back and repeated, 'We'll see about that.'

He did. Within an hour military police boarded the *Sandringham*, the coolies were ordered off, and the ship was placed under police guard. I never did find out when or if she was unloaded. Eventually we got our rubber away on an Australian vessel.

Red-tabbed colonels were not the only bloody-minded and obtuse people. Civilian government was equally stupid – as Gilmour, the deputy municipal engineer, discovered. I met Gilmour that same night in the club. He was seething with rage. He had been asked to dig lines of trenches on the padang of the Cricket Club and other sports grounds to prevent Japanese aircraft from landing. Somehow he had rounded up several hundred coolies, but when the trenches were half dug an official from another government department insisted they must be filled in and dug again in a zigzag pattern. Solemnly he warned Gilmour that straight trenches made easy targets for machine gunning. The coolies filled in trenches they had dug in the heat and dug new staggered trenches. When Gilmour asked what to do with the displaced earth, he was told, 'Leave it there.'

'You'll find it hard to believe,' said Gilmour bitterly, 'but within an hour another bloody busybody told me to take all the earth away because soft soil would make an ideal dropping zone for parachutists, so I arranged for the earth to be carted away. We'd just finished doing *this* when along came the health authorities. They told me that trenches in low-lying ground were breeding grounds for mosquitos, and ordered every trench to be filled in. I argued like hell and finally they agreed that they could be half filled so we had to bring half the bloody earth back again and fill in the bottom two feet of each trench.'

*

I had stayed later than usual at the club because Julie's shift ended at eight p.m. and her car was being serviced so I had arranged to pick her up. I reached the Alexandra just before eight, parked the car and walked into the big square entrance hall. It was a pleasant, spacious hospital, built before architects started planning small air-conditioned cubicles. On either side of the front entrance hall ran a long ward, with the doorways kept open, no doubt to increase circulation of air.

In the dim light I could see rows of beds, ceiling fans turning, nurses moving quietly. A hidden radio hummed soft music. The big rectangular room had a balcony all the way round, high above the beds. In front of me broad wooden stairs led to an upstairs hall between two wings. I was waiting when a nurse bustled out of one ground floor ward and said officiously, 'No visitors are allowed.'

'I'm waiting for –'

'Sorry, you must go now. Immediately.' She didn't wait for an answer, and as I didn't see why I should go I nipped up to the first floor where the entrance hall was lined with benches for visitors.

Another nurse came out of an upstairs ward. 'What on earth are you doing here? No visitors.'

'I'm waiting for Miss Soong.'

'Ssh!' she whispered. 'Security. This is an army hospital, and a major in the RAMC is just finishing an inspection. All hell will be let loose if they find a civilian here – a *man*!' At least she had a sense of humour.

At that moment I heard male voices. 'Quick,' the nurse whispered, 'hide in here.' She almost bundled me into a cubbyhole near the entrance to one of the upstairs balconies, whispering, 'I'll let you know when the coast is clear.'

It was ridiculous – like hiding at school. Through cracks and ventilation holes I could look down over the balcony on to the rows of beds on the ground floor. I heard voices almost next to me, separated by only a panel of wood, strident, bristling with authority, snatches of conversation, 'Thank you Matron,' and another, 'I think that will be enough'. And then the clump of heavy boots going downstairs and a voice, perhaps the matron's – 'Thank you so much, Major.'

I waited a couple of minutes, sweating like a pig, until I heard a warning knock and the nurse slid open the door. 'Matron's gone to her room. The coast's clear,' she almost giggled. 'That was a narrow shave. Who did you say you were waiting for?'

'Miss Soong.'

'Oh! Julie. She'll be ready in a couple of minutes. She's such a sweetie – and she works so hard. Are you her husband?'

She was obviously an army nurse, new to Singapore. 'Not yet,' I smiled.

'Here – you can take a peep – watch her at work.' Julie, in uniform, a white nurse's cap and rubber gloves, was carrying a kidney-shaped enamel dish in her left hand, and in her right hand was what seemed to be a pair of tweezers. She went from bed to bed, bending over each patient with a smile.

'What's she doing? I don't understand,' I whispered to the nurse.

'It's the last job she does before going off duty. She'll soon be through.'

'But what's she doing?' I whispered.

'Just routine.' The nurse didn't sound the least upset, 'It's the flies, you know. We can't keep them out and they never stop laying eggs in open wounds. They turn to maggots in no time. Every night and morning the nurse going off duty has to make the rounds and pick the maggots out of the wounds.'

In a few minutes Julie arrived. 'Sorry if I'm late.' She cuddled up to me in the car. 'We all have to take a shower at the beginning and end of each shift. Hygiene, you know.'

I could hardly talk on the drive home. Though I tried and tried, I could not erase the picture of Julie, smiling as she bent towards each patient, and the sweep of her right arm as she moved, tweezers gripping something I couldn't see, dropping it into the kidney bowl. I wanted to blurt out that I had watched her at work, tell her what I had seen, but I knew it would only upset her; so, when she remarked on my silence, I just said I was tired.

Two days later I had an unexpected visitor. It was on one of the rare occasions when Julie and I were unable to synchronise our shifts — or rather, when her night shift at the hospital lasted longer than mine. We had agreed that at times like this each would creep into the Cadet House quietly. Li, who lived in the compound at the back, had been told not to wake if he heard one of us. The Sikh jagger, armed with the usual stout pole, guarded the front door by sleeping on a trestle bed in front of it, but always woke at the sound of my car, and pulled the bed away from the door just enough to allow a person to squeeze in.

I had spent four exhausting hours at the YMCA and was dropping with fatigue. Certainly, as I climbed the stairs, lighting the way with my small pencil torch, I was quite unprepared to find anyone in the house. Suddenly I froze, halfway up the stairs, as the lights in the hall were clicked on, as though by an unseen hand. I was even more astounded when I saw who was standing at the top of the stairs.

'Tim!' I had not seen my elder brother since we smashed each other up in the terrible fight at Studio Z. I ran up the stairs to greet him.

'It's a bit late but — happy New Year!' I said.

'Happy New Year.' The greeting was hardly warm and brotherly. In fact, standing there in the middle of the night, he looked distinctly off-putting. He was dressed in khaki shorts, with a captain's pips on his lightweight tunic. He had lost weight, I could see that; he looked older, strained, perhaps because his hair was cut very short. But it was not the past that made his greeting cold. It was the present. The moment he started talking I sensed that he knew I wasn't living alone. The temperature was chilly, the voice drips of ice.

'I hope I haven't barged in,' he said. 'I went to the club first — they told me Tanamera had had a near miss and that

375

you had moved in here. Very sensible of you. I'm afraid I started looking around, and —'

'Sorry I wasn't here to meet you.' It was ridiculous really, like apologising to a house guest.

'You mean so you could hide the evidence?' He gave me a thin smile.

'Come off it, Tim. How long is it since I saw you? Have a beer. Tell me everything that's been happening.'

'Compared with your life — very dull, I'm sure.'

For a moment or two we stood there on the landing, sparring. Finally I said, 'For Chrissake Tim, be your age. I'm going down to the dining room for a beer. There's one for you if you can stand my company.'

He did accept a Tiger — but the curl to his lip grew even more supercilious when we went to get the beer from the refrigerator in the dining room and he saw the rough shelter we had arranged under and round the dining room table.

'You think of everything,' he said.

'Tim,' I said desperately, 'just let me lead my life, okay? Tell me about Papa Jack.'

'I notice you didn't ask for news of Irene?'

'I heard from her in New York,' I retorted, 'only the other day. And as for this,' I shrugged my shoulders, 'I'm delighted to see you, Tim — at least I *think* I am — but mind your own bloody business.'

'Perhaps I'm a little old-fashioned,' he said, 'but I always thought company flats were not supposed to be used for screwing. Isn't that a house rule? Wasn't that why old Cowley got sent back to England?'

'Balls, Tim — this isn't a company flat any more. We offered it to the forces. I'm just like a lodger here.'

'With services provided.'

'Please! Tell me what you've been doing.' I put my hand on his shoulder but he moved away, not aggressively but quite deliberately, as I added, 'Li will be here soon with breakfast. Things are never quite what they seem. Try to understand.'

Tim had always had a foul temper. Now he looked me

full in the face and snarled, 'Understand? Understand what?' I knew what was coming next. 'Understand that you pinched my girl, that you married her when she'd agreed to marry me, that you had a son by her' – he hardly stopped to draw breath – 'and then at the first opportunity you pack her off, and move into bed with another woman.'

'I didn't pinch your girl, as you put it – and you bloody well know it,' I retorted.

'Oh really,' he said sarcastically. 'So now you *didn't* pinch her. That's news anyway. Then why did she turn me down and marry you?'

'You know damn well. Don't play the martyr with me.' I was praying for Li to come in and announce breakfast. 'She didn't want to marry either of us. Irene loathes Singapore. The reason she married me was that you didn't go to bed with her – and I did, and I got her pregnant.'

'God, what a shit you are,' he said.

I felt so angry – the anger perhaps exacerbated by fatigue and a touch of guilt about Irene – that I lost my temper.

'Don't feel sorry for what you've missed,' I said. 'You're my brother – and since I was pushed into marrying Irene, I've got a right to tell you this.' I drew a long breath. 'Irene is a good mother – right. She's a good wife – right. But she's lousy in bed – and if that doesn't go right nothing matters. But even so – Irene doesn't know what's happening here and she never will.'

For a moment I thought Tim was going to hit me. Instead he said, 'Don't you ever think of anything but bed?'

'Why the hell do you think Irene and I are still married?' I shouted. 'Because I *do* think of other things than bed.'

'Not at present,' he looked round with distaste.

'No, not at present, you're right. It may sound corny, but fate – that's what it is, fate – has given me a break. And I'm grabbing every single moment of it while it lasts.'

Thank God Li chose that moment to come shuffling in, carefully pretending not to see our tight, strained faces. 'Breakfast, *tuan* Tim?' he beamed. 'You like cook bleakfast?'

'No thanks, Li.' Tim turned to me, looked at his watch,

and added, 'I've got an army car coming in a few minutes to take me to the mess.'

Looking out over the green garden, wet, still sparkling with dewy diamonds in the first few beautiful moments before the heat of the day sucked every drop away, he added, 'I'm sorry it hasn't turned out to be a pleasant reunion. But your sort make me sick and there's nothing I can do about it. Especially when I think of you cheating on Irene like this – her of all people. What the hell would *you* think if you discovered she'd been unfaithful to you?'

'I'd hope she'd be enjoying it,' I replied cheerfully, knowing that even if I didn't love Irene I wasn't speaking the truth.

'You've done very well for yourself, haven't you?' He was being sarcastic now. 'First you almost wrecked Papa Jack's partnership with Soong. Then Irene. And now?'

'Does it matter what I'm doing?' I suddenly felt very tired. 'Don't you realise that a war changes things? You do things in a war you wouldn't do in peace.'

'War!' he almost shouted. 'War! You don't even know what war's about. I've spent a whole bloody year of my life living like a peasant in China – without one single square meal. And I arrive in Singapore and they give me so much turkey at the club, I'm sick. Physically vomiting. War! *You* don't even know there's a war on.'

'I thought you were in Cairo.' I was feeling so tired after my training session I could hardly straighten my back. 'The letter you sent to Papa.'

'That was a blind, deliberate, just to put you off the scent. Do you think I'd deliberately try to beat the censor?'

'Okay, so you're a genius! And I still say war makes a difference – to all of us.'

'You civilian jerks make me sick with your excuses. And if it comes to that, half the men in Singapore ought to be in uniform.' Though he didn't mention my name, I knew he meant me. It was hardly the moment to mention that I also held the rank of captain.

'You're a Singaporean – you know that rubber and tin –' I began.

'Come off it. I'm *not* a Singaporean – not any longer.' Leaning forward, he jabbed my chest and raged, 'When I look at you bums playing at war I'm ashamed I've ever lived in this rotten dump.'

'Then why did you come back. To spy on me?'

'Don't ask bloody stupid questions. It may interest you to know that I've come back for one reason only – to find one man, and if I do to kill him. I'm in Intelligence, and that's why I'm here. I've been trained as a killer.'

Suddenly I felt almost afraid, the anger evaporating at his words. 'Are you serious, Tim?' I was not only horrified but almost sorry for him – sorry for his drawn face. 'Is the army really like that?' I asked. 'You're here specially to find one man? Do you know him, who he is?'

'It isn't Hirohito, if that's what you mean.' And then, just as I was about to say 'Sorry,' to try to explain that, with all my faults, I understood his point of view, he spoiled everything as he always had done, every time we quarrelled since I threw the tennis racquet at him in Tanamera. 'Don't worry,' he sneered. 'I'll have plenty of time left to save people like you and the tarts you're sleeping with.'

A car driven by a soldier crunched round the gravel drive and braked in front of us. With a stony face Tim said, 'I'll give you a ring at the office when I've calmed down a bit.'

He felt underneath one of the ugly old chairs for his cap, put it on, and smiled – with thin lips, but not his eyes.

'We'll have lunch perhaps. You might be able to help me to find a man I'm looking for. But we won't lunch here. I've no particular wish to meet Miss Soong again.'

My mouth dropped open.

'You should tell your girlfriends not to leave their ration books hanging around in your bedroom.'

25

In January the raids returned, and the Japanese were soon killing more than two hundred civilians a day. The effect of savage, round-the-clock air attacks was catastrophic. The fires, the explosions, the awful suddenness of death were probably not as severe as they had been in Britain; but the basic problems were magnified by all that the tropics imposed on us – the flies, the heat, the rain, the sweat. It was not the heat of the fires that wore out the ARP men, but the damp enervating heat that never let up, adding a burden which only the toughest could withstand.

The Chinese and Malays in the ARP worked as heroically as their brethren in Europe; but the ARP was understaffed, and all it could do was provide the equivalent of first aid before moving on to the next victim.

Soon the most urgent problem was not so much keeping people alive but finding live people to bury the dead before they rotted. I tried to persuade some of the coolies who worked for us to volunteer, but like many others they refused – not because of the stench of decomposing flesh, soon even worse than the stink of durian, but because more and more men refused to leave their families. A family huddled together in a rickety shack gave an illusion of safety, an added shelter against fear.

One half of Singapore had no idea what the other half was doing. Eric Pretty, the Acting Federal Secretary, and his staff were solemnly burning five million dollars in notes in the government vaults in Empress Place 'to prevent it falling into enemy hands', while round the corner Tommy Kitching, the Chief Government Surveyor, received an urgent request from the army to print new bank notes. The army paymaster was running short of money to pay the troops retreating to the island.

With the monsoon adding to the humidity, with people dying in every street, with the danger of plague from foetid bodies, with the enemy approaching closer every moment, daily life took on a nightmarish quality. It was not fear so much as bewilderment. The fiasco over bank notes was typical, though known only to a few; but all of us could see other examples.

When by chance I met Ian Scott in the Tanglin Club he was reading a bold government advertisement in the *Straits Times*. 'Look at this,' he said. It contained a fervent appeal to everyone to start growing vegetables. Supplies of fertiliser, the advertisement promised, would be distributed by the Food Production Office. 'Don't put it off until tomorrow – start growing vegetables today,' said the ad.

On the next page an advertisement for the New World promised 'Non-stop dancing and cabaret and the usual tiffin dance on Sunday.' This was not the only bizarre advertisement appearing in either the *Tribune* or the *Straits Times*, and as the staff which normally handled these advertisements had shrunk, George Hammonds often had to help out – and was staggered when one came in:

For sale – European guest house in select non-military area. Good business proposition. Reply with bank references.

The Alhambra Cinema offered Greta Garbo and Ramon Navarro in *Mata Hari*. The Cathay cinema advised readers to 'Fling your troubles away and have a fling at love and laughter' by watching their latest comedy.

The personal column adverts of the *Tribune* began to fill up with heart-rending advertisements:

Mrs. J. Norman Miln of Lower Perak and her two children are staying at 27 Newton Road and are anxious for any news of her husband. Sgt. J. N. Miln.

Can anybody give me news of her husband to Mrs. Wong R. Chan, c/o Maynards, Battery Road?

There were other significant signs. The Cold Storage stopped baking its delicious French bread and produced, in common with all bakers, a new government 'Health Bread' which resembled a wholemeal brown loaf. As the army fell back into Johore, north of the causeway, Bill Jackson of the ARP drove to his Store Headquarters to collect some picks and shovels. He found the place deserted, the doors locked. A sign pinned to the door announced, 'Back in four hours'. The man in charge had gone to the cinema.

News of these disasters must, I suppose, have somehow reached people abroad despite censorship; and their anxiety was reflected in the letters I still miraculously received from time to time. There was a change in emphasis. Until Christmas I had been writing worried letters to Mama begging her to take care in England, feeling embarrassed at my own comfort and safety and my inability to help, even with a food parcel. But now Mama wrote to tell *me* to be careful, while Father's business cables included messages of love and anxiety between the humdrum lines of commercial intelligence.

Irene wrote more often too. She was still homesick. Her brother Bill had not been officially reported missing, but the Bradshaws had not heard from him for several weeks, and she wanted to be with her mother, specially as Natasha could look after Bengy. 'But I can't go yet,' she wrote, 'because I'm five months on the way, and not only would it be wicked to bear a child in London now, nobody would let me go. But Roosevelt says we are on the turn – so perhaps I'll be able to get there by the end of the year. Singapore sounds horrific, darling – do take care. I want our daughter (son?) to see his (her?) father as handsome and as healthy as you were when I kissed you goodbye.' There was a PS: 'I won't ask you if you are behaving yourself. But do be discreet!'

I read the letters in the office as I always did, fearful that one might contain an accusation. I always left them there. A guilt complex? Of course. Yet I never felt guilty about Irene in the way I did about Ben. Irene not only hated Singapore and Tanamera; she actively loved her home in Wimbledon. If the two of us had been childless I am sure she would have been delighted at the prospect of divorce – and I knew it would be genuinely amicable.

Compared with mine, Julie's attitude was very straightforward. 'I love you and I always will – but this is only for the duration.' She robbed the words of any offence. 'I don't think we *are* doing wrong – only if we are found out, because then we'll hurt people. But in times like this – I know it sounds an easy excuse, but it isn't meant to be. We've loved each other, you and I, since we were childhood sweethearts. Now's our chance – it may never come again.'

'Really, it's the fault of our parents!' I said. 'If only they had left us alone.'

That was the day she took a long time to reply. I watched her undo her lipstick, unscrew it and dab her lips and then say seriously, 'If I hurt Irene I'm very sorry. Truly I am. But it's strange: I have no *real* sense of guilt. I don't feel as though we are sinning.' She put her lipstick back in her handbag. 'When I was studying philosophy at Berkeley we had to read about an old monk called Pelagius who didn't believe in sin. That's how I feel. Everything's too beautiful to be a sin.'

'Never heard of him.'

'I'll tell you about him one day. He started the Pelagian movement oh, seventeen hundred years ago.'

But somehow she didn't for many years.

I did not see anything of Tim for some time after our last unpleasant meeting, and since I had no idea where he was stationed I couldn't have discovered his whereabouts even had I wanted to. Not that I cared much.

Then in the middle of January, Tim walked into my office. As usual he looked well turned out, uniform pressed – civilians were by now having trouble getting their laundry done.

A thamby came in with some iced lime juice, but as I poured out a glass Tim shook his head.

'It's fresh —' I remembered how as a boy he used to sneak into the kitchen for an extra glass of lime juice.

'No, thanks.'

'Am I allowed to ask what job you're doing?'

'I told you — Intelligence in the Commandos.' He was sitting back in a chair on the other side of my desk, facing a large sepia photo-cum-picture of Grandpa Jack, eyes glaring below bushy eyebrows.

'I popped in to see Grandpa Jack,' he said. 'He seems happy in the General. How old is he?'

'Must be eighty-nine.'

'In Singapore — where you're not supposed to live over forty? He's a marvel. Healthier than Father.'

He was looking again at the sepia photograph. 'Nothing changes here, does it?' He looked around — with a touch of envy, I thought.

'I'd hardly say that. With two hundred civilians a day being killed. *And* an office in which we have to do exactly what we're told. The firm's become nothing but a group of office boys — me included.'

'Sounds as though your reserved occupation isn't quite so essential as it might be.' He toyed with a thin Jensen silver paperknife which Mama had bought for me years ago after a trip to Copenhagen. 'Don't you ever feel you'd like to do *this* to a Japanese?' He gave the paperknife a sweeping, bayonet-like thrust.

'That wouldn't get you very far.' The words slipped out as I thought of my lessons and his amateur attempt to stab thin air.

'Who are you teaching how to kill?'

I forced a laugh and told him I'd read some article on the latest methods of killing.

'Anyway,' he said, 'I'd rather fail in an attempt to kill one bloody Japanese than try to win the war by signing bits of paper.'

I didn't want to provoke an outburst — and anyway, I had to be careful. 'I agree with you,' I said quietly. 'I did try to volunteer, you know. They turned me down flat.'

'Flat! Flat what? Feet?' Then he did have the decency to cry out impulsively, 'Sorry, slipped out. I know you've got an important job – but even so, how can a tough, healthy man like you have the nerve to walk around this place, surrounded by soldiers? Don't you ever feel a sense of – well –'

'Shame?'

'If you like. Yes. After all, it is your city.'

'Yours too.'

'Never. Never again. Was, not is.' He stood up, examined the air conditioner humming in the corner of the room and ran a finger along one of the brown fluted metal vents. 'I'll never come back here after the war. Never. I hate the place and everyone in it – and what everyone stands for. Rotten to the core.'

'Thanks.'

'Well, I wasn't talking about you; but, let's face it, you are one of the people who's been living on the golden eggs hatched in Singapore, and now – well, none of you is doing a damn thing to save the goose that lays them.'

'You oversimplify everything,' I muttered. 'If you hate us all so much why don't you go back to your buddies in the mess?'

'All in good time. I do prefer the mess. But this isn't a social visit. I came to ask advice.'

'On how to win the war?' I couldn't help it.

'All right – have your fun.' For a moment he was silent, as though pondering. And then he said something which staggered me – not only the reply itself, but the ice-cold, casual way in which he delivered it.

'I'm looking for a man I've never seen and I can't find him.'

'The man you were sent to kill?'

'I never said that. Someone I want to talk to.'

'Why come to me? Do I know him?'

''Fraid it's very likely. But it's not going to be very pleasant. I've searched his flat but the bird's flown. However' – he paused – 'I found a fragment of a letter, just a bit

385

of a page, in the bottom of a dustbin. Obviously the rest of the letter was thrown away when the dustbins were emptied. This must have stuck inside the bin.'

'Sherlock Holmes,' I murmured.

'Look, you may hate my guts but shut up – this is serious. It was part of a love letter – and it was just signed with one initial: N.'

'So?'

'I hope I'm wrong, but I'm convinced I recognise the writing. I ought to. I saw it often enough when we were kids.' He fished in his pocket and handed me a torn piece of blue notepaper. 'Here it is – I brought it along for you to look at. That's Natasha's writing, isn't it?'

I felt my guts writhe as I looked at the blue paper. There was no doubt about it. We had always joked about her upright, almost squarely-formed letters, as though she had never outgrown her schoolday lessons. The letter bore her hallmark even without the N.

Playing for time, as the awful possibilities raced through my mind, I asked dumbly, 'Can I read it?'

He handed it over silently. There was nothing to the letter really, no torrid prose, no desperate yearning, just a note so practical in its information that it had clearly been written by a man's lover. 'I'll be along at seven tomorrow evening, but I *must* leave before eight a.m.' And the word 'love' before her one-letter signature had a heart in place of the o. Of course it could only have been written to one man, even though it was undated. The man nobody could find, the man·who seemed to have vanished.

'No doubt about it.' As I handed the letter back I was gripped by such a sense of shock that I felt quite cold, the shirt clammy on my back. 'Do you know who the man is?'

'Do you?' He had obviously asked the question idly, never expecting an affirmative answer, and his mouth dropped with amazement when I nodded. 'You *do*?'

'I imagine it's a man called Bonnard – Bertrand Bonnard.'

Tim whistled. 'So that's what he calls himself,' he said softly.

'He's a Swiss.'

'Is this him?' He took a photo out of his pocket and handed it to me. One look was enough for me to nod.

'He's no Swiss, he's a German,' said Tim grimly. 'A German agent working with the Japanese.'

'He can't be – we're all friends –'

'Christ! Don't be such a bloody Boy Scout – he's one of the top men in the business. He's a killer. He handled Prague – prepared everything, arranged to liquidate any-one who was a nuisance before Hitler marched in. It's said that he was the secret lover of the Countess de Portes – and *she* was the mistress of Reynaud, the French prime minister, and she was the one who persuaded him to give in to the Germans. His speciality is using women. Very attractive, I'm told. But how the hell did Natasha get involved? I thought she and Tony Scott. . . ?'

'She started with him before they got married,' I muttered.

'Christ!' he said again. 'Does no one do *anything* but fuck in this place? And do you mean to tell me she carried on with this – this bloody monster *after*. . . ?'

He sighed, mopped his forehead and asked, 'How are *you* involved?' This was the moment I knew I had to tell him everything – how Miki had introduced Bonnard to Dexters, the deals we had made with the Japanese, his visits to Tanamera. The only detail I didn't mention was Natasha's abortion.

But Tim had been trained, honed sharp as a razor to detect any hesitation, and he pounced. 'You're holding back something. Look, brother – sonny – great lover – call yourself what you like – but tell me *everything*. There's something more about Natasha, isn't there? Can you get it through your thick skull that this bloody man is plotting the fall of Singapore *now*? This very minute. *Here*. We're certain he's in daily contact with the Japanese – telling them how we're doing – or rather, what we're not doing. My job is to find him. And for that I need to know *everything*. What are you holding back about Natasha? I'll give you two minutes, Johnnie.'

'She's innocent. You must promise not to let her know.'

'I promise nothing,' he said harshly. 'If you don't tell me *everything* I can't afford to take a chance on her. One word to the Americans about Natasha's connection with this man and she'll be arrested in New York within an hour.'

'You wouldn't dare.'

'Try me, little brother, just try me. There's a war on. Remember? You're the one who said it made a difference to people's lives.'

'Okay,' I sighed. 'Natasha is expecting a baby. And she says it's Bonnard's.'

Tim said nothing for what seemed a long, long time. Finally he asked, 'Did he know?' And when I shook my head he asked, 'And Tony?' I shook my head again.

'I'm worried about two things,' he said. 'Was Natasha involved? No, no,' he stopped me speaking. 'It's easy to say she wasn't – but when a girl falls for a man – well, look at *your* girlfriend. Natasha probably wasn't involved – but you can never really know.'

'And the other thing?'

'Where is he – where *is* the so-called Monsieur Bonnard?'

'No one's seen him for ages. My bet is he's left the island.'

'He's here all right. He's a pro. He was sent here to work with your Japanese chum – the one you mentioned – and to prepare for the Jap attack on Singapore. No. He's here.'

All the time Tim had been talking – every moment since I first held the piece of blue notepaper – my mind had been whirling round one thought, one location, hidden from everyone in Singapore except secret lovers – and surely Natasha must have been there as well as me. The Love Club of those long-lost wonderful times.

'Did you know Bonnard had a second flat?' I asked.

'I thought he might have. A bolt-hole. Know where it is?'

'Abingdon Mansions.' I told Tim everything – well, nearly everything. I didn't involve Julie, just said I had visited it occasionally, and that Bonnard had told me he used it to entertain girlfriends. If brother Tim elected to think I had used it – well, there was nothing I could do about that. For once his response was almost agreeable.

'Could be just the lead I'm looking for.' He made a note of the number of the flat on the fourth floor. Then he couldn't help adding sarcastically, 'You might get a gong for this.'

I let it pass, for one thing puzzled me. 'Surely you should call in the police?'

'Never. My job is not just finding this bastard. We know he's transmitting to the Japs, and it's essential that they don't know his cover's blown. I've got a replacement standing by, ready to send the information *we* want the Japs to get. I'll let you know what happens.'

As he reached the door he stopped and said, 'I'd almost forgotten – there's something else I want to ask you.' He looked at me hard. 'Have you seen your girlfriend's father lately?'

'You leave Julie out of this,' I said.

'Don't be so bloody touchy. This is also a serious matter. We both know you're living with Soong's daughter – okay, you may think it's a great love saga, but that's by the way. I want to talk to you about her father.'

'What about him?'

He lit a cigarette, inhaled deeply and suddenly became business-like. 'Do you think there's any chance that Soong's a Communist?'

'That's ridiculous,' I almost laughed. 'I'm sure he's not. He's the most die-hard, money-grubbing capitalist in Asia.' As I spoke I had a niggling memory of a conversation on Christmas Day. 'I do remember,' I added, 'one day at lunch Soong asking why we didn't use members of the Communist Party to fight the Japs – but it was only a casual remark.'

'Can you remember when?'

'That's easy. I've only lunched with him once – when he invited me on Christmas day.'

'Did you know that this die-hard Chinese capitalist is paying regular visits to Communist headquarters?'

I recalled Colonel Chalfont – or rather the Oxford professor-cum-brigadier who had interviewed me at the YMCA and who had told me about Julie's father. It was on the tip of my tongue to cry, 'You mean Loi Tek?' Instead I looked (I hope) suitably inscrutable.

'Perhaps you don't know that Soong has been visiting Loi Tek. You know who I mean?'

I nodded. Loi Tek might be a shadowy figure known only to a few intimates, but everyone knew he had galvanised the party in Singapore and Malaya.

'I still can't believe it.'

'Who knows? Soong is a slippery customer. He might be taking precautions – making sure he has friends on every side,' said Tim.

He picked up his cap and prepared to leave. 'If you get any news,' he said, 'phone this number and leave a message. Something innocuous, like Mr Dexter wants to speak to his brother. Something like that, then if I can I'll get back to you. And if I have any luck at Abingdon Mansions I'll let you know.' He closed the door behind him.

Sitting there I thought of everything that had happened. I realised that Tim must be right about Bonnard, but Soong – that was different. I didn't for a moment believe P.P. was a Communist. But if somehow a rumour had started that he was visiting Communist headquarters it might have reached two separate branches of army intelligence, and each might be pursuing separate enquiries. After thinking matters over I decided that, as a member of Force 136, I should report the news to Colonel Chalfont.

I met him at the Adelphi.

'Jolly decent of you,' he offered me a stengah. 'Not really my pigeon, old boy, but I'll tell the brigadier. Sure you didn't let anything slip out?'

I shook my head. 'I'm too frightened to give myself away,' I smiled.

'Good show.' He hesitated. 'I *can* tell you, since it looks as though you'll be passing out soon with flying colours – this man Soong *is* behaving oddly.'

I asked how he could be sure.

'There's nothing to pin down. But it's a fact that he's made several trips to Loi Tek. Don't know why. Ever seen this feller Loi Tek?'

I shook my head again. 'I don't know anybody who's *ever* seen him.'

'Might be nothing to it – perfectly harmless – but I think I'll get the brig. to pull a bit of rank and get your brother's lot off the scent. Otherwise, might just end up arresting each other, what?'

I was dying to ask one question and he knew. 'No,' he shook his head. 'There's nothing to incriminate Miss Soong. We've kept her under surveillance –'

'You mean she's being spied on?' I must have looked horrified, for Chalfont laughed.

'My dear feller – of course! All our lives depend on keeping a secret. One stupid man or woman can betray us, even unwittingly.' He shrugged his shoulders. 'Much better to be on the safe side, old boy. I want to enjoy life when this show's over.'

I was not really upset after talking to Chalfont, because I refused to believe Soong was a traitor. But I did feel guilty about Julie – knowing that her father was under suspicion, yet unable to tell her. I just had to blot out everything I knew, pretend the conversations had never taken place, just as I had to blot out the fact that I was an army officer. It was not easy, except in the gentle isolation of the Cadet House, still empty except for the two of us and Li, who clucked conspiratorially at the presence of Missie for breakfast.

The house did not seem to be in the flight path of the Japanese bombers making their way to the docks day after day. Nassim Hill, the curling, quiet lane at Tanglin, was half a mile on from Orchard Road which in those days was not a shopping centre like Raffles Place, Battery Road and High Street. The bombers usually left Orchard Road alone, though they did fly along it as a guide. But they always flew from the Tanglin end to the dock areas – away from us – so the district round the Cadet House was not in a target area.

Our life there was so perfect that it never occurred to me to try to persuade Julie to be evacuated. Hundreds of women and children were leaving – what Churchill called 'the useless mouths'. Julie wasn't useless, but even so was I being selfish – holding on to an excitement I knew could never last, would probably never be repeated? Perhaps I was, though it wasn't as simple as that. It just never entered my head. Her father was staying, Paul was staying, and despite the suspicions Soong was one of the most influential Chinese in Singapore. Every snippet of news trickling down the peninsula, every detail of every atrocity, indicated that Japanese vengeance was being reserved for the white man. The Japanese would leave families like the Soongs alone when they started to build their 'Co-prosperity Sphere of Asia', if only because they would need them.

I *believe* I felt like that. But I was also conditioned to a spurious sense of safety by the beauty and isolation of the Cadet House. Sometimes, specially in the early mornings, it was hard to believe it was part of a dying city and a dying era. I was thinking like this on the morning of Tuesday, 20 January. I woke at six and crept quietly out of bed, leaving Julie sleeping. I slipped on a pair of old shorts, a shirt and sandals, grabbed a tin of cigarettes, closed the door quietly and walked into the garden. It was the time of day I loved best. Feeling the lush, wet grass under my feet, I crossed the lawn towards the clumps of roof-high bamboo and two casuarina trees with their whispering, lacy foliage, all shielding us from Napier Road and stifling the murmur of the early-morning traffic. It was still cool. The distant gun-fire was no more ominous than far-off thunder. I walked round the gravel path circling the garden, watching two monkeys, tails down. They had ambled in from the nearby Botanical Gardens, and I think they came for company once they knew a human being took regular morning walks.

Half an hour later I returned to the house, showered and shaved. And then, knowing Li would serve breakfast sharp at seven thirty, I crept quietly back into bed, under the single sheet, snuggled up, and gently turned Julie over and started to make love. It was wonderful this way, for this was the moment when I was in control. In the afternoons or evenings, lovemaking was a fight – a fight between two people, each wanting everything, to give everything yet take everything, battling for victory, timing it so both were victorious at the same moment. But in the mornings it was deliciously different. Her eyes were closed, her face framed in black hair. I knew she was half awake, but she pretended to be asleep. I didn't kiss her, I didn't caress her with intent to arouse, just gently moved, forcing myself to make the exquisite moments last forever, almost succeeding, until she made one small movement – no, not the loins; she smiled, eyes still closed, and a sleepy hand gently stroked my neck. It was enough and it was all over.

'You love your personal ones,' she smiled sleepily. 'I love it when you do it like that in the mornings. It's like being raped – by a friend, of course.'

'It's selfish of me,' I kissed her now. 'But it gives me a feeling I can't begin to describe.'

'And me. If she really loves someone there's nothing in the world that makes a woman happier than to feel her man is really enjoying himself.'

I could hear Li shuffling and singing softly outside near the verandah. 'And it does something else.' I looked at her stomach, splashed with black, and turning her over gave her pale gold bottom a smack. 'It gives a man an appetite for breakfast. That's the only reason I do it, really.'

After breakfast on the balcony I stood looking down on the garden in the quickly warming morning sun. The Java sparrows were feasting on the lawn, a couple of mynah birds were chatting away: it was beautiful and strangely peaceful.

Suddenly Julie put her two hands on my cheeks, cupping them, stroking the beardless chin, saying 'You've shaved well – no stubble!' Then she pressed herself against me. We were alone, the door to the room behind closing us off, no one in the garden. She was wearing a long thin white dressing gown and it was not properly fastened round the waist so that by accident – on purpose? – a narrow band of the front was open, and I had the feeling, looking down as she pressed harder, that I was peeping at something forbidden.

As my hand slid down below her waist, so did hers, and she whispered with a tiny laugh, 'Have *I* got the right to rape you? To a personal one? Or is that the prerogative of the lord and master?'

I started to return to the bedroom, but she stopped me, whispering 'No. Here. In the open air.'

I was terrified someone would see us, a gardener, a syce. 'Never mind,' she said urgently. 'It'll only take a minute. And if they do see us we'll never know. Now, on the rattan sofa or up against the wall. But in the open.'

It certainly didn't take long, and I could feel her suddenly droop, exhausted, when it was over. 'Funny girl,' I said after she had insisted on sharing a shower with me. 'What was all that about?'

'Just to show you that we get as randy as men! And because,' she was still smiling, 'I wanted to see your reaction – that of a stuffy English *tuan bezar* when a girl makes all the running.'

That was how Tuesday, 20 January, started, when everything changed, when I knew that I had to get her away, for it was on this Tuesday that Orchard Road was bombed for the first time – just as I was driving Julie down to the Cold Storage to do some shopping.

'I'll get out at the corner of Clemenceau Avenue,' I suggested, 'and you keep the car and go home after you've finished. I'll walk to the ARP station in the YMCA and get a lift back. Promise you'll drive straight home to the Cadet House?'

'Promise. I'm on duty at the Alexandra at three. I'll stay at home until half past two.'

But we never got as far as the Cold Storage. We were almost opposite Wearne's garage when the anti-aircraft guns opened up. There had been no siren. Julie cricked her neck to peer out of the Morris window.

'My God!' she whispered. 'There must be a hundred of them.'

'They're making for the docks,' I said. They looked like silver fish, floating very high, glinting in the sun.

Because her head was half out of the window, Julie heard the first faint whistle above the sound of the car's engine. 'They're bombing *us*!' she shouted.

The whistling grew louder. As I jammed on the brakes, our ears were blasted by a terrifying mixed sound – the crash of impact, the roar, the faint noise of the sirens – everything sounded on top of us, though it wasn't. The car rocked, that was all; the bomb must have landed some distance away.

People ran across the street as we dived for shelter in the nearest drain before the next lot fell. I pushed Julie in, but as I was about to jump on top of her three Indians slithered in before me. There was no room for me. I ran for the shelter of Wearne's garage, twenty yards away. The solo whistle was followed by a concerto – different whistles, different percussion as a stick of bombs cracked the street wide open.

They seemed to straddle us. One tore into a Chinese shop house near me – one minute the house was there, the next there was a gaping hole, as though a dentist had pulled out a tooth. A mysterious current of air plucked me from the shelter of the doorway, floated me across the pavement and deposited me in the roadway. Two bodies sailed past me through the air. An old-fashioned lamp post and a car hurtled by, plunging straight through the plate glass window of the garage from which I had been lifted away. Two more bombs fell. A spume of dirt, dust and fragments jerked into the air just near the drain where Julie was sheltering. I groped my way, spluttering through the acrid fog of dirt and smoke to find her.

Three cars in front of me suddenly blew up with twisting tongues of flame. Next to them a smashed petrol tanker sprawled its ungainly bulk across the road. At first I couldn't see anything clearly, but then a man jumped out of the partly wrecked cab and screamed at me, 'Get this bloody tanker away!' He was a European civilian, I had no idea who, but I saw one thing: his right arm had been blown off above the elbow – the stump was bleeding, his face was bleeding, he couldn't drive. I shouted, pointing to the drain, 'There's a girl –'

'Fuck the girl,' he yelled. 'That tanker will blow up any minute if you don't get it away from the blazing cars.'

I fought my way past the cars. I had never driven anything like this monster before. I climbed into the high cab, found the switch and crashed the lever into the massive gear-gate. I had no idea where the gears were, but I knew I had connected when the tanker gave a spasm. But I was in reverse. And I couldn't get the bloody lever out. I pressed gently on the accelerator, though I had no idea where I was going. We heaved and jerked backwards, rocking, until there was an enormous crash and the engine stalled. I had backed her out of danger – but straight into the front display window of Jasmine's Lingerie. I climbed out. The man with one arm was either dead or unconscious; I never found out.

The drain was choked with rubble, even soil – or it looked like soil. I started scrabbling with my hands. I turned over the top Indian. He had been almost cut in two by the blast or by a bomb fragment, sliced open from the neck to the stomach with all his insides falling out as I held him. I was pulling him clear, hands, clothes, face covered in blood, when a tiny tot of a Chinese girl ran across the road wailing bitterly. She stopped a few yards away, bent down, picked up a rag doll she had been looking for, and instantly stopped crying.

I managed to get the first body out. He had cushioned the other two Indians but both were dead, though not so terribly mutilated. After I had got the third out, but even before I saw Julie, I felt her as my hands probed to push aside the layer of dirt. I could feel the soft, invisible flesh. Carefully I dug with my hands.

A piece of wood – it might have been half a door – was jammed in the drain, and this must have stopped the rubble from choking her. Her face, once I managed to tear the wood away, was the colour of ashes. Some of her clothing had been ripped off her body. Dirty water lined the bottom of the concrete culvert. I cupped some in my hands and splashed her face until finally her eyes flickered open. She owed her life – and I owed mine – to the Indians killed by the blast. When they jumped on top of the ditch, just before I tried to get there, they made a perfect air-raid cushion for Julie. And if they hadn't jumped in I would have been there.

The heat was fearful. So was the smell of death, of open stomachs. Sweat and blood and dirt threatened to close my eyes, and when I tried to wipe my face with my shirt front I found the cloth had been ripped away. I tore the tail from inside my trousers, wiped my face, and then, carrying Julie, made for my car. Miraculously, it and two other cars near it seemed undamaged. There was no selection between life and death, between damage and normality. Wearne's garage was smashed beyond recognition, but the buildings on either side were untouched. Orchard Road looked like a film of no man's land. Flame trees, lamp posts, telegraph poles – anything tall and slender had been uprooted. Windows, doors, flights of stairs hung crazily from walls that still stood in the gaping shells of bombed houses. Some attap huts were burning in a kampong behind the main road. In the half-fog of smoke and dust the stark evidence of the one-sided battle was everywhere. A café at the corner had received a direct hit and the pavement in front was littered with hundreds of smashed-up chairs. A burst main gushed water with the exuberance of a fountain out of control. In front of it huge paving blocks and the deep concrete ditch had been smashed as though a giant had wielded a monstrous sledgehammer, or a thousand bull-dozers had forced their way through, driven by maniacs who had torn the area apart in a moment of unbridled frenzy.

I carried Julie to the car and put her into the left-hand seat, just as the all clear sirens sounded. To my immense relief the Morris responded to the first touch of the button, but as I edged forward gingerly she stopped with a grinding snapping noise. It wasn't the car. I hadn't realised that at the side of the road the uprooted telegraph poles had produced a curtain of hanging, trailing telephone wires and electric cables. Somehow I managed to back the car a few feet, get out and untangle the wires which had become twisted in the front wings and bumper. Only then could I make for the middle of the road and comparative safety. I had just reached it when a British army truck filled with soldiers dodged its way past. One tall, blond boy was stripped to the waist. He held a tommy gun crooked in his arms and shouted, 'The lady okay, mate?'

'Yes, thanks,' I shouted.

'Better not come back!' he cried cheerfully, 'The Japs are coming – they must have seen that sign!' He jerked his gun in the direction of an enormous street hoarding that still stood amidst the wreckage. It bore the slogan, 'Join the army and see the world.'

Back in the Cadet House I put Julie to bed. Li heated a large bowl of Chinese soup, thin but strong and very hot, pieces of white chicken and barely cooked vegetables forming a solid base to the liquid.

His crinkled face was etched with concern, and it gave me a tender yet almost proprietorial feeling to see him in his carpet slippers, tall because of his ramrod straight back, moved by gentleness at the sight of Julie. He seemed to swell with pride every time he had to do something for her, to shrink with worry if anything went wrong.

'You're making too much fuss of me.' Julie, covered by a sheet, pillows propped up behind her back, smiled at him. 'I'm feeling fine – I was safe in a trench. It's the *tuan* who was nearly killed.'

'I bring medicine for *tuan*.' Li's face broke into a beam. I hadn't noticed, but he had also brought a glass of liquid on the tray which he had left on the green-topped table by the door. 'Whisky.'

'Christ, Li, it's only eleven o'clock.' Could the morning really be only half gone? I looked at the Scotch – and immediately I could see my father, warning me, 'Never drink whisky before sundown. Bad for you – and makes your breath smell too. Gin or sherry before lunch, a stengah in the evening.'

'Medicine, *tuan*,' Li coaxed me.

'There's a first time for everything.' I gulped the whole glass, then screwed up my face. 'It tastes foul at this time of day.' But it did send a tingle through my body which I suddenly realised was aching all over.

'I'll have a quick shower,' I said, and in the bathroom

398

peeled off my shirt and the rest of my clothes. Only then did I catch sight of myself in the long mirror on the door. My entire body was one great bruise. My chest was purple, or a mottled green and yellow from one side to the other, across the shoulders and down the arms. That was only the beginning. The sight that really staggered me – and for a moment terrified me – was further down. Not only were my legs bruised, but my testicles were a vivid purple and the size of grapefruit. Yet I didn't feel any pain; in fact, after the first shock, I was so fascinated – and even amused – that after drying gently I put on my white boxer shorts and then, to an audience of one, announced to Julie in the manner of a busker, 'Wake up! Wake up! Your one and only chance to see the engines of Singapore's greatest stud!'

I stood there, posing Atlas fashion, as she turned over in bed. I had forgotten that my chest, streaked like a rainbow, was showing. That was enough. She burst into tears – real salty tears, brought on by bottled-up shock and the sudden sight. 'What have they done, darling?' She jumped out of bed, naked. 'Does it hurt? Can I touch you?'

'It doesn't hurt a bit.' I took her arms and put them on my shoulders – gently. 'It aches – a sort of toothache. But darling – look at *this*!' I took off my shorts.

The tears stopped – turned off by fascination. 'Oh no! My poor darling. Do *they* hurt?'

'Well, I wouldn't like you to squeeze them.'

'Can I stroke them?' She did – very gently. 'Aren't they beautiful? Like pomelos.'

'And about as much use,' I grinned. 'That's enough. I'll let you stroke them again this afternoon if you're a good girl.'

'This *evening* – I won't be here this afternoon – my day at the Alexandra – remember?'

'Are you crazy? Of course you're not working this afternoon after the shock you've had.'

'I must.' She put her arms round me, and was suddenly very serious, the large dark eyes slightly worried, the face framed in black, puckering with secret thoughts, the mouth tremulous. I could never fight with Julie because I just couldn't bear to see her angry, worried or even upset.

'You really *shouldn't* go,' I said weakly. 'You've had a hell of a shock –'

'I'll get off early, I promise – but there are one or two problems I've got to clear up. There's a report on some tests that I must check. *You're* the one who'd better stay in bed – and get those enormous footballs back to normal.' She looked really anxious, or was she just teasing, 'Will you ever be able to make love again?'

It wasn't the lovemaking that worried me, though I would have to wait a few days. It was the prospect of spending four hours at the YMCA. Perhaps they would put me on light duty.

26

I was right. By lunchtime I was stiffening up. No real pain, but I would have been useless in the mud pit, and I doubt if I could have climbed a tree. I wasn't sick; I felt like a boxer must feel, win or lose fifteen rounds on points. But I had to report – that was obligatory. One look by the sergeant, however, and I was excused duty, so I decided to go to the office.

I found it difficult even to walk up the stone steps to the first floor. Some bombs had dropped in Robinson Road, and the office was showing signs of wear and tear. A few more windows had been smashed by blast. Three were boarded up in my office, but the air-conditioner worked, even if some cool air leaked out through the broken glass panel in my office door. Still, after the sweat and heat of the drive the cold air hit me like a needle shower, pumping new life into me the moment I stepped into the room. Ball came in, fussy in the way his type of man so often is.

'I thought you were on ARP duty, sir.' He looked surprised as he leaned in his special confidential manner over my desk – sober, but with a whiff of Scotch on his breath. My father was right – Scotch does smell. I told him what had happened in Orchard Road.

'It's an ill wind.' He sounded relieved. 'I was coming to see you. There's a very strong rumour that Shenton Thomas is going to order the destruction of all liquor stocks.'

'Better hide some Scotch if it's true.' He looked startled and drew back a little, perhaps wondering if I had smelt his breath – or maybe, for once, he had smelt mine.

'We've got a large consignment on the *Willerby* – she's waiting in the roads to be unloaded. What's going to happen if we get it off the ship and then have to smash it all up? Do you think we should refuse delivery? There's a big financial responsibility involved.'

'Don't worry. It might be bombed on the ship,' I said facetiously. 'This liquor-smashing lark, how strong is the rumour?'

'I heard it at the Swimming Club.'

'Don't do anything until I've checked. Phone George Hammonds at the *Tribune*, will you, and ask him if he's going to be at the Cricket Club around five o'clock. Then you might ring Mr Paul Soong – and ask him if he'd like to meet me at Raffles at half past six.'

Rawlings came in a moment later, peering through his glasses.

'Geyland godown is filled with rubber,' he said.

'What's the shipping position?'

'The *Anlaby* is ready – but there are no coolies to load her. And I've just heard from Johore – a miracle, sir, the phone was clear as a bell – they've got four loads. Can we accept delivery if they can get it across the causeway?'

'Well, can we?'

'There's no room, sir, but maybe we could rent some godowns. The commission would be enormous.'

'What use would the bloody commission be?' I tried to keep the harshness out of my voice as I looked at him – and at my office: the Thermos of iced water still changed religiously each morning and afternoon, the boarded windows behind my oak desk, the scribbled doodles on the blotting pad, the broken glass in the door, through which I could see outside, in the general office, the girls and clerks typing or entering figures in books, working as though their lives depended on it when, in fact, their lives depended on graver issues beyond their power to influence.

One of the typists in my line of vision through the broken door was a pretty Chinese girl. I was looking at her – through her, really – when she looked up and caught my eye. She looked positively alarmed – not afraid, but the alarm of anyone whose only objective in a white-dominated society is to remain unnoticed and therefore out of trouble.

Why did she look alarmed? I wondered whether perhaps she thought I had suddenly taken a fancy to her, and that, since she needed her miserable salary to support her crippled husband, she believed she would have to go to bed with me, hating me, to make sure she kept her job. All fantasy, of course; but I remember a Chinese once telling me that most Chinese office girls who were pretty expected the white boss to exercise his *droit de seigneur* eventually. It couldn't be true, I thought. Did the white man really behave so badly to the people of the country he had settled in? Did Rawlings regard the occasional horizontal exercise with Kitty Lim, the newest young filing clerk, as one of the perks of his job? Surely the British weren't as crude as that? Or if we were then Papa Jack had been right to say we needed great changes if we wanted to stay in Asia.

My mind jerked back to reality as Rawlings repeated, 'The commission, sir?'

Ball had just come back in to say he had set up the meetings. All this talk about commission – rubber – Scotch – work – the attempts to carry on as though nothing had happened: it was pathetic. Rawlings, with his pretty, ordinary little wife Rosie and their baby, and Ball, pompous because he had a title instead of being called a shipping clerk, which is what he would have been called in England – couldn't they realise they were helpless on-lookers, watching in slow motion, blow by blow, the end of an era? Whatever happened the present was all over.

Chalfont was right. Nothing could save us. So what difference did it make if we or someone else had to pay for a cargo of smashed-up bottles? It couldn't make any difference if no one had any money.

'Well, will it make any difference?' I asked Ball.

'What difference?' The poor devil looked baffled, as well he might; I had started voicing the end of a train of thought. I tried to explain.

'But we *must* think of the future,' Ball sounded shocked.

'We can't let things *drift*, sir,' added Rawlings.

'But if the Japs take Singapore?'

'Even if they do,' Ball conceded, though doubtfully, 'Japan and Germany can never win a war against the rest of the world – including America. So we're *bound* to defeat them in the end.'

'I agree, sir,' said Rawlings. 'And it would be very embarrassing if the books and records weren't in order when we came back.'

There was no point in arguing, in telling Ball that maybe the Japanese would burn all the books and records. And that if or when we returned Singapore itself would be radically changed, like a man miraculously cured after a traumatic operation. The city would not even *look* the same – and as for a welcome, who could foretell what *that* would be like, after the real people of Asia had watched their fellow Asians thrash the hides off the *tuans*?

Ball was typical of the Britons who assumed that nothing would change. He had sent his wife home long ago, but without ever doubting that when she returned their flat would be untouched, the food on the shelves of the Cold Storage exactly the same. Ball had no children, no relatives in England, even though he was under fifty. 'And I don't really like Mrs Ball's family,' he had once told me primly, hinting at hidden, mysterious in-law forces with which he did not want to be involved. Rawlings was leaving shortly with his wife because of his physical condition. His bad eyesight would make him a liability in Singapore, whereas he could help Papa Jack in London.

'You've got your passage booked?' I asked him.

'I've got to collect the tickets in a few days,' he said, adding defensively, 'it *was* your suggestion, sir – I don't like it.'

'We've been through all that. If you stayed here with those pebble glasses of yours you'd be mistaken for a Jap.' I tried to dispel his guilt complex with a joke – the guilt of leaving, of being forced to leave, was a terrible weight on men, however much they might be secretly afraid of the consequences of staying. 'I applied for your exit visa because we need you in the London office – and you'll be no good here.'

Ball, just because his wife had gone, said sententiously, 'All women should have been shipped out long ago. They would be an added burden if the Japanese arrived.'

Suddenly a face with a trim beard appeared in the broken doorway, as though framed.

'Wilf! I don't know why you're here, but it's great to say hullo.'

I had hardly seen Wilf Broadbent for weeks, though I had caught many glimpses of his sturdy figure sitting upright in fire engines clanging through the streets.

'Saw your Morris outside. I'm on the way to the docks. I was going to phone you anyway.'

The foundations of Tanamera, he explained, had been badly shaken by another bomb, and might now be dangerous.

'It was a near miss,' explained Wilf. 'It *looks* the same – the front, I mean – but a lot of water from broken mains has seeped in, and for the moment we've put up No Entry signs. I thought I ought to warn you. Don't send your man or anyone from the office there. It *might* be okay, but the whole damn lot could fall on top of you. Plaster is a damn funny substance. Sometimes it's only kept up by the wallpaper that covers it.'

'Thanks for letting me know,' I said. 'If I do go and have a look I'll be careful.'

Another face appeared framed in the broken glass – one of the Chinese girls from the outer office. Though I could see and hear her, she automatically knocked on the lower part of the wooden door as she announced that brother Tim was on the telephone.

'Morning Tim,' I said.

'I've only got a second.' Tim never did waste words. 'Just wanted to tell you I drew a blank at Abingdon Mansions. It was his place all right, but not a sign of him.'

'Perhaps he's left Singapore after all?'

'Doubt it. I *know* he's somewhere around. I'll keep you posted.' He didn't even bother to say goodbye, just clicked down the phone.

'I'm off to the Cricket Club,' I told Ball. 'But you may have to help me into the car.'

He looked startled. 'Don't worry – but take a peep at this.' Both men gasped as I undid my shirt front. 'And my balls are the same colour. No, I'm all right really, just stiff.'

Ball *did* have to help me – even down the stone steps, which in places were dangerously worn, and then into the Morris. But once in the car I somehow managed to set off for the Cricket Club. I wasn't in pain, but I was so stiff I found it difficult to coordinate.

Driving slowly, I started thinking again about Ball's remark that all women should be evacuated. I realised I had been thinking more and more about it since the bombs in the morning. Until then I had never thought about Julie leaving. But those bombs – God, how close they had been! It wasn't only that, though. Now we had been living together I realised how deeply I loved Julie, how – simply – *happy* I was. If we ever did come back to Singapore, if the Japs were beaten, then nothing *could* ever be the same again – not only for Singapore, not only for the white man's so-called supremacy, but for Irene and me.

It might be wrong to say that I didn't feel guilty for what I was doing to Irene because I did; but not deeply. I worried more about Bengy. But Irene? In a way Julie was right when she said that I had paid my debt. Julie had come first, and we had only been separated by stupid (loving?) parents. Now that we were together I knew we would never be parted.

I had talked often to Julie about it, but her attitude was different. Though we were both, so to speak, living for today, I kept on thinking of tomorrow; she insisted on using 'today' as a yardstick. After the bombs had fallen in Orchard Road, and she wondered why the Indians had died while she was spared, I said, half facetiously, 'Perhaps it was a warning – the sort of punishment we face if we don't stop behaving like this.'

'We could have been killed at that moment,' she said, 'and if we hadn't come to live in the Cadet House we would have died without ever knowing the wonder of all this. But we have known it now, so if we do die tomorrow at least we'll have known this happiness.'

She wasn't being morbid, only determined to extract from the prospect of death every ounce of life she could. But I was worried about the future – not Irene; I had a feeling she would understand; even a feeling that if – when – whether – Singapore came alive again and the smoke and bombs gave way to the peace we had known, she might even give a sigh of relief, she might prefer to use my misbehaviour as an excuse to stay in London as a divorced woman rather than return to a city she hated. Secretly I hoped so. And it was because of my concern with the future, because I was actually *living* with Julie, that I did think of the future – a future for Julie and myself.

I had been given a second chance at life; it had taken a war, men and women uprooted, tortured, killed, to give me that chance. I remembered a sentence by Anatole France, 'Chance is the pseudonym God uses when he doesn't want to sign his own name.' He had gone a long way round to offer us that chance – wouldn't I be displaying base ingratitude not to take advantage of it?

I knew now that I could never put the clock back at the end of the war. And now that I realised this, shouldn't I show Julie how much I loved her by begging her to leave, to be evacuated to safety?

I swung the Morris through the broad gates of the Cricket Club, with its lion shield emblazoned on the noticeboard by the front entrance. It was incredible: despite all the guns and bombs and black, bitter news, there was hardly a space to spare in the parking lot. I was not only aching all over; I was drenched in sweat after the effort of turning and twisting the car into a vacant slot. I walked, bending like an old man, through to the verandah. Every long chair was filled. Every small bamboo table was loaded with glasses, empty or full, under the whirring fans. Boisterous voices bellowed in the billiards room behind the verandah, 'Have a go, Jim!' or 'Don't be a bloody fool!' – a sign that a foursome was engaged in that most dangerous of gambling games, volunteer snooker. The drinkers on the verandah were just as boisterous. Many had arrived directly from offices or ARP duty because burst mains had cut off some water supplies but you could still get a shower at the club. I looked out over the padang. The tennis courts had gone. In front of the verandah steel pylons sprouted as a deterrent to gliders. By their sides were the half-filled trenches. It all looked very messy.

While I looked round for George Hammonds, I asked Chan, the head steward, for a stengah. When he brought it, the soda still bubbling gently in the tall glass, I automatically looked for the usual proffered pencil and pad to sign.

'No more chits, *tuan*.' Chan looked unhappy.

I was so astounded I almost dropped my glass. 'What the hell do you mean, Chan?' I asked. I had been signing chits at the club since I was old enough to be elected. I signed chits *everywhere*. Nobody in Singapore ever carried cash – youngsters even signed chits at the local bordellos.

'Haven't you heard?' I turned at the sound of George's voice over my shoulder. 'It's cash only from today.'

'But you must be joking – it's bloody crazy – I've no money – I never have any!'

'Be my guest,' Hammonds had a soft agreeable voice, always lightly hesitant, though there was nothing hesitant about the way he ran the *Tribune*.

'But what's this all about?' I asked. 'Don't tell me the governor –'

'No. Not him for once. Cheers!' He ordered refills. 'You're drinking to an historic moment in the life of Singapore. The Chinese have decided we're going to lose – they're the ones who decided it's to be cash only from now on. How they did it beats me – their grapevine is incredible – but they *know*.'

When I echoed the word know he nodded, 'Yes – know. They know we're sunk.'

Did it apply to everything, I asked George. Apparently it did, though no one ever discovered how the move had been coordinated. The whisper had travelled round like a Chinese wind, telling everyone the Japanese were going to win, and – with the prospect of unhonoured chits – a system which for decades had worked smoothly was abolished overnight.

'Better get some cash from the bank before it's all gone,' sighed George. 'If you want to continue drinking, that is.'

George was one of those journalists who knew everyone, and everything, because his informants could trust him not to print news they shared with him in confidence. 'I'm not after the old-fashioned scoops,' he once told me, 'but I do like to see into the future, so that without breaking any confidence the *Trib* doesn't make a fool of itself.'

'But will we be *able* to drink?' I told him about the rumour I had heard of a ban on liquor.

'The Order in Council has already been drafted,' he admitted. 'It's bound to come any day now. But I can't print a word – the government is scared stiff that if the news gets out there'll be a rush to hoard drink. For once Shenton Thomas is right. The Japs went berserk in Hong Kong after they'd looted the liquor stores there.'

Paul was already at Raffles, propping up the Long Bar, when I arrived. As usual he looked elegant, his sharkskin suit as pressed as though he had just stepped into it, his dark hair neatly brushed, his shirt unruffled, his brown and white co-respondent shoes spotless. As I walked through the entrance and across the huge room, he looked as if he were living in the midst of perfect peace without a care in the world. Paul, even in the midst of war, looked what he was – a young rich Asian, a member of a noble family, a man who knew that the war, however distasteful, would pass him by. He was almost urbane – with a confidence that gave him a certain disinterestedness. I couldn't help comparing him with the barman, for they both had one characteristic in common – victory by the Japanese would no doubt be annoying, but each would carry on; the bar would still remain open and, unless he behaved stupidly, the barman would be serving gin slings or stengahs to Singapore's new masters once the hubbub had died down. And Paul Soong, his powerful family steeped in prestige and wealth, would no doubt carry on too, missing his old friends, habits changed, but still making the best of it. I wondered if Paul would ever *feel* the war. I knew he hated the Japanese, I knew he loved the British, but the Chinese have a great facility for adapting themselves to change.

At least a couple of dozen men were propping up the Long Bar. 'Amazing really, how war seems to make no difference to drinking,' I told Paul. In one corner the click of liar dice was followed by mock howls of anger from the loser. The Chinese boys served drinks swiftly, politely. The first mosquitos were invading the room.

'You'll have to pay, Paul,' I said. 'I only heard about this chit business an hour ago. And I've got no cash with me.'

'Don't worry, just watch.' Paul gave his low chuckle and the tremor of a wink as the stengah appeared and the barman gravely handed him a chit and pencil.

'Ah! Good old Raffles – the exception,' I said. 'Now I can stand *you* a drink –'

'Not so,' said Paul. 'I heard about the chit rumour early this morning – and as this is about the only place where I can drink with my European friends I brought five hundred dollars along and left it here so that I can sign against it. I'm damned if I'm going to start filling my pockets with loose change just because a handful of Japs –' He shrugged his shoulders, picked up some nuts and asked, 'How's my kid sister?'

'Julie's fine, but only just.' I described the morning's narrow escape. 'I've been thinking, Paul – she ought to get away – home –'

'Home! That's a good one.'

'You know what I mean – Australia or South Africa – it's

going to be panic stations here for a woman if the Japs take over. You've heard what happened in Hong Kong. The Japs went crazy with the women. And there's something else,' I hesitated and then said very slowly, 'I don't know how – or where – but Paul, I'm going to marry Julie when all this is over.' I stayed his interruption. 'I know you're going to say I'll feel different when Irene comes back –'

He laughed. 'I wasn't going to say anything of the sort. You're an idiot, Johnnie – of course you think you're going to marry her. I know you're mad about her – and you're the marrying sort. Besides' – with mock disapproval – 'do you think I'd let my sister go to bed with somebody who wasn't serious? But marriage? It's amazing how men fall out of love when a war ends.'

'You're wrong about Julie and me. I don't know what the hell's going to happen, but I'm serious.'

Suddenly quiet, he put a hand on my shoulder and said, 'Johnnie, I'd love you two to get married. Mind you,' he gave his slow, disarming smile, 'I don't think you ever *will*. You're up against an enemy much tougher than the Japs. Our fathers are like two immoveable objects.'

'To hell with them!'

'I'll drink to that,' he laughed, 'but though *we* can say it, Julie never will. She may worship you – I really think she does, crazy kid – but you know as well as I do that with the Chinese, family comes first. She'll never disobey her father.'

'What's she doing now, for Christ's sake?'

'Working at the hospital – that's our story, and we're sticking to it. My father is probably the only man in Singapore who doesn't know she never sleeps at the Alexandra. Lucky for you everyone is too afraid to tell him. War gives young ladies a lot of extra liberties – and not only for the men.'

'Your father couldn't forbid her to leave. I'm going to ask her tonight.'

'She'll say no. Bet you ten dollars – cash, remember, no chits.'

'Done,' I said, even though I felt I would lose.

But Julie didn't say no. I broached the suggestion gently, expecting opposition, as we sat on the verandah after supper. Late evening in Singapore was almost as blissful as early morning, not quite so cool, but the windless night was alive with noises: the hum of mosquitos, the fluttering of moths, the croak of bullfrogs, the endless crack–crack of cicadas. Every now and again the thick clumps of bamboo at the bottom of the garden were lit up by a blaze of silent sheet lightning.

'This morning really gave me a fright – for you,' I started warily. 'You know how much I love you, Julie – and I beg you, if you really love me – will you get out of Singapore while you still have a chance? For my sake, if not for yours.'

She was very thoughtful for her – and under the light of the yellow–shaded lamp, noisy with moths banging against it, I could see her 'sad look'.

'Just think of one thing,' I begged her with a white lie. 'I suppose I'll be interned. Perhaps for years – just think how relieved I'll be, happier – with more courage if you like – to face the years ahead, if I know the one I love more than anyone in the world is safe. Imagine the difference it'll make to my morale, and think of the alternative – wondering what's happening to you – with me in Changi, I suppose, next door to Tasek Layang, and you next door, yet a million miles away.'

'I've thought of that – and of other things too.'

I started to talk, but very quietly she said, 'Don't interrupt me. You don't have to persuade me.'

I gaped at her, speechless.

'I want to leave – for my sake as well as yours.'

'Julie, what on earth do you mean?'

The sad look was replaced by a tiny, slightly mischievous smile, just a twitch at the corner of the mouth, the smile of a naughty girl found pinching the jam.

I must have looked astonished, and when I asked, 'What made you decide?' she laughed, 'Now – don't try to make me change my mind back again!'

'Why *do* you want to leave?' I persisted.

'Before I tell you, will you promise me one thing – on the

Bible, so to speak – promise you'll never tell anyone, and especially Paul.'

'Of course I promise.'

'And will you answer one question – really honestly?'

I nodded again.

'These weeks have been the happiest of all my life,' she said. 'Tonight, it's as though I'm your wife. I know it's only pretending – supper at home, coffee on the verandah, then bed – does it mean that to you? Do you feel like my husband? Or is it just a war-time adventure to you?'

'I've *always* said I wanted to marry you. Do you know what I told Paul earlier this evening? I told him that when this bloody business is over I am *going* to marry you.'

'Thank you for telling Paul. It makes it easier.'

'Makes what easier? For God's sake stop talking in riddles.'

'I was afraid to tell you – why I've decided to go. But I'm not afraid now,' she stroked me gently on the cheek. 'Can't you guess? Didn't I hint this morning when I told you that I had to check on a report at the Alexandra? Some tests on a patient – remember? Well, darling blockhead, the tests were about *me* this morning, and they were positive. We're going to have a baby.'

27

What twists of irony fate gleefully keeps up her sleeve. I remembered the dull sickness that twisted my guts when Irene whispered that she was pregnant. It wasn't fair! Marriage? It had never entered our heads. I liked Irene; I just never wanted to marry her.

Now someone had spun a coin and it had landed the other side up. As we sat that night on the verandah talking it over, we both faced untold problems, a long separation, the prospect of death, angry parents, chains of marriage that would be difficult to break however much I wanted to. And yet, with all this, and the Japanese almost at the southern tip of Johore poised for invasion, we sat on the verandah drinking in the warm night with its slight breeze, the sweet smell of the tropics, the Milky Way like a curtain above us, and we were suffused with our happiness.

'There must be something wrong with us,' I said, as Julie sat on the rattan sofa leaning close to me. 'We *should* be terrified of the future. Our families are never going to forgive us.' A distant growl of gunfire rolled like thunder. 'Listen – even the world won't forgive us!'

She snuggled up, forgetting my bruises. 'But nobody's going to know for years – and nothing can ever be as bad as it is now.'

'As bad – and as wonderful, Julie. The only thing I'm worried about is you.'

'And the only thing I'm worried about is you,' she kissed me lightly. 'Remember Johnnie, I'm one of the lucky ones. I *hate* leaving you, but at least the Soongs have money tucked away abroad – South Africa and London, I think. At least I'll be able to have our baby in peace – and in secret.'

That was true. Normally the dutiful daughter of a strict Chinese father could never have travelled abroad even for a week without his permission. Now, a war which had been partly responsible for the problem might also be a war which would solve it. Given money – Paul and I would see to that – Julie could disappear for months, and war could always be the scapegoat, blamed for lack of communication, for censored letters.

'Will you try to get away, Johnnie?' she asked. 'For my sake? Try to escape? You can't just wait here and let the Japanese take you to Changi.'

I couldn't tell her that my future was already being organised by others. If only I could whisper that I was training for the biggest battle of all. Did she even wonder if I had a yellow streak? Chalfont had been right; keeping my secret was the toughest part of the job. 'I'll be fine,' I answered evasively. 'And by the time the war's ended everything will slot into place. I'll have no trouble getting a divorce. War changes everything, you'll see.'

'You still won't be able to take me to the Cricket Club,' she teased.

'Care to bet? If we lose Singapore – and then get it back – nothing'll be the same again.'

'I wonder,' she said. 'Having a baby brings me closer to you than I've ever been. Now I have a part of you living inside me, and when I do leave some of you will be going with me. It's a wonderful feeling for a woman – whatever happens, even if – well if we're parted forever, there'll be a bit of you. It's sloppy, I know . . .'

I could see that she was almost crying with happiness, but I had to stop her tears. 'Tonight of all nights you make life sound so morbid – so final.'

She snuggled closer to me. 'I didn't mean to. But I wonder sometimes – we *did* say that first night – when the war's over –'

'That's nonsense,' I shouted. '*That was then*. Now you're going to have a baby everything's changed.'

'Darling Johnnie, you're so naive. How you make money at Dexters I don't know. Why has everything changed? How can the baby that I'm going to have change your feelings for your beloved Bengy? He's your first-born.' She paused to light a cigarette. 'I'm deliberately not thinking about Irene. I feel no *real* guilt about her; I'm only ashamed of the way I've pinched her husband. But I did vow to give you back – to your son too. Why should my baby take preference over him?'

I said nothing, for there was no answer I could make.

'One of the things I learned when I took philosophy at Berkeley was that the great thinkers always faced their problems one at a time. So wait, my darling. The world has a way of sorting things out on its own. Let's win the war first and then see what happens. Until we do win – until I go – we belong to each other. As we have always done.'

There was much to do in those days. We decided to tell no one, though my first instinct had been to confess everything to Irene by letter and so prepare the way for any postwar action.

'Absolutely not!' Julie was adamant. 'You gave me your word. You promised, and I'm going to hold you to it. First of all, if you *did* tell Irene it would get back to my father. Then you'd be hurting lots of people without any need to.'

'They'll have to know sooner or later.'

'Perhaps – but you might never have to tell them. After all, girls do have miscarriages – and then you'd have shattered everything for nothing.'

I was suddenly tormented by suspicion. 'Julie, *you* promise *me* – you'll never, never do anything – have an abortion – or anything?'

She smiled. 'Don't worry about that. I want my baby more than anything I've ever wanted in the world. Even if you –'

'Now, Julie, don't get morbid –'

'No – if you change your mind, I would always want the baby.' Then, with her teasing look, 'but don't change *your* mind or I'll come after you with a parang!'

There was no danger of that. I, too, wanted her to have the baby – but for other reasons as well. I suppose in a closely knit family like ours, with a dominant father once dominated by his father, sons tend to behave weakly towards their parents; or perhaps a better way of putting it would be that we were chained by a kind of loyalty, sometimes unnecessary. I don't think I was actually afraid of standing up to my father, but I knew I would be grateful for some positive assistance in the event of a showdown. In other words, when the time came I knew it would be difficult to tell him I was divorcing Irene if I merely said that I loved Julie and wanted to marry her. But if I could confront Papa Jack with the fact that we already had a child it would be easier. And Irene would never stand for it.

I had to tell Paul – not about the baby, but that Julie had agreed to leave, because we needed his help.

'You owe me ten dollars,' I said. 'Cash, remember?'

'Damn it, she *must* love you!'

Paul felt that if possible Julie should go to America.

'Won't her mother be upset?'

'I don't think so,' said Paul. 'Life is so topsy-turvy she'll have to take things as they are.'

We both agreed to check on the shipping, but soon discovered that no more boats were sailing to the States. She would probably have to go to Colombo or India, Australia or South Africa.

I had been meaning to ask Paul one question for a long time. 'Why don't you go?'

'And leave Father?'

'He could go too. I'm sure it could be arranged.'

'For a start, he won't. He refuses point blank to budge – and I can't say I blame him. Papa Jack had a *reason* for going – to take the place of someone who was killed. But this is the Soongs' home. And there's a business to run. Come to that, why don't you get Grandpa Jack away? That's even more crazy, him staying here.'

I sighed. 'You don't have to tell me that. It's absurd. But you know, Paul, he's actually enjoying himself for the first time for years. He's revelling in everything.'

The last time I had visited the General Hospital my grandfather was holding court with his fellow inmates, as he called them, and all sorts of crazy plans for his own good had crowded my thoughts. I had even wondered if we could arrange for a doctor to give him a shot, put him to sleep, while we got him on board a ship. Crazy, of course; and anyway, with ships being sunk, hospitals being bombed, women being raped, men being tortured, how dare I presume to know what was good for a happy old man? My father had decided what was good for me, and what a sorry mess that had turned out to be.

'But what are you going to do?' I asked Paul.

'Oh,' he said airily, 'I'll melt into the scenery. Come to that, have *you* ever thought about going? With Julie?'

'Not allowed to,' I said shortly. 'No men can leave without special orders. And I couldn't anyway.'

'Not even for Julie? Isn't she' – his smile robbed his

words of any offence – 'worth more than a point of honour? And apart from Julie, which is worth more: to obey orders from an old buffer like Shenton Thomas whose government has let us all down, and be interned, or escape and live to fight another day?'

'There's no answer to that.' I could not tell him what was really going to happen to me. 'But you? I'm worried about *you*.'

'Wasted worry! I've got plans.'

'Such as?'

'Well – I see it this way. If you lot are all bundled off to Changi there's bound eventually to be some leak from the camp to here – some way of making contact. I might be useful. I'm above suspicion here. I'll be able to move freely.'

'That's what you think. The moment you start poking your nose into the world of the rising sun yours'll start setting.'

'There'll be something for me to do. Apart from anything else I've got a short-wave radio stashed away. Transmitter and receiver. I'll make myself useful.'

I was horrified. Didn't Paul know that direction-finders could trace any transmission? He hadn't been trained to get mixed up in a war. 'Don't do anything stupid,' I begged him. 'I expect you to greet me with a large Scotch when I come back.'

All this lay in the future. The present was more pressing.

As the Japanese prepared for the final onslaught an utterly different, more menacing element tore into our lives – shelling. There was something almost inhuman about this new sound – a low whine in the distance which slowly crept up the scale until it reached a wild, screaming noise culminating in a piercing crescendo. And no one knew where the noise would end. Bill Jackson's wife Marjorie heard one of the first shells in Orchard Road. 'At first nobody had any idea what the sound was,' she told her husband. 'The noise seemed to hang in the air. I felt as though I'd been hypnotised – I can't describe the terrible scream. Then a soldier shouted that it was a shell and we all dived for shelter.'

The raids were being stepped up, too. Using four airfields which they had repaired in Johore, the Japanese were sending not only dive bombers but fighters to cruise low over Singapore city, machine-gunning the streets or dropping showers of small anti-personnel bombs which burst in the air into hundreds of tiny, sharp fragments of shrapnel. The pockmarks of war showed everywhere. Hardly a street was without a gaping hole or jagged ruin to mark the path of bomb or shell, though some places seemed to bear charmed lives. The Cricket Club had only been bombed once. Robinson's was never hit again after the first night. The Singapore Club down by the waterfront was untouched apart from a few shrapnel scars. But in some parts of China-town entire streets had been badly damaged, and the docks always seemed to be on fire.

Each day also brought mounting evidence of an uglier mood, particularly among battle-weary soldiers who had retreated from Malaya, fighting every inch of the way. Time after time I came across bewildered knots of men wandering, grimy and leaderless, apparently without any-one to direct them. Ian Scott found the compound of his bungalow filled with convalescent soldiers – who didn't look very sick. The road from his bungalow was blocked for hours because a column of troops couldn't find an officer to tell them whether to take the left or right fork. Many troops were desperately tired, yet often they couldn't find their units and had to sleep on the floor of a requi-sitioned building after a supper of tea and buns. Others who did manage to find their commanding officers still had nowhere to sleep – because there were not enough tents, and billeting officers had been unable to find enough rooms. We had rooms at the Cadet House that we would cheerfully have given to any troops, but every time I offered them to someone in authority they made a careful note of the address – and nothing happened. It was chaos. Gunners couldn't find their guns, army cooks couldn't find their food, pay-masters couldn't find their money. Inevitably drunken, dishevelled troops appeared, reeling round the main squares, waving bottles of cheap liquor. Their mood became more bitter, and more belligerent, with each new raid or rumour. Looting was widespread.

Broadbent was clanging along to a fire when a bunch of drunks, amused by his beard, jeered, 'Let it burn, dad! It's too late.' They started to pelt him with – in his words – 'big oblong missiles', two of which landed by the front seat. They turned out to be cartons of cigarettes.

Paul told me that one evening on his way home he noticed a Chinese boy laboriously trying to ride a brand-new bicycle which was far too big for him – it had obviously been stolen. A group of children in nearby Beach Road were playing in a big, abandoned American car. Further on, a family outside a smashed dwelling was eating rice when a tiny naked girl ran breathlessly towards them carrying a chicken. The mother guiltily bundled it under her clothes and hurried inside the ruins.

In Government House Shenton Thomas struggled to 'live according to his station'. Each morning after breakfast – which inevitably ended with toast and marmalade – the cook brought the day's menu for his approval, though lunch was largely reduced to cold cuts. Shenton Thomas, however, insisted on guests wearing collars and ties. The shells had now found the range of Government House. Firing from Johore, at twenty-four thousand yards range, and aided by an artillery-spotting balloon floating high in the sky, the Japanese bombarded the residence with devastating accuracy.

I might have felt more sorry for the plight of the governor and Lady Thomas had I not been suddenly summoned to Government House. The phone rang one morning and Archie Goodman, of the Public Works Department, who was very close to the governor, said, 'You're wanted up at GH. Twelve thirty tomorrow morning – a conference with a gin thrown in if you're lucky. He wants to discuss a scorched earth policy.'

I had my own reasons for going. I could not disguise the fact that with the growing shambles in Malaya Dexters was losing vast sums of money. We had luckily always kept cash in the bank, but cash *flow* was a very different matter from cash in hand. Our highly profitable lumber business, with its ready-to-wear huts and barracks, had been overrun by the advancing Japanese, though on my orders all stocks and machinery had been destroyed. Those of our ships still afloat were virtually under the control of the military (though they often left us to pay the crew's wages). When we managed to get a cargo of rubber or tin away we received a credit note from the military authorities. But there was no way of cashing it, even at a discount. Our insurance business had vanished, and the only thing that seemed to remain unchanged was the cost of running a business which had no business to transact. The wages had to be paid, not only in Robinson Road but at our godown and lighter complex on the river at Geylang.

Of course my troubles – echoed by every businessman in Singapore – mattered hardly at all in the context of the war; that I realised. And I knew too that Papa Jack would be the first to sacrifice the entire Dexter fortunes if it became necessary in a last-ditch stand to beat the Japs. Still, if any offers were made, commitments entered into in the case of a scorched earth policy, I wanted to know where Dexters would stand, how much they would be paid after the war was over. It was not unlikely, for instance, that the navy might order us to scuttle our last remaining vessels. Who would pay to replace them?

I had for years been a regular visitor to Government House. The Dexters, as one of Singapore's most respected families, were always 'on the list', whoever happened to be governor. I drove up past the trim, tree-studded lawns to Government House, which was built on a rise, and was taken straight up to the first-floor balcony with its superb view over Singapore. Several other men had already arrived, including Brigadier Ivan Simson, Chief Engineer, in charge of defence works. I had met him before and admired him, though I knew he didn't get on with Percival – which was understandable.

The conference opened with decorum. Whatever the

pressures, Shenton Thomas was determined to uphold the dignity of his position. All of us wore ties, despite the heat. The governor's head boy dispensed gimlets or pink gins, while other boys laid out assorted cold (and tinned) meats and salads for a working lunch.

Thomas's authority was rapidly dwindling as the military virtually ignored him. Despite his treatment of Papa Jack, at first I felt rather sorry for him, for he was in an invidious position, especially as the military generals like Percival and Gordon Bennett, the Australian, who were whittling away his authority, were hardly proving to be military geniuses. But I felt only a burning anger by the time I left.

Simson spoke first. He had only one thought: to avoid a repetition of the disaster in Penang where, in the hurried British flight, the Japanese had been presented with equipment ranging from a radio station in working order to a fleet of small ships which they had gratefully used to invade Malaya further south. And Simson knew (as he told me) that Churchill had cabled the Singapore command that he expected 'every scrap of material to be blown to pieces to prevent capture by the enemy'.

But the brigadier faced a problem. Though the governor was by now little more than a figurehead, he *was* still responsible for civil affairs, and he was determined that if the Japanese took Singapore the Asian businessmen would be able to carry on as best they could, for they would merely be changing masters.

Simson, however, wanted overall *advance* permission from the governor to destroy about a hundred major installations on the island – though, as he insisted, only if it became necessary. As Simson pointed out, the army could not destroy civilian equipment – he cited a tin dredger as an example – without government permission, and so the Japanese had time after time been presented with valuable equipment during their advance down Malaya, simply because it had been physically impossible for the army to get permission to destroy it in time. And if the army did destroy equipment without government authority they would face post war claims for damages. It was absurd, but there it was.

'And it has to be changed,' said Simson.

Together the governor and Simson went through the list of major installations on the island. But then I saw the governor hesitate. Finally he dropped his bombshell. He refused to sanction the destruction of forty large Chinese-owned engineering works. I watched Simson. His mouth literally fell open with dismay as Shenton Thomas took the list and calmly crossed out the names of Chinese-owned businesses. And these were not unimportant back-street garages. There were big workshops, many equipped with the latest and most modern machinery. Others, I knew, were stacked with new vehicles which had been ordered through us before the war broke out.

Simson, who could hardly believe his ears, cried, 'But they'll be invaluable to the Japanese! Why sir? What's the reason?'

The governor, I remember, was sipping a drink. He held his glass up and gazed reflectively into it, before uttering, quite calmly, a phrase that seemed to haunt officialdom – both military and civil – during the entire campaign. Turning to Simson, he said simply, but with complete finality, 'It would be bad for morale.'

'But we can't make a present of all this to the enemy!' cried Simson.

The governor gave Simson what I can only describe as a hard, long look, and said coldly, 'I would remind you, Simson, that we haven't lost the island yet.'

And that was the last word on the matter. Most of the important Chinese engineering works were to be left in running order for the enemy – and Simson could only study the names still left on his list, about forty-seven British-owned plants. These he was allowed to deny to the enemy if the moment arrived.

Within a few hours the repercussion from infuriated British businessmen started echoing across Singapore, causing more bitterness and anger than even the bombing and shelling, and none of this bickering helped civilian morale, especially as there was a complete lack of any inspiration to civilians, no direct appeal to us, exhorting us to prepare to fight to the last man in the last corner of the last street. There were more than a million civilians in Singapore by now – civilians with their backs to the sea – yet the army, to say nothing of the government, seemed to contradict themselves with every official pronouncement.

General Percival talked (publicly) of 'the enemy within our gate', 'loose talk' and 'rumour-mongering', all calculated to alarm – when in fact there was no fifth column in Singapore. A few days later General Wavell issued his Order of the Day stressing that our job was to gain time for the great reinforcements which he promised would arrive. Yet in the next breath he demanded that 'We must leave nothing behind undestroyed that would be of the least service to the enemy. I look to you all to fight this battle without further thought of retreat.'

As George Hammonds put it, 'It isn't clear to me how anyone can retreat from a beleaguered island, nor how the scorched earth policy Wavell is demanding could help the reinforcements which he says are on the way.'

Since there was no one to inspire people, no one to lead them, tell them what to do, our unreal existence developed into a spending spree greater than anyone could remember. The thousands of soldiers on the island – who presumably never contemplated defeat – spent all their spare cash buying souvenirs to take home. The small shops and stalls in Change Alley – the traditional bargain-hunter's paradise off Raffles Place – were jammed with more customers than in peacetime. In Raffles Place itself Robinson's couldn't cope with the shoppers. When I walked into Kelly and Walsh, the booksellers, I found they had almost run out of 'serious books'. Round the corner in Battery Road, Maynard's the chemists still had a waiting list for their Elizabeth Arden beauty treatments. Fraser and Neave still bottled their soda water. Tiger beer was still being brewed. The brickworks were making bricks. Wearne's garage in Orchard Road, where I had so nearly been killed, was inundated with minor repair jobs because cattle from the dairy herds had reached the outlying districts of the city and motorists regularly hit them in the black-out.

If you wanted to dine at Raffles you still had to book a table. At the Great World, a soldier had to queue for half an hour before he could get a dance with a taxi girl – unless he invested in a complete roll of tickets and waved them, whereupon the girl, who got a percentage, would attach herself to him for the rest of the evening. For the taxi dancers and prostitutes this was their biggest boom ever.

For me there was a personal agony now I knew Julie was leaving. I was the one who had to make the arrangements, the life or death decisions, and I was haunted by terrible fears that I would make the wrong ones. I would perhaps have to choose the ships, the destination (if any choices were left by the time she sailed) and from time to time I would suddenly feel certain I was sending her to her death.

I wasn't tortured by thoughts like this all day long, and they melted away when we were together, but I woke one night sweating from a nightmare: I was standing on a beach with Miki and he was machine-gunning a rowing boat in which Julie and her baby were sitting. I begged him to stop, but all he hissed was, 'You put Julie on wrong boat. Other boat already arrive.'

I wanted her to go, of course. Now more than ever. But wanting to do something for someone doesn't necessarily mean a lessening of grief. I might feel a profound sensation of relief when she sailed, but that wouldn't lessen my loneliness or pain.

At least one selfish thought helped to lessen my gloom. It had nothing to do with her safety but with my pride. I had become increasingly haunted by one thought: when Singapore was about to fall I would certainly receive secret orders. Equally certainly, they would instruct me to sneak away like a thief in the night, without telling anyone. If Julie *had* decided to stay in Singapore what would she have thought in the years ahead of the healthy young man who never fought, but at the last moment ran away without saying goodbye to the girl who was carrying his child?

2

I had returned to 'ARP duty' after two days and by now Julie was sometimes working twelve-hour shifts at the Alexandra Hospital. After some raids, when the water mains were hit, water was so short that doctors and nurses had to wash their hands and instruments in soda water before operating. Sometimes she snatched a little sleep on the floor of a corridor overflowing with wounded and other nurses.

I, too, was working flat out. Three of our ships had been bombed by now, and in addition to office work I still had to spend my four hours a day at the YMCA. Each of us snatched sleep wherever and whenever we could, falling exhausted into the arms of the one already in bed.

28

The time was fast approaching when Julie would have to leave, for we both realised that a Japanese attack on the island was inevitable, even imminent. Some still believed, or half-believed, that Singapore could go down in history as another Stalingrad, that, with the cream of our troops back on the island and reinforcements on the way, we could repel any invader. But it would be a bloody task — and though the prospect of Julie's departure was like a bad dream I was also terrified she wouldn't get away in time, for her sailing depended entirely on the arrival of ships bringing in the 18th Division.

Julie had already obtained her exit visa, but we had to wait to get her ticket until the shipping position was known. Finally she was told to collect it on Friday, 6 February. In all probability she would sail the following week.

Soon after a hurried breakfast I started up the Morris. The ticket allocation arrangements for women and children — and the few men who were allowed to leave — were simple, but tiring and irritating. All bookings had been centralised through the P&O which had moved its offices from the centre of Singapore to the less dangerous Agency House at Cluny, five miles out of the city.

The house lay up a long, uphill drive. Scores of cars lined the grass verges where the main road met the drive, some with wheels jammed in ditches, some pitted with machine-gun fire. A few Malay policemen struggled to keep order among the long, slow-moving procession which stretched to the house at the top of the hill.

'It's like a picture out of the Bible,' Julie said, wiping the drops of sweat from her brow; and it was. The slowness of it, children tugging at their mothers' skirts, the sharp words mothers used to mask their fear. The heat was pitiless, and the trees lining the drive gave only a little shade.

At first I suggested that Julie kept her place in the queue – after all, I was only there to lend moral support – while I would go ahead and see how long it was going to take. Though I knew Frank Hammond (no relation to George Hammonds), the boss of P&O, I didn't want anyone to cut corners for me.

The queue lined the left side of the drive. Down the opposite side others moved more quickly, more decisively, in the opposite direction. They had been to the bungalow, they had got their tickets, they were off. They almost ran to their cars at the bottom of the drive, eager to be on their way. I recognised one woman walking along the exit lane. She was followed by an amah carrying a baby.

'I didn't expect to see you here, Mr John.' It was Mrs Rawlings, out of breath, her perspiring face pink with triumph. I introduced Julie (wondering if Rawlings's wife had heard any gossip) and explained that I was giving her a helping hand. 'It's going to be a long wait,' I said.

'I started queuing before dawn.' Like all women who have succeeded in a difficult enterprise, Rosie Rawlings was eager to impart information, to show how it was done. 'I'm booked on the *Ban Hong Liong*,' she added. 'Bill says it's got a very good captain – I should try to get aboard her if you have the chance, Miss Soong.'

There was nothing I could do really to help – and in fact I felt conspicuous among so many women, specially when I learned that Bill Rawlings, thinking of the office and business as usual, had dumped his wife there and left her to queue for his ticket as well as hers.

Apart from anything else I could see in the waiting women, reduced to a sweating, bedraggled, impatient line, the epitome of all the misery and futility of civilians at war. What had they to do with war? Why should wars between men, engineered by men, not be fought on battlefields instead of spilling over into kitchens and boudoirs? While this queue waited in Singapore, women lined up for bread in London, other women stood in line for rice in Tokyo, a fourth queue waited in Berlin for a ration of ersatz coffee. It was mad!

For the men – even in a subtle way for people like me – there was an undercurrent to war that stimulated; it clothed the degradation of war as easily as a uniform clothes a civilian. History, legend, the blowing of bugles, the waving of flags, somehow seemed to invest war for some men with thoughts of heroic deeds, it gave men a camaraderie often denied to women in adversity. But women? Through no fault of their own they were standing there, waiting patiently in the sun, moving forward like snails. Not one could be blamed for the predicament that had brought them to this quiet drive on the outskirts of Singapore, yet all of them, including Julie, had become common denominators, of no more account than a drudge, the lowliest coolie.

I had been relieved when the family left for America, but it had been a different relief, for even if those were days of anxiety they were also days of peace. Now my only fears were that Julie might not get away in time – the fears mingled with a prayer to make every remaining moment together last forever.

'I know what you're thinking,' she said. 'It's terrible, isn't it, all these people here and the same thing's happening all over the world. I'm dreading the last moment' – she could not force out the words –; when I have to leave.' She added, 'If it wasn't for the baby, nothing would make me go.'

'I hope you still would.' I mopped my face. 'It's the only way you can give me the one gift a man in love wants in time of war – peace of mind. I've never felt so miserable, not even when you went to America that first time. We were younger then, but now, I feel desperate, and yet, I have to say it, thank God you're going.'

'But what about me? If you were fighting in say, North Africa or somewhere, I could only have vague pictures of you. But now, after all that we've been through these last heavenly months, I'll be sitting somewhere safe and sound, and be able to picture you in every street we've driven in, every room of the Cadet House, your funny little car. Darling, it's going to be even worse for me.' I could see the start of tears.

'Nonsense,' I said with deliberate cheerfulness. 'You're not the sort who's ever going to see the inside of a prison, so you'll never be able to imagine me.'

'I don't understand.'

'Changi, darling. I can't believe Singapore will hold. I certainly can't get away. I'll spend the next few years with all my chums growing vegetables in Changi.'

I had to tell her that, I had to dispel the idea of me in Singapore. I already had a hunch, gleaned from discussion at some training sessions, that I might easily find myself near Kuala Lumpur. Time and again Chalfont and others stressed that the great strength of Force 136 would lie in trying to place officers in locations with which they were familiar. I had already spent hours explaining, with dividers and Ordnance-type maps, the area around KL, the Ara estate, even the old club house on the Bentong Road.

Standing by Julie's side, knowing that every shuffled step forwards in the queue was a step that would eventually lead to a parting, I suddenly thought that if the war dragged on and on, I would never be able to discover where she was, and she would be spending years bringing up our baby with a totally wrong picture of me, imagining me in Changi when in fact I would, if I were still alive, be living in the jungle. I had an overwhelming desire to tell her my secret.

I don't think I ever would have done – I was too scared of

Chalfont's all-seeing eyes, all-hearing ears – but I had no time to be tempted. There was a sudden blinding roar, a shadow across the brassy blue sky, the quivering death rattle of machine guns, and even as we all ducked in pandemonium into the ditch the babble of guns ceased and the motors changed their pitch into a scream as the two Zeros climbed up and away, wheeling like birds. They must have come across us by accident and I wondered if the two young pilots had beaten up the queue for a lark.

We picked ourselves up, helped each other, dusted ourselves down. I had fallen on top of Julie, held her tight, felt her heart pounding with fear, and now she looked at me, biting her lip to hold back the tears, and she said, 'I must help that poor woman over there, with the two children.'

I couldn't bear it any longer – and I thought that for Julie's sake too I should go. It seemed terrible deliberately to waste precious time we could have had together, but she made no attempt to disguise her relief when I suggested, 'I'll come back at tiffin time. If you're through before that, get a lift from anyone you can.'

I returned at lunchtime. Twice more Japanese planes had forced the women to take to the ditches, though the aircraft had passed over on their way to the docks. At one o'clock Julie had just reached the house, which in normal times had been the pleasant residence of Hammond, the head of the P&O, and I had often dined at the big bungalow, with its handsome porch and large verandah with rattan shades.

Now it had the frenzied atmosphere of an evacuee transit camp. True, dozens of orchids in their ochre pots still hung from the trees in the garden, but the clipped lawns had been churned into a quagmire. As we moved inside I could see that all the 'best furniture' had been replaced by rows of cane chairs and two large trestle tables.

Distracted P&O officials struggled to cope with the horde of women, some half-fainting in the heat, many on the verge of hysteria, and undecided really where they wanted to go or what they wanted to do. I reached Julie almost at the moment she stumbled into the welcome shade of the big room. By the entrance a shy Malay boy, with shiny teeth and shiny hair, wielded a metal soup ladle, filling glasses with fresh lime juice out of a zinc bucket. It may have been warm but it tasted like nectar.

Julie took a long drink and as she reached the top of the queue, looked round the crowded room, not sure where to go in the bustle and movement. I could see that two small queues had formed behind two flat unpainted trestle tables, each one with a man behind entering names in a big book. I went across to examine cards with large letters prominently displayed on each table. One read Colombo, the other UK.

She was the last girl in the world to give way under stress, but now she burst into tears. It wasn't only the desperation we both felt at parting, it was the raids, the morning machine gunning, the suspense, the heat – and God knows what Julie had suffered without saying anything during her shifts at the Alexandra Hospital. I could see that she didn't care any more. In a way I didn't either – I had the sudden thought of how wonderful it would be if we both bolted to Tasek Layang and stayed there until the last moment and then romantically died in each other's arms. You can't stop thoughts like that, however absurd they are. Instead of voicing them I said, 'Come on, darling, no problem.'

Suddenly irresolute, in a flood of tears, she buried her head on my shoulder and wailed, 'I don't know where to go. I don't want to go – I don't want to go *anywhere*!'

'Please, darling, don't miss your place in the queue.'

'I don't want to go, I tell you.' The eyes were suddenly angry. 'And you can't make me.'

'I don't want you to go either. But I can make you – by asking you, by begging you.'

'But we promised each other we'd stay together until the end of the war. It isn't the end yet.'

I would have given anything to agree with her, yet I knew that to do so would be a wickedness that would live with me for the rest of my life. 'Much better to leave now,' I said gently, 'remember – all's changed now. It won't stop with the end of the war. I'm going to come back to you as soon as it's over. You and – what shall we call the brat?' I was trying to make her think of something else. A new voice joined ours.

'Come now,' Frank Hammond had seen me and looked kindly towards Julie, understanding her agony. 'Having a bit of trouble, Johnnie?' And without waiting for an answer, 'It's Miss Soong, isn't it? Take my advice – go to Colombo. From there if you want to you can make for South Africa or Australia. But once you're in the UK you're stuck there for the duration. Besides, Colombo's a shorter trip – and that means a safer one.'

'Thank you, Mr Hammond.' Julie took hold of herself, remembered she was a Soong. 'But I thought all journeys to the UK had stopped?' She was asking questions really as a kind of therapy to keep her self control.

'Normally yes,' Hammond explained. 'But these are the troopships due into Singapore soon with the 18th Division. They'll be going back to Britain to bring more troops out, I suppose.'

'What do you think, Johnnie?'

'I agree with Frank. Colombo every time.' I was suddenly wondering if I might be able to tell Chalfont where Julie was heading for, whether he might be able to help Julie get a job in a Ceylon hospital. There must be wounded there. It wasn't the money; I was thinking of work as a way to occupy Julie's mind during the months she would have to wait alone to have our baby.

'All right,' she said briefly. 'And` thank you, Mr Hammond.'

As the young man at the Colombo table thumbed through her passport he asked her politely, 'Your evacuation order, please?'

Julie handed over the authority with its government stamp and scrawled signature. Attached to it was another certificate – from the doctor. He studied it, wrote in his large book then automatically, without looking up, asked, 'Name of father?'

I must hand it to Julie. She must have been unprepared for the question, shocked by it, but without a moment's hesitation she answered, almost defiantly, 'I haven't the faintest idea.'

The Soongs are not names with which to trifle, and perhaps the clerk knew this. Or perhaps he was just a very nice young man. I saw him write carefully in the end column, 'Father unknown,' and then fill in her ticket. It consisted of nothing more than a slip of paper copied on a duplicating machine, with a place for her name on it, an official stamp, and a few embarkation instructions.

'You should be going on the *Ban Hong Liong*, Miss Soong.' He handed her the paper. 'We'll let you know the sailing date some time next week. You'll find all the details on the ticket. Good luck. Next, please!' He held out his hand smilingly for the next woman to offer him her passport.

We walked out into the blinding sun and down the right-hand side of the drive to my car. Julie made a brave effort to hold back her tears but once in the car they flooded out.

'I'm so silly,' she sobbed. 'Give me a handkerchief, darling. I hate myself for being so silly, but I just don't want to leave you.'

As she dabbed her eyes I stopped the car by a large clump of mango trees that shaded the side of the road, and switched off the engine. Because the P&O Agency House was well out of the city – and away from the normal path of the bombers – the ugly scenes of the morning seemed easy to forget in a sudden oasis of peace, as though the clock had been turned back. The heavy mango tree branches, each with their clumps of thick green leaves, kept out the sun, and as I tried to comfort her we might have been in the Singapore of 1940. A couple of rickshaws passed us, the skinny, taut pullers between the shafts, each with a sweat rag round necks in which the veins stood out like cord. They loped along mechanically, their fat human cargos lolling behind. Two Malay children with wide eyes darted out inquisitively from behind the mangos to see why we had stopped. There must have been a small kampong be-hind the road, for a dog appeared, saw there were no scraps to be had, yawned and started scratching for fleas with an energetic paw.

'The thought of leaving – it's like a death sentence. I've grown to depend on you, Johnnie. This is the first time in all my life that I've been – like a married woman, with a man around, helping, loving. And now I'm carrying your baby. I can't go, Johnnie, I can't. When the ship sails to Colombo – is that going to be the end of everything for us? I always said –'

'Julie, darling, it'll never be the end of us.'

'It will be, I know it will. For our sake I have to make it that way. Otherwise you'll end up hating me. I have to be the one to end it – but only when the war ends. Now' – almost savagely – '*you're* shortening our time together. *You're* cutting into the only life we'll ever have together.'

'Beloved, I'm trying to save your life. That's more important to me than anything. Especially now.'

'But the war could go on for years – and you're going to sacrifice them, throw those years away, part us when we could be together.'

'There'll be no together in Changi, Julie,' I said.

'All right, then. I'll hate myself later for saying this – no, I won't – but Johnnie, I'm scared. For the three of us. Come with me, darling, come away. You can, I know you can. Join up somewhere else.' She was in tears again. 'So that our life can go on until the very last day of the war. Just give me that. All right? Till the baby's born. Is that fair? I'll give you up, I swear I will later – but don't throw it all away now. I'm frightened and I can't leave you. I won't.' She rummaged in her handbag to find her ticket, forgetting that I had it. I am sure she was going to tear it up. 'Come with me,' she begged, 'I know you could pull strings – or else, darling Johnnie, let me stay, even if I have to stay here and die with you.'

'Listen, my beloved Julie,' I kissed her gently on the lips and held her hand. 'If I *did* come with you, you'd end up despising me. Yes, you would. And if I tell you that there are good reasons why I can't –' I held a finger to her lips as she started a question. 'No questions from you mean no lies from me. I couldn't go. If I pulled rank and bolted I could never look any of my friends in the face again — your father, Paul. I couldn't.'

'Then I'll stay,' she pleaded. 'The Japs wouldn't touch a pregnant woman. I'll stay and take my chance.'

'Darling, they'd rape you until you died. Or lost our child. And we've been through all this before. If you stay you are dooming me to years of agony, wondering about you, frightened for you. By going, you're giving me the greatest gift a woman can give to the man she loves. The knowledge that you're safe and sound — and waiting.'

'I know you're right,' she said, 'but why, oh why, do people have to spoil everything? It was so beautiful before.'

'Here, wipe your eyes, or those kids' — who had returned with more giggling friends — 'will think I've been beating you.'

She laughed ruefully. 'If only that was the worst of our troubles! I'm so silly, Johnnie. You can drive on now.'

There had never been any doubt in my mind that Julie loved me as much as I loved her, but those moments under the mango trees somehow seemed to sum everything up; moments for us both to remember in the years ahead.

'Don't be sad, Julie,' I said. 'If it hadn't been for this mess we wouldn't be together.'

I didn't go to the office that afternoon, and since both of us were off duty we relaxed at home. The ticket — that miserable piece of paper that was to part us — had been put away, out of sight, even if never really out of mind, and because our phone was down again nobody could reach us — or so I thought until I heard the sound of a car, the crunch as it turned into the gravel drive round the side of the house.

'Who the hell's that?' I listened. My first thought — fear? — was that it might be Tim, though of course everyone knew where I was living — I had had to tell the YMCA and the office; but everything was quiet, I had done my stint at the YMCA, and I had told the office I wouldn't be returning until the next day.

'Don't make a sound,' I whispered, 'until I see who it is.'

The ancient office truck was parked on the drive next to

my car and Julie's. I couldn't see who was inside.

'Who is it?' I shouted.

'It's me, sir,' the voice sounded scared. A head appeared through the truck window.

'Rawlings!' My first reaction – but only for a second – was anger. But then I realised that Rawlings would never dare to come to the Cadet House unless the matter was desperately urgent. 'I'll be right down,' I shouted. 'Li! Tea please.'

Back in the room I told Julie, 'Won't be long, darling – but it must be something really important to bring Rawlings up here.'

He was standing outside the porch, waiting for me. He was looking at Julie's two-seater MG sports car. He must have known it belonged to Julie, and I wondered whether I looked dishevelled, interrupted in illicit pleasure. And had his wife, I also wondered, told him of my presence with Julie that morning at the P&O house?

Aloud I said, 'Come in – I hope it's worth it. I was on duty all last night.' I led the way into the old-fashioned dining-room with its makeshift shelter.

As Li put the tea on the teak table and switched on the creaking ceiling fan Rawlings seemed almost afraid to open the conversation; for a moment I entertained a wild notion that he knew about us and had come to blackmail me. Nonsense, of course. Rawlings was typical of hundreds of men who came to Singapore to make their fortunes and never did – yet proved invaluable in minor jobs, and in fact carved out for themselves far better livings than they would have enjoyed at home. He probably got slightly tiddly once a week at the Swimming Club, he was never unfaithful to his wife Rosie (except when she went on home leave, of course) and like most of those who stayed – who weren't shipped home – he was honest and loyal.

'I'm awfully sorry about this, Mr John, but I did try to phone. I didn't want to intrude – you're not busy, I hope?'

I tried a little misplaced humour. 'Well, I can't exactly pretend I'm otherwise engaged. What's the trouble?'

He got up, carefully closed the door behind him, sat

435

down and shifted his feet uneasily. I knew he was booked to go home within a few days, and it struck me that he might want to ask me if he could stay.

'You ought to be bloody glad you're leaving,' I tried to put him at ease. 'For Chrissake don't get any guilt complexes.'

'It's not *that*, sir – though I do feel pretty awful –'

'Well, come on – out with it!'

He took a deep breath. He really did, as though to gather courage before making a momentous pronouncement. It *was* momentous.

'I've been offered a quarter of a million US dollars,' he blurted out.

'You *what*!'

'Yes, sir,' he looked miserable. 'By four Chinese. They're coming to see me this evening, with the money in notes. That's why I had to come now – to see you.'

'Have you gone crazy?' I looked at my watch – three o'clock – and swiftly strode to the drinks cabinet. I poured out two large Scotches. 'Here, take this.' I offered him one. 'I don't know who needs it most, you or me.'

He gulped half the glass gratefully. 'I thought I should come and tell you – because it's the rubber we're holding in our godown at Geylang for Mr Scott.'

I remembered. Scott could find no shipping, and worse, he had also run out of godown space as more and more warehouses went up in flames. We were storing the latex, hoping to ship it. A faint hope!

'Start at the beginning,' I suggested. 'Take your time.' I needed him to, because he was talking about a great deal of money. My immediate thought was that a quarter of a million American dollars would come in very handy to rebuild the Dexter fortunes when the war was over. The second thought was that it wasn't our rubber. My third was: did that matter, with the whole place going up in flames?

'What's the deal?' I asked.

'I've been approached several times recently,' Rawlings began, 'by a very well-dressed Chinese. He came to see me at home one day. He didn't say anything except that he had a business proposition. I thought he was half-baked so I didn't bother you with it, but he came at odd times and for no special reason — then the night before last he asked me to meet him in the lounge of the Goodwood Park Hotel.'

'What sort of man?' I began.

'Very well-spoken, Mr John, a gentleman, and he told me he and his associates have a ship leaving for Java and he wants to buy the rubber. He knows all about it — exactly how much there is. He says they could get it away.'

I didn't see how they could — but that was none of my business. Yet, if they had the lighters? Or our lighters? It was possible.

'I told him it wasn't our rubber,' Rawlings continued, 'that of course it was impossible — but he said that if we didn't do something about it, if we didn't let them get it away, the Japs would get it and that would be even worse.'

Too right. 'I refused,' Rawlings continued, 'but he told me to think it over so I thought I'd better come and tell you.'

'Good thinking, Bill.' My mind was racing with possibilities. 'The godown on the Kallang River won't last much longer,' I added. 'Half of the village of Geylang is in ruins. Did you make a date to meet your Chinese friend?'

'Tonight at nine o'clock,' replied Rawlings. 'He won't wait any longer. I tried to put him off. But he said he would come to the Kallang godown with his colleagues anyway, and he'll have the lighters in the river, and the money.'

I poured out another drink — and another one for Rawlings too. I began to try to figure out how they could possibly manage to get the rubber away. Shenton Thomas was ordering all British firms to destroy their machinery and stock as part of the scorched earth policy. But, as I had been told at Government House, nothing must be done to interfere with the livelihood of the Chinese and Malays — the real people of the island — for if or when the city fell they would have to carry on. This meant of course that a British boat would have to be blown up if it couldn't get away, but a Chinese vessel — or even a lighter — might be left untouched. One of the reasons for British anger at this stupidity was the knowledge that many unscrupulous Chinese would stop at nothing to take advantage of this – and might even sell to the Japs.

A shell came whistling overhead. I could hear its whine, slowly descending the tonal scale, until it ended in a mighty crash maybe a mile away.

'A near one,' I said, suddenly noticing not sound, but the *absence* of sound. The fans had stopped and in a minute I was drenched in sweat, sitting in a room with hardly a breath of air. Rawlings took out his handkerchief and wiped his neck.

'Okay,' I said. 'Take it.'

'But sir,' he gasped. 'We're only holding it for Mr Scott! It's not ours to sell. If we did it would be stealing.'

'Shut up! There's something called a war going on. You work for Dexters and you do as you're told. And when you leave Singapore next week you'll have a bonus of fifty thousand Singapore dollars in your pocket.'

'But sir!' He was even more indignant. 'Are you trying to bribe me into becoming a thief?'

'Stop shovelling the shit at me,' I snarled. 'And if you suggest again that I'm a thief I'll kick you all the way down Robinson Road.'

'But it *isn't* our rubber, sir –'

'It will be by tonight,' I reassured – and mystified – him. 'I'm going to buy it from Ian Scott. Now – for a quarter of a million Singapore dollars payable in London. Nothing illegal about it. I'm giving them a break. We're only the agents, but if they don't sell or get it away they'll lose the lot. They're *British*, remember – they'll have to destroy the rubber to prevent the Japs getting it.'

I had to trust Rawlings, for I did not dare to handle the deal myself. With the reputation of our firm at stake – to say nothing of my army status – I couldn't be seen to negotiate with crooks – and they had to be crooks. Nor could I show them I was on the level by telling them what I was doing. If they knew their price would plummet. Rawlings would have to pretend to them he was making a deal behind my back.

'You've got to be the go-between, Rawlings – and I'm

going to use that money to restart the business when we kick the bloody Japs out.'

I had to see Ian Scott. But first I told Rawlings that we would drive separately to Geylang and meet there at eight. We had to use separate cars in order to return at different times. At one end of the shed, high above the piles of latex, was a small balcony with the standard glassed-in cubicle of an office for the foreman. How many hours had I spent there when learning the business! It had curtains and a window that opened. It might be a good idea to see for myself what happened.

It meant a tremendous rush. It was now four o'clock. I asked Rawlings to drive to the nearest phone and make a date for me to see Scott – and Vicki – right away. I particularly wanted Vicki to be there.

'While you're doing that I'll change from these shorts into some proper clothes,' I said. 'Then – as you can't phone me – perhaps you'll come back and tell me what arrangements you've made. It shouldn't take you more than ten minutes.'

As I reached our bedroom the fans started up again. Li had mended the fuses which must have blown with the shock of the shell. I told Julie the truth – and promised to get back as soon as I could. Then, after Rawlings returned to tell me that Scott would see me right away, I set off for their bungalow in Keok Road.

Ian Scott was a rubber man through and through. But his firm Consolidated Latex did not have the resources of a firm like Dexters and I had the feeling that he was short of money. The war had hit him hard. And he also had to look after Vicki, fun-loving and eager, a big spender, even in the days when I used to take her out. Perhaps that was why Scott, who had at first refused to evacuate her, had changed his mind and was sending her away.

I bought the rubber in twenty minutes – though I did have to pay three hundred thousand Singapore dollars for it after Scott produced a piece of paper – more government waffle – which guaranteed him that amount if stocks were destroyed to deny them to the enemy.

It was touch and go – and I might never have succeeded if Vicki hadn't been present.

'I don't think I ought to sell without knowing who you're going to sell it to,' said Scott doubtfully.

'I'm not going to sell it,' I tried to look outraged. 'I'm going to get it away.'

'You can't!'

'That's what you think – I've got ships. You haven't.'

'Well, in that case – since you say you *do* have the ships – get it away for us. There's no need for me to sell it to you. Just send it – as you agreed to.'

'Listen, Ian, our shipping is limited. We've lost three vessels. And we've got our own rubber – stocks from Ara. Can you give me one good reason why I should ship someone else's rubber before shipping our own?'

He hummed and hawed. What about guarantees of final destination? How could he be sure it would not fall into enemy hands? Patiently, I explained that it *would* fall into Japanese hands if he did nothing. What finally clinched matters was my final offer.

'I'll give you a draft on London for the amount in sterling,' I said, 'and that by itself is a fair price. And then tomorrow morning I'll give you fifty thousand Singapore dollars in notes. That money could be useful to Vicki for incidental expenses when she leaves.'

Vicki got up and untwisted those slim legs of hers. She always looked beautifully dressed, and as though she has just come from the hairdresser. She kissed me – on the cheeks of course, not as she used to. 'You really are wonderful, Johnnie,' she said.

'Of course I know my partners in London would want Vicki to have some cash when she leaves,' admitted Scott. And it was then that I knew the deal would go through.

I met Rawlings as arranged at eight o'clock, leaving my car in a smashed-up side street in Geylang village; I let him drive me in the office truck to the godown. By now the area was a jumble of potholes, craters, twisted wires, trees torn up by the roots. The open country spaces were littered with abandoned cars and in the eerie silence, broken only by distant gunfire, it reminded me of a film I had seen in which the earth had almost ended, with nothing moving except a few lonely, dazed survivors. When we reached the bank of the Kallang River Rawlings took out his torch and keys and opened the big sliding door that guarded the squat two hundred and fifty-pound bundles of stinking latex covered in talc.

They were stacked in regular columns, and looked like giant bricks piled symmetrically to make dividing walls, leaving a maze of spooky corridors. The smell was enough to make one vomit. At one end of the godown stood the same old scales and a small desk as ancient and as used as a children's school desk, with a small light which Rawlings switched on. I climbed the stairs to the overseer's office. It had no ventilation and a single mosquito hummed unseen. I prepared for a long, sweaty evening. Despite the mosquito, I took off my shirt and trousers and waited in my boxer shorts for the Chinese to arrive. By opening the curtains an inch or so I could see everything below.

Until now I had blithely taken Rawlings's word for everything. But as nine o'clock passed, then another half hour, I began to feel uncertain. I had bought the rubber, I had promised to pay; and in our line of business words were all that mattered in buying and selling. Often there was no time for written documents, but a handshake was as binding as any legal document, at least in the agency business. No one could take you to court, but if you broke your word no one would ever deal with you again. Supposing the Chinese got the wind up? On the threshold of panic I had almost started climbing down the stairs when the sliding doors opened. It was a quarter to ten. A Chinese face peered into the dark hall. Rawlings called out and waved to it. Three more faces appeared. The men looked neatly dressed, almost smart, and two of them each carried two bulging briefcases. One – presumably the man who had earlier contacted Rawlings – said in a quiet, almost casual voice, 'Have you decided, Mr Rawlings?'

As loud as he could – for my benefit – Rawlings replied

in a quavering voice, 'Have you got the money?' The Chinese motioned to two of his colleagues. Without a word they disgorged the contents of their briefcases. The effect was incredible. Hundreds, thousands of bills in packets spewed over the ancient desk, some falling on the floor. I swear I heard a gasp from Rawlings. I nearly gasped myself.

'Do you wish to count it?' asked the Chinese. Dumbly, Rawlings shook his head. 'Then if you will give me the keys you can take the money. We have our lighters waiting and a ship in the roads, and fuel — thanks to the governor's consideration for the Chinese — so we start loading as soon as you leave. Have you any transport?'

Rawlings nodded. He was still speechless.

'Then my colleagues will carry the briefcases to the car for you.'

They might have been discussing a normal business proposition. Their courtesy was amazing, unbelievable. The deal was made, of that there was no doubt.

I could hardly contain my excitement, cooped up in the high, hot office. I had to remain, to stick it out because there was no way down from my cubbyhole perch. Rawlings quite rightly felt he must drive off as soon as he got the money, if only not to give the Chinese grounds for suspicion of a double-cross. I had deliberately driven in my own car to Geylang for that very reason — so that I could let Rawlings go.

Hardly had he left before the old godown was alive with coolies. Using their old-fashioned iron hooks, they prised the tacky bales of latex on to their porters' trucks and wheeled them towards the side door leading to the river. Soon I could hear the rattle of the tiny rollers as the bundles were pushed along the conveyor belt leading down the bank to the open holds of the lighters.

After three hours I was able to sneak out during a lull, for I realised the operation would take all night. Once out, I walked to Geylang, picked up the car and drove the four miles to Robinson Road where Rawlings had promised to wait for me. I wanted to put the notes in the office safe right away.

'Shall we bank the money tomorrow?' he asked.

'Are you crazy? The Japs are going to steal every bit of cash out of every bank in Singapore if they take the city. This is our stake for the future. I'm not going to put this money in the bank, I'm going to bury it. Buried treasure, that's what it is. This is for the future. When we come back the one thing we'll need is ready cash – lots of it.'

As far as the books were concerned I sent an enigmatic cable the next day to Papa Jack telling him Rawlings would explain everything. Then I deducted the equivalent of $50,000 for Vicki Scott.

'Not a word of this to Ball and the others,' I warned Rawlings. 'What I have done is unorthodox – but I've done it for the firm, not for me. As soon as you reach London tell Papa Jack *everything* except,' I added, 'what I've given you and Rosie. Forget that.'

'Where are you going to hide it?'

'You'll be the only one who knows – in case anything happens to either of us. But we're going to bury it together.'

I had a sudden idea where I would hide the cash – in the dogs' cemetery near the lime trees at the back of Tanamera. We packed the notes in oilskin, put them in three old-fashioned stainless-steel deed boxes lined in camphor wood, and dug a grave near those where as children Tim, Natasha and I had buried our pets when they died. Their graves were still marked with wooden crosses.

It was hard work, but we did it. After we had filled in the grave and replaced the lallang – which in the climate of Singapore would knit in days – I fashioned a rough wooden cross. Using a thick black marker pencil from the office, I wrote in neat capital letters, 'In memory of Vicki'.

Rawlings, dripping in sweat, wiped the mist off his pebble glasses, peered closely and said, 'That's a funny name for a dog.'

'It's a perfect name for a beautiful bitch,' I said.

Julie and I had missed our night alone, but we did spend the whole of Sunday together – a lazy morning, most of it in bed, and then in the afternoon I took Julie to the Alexandra, arranging to pick her up in the evening after I had gone with Jackson and Broadbent to see their wives off on the *Felix Roussel* which was sailing that afternoon. As we left Keppel Harbour Broadbent asked if I would like to have a drink at the Fire Station. Both men were feeling desperately miserable – a foretaste of how I would soon be feeling – but I had to pick up Julie and told them so. Julie and I had become reconciled to the fact that we couldn't keep *everything* secret. Nobody could prove we were living together, might never suspect it, but I couldn't spend my days squiring one of the most beautiful girls in Singapore to and from hospital without a few tongues starting to wag; and anyway, both Broadbent and Jackson knew Julie, because both frequently had occasion to visit the Alexandra.

'Bring her along,' said Wilf Broadbent.

'I'll tell you what,' Bill interrupted. 'You go to the fire station and I'll go with Johnnie to the Alexandra. I have to go there anyway. They're running out of lime. Then we'll all join you later.'

'Lime?' I asked.

'I'll show you,' Jackson promised. 'If you are not queasy, that is.'

We set off for the Alexandra before it was time to pick up Julie, and when we reached the back gates Jackson said, 'Come and see – but you'll need a strong stomach.' He drove along the neat drive until he reached a corner of the grounds out of sight of the building. A melancholy procession of orderlies was carrying corpses. They moved towards a place where the once-beautiful gardens and lawns had been slashed open to make two huge pits, each forty feet long.

It was one of those moments in which you want to turn away, and yet can't. Impelled by a morbid fascination, I watched. The nearest pit was half filled with bodies, neatly laid out in tightly packed rows. Bill turned to me and said, 'It's like a gigantic tin of sardines.'

As we stood there, rooted, with handkerchiefs over our noses to shut out the stench, half a dozen Chinese orderlies came down towards us carrying more bodies. They laid the

European bodies at one end of the pit, the Asians at the other end, and sprinkled them with spadefuls of lime to try and stop the smell.

'That's what they need the lime for,' said Jackson.

A nurse was standing beside us and she just made one remark, 'They bury Christians at one end, other religions at the opposite end.'

I felt I couldn't stand another minute there, the stench was so overpowering, and the mass grave itself so tragic. As I was about to turn away an army car arrived, bouncing over the grass, ignoring the paths. Two sergeants jumped out briskly, indifferent to the awful scene. From the back they unceremoniously pulled out a corpse. It wasn't even covered with a shroud – material was unobtainable by now. One of the sergeants saluted the nurse and said, 'Found this poor chap in a bombed house. Can we bury him here?'

She nodded. 'Over there.' She indicated the 'Christian end' of the grave.

'Sorry we didn't have time to wrap it up – just found it.' They lay the corpse on the green lallang, and without thinking I waited for the two men, their good deeds done, to return to their vehicle. One looked vaguely familiar, though I couldn't place him. I was also puzzled because instead of leaving they stood by the grave, waiting. They must have noticed that I was puzzled, for one said, 'Seeing as 'ow we brought 'im 'ere we'd like to pay our last respects.'

Two hospital orderlies picked up the body, and as they turned it over I saw the face. It had not been torn by bombs. Instead, it was contorted with the fear of a man who had died in a moment of terror. It was the face of Bonnard.

I was so stunned that I hardly remember picking up Julie. I said nothing as the three of us drove to the fire station, but when Wilf Broadbent served the drinks I couldn't get Bonnard's face out of my mind – or the strange circumstances, or for that matter the face of one of the soldiers. I was filled with doubts. Everything was too pat, too contrived. Soldiers didn't go around Singapore picking up bodies and taking them to burial pits; they certainly didn't wait to see what happened to them, to make sure – as though they had been detailed as official witnesses to a burial.

Then I remembered the soldier's face. He was the driver who had collected brother Tim on his first visit to the Cadet House. And Bonnard's face. It had a look of shock, yes, but it was unmarked.

'Mind if I use the phone?' I asked Wilf. I still had the number Tim had given me, and he was in.

'I've seen Bonnard's dead body.' I etched in some of the details, including the fact that I recognised his driver. 'Bonnard's face was unmarked and as far as I could see so was the body. He didn't look like someone who'd been killed in an air raid.'

'Let's just *say* he was,' said Tim shortly.

'Where did you find him?'

'I'll tell you after the war.'

'And I suppose you –'

'Forget everything. It's not a story for civilians. The way you've seen it, you can write to our beloved sister Natasha and tell her that her hero was killed in a raid and that you went to his funeral. Sounds much better than the truth, doesn't it?'

The invitation to a drink turned into a scratch meal, for nobody really wanted to leave the others. In fact Bill Jackson stayed the night rather than return alone to his bungalow in Stevens Road. I too felt low – for what I had seen at Kepple Quay was a preview. Soon it would be my turn to say goodbye.

After a meal of sardines and bully beef we sat on the balcony of the fire station drinking a last stengah. It was the kind of warm, starry night that normally made life in Singapore so wonderful. A faint breeze blew the mosquitos away. The night was crowded with stars. From time to time sheet lightning lit up the slim spire of the cathedral in front of us. Then, as nature switched off the lighting, the cathedral silhouette stood out starkly against the Milky Way.

'They're bad times,' Bill Jackson was missing Marjorie, who was a wonderful woman.

'Absent friends!' toasted Broadbent.

As he spoke – it was shortly after ten o'clock – the black sky was broken by a red and then a blue rocket bursting far to the north. The stars seemed to hang in the air for a moment, then the sky was black again.

'It reminds me of the time Grandpa Jack had a stroke,' I said.

'Maybe distress signals,' said Jackson.

In fact, though we did not know it until the next day, those red and blue rockets had been fired by the enemy – to announce that the first crack troops of the Japanese Chrysanthemum Division had crossed the Straits of Johore and landed successfully on the island of Singapore.

29

The phone rang in the office on the morning of Wednesday, 11 February. Hammond of the P&O was on the other end of the line: The *Ban Hong Liong* was leaving in two days, on – of all dates – Friday the thirteenth.

Until he gave me the actual details I had somehow dreamt that perhaps the vessels would never actually leave Singapore, that the decision for Julie to go would be annulled by fate, so that whatever the consequences our consciences would be clear. I had the same reaction as a man suffering from a deadly disease who is terrified of having the operation which he knows is the only hope of saving his life. The feeling of relief when the doctor can't make it and everything is postponed!

I felt physically sick as I muttered my thanks to Frank Hammond and hung up. Julie was working the morning shift and wouldn't be free until four p.m., so I had decided to get rid of my training session that morning. Now I decided to go and see Grandpa Jack after leaving the YMCA so that I wouldn't need to go again on Thursday. And I would ask Chalfont for the day off, hoping Julie could make similar arrangements at the Alexandra. That way we could spend our last day together quietly at the Cadet House.

Wednesday was a terrible day. On the way to the YMCA I saw a long file of men queueing outside an address I did not at first recognise. They seemed oblivious to occasional bursts of machine-gun fire from solitary aircraft flying over. Then I saw Jackson with his two spaniels on a lead. Like the others he was taking his pets to Forbes the vet to have them put down. None could bear the thought of the ill treatment their pets would suffer under the Japanese.

Jackson didn't see me as I made my way forward inch by inch in the Morris. It took me nearly an hour to complete the trip from Robinson Road to the YMCA, and I arrived there just as a small bomb landed in the mud pit where I had spent so many miserable hours. Chalfont was there, unmoved by the near miss, and happily agreed to my request for Thursday off.

'No problem, dear boy,' he said languidly. 'We'll call it compassionate leave.'

I had explained that Julie was leaving on the *Ban Hong Liong*, and I also asked him if he thought she might be able to get a military job in or near Colombo. 'She's a trained nurse,' I said, 'and she's been through the mill. I imagine you must have hospitals in Ceylon?'

'Seems quite a possibility,' he agreed, and took a note of the name of her ship. 'Will see what can be done.'

I was worried about my Friday training session, for the roads were now so clogged, the raids sliding one into the other, that I knew I might not be able to get back from the docks to the YMCA in time.

'Don't worry,' said Chalfont. 'I think we can call you a fully trained operator by now. I hear you've even mastered the throat-slitting technique. Forget the training.' I would still have to report twice a day to the YMCA to see if my orders had come through. Nobody knew when that would be, and nobody knew for how long the telephones would work, so reporting in person was the only way.

'Things are pretty bad, aren't they?' I asked Chalfont.

'Couldn't be worse, old boy,' he drawled. 'All over bar the shouting. It's only a matter of days before we send for you.'

'Is there *no* hope?' I still couldn't believe the worst.

'None.'

Chalfont told me something else. General Tomoyuki Yamashita, the Japanese commander of the attacking forces, had dropped a letter from an aircraft addressed to Percival, telling him to surrender. 'I bet Percival wishes he could, but the old man – that's Churchill – sent a message which makes it impossible. I've seen it, and he's told Percival there must be no thought of saving the troops or sparing the civilian population. I remember two sentences, "The battle must be fought to the bitter end at all costs. With the Russians fighting as they are and the Americans so stubborn at Luzon, the whole reputation of our country and our race is involved."'

'He's right, I suppose – but it's a forlorn hope, isn't it?'

'Absolutely, old boy.' Chalfont sounded almost bitter. 'But people don't matter in war. World leaders are writing tomorrow's history today – and they're going to take damned good care they're the heroes.'

He reached behind him and plucked a sheet from a small pile of what looked like typing paper. 'Take a dekko at this – today's history,' he smiled sardonically. 'The governor has gone into the newspaper business.'

In fact, the *Straits Times* and the *Tribune* had been closed and Shenton Thomas had taken over the *Times* office as a government printing press. A member of his publicity department had been appointed acting editor, and seven thousand copies were produced of the first issue, most of them sent by despatch riders to ARP posts.

The newspaper, a quarto sheet, contained only six items. The splash consisted of eight unadorned paragraphs consisting of the latest communiqué, which was studded as usual with meaningless phrases that no longer registered with anyone in Singapore. 'Enemy pressure slackened during the night . . . It is hoped to stabilise our position . . . Elsewhere there is no change in our position . . .' There were five other brief news items, one containing details of cash contributed to the Malayan war fund. Two had absolutely nothing to do with the war.

'Makes you wonder whether all this enterprise is worth it,' said Chalfont. 'See you.'

I found it almost impossible to get from the YMCA to see Grandpa Jack in the General. Orchard Road was a waste-land. The Asians had given the city up, and were clogging the roads in long lines, most of them making for the east coast, impelled by an almost dumb instinct, knowing that now it was only a question of days. Japanese tanks were already threatening the village of Bukit Timah, barely four miles beyond Tanamera. The village contained vast stores of material, food and fuel. Hand to hand fighting was flaring up in places whose very names were evocative of my child-hood, of the good old days, of places where Julie and I had first played together. There was a pitched battle on the racecourse, another on the greens and fairways of the golf club where once we had sneaked late at night, a third at the Dairy Farm.

The governor still refused to evacuate Government House, even though it was now being shelled system-atically. Already twelve members of the staff had been killed by shellfire. To make matters worse, Lady Thomas was so ill – with amoebic dysentry, according to one re-port – that she could not be moved to the shelters during bombing raids. General Percival begged her to go. He could, he said, arrange transport by air to Java. But she refused to leave her husband's side.

It started to rain – heavy, slanting rain – as I reached the General Hospital. The grounds were pockmarked with bomb craters, the entrance and loading bay a chaotic mess. Ambulances – makeshift or otherwise – jammed against each other and private cars. As I looked for a place to leave the Morris I saw one heavy ambulance, trapped between two cars, simply back against one, crumple its bonnet like a concertina, and push it out of its path before roaring away to pick up more casualties. I reversed and left my car halfway down the drive. I was almost down to the last tank of petrol I was likely to get, and I wasn't going to risk losing it if someone banged into my back and split open the tank. Derelict cars were two a penny on any roadside, but petrol was more precious than gold.

I suppose there is no shock so utterly traumatic as the totally unexpected. I walked into the hospital, picking my way along the corridors, the floors crammed with wounded on stretchers or mattresses laid end to end on the floor. I knew exactly where the ward was, and I was thinking to myself what hard work it was keeping a conversation going with an old man in a public ward, but that I would stay half an hour. I knew he relished the company of the 'feller-me-lad' he always insisted was his favourite grandson.

Three minutes later I stood aghast at the door of the ward, unable to believe what I had learned. Grandpa Jack had vanished. He had left two hours or so previously.

The ward sister looked at me as though I was mad not to know, and said coldly, 'After all, Mr Dexter, he told me you had arranged everything. You even sent that big car to take him home. I helped him into it.'

'I arranged *nothing*!' I couldn't control my voice.

'Please don't shout.' She was a prim army nurse used to discipline. 'Keep your voice down. There are people here wounded in battle, much more upset than you.' The inference being that a civilian was of less consequence than a brave soldier.

'I'm sorry sister – but it's unbelievable. I gave no orders at all. What a crafty old man! He must have been plotting this for days. How did he go?'

It seems that old Li, who stayed with him in the ward, arranged with the syce to sneak the Buick from the office godown and then my grandfather calmly told the nursing authorities that everything had been planned by me.

'But he's so old – couldn't you stop him?' I blurted out.

451

'Why should I? This is a military hospital. Every bed is desperately needed. If he has a home and people to look after him –'

'But he could die!'

'Quite a few people are going to die,' the nurse said dryly. 'With the Japanese killing our troops all over the island it seems a little incongruous for a civilian to be talking about that. I suggest you look after him at home – until the Japanese intern you.'

What a bitch; but I couldn't blame her. To her I suppose I was just another whining, whisky-swilling British civilian. And there was no way I could tell her – if only to salve my tattered pride after her dressing down – why I was the one person who would be unable to look after Grandpa Jack.

There was nothing else to say. I dashed back through the blinding rain, jumped into the car and set off for Tanamera.

I was drenched when I walked into the ballroom, forgetting the possibility of structural damage, and shouted 'Grandpa Jack!'

I didn't have to shout. He was sitting there in his wheel-chair in a corner of the vast room; and though old Li carefully avoided my eye Grandpa Jack had a kind of artful look, saying without words that he had put one over on me, and he was delighted about it. As though nothing was amiss, he grunted, 'Better go and change. You're wet through.'

'It *is* raining.' I was still angry.

'Aye, that's true. It's pissing stair rods.' It was one of his favourite Yorkshire expressions.

I did go and change, finding clothes that had been left in the married quarters, and when I came downstairs and drew up a chair I said to him over and again, 'But *why? Why,* Grandpa Jack? I thought you liked it there.'

We must have argued for half an hour before I realised that it was all to no avail. The old man was by turns obdurate, sly, even arch. With the cunning that often ac-companies old age, he knew – and I knew – that there was nothing I could do. Even had I been able to persuade him no hospital could have found a bed for him now. The other reason that made him stand up to all argument was more worrying: with a touch of senility, he seemed convinced that I would stay with him if Singapore fell. A mental block seemed to make him incapable of understanding that the Japanese would intern civilians – and though they might make an exception of Grandpa Jack because of his age they would never do the same for me. And anyway, I wouldn't be there, though this I could not tell him.

Trying to scare him, I leaned over him and said, 'The Japs are less than five miles away. They could be here to-morrow.'

'If I die, young feller-me-lad, I'll die here. And I'll die happy.'

The trouble was that his obstinacy had increased as a result of his new life in hospital; he was swollen with pride at the success of his daring escape, and I had to hand it to him. He *was* a card.

'This is my city and my home,' he grunted. Even his voice had improved, lowered into something more like his gritty old growl; and though he still sat in his invalid's chair I had a sudden thought of the good old days when he was hale and hearty, of my eighth birthday when he strode into the Sick Bay and gave me a hundred dollars, telling me not to spend it all on women. He was so proud of his achieve-ments, it would be criminal to send him back to the wartime equivalent of an old folk's home, and equally wicked to leave him alone in this vast, unsafe house. Yet I could not look after him.

Then the solution came to me.

'Grandpa,' I said sternly, 'you can't stay here alone, and that's final. The house is unsafe and there'd be no one to look after you. Get it into your head that I'll be taken away the moment the Japs enter Singapore. But I've got an idea – I'm going to ask Mr Soong if you can stay with him for the time being. Just until things settle down. They've got bags of room, and you can take Li with you. But you can't stay here alone.'

He hesitated, gave me another sly look and said, 'Mebbe.

Makes sense. Two old fogies together. But on my conditions.'

'No conditions. If you don't agree I'm going to fetch the police.'

He did not reply. He knew as well as I did that no police could ever be spared to come to Tanamera, even if I could find one. He also knew that I couldn't manhandle him. 'Well,' I said wearily. 'What's your condition?'

'We stay here for a short while,' he smiled almost beatifically, 'while we finish my bottle of Scotch.'

'Scotch! You must be mad. First, you're not supposed to have any – and, second, it'll kill you.'

It must have been five years since he had been allowed to touch strong liquor – at least that was what I thought. 'Bloody doctors,' he confided with a leer, 'telling me I'd die if I took a nip. I've been drinking ever since I got my right arm back again.'

'You mean it?'

'Of course I have. Only thing that's kept me alive.'

I thought it better not to enquire where he had got his stocks over the years.

'Well, I'll have a drink with you,' I said to cheer him up, and because I did admire the old boy.

'That's my boy,' he clapped a hand on the side of his chair and even though Li was only feet away cried, 'Li! Two stengahs!'

We drank not only two but three or four – each. With our world crumbling around us, why not let him enjoy what might be our last-ever meeting? I knew in my bones that even if I lived through defeat he would not. He was too used to an imperious way of life to kowtow to any conquerors. He would rather die – and he knew it; and that, I thought, was why he was relishing his life so much now, with me. He was like a condemned man who orders a hearty meal before the hangman arrives.

It was the drink that loosed his tongue and undid the secrets of his mind. It started with a casual remark I am sure he did not intend to make. 'What are you going to do about Julie?' he asked.

'Julie?' I felt my heart pound.

For a second he looked embarrassed, then his excitement got the better of his earlier emotion. 'Didn't think I knew, eh? Good young feller-me-lad! Always did fancy her, didn't you? Can't say I blame you. Did the same when I was young.' His eyes lit up with remembered pleasures.

Oh God, I thought, how has he found out, this old man tucked away in a hospital? Julie had never even been to see him. Broadbent and Jackson might have suspected – *must* have suspected – but they would never tell Grandpa Jack a thing.

'Shouldn't tell you' – he was enjoying my discomfiture – 'but God help you if old Soong finds out – or that monkey Kai-shek. Cut your balls off,' he cackled with glee.

'But – how did you find out? Please, Grandpa, it's important if you want to help Julie and me not to let anyone else know.'

'You've got a point there,' he ruminated. 'Shouldn't really tell, but what's the phrase? Forewarned, forearmed? Yes, you're my favourite, got to help the family.' He was wandering.

'Do you want another drink?' I asked. Two could play at being crafty.

'Ye'll give me another one, young feller-me-lad?'

'If you tell.'

'Why not? This ain't no time for secrets – all be dead and buried soon. Nice to know everything before you pop off. You can't guess, eh? Captain Dexter mean anything to you?' He almost laughed at the horror on my face.

'Tim!'

'None other. Though I'll grant you it was by accident.'

'Accident on purpose,' I snarled. 'What a bastard. What a bloody shit that man is, always fucking up my life.'

'That's good!' he cackled. 'That's good – after the way you fucked up his life.'

'I suppose that's why he hates me,' I said, 'though he seemed to hate me before I married Irene.' Grandpa Jack gave me an odd, almost an uneasy look.

'You called him a bastard,' he shook his head. 'Nasty

word that, m'boy. Not unless you mean it. Did you mean it?'

'Tim?'

'Why not tell all, eh?' cackled the old man. 'One bad turn deserves another. But first' – with a crafty look – 'one more for the road eh? The Soong road – that's a good one.'

'The doctor said it would kill you.'

'It's worth dying for, m'boy, but it won't be the drop of hard stuff that kills me. I've had my chips, Johnnie, I can feel it in my bones. And I ain't sorry. I'm tired. And I'm glad you're here. And that's why' – he gave an enormous hiccup – 'I'm telling all, as they say in the story books. It's my last gift to my only grandson.'

'Youngest one,' I corrected him.

'Only one,' he insisted. 'Damn funny, wouldn't it be, if you were the first Dexter to marry a Chinese girl? Could happen if Irene gives you leave. Could happen. When this blows over – if the British ever return to Singapore – it'll all be changed. Why not?'

'It's a nice thought, but I'm afraid there'd be the most unholy row among the parents.' I hesitated, then asked, 'What did you mean – the only grandson?'

'What I said. You deserve a break, young feller. Knowledge is power, and if you know what I know you'll have all the power if you ever have a showdown with the parents.' He slurred his words a little, but still made sense. 'Ever thought why you're such a spunky feller, Johnnie? Ladies' man? Full of piss and vinegar? That's my boy. Take right after your darling Mama.'

'I give up,' I said – and I *was* just about ready to give up. His mind was wandering; after all, we had both knocked back quite a few stengahs. It was time for me to go and see Soong.

'What's all this got to do with Julie?' I humoured him.

'Because, m'lad, if your mother and father find out about you two, just you tell them –' he stopped, looking crafty.

'Come on, Grandpa Jack, tell what? It's time I went to see Soong.'

'Just tell them,' he said softly, 'tell them nicely, not vindictively, not nastily, because you're a good boy at heart. Just tell them you know all about Tim.'

'Know *what*?'

'Just tell them the secret.'

'What secret?'

He looked astonished. What tricks age plays with the mind! 'Didn't I tell you?' he asked. 'Didn't I tell you Tim's not your brother?'

I dropped the glass, shattering it.

'You can't mean it,' I whispered. 'Grandpa, that's a wicked, horrible thing to say. And you know it's not true.'

He chuckled, almost with a touch of obscenity. 'They're all alike. You think kids of your age are different from mine – or your parents.'

'But –'

'It's true, lad – you'll find out if you have a showdown over Julie.'

'But Tim – he's always been at Tanamera. He's part of the family.' The suggestion was preposterous.

'Does he look like the others? Pretty dark hair for a Dexter, eh?'

'But, Grandpa, what you say just couldn't happen. Not with Mama. Did you mean Mama – or what *did* you mean?'

He ruminated, demanded another whisky, and I would have given him the bottle if necessary to force the story out of him – *force* being the operative word, for though he wanted to tell me it was almost impossible to keep him on the track.

'It's all a long time ago.' He suddenly seemed sleepy.

'Keep awake, Grandpa Jack' I shouted. 'Li! Bring some more water.'

'Where was I? Ah, your mother. High-spirited girl, I can tell you. Most beautiful girl in Singapore. But at first she hated the place. After Natasha was born – well –'

I had a sudden recollection of my father telling me how Mama had disliked Singapore and how she had gone to America – for what I assumed was a normal holiday. I hadn't dared to ask if there was anything more than boredom behind her decision to leave Singapore.

'I'll say!' chuckled Grandpa Jack. '*Her* father had always been against Papa Jack. She'd been going steady with some posh American, they'd planned to get married, and then she defied the lot and upped and married your dad. And' – with a chuckle – 'Natasha was born seven months later.'

Shades of Irene! And no wonder Natflat was such a high flier, such a girl for getting into trouble. I couldn't help thinking, didn't *anybody* ever get married unless they were pregnant? Darling Mama. No wonder she smiled so knowingly each time she found me out. But where did Papa Jack come in.

'He's always loved her. She was away in New York for over a year, I don't know what happened, but I've always thought she met her old boyfriend, had a fling, and your father took her back. He's got a heart of gold.' I wondered whether he was being facetious.

'And all wasted!' He was thinking aloud. 'All that crafty concealment and then –' He shook his head, looked at me with one bleary eye and asked, 'Any more Scotch? Just one small peg for the last road?'

'Not another drop.'

'Just one. To celebrate Tim's sudden departure from Singapore.'

'What do you mean, all wasted?'

'Tim had to leave – had to get out.' He was almost asleep now. 'Preferred the boys. Damned nearly a court case. Papa Jack only stopped it by getting him out – plenty of boys in the army.'

Could it be true, or was this the revenge of a jealous old man? But I knew it was. Suddenly I felt very sorry for Tim. What Grandpa Jack said explained a lot: Tim's bitterness – it was a kind of envy because I enjoyed more normal pursuits, ones that had no need for boys. But if he was homosexual what about Irene? In a way that made sense too. The very fury that made him nearly kill me was due to the fact that at long last he had tried to throw off the yoke of homosexuality by finding in Irene a girl who might have been able to help him. Wasn't that why his fury had boiled over? Not because I had robbed him of the girl he loved, but of the chance he had hoped for. Poor Tim. And, despite my treatment of her, lucky, lucky Irene! For Tim might never have made it with her, though I knew he would have tried. She had done better marrying me.

And that of course explained something else. The love showered on Tim by Papa Jack and Mama. Papa Jack *had* to take his side, if only to bolster his own false position, and once my parents realised that Tim was a homosexual, Mama had the protective feeling for him that all mothers have for children that aren't quite right in the head. And even though Tim's sickness manifested itself in his trousers, it was the head that needed attention.

The effort – and the drink – had taken the stuffing out of my grandfather. Suddenly his head rolled down on to his chest and he started to snore. I knew that this time there would be little hope of waking him.

I was exhausted with argument, but even more shattered with knowledge. I knew I must go soon so see Soong, but first I had to gather my wits. I needed a breather. The rain had stopped, but the afternoon heat on the wet lallang produced an eerie kind of ground fog, steam rising from the wet earth, coiling around my ankles, hiding the lower branches of those plants that had not been torn up by war.

Mama, of all people! I wasn't shocked in the sense that I disapproved: that didn't enter into my thoughts at all. I just couldn't take it in. And yet, was it really so unexpected – now that I knew? Didn't her whole attitude to life, the way she quietly ran Tanamera behind the backs of the men, so to speak, didn't it indicate a woman of enormously strong character hidden behind that deliberately vague exterior; a woman who not only knew what she wanted, but got it – quietly?

And her warm tolerant love for Papa Jack. Was that real love, or was it a love like Irene's and mine? Or – how incredible the whole thing seemed! – a love like that of Natasha for Tony? Or, for that matter, a marriage like that of Ian Scott, so proud of the wife who had tried me before she married him — and again after?

My first sensation had been one of enormous shock, coupled with a kind of anger that Grandpa Jack should tell me things I felt I had no right to know. He had watched me as he prattled on, lapping up my reaction as he betrayed a secret which he was passing on to me only because — aided by a few drinks — he felt he was going to die. It was wrong of him to tell me, though it had slipped out as an addition to the first secret — that he knew about Julie. I had the feeling that he was just possessed of an overpowering desire to get rid of the burden of secrecy.

Well, it was told now. But was it really so shocking? Or did it only seem shocking because the central character was my mother, and all children are conditioned from birth to assume that their own mother is different, that she could never indulge in the wickedness so prevalent among other people. The funny thing is that, as I stood there on the wet lallang, looking at the white walls of Tanamera, with black smoke from burning oil dumps darkening the sky behind the palm trees on the jungle fringe — and always the incessant growl of gunfire or bombs — I thought not of the rights and wrongs, the sadness or tragedy, but of the actual dramas that must have been enacted in Tanamera so many, many years ago.

What agony for the players! And all before I was born, when Natflat was a squalling brat with a red face and nappies. My Mama — to me so gentle, so grown up, so mysterious with her billowing dresses, so vague in her Billie Burke moods — darling Mama, what a moment it must have been when she faced my father and told him she wanted to go home to New York — the same father who had shouted at me for a crime no more heinous than my mother's.

What had my poor father said, how had he let her go? A trial separation? ('And not a word to our friends until we've decided . . .') My mother, ten thousand miles away, back in the arms of her first lover. Poor father here, walking where I was standing, a young man torn between love of a spirited woman and his pride, tormented as he decided what to do.

What had he said, done, in this house when Mama finally returned over a year later? With Grandpa Jack knowing all, seeing all, chuckling at the vagaries of human life.

I would never know, of course. For though Grandpa Jack had thought in his senility that he had given me a weapon I knew I would never use it, never by a breath let my parents know what he had told me about them.

On the other hand, as I looked at my watch, realising I must go, it came to me just how much they were the same as I. Not only the same blood, but the same problems. They were — they were *human*. At last! They seemed different to me at that moment, more understandable than they had ever been. Mama might prattle on about my sense of honour as she tried to warn me off Julie, but after all, somewhere, some time — when, where, how? — the same passion that tore into Julie and me at Tasek Layang the night the war started had torn one night into my father's wife, and somewhere she must, like Julie, have stripped off her clothes, breathless with impatience and desire, and begged her lover to take her body.

'It's a funny bloody world!' I said aloud — just as a huge crash split the air to remind me there was a war on. The bombing sounded very close, but even so I couldn't stop laughing and laughing and laughing. And when finally I stopped and wiped the tears from my eyes, I knew one truth for sure: there would never again be any bullshit where Julie and I were concerned. If we came through this war nothing would ever separate us again.

As I expected, P.P. Soong was horrified when I told him of Grandpa Jack's escape from the hospital. 'Of course he can't stay alone in Tanamera,' he said. 'And we won't even realise he's here, we have so much room.'

He called the head boy and ordered him to prepare a spare suite at the back of the house, explaining to me, 'It has its own servants' quarters, so Grandpa Jack can bring his boys with him. Then, when things settle down, we'll see. I imagine you'll be interned, but they'll let an old man like him stay free. The main thing — don't *you* worry, Johnnie. We'll take care of him.'

461

I was always slightly nervous in P.P.'s presence, wondering if he knew anything about us. I felt sure he didn't, but if your own grandfather knows about your love life – well, who can keep *any* secrets in wartime? But I didn't think he knew, though I was immediately on guard when he asked me, apparently innocuously, 'Have you seen Julie lately? I have hardly seen her since Christmas. She's working too hard at the Alexandra.'

Half the truth, I thought, was better than a lie. 'Yes,' I replied. 'Actually I saw her for a few minutes at the Alexandra, but in the most terrible circumstances, with Bill Jackson, the ARP warden.' I started to tell Soong the gruesome story of the lime pits.

I never ended it. Without a moment's warning the dull rumble of gunfire or distant bombing – so much a part of the background to our lives that we hardly noticed it – erupted into a terrifying crash. It seemed on top of us: for a moment I thought we were actually in the process of being killed. I couldn't believe any noise could be that close and not annihilate us both, standing there in the huge grey circular room. Everything shook. Plaster trickled down like the beginning of a waterfall. Even Soong's normal composure seemed shaken, as he said, 'A near miss. That must have been very close.'

Through the open back doors leading to the pool I could see a pink cloud lighting the sky, smell the pungent stink of burning wood, hear faintly the crackling of fire.

'Tanamera!' I shouted. 'My God! Grandpa Jack!'

I raced towards the massive front doors without saying a word to Soong. Paul ran into the room crying, 'I'll come in case you need help.' He barely had time to open the front door of the Morris, just threw himself in as I put my foot down.

Outside the front gates an old gardener stopped me. The flames shot up against the backdrop of dark trees, so bright I could have read a newspaper. The old man was dressed only in shorts and a singlet and was wringing his hands and crying over and over again, like a dirge, 'All die! All die! All die!'

'Shut up!' I said savagely, and raced the Morris down the drive. As I turned the bend the full facade of the huge house stood directly in front of me. 'Oh God!' I said to Paul – or to no one.

The great front walls of indestructible plaster still defied the heat and flame, and because of the raging fire behind, with flames set against black, billowing smoke, the walls stood out in a glaring white, with all the unreality of a set piece on a stage, walls that – just for a second – reminded me of a piece of scenery without any depth, with nothing behind – no lives, no family, no Grandpa, no boys, no cooks, no amahs, no syces; just a brilliantly conceived theatre set, out of which I half expected an actor to emerge and take a bow.

Only this wasn't make believe. I didn't dare to drive the car any nearer. The two of us ran towards the side of the house, round by the east verandah, hoping that perhaps the damage was less severe there, that someone might still be alive – if we could get to them.

In fact the damage was worse behind. Though I was no expert, I could see that the bomb had hit the rear of the house, making a huge crater, and the fire we had seen was in reality a by-product and not as severe as it appeared viewed from the front, its flames exaggerated by the drama of the white front walls setting off the blood-red flames.

'Even if we could get in it would be hopeless,' gasped Paul after one look at the crater, the twisted beams, the half-standing walls, and he was right. Yet I had to try – despite the dust that hung over everything like a cloud, despite the smoke which was worse than the dust – partly because torrential rain had saturated the exterior, producing a wet, evil-smelling smoke you couldn't escape. I held a handkerchief to my nose – but I might as well have tried to wave the smoke away with my hand.

At that moment I heard the clang of a fire engine and an engine with a trailer pump came tearing across the lawns, leaving a twisting snake of hose unwinding behind it. Miraculously the first jets of water appeared within a couple of minutes – a miracle not only of speed but also because so many mains had been bombed that water was scarce.

'We're lucky,' shouted the fireman. 'We're drawing water from the canal.' Bukit Timah Road had a canal running down the centre – a big canal, but until now I had never thought how useful it would be to us. I knew one of the fire chiefs slightly, a colleague of Wilf Broadbent's. He was called Wise and he shouted, 'Was it occupied?'

I nodded. 'Grandpa Jack. I don't know how many servants.'

'I can't believe it – what the hell was an invalid doing here all by himself?'

I explained that I had been with him barely ten minutes previously. 'We'll soon have the fire under control,' he shouted above the noise. 'Worse than it looks. But I'm afraid –' he left the sentence unfinished, and shouted to firemen to lug the hoses round to the side of the house so the water could play on flames behind the front walls.

Almost roughly I shook the gardener's shoulders and asked him, 'Who was in the house?'

At first I couldn't get an answer out of him, just 'All die, all die.' I stood there, unable to move amid the mud from leaking hose junctions. The hoarse, shouted instructions of the firemen mingled with the crackle of Tanamera's death throes, the actual noise of the spreading flames.

'Who was inside?' I shook the gardener again.

'*Tuan* in sitting room. Cookie and two children in kitchen. Li there – not know where – and one amah.'

Six people! My wonderful Grandpa Jack and five faithful friends, some I had known since I was a child, all dead. Without warning I retched, then vomited, powerless to control myself, even to lean forward, so that I was sick all over my shoes. Before I could stop him the gardener took off his vest and made a pitiful effort to clean me up.

In the end, after the fire was reduced to smoke they found all the bodies – or bits of them – including a few scraps of twisted metal that had once been Grandpa Jack's wheelchair.

Wise, the fire officer, said to me, 'I think you should go home for an hour or two. It's been a hell of a shock, but the fire's dying out now, and we'll arrange with the ARP to bury the remains.'

'I can't do that,' I said. 'I must be there when you bury him.'

He hesitated. I knew he was trying to tell me that there wouldn't really be much to bury.

'I know what you're thinking,' I said, 'but let's do this. Put all the bodies' – I couldn't bring myself to use the word bits – 'into a coffin or shroud or whatever we can find, and we'll bury them all in the same grave. I think Grandpa Jack would like that. He loved his Chinese.'

That was how we arranged it. I asked the gardener to round up some coolies and dig a hole in readiness for the next morning. For once I felt I couldn't go back to the Cadet House and tell Julie the story. Paul offered to go in my car and then return with Li – for, after all, old Li was his father – and he would have to attend the funeral. I thought I might sleep in the tennis pavilion.

I asked Paul to do one last favour: phone Tim from the Cadet House, using the number he had given me. I had hesitated at first – I really didn't owe him a thing – but then I thought: what happened with Mama years ago (if Grandpa Jack had been telling the truth) was not Tim's fault. He was only the end product, and Tim *had* been brought up with Grandpa Jack. And what Tim chose to do with his life wasn't my affair. But if I didn't let him know then I would be acting in the same way he so often treated me.

Tim arrived directly from the Singapore Club, where he had seen Shenton Thomas and his wife arrive. She was so ill that the governor had finally agreed for them both to be evacuated. They had only one room, with no running water.

It seemed almost indecent standing there talking to him, knowing all about him. *He* was the one who had always criticised me, but now I had a curiously powerful hold on him, even if I never boasted of my knowledge. I knew I would never be afraid of him again.

I explained what had happened, how I had been trying to arrange for Grandpa Jack to stay with Soong, and then on an impulse I blurted out, 'Julie's leaving Singapore'.

He seemed surprised. 'I never thought P.P. Soong would pull out. Will Paul go?'

'Old Soong isn't going.' I shook my head. 'The old man refuses to budge – and Paul's with him.'

'Soong would never allow his daughter to go on her own. After all, the Chinese are in no danger – not really – as long as they behave themselves.'

'I got her away. I heard that all the nurses were going to be treated as members of the forces –'

'You have been busy. And didn't Kai-shek have something to say about that? I always understood P.P. was hoping they'd get married.'

'No longer,' I said shortly.

'Your guilty secret been found out?'

I ignored his edge of sarcasm.

'No. Kai-shek doesn't know because nobody's seen Kai-shek recently.'

'So that leaves the coast clear for you – apart from Irene?'

This was hardly the moment to mention Irene. All I said was, 'We'll just have to see.'

'You civilians certainly live it up,' said Tim.

We buried Grandpa Jack and the others near the edge of the jungle fringe within sight of the empty space of the east verandah where we had so often greeted the dawn with huge breakfasts in the good old days. We couldn't find a Bible.

Before I returned to spend my last whole day with Julie I took a final look at the house in which I had played hide and seek as a boy, dreamed as a young man, crept home as a furtive lover, settled down as a married man and father.

The nursery had been near the end of the main corridor leading to the back of the house, and it was here the bomb had exploded. The fearful chaos stunned me. Bedrooms, bathrooms, store rooms, kitchen, pantries – all had vanished, not cleanly, not neatly vanishing, but crumbled into fragments as though a giant fist had pounded everything together. The smell of wet, charred wood almost made me vomit again. I stood there rooted to the ground, just staring at the thin spirals of smoke, at the puddles of water, at a whole part of a world that had come crashing down. The Sick Bay had vanished. It had just ceased to exist; not a trace, a sliver of wood, a piece of plaster remained to remind me of that birthday where Mama had come to wake me up, the day Julie had come to the party and I had fought with Tim.

As though cocking a snoot at the enemy, half the first floor nursery still hung, suspended against the grey morning sky, kids' pictures still stuck on the wallpaper of big red roses and a row of children's books in their case still untouched. Yet the front had been savagely torn away, ripped out so that I had the feeling I was looking into one of those expensive dolls' houses in which the entire front opens, revealing every secret to outsiders, including a teddy bear sitting grinning near the jagged edge of the twisted floor which hung perilously, apparently attached to nothing. The toilet next to the nursery had been blasted away, the floor had vanished, but the old-fashioned lavatory hung glued to one plaster wall by its plumbing pipes.

Below it nothing was left of the kitchen, where at party times scores of boys queued for the trays of food which made Dexter parties famous all over Singapore, and where at other times, alone, I used to creep in and wheedle an extra slice of cake out of Cookie who was now dead.

The fire had spread towards the front of the house, but the damage was less severe, and the iron-hard walls which Grandpa Jack had promised would last a hundred years still stood proudly, the dirt a kind of battle scar. Some flames, creeping along the wooden roof structure, had reached the front, but the double staircase still stood, and so did the staircase leading from the west verandah. The side staircase was rickety but I managed to climb up to the landing. Several rooms over and just behind the ballroom, including part of our married quarters, were not badly damaged.

For the rest – it was terrible. I began to think of letting Papa know. There was no way to soften the blow in a cable. And what about Tanamera? Would I be allowed to report damage in wartime? Perhaps I would have to disguise the message with some sort of code. What words could I use? The news would hit Papa Jack like a body blow. To him Tanamera was a way of life. He identified his father and Tanamera with everything the British Empire stood for; it *had* been a great empire in the days when the house was built. Years ago Paul had remarked jokingly, 'I think Papa Jack regards Tanamera as the centre of the Empire,' and the remark had a germ of truth in it. So long as Tanamera stood and flourished so would the British Empire. But Papa Jack had warned me that times were changing, and as I scrambled across the debris, watching firemen throw smouldering lumps of wood into a central pile, poking in the smoke, I wondered if my father who loved Singapore so much would think of this as a symbol of that change.

30

I woke early on Julie's last day. The date alone was enough to make anyone sick with fear – Friday the thirteenth of February.

We had spent the previous day quietly; it had been tinged with sadness because of Grandpa Jack, but the terrible chaos all around us helped to put grief into proper perspective, for after all death could have advantages. What old man wouldn't rather die painlessly without any foreknowledge than be left to the whims of a beastly and cruel conqueror? And Grandpa Jack had died in the home he had built. No, once the shock had passed – well, poor old Grandpa Jack was better off than many others would be.

Until this morning I had hoped for a miracle, for a last-minute change in the island's fortunes, with relief coming, as it does in western films, with the cavalry galloping to the rescue. But there was no hope now. The Japanese were everywhere, as unstoppable as ants.

The once beautiful city looked as though it was suffering from a monumental hangover after a drunken orgy. Water gushed from broken mains, drunken soldiers reeled about, shoes crunched on glass.

Yet, as we watched the thin spirals of bluish smoke rising from crushed buildings where fire lingered on, there was a moment or two of quiet in the side streets, for it was a beautiful morning of a kind which only the tropics can produce. Then the illusion of peace was shattered and the present impinged as people emerged dazed from blackened ruins like rabbits coming out of their warrens.

I had gone down Orchard Road hoping to find some milk, but it was hopeless. However, I did manage to get hold of a morning newspaper, but now reduced to the third issue of the government's single sheet, several copies of which had been delivered to the ARP post. The main headlines read: 'Japanese Suffer Huge Casualties in Singapore.' It was a pathetic, evil lie. The story that followed – a bare five paragraphs – consisted of extracts from British and American newspapers. The rest of the contents looked as though they had been edited by a moron ten thousand miles away. Here we were, in the thick of savage fighting, with defeat only a matter of days away, yet the government's only attempt to inspire the embattled people consisted of a few slogans under the masthead: 'Singapore Must Stand! Singapore SHALL Stand!'

There was virtually no local news. Instead, great prominence was given to a meeting between Nehru and Chiang Kai-shek – as if we cared! – while another report described a long-term American plan to raise an air force of two million men.

Bill Jackson waved to me and came over. He too had been trying to buy some milk for his ARP staff. 'If that's the best Shenton Thomas and his chums can do to whip up morale we deserve to lose.'

Before going back I had two calls to make – the first to the office, the second to the YMCA where I had been told to report twice daily. In the office I leafed through a bundle of unimportant letters. One reminded me that I hadn't paid

469

my Tanglin subscription; another asked me if I would sit in a panel of judges at a forthcoming beauty competition. And then, right at the bottom, I saw a flimsy, blue envelope. It was a cable – and I knew it couldn't be from London, for messages from Papa Jack all came through military channels.

I had forgotten how long it was since I received a letter from Natasha or Irene in New York, though I had tried to get in touch with them by sending a carefully disguised 'office cable' to Papa Jack because I wanted to tell Natasha about Bonnard. I had had to make it look businesslike and it had taken some time to compose, but finally I had sent: 'Please inform New York office our Swiss contact killed in air raid.'

I was sure Papa Jack would know who the Swiss contact was. And since we did not have a New York office, he would surely realise that the message was meant for the family.

I had heard nothing from America until now. Lying in front of me was an ordinary civilian Western Union cable.

I tore it open. It was from Irene. It had been skilfully written to contain a great deal of information:

ALL JOIN ME IN SENDING LOVE PRAYING FOR YOUR SAFETY STOP NATASHA RECEIVED MESSAGE STOP SHE'S ENVIOUS BECAUSE I AM PREGNANT AND SHE'S NOT LOVE IRENE

Had Natflat decided not to have the baby after she received the news about Bonnard? I wondered.

I had been told to report to the YMCA again before lunch on the Friday, and it was now that I was given my firm orders.

'Between you and me, old boy,' said Chalfont, 'my bet is that we'll start negotiating a surrender some time on Sunday. Churchill's finally agreed that we can't go on any longer.'

My orders were to report to the YMCA at ten p.m. on Saturday, from where I would be taken to the rendezvous. I was to arrive with nothing but the clothes I was wearing. I must not bring even a watch or a pen with me.

'You'll find everything you need waiting for you,' said Chalfont. 'Not only your uniform, but weapons, a watch — everything when you reach your final rendezvous.'

'Where?' I asked innocently.

'A submarine off Keppel Harbour. It's going to land you on the east coast. If I don't see you again — good luck.'

I had the awful sick feeling that comes when you are on the edge of the unknown. I had no idea where I would have to go, what I would have to do. I was scared stiff — not of the *real* future, but scared in the way one is afraid when a nurse wheels you along an impersonal corridor smelling of antiseptic to the operating theatre. What makes your heart flutter is the knowledge that you have no control over what is going to happen to you. One stupid move, one error of judgment, by some stranger who suddenly controls your life — and your life could be blotted out.

'I'll be there on time,' I promised.

As I drove home, dreading the goodbyes, it was almost a relief to see Paul's car outside the portico.

'Come to say goodbye to my sis,' he said, adding, 'You look all in.'

'The bloody date is enough to give you the creeps.'

At first Julie had insisted on going to say goodbye to her father, but Paul advised against it.

'Let him think you're at the Alexandra until you've gone. Then I'll break the news to him — that as a nurse under military orders in an army hospital you were evacuated without warning. It'll save his pride — which is already dented.'

'What do you mean?' asked Julie.

'Kai-Shek has vanished,' replied Paul abruptly. Apparently he had been seen setting off in a launch with some other young Chinese. No reason why he should not try to escape. 'Only as a member of the family,' said Paul, rather primly, 'he should have told my father.'

There was a curious incident just before Paul left. 'There's another reason,' Paul languidly sipped a Tiger from my dwindling stocks, 'my respected father is behaving very oddly. If I didn't know he was a dedicated moneymaker I'd say he was flirting with Communism.'

'That's ridiculous!' Julie laughed out loud – but I didn't, because I knew what Paul was going to say.

'I'm serious,' Paul insisted. 'He's mysteriously vanished several times recently, so I've had him followed.'

'Your own father!' exclaimed Julie.

'Yes,' Paul sounded a trifle defiant, then turned to me. 'Do you know Loi Tek?'

How that name kept cropping up! The man the brigadier had asked me about, the man Tim had mentioned, the mysterious, shadowy, all-powerful head of the Malayan Communist Party.

'Well, I believe my father knows him,' said Paul. 'He's made several secret visits to the MCP headquarters – and my father isn't the sort of man to go *anywhere* unless he sees the top brass.'

For a moment I was tempted to tell him of Chalfont's suspicions, but I didn't. There was probably a very simple explanation – that Soong was taking steps to protect his financial empire in some way I couldn't pretend to understand. But I was certain about one thing – the old man was never a Communist, and never would be.

'Well, give him my love when I've gone.' Julie gave a little sigh.

I looked at my watch, for we had to leave early, not only to catch the boat, but because Julie insisted on saying goodbye to the matron and her patients at the Alexandra Hospital.

'Don't waste too much time there,' Paul warned us. 'The Malay Regiment is holding Pasir Panjang Ridge by the skin of its teeth, but they can't hold out much longer, and then the Japs'll make straight for the Alexandra area.'

'I've been looking after the wounded there for weeks,' said Julie defiantly. 'I'd be a coward if I just walked out on them without saying goodbye. Matron's the only one who understands.'

472

'Understands what?' asked Paul.

She turned away, confused. 'Nothing, really. She's the only one I've talked things over with.'

Paul left. Julie said goodbye to Li whose face was crinkled with misery.

'And now, my beautiful Julie, it's our private goodbye,' I said as soon as we were alone. 'I'm not much good at long farewells in public. Be brave, darling.'

She didn't cry. I don't think either of us could quite grasp that the most important part of our joint lives was about to end, never to be repeated in just this wonderful way, whatever the future might hold.

I pulled her close to me, running my fingers through her jet black hair, standing at the foot of the Cadet House stairs in the old-fashioned hall, the dining room door open, the heavy chairs and table, the mattresses still arranged to form a makeshift shelter, with the fridge in the corner of the room. 'It's been a wonderful home,' I said. 'We'll never have a better one wherever we live when this is over.'

'Take care of yourself, darling Johnnie,' she said. 'I can't really think I'm going at last.'

'The months will fly by.' I knew they wouldn't. 'And then –'

'Don't say anything, Johnnie. Don't make any promises. Just kiss me once more before we get into the car.'

She clung to me, wordless, tearless, but with a desperation she couldn't disguise until I gently pushed her away. I held her at arm's length, my hands on her shoulders, then leaned forward and kissed her gently. 'We've a long way to the Alexandra and then the docks. God bless you Julie – and keep you for me.'

'I hope so.' She was still dry-eyed. I picked up the one suitcase she was allowed to take with her, put it on the small back seat of the Morris and we set off for the Alexandra. I was getting anxious, for the trip to the hospital involved a detour, though it was in the general direction of the docks and, as I had expected, the congestion was terrible. Apart from military vehicles, streams of Chinese and Indians were heading for the east coast, presumably to escape the bombing. All the pathos of early newsreel films we had seen of French civilians fleeing the Germans was being re-enacted, as though the film was being repeated. Wrinkled old men staggered under immense loads – beds, bedding, pots and pans. Women followed carrying food – a sack of rice perhaps. Every child was burdened. One wizened old grandma had been put between the shafts of a rickshaw and was physically unable to pull it out of the path of my car. I had to get out and help. Near the Memorial Theatre one family had acquired an empty coffin which they had loaded up and were now carrying by its brass handles.

It took us nearly an hour to reach the hospital, shortly before two o'clock. After driving Julie to the entrance I decided to drive back to the rear gates.

'I'm scared the car might be requisitioned by some army doctor,' I explained. 'So I'll wait outside. Shout when you're ready then I'll drive in and fetch you.' It was only a hundred yards away.

I parked the Morris near the back gates under the shade of a huge Tempusu tree, one of the giants of the Malayan forests, and sat down under its shady branches, anxiously looking at my watch and the front entrance. My only fear was that Julie might not be able to get through to the ship in time. Pasir Panjang, where I knew there was heavy fighting, was some distance away, and of course the hospital would be evacuated the moment any danger became acute. But the traffic was hell.

I was almost dozing when a chilling scream froze all thought. A shambling Indian jagger was running towards me shouting in terror, gasping, 'Japs, *tuan*! They coming! They here!'

'Where?'

'Not knowing, *tuan*.'

Some instinct made me leave the car where it was – and we both owe our lives to that instinct. I jumped out, ran the hundred yards in even time – or damn nearly – and barged into the main ward.

'Julie!' I shouted. She was talking to the matron who started to protest, making an expelling motion, but I pushed her aside and gasped, 'The Japanese are coming!'

I pulled Julie towards the door and into the entrance hall, but as I prepared to bolt I heard shouting in Japanese outside in the grounds. I ran up the stairs, half-pulling Julie, shouting blindly, 'For God's sake, come on! If they find us here – two civilians – they'll kill us!'

In a curious way the immediate and terrifying danger made me forget where I was. The weeks of weary training took hold of me. I was no longer in the Alexandra – I was in the YMCA, with a Scots sergeant shouting, 'Move quickly, sorr! When the Japs come you'll na ha a second to spare!'

'We've got to hide.' We reached the top of the stairs. I could hear more Japanese shouting outside. Banging – rifle butts or feet on concrete floors. I looked round frantically. I had five seconds to decide how to save our lives in a hospital stripped of nonessentials, with not a screen, not a sofa to give us some cover, however flimsy.

Then I remembered – the tiny cupboard at the far end of the first-floor landing where the nurse had hidden me during the military inspection. Without a word I pulled poor Julie along. The tiny closet had an almost invisible sliding door. I wrenched it open and pushed Julie inside. There was just room for me to squeeze in after her. Through a crack in the door I could see down the well into the ground floor ward where I had once watched Julie. If we could hide in the cupboard until the Japanese had moved on perhaps we could climb down the fire escape at the rear of the building and make a dash for the car.

In ten seconds we were drenched in sweat. The only light came through the crack. Through it I could make out a British officer talking urgently to orderlies and nurses. I heard a tearing sound as someone ripped a sheet in two, to make a flag of truce. The hospital was surrendering – which seemed the only sensible thing to do. One young officer set off, carrying the home-made flag.

For a few moments there was silence, a deathly, frightening silence. Then shouts in Japanese splintered the outside air – orders, punctuated suddenly by one fearful scream of agony. Before the scream ended half a dozen Japanese with fixed bayonets charged into the ward below us. They rushed in half crouching, bayonets on the ends of their rifles. For a second they paused, looking round like beasts about to select their prey. I held a hand over Julie's mouth in case she screamed, and managed to twist her body round in the cramped space, hoping she would not see as much as I could. Through the crack I saw the senior British officer and two others step forward. One man saluted, another pointed to his red cross brassard. With animal grunts the Japanese waved and pushed them into a corner at the far end of the ward.

I couldn't see all the patients, but one sat up as though to protest, squeaking out words I couldn't hear. Almost nonchalantly, almost like a scene in slow motion in a film, a Japanese soldier turned, twisted his rifle so that he held it by the barrel and brought down the butt on the patient's head, splitting it open. The man fell to the floor, his legs still tied to something on the bed underneath the cover. Blood spurted everywhere. One of the British officers who had been herded together at the far end of the room sprang forward, shouting: it was the signal for murder.

Julie couldn't see anything, but she could hear the screams of agony. I held her close, head down in my stomach, to stifle her screams. I didn't really want to see anything, but I couldn't move. My face was up against the crack and I couldn't twist round. The senior officer who had tried to move was bayoneted twice through the throat. As the two other British officers fell, the Japanese thrust their bayonets into them with almost diabolical relish. Three orderlies rushed in to the rescue. The Japanese set about them. One fell screaming, and I saw a Japanese soldier with one foot on the man's face as he tugged to pull his bayonet out of the body.

That, I thought, might be the end, but now the Japanese started ordering patients out of their beds, signalling by waving their rifles, prodding them, shouting, while the bodies on the floor gushed blood. Many patients were awaiting operations and couldn't move. Those who could stumbled off their beds, some with bandaged heads, others too terrified to feel what must have been excruciating pain when they were suddenly ordered to walk on a broken leg. They were herded out of the room. Any man who couldn't get up quickly was bayoneted on his mattress. It was all over in a few minutes.

I had always imagined that soldiers ordered to attack with bayonets would do so with hate perhaps, but never with pleasure. Yet now, as I looked down on the blotches of scarlet everywhere – on the floors, on the curtains at the end of the room, on the mattresses – I realised that the Japanese were in a frenzy of excitement, of enjoyment, that every thrust of a bayonet into a defenceless man, every twist before the steel was withdrawn, was a personal act of revenge.

As suddenly as it had started the massacre ended. While Julie's body shook with sobs which I tried to stifle, I heard a whistle blow three times outside in the garden. Only one of the soldiers remained behind in the ward – but only for a few seconds, to wipe the blood off his bayonet on the pyjama trousers of a dead man before he too ran into the garden. The others, without a backward glance, made for the door, and I suddenly realised that perhaps the Japanese had not been ordered to attack the hospital – there were too few for a full-scale attack, anyway – but had stumbled across it by chance. As quickly as the ward had been invaded so it was emptied, except for the dead and dying – and the screams. For a few moments I waited and then, heart pumping, slid open the door and listened. Not a soul on the long landing. Not a sound.

'Stay here,' I whispered, 'and whatever you do, whatever you *want* to do, don't look through the crack.' I could feel the sweat wringing in my clothes, down my forehead and into my eyes as I crept to the top of the stairs. I knew there were no wards above us, only nursing quarters and store rooms. On either side of the stairs leading down to the main hall were big windows. Raising my head carefully until I could peep out, I saw a squad of Japanese troops being formed up, heard guttural shouts, obviously orders – and then a final shout, and I realised they must be leaving a sentry to guard the front door.

I tiptoed across the landing and peered out of the twin windows at the rear of the hospital. The lawns, studded with flowering trees and some frangipani, edged with a line of ceremonial, carefully-trimmed palms, were empty. And just outside the back window was the fire escape. If we could climb out of the window and down the escape we might be able to run to the back gate, with the building shielding us from the front door where the sentry was posted.

I half carried Julie to the top of the stairs – and there I had to stop for a moment while both of us were violently sick. The screams of the dying men below masked any noise we made. I knew how guilty she must feel, guilty that she hadn't been there to die with them.

'Don't worry,' I whispered. 'They didn't touch any of the women.' I didn't mention the terrible fate that probably awaited those nurses who had been herded away.

'My poor patients,' she sobbed. 'Oh Johnnie, how can people do this to each other?'

'Easy, darling.' I tried to clean up the front of her dress. 'Now you know why I want you to leave. But we must rush. They might come back – and there's a sentry at the front door.'

All I had to do was push open the window, climb on to the iron ledge at the top of the steps. The ledge ran the length of the back of the hospital in the way ledges lead to fire escape steps.

There was no problem – except one: the window was jammed. I heaved, I pushed, but it was stuck fast, immovable. I didn't dare break the glass because of the noise it would make.

The roof sloped, and there was a circular skylight almost immediately above the window. I lugged a bench – the sort visitors sat on whilst waiting – to the window, and by standing on it was able to open the skylight. There was only room for one at a time to creep through, but I hoisted myself up and peered out. No sign of anyone, and a hundred yards away I could see the back gate. The patrol had obviously marched away in the other direction. The more I thought about it the more I was convinced the Japanese we had seen were members of an advance patrol which had lost its way, had stumbled on the hospital by chance, and had panicked when they thought somebody was going to attack them.

The roof below the skylight sloped gently for perhaps four feet to the iron ledge. It would be quite easy for us to lower ourselves down, but first I had to get out in order to help Julie through the window. I climbed out, and by holding on with one hand I was able to help Julie halfway through.

'Now you'll have to pull yourself through,' I whispered. 'I'll hold you until you touch the ledge.'

She wriggled half out of the skylight, and I lowered myself on to the ledge which was three feet wide, a firm, solid foothold. Arms upstretched, I waited. As she came out she had to get her feet into position so she could make contact with the ledge, guided by my hands on her body. She had almost made it when she lost a shoe.

It hit me in the face. I grabbed wildly for the edge of the escape stairs, then fell straight over the edge of the iron ledge – and landed right on top of an unseen Japanese sentry.

Every prayer I had uttered in my life must have been answered in that split second as I hurtled downwards, for though I had no idea a sentry was there, he had no idea there was a man on the roof, and the one place he wasn't looking was upwards. My feet crashed on to his head. As I hit him his rifle fell on the lallang. He uttered the beginning of a scream that mingled with the moans from the ward, but then I had my fingers on his throat.

Again I had the curious sensation that I was back in the YMCA. ('Always go for the windpipe, sorrr!') Everything I had learned made my actions automatic – all based on the need for self-preservation. There was only one problem – the difference between practise and the real thing. I suppose everyone, from a bullfighter to a racing driver, faces once in his life that awful first moment of reality, when there is no one to say, 'Not bad, sorr! Ye'll be doin' better next time.'

With my fingers round his throat, I should, in theory, have been able to kill him almost instantly, even effortlessly. But nobody had told me how the sweat would make my hands slide; that his neck would not be bare, but covered by a piece of knotted cloth.

I knew I couldn't hold on for long. Dazed at first, the khaki-clad figure started squirming, boots flaying, legs kicking. At all costs I had to prevent him from screaming in Japanese. I tried to tighten my grip round his throat. I called to Julie, 'Jump! Slide down and get his rifle.'

The terrible screaming from inside the hospital hid our noise, but I knew that one shout in Japanese would mean the end of us. Yet I could feel myself losing the battle against him. My fingers round his throat prevented any screams, but he tried to twist and turn as Julie landed with a thump next to me. She grabbed the Japanese rifle and made as though to hand it to me. But I didn't dare to release my grip on his throat. And shooting was out of the question, even if Julie knew how to handle a rifle.

'You do it, Julie,' I gasped, holding on to the man's neck, 'The rifle! In the face. In the face.' Terrified, she hesitated. I got him on his back, and shouted, 'Now! Before he gets us. Do it, Julie! Do it! The rifle! Bash his face in!'

Like a shadow I saw her in front of me, all of this happening in seconds. I saw her lift the heavy rifle, saw her fingers gripping the barrel. 'Now!' with one last effort I held him still, and actually saw the terror in his eyes. Then she hit him, again and again, while I held him there, legs and feet kicking me, but I couldn't feel them as she lunged at him, grunting and gasping, each hit, I knew, from one of her patients. I didn't dare take my fingers off his throat. He gurgled for breath, and dark red, almost black blood poured out of his mouth and over his face, dirty, foaming like the head on a bottle of Tiger beer. Then his legs stopped thrashing and I knew we had won.

I managed to get my fingers, which had become locked with cramp, from his throat. They were set and red. I wiped

them on the lallang, and hoarsely whispered, 'The car –
run for it!'

She started to run – but then toppled over in a dead faint.
I slung her over my shoulder and somehow reached the
car. How I started it I shall never know, for the YMCA
instructors had forgotten to tell me that if you grip a man's
throat for any length of time the fingers are virtually useless
for several minutes. At first I just couldn't switch on the
ignition with my left hand, which for some reason was
more locked with cramp than the right. I finally managed it,
but then I couldn't shift the gears. So I had to lurch forward,
lean over – with Julie still unconscious – and use my right
hand to change gear on my left. Once we started it was all
right.

Everything was covered in blood. Not only our hands
and faces, but our clothes, our shoes. The smell of drying
blood, sweat and vomit was overpowering, and as Julie
began to stir I realised that she couldn't get on the boat like
that. We had to do something. Time was running out, so I
decided to skirt Keppel Road and drive to Robinson Road.
We had an office shower and a loo, and since the war I had
kept a change of clothes there, so I could go straight to work
from the YMCA. Julie could have a shower and change into
a spare dress from her suitcase.

She was awake, but staring blankly as I braked in front of
the office. I tried to lift her out of the car, but the shock had
set in: I was so weak I could hardly move. For a second my
mind flashed back to the hospital – and then I smelt our
smell in the car, and got out and vomited. I crawled to the
bottom of the stairs and shouted. 'Ball! Ball!' A frightened
thamby at the top of the stairs took one look at me, disappeared, and Ball came into view.

'Japanese – help us –'

Ball almost slid down the stone steps. For a short man he
was tough. Though we were both drenched in blood he
never said a word. Resting on Ball's shoulders, Julie
managed to drag her feet up the stairs. We got into my
office.

'No time to be fussy,' I muttered, 'Ball, get a towel from

the shower room and help me to take her clothes off – burn them – and wrap her in a towel and let her rest on my sofa. Give her a Scotch while I have a shower and change – burn all my clothes too.'

Between us we stripped off Julie's clothes, and when I returned from a shower there was Ball gently washing her, with two dishes of water, one clean, one bloody, by his side.

At the first sip of Scotch she vomited, but I forced some more down her throat, and it did give her a little strength. I took her to the shower, helped to soap her down, holding her each time her legs started to buckle. Then, wrapped in a towel, I led her back to the office, with the remnants of the staff goggling, found some clothes in her suitcase, helped her to dress, and prepared to set off for the docks.

All the time in the office she was in such a state of shock that she hardly said a word. And I was thinking not of the beastliness of the Japanese butchery but of the delight – that is the only word for it – that had shone in their faces when sticking the steel into helpless invalids. Was that pleasure a kind of revenge for the way in which the white man had ridiculed, despised, exploited them? I wondered because, though I had been horrified as I watched them, when Julie struck the soldier – little more than a boy – time and time again in the face, in the eyes, I was urging her on, not only to save our lives but with a sadistic pleasure in getting our revenge. Thank God Grandpa Jack is dead, I thought. Thank God!

'We've got to go, Ball,' I cut into my thoughts. 'Thanks for your help. I'm seeing Miss Soong off – I'll be in the office tomorrow.'

All through the night and morning the docks had been attacked by Japanese twin-engine bombers with Zero fighter escorts, and after a short respite – almost, I thought bitterly, as though the pilots had knocked off for lunch – the raids were resumed with even deadlier ferocity. As we came to the approach roads we could see flames ahead. Nothing could keep the acrid smoke of burning rubber or wood out of the car, but at least the boys at the office had wiped the car fairly clean while we showered. Half the sprawling godowns were in flames by now. Every few feet I swerved or braked to avoid bodies, not always in time. When I hit a fallen tree or some debris the car jolted, but I could always tell when I hit a body because when the wheels made contact with yielding flesh it was a different kind of bump.

Cars of all makes, sizes, vintages, formed a long snake along the roads leading to the large, rectangular Empire Dock. Waves of planes roared over, sometimes strafing, usually making for the docks ahead. 'I can understand why soldiers haven't time to be afraid,' I shouted to Julie, trying to take her mind off the horrors of the hospital. 'They're too busy doing this to have any time.'

At one corner a building had received a direct hit and three ambulances, motors running, waited while those still alive were pulled out of the crackling wreckage. At one side was a pile of bodies – there was no time for ceremony with the dead. A doctor made a quick examination of each victim and pointed either to the ambulance or the pile of corpses.

We were jammed at that corner for twenty minutes. The police and army had long since stopped trying to marshal the traffic. They couldn't have done anything anyway, for the roads leading to the three–mile dock area were not only filled with cars like ours *going* to the ships, we were clashing head–on with convoys of army vehicles racing to get military stores, equipment, weapons, *away* from the docks so the ships could sail before the Japanese sank them.

Trucks rattled towards us, came abreast, lurched past, piled high with army stores on top of which eager, grinning youngsters, often bare to the waist, held on precariously. Many had obviously never seen a tropical island before, all seemed cheerfully convinced that victory was on the way now they had arrived.

'Don't worry, lady,' one shouted to Julie as our two vehicles were stuck abreast. 'We've arrived – your troubles'll soon be over.' Then he was off with a harsh clank of gears, rumbling and clattering away. Everyone had a cheery grin, a wave and a greeting for a pretty girl. 'Don't let her go, Mister,' shouted one wit. 'She's too pretty to be left alone.' Another bellowed, 'Any more like you around, Miss?'

I was worried about the time. We had hardly moved fifty yards in fifteen minutes. Twenty yards ahead of me I saw an elderly man suddenly jump out of his car, pull out a suitcase, and then his wife got out of the other side. They banged the doors and set off on foot. That meant the car was immobilised. Immediately the people in nearby cars did the same.

'Come on,' I told Julie. 'We'll have to walk.' Everywhere people were abandoning cars. A hundred yards further on I saw Wilf Broadbent. 'Hello, Julie,' he said, '*Bon voyage*. No good keeping to the main roads. There's a direct hit on the water main round the corner. Cut through here.' He indicated a way round the back streets. 'See you at the docks,' he added. 'I'll be there in any case. The others are trying to get the fire engine around the other way – by Mount Faber and down again; less traffic that way.'

'Can you make it?' I looked at Julie. Beyond words, she just nodded. Not only was the stench of bodies terrible, but each corner was an echo of the hospital, the writhing, screaming figures of wounded left to die, some with arms torn off, others sightless, others with faces drenched in blood. And with all this, as we struggled to reach the quay and the boat, there was constant choking as we inhaled burned-up air. Julie's eyes were red-rimmed and streaming.

'We've got the ARP here,' said Wilf bitterly. 'But we can't get the ambulances past the abandoned cars.'

I would have given a lot for a sudden tropical downpour, to wash away the blood, to break the sultry, clammy, steamy air. As we reached the quays a seething mass of human beings covered every inch of hot ground. I could feel the heat coming up through my shoes, and from time to time I had to move my feet as we stood pressed together, edging forward slowly, in the streets between the gaunt godowns, all leading to the vessels behind. Everywhere gasping women jostled or just waited patiently until it was their turn. Not until we moved in the queue could I see the reason for the bottleneck.

The passengers had to pass through a small gate in the centre of some makeshift but stout fencing that had been erected. By the gate sat an official from the P&O at a very small table. Slowly, methodically, he was writing down in a book particulars of every passenger.

Just ahead of us I saw a familiar figure.

'Rawlings!' I shouted. His wife Rosie was clutching two suitcases while Rawlings held the baby. I managed to get near him.

'Try to keep an eye on Miss Soong, will you?' I asked him. 'She's on the same boat as you and your mem.'

'Of course, Mr John.' He didn't display any more guilt feeling – in fact I found myself wishing to God I was going along too. But I just squeezed Julie's hand as hard as I could. It wouldn't be long now.

There were several male passengers in the crowd. No doubt many would be useful continuing the fight in Java – I saw one who I knew was an expert demolition engineer – but I also saw several others whom I recognised as members of the PWD – the Public Works Department. Why were they going, I wondered – but not for long, for suddenly the man at the gate refused to accept one man's pass, and several men near the front tried to smash down the barrier. At that moment two Japanese planes zoomed low and opened up with machine-gun fire. Twenty or thirty women pushed through the barrier, but half a dozen soldiers rushed to the other side of the fence and kept the men back while an officer checked on the passes of the women who had burst through.

As the planes vanished I heard the P&O shout through a loud hailer, 'Passes without government stamps aren't valid for today. Only P&O slips are valid here.'

It was the signal for panic. As I discovered later, the men from the PWD had been issued with phoney passes by someone in the PWD who wanted to get away too. They had no government authority. Somebody had been fiddling. Men shouted and yelled that they had their passes and should be let through. Whenever the gate was opened to admit a passenger with a legitimate pass there was a concerted surge towards it, and the fence seemed to buckle. The psychological effect of having got a permit — whether valid or not — and then being refused permission to leave was too much for many men. Some were crying. Others tore at the fence, trying to break it down. Yet others — men like myself seeing their women off — shouted obscenities at them, hurled words like 'Coward!' and 'Women and children first!' There were several scuffles — until a young lieutenant in charge of the troops ordered them to fire over the heads of the crowd. It calmed the situation a little.

Just as Rawlings and his wife, ahead of us, reached the desk by the gate — after we had queued for untold hours — the Japanese planes returned. They were obviously trying to sink the boats. Plumes of water from behind the end of the godowns shot into the air — some so high the spray doused us. Then, their bombs away, the planes wheeled in a large arc like swallows, and dived straight towards the quays, guns spattering. It was impossible to seek cover — impossible even to fall on to the ground, for there were too many bodies standing pressed together. People stumbled on each other like dolls trying to fall. With an ear-splitting shriek the planes were directly over us, then with a whine they zoomed upwards and away, leaving only the shrieks and cries of the wounded.

How many were killed in those few seconds I never discovered. I saw one man stand up clutching a baby. He was screaming, blaspheming. For a moment I didn't realise who it was. Then I saw it was Rawlings. I pushed through, elbowing viciously. His wife's face was a pulp. She must have died the second the bullet tore into her, but even in death she was half standing, unable to fall down. As I reached her she crumpled to the ground. Julie grabbed the baby. The P&O man shouted at Rawlings to get a move on and pass through the gate. Others were waiting, pushing. A sailor on the other side of the barrier shouted, 'For Chrissake get a move on, mate. These buggers don't give you a second chance.'

In an agony Rawlings looked at me — and I could see that he was going to try to pick up his wife's body. The pebble glasses hid his eyes, the tears streamed, he just moaned, 'Rosie! Rosie!'

'Come on!' I tried to be stern, though I felt terrible.

'I can't. I can't – I can't leave her like this –'

'Get on board. Not for yourself – think of the baby.'

For a second I thought he was going to fight me. Then he shouted, 'Will you bury her, sir? Promise?'

'I give you my word,' I said. 'But go, man. Go!'

He stumbled through the barrier before Julie had a chance to hand the baby to him.

'Your passes,' the P&O man shouted. Rawlings was clutching the three tickets – and then, before I knew what was happening, before I could do anything, before I could kiss her, touch her, Julie had gone. She had been standing just behind Rawlings, holding the baby. Rawlings still clutched his three tickets, and the P&O man must have thought the tickets were for Rawlings, Julie and the baby. He pushed her through, assuming she was Mrs Rawlings.

I saw Julie turn towards the man. As she gave him *her* ticket she waved to me. And as she had passed through on Rawling's ticket the man misunderstood, looked at me, thinking that Julie had taken my ticket.

'Come on, for Christ's sake,' he beckoned me.

For one awful moment I hesitated. No, in that moment of cowardice I *didn't* hesitate. I stepped forward, ready to join her, given once again a chance in life – this time to escape from the hell around me, to leave it, to be with her. I saw her looking at me, arms outstretched like a supplicant, and then I stopped. I don't think I was swayed by the knowledge that if I did go on board I might be posted as an army deserter; I didn't have time for thoughts like that. I just knew I couldn't.

The man at the desk looked at me and cried, 'Well, make up your fucking mind.' Then vicious elbows dug into my ribs as those behind – who did have tickets – forced their way past me.

I caught one last glimpse of her. 'See you!' was all I had time to shout as she blew a kiss. Then she held her hand out with her eternity ring on it and kissed it so that I could see her. A moment later she was swallowed up in the rectangular iron doorway leading to the bowels of the ship.

I don't know how long I stood there, just staring at the side of that bloody ship, a vaguely neutral colour, the tiny door opening; oblivious to elbows pushing me, feet stamping on mine, people pushing, oblivious even to the Japs who returned for two more hit-and-run raids. No, I wasn't oblivious to *them*. When I heard them wheeling in, zooming down, I waved my fists defiantly, hurled curses at them, hoping they would see me, hoping they would kill me. Lucky Grandpa Jack!

She was inside that ship behind the fence, the *Ban Hong Liong*, a few yards from me, a million miles from me. I prayed the old tub would live up to her name, 'Good Progress'.

As I looked around, wondering how to get back to the city, I realised that the hot suffocating day had changed into a sunset the colour of blood, followed by the swift pink of tropical twilight before a blessed curtain of darkness. Standing there by the body of Rosie Rawlings, wondering what to do about her, I was thinking also of Julie, one of hundreds of women who would soon be lining the rails of the ships when they departed. A bright moon had broken over the edge of the city, lighting the sky, perhaps to give them a last indelible picture of the waterfront of Singapore, of home, of men left behind, in a once proud and thriving port, now a warren of public holes and private hells.

It was at this moment I saw the sergeant who had been largely responsible for my YMCA training, and the sight of this burly dependable Scot, whose job had been to turn me into a reluctant killer, made me forget for a moment my own worries. He was at the wheel of an army vehicle.

'That's a coincidence, sergeant,' I cried. 'Any chance of a lift?'

'Jump in, sorr! But it's na a matter o' coincidence, sorr. I came here tae look for ye.'

'What's happened? How did you know I'd be here?' I had an instant premonition of the unexpected.

'Colonel Chalfont, sorr,' he said, as though the name

would explain everything. 'He told me ye'd be seeing some-one off on the *Ban Hong Liong*. And he told us na to hurry, but to wait.'

'Well, I'm here. What next?' I jumped into the vehicle and nodded to another soldier I vaguely recognised.

'There's been a change o' plan, sorr,' said the sergeant. 'The date's been advanced a wee bit. Ye're leaving tonight.'

I felt a sudden awful sickness, almost ready to vomit with fear, a surge of panic. I said nothing. The other soldier lifted up Rosie's body, wrapped it in a tarpaulin and put it in the back of the carrier. 'Aye, sorr,' said the sergeant. 'I saw what happened and it's a terrible thing, war. We'll be seein' she gets a decent burial, poor wee bairn.'

'I didn't enquire how, or who would do it. All I could say was, 'What time?'

'Ten o'clock, sorr. Is there anything ye'd like to be doing before ye gae fra Singapore?'

I *had* planned to take Li to Tanamera. The married quarters were habitable, if rough, and I felt that when Singapore came under Japanese rule he would be safer there than in the Cadet House which would surely be requisitioned. Li would also be near the Soong house. He might even work there. But how could I get him there now that my own car was abandoned?

'I'll take ye where ye want, sorr,' said the sergeant. 'We'll take the body of this lassie to the YMCA on the way, then ye'll tell me the direction ye want to gae.'

We did this. I was delighted to sit next to him, for somehow his cheerful presence helped to settle the butter-flies dancing in my stomach, for I *was* very frightened.

'I'm glad you happened along, sergeant,' I said, and I could sense that he knew I meant it.

'It's an honour sorr,' he replied. 'The colonel says ye're our star pupil, sorr.'

We drove first to Nassim Hill. I climbed the stairs to the white and green bedroom which had been our home – really our home. Everywhere Julie haunted me. It was hard to believe that she had only left earlier that day and that so much had happened since we kissed each other in this room, such a terrible, bloodstained afternoon, her patients slaughtered.

I opened the wardrobe to get a pair of socks, which I always kept in the bedroom. Her dresses were still hanging there. I could hear like a metronome the tick of the alarm clock which used to wake her up when it was time to go to the Alexandra. There was a faint smell of her – a smell of woman, a compound of odours, the powder she used, her toilet water, her soap, her body. With a sigh, determined to leave as quickly as possible, I slipped on a shirt.

Something stiff crackled in my breast pocket. It was a last letter from her, a last poem. I read it alone in the room. She had written,

Beloved, Faithfulness is a pearl beyond price and however much a woman loves a man it is too much to demand. But when (if) in the years that separate us and it ever happens, and you still truly love me despite what you do, we will both take heart from this poem:

All night upon mine heart I felt her warm heart beat,
Night-long within mine arms in love and sleep she lay;
Surely the kisses of her bought red mouth were sweet;
But I was desolate and sick of an old passion,
When I awoke and found the dawn was grey;
I have been faithful to thee, Cynara! in my fashion.

I read the letter twice, folded it up and put it in my pocket before packing up everything portable that was of intrinsic value – the clock, my watch, a radio, other trifles – put them in a canvas bag and gave them all to Li.

'Sell everything, if you have to,' I said, as he looked amazed. 'Missee and I will never need them again. They'll be more useful to you if you run short of money.'

From Orchard Road we turned left up Scotts Road and drove past the Goodwood Park Hotel, with Li in the back seat. The journey took only a few minutes, and as we passed the Soong house I warned the sergeant, 'Next on the left – about three hundred yards up the road.' When we reached the gates, which were open, the driver swung the vehicle round with a rattle and a crash of gears. The headlights cut a swathe of light on the gravel path curving towards the massive gleaming white walls, the beams shining on them like theatre spotlights.

We climbed out and I just stood there, looking at the walls and the pillars. I didn't want to go behind, poke in the ruins, I just wanted to look, to remember the early days in the Sick Bay, the first birthday party which Julie had come to, the dance when Grandpa Jack had his stroke, Julie in my arms in the dark, gasping; Vicki – and the strange look she gave me as I came in from the tennis pavilion that night – the knowing look that only ex-lovers can exchange; Mama teasing me, 'Why are you always so hungry on Friday mornings?' Irene – how she disliked the house! – the day Bengy was born; everything mixed up, memories tugging details from a half-forgotten past in a home rich in memories of a happy and wonderful life, torn into shreds now, so that as I looked the nostalgia was invested with a curious unreality. They were like the memories that are stirred when in a dusty attic you find a forgotten toy that once, a long time ago, was the most important thing in your life. It was like opening the door of the cupboard of my life.

A broad Scots accent interrupted my dreams. A cough, an apologetic, 'We dinna ha much time, and I've got a lot to do before we rendezvous, sorr.'

'We? Are you coming, sergeant?'

'I'll na be letting my favourite pupil go alone, captain.'

'Why, that's wonderful!' In an instant the last of the butterflies in my stomach disappeared. 'Thank God,' I cried, adding, 'I was told never to ask questions at the YMCA, but now don't you think I should know your name?'

'Sergeant Macmillan – sorr,' he replied. 'Aye, I'm glad we'll be gaeing together. Colonel Chalfont says it'll be a rough trip.'

A sudden thought struck me. 'Shouldn't I go and pay my respects to the colonel?'

'He's gone, sorr.'

'Gone!' I was astounded. 'Just like that — *gone*?'

'Aye, sorr. Now that we're on our way, so to speak, no harm in explaining matters. The colonel has left. He's parachuted down in Malaya — a sort of welcoming committee for us. Getting the camp ready, lookin' after the heathen Chinese who're already there.'

'So we'll be seeing the colonel?' I could hardly believe it.

'Och ay, sorr. That's been the idea all along, only it was nae possible to say so. The colonel he picked you as his number two — he wanted a man with local knowledge — and the three of us — we trained to be a team on our own, sorr. There were a dozen other teams training at the same time. The colonel says it could take us three months to reach our base camp.'

I was still looking at the white walls of Tanamera, my thoughts jumbled — Julie, Irene, Ben, my father and mother, even Tim — and now? What lay ahead, and would anyone ever know where I was, what I was doing? The sergeant interrupted me.

'Excuse me, sorr,' he asked after a moment's hesitation. 'Would this great pile of masonry ha been your hus, sorr?'

'It was,' I sighed. 'My grandfather built it. He was killed instantly when the place was bombed two days ago. I was born here. It was the greatest house in Singapore in its day, and my grandfather built the walls out of coconut husks, eggs and sugar and swore they'd last for a hundred years. They're still standing, you see.'

'It must ha' been as big as Edinburgh Castle!' Then, changing the subject, he asked, 'May I ask, sorr, what are ye going to do with this Chinese man?'

'Li? Leave him here.'

'Alone, sorr?'

'Why not? He'll be safe here.'

'You're sure he's na a spy?'

'Li a spy!' I almost burst out laughing. 'Li was born here, the same year I was born. He was my first friend. We grew up as boys playing here in this garden.'

Macmillan seemed puzzled. 'I thought he was your servant — your boy.'

'He is,' I laughed. 'His father was my father's boy.'

'It's a wee bit puzzling, sorr, the way ye live in these heathen parts.'

'Sergeant,' I tried to explain, 'Li is the most faithful and honest man in the world. I love him like a brother – even more perhaps. He *likes* looking after me – he's proud that he can do it better than anyone else in the world. One day it may all change. I wouldn't be surprised after all this mess is over if Singapore doesn't one day belong to the children of men like Li. Perhaps it should.'

'That's blasphemy, sorr!'

'Not really,' I laughed. 'And' – pointing to the white walls – 'it doesn't apply to Tanamera. That will always belong to the Dexters, and when this war is over I'll come back and I'll rebuild it again, stone by stone.'

'Well, sorr' – as I said my farewells to Li, Macmillan became suddenly practical – 'the sooner we start to kill these little yellow buggers the sooner ye'll be hame, sorr. And perhaps it'll nae be as long as ye think. What's the house called, sorr?'

'Tanamera.'

'It's an unusual name, sorr.'

I explained what the two Malay words meant, and then, bending down by a trampled bed of cannas – just as Grandpa Jack had done – I picked up a handful of the rich red soil. Under the light of the headlamps I showed it to Macmillan.

'That's our heritage,' I said. Then I looked at Li. For the very first time in my life I saw tears staining a face that was crumpled and shrunken with grief.

On an impulse I held out my hand with the red earth in it, gripped his hand so that both of us were clasping the soil between our palms – a bond of friendship – as I said, 'Take care of yourself, Li. I'll be back.'

To Macmillan I said, 'That's why I volunteered to join Force 136, sergeant – to fight for Li, for the good red earth of Singapore – and for Tanamera.'

PART FIVE

Malaya, 1942–1945

It was like reaching a haven, the moment when Sergeant Macmillan and I – and Ah Ki, the tracker who had guided us from the east coast – finally reached camp, and there was Colonel Chalfont in tattered jungle greens striding towards us in the jungle clearing.

For this was *my* territory. Though the Ara base camp, as it was known to Force 136, was not actually on the estate – the bungalow once occupied by Tony and Natasha had become a Japanese officers' mess – we were only two or three miles behind it, hidden in deep jungle, where an astonishing transformation had taken place.

Long, long ago, in the different world of the YMCA, when I thought of my future as a guerilla fighter, I had always visualised myself as one of a group of four or five dedicated men, living in caves or hastily erected bashas, the temporary shelters that could quickly be constructed from attap. There, I supposed, we would wait and cower between assignments.

How different it was! The camp had begun to take shape even before Malaya was overrun. A group of hand-picked Chinese had been left there, posing as coolies or tappers before Singapore fell, and the retreating British army had left them buried caches of arms, explosives, radio equipment. When it became obvious that defeat was imminent Chalfont had been parachuted down to take command. His was the last plane, so Macmillan and I had walked to Ara. That's the sort of nightmare journey I prefer to forget – if I can. It was thirteen weeks before we arrived, two worn-out skeletons, in the middle of May, 1942.

That was four months ago. Now we were an integral part

of the camp which consisted of solidly-built huts encircling a parade ground of beaten earth, the huts at the jungle fringe so they would be invisible to the prying eyes in any low-flying Japanese aircraft. At one end were the admin offices, a command post and the office of Colonel Chalfont, with another office nearby for Tan Sun, the chief of the forty-two Chinese guerillas – each one a dedicated Japanese-hater, each one a dedicated Communist. The camp was sited on an incline, with a small mountain river trickling along one side. Washing and bathing areas, kitchens and latrines had been easily arranged in descending order on the banks of the water that eventually tumbled into the Klang near KL, ten miles or so to the west.

Security was vital, and it depended on a simple Chinese system that had bewildered me when I first reached the parade ground and was urgently warned not to step on the lengths of thick rattan rope that crisscrossed it and which led to sentries circling the camp. In the event, all they had to do was give the rope several vigorous tugs to sound the alarm.

The only way to reach the camp was through thick jungle that reached down to the KL-Bentong road – a road I knew backwards, but though I had lived in the area I could never have found my way unaided to the camp. Even the entrance to the secret jungle paths was impossible to find without the aid of the sentry always on duty near the road itself, a sentry whoe disguise was perfect – black tapper's clothes stiff with years of spilled, congealed, stinking latex. He was the man who had first led me through the jungle, then through rows of identical rubber trees, along untended paths, the precious trees now neglected, the diagonal cuts in their bark dried up, empty cups still tied to mottled trunks; then back into the jungle, where the light filtering through the trees faded and the sun vanished. A rough path had been hacked leading to the camp, and along it a succession of sentries waited to greet – or kill – any intruder. It had taken us nearly two hours to make the jungle trip, with visibility at times down to fifteen feet. Each step was agony, not only because of thorns and leeches, but because the sweat refused to evap-orate in the saturated air until, without warning, two

Chinese brandishing tommy guns rose like wraiths from the undergrowth barely two yards ahead of us, and we had reached base camp.

Chalfont had changed, of course. He still bore traces of the old flippant manner which, at our first meeting at the Adelphi, had convinced me he was homosexual, but this didn't matter once I realised that it was not an affectation. He had actually spoken and behaved in this manner since he was a child. But underneath there was a hard, tough fibre that he had not needed to show me in the comfortable days of war in Singapore. It was weeks before he let slip what Macmillan had already told me: that earlier in the war he had once landed on the French Channel coast with some commandos.

In Singapore I had, I suppose, stood a little in awe of everyone connected with Force 136, but here, though discipline had to be strict, life was more informal. It was impossible to be second in command without knowing that the CO's Christian name was Robin, or that he brushed his teeth three times a day, and always slept in a sarong instead of pyjamas. I liked him more each day we shared Ara.

Though he was a friendly man, we usually ate only one meal a day together. He felt that we had to show the Chinese that British officers never forgot they were commanders. And the bosses. It was crucial to impress the Chinese with our authority because they were always trying to persuade Chalfont to allow them to set off on crazy missions – always with our explosives and grenades, of course. So, to keep up appearances, Chalfont and I always supped in splendid isolation outside his 'office'. But we had to consider Sergeant Macmillan, the only British NCO. So though Chalfont and I 'dined' together, I 'lunched' alone, for at midday Chalfont and Macmillan had a daily working lunch – 'lunch' being a comparative term, for it consisted of whatever supplies reached camp from sympathisers – often relations of the Chinese fighting by our side – and which were smuggled in to Ara by would-be recruits who were given these assignments as trials in outwitting the Japanese before they were accepted into the Chinese forces. It was a method that suited all of us — we got the food, the eager young men got a training. Of course the training was one in which if he made a mistake the recruit was killed; but we only lost a couple of meals.

The most extraordinary aspect of camp life was the feeling of complete security. Chalfont used to say, 'Unless a soldier can relax in his base camp, he'll never relax on a raid.' We were surrounded by Japanese troops — thousands of them. Ara was only two or three miles away; KL barely ten, and the city was swarming with Japanese. But an army could never have found us, could never have penetrated the jungle into which we could melt at will. Even *we* could never return to camp without our sentry-guides. It meant that after every dangerous raid we knew we would be able to return to a safe 'home'. In war that is a great bonus.

We bathed each day at dawn, that magical grey moment when the sounds of the night ceased and the noises of the day had not begun, and the silence was broken only by the whisper of the river. This was the only time when the river was even moderately cool. It was never cold.

There was no chance for anyone to take normal exercise so it was essential for us to do regular PT each morning, much to the amusement of the Chinese — until they joined in and loved it. Macmillan and I certainly needed to exercise — carefully, though, for I must have lost twenty pounds on the trip across Malaya. I needed to put on weight but in the right way: muscle not fat. And with careful exercising I did, though for the first few weeks Chalfont would not let me do my stint on the bicycle which someone had to pedal once a week to raise power for the short broadcast to base in Colombo. Every broadcast was a long and exasperating procedure. We slung an aerial between two trees. We composed our message. We then had to code it, using five-letter twin-group codes, the keys in two precious books which Chalfont always kept hidden. One letter wrong in the code and we might as well have stayed in bed.

Sometimes every attempt to get through was foiled by atmospherics, yet we had set times when we had to try, if only because we knew that, thousands of miles away, someone was waiting to take down our message, perhaps just to be sure we were still alive, that the base had not been wiped out. And when we did get through, when we received a brisk message in reply, it made all the effort worth while.

The first months were a time of waiting, of making sure the Japs had settled down, that they believed they were safe, that no enemies were left – at least enemies of any consequence. For this reason we launched only sporadic raids at first, blowing up bridges or derailing trains, because Chalfont felt the Japanese would not believe them to be the work of British-led saboteurs but of local partisans who presented no serious threat. Besides, they provided what Chalfont called 'acclimatisation exercises'. I went on every one I could, not only for experience but because the days of inactivity in camp were terrible, and action was the only way to forget the outside world. I wasn't homesick in the accepted sense of the word; I didn't have time for that. But I did have moments when I thought of the others. Was Julie safe? She must have arrived in Ceylon long ago – and I would sometimes imagine her, almost with a touch of bitterness, perhaps dancing at some officers' mess. It was all nonsense, of course. And I thought of Irene and Bengy – and who else? Was I the father of a son or daughter? It was a curious sensation, being totally cut off from all the family – all of them carrying on, business as usual, scattered over the globe, and I couldn't find out one damned thing about any of them. And, as far as I could see, for years I never would.

If the days in camp dragged, the evenings were worse, for the real bane of our lives was not the Japs but the flies and midges. Though the mosquitos were never absent, the midges didn't come every day – they must have alternated Camp Ara with other hunting grounds – but when they did come I could sometimes see them like a lacy cloud, millions and millions of them zooming into the attack in the brief moment before dusk thickens into dark.

There was no escape. We did have a mosquito net each, but there was no way we could take that from our bunks: that space had to be protected day and night. And we had no

501

defence against midge bites and other flies. The only thing to do was to turn in early.

During my first months at Ara we were trying to perfect a new type of bomb – with one victim in view, a notorious Japanese commander of horrific cruelty. His name was Captain Shinpei Satoh, and he had the unsavoury reputation of leaving camp in his small car almost daily and picking out at random some luckless Chinese or Malay for torture or, if the victim was lucky, execution. It was his way of instilling local obedience through fear, and the entire area was wrapped in terror.

The trouble was, although we knew his name we didn't know his face, or the exact location of his camp, and we didn't have the right kind of bomb to blow him up. Though I didn't know it at first Chalfont was giving me postgraduate training for the moment when we did have the right kind of bomb and I could lead the attack.

The army had left us enough explosives to blow up a fair-sized town. They ranged from grenades to plastic high explosives which were not affected by water and which we could – and did – bury and connect to a pressure switch which would trigger off the bomb with the weight of a vehicle passing over it. This was fine for derailing trains or blowing up bridges, when we could hide the PE, knowing that the next vehicle passing over the fuse would blow up the target; remembering also that the objective in these cases was not to blow up the vehicle, except incidentally, but use the enemy vehicle to blow up a bridge or smash up a stretch of track. Such a method couldn't be used for the assassination of a particular individual. On a road a pressure switch was very much a hit-and-miss affair, for we could have no guarantee that the man or vehicle we wanted to destroy would ever arrive on the scene. So with a man like Satoh it was a chance we couldn't take, if only because it was hard work making a jungle journey carrying thirty pounds each of high explosives in addition to our other gear.

Nor would we use time pencils, for they also tended to hit the wrong road targets. These were ingenious delayed action fuses in which we placed HE or gelignite where we wanted to, then squeezed a tube fuse which forced acid to burn its way along a thin wire until the wire dissolved and the charge blew up. Time pencils were light and easy to handle and gave us plenty of time to get clear, but again their use lay in blowing up bridges or tracks.

So far we had found no way of producing a bomb which could lie in the target area for a day or two if necessary and be detonated at the exact moment when the man we wanted to kill arrived. Now, after months of experiments we felt that Tan Sun, the guerilla leader, had solved the problem.

Tan Sun was the last man I would have expected to be a guerilla fighter, let alone a Communist. When he had agreed to serve under the British and help form the Ara base, he had arrived with only one item in his possession: a well-thumbed copy of Shakespeare's plays. He was a tall, skinny man with a drooping moustache and an unhealthy pockmarked skin. But he knew his Shakespeare by heart, and he was the only man to discover the perfect way to pass the time in the jungle, for he could go on rereading that one book until the war ended.

Chalfont told me Tan Sun had once worked in a garage, and later as a schoolmaster, and he certainly had a way of working with his hands. His idea for what became known as the Satoh bomb was, like most Chinese devices, ingeniously simple. He had hollowed out a length of thick bamboo – the sort you could pick up anywhere near any target area – and stuffed it with gelignite – not the lighter PE, alas, but the old-fashioned high explosive which had been left in bulk, and which we had been ordered to use up whenever possible. The bamboo bomb could be left, innocuous looking, in the middle of any road, strewn among other bits of wood that might easily have fallen off the back of an overloaded bullock cart. It would never excite curiosity.

Inside the gelignite Tan Sun had buried an instantaneous fuse, connected to a long length of the thinnest wire he had been able to smuggle into camp – in fact it was piano wire – and which was virtually invisible to the eye. One tug from a safe distance – with one man watching the target through field glasses to make sure when the right man was in the right place – and the bomb exploded instantly, at the exact moment you wanted. The bomb had the additional advantages that it could be manufactured in the killing area – we didn't have to carry long stretches of bamboo through the jungle – and also that dozens of heavy vehicles could grind over it without any effect unless the wire was pulled.

Now the only ingredients needed were a detailed description of the life style of Satoh, the exact location of his camp and someone who could be sure to recognise him. Despite repeated pleas by Tan Sun to send out an extermination squad Chalfont was adamant that we would not act until we knew for sure that we would kill the right man.

The opportunity came unexpectedly with the arrival of a new recruit in camp. Would-be guerillas underwent a strict form of positive vetting by the Chinese officers and started life in camp as cleaners or food carriers and in other menial tasks, while discreet enquiries were presumably made in the kampongs. This man was a Straits Chinese called Ah Tin, and he had actually worked in Satoh's camp after being pressed into a work force by a Japanese patrol sent out to round up civilians.

He looked sixteen or seventeen, though he was several years older. He seemed pathetically inoffensive, small, dark, watery eyes permanently alarmed, even when he was asked the most innocuous questions. It was the shape of his unwrinkled, moonlike face, with its two small startled eyes, that gave one the impression he was afraid of his own skin. But Ah Tin could not only recognise Satoh easily; he knew a great deal about his habits and movements.

'We might be able to do it.' Chalfont and I were having supper, the name that dignified a little soggy rice, an ounce or two of salt fish and, to make up weight, a plate of ground-up root from the tapioca that grew in every kampong and which was served day after day, just as it had been (though rather better cooked) in the nursery days at Tanamera.

'Certainly we can make the right bomb now. It's brilliant,' I said.

'It's a trifle dangerous for the chap who pulls the wire,' drawled Chalfont with typical understatement.

'It's all right if you're far enough away — if the wire's long enough.'

'*That's* not the problem. How are you going to make your getaway from the killing area? I don't want to cut you off in your prime, Johnnie! After the sort of bang we hope you make the area will be swarming with Japs. Nobody will stand a chance of getting away.'

I disagreed. More than once during the past months I had hidden in secondary jungle only a few yards from Japs searching for me, Japs who knew I was in the area. With one's face blacked it was virtually impossible to be discovered except by sheer bad luck — say, by a man sticking a bayonet haphazardly into jungle undergrowth. At which moment any of us would have taken our L pill — L for lethal — before any Jap could grab us. It was swift; Japanese torture was not.

'It's a chance we've all got to take, and I don't think any of the Chinese would mind,' I said. 'But of course your chances of survival are doubled if you really know the terrain.'

'Do *you* know exactly where Satoh's camp is?' he asked me almost lazily.

'Come off it, Robin. You know I haven't the faintest idea — except that it's not far away.'

'Well, I've found out the *exact* location from Ah Tin. And, Johnnie, I'm sure you know every inch of the place.'

'Well? Stop teasing!'

'It's the Country Club — the one on the road from Ara to Bentong. You do know it, don't you?'

Know it? How often, as I sat in the jungle, the past seemed to catch up with me. 'The Club': sausages and mash in the long, tatty but homely room; the old copies of the *Daily Telegraph* and the *Illustrated London News*; and, before that, Natflat standing on the verandah, twisting her glass nervously as she confessed that she was expecting a baby —

and that Tony wasn't the father. That was the night the Indian lunatic fired a shot into the room where Irene was playing bridge. I could see every inch of the scene: the chirpy little secretary telling everyone to keep calm. And Irene – earlier that same day, that afternoon, deliberately setting out to become pregnant. And by now? What had happened since that day?

'Well – do you know it?'

'I was miles away.'

'Obviously.'

'Light miles, I mean. Time-machine stuff. I was thinking of the last evening I spent there. God, it seems a different life. Do you think it'll ever come back?'

'It might speed up the process if you manage to knock off Captain Satoh,' he said laconically.

'Soon?' I hope my voice didn't betray any 'un-British' excitement, for I had long since discovered that acute danger was preferable to acute boredom.

'Sure. The sooner the better. Take Jock Macmillan and the Chinese – he's the only one who can recognise Satoh.'

'Ah Tin? You think he can make it?' I had my doubts, he looked so scared. 'If he lets us down – if *anyone* isn't up to it – well, you know, it's curtains for the rest of us. I wonder about him.'

'He'll be okay,' Chalfont drawled.

'He looks scared.'

'He *is* scared. But there's one emotion that always conquers fear, and that's revenge. Ah Tin's father fell into one of those Jap traps – you remember them at the YMCA? – and Satoh just poured petrol in, a bit at a time, and burned the poor sod alive. Slowly. I wouldn't worry about Ah Tin, Johnnie. In fact, since he's the one who's leading you to Satoh, you might even let him have the honour of pulling the wire.'

32

Three days later, dressed in khaki drill trousers – partly as a precaution against leeches – rubber-soled boots, khaki bush shirts and wide-brimmed Australian bush hats (useful for collecting rainwater or even as a washbowl to say nothing of shading your head) we set off for the club: Macmillan, Ah Tin and myself. We carried between us nearly eighty pounds of gelignite, in addition to a change of clothes, groundsheets, a primitive first-aid kit, an ordnance map of the area, a compass, a parang each (for the jungle more than for the Japs) and several boxes of matches, each box in a separate taped tin. Macmillan and I also carried tommy guns with six spare magazines and six grenades each, while I also carried field glasses. We took little food, hoping Ah Tin would forage rations from friendly kampongs, because we just couldn't carry another ounce on top of the weight of explosives. I carried something else – a tin of lamp black made from soot and a bag of that old tropical standby used to stain a thousand floors in the east as well as for the more private treatment of VD – crystals of potassium permanganate. I knew that a solution of this, plus the lamp black, touched up with a little local dirt, would be enough to darken our faces.

We made our way without mishap through the jungle surrounding the camp then into the rubber trees, finally arriving at the edge of the Bentong Road – the point where the pseudo-tapper marked the entrance to the route leading to our base. We crouched in the undergrowth while the sentry and Ah Tin held an earnest discussion.

'The sentry say road very busy with Japanese trucks,' explained Ah Tin.

I had expected this, and had been prepared to make our way through the jungle rather than risk being suddenly caught in a Japanese ambush. And the jungle wasn't far away. The point where we emerged was beluka, as the Malays call the secondary jungle; it was not difficult to get through. But the other side of the road was very different. Within a few feet of us loomed the real jungle, the tough, almost impassable rain forest, so dense it blotted out the sun, so that it was like walking from day into night as we crossed the road. Every thrusting creeper stretched upwards, searching for the sun that filtered through in faint streaks here and there, like the shafts of dusty light in old religious pictures. Many trees were as straight as pillars, some a hundred feet or even taller.

'We canna make more than five miles a day, laddie,' Macmillan tried to console Ah Tin who was anxious to push on quickly. 'But dinna fash yoursel, your turn'll come.' And though Ah Tin's English was too limited to understand this startling brogue, he added, 'I dinna care if it takes a year, I'll nae let that bastard Satoh off the hook.'

Almost the moment we crossed the road and plunged into jungle it started to rain. It lashed down, a curtain of pelting water that drenched us, hemming us in. We hacked our way forwards for perhaps half a mile and then, soaked to the skin, decided to halt for the night. Ah Tin soon had a fire going. Like many Chinese from the countryside he never travelled without a piece of resin or rubber with which to start a fire, but before he set light to it he foraged around for wood. There was no dry timber but that didn't matter. With his parang he hacked down several lengths of wet bamboo, carried them to the small clearing where we had set up camp and only then set fire to the resin. Soon the bamboo was alight. It always amazed me that when no other sodden wood could produce a fire bamboo always burned, no matter how wet it was. However, it was smoking badly.

'No danger?' I looked at the grey trail wafting upwards.

'No, *tuan*. All smoke lost in jungle before reaching heaven.'

Macmillan produced some soup cubes and water-purifying tablets, and asked me, 'I'll start cooking, sorr. Will ye be good enough to cut down some branches, and then we'll make a basha with our groundsheets.'

Even cutting down branches for a lean-to was hard work. In the hissing rain the trees, with barks of a dozen hues – some as white as marble, others the scaly green of a python – thrust their way upwards all round the tiny square of open ground where the fire smoked, ringing us like a cage; some were laced with tortuous creepers like the Ara, other vines hung like the rigging of a doomed schooner. In the forks of smaller trees tufts of fat leaves sprouted like overblown mistletoe, parasites born in the tree, strong enough to live off it yet never quite strong enough to kill the tree itself.

I returned with an armful of brushwood just as the soup was ready, though there was one chore awaiting us before we sat down for supper, one hateful, sick chore that always awaited anyone who stopped in the jungle to cut wood. I was used to it by now, but I could never master my disgust. Though I had laced my boots over the bottom of trousers tucked into them, somehow two fat, unseeing leeches had managed to find a way in and were squirming towards my toes – a favourite spot, along with the fingers and the crotch. At least a dozen hung like slugs on my clothes. Another four had managed to reach skin – two on my left arm above the elbow – the arm I had probably kept more still when slicing off brushwood. Another two had fastened themselves on the back of my neck without my realising.

Smokers burn off the leeches with cigarettes, but neither Macmillan nor I smoked (I had given it up when Singapore fell, rather than face the craving of a rationed supply). I always carried salt which, when sprinkled on leeches, makes them fall off, but I hated to waste it – and I had no need to, for Ah Tin smoked like a chimney, rolling his own cigarettes. He calmly touched the first leech on my neck with the burning end, and after it contracted, squirmed then dropped away he took another long drag until the cigarette was burning and repeated the process until I was leech-free. I couldn't help wondering if it made his cigarette taste any different. It was better, anyway, than pulling them off. I had done this once, only to find later that the tiny teeth remained embedded in my flesh, and we had to cut them out before they festered; for if that happens in the tropics a sore can kill you in twenty-four hours.

'They're nae very pretty buggers,' Macmillan observed. Like me, he could never get used to them.

'But good joss,' Ah Tin beamed happily and started to pour out the soup.

We passed a wretched night. The cicadas never ceased their chatter, while the croak of bullfrogs rumbled on until dawn. I had known these sounds all my life, but had always been able to avoid them when bedtime came. Not now.

I was suffering from an added vexation – catarrh. Perhaps it was only a dry cold but it persisted, possibly because our clothes were so often wet, so that I found it difficult to breathe through my nose at night. This in itself would not have mattered had I not been chronically afraid of insects, earwigs or beetles creeping into my mouth while I was asleep. All around us spiders' webs glistened after the rain like symmetrical diamond necklaces – and the spiders were there too; sometimes giant brutes with hairy legs and beady eyes.

The next morning we set off, taking a compass course, but it took us five hours to reach the kampong, for at times we had to hack our way through thorns, bushes, or the clammy hands of jungle vines – and though I had been using a parang now for several months I still found it a highly dangerous weapon. If the downward sweep was not timed properly it would slither off a wet branch, or even sometimes off a chunk of rock that looked like dead wood.

Then, without warning, Ah Tin held up a hand and stopped.

I couldn't understand his Chinese accent, so asked him why in Malay, '*Lekaslah! Mengapa kau berhenti?*'

'Smell smoke, *tuan*.' He sniffed the air. 'No *lekaslah*,' meaning, 'No come along.'

'Let's wait for a minute. Are they friendly?'

'Not knowing, *tuan*. I go see.'

'*Hati-hatilah!*' I warned him – 'Have a care.' I was always afraid of betrayal, so we arranged to wait for thirty minutes, and if he did not reappear by then we would push on. That was standard procedure. It was in Ah Tin's interest as much as ours that he should not be found with us if the Japs were around. Alone he could always melt into the local scene. Macmillan and I gratefully slumped out of our packs – which grew heavier with every mile – and I said, 'Let's hope he can scrounge a chicken or something.'

Within fifteen minutes Ah Tin was back, actually smiling for once, and said to me in Malay, 'My sister live here. She say quite safe for *tuan* to come into kampong to eat.'

'Come on, sergeant.'

The kampong was small, a dozen thatched huts on stilts – the sort of village duplicated all over Malaya – but after the jungle it was like entering paradise to see the leisurely life of the Malays and Chinese families, the lack of *want*, with coconuts, heavy papaya on their thin stems, pineapples, bananas, the inevitable hedge of sago and even a few flowers, some cannas reminding me of Tanamera, and a small paddy field near the river in which I could see a buffalo bathing, shaking its ears to frighten flies away. Naked children played cheerfully among the chickens, goats, squealing pigs, half-starved dogs and cats.

Ah Tin's sister, in direct contrast to her skinny brother, was a fat, heavy-bellied woman, with sagging breasts and the sort of smile that never lit up her brother's worried face. I was puzzled at first until I suddenly realised that she was not Ah Tin's sister but his sister-in-law; and when his brother arrived I could see immediately that they were twins. Like Ah Tin, the brother had the same startled, almost frightened appearance; I found myself wondering how he had plucked up courage to ask the healthy woman to become his wife. Perhaps she had asked him! The two men looked uncommonly alike and were obviously very close. They talked earnestly as we waited for lunch, picking tiny bananas from the nearest tree, while the wife sliced open two coconuts to give us a cool, sweet drink. And if the curry wasn't up to the standards of tiffin at Raffles no chicken cooked Malay-style ever tasted better. We ate squatting on our hunkers, tearing the flesh off chicken legs held in our fingers, after dipping it into the sweet, hot, dark-green coconut-flavoured curry sauce, as thick as gruel. And after that, fresh pineapple.

We reached the killing area on the evening of the third day, my face and arms torn with thorns and bearing the ugly scars of at least fifty leeches we had burned off my body. Most sores were harmless, though a couple were beginning to fester and one was suppurating; but they seemed to dry up after liberal doses of iodine.

Our first task was to recce the area. The club lay on the south side of the Bentong Road. On the north side along which we had travelled the jungle fringe ended in a steep bank that reared up for fifty feet, covered with beluka, in which, unless the Japanese were actually searching for us, prodding the undergrowth with bayonets, we could hide and look down on the main KL-Bentong Road.

On the first night, under a risen moon, we crept to the top of the bank to study the night life. Soon we heard the distant clatter of trucks approaching from the direction of KL. They could only be Japanese at this time of night. Macmillan cried, 'Into the ground, sorr!' We both dived into the matted, wet undergrowth, stumbling and swearing. Ah Tin slid into hiding with no apparent sign of haste or fear or clumsiness, more like a nervous animal melting into its natural surroundings.

Beams of light, still hidden by the corner, leapt into the moonlight like miniature searchlights until, the corner reached, they flattened out, stopped darting aimlessly around and shone directly on to the glistening road a few feet below us. Then they turned right into the entrance of the country club. The Japanese had no need for darkness, of course, or silence, for to them Malaya was at peace. The war was over, the Co-Prosperity Sphere was already an established fact, and we, lying hiding in a clump of fleshy leaves oozing sap, were the hunted.

Just after first light the next morning I returned to examine in detail through my field glasses the old clubhouse which had now become the headquarters of the hated Captain Satoh. I hadn't realised before that the back door of the club house was actually at the end of the building, so that I could see both the front entrance where I had arrived the night the Indian fired his rifle and the back door which was nearer to me. A couple of Japanese soldiers in underpants and singlets, smoking what was obviously their first cigarette of the day, came out and started urinating against the wall. Three more followed. I remembered that the toilet facilities at the club were confined to a small ladies' loo and one for the men, and of course it had never been built to accommodate overnight guests. No doubt that was why a young Chinese woman came out to relieve herself in the garden.

The coarse laugh of a Japanese soldier floated across the still air as she pulled down her black trousers and squatted. She must have been one of the impressed workers or cleaners. One Japanese went up to her and squatted beside her. He offered her a cigarette which she accepted with her left hand, putting it behind her ear. Then he did an extraordinary thing. By sign language he told her to pull down her trousers still further and without changing expression or speaking she did so. He tore open his fly and started playing with himself. Watching her, he came quickly. Then with another laugh he gave her a second cigarette, stood up and adjusted his shorts. As far as I could see through the glasses she never changed her expression.

At first I couldn't believe what I had seen. A kind of horrible fascination outweighed disgust and kept my eyes riveted to the cynical beastliness. I am sure I was not the only European officer in the jungle who enjoyed himself secretly on occasion, though I always regarded it as a private time to relive remembered pleasures. But the Japanese! My God, he did it almost as though it was an exercise.

I was not the only one who was disgusted, for as the Jap swaggered away, still laughing, there was a bull-like roar from the front entrance. A man in baggy riding breeches and a vest, and wearing a white helmet, charged out, screamed an order at the soldier as he banged the door behind him. The soldier stopped in his stride.

'That Captain Satoh, *tuan*,' breathed Ah Tin.

It was my first chance to study, however remotely, the man I had come to kill. He was thickset, powerful; taller than the usual Japanese, obviously a man of violent temper. I could hardly see his face, for he was striding angrily to the back door – and the errant soldier. Satoh must have witnessed the sordid scene – perhaps from an upstairs window while dressing – and had charged apoplectically down and into the grounds. That much I could see. For a moment I felt almost sorry for the Japanese as he stood there, as transfixed as a rabbit caught in the headlights of a car.

I could not understand what the captain shouted, even had I been able to hear, but as the man stood stiffly to attention Satoh brought the butt of his revolver down on his skull with all his force. The man crumpled. The squatting woman had already started to flee. Satoh roared at her, fired two rounds but missed as she scuttled to safety. Then with one last disgusted look at the soldier on the ground Satoh swung back his foot as though preparing to take a penalty at soccer and kicked the soldier full in the face before striding indoors.

During the morning Ah Tin, who disappeared regularly on mysterious errands, confirmed that Satoh made four or five trips a week to KL, always leaving at about eleven o'clock in the morning, to have lunch at the Spotted Dog, as the Selangor Club had always been called since one of its founder members tied his Dalmatian near the front door when lunching there.

The Spotted Dog stood on the edge of Kuala Lumpur's beautiful padang; in fact both had been constructed at the same time so that members of the club could walk out to play their games. It was a fine stretch of green, bordered on the opposite side by KL's ornate, Moorish-style government offices and equally baroque railway station. By now the Spotted Dog had become the Japanese Officers' Club, and I could well understand that Satoh would visit it regularly, for he must have been fed up with the limited facilities at his own headquarters. Even I didn't think much of the Planters' Club! And after all Kuala Lumpur was only twenty miles from the club – with Ara midway between the two – along a main road, metalled and well kept.

I was concerned with only one worry: where and when to plant the bombs. Obviously each time Captain Satoh decided to visit KL he would have to turn left when he set off from his headquarters and reached the road. This being so we decided to lay the bombs about quarter of a mile west of the club entrance. The bank was even steeper there, giving us better cover for our escape into the jungle, and there was a slight bend in the road which made it much less likely that anyone would discover the piano wire.

Making the bombs was difficult, not only because of the oppressive heat and humidity, but because the danger of detection was always present. From time to time Japs came roaring along the road directly below us, to say nothing of occasional foot patrols or peasants sitting in bullock carts. Anyone of them, looking upwards by accident, would certainly have spotted us if we were sitting up.

Thus before we could even start to make the bombs we had to devise an alarm system. Macmillan or myself always had to mount guard during daylight hours some yards nearer the club, by the bend in the road, so we could be warned of any approaching Japanese. The other one in camp had a full view of the straight stretch of road to the right as we looked down – the road leading to KL. We had to be able to warn each other at the first signs of danger. Yet the slightest movement could be fatal. Noise – a shouted warning, even a hiss – was out of the question. So we had to fall back on the warning system used by Chalfont at the Ara base camp.

Before making the bombs we returned to the jungle and in the sweating heat cut down as much rattan as we could carry to the fringe of beluka. There we sliced off the outer, shell-like bark, knotted the resulting 'ropes' together, finally making one long enough to reach from the sentry to our bomb-making camp – about fifty yards. It wasn't foolproof, for the rattan lay along the ground, but it was the best we could do. However, since the rope alarm did not end on a square of flat, beaten ground, as in the Ara camp, where every twitch was visible, we had to make more certain we would not miss a tug of alarm: the one who remained behind working in camp looped the end of the rattan loosely round an ankle.

There were several false alarms, including one when an inquisitive monkey started playing with the rattan, but it didn't really matter, for the alarm was not a signal to bolt but a warning to take cover where we were, to lie down and peer through the ferns and undergrowth to the road below until the danger passed.

We faced another hardship – no fire – and that meant no cooked food, not even a cup of tea or soup. It didn't matter in one way for the heat was overpowering, but the only iron rations we carried consisted of soup tablets and two tins of corned beef. We couldn't wash, of course – not with soap, anyway, though there was a brackish water hole fifty yards into the jungle. But soap in some mysterious way has a smell that carries as far and as pungently as tobacco. That also meant that poor Ah Tin could not smoke, but in a way this helped us for he craved cigarettes so badly that from time to time he whispered, 'I go get food, *tuan*.'

I knew he was off to the nearest kampong to smoke and talk to his chums, but I also realised that had Ah Tin been a non-smoker he would not have bothered to make these tiresome forays. And I also knew that, in order not to lose face, he *had* to return with some loot, so we got unexpected windfalls of cold rice, bits of fish and fruit wrapped in banana leaves. I was still afraid he might talk, for sharing secret information is one of human nature's easiest ways of displaying ego. But it was a chance we had to take.

It was very hot. The rain had given way to a pitiless sun and at times our bush hats were hot to the touch. With our parangs we cut down several lengths of bamboo, picking two, each about three feet in length, for our bombs. The other pieces we planned to strew haphazardly on the road-way, some of them between the killing area and the club so that if a suspecting Japanese picked one up he would find only the harmless by-product of a tropical storm, or part of a badly lashed load that had fallen off.

When we had half-filled two sticks of bamboo we inserted small detonators which were attached to five-foot lengths of piano wire. Then we packed in the rest of the explosive.

Obviously we could not pull a wire only five feet long or we would have been blown up with Satoh. We would need a much longer stretch of wire, one that would reach from the roadway to the top of the embankment. But if we attached such a long piece of wire to the bombs before carrying them down to the edge of the road we faced terrifying risks. The ground itself was rough and tricky; it's no fun anyway climbing down a steep bank carrying two lethal bombs which could explode if tampered with. The danger would be magnified if those bombs were attached to long wires being laid out behind us. Anything could happen; even a tiny inquisitive jungle animal, tugging at something never seen before, could blow us up.

I proposed that in the first instance when we manufactured the bombs each one would have only a five-foot length of wire leading from the buried detonator. This would mean much safer handling. Once on the edge of the roadway we would join up the ends of each short wire, thus in a way making a double-barrelled bomb.

In the meantime Macmillan would make his way separately down the embankment, laying the long length of wire from our camp at the top of the embankment and only when we had safely carried the bombs down would he join the long length to the junction of the two five-foot wires. One long, hard pull from the top of the embankment and both bombs would go off.

There was one other hazard – the danger of stumbling into the unseen piano wire on our way back up the embankment in the dark after laying the bomb. To avoid this danger Macmillan would lay another trail down the embankment, this time made of rattan, and well to the right of the piano wire. Thus, when everything was ready and the bombs in place, we could use the rattan as a guide back up the embankment.

All this took three days. We were able to watch Captain Satoh drive out of the club in an open Morris – one of dozens of cars obligingly left as free gifts by the retreating British troops. He always sat in the back seat, with an aide next to the driver. He apparently couldn't see how ridiculous it was for a bulky, important officer to squeeze into the tiny rear seat while his subordinates stretched their legs comfortably in the front.

For two days Satoh didn't drive in a westerly direction, but turned right at the club gates.

'He go other way for big officer conference at Bentong,' Ah Tin discovered. 'Tomorrow he go KL. Tomorrow kill, yes?' I patted his shoulder, and at the promise he smiled.

This meant that we had to lay the bombs that night, though we had to go down at dusk because we didn't dare show a light after dark, yet we couldn't risk scrambling down the bank in total darkness carrying two primed bombs. Both journeys – down and then up the bank – would have to be made wriggling on our stomachs.

Just before dusk Macmillan and I blacked our faces, arms and hands. The blacking was fine, and the permanganate sealed it into our skin for a few hours. We looked like a comic turn out of a minstrel show. I could never get used to the way a blackened face made the eyes shine out startlingly, like cat's eyes in the dark. It seemed impossible that nobody could see them.

In the end I decided that I would make two trips, carrying one bomb each time.

The trip down took nearly an hour. I had to make it crawling on my stomach, stopping whenever I heard the sound of a car or other traffic. Once a motorcycle turned the corner and the beam of a badly adjusted headlight seemed to shine right on my blackened face. I was sweating – with fear as much as heat. I had already earmarked a hiding place, a declivity in a mass of thick juicy ferns a few yards from the edge of the road. I left the first bomb there, then returned with the second. Meanwhile Ah Tin brought some safe bamboo down to be left later on the road so that our two live bombs would be less conspicuous.

Once both bombs were down Macmillan, who had already laid out the rattan guide, followed with the piano wire. Before dark he fastened the end to the joined wires protruding from the bombs. Then we settled down to wait.

At midnight Ah Tin crept into the roadway and distributed his armful of innocent pieces of bamboo over a fairly wide area; then I crept out, one bomb in each hand with the wires – which made a kind of V where they joined – behind me. I knew they were invisible, but they seemed so large to me I was sure they would be spotted in daylight. Macmillan came out on to the road with me, paying out the main wire in case I stumbled in the dark and jerked it.

Despite our safety line of rattan I was nervous of the short trip back up the embankment. It is hard to explain how easily one can lose every sense of direction in the jungle after dark, and how easily one can trip over unseen objects. The way up the embankment was not smooth but rough, with shrubs, roots and holes in which anyone could twist an ankle. But most of all I was frightened of tripping over the piano wire – until Ah Tin lit the way for us – literally, though without showing a light. We were about to climb up when he whispered, 'You wait one minute, *tuan*.'

Each moment by the roadway seemed an added danger, but he was fishing something out of his pocket.

'*Lekas!*' I whispered. 'Hurry up!'

Without a word Ah Tin took a tin out of his tunic, turned me round and I felt him fastening something to my back.

'Silk worm! Now we follow each other up hill.'

And we did. We had the rope to guide us, but in addition we had the tiny winking lights to help; the first one on Ah Tin's back after I had fastened it, the next on mine.

All we had to do now was wait – and be certain the next morning that we got Satoh and not the wrong man. I don't think I slept at all that night. I don't remember sleeping anyway, and as soon as dawn turned the roadway into a grey shadow we ate the remainder of some cold rice. We had four hours to wait.

At nine a.m. the unexpected happened. Two Japanese soldiers with fixed bayonets came striding along the road towards the bamboo, accompanied by four Chinese labourers carrying chongkols, the large hoes often used in Malaya instead of spades. Hidden behind a bunch of fat, oily leaves, I looked down, watching them through the glasses. They stopped almost directly below us, then moved on a few steps, perhaps ten yards. The first soldier ordered the men to the far side of the road. He glanced up and down, bored, and I caught my breath as I saw him look at a piece of bamboo in the road. He bent down, as though to pick it up, thought better of it, gave it a kick. By now I didn't even know which were the live bombs and which were dummies. And he hadn't seen the piano wire. My field glasses actually misted over; my shirt was drenched.

The other soldier ordered the Chinese to start work clearing the ditch by the roadside – and at that moment Ah Tin pointed and whispered, eyes wide, 'My brother! My friends from kampong!'

I thought I had recognised the frightened look of one of the labourers, but imagined the field glasses were playing tricks. The twin brother!

'*Tutup mulutmu!*' I hissed angrily – telling him to shut up, not because I *was* angry with him, not because I knew that sound always seemed to travel more dangerously in the still tropical mornings, but because I had a sudden sick feeling that everything was going wrong. We had worked for days, had suffered the tortures of the damned, and now a bunch of Chinese forced labourers had come on the scene at the very moment when Satoh was expected. And one of them *would* have to be Ah Tin's twin! We might end up having to scrub the operation if those bloody coolies didn't get out of the way. I wiped my glasses clear with my shirt tail and studied Ah Tin's friends.

The two Japanese soldiers were smoking, shouting lackadaisical orders, occasionally threatening the four Chinese. It seemed to me that perhaps some drain or pipe had become blocked, perhaps the pipe bringing water to the country club. I never found out. The Chinese worked indolently. Why didn't they get a move on, why the hell didn't they get the job done quickly, and bugger off back to the club?

What was it Chalfont had kept repeating during my training? 'The objective must always come first?' But I knew that the uncomplicated mind of a Chinese peasant like Ah Tin would never understand that. I knew he would never have the guts to pull the wire and kill his own brother. The question was: would I?

As I watched — and as the time crept towards ten-thirty — I whispered to Macmillan, who was lying next to me, tommy gun crooked in his arm, 'Maybe they'll go.'

'Not them,' he whispered back. 'They're having too good a time.' They were probably enjoying a day in the open and determined to make it last as long as they could. The guards too seemed relieved to be out and away from the more humdrum chores in camp. I found myself praying under my breath, 'O God! Get them out of here — get them away!' And all the time Ah Tin's face was growing more alarmed — or was it bewildered? — as though he couldn't understand the tortures that I faced, as though we ought to be moving off. But he still had his hand on the wire.

The minutes, even the seconds, ticked by in the hot sun until suddenly everything looked as though it was going to be all right, when one Japanese barked an order and the four men climbed out of the ditch, chongkols over their shoulders, ready to march off.

As they stood there, the other soldier cried 'Hai!' He jumped back into the ditch, shouted to the Chinese and gesticulated. They remained where they were, ready to move on. The second soldier made for the ditch, obviously to see what was the matter. I had an almost irresistible desire to scream to the Chinese, 'Run for it! Run!'

The soldiers held a whispered conference. One pointed into the ditch. The second shrugged his shoulders and pointed to his watch. The first examined *his* watch. I looked at mine. Almost eleven o'clock.

For a moment I thought they might still go, but then I realised what must have happened. One soldier was telling the other that Satoh was due at any moment – and surely it would look better if they remained, so that the captain could see them shouting at the Chinese.

It must have been that. Orders were barked, for the first time I saw one soldier hit a Chinese across the back as they hurried them into the ditch. Now they stood over them, shouting, arms raised, rifle butts threatening. Then I heard the sound of a car approaching behind the bend in the road.

'It's now, laddie,' muttered Macmillan to the terrified Ah Tin, as he pulled back the breech of his tommy gun and pulled the pin out of a grenade. I clicked my tommy gun into the firing position.

The car came round the corner. It approached slowly, and I could clearly see Satoh in his white helmet sitting upright in the back seat. I turned to Ah Tin. 'Ready?' I asked, hating myself.

'No, *tuan*! My friends, my brother.'

'Ah Tin, I know – but Satoh very bad man.'

'No *tuan*, no. Tomorrow we try again. I help.'

I knew there could be no other time. I knew we would be risking our lives if we tried to retrieve the bamboo bombs, that every moment counted, that we had to get away. The car was only a few feet away. I saw Satoh lean forward, tap the driver on the shoulder as though giving an order.

'You must,' I whispered. 'You must do it!' Safe in the knowledge that it wasn't I who was going to have to kill any of our allies including those who had fed us while we waited for this moment.

'No can do.' Ah Tin took his hand off the wire.

'Damn and blast! Too late!' growled Macmillan for the car was about to pass over the bamboo. But then I realised that Satoh must have ordered the driver to stop: he wanted to see what was happening.

I grabbed the wire as Satoh stood up by the side of the car. To me it looked as though he was actually standing on the bomb.

'Ye canna miss this chance, laddie.' Macmillan squeezed

my arm. 'This is what we've trained ye for. Ye've got to do it.'

'I can't,' I hesitated. 'These poor bloody Chinese.'

'Ye've got to, laddie – sorry, sorr. Ye're the boss, but if ye dinna want to do it – give *me* the wire.'

'I can't do that.'

'Then do it, laddie – *do it*.'

I caught a glimpse of Ah Tin's puzzled face, a bewildered moon, as though the urgent argument in undertones was beyond his comprehension.

'Now, sorr.' Macmillan whispered. 'The objective always comes first.'

I suppose the thoughts that crowded my brain all flashed past in a split second, for this was a situation which my training had never warned me about, a gap in the endless YMCA sessions, a gap which left me on my own to make a momentous decision in the time it takes to sigh. Do you murder your allies to kill one beastly Jap? Do you ignore the brother of the man who led you to that hated Jap – just to chalk up a partisan victory that would never make a scrap of difference to the outcome of the war?

If I refused now to murder Ah Tin's brother in order to liquidate Satoh – if I refused, then Satoh would live a little longer, and kill a few more innocent people – until someone else came along to undertake the execution I had failed to carry out. Was there any difference between letting Satoh live to kill a few more unknown Chinese or my killing him now, knowing that in doing so I was killing the innocent? I found myself almost praying that Satoh would himself shoot one of the Chinese – it was the sort of thing he was reputed to do – and so absolve me; for I knew I would have to do it. But I also knew that if my brother or sister had been down there on that stretch of road, nothing on God's earth would have made me kill Satoh.

'Now sorr! It's the last chance.'

I looked away – and gave the wire a savage tug.

The earth seemed to shudder. Even though the sun by itself was strong enough to hurt the eyes, the searing flash transformed the yellow light into a blue-white flame that soared upwards, so intense that for a second I instinctively shielded my eyes. Then I turned to look, in the few moments before flight. Bits of Satoh's car had been hurled halfway up the bank. Bodies, caught in the agonising postures of unexpected death, sprawled across the road, half out of the ditch, one of them actually in flames. As the white flash disintegrated a second explosion rocked the road, this time as the petrol tank blew up and the tangled wreckage of the car burned furiously, a yellow flame with black smoke loitering in a sky reeking of gunpowder.

I heard whistles, shouts; a siren wailed from the direction of the clubhouse. Half a dozen Japs clattered round the corner, screaming. I could hear the clink of weapons.

'Let 'em have it,' said Macmillan, and for the first time we stood up, hurled grenades down the bank, our tommy guns stuttering as we fired down the hillside, killing every man.

'That gives us a breathing space,' said a grimy Macmillan.

There was no point in hanging around. Though most of Satoh had disappeared – he had taken the full force of the blast – I could see his white helmet with a mass of torn flesh inside it, and that was identification enough. Everyone was dead. Only the crackling flames and the black smoke moved, and they were dying too in air suffocated with the stink of cordite and burned flesh.

'Let's go!' I started off towards the top of the bank. 'Once in the jungle they'll never find us. Then it's home, James –'

'And dinna spare the horses!' added Macmillan. 'And may I say, sorr, I'm proud of my favourite pupil.'

I, too, felt a glow of pride. Strange in the flush of killing how swiftly the racing adrenalin pushes away conscience. I felt terrible in one way, yet I had for the moment almost forgotten the innocent. I had a sudden childhood memory of the day a rat was discovered in Tanamera and I burst into tears as Papa Jack and the servants tried to kill what to me in those innocent days was just another small animal – until my father shouted angrily, 'Don't be so stupid. Rats spread disease – they could kill any of us, even your mama.' In a second I was transformed from an animal lover and was screaming, 'Kill it! Kill it!' as Papa Jack and the boys tried to corner it.

Now, just as swiftly, I had almost forgotten the torment of a few moments ago in the luxury of legalised killing. Then I remembered Ah Tin.

'Come along,' I said, and putting a hand on his shoulder in the seconds before departure, added, 'You know I'm sorry, Ah Tin, but you realise that Satoh would have murdered many more men if we hadn't killed him.'

His face was a mask of horror, looking at me as though I were a monster. The timidity that had always etched his face had slid into a new set of lines and creases. He looked at me with loathing, as though the hand I had placed on his shoulder was dirty.

'I no come,' he said. 'You bad man like Captain Satoh. He kill my father, you kill my brother.'

Before I could say anything, he was scrambling upwards but to the right, in the opposite direction we planned to take. I could hear cars grinding into gear as they approached, then machine-gun fire seemed to be all around us — though in fact the Japs were firing blind and nowhere near us. As I saw the small figure of Ah Tin flitting towards the jungle, Macmillan slid back the breech of his tommy gun, crying, 'Christ! I'll have to kill him.'

'No!' I screamed out loud.

'He knows where the camp is — Ara!'

As he brought his tommy gun into the firing position, I pushed the hot barrel gently downwards. 'No, Mac,' I pleaded. 'We've done enough to the poor bugger already.'

Before he could argue Ah Tin had disappeared.

'I hope you've done the right thing, sorr,' muttered Macmillan.

33

In December 1943, after nearly two years of assaults that had made Chalfont a legend in Force 136 – this we could tell even from brief radio messages – a miracle happened. I received a letter from Julie.

Until that moment arrived I had had no word from her, I did not know where she was, even if she had ever reached safety in the *Ban Hong Liong*. How many times had I thought of her, imagined her, and fallen dog-tired on my bed and dreamed of her. And here, in hands that trembled, I held a blue envelope which even *felt* full of packed pages of love.

A European officer brought it. He had been landed by submarine with a long, top-secret coded policy document to distribute to commanders like Chalfont. He stayed three nights in the camp before striking northwards, and it had taken him many months to reach us.

'The letter's been passed by censor – special dispensation,' said Chalfont. 'I got a radio message telling me the courier was bringing it.'

'Jesus. You might have told me!'

'I didn't know who the letter was from – and anyway, I didn't want you mooning about for months like a lovesick swain. Now, off you go and moon.'

Julie was alive! As I tore open the envelope in my tiny hut a photograph fell out – Julie smiling, long black hair unchanged, beautiful oval face the same as when I had last kissed it. She was holding up, as though presenting it to me, a bundle of dark-haired baby, dark eyes wide open, chubby fingers outstretched as it tried to clutch Julie's eternity ring.

On the back Julie had written, 'Your girlfriends, June

1943.' My God! It was nearly six months since she had written those words. Six months in which she had heard no news of me – or so I thought until I spread out the thin blue writing paper, patting the creases away.

She wrote:

Beloved (I cannot use your name),

Never an hour of daylight passes without me thinking of you and praying for you, not only for the man I love more than life but now the father of our beautiful daughter Pela, who was born on 4 September 1942 and is ten months old as I write this letter, hoping it will reach you, taking my heart with it.

I wait for you, resigned to your terrible dangers, seeking comfort in the fact that fate, in the shape of the message which you arranged behind my back to send to [blacked out by censor] has meant that from time to time I hear news of you from colleagues in your outfit.

It seems so strange when men and women whisper about your latest exploit – I want to shout out that we were lovers, we have shared the same bed, we have produced the beautiful child sleeping next to me! When we *really* fell in love, the second time, the day war broke out, the time when we knew it was forever, I thought that I was in love with a man who was famous for his ready-to-wear houses, not someone whom everyone here regards as a hero!

There were times in those happy days in Singapore when I *did* wonder what you were up to behind my back. The sudden disappearances, the times when you were so tired. You even went to ARP practice on Christmas morning behind my back – and there was the time when you couldn't do anything! Well!!

But in a way I too was deceiving you. I promised you that when the war was over I would fade away – remember how you hated that phrase! – but I knew I wouldn't. I wanted to prevent you from being tortured over your son Ben and worried about Irene and the future. But I had already made up my mind that if *you*

527

wanted me for the rest of *your* life, I would agree, because I knew that you would be unhappy living a lie with someone else.

I live in a small flat to which no man has ever been admitted. We Chinese mothers are very very prim and proper! Over the bed is an old-fashioned picture poem on vellum consisting of one verse of a poem by Francis Thompson, and the woman who wrote it out in beautiful script and then painted flowers and borders on the vellum must have been very much in love. Like us. I bought it because I had a sudden mysterious feeling that years ago, around the turn of the century, before we were born, Mr Thompson had written it specially for us, both of us:

> Leave thy father, leave thy mother
> And thy brother;
> Leave the black tents of thy tribe apart!
> Am I not thy father and thy brother,
> And thy mother?
> And thou — what needest with thy tribe's black tents
> Who hast the red pavilion of my heart?

Each day I seek news of you, but wherever you are, wherever I am, we are in each other's red pavilion.

I hope you like the name Pela. I don't think it existed before the christening, but I chose it because – do you remember? – I told you that when I studied at Berkeley I came across the Pelagian theory while reading philosophy. You had never heard about it or the monk Pelagius. I promised to tell you! Pelagius refused to accept the doctrine of original sin, but believed that man was inherently *good*, not inherently *evil*, and I thought of you and me.

We broke all the Singapore rules, but when we first made love we were innocent and only our parents turned our love into a sin, so *we* didn't really sin, did we? I like to think we are both Pelagians, now blessed with an unsinful and beautiful Pela.

I wish I could touch you, my beloved, if only for a little while. Sometimes at night alone – do you? And then as

528

ecstasy floods out of my insides I am in your arms again for a few minutes. God bless you. I am here, yours, faithful, loving you as someone else wrote, more than yesterday but not as much as tomorrow. Julie.

As I reread the letter – and then again – sitting there, holding the flimsy pages as the first midges winged in with the dusk, I thought of the times we had spent together, the times we *would* spend together. The present was a prison – the circle of tall, straight jungle trees slowly darkening were like prison bars shouting 'No Love Allowed Here!' But now at least I could picture Julie in her small flat, which I immediately coloured white and green. I could see the poem over the bed, and Pela – and then I could picture Julie undressing for bed.

The letter banished the one niggling fear that had occasionally haunted me: that love could be lost, that in a new world, not knowing whether I was alive or dead, the temptation to run from loneliness might have been too much for Julie.

Sometimes in the jungle I had wondered – was I waiting, enduring, surviving against all odds in order to return from a kind of death in life to reality, only to find she had gone? After all when, as Julie put it, our parents told us we would never meet again I had married another. Suppose Julie felt that she should fade away so that I could return to Irene and Ben? Until the letter arrived I had never been absolutely sure.

Lieutenant Kirk, the courier who brought Julie's letter, had in civilian life been a junior in the Chinese Affairs Office at Ipoh. He had escaped and his fluent Cantonese and knowledge of the area made him an automatic choice for Force 136. The next morning, knowing he would not be staying long, I eagerly asked him if he had ever met Julie.

'Oh yes, sir,' (how old that 'sir' made me feel), 'everybody adores Julie Soong.' Perhaps my face showed my surprise for he added hastily, 'You see, sir, we all have a reason to know her – and be grateful. She's the sister in charge of the Force's own hospital. It's always filled with trainees breaking legs or arms or spraining ankles. The training's *very* rough, sir.'

He was a pleasant lad and almost shyly he filled me in with yet another picture of Julie's life – only crumbs really, but I hungered for them as greedily as a starving man. The hospital was at Kandy, the HQ. Until now HQ in Ceylon could have been anywhere from the Galle Face hotel to Adam's Peak. Now I could see it – and the hospital – in the peaceful, green tea-clad mountains of Ceylon's loveliest hill station. The hospital was small, he said, barely a dozen beds, adding wistfully, 'Reminds me of a cottage hospital in a Cotswold village.'

Kandy itself had been mysteriously filling up with red-tabbed colonels who treated the other officers like dirt. 'They were all over the place,' he said, 'picking all the best houses as billets. They even bundled everyone out of a big hotel, and it was still empty when I left. Made one boil at the time, sir, it seemed such bumbling.' Not until the day before he was landed at night on the east coast of Malaya did the submarine receive a signal that Mountbatten had moved in as Supremo for Southeast Asia. 'Rather puts a different complexion on the affair,' he grinned shyly.

I asked for more details of Julie. 'Well, sir, she didn't circulate much,' he said. 'After I'd been in hospital for ten days I spoke to her once or twice when she was out shopping. She has a –' he hesitated, a little unsure of the depth of my interest.

'A baby.'

He nodded. 'And Miss Soong – sorry, sir, Mrs Dexter – she's a real corker! You should hear the wolf-whistles from the other ranks when she walks down Robertson Street.'

Ah! Those wolf-whistles. It was as though Julie had her own orchestra, following her wherever she went. I thought of that last afternoon of peace, when she and I walked down the main street of Changi looking for eggs and a bottle of Scotch. The wolf-whistles had never stopped. What a long, long time ago. But strangely, after talking, I didn't feel sad or lonely or longing for the clock to turn back: just the opposite. After I took a dip in the tinkling river I realised I was singing lustily as I towelled myself down with a filthy bit of ancient cloth. The song was 'My baby loves me.'

Chalfont's pile of bumf might not have been as exciting as my letter but it was vitally important, and it took him the best part of three days to decode. It amounted to several policy decisions which had been made because of the increasing number of Chinese guerillas. And it gave us for the first time an overall picture of problems present and future that we could never have received on our ramshackle old bicycle radio.

The fighters of the MCP, the Malayan Communist Party, now called themselves the Malayan Peoples' Anti-Japanese Army, MPAJA for short. By now they numbered three thousand and were increasing weekly. Though they were still under the direct command of Force 136 the Chinese were formed into separate regiments with Chinese commanders answerable only to us. The transformation had been largely due to their guerila leader, Chin Peng, the Straits Chinese son of a bicycle repairer in Sitiawan.

'The real problem,' explained Chalfont, 'is that we will soon be getting brand new weapons dropped by parachute. And this is coming at a time when the Chinese are becoming more independent, demanding more, telling everyone they are the only ones fighting the war. That's the political problem – to make sure the Chinese don't grab all the credit when the Japs are beaten –' he let the rest of the sentence trail off.

'But that's a hell of a long way off.'

'Don't be too sure. There's something in the air. And in a few weeks we'll be getting supplies parachuted down by the ton. Colombo's waiting for a new long-range Liberator – an American kite – that can make the round trip, Ceylon and back. That will mean unlimited supplies – food, ammo, drugs. But it presents a danger. We've got to make sure that arms canisters aren't picked by the Commies and then conveniently lost.'

'How do you mean?'

'Lost. Pinched from the DZ areas and hidden – to be used against the British after the war. The Commies are already planning this.'

'It's not feasible.'

'It is. HQ has been tipped off – secret documents and all that stuff, leaked from the MCP. God knows how. When the arms come pouring in we've got to watch the Commies as well as the Japs. It's hard to believe, but we're reaching a turning point in the war. I'm sure of it. With America giving the enemy hell in the Pacific, the Japs are beginning to realise what they're up against. And the Commies are getting ready to make the most out of an allied victory.'

Of course I could see the dangers ahead, but at the same time the Communists *had* suffered two shattering blows at the hands of the Japanese, even though Loi Tek, the shadowy secretary-general of the party, had survived on both occasions.

In the summer of 1942 almost the entire Central Committee of the Communist Party had been killed. It was as though the Japanese had been tipped off, for the committee members arriving from different parts of Malaya were arrested as they reached Singapore. Loi Tek arrived later than expected, and the delay saved his life.

Worse was to follow. In August delegates held a secret meeting in the Batu Caves, a well-known limestone outcrop a few miles outside KL. We had known of the meeting because Tan Sun, our Chinese commander, had asked Chalfont if he could attend it.

Tan Sun never returned from the Batu Caves, for as he and the leaders were assembling the Japanese struck. Obviously they had been tipped off again, for they surrounded the area, and as soon as the meeting was ready to start they moved in. Eighteen top Communists, including four political commissars in the MPAJA, were killed, together with almost every member of the old guard of the MCP. In all, eighty communists were killed or taken prisoner in the massacre.

Loi Tek was again lucky. His life was saved because he was delayed while making his way through jungle paths.

Chin Peng, the guerilla leader, had decided not to attend the conference.

The loss of Tan Sun had been a grievous blow to us. Our Chinese force now totalled nearly two hundred tough fighters, and Tan Sun had been the perfect leader: intelligent, a man able to keep hotheads in check.

His second in command succeeded him and he was a hopeless demagogue always spouting Marxist propaganda, forcing the men to spend long hours listening to dreary drivel disguised as lectures. Morale plummeted.

'In the end I radioed Colombo telling them I must have a replacement,' said Chalfont. 'And they told me to wait until I had read a report that was on its way. I radioed yesterday that it had arrived, and now we have some startling news. Some you'll like, some you won't. First, we're getting a new Chinese Commander, chosen specially by Chin Peng who regards Ara as one of the top outfits in Malaya. Second, Chin Peng and Loi Tek are coming to honour us with a visit.'

He hesitated for a long time, sitting there on the narrow verandah of his hut, until finally, almost heavily, he said, 'There's going to be another replacement – haven't told you yet, old boy.' We were having a rare treat, a supper of *mahmi* – Chinese noodles – which had been brought up by food bearers and reheated. The dish was spiced not only with bits of old dried fish but with tiny *ikan bilis*, a kind of local whitebait which you eat whole – eyes, heads, tails – after they had been marinated in chillies until they could blow off the roof of your mouth. They provided a rare treat for jungle-jaded palates.

'Don't tell me I'm being fired,' I laughed.

'Never. You're a natural for this life.'

'Macmillan?'

Chalfont carefully extracted a fly from his *mahmi*. Even when the food was rough he always ate as delicately as at a banquet. Then, pushing the plate away from him and wiping his lips on a square of glossy banana leaf, he almost grinned as he asked, 'Can't you guess?'

'Who?'

'Me!'

I was so taken aback I spluttered out a mouthful of *mahmi*.

'Hey! Don't waste good food!' Chalfont laughed – but not very convincingly.

'Have you gone off your rocker, Robin? You *going*? You can't just walk out on us!' My outburst came from the heart. I had never realised how much I depended on the man I had at first dismissed as an incompetent queer; not only as a leader, but as a friend.

'I know I'm irreplaceable,' drawled Chalfont.

'But what's happened?' I slapped my face and actually killed a mosquito. 'When did all this happen?'

'On the latest radio session. Only heard yesterday,' he said, adding with a grin, 'I knew you were having your favourite *ikan bilis* for supper and I didn't want to spoil your appetite.'

'But who's my new boss going to be?' I couldn't keep the hostility out of my voice.

'Well, there are – er – compensations. The new boss is a major. Decent sort of feller I believe.'

'But *Major* who?'

'Major Dexter, you dumkopf.'

Rather like an old Colonel Blimp in a Victorian novel, Chalfont rose from the table with a touch of ceremony, and solemnly shook hands, taking my right hand in both his.

'Congratulations, old boy! It's overdue – and you should have got a gong as well!'

'I can't believe it – you going.' I slumped down again in the uncomfortable rattan chair, made, like all the other furniture in the camp, by guerillas who happened to be carpenters in peacetime. 'I *can't* take over, Robin. My job is in the field – always has been. You've got to cancel the transfer,' adding rather pathetically, 'we've got on so well together. In all this –' I waved an arm to take in the dusk, the tall trees on the other side of the parade ground, the sounds of insects starting their nightly cacophony. 'All this!' I cried. 'We've got used to it – you, Mac Macmillan and me.'

The prospect of his departure – the suddenness of the announcement – made me at first forget my own preferment. The news *was* shattering, largely because of the curious nature of jungle warfare, when you killed but could never be seen, when you depended for your life on others who could never be seen. Because the initial training had been so thorough, none of us realised how indispensable was each member of the team. We were either so busy or so frightened (or so lonely?) that each of us regarded the work of the others as a perfectly normal backup. Only when that backup was suddenly removed did we realise its value.

'And where are you going?'

'Back to HQ first. We're expanding, Johnnie. The MPAJA will soon be nearly four thousand strong — and that means four thousand dedicated Commies ready to play hell when the war's over.'

'But why you?'

'I told you at that first meeting at the Adelphi, remember? I said I was just a recruiting wallah.'

'When?'

'I'll be given a date to rendezvous on the coast. It should allow me to stay here long enough to welcome your Number Two.'

'But I don't want a bloody Number Two! Some bloody man I've got to get used to working with. Macmillan and I can carry on.'

'You might just change your mind, old boy — sorry, Major! — when I tell you who this chappie is. You know they're insisting on sending in blokes with local knowledge. They also want blokes who speak the local patois, and this feller used to be a planter. Escaped from Singapore, swam to Colombo — nearly! — and volunteered. Name means nothing to me,' he added slyly. 'But maybe it rings a bell in the Dexter brainbox, eh? It's Scott.'

'Tony!' I cried. 'I thought he was a POW. My God! He married my sister, you know. How wonderful!'

'You see,' Chalfont sighed with mock despair, 'how ephemeral friendships are. Already I'm half forgotten.'

'Don't even joke about it,' I could feel the tears behind my eyes. 'Don't ever say that, even in fun. Never where you're concerned.'

Dark had fallen and we had lit the ancient fat-burning and evil-smelling lamp that gave our only glow between supper and bedtime. The mosquitos were zinging around – harmless, for we were immune to their poison now – the first moths were banging against the meagre source of light, the cicadas were out in force, the first bullfrogs were croaking their guts out by the river. At the far end of the parade ground a dim light shone in the Chinese 'common room' where, as on every night, the troops were being indoctrinated with, as Chalfont once put it inelegantly, 'doses of Communist crap'. The jungle was a tough place to forge friendships – and an even tougher place to cement them, to make them last.

'Specially as I was the chappie who got you into this mess,' said Chalfont.

'I *did* volunteer, Colonel,' I grinned back. Tony Scott!

Loi Tek and Chin Peng arrived on their 'state visit' a week later, and to the two hundred Chinese guerillas in our camp, daily becoming more aggressively political, it was an epoch-making event.

Loi Tek was dressed in singlet and khaki shorts, with sandals and short socks, and was enormously impressive even though he had none of the hallmarks of power. He was rather slight. He did not strut but was extremely polite, with a soothing voice. He had brought along a few medals to pin on the chests of Chin Peng's troops, but what I found curious about this enigmatic man was that, though you would never pick him out in a crowd, he still radiated an almost uncanny magnetism. He seemed to take obedience as a matter of course. He rarely asked questions, just listened and made statements, as though he was totally convinced that anything he said or did was right, the only thing to do, the only way.

Not even the dirty vest could disguise the fact that he was a man of the world, educated, speaking perfect English (as well as several other languages) a man who had left his home in Saigon to travel extensively all over Europe, seeing for himself how others lived. He smiled easily. Looking at him on the verandah in the jungle – just another Asian – I had the feeling that he was highly sophisticated, the sort of man who would never listen to the dreary Communist fodder spewed out for hours by political commissars but who was intelligent enough to know that they had a value for the rank and file.

Chin Peng was different. I had heard that Spencer Chapman, who had really started Force 136 and was still somewhere in the jungle, regarded Chin Peng as our finest guerilla leader. He was dressed in uniform – a khaki tunic, slacks and, incongruously, a Sam Browne. He wore a khaki military cap with two gold bands and three stars above the shiny peak. He was in his early twenties, with a pleasant round face, though inclined to pimples; he seemed to be a gentle, quiet, bookish man with a polite voice. He would have been perfectly at home running a mobile library among the villages surrounding his native Sitiawan. I found it hard to believe that he had started life in humble circumstances, yet was reputed to speak six languages fluently. He had joined the Party when he was eighteen, cutting stencils for the propaganda department.

When the flurry of official inspection, official speeches and presentations was over Chin Peng spoke to the men. He lauded their exploits and courage and the skill of 'the Ara Regiment' – his description – under its brilliant British officers. We left the Chinese alone for an hour or so, though Chin Peng had warned us that on no account could Loi Tek stay for long. He never, apparently, remained *anywhere* for more than a few hours at a time: it was too dangerous.

When eventually they did return across the parade ground and towards the command post, where someone had prepared some Chinese green tea, I received a second jolt of bad news – far more sickening than the shock of Chalfont's impending departure. Chin Peng addressed me as major, and despite his gentle voice it was clear that he was a little hesitant.

'I want you to know, Major, that we have lost the cream of our operational commanders in several tragic ambushes – specially the one at Batu Caves. What happened there was a disaster; it will take years to repair it. Yet Ara, because of its vital position, is a central pivot for our operations, so I agree you need a better commanding officer for the Chinese troops. This is why I am prepared to give you my number three commander.'

'Sounds splendid,' I murmured.

'I fear not, but he's the only man of that calibre we can spare. Unfortunately, Major, he doesn't like you.'

'What the hell – do I know him?'

'He's been a secret member of the MCP since he was sixteen, and now he's had a brilliant military career in the jungle. And yes, you *do* know him.'

'But – who?'

'His name is Soong. Soong Kai-shek.'

'*Him!* Never!'

'Major!' Chalfont interrupted sharply – the stern voice put on for effect, so that we didn't lose face before the Chinese.

'Sorry, sir.' I turned to Chin Peng. 'But it's not on. Why – he even threatened to kill me.'

'I know. He told me.' With a faint smile on his face, he added, 'He doesn't *want* to come and serve under you, Major.'

'Well, then –'

'I've ordered him to report to Ara. I don't have another man of his experience. We are at war, Major, and may I remind you it's quite normal for officers who dislike each other to work together.'

'Kai-shek is not the only member of a rich family who has become ashamed of its wealth,' said Loi Tek smoothly.

'I still think' – I turned to Chin Peng – 'that there must be *someone* else.'

'Comrade Soong is already here,' Chin Peng's voice was final. 'He will be sworn in as the officer in command of your Chinese forces, and he will swear obedience to your orders.'

'Will he keep his word?'

'Major, we members of the MCP have our own code of rules. And one of them is unquestioning obedience to European officers. Not necessarily' – again the faint smile lit his pudgy face – 'because we agree with your political views, but because only the British can supply us with arms to fight the enemy who is savaging our homeland, mainland China. If Comrade Soong disobeys I shall hear of it – I hear about *everything*, Major – and he will be shot. The defeat of the enemy is more important than private squabbles.'

And that did close the matter. Loi Tek left shortly afterwards, and Chin Peng sent for Soong who was in the Chinese camp. Not even the khaki drill, the two red stars on his cap, the stiff salute, could make that hated face look agreeable. I could see his hatred, feel it. He wore it visibly, unable to disguise it.

While we stood on the verandah Chin Peng read the riot act to Soong; both men spoke fluent English, so I knew what was being said. Chin Peng forced Soong to state categorically that any quarrels between him and me would be forgotten until the war had been won, and that as commanding officer I would be entitled to unswerving loyalty and obedience. Sullenly, but at least looking me in the eyes, Kai-shek agreed and held out a hand. I hated taking it but I had to. I couldn't look petty in front of Chin Peng or Chalfont.

'And if there *is* any trouble' – they were Chin Peng's last words – 'the political commissar in this camp works for *me*. And I am sure you realise that he tells me *everything* that happens.'

34

Events didn't occur in quite the order Chalfont had envisaged. A hold-up in the delivery to Colombo of the long-range American Liberator postponed Tony Scott's arrival and Chalfont had to leave before Tony arrived in order to keep his rendezvous with a pick-up submarine.

By then it was early 1944 and over the radio we had learned, in headline fashion, snippets of the latest allied successes. In Russia the last Germans had been thrown out of Stalingrad, and in Italy we had landed at Anzio.

'In fact, as far as I can see,' said Chalfont, 'there won't be anything for you and your brother-in-law to do.'

On the last night the Chinese guerillas gave him a farewell dinner. It was bizarre. Food bearers, often within yards of hostile Japanese troops, managed to smuggle in a sumptuous meal, and even some saki. We toasted '*Yam seng*' until there was no more liquor for 'bottoms up' and after it was all over, warmed by the rice wine, Chalfont told me something that did surprise me. I knew little about his private life – though he had told me he was unmarried – but it had never occurred to me that he was not regular army. He had displayed in Singapore all the spit and polish of an officer to whom the military was a chosen way of life.

'I say!' He pretended horror. 'What a terrible judge of character you are. Do I really look as bad as that?'

'I'm sorry,' I laughed. 'Didn't you go to Sandhurst?'

'Oxford,' he murmured, 'Oriel.'

That was a surprise. I enjoyed the rare luxury of picking bits of almond out of my teeth – a luxury because the chicken and almond of the Chinese meal was the first 'pickable' food I had eaten for months.

'Give you three guesses,' said Chalfont.

I shook my head. 'No go, I'm no good at crosswords or any other puzzles.'

'A copper,' he grinned.

'A *policeman*?' It was the last thing I would have expected. '*You?* It's not possible.'

'To be truthful, I'm in Special Branch.' He spoke the words carefully, with capital letters. 'I joined up when they asked for volunteers with special skills. Didn't quite realise what I was letting myself in for.'

His special skills, he explained, consisted not so much of jungle fighting but, as a university-trained police officer, of recognising and dealing with Communist infiltration.

'Sounds absolutely mad,' he drawled, 'but the powers that be are more worried about the peace than about the war. They're scared stiff the Commies will take over. I'm sort of studying the terrain – sorting out the prospects – meeting blokes like Chin Peng and your horrible chum.' He jerked his head in the direction of the Chinese barracks. 'And to be frank, I just sort of got drawn into this mess. But I'm glad I came. There *will* be trouble after the war ends. Wouldn't be a bit surprised if I don't come back and bore the pants off you again, old boy.'

This was our last night. We had both spent so much time together that each was afraid of the parting. I had one last favour to ask of Chalfont. Would he carry a couple of letters for me? I wanted of course to write to Julie. But now that I had heard from her, now that I could be sure we would never be parted again, I knew I must also write to Irene. She had presumably had her baby. He or she must be two years old by now. And Ben was five. My God, five years old! I didn't even know whether Irene had gone to London to see her parents, so I would write to Brewster in New York State. But it would be wicked of me not to warn her that I wanted a divorce, even though we had two children. Ours wouldn't be the first family to be split up, and after all the preliminary splitting had been undertaken by others. But I knew that even if I had decided to return to Irene I would have to tell her about Julie – and her baby. And after such a confession we could never live together without bitterness – especially as I wanted to live in Singapore for the rest of my life, and Irene hated it.

'Course I'll take your letters,' drawled Chalfont. 'But until I leave I'm your CO, I suppose – so I'll have to censor them.'

'You know the contents before I write them,' I said.

'I'm pretty sure I do. Divorce is always a bit messy but – well, Julie's quite a girl. I suppose that's what you're gong to tell your wife – if not in so many words.' He hesitated. 'As for Julie, I'll be able to *tell* her all about you.'

To Julie I wrote a long screed of love, pouring out my soul, but saying nothing of my work or danger, and trying, through the medium of words I knew others would have to read, to tell her how much I loved her, that I was writing to Irene asking for a divorce, and sending my love to Pela.

The letter to Irene was more difficult. I couldn't write anything about myself except that I was alive and well, and then I told her that I loved Julie, that she was the mother of my child, and that, despite our two babies, this was for the best. It was a difficult letter to write, and I can't remember the exact wording. But I had the feeling – the hope – that when, if ever, the letter reached New York, Irene might give a sigh of relief.

Tony Scott didn't arrive until the summer of 1944, and despite the company of Macmillan those waiting months were my loneliest spell of the war. Despite the victories now being trumpeted it seemed to me physically impossible ever to *invade* Japan. The magnitude of the task was fearful. Europe perhaps – the people of Europe were in chains, begging to be liberated – though even that was an awesome task. But Japan? Never. It was peopled with fanatics, kamakazis. They revelled in death. Meanwhile we were stuck in this bloody jungle – forever.

Kai-shek, thank God, had settled down. He was not exactly a ray of sunshine with his brooding, saturnine face, but he was a good soldier and not only a stern disciplinarian among his Chinese troops but fanatically brave. He led at least two bridge demolition sorties with such an utter disregard for his own safety that I had to explain politely that his duty as a leader was to inspire others, and that if he were killed on a foolhardy mission he would receive no thanks from Chin Peng. He agreed – equally politely, but since I never knew what he was thinking, it made no difference.

Macmillan was a tower of strength but now, after the departure of Chalfont, he could no longer come with me when I led a raiding party. Since there were only two members of the British army at Ara – until Tony arrived – one of us always had to remain in camp. I missed him on those sorties – specially when we learned that the Japs were opening up the factory on the Ara rubber estate and I had to go and blow it up with time fuses and PE. Without Macmillan! It didn't seem right. But what a bang the explosion made!

Early in May 1944 our radio crackled out the news that Tony Scott was ready to parachute down. Were we ready to receive him, over? Yes we were, over. Damned impatient, over. It was impossible to contain our excitement, not only at the prospect of the new arrival, but of food, drugs, new weapons.

We had only one available DZ – dropping zone – and that was our so-called parade ground. It was two hundred yards long and fairly wide, which at least gave room for error – which was always possible because the aircraft had to be over the DZ either at dusk or first light or in full moonlight.

A dusk drop presented an extra hazard. To be over Ara on time, in a tropical country where the magical moments between day and night – between light and dark – never add up to more than twenty swiftly disappearing minutes, the plane would have to cross the coast in daylight; otherwise it would never have time to locate the DZ – which could only be done by extremely sharp eyes.

When we were finally notified of the ETA – the estimated time of arrival – and the date, we made a huge cross of ferns and bamboo in the centre of the parade ground. After tearing them out of the surrounding jungle, we weighted them with stones, the main line running half the length of the parade ground, though the cross line was smaller.

We chose this method of identifying our DZ for several reasons. The most obvious was that we had nothing better – no white paint or lime to mark the ground. Second, we were always afraid that Jap planes would spot our camp; and if we heard the throb of a small plane – a very different sound from that of an approaching Liberator – we would have time to brush the cross away and make the space appear just another dirty jungle clearing. Third, if our plane failed to pinpoint the DZ we could (if the rain kept off) set the ferns alight and make a fiery cross simple to identify.

All these details were discussed in our radio transmissions with Colombo, and we were also told that in addition to weapons we could expect new high-powered radio sets that worked off batteries or accumulators, some European food, and even new clothes – in a way perhaps the items we longed for most of all.

For me of course there was the excitement of meeting Tony. He had presumably been training in Ceylon; he must have met Julie, and my heart was beginning to flutter at the prospect of hearing about her.

Late that first evening after the drop, Tony and I sat on Chalfont's verandah – it would always be 'Chalfont's verandah' to me – and I felt happier than I had been for months.

'What a stroke of luck,' I said dreamily, 'that you of all people came here.' We had made an agreeable hole in a bottle of Scotch Tony had brought.

'Luck be buggered,' retorted Scott. 'You're a bloody hero in Colombo! When I heard rumours that a new Number Two was needed for Ara camp they couldn't refuse me. I was waiting for a posting and, after all, local knowledge of the terrain is rule four in the Force manual. And I know this bloody countryside even better than you do. After all, I *did* plant Ara.'

'Tony, *please'* – I leaned forward – 'before anything else, tell me about Julie. How is she? What's she doing?'

'She's in great form. Sends all her love. I've brought a letter for you.'

'And the baby?'

'Super! Sounds crazy, but I saw Julie earlier today.'

Today? *This morning!*

'I went to collect the letter,' Tony explained, 'and to say goodbye to Pela. When she was christened you weren't around so we couldn't ask you, but I'm her godfather.'

'Julie managed to get one letter through to me, but she didn't tell me that.'

'She couldn't. I was on secret training. All of us were

bound to secrecy the same way you must have been.'

Of course. I remembered the days when I had longed to tell Julie what I was doing.

'Julie had an idea that I was in Force 136,' added Tony, 'After all, she's in it too. So I had to tell her not to mention my name.'

Tony peered into his half-empty glass of Scotch, twirled the golden liquid round, and said, 'She told me you two had become lovers again. You've got the most adorable baby daughter – poor little bugger, she's doomed to a miserable life – looks just like you.'

'And Julie?'

Did he hesitate? 'She's changed. Not about you, she's potty about you, can't see why. No, she's gentle and kind, and wonderful in the hospital. But you know, Johnnie, she had a terrible time – it'll take her years to get over it. Two bloody ships sunk underneath her – I was in the second – eight of us in a bloody life raft – the only girl – and no one knew she was pregnant. Perhaps she *has* got over it – but she'll never *forget* it. She's more serious.' He had said his piece, and now felt he could relax. 'Too bloody brainy for a madcap bugger like you.'

Poor Julie. All these months I hadn't realised the awful journey she had made. She had never mentioned a word in her one letter; perhaps she didn't want to worry me. And I had somehow thought of her as taking an uneventful trip across the Indian Ocean . . .

'Don't worry,' said Tony. 'She's yours for life. Everybody in the Force adores her, but she's built a fence ten feet high around her,' adding with a sigh, I wish I had a woman who loved me like that.'

'And the baby? How does she explain her?'

'Right from the start Julie stopped any questions with a bang, and people long since ceased asking. As for you – no one knows what you look like. Anyway, I exaggerate. She's not a bad little reptile, your daughter. There's a photo of her in the letter. I've got scads of mail for you. Some of it – addressed to Army Post Office – has been hanging around in Colombo for months. No way to get it to you until they offered me the job of postman. God, it's good to be here!'

'I wonder what the family would say if they knew we were together,' I said. 'It'd make them very happy.'

'I couldn't tell them what I was doing. But I have been in touch with them.'

From Colombo Tony had been able to piece together fragmentary news of the family. Now that victory was nearer Irene had moved to London, leaving Bengy with Natasha. That was the first I had heard of that.

'Natasha stayed on in America, got some sort of war job,' he said. 'Maybe it's for the best. Give her some sort of chance to build a life away from Malaya. You know,' Tony added, 'she wasn't very happy at Ara before the end. Restless. I often wonder if she had a boyfriend. She was always a bit of a flier – took after you.'

'Balls! Anyway, I must read my letters.' I could hardly wait.

'Sure. But before you go I must tell you who has done a wonderful job. Paul Soong.'

My mouth must have fallen open, for all I could see of Paul in my memory was an immaculate young man of great charm, always beautifully dressed, a man who I could have sworn would take the war in his stride and with as little discomfort as possible.

'He's one of the unsung heroes,' said Tony. 'He started out running a secret radio station but the Japs discovered it –'

'I remember – I told him about the danger of direction-finders –'

'They roped him in and beat him up for a month, but he managed to get released. Perhaps his old man helped; I don't know.'

'I'm glad of that.'

'That's not the end. Remember Coulson in Singapore? – Norman Coulson, a water engineer with the PWD?' I remembered him vaguely, one of dozens of Public Works Department workers I met from time to time.

'Well, as far as we could find out on our secret radio contacts the water pipes at Changi kept on going wrong –

sabotage, of course – and finally Coulson – a very brave man – was put in charge of repairing them. He used to go under guard to Singapore to collect spare bits – he was the only man who knew where to get them – and his supplier was – you've guessed it – Paul Soong. Apparently he hid hundreds of family messages written on rice paper, stuffing them into the pipe joints that Coulson took back with him. He kept Changi filled with news for nearly two years – until the Japs picked him up. And poor old Coulson. By the Kempetei – and I'd rather have the German gestapo than the Jap Kempetei.'

'What happened then?'

'No idea. Last I heard was that Coulson had been arrested. That was months ago.' Then with a mock sigh Tony said, 'Okay, go and read your letters. Tomorrow I'll tell you the saga of how Julie and I met in Java and managed to reach Ceylon. It was hell, I can tell you: we were sunk again almost within sight of Colombo.'

'Tomorrow,' I said thickly.

35

The letter from Julie was tender, loving and long. I will not put down all she wrote, only the gentler passages which stuck in my mind:

> My Beloved,
> Pela's godfather, who is very circumspect, phoned last night to say that he hoped to meet her father within twenty-four hours. Though I do not know where you are, I see you before me every day, I dream of my loved one every night, and talk about you to Pela who will soon be two and is so much like her father that sometimes when I feel sad it almost hurts me to look at her.
> I hear so much of what you are doing – discreet and

carefully worded, from patients who visit me – that in a way I seem to be sharing your life and waiting each day for news of you which you yourself can never let me have. Isn't it sad that you cannot write to me and yet I sit here in my small flat, Pela asleep, writing with the knowledge that you will read these words tomorrow.

Oh! Darling husband-to-be, when will this war end? When will we be in each other's arms again? The only consolation I have in these terrible times is that I love you with such a full heart that I don't see how you cannot sense it and love me in return.

Sometimes after Pela has been put to bed and I sit and think, I feel a loneliness that hurts physically, just as though you *have* taken my heart for safekeeping. And then I think that this horrible war cannot go on forever, and that one day the only man I have ever loved will be back in my arms.

She did give me some news. She had (understandably) not heard from Paul or her father, but she had written to her mother in San Francisco telling her about Pela – and that we planned to marry after the war. 'I *had* to talk to *someone*,' she wrote, 'and Mummy wrote back such a sweet letter, sending her love to you if I could ever write, and even a kind of apology for telling you not to write to me when I was in San Francisco. So, whatever Daddy thinks and does, we have *one* friend in the family!'

Inside the envelope were half a dozen photos of them both; Pela struggling to walk, Julie looking very prim in her sister's uniform and obviously taken near the hospital. Another showed Julie sitting in a deck chair in front of a bank of flowers that would have looked beautiful in a coloured photograph. Pela was at her feet playing with some bricks. She mentioned this one in the letter. 'Because of Pela I can't live in the hospital mess, but my small flat – in a requisitioned hotel – has a communal garden where Pela's godfather took the photo of her playing with her bricks.'

I looked at the photos, the black and white shading suddenly coming alive with the warmth of mother and daughter, *my* wife – almost – *my* daughter. I reread her letter two, three, four – I don't know how many times, knowing I could never spoil my pleasure by reading any of the others until the following day. The sulky, unwilling flame of the foul fat-lamp spluttered and grew smaller as though it, too, was tired.

Some of the letters which I read the following day were two years old. Many referred to previous letters which I had never received. I opened the four letters from Irene first, not without a touch of apprehension. I noticed that all the letters were addressed to Captain Dexter, APO No—— but the number had been blacked out, presumably before the letters were handed to Tony, in case they never reached me.

Normally it would have been wonderful to hear from home, but after reading Julie's letter, which dealt with realities, because she knew about my work, it was almost comical to realise that no one else writing to me knew where I was, what I was doing, how I was living. Of course they couldn't know; the vagueness was not their fault, but it lent a curious unreality to the words penned so long ago and so far away. One letter from Irene actually said how pleased she was that I was on active service because, 'I've heard reports that conditions in Changi are terrible and we believe poor Tim is there. I fancy the poor dear must be having a hell of a time of it.' I am sure she believed – and I hoped she did – that I had wangled some cushy billet at divisional HQ miles behind the lines, probably in India with a dozen native bearers and polo every afternoon.

That was her first letter, written in early 1942. The new baby hadn't arrived and she didn't elaborate on how or why Natasha had lost her baby, only made the cryptic remark, 'Natasha has really fallen in love with America and I don't think somehow she would ever go back to Tony even if he's alive. No one has heard a word since he dashed off with the Volunteers.'

They must have heard since then that Tony was alive. I wondered what Natflat thought now.

I scanned the closely written pages for news of my son.

'Ben is in great form, but he is already picking up horrible American words. He says "Mom" and "Gee". You'll have to take him in hand when you come back. Oh dear, when? It's only a couple of months to Ben's birthday on 8 May. Four years old!'

After the March letter, written soon after the fall of Singapore, there was a gap. Obviously several letters had gone astray because the next letter, dated March 1943 – a year later – took for granted that I knew all about my new daughter who, I had learned, had been christened Catherine. It was the first I had heard about the birth, and because presumably I had been told all about her in previous letters I was merely told that the children were well, and that Ben wanted a tricycle for his fifth birthday.

The next was a cry of distress. It was written in April of the same year. Bill, her brother, had been killed. Shot down in his Spitfire. No details. 'Mummy and Daddy are heartbroken and I must go to see them. If Natasha hadn't promised to look after the kids nothing would persuade me to leave them, of course, but she really does love the family house at Brewster up in New York State, and they will be safe and happy there with Victoria while I go and see Mummy and Daddy. They're old and with Bill gone they need me – especially in that rambling old place.'

That house! The letter took me right back to the days of Sunday tennis parties at Wimbledon, Sir Keith playing with Bill – who had been a bloody good player – and Miki – I wondered what had happened to *him*? – the butler serving drinks between sets and Lady Bradshaw still convinced that Singapore was in India. Poor devils, to lose their errant son like that. I sometimes felt that war had been cunningly devised to cause discomfort to the young but grief for the old. They were the ones who suffered most, left behind, their world vanishing, all the things they had striven for.

I was thinking of earlier, happy days, remembering with half pleasure the times when I had first known the leggy girl who hated the idea of marriage, so that I was totally unprepared for the naked savagery of the next letter. It had been written in cold fury at the very moment Irene learned about me and Julie. There was no beginning, no end:

I didn't expect you to be faithful. But as your wife I at least expected discretion. But to set up house in the city where I lived – openly with a Chinese half-caste! My God, what a beast you are! Even your own parents are ashamed of you. And when this war is over, won't *you* be ashamed, knowing that your son and daughter will learn when they grow up about their despicable father who was putting a Chinese girl in the family way while their own mother was pregnant. When I think of the day I denigrated poor Bill in front of *you*. Poor Bill who is dead while you – you are alive – an animal with the morals of the farmyard. No wonder I hate Singapore.

That was all. No signature. My hand was shaking when I finished reading it. Only a few minutes before I had been dreaming so happily of Irene – and then this! I had known that some day, somehow, she would learn about us. But I had also vaguely hoped that I might be able to tell her after the war, that we could discuss what had happened in a so-called civilised way. What a letter! Would a wife write a letter like that even to a prisoner in a condemned cell? Perhaps. I was not *proud* of what had happened! I wanted Julie's child, I did. But I did feel a sense of wrong – in hurting. That is always the unforgivable. Hurting.

I went to get a beer in one of the newfangled tins that Tony had brought. It was called Budweiser, and Tony had given me a small strip of metal, pointed at each end, with which to pierce holes in the tin and pour out the beer. A church key, he had called it.

The beer was warm, not as good as a Tiger, more frothy, so that when I poured it into my tin mug it brimmed over. I took a deep gulp – and the old familiar sweat came seeping out of my shirt almost instantaneously. At least a drink took my mind off that letter. I wondered how she had found out. Not a clue in her letter. How strange. Could it have been Tim? Out of revenge? The note gave me a curious reaction after the first shock. I *was* beset with guilt, especially when she taunted me with Ben. But then, I reflected, sitting on my rattan chair alone in my hut, flicking the flies buzzing round my head, but then he might never know. Irene had written in a rage, but secretly and on second thoughts, she might be glad. She hated Singapore. Well, though I had happy memories of that nice old pub, the Hand in Hand, I hated Wimbledon. So why was I worried? I might be killed. Ben's mother might be killed. London was still being bombed.

And anyway what *was* my crime if you analysed it? I heard Papa Jack shouting years ago in Tanamera, 'You're not sorry. You're only sorry you've been found out.' I heard Julie's calm gentle voice telling me her old Moslem proverb – what was it? – something like, 'A sin concealed is two-thirds forgiven.'

I kicked the empty beer tin savagely and the unaccustomed noise startled the birds in the tree above. They started a noisy quarrel up in the branches. Damn it! My *real* fault lay in doing what my father had always taught me to do: in behaving like a gentleman. I should never have married Irene in the first place. I should have shunted her off to some back street butcher and let her have the same treatment as Natflat. Bloody parents! If they had left Julie and me alone in the first place, none of this would have happened. Julie was right – they had turned our beautiful innocence into sin.

I tore open a letter from Mama, every word a tear of reproach, or 'where have I gone wrong?' Early 1944. 'We really prayed that you had settled down, the father of two lovely children. Papa was so proud when he was told of your war service. And then to learn that you had taken up again with that awful Soong girl. And while poor Irene was suffering, pregnant. You will regret that Soong baby all your life.'

Would I? Would I, darling Mama, I thought. Did you regret New York? Tim? And don't you know about Nat-flat, Mama, screwing her arse off with a German spy? Maybe we kids inherited something from you? Some wild streak. It's not our fault, we're not to blame. At least if I was wrong I wasn't a bloody hypocrite, going back home after

I'd had a fling. I wanted some one, I loved her, I took her. I didn't preach sermons, I didn't live a married life of pretence.

My father's letter was in much the same vein. All about family honour! At least he couldn't tell me I had ruined the business. The war had done a hatchet job on that. *And* dumped me in this shithole.

'Tony!' I shouted. 'Come and bring some beer over. And ask Sergeant Macmillan to join us for a celebration. I'm in the shit. All is discovered.'

Tony arrived, wearing a sarong. We opened some beer and I began to feel better. Who gave a fuck anyway! They all had to know sooner or later. And I would always have Julie. I fished the photographs out of my pocket and showed them to Macmillan.

'Look at my daughter Pela,' I said proudly. 'Isn't she beautiful?'

'The mother's a rare beauty too, sorr.' His brogue was thicker than ever, and I knew that he had watched me seeing Julie off. But he was a bloody good sergeant, and all he added was, 'Pela? It's nae a usual name, is it?'

'I didn't tell you before, Sergeant' — I held up my brimming tin mug in a toast — 'but I'm a Pelagian.'

Over the next few days — and sometimes as I listened in our jungle hut the recital seemed like a nightmare from which I would suddenly wake — I heard from Tony how he and Julie reached Ceylon. It was told to me in fits and starts, much of it prised out of Tony by questions; but now, when I retell it, I have ignored my queries which only make the narrative less smooth, when all I wish to do is tell this terrible episode of Julie's life as simply as possible.

When the *Ban Hong Liong* sailed on the night of Black Friday she was one of a flotilla of Singapore 'Dunkirk' ships of all sizes and shapes that were trying to escape; some, like the ship carrying Julie and Rawlings and his baby, were fairly large, others pitifully small — junks, even a tourist launch ('Round the Harbour $5') or boats with puttering outboard engines seized from the few seaworthy craft left at the Singapore Yacht Club.

Though Julie had opted for the Colombo desk when getting her ticket at Cluny the first objective of every vessel was to reach Sumatra or any of the hundreds of islands sitting astride the equator. Every stratum of humanity crouched in the vessels. On the *Ban Hong Liong* alone there were two hundred women and children. Yet no one in the armada had formed any real plans, though all were bound by one compelling instinct: to put as many miles as possible between them and the enemy. At first all seemed well. Unseen currents of the northeast monsoon, now on the wane, guided them steadily in the direction of Sumatra or Java through the Banka Strait, a strip of water separating Sumatra from Banka Island. With each hour that passed in the flat, still waters, with the wash astern putting them farther and farther from Singapore, fears began to dwindle. What no one on board could know was that Admiral Ozawa of the Japanese navy was waiting for them, and had sworn on Tokyo Radio, 'There will be no Dunkirk in Singapore. All ships leaving will be destroyed.'

Ozawa had the might to back up his threat – two eight-inch cruisers, a carrier and three destroyers. He planned (as we know now) to lurk under cover until the convoy became scattered, with the slow ships lagging behind, then pick them off at his leisure. Secrecy was important, but then the allies had a stroke of luck. A Dutch plane from Sumatra spotted Ozawa's task force only a few hours after the de-fenceless convoy sailed from Singapore. The pilot radioed his base. Base sent an urgent signal to Singapore, begging them to warn the convoy to change course while there was still time.

The warning might have succeeded but for one dreadful fact, fortunately unknown to anyone on the ships sailing to their doom. The messages *were* received on the only Singapore radio set still working. But, as always, the messages were in code and – irony of ironies – the man with the code book had been evacuated, taking the code books with him. He was in fact on the *Ban Hong Liong*, and so back in Singapore nobody could unravel the ciphers.

The Japanese launched their attack almost as the vessels reached the Banka Strait and sank forty vessels with either bombs or gunfire. Yet – though unrealised at the time – hundreds of lives were lost simply because the fleeing vessels were unable to make any form of contact or understanding with the Japanese. The *Ban Hong Liong* was only one ship among hundreds frustrated by an insurmountable language barrier. Despite repeated air attacks she managed to survive until she was nearly two hundred miles south of Singapore, when two Japanese destroyers appeared on the horizon; the British captain ordered the white ensign to be lowered and told all the women and children to parade on the decks. Julie was among them, carrying the Rawlings baby. As the destroyers approached they signalled in Morse code, but nobody could understand the message. The *Ban Hong Liong* signalled that she wished to surrender. After some delay the Japanese appeared to understand, for a launch was lowered from the nearest destroyer and made for Julie's ship. It was within a hundred yards of the *Ban Hong Liong* when an RAF bomber from Sumatra suddenly appeared and started circling over the two destroyers. The Japanese opened fire, the plane flew off – and the Japanese launch abruptly turned round and raced back to its destroyer. The British lost their only chance of making contact with the enemy. The two destroyers remained about half a mile away.

What happened next was extraordinary, and emotions must have been stretched to breaking point. For the Japanese ships just sat there, guns trained on the *Ban Hong Liong*, for hour after hour, all through the day.

As the heat of the day mercifully cooled off and the red sunset turned to dusk the Japanese destroyers trained powerful searchlights on the *Ban Hong Liong* – and continued to sit there, waiting. Still nothing happened.

Finally, around seven-thirty p.m., the captain decided to order all women and children into the boats, for he was convinced the Japanese would sink his ship. In the darkness, lit by the gleam of enemy searchlights, the crew started to lower the boats, packing the women and children in, fifty to a boat.

Disaster followed disaster. No one could make sure that families were not separated. Julie met one Asian mother with eleven children. In the panic it was impossible to get them into the same boat, and there was only faint hope of finding them later, for a heavy sea and a strong tide swept the lifeboats astern as soon as they cast off. Worse was to follow, as damage caused by earlier air raids came to light. The ropes supporting one lifeboat parted as she was being lowered, spilling fifty women and children into the darkness. Another lifeboat was lowered, but once in the water it was discovered that she had been holed by gunfire and Julie could hear cries of 'We're sinking.' There was nothing anyone could do. Julie found herself in the same lifeboat as Rawlings and his baby and was perhaps a quarter of a mile away when without warning the Japanese destroyers fired six rounds at the *Ban Hong Liong*. She glowed red from stem to stern and sank a few minutes later. Then the Japanese doused their searchlights, and when dawn broke they were nowhere to be seen.

Julie never remembered how her lifeboat reached land, but it did – beaching on the sandy shore of Pompong Island in the Java Sea. From there friendly natives ferried them to Sumatra, where she found Tony Scott languishing after an equally dramatic escape from Singapore.

The Japanese had not yet occupied Sumatra, and Julie and Tony might have thought their troubles were over when on 26 February they sailed for Colombo in a Dutch ship, the S.S. *Rooseboome*. She was a sturdy old tub, and on the last night before they were due to reach Colombo the passengers met in the saloon to celebrate their impending arrival. At ten minutes to midnight a Japanese submarine surfaced. She fired only one torpedo, which hit the old Dutch steamer amidships. Three of the four lifeboats were smashed and the *Rooseboome* sank in four minutes. Julie, Tony and Rawlings, who were all together in one corner of the saloon, were hurled out through a huge gash in the side and found themselves floundering near a Carley float that had automatically been released with the impact. Poor Rawlings never saw his baby again.

Eight survivors managed to clamber aboard the rubber dinghy in the darkness. Five died of exposure before the raft was spotted by a British plane four days later. A destroyer raced to the rescue, picking them up later the same day.

All went to hospital. Tony, as a soldier who knew Malaya, was welcomed into Force 136. Rawlings had a priority ticket to England as a rubber expert. Anything might have happened to Julie – except for the fact that Chalfont had kept to his promise and sent a message, and when her files were being checked as a matter of routine someone spotted her name on a list and she was asked to join the small hospital attached to the Force.

36

Everything changed once we started receiving supplies by parachute – goods we had only dreamed of, a new weapon called a Sten gun, canisters of ammo, food, clothes, drugs – including a new one guaranteed to cure the malaria from which Macmillan and I suffered regularly.

I had been radioed the number and details of packages to be dropped, and as we peered upwards the heavens seemed to be showering down confetti. Some fell on the DZ, others missed and went plummeting into the jungle. The Chinese rushed off to retrieve them.

Alas, we only recovered an average of seventy per cent, but that was enough to give us a new up-to-date armoury; and the Sten quickly proved to be a far more efficient killer than the old tommy gun. The Chinese loved it. But the food! It was fantastic – some new tinned meat I had never heard of called Spam, even more beer in tins.

I was disappointed that we lost so many of the dropped

canisters, but Colombo replied cheerfully that our recovery rate was better than most; and I réalised – or thought I did – that it was impossible for even the most agile Chinese to climb the tall, smooth pillars of jungle trees to retrieve packages trapped in their uppermost branches. Not until much later did I realise that all over Malaya every canister of arms that was missing had in fact been quickly found and hidden in jungle caches for use in the insurrection that Chin Peng was secretly plotting.

Not only did life in the jungle become more comfortable with each passing month, but by 1945 there was a noticeable shift in the attitude of the Japanese. They seemed anxious to avoid trouble, instinctively reacting to the growing allied victories. During the first three months of 1945 their 'invincible' allies the Germans were in full retreat. The Russians had liberated Warsaw, Budapest and Vienna, and their tanks were rolling closer to Berlin. The British and Americans had liberated Belgium and France and had crossed the Rhine.

Nor could the Japanese take heart from news in the Pacific for American forces had liberated Mânila, while north of Malaya the British had driven the enemy out of Burma. Though we might have to wait a long time before mounting an invasion of Japan itself the tide had turned, and isolated as we were in the jungle – waiting for *our* liberation armies to arrive – we knew it; so did the Japanese.

There were also marked differences in the attitudes of our Chinese guerillas. It had been specifically agreed with Loi Tek that Chinese troops of the MAJPA would remain under British command not only until the war had been won but – and this was vitally important – during the immediate postwar period before civilian rule could be re-established. And Loi Tek, together with Chin Peng, had agreed that all political questions would be left in abeyance until that moment arrived.

However, the Chinese at Ara were becoming more restive politically. They too knew what was going on in the outside world – Soong Kai-shek made sure of that, particularly dwelling on the heroic exploits of the beloved Red Army which would, he assured his troops, reach Berlin long before the second-rate troops of the West. He knew, too, that China – still the revered homeland to millions of Straits Chinese who had never been there – would soon be freed from the Japanese yoke. He did not feel it necessary to explain that this had only been possible by pouring in millions of dollars-worth of American arms and troops. Like many others in Malaya and Singapore he was determined to make sure the Chinese received all the credit for victory in Malaya – as the men who had stayed behind, suffering intolerable hardships, after the Europeans had run away.

Kai-shek and I maintained a polite if reserved relationship, and all our forays were examined at a joint war council. Without doubt Kai-shek had turned into a magnificent guerilla leader. He was a born killer, even enjoyed it – perhaps practising for the moment when he would face me.

I could not speak for other camps – for by now men and arms were being poured in by parachute or submarine – but Colombo was warning us more and more to keep discipline tight, concerned about the resurgence of a Communist spirit among the guerillas.

Our lives had changed too. We had long since dumped our hateful bicycle and were being supplied with powerful radios that could keep running with a small petrol engine. Drugs helped to keep us fit and, most wonderful of all, I now received letters once every two months or so from Julie. If only I could have sent one to her, but there was no way. We also received regular drops of clothes, soap, toothpaste and so on. Our food had changed. Though I had grown accustomed to local food it had always been scarce – a durian or a cup of unsweetened Chinese tea was a rare treat – but now food, even the occasional bottle of whisky – with cigarettes for those who smoked – poured down on us like manna from heaven.

Then came 30 April – and the unbelievable news on the radio that Hitler had committed suicide in his Berlin bunker. On *that* day I even felt kindly disposed towards Soong Kai-shek and invited him over to our command post for a celebration dinner of Spam. The good tidings poured in almost daily. A week later came the greatest news of all – unconditional surrender by the Germans. The war in Europe was over.

It was a moment to think back, with remembered pleasure, of those days so far away – my father and mother, what must they have been through! Would Irene now be able to send for Ben and Catherine? They all seemed so remote, part of another world, whereas Julie seemed close because of her letters – and photos. I had heard no more from Irene; not that I expected to. Father and Mother wrote occasionally, letters of parents who felt it their duty to keep in touch with a wayward son who might be suffering. They had, they wrote on one occasion, received a POW card from Tim in Changi. At least he was alive.

Though the news from Europe was good I still found it hard to visualise an end to the fighting in Asia. The liberation of Malaya might arrive sooner than we dared hope, if only because the Japs would surely have to concentrate more troops on their home islands in case of attack. But how *could* we invade Japan? The fanatical spirit of the Japanese, in which death was preferable to dishonour, would present a baffling problem to allied commanders. We had lost Singapore because we did not fight to the last man; but in defence of their homeland the Japanese *would* fight to the last man. No doubt about it.

Still, I would settle for the liberation of Malaya.

Then, early in June, a whole series of unfortunate events led to a crisis at Ara. It started with information from Colombo that on 6 July – barely a month ahead – the Japanese were staging a series of high-level military conferences. Colombo could only guess at the reason for the meetings, which would take place in six different area headquarters, but they feared it might be to coordinate plans for large-scale massacres of POWs or internees as a final savage gesture of revenge if the Japanese in Malaya found themselves cornered.

Personally I doubted this reasoning and told Colombo so. Much though I hated the Japanese I felt they would remain a disciplined force ready to obey without question an order to lay down their arms if told to do so. I knew that the appalling savagery of many Japanese was really only a reflection of their way of life, a code of justice in which a man could not be judged guilty until he had confessed, so that torture became a weapon of justice. Nothing could excuse their beastliness and yet – perhaps because I had lived all my life in the East – I could see a dim reasoning behind their actions. And though that was no excuse, I felt that the barbaric behaviour of the so-called civilised Germans was far more horrific.

Long before I had decoded the message telling me of the meeting place in our area, I knew where it would be. I had to be the Ara estate bungalow. A high-ranking Japanese officer had made it his headquarters by now, and he would presumably host the conference. It was an ideal spot, for the coolie lines would provide barracks for the extra Japanese security guards. And I was right. Ara was the meeting place.

I now faced a problem. Because of Tony's and my intimate knowledge of the people at Ara we had organised a small but highly efficient group of agents among the estate workers. For months they had been feeding us information which I had relayed back to Colombo. Our camp in the jungle was perhaps three miles behind Ara but we never attempted to reach it – except for the time when I blew up the factory. Our agents met us at a safe kampong three miles from the estate.

I knew that if we launched a major attack on Ara my informants would surely be massacred in savage reprisals. But there were other reasons why I didn't want to do that. We could all scent ultimate victory; it seemed wrong to sacrifice scores, maybe hundreds of innocents. For, without words ever passing between us, the Japanese had in some undefined way compiled a ratio of reprisals. I didn't know who the local commanders were, of course, but it seemed as though they were realistic enough to admit that guerillas had to be kept busy, and that if they were not *too* busy the inevitable reprisals would be of a modest nature – if one can ever call killing innocent people modest. There was no doubt that the bigger the attack the more brutal the reprisals. A derailed train or a blown-up bridge was one thing; assassinating a bunch of generals would be a very different matter.

Any one of these factors alone would never have influenced me if I felt the job had to be done, but taken together they presented a more cogent argument. The matter had, however, to be discussed in council at the Command Post. Ostensibly this recent innovation was to discuss with the Chinese, who were doing brave work, what events were being planned. The real reason was different: by my arranging for Soong (and his counterparts in other squads) to attend all 'action councils' Soong on his part had come to us with any proposed all-Chinese action; and this was vital, for we had discovered that some Chinese with private grudges had gone off in small groups without letting us know. Liaison sometimes slipped, and in one case two of Soong's men had murdered a wealthy Chinese near KL who had long been reviled as a fifth columnist, whereas in fact he was a British agent.

Kai-shek was furious when I proposed that we should decide not to attack the officers' conference at Ara.

'If I was in command I would kill every Japanese dog I could find,' he said savagely. 'If we are ready to die let us go.' And then with a barely concealed sneer he added, 'Leave it to me, Major. Just leave it to me.'

'It's not as easy as that,' I explained. 'It's not our deaths I'm worried about – it's the others'.'

Colombo had in no sense ordered an attack, nor even suggested it. Final decisions were always left to the officer in charge of the Ara camp. However, after radioing Colombo that I was not going to attack I did decide to go with Macmillan – by now sergeant-major – to meet our Ara contacts at a safe kampong. It was by now the middle of

June and I had in mind some sort of compromise action. If I could learn the planned movements of some high-ranking general – say the time he was due to arrive at KL, the make of his car – perhaps Kai-shek could ambush him before he reached Ara, blow up his car with bamboo bombs as we had killed Satoh.

'It's worth a try,' I said, and turning to Tony added, 'You stay here in command. I'll take Wung with me and we should be back in two days – even less if we make contact quickly.'

Wung was an aged Chinese-Malayan baba who lived in the safe kampong and who had been lent to us as liaison officer, simply because he could track his way through the three miles of jungle paths between our camp and the kampong as though they were broad main roads. Alone, or with an ordinary guide, using compass bearings, I might have taken an extra twenty-four hours to cover the three miles. With Wung's uncanny knowledge we could perhaps do it in ten, even less.

In fact we reached the kampong nine hours after leaving our base camp, despite pitiless rain every inch of the way. It was with a huge sigh of relief that we saw the edge of the village.

'Packs off!' I cried to Macmillan. 'I'm feeling whacked. 'Fraid I've got a touch of fever.'

In fact I felt like death. My hands were sticky with sweat and I had a burning sensation all over my body. It couldn't be malaria – the drug mepacrine had stopped that – but it might be dengue, a nasty (though curable) fever. 'I'll have to rest up a bit now we're here,' I said.

The village was little more than a collection of attap-roofed houses dominated by the long house on stilts where the head man and his four wives lived with their innumer-able children. But there were fruits and flowers and one could sense the contentment of people living off the free produce of a bountiful nature. The only work they did was in the paddy fields, which shone like sheets of glass after the rain. Behind the paddy was the river, yellow and turbid, in which I could just see the red nostrils and horns of a buffalo, contented, the world forgotten until his next stint of duty.

The villagers knew we were coming — news travels fast in the jungle — and two girls climbed down the steps leading from the long house. One carried tin mugs of fresh lime juice, the other a banana leaf with some sago and coconut scones laid on it.

Groggy though I felt I knew I would have to spend several minutes exchanging courtesies with Yeop Hamid, the village leader, who half tumbled down the steps in his eagerness to greet us. He was tall, a little fleshy, and was dressed in a dark purple checked sarong and nothing else. The beginnings of a fat roll spilled over its top, a tribute to his enjoyment of life, which consisted of having, besides his four wives, innumerable other girls and most of the village land. As Macmillan and I munched our cakes — two each had to be eaten as a matter of politeness — I watched him roll a piece of spiced betel into a leaf from the same tree, pop it into his mouth and start to chew it. It was a filthy habit, for the scarlet juice made a man's mouth look as though it was bleeding; but who could blame them for using a drug which grew on the trees around them and could be picked for nothing, specially by the devout to whom alcohol was forbidden in the Koran? (The less devout didn't bother with that injunction.)

Yeop enjoyed everything — the pleasures of the chase, the bed, the bottle, the pipe. He had but one peculiarity. Presumably after spending a few months at some mission school, he had learned to read English. Unfortunately, he possessed only one book, a dog-eared Tauchnitz edition of *My Life and Loves* by Frank Harris. It had become his bible, and for one who thought of lovemaking as an exercise to be enjoyed it had done a great deal to stimulate his belief that a village leader had automatic rights over all the girls in his village.

We climbed into the long house where Yeop lived with his family. I had been there before. It was built on stilts, as usual, near the river, covered with thatch, and consisted mainly of one long room in which nearly everyone lived, ate and slept. At one end, the house branched into an L-shaped extension actually built over the river: you could see the water through cracks in the planks. It must originally have been a storeroom from which rice was perhaps loaded into sampans directly below, for there was a trap in one corner, and along two walls a shelf arrangement four feet above the floorboards which made a splendid place for Macmillan and me to sleep on straw mats already laid out for us. The house was not mosquito-proof, and the smoke from the greasy lamp, together with the faint, sickly-sweet aroma of opium, did nothing to purify the air. Still, the people were wonderful, and I did not forget that Yeop and his villagers were risking their lives – and even worse, torture – by helping us day in, day out. It was a very brave village.

I had planned to discuss the forthcoming Japanese conference at Ara with Yeop – to see if he could find out who would be attending, or if we could ambush anyone as they approached Ara – but I was feeling so ill that I asked him to let me sleep first. My head felt as though it would topple off at any moment.

'You sleep first, *tuan* blond. You all right soon,' Yeop tried to comfort me. 'My fourth wife look after you. Siloma only seventeen, but give me a son and she speak good English.' He was obviously very proud of her, and though his words tired me I had out of politeness to listen as he added, 'I teach her. Three words a day. She learn or I beat her. Then' – with a sly smile – 'make love. Violence and love go together very good. You like I lend you Siloma?'

I gasped that with the best will in the world I couldn't have obliged even the most beautiful girl alive, but Yeop laughed and said, 'Another time okay. I have to keep four wives happy, so if you wish to help me you my friend as well as my war colleague.'

At first, in a half daze, I had hardly noticed Siloma. She was much younger than the other wives, a round face, shy smile, dark eyes – large ones – a mass of hair down to her waist and a sensual body, I thought, a kind of freedom in the way she moved. Her baby clutched one of her breasts, gripping it so tightly with its mouth it reminded me of a trapeze artist hanging on to a high wire by his teeth. She did speak a few words of English, but at first I was too ill to understand her except in Malay.

'This bad war, *tuan*.' Yeop puffed at his long-stemmed pipe, the tiny ball in the bowl glowing red from time to time. 'Maybe Japanese never leave Malaya.'

'Bad war,' I agreed. 'And bad men, the Japs. War is one thing, but even in war men don't have to be beasts. Remember Satoh? Well, anyway,' I tried to grin, though I was feeling really bad, 'we bombed *him* to buggery.'

'That good phrase to teach Siloma,' Yeop shouted to a daughter for paper and pencil. 'How you spell buggery?'

'That's nae a word to teach a lady,' I dimly heard a shocked Macmillan say.

'I only teach Siloma sexy words used by Mister Harris. Fine man, he have horn of plenty, always standing up ready for action. I try to be like Frank.'

Lying on my shelf bed, drifting between sleep and spells of wakefulness, slightly delirious, I was hazily comparing the simple philosophy of Malay village life – enough food to eat, enough fish to catch, a simple family life of work and sleep, love and death, no tensions – with family life at Tanamera or the Soong mansion. Of course we had all the advantages of civilisation and yet what a price we paid! Yeop and his girl-wife with the baby set me thinking of the fury of the Dexters and the Soongs when they discovered that Julie and I were lovers.

'Japanese tried to take my book away,' said Yeop.

'The Japs? They've been here?' A sudden prick of alarm roused me for a second.

'Only one time. Looking for spy. They find him, tie him to tree. Then they line up entire village except Siloma who is ready to have baby inside hut. Officer hears her cry and I explain. He blows whistle, and shouts – Japanese always shout, eh? Then he say to me "Your daughter okay – I send for doctor." Doctor arrive, help Siloma, baby born, then Japanese shoot spy while all village lined up to watch. He think she my daughter! Funny people Japanese.'

*

I must have drifted off without undressing, and I was wakened by Macmillan offering me a cup of green tea. He was just about to hand it to me when without warning he spilled half of it and cried, 'My God, Major! Ye're crawling with leeches. They're all over your pants. Let me burn the buggers off, sorr.' He beckoned to Yeop to come with a cigarette and whispered, 'God forgive us, sorr. They're inside – a dozen or 'em – more. They're all over your leg.'

I had never noticed them. By now we all had the latest type of jungle boots and I was always doubly careful to tuck the bottoms of my jungle greens into them as a precaution. But I had ripped a long tear down one trouser leg as we battled our way through thorn bushes. The leeches noticed it before I did.

With the help of Yeop he unlaced my boots and tore off my trousers; without a word Wung took them outside, running down the steps of the long house.

'He'll burn them,' said Macmillan. 'It's mortal risky to leave them in the hut. And now we'll start burning you, sorr.'

I suppose I was so exhausted I couldn't even feel them. 'There's twenty or thirty, sorr – at least. And there's five on the soft skin of your private parts.'

I looked down – and was nearly sick. My scrotum was half-covered with black, slug-like leeches, some as thick as my finger. One was sucking at the base of my penis.

Yeop drew on his cigarette and started applying the cigarette end.

'Dinna move, sorr,' cried Macmillan. 'We dinna want to burn off your waterworks.'

It must have taken half an hour before the last filthy, satiated slug had twisted, writhed and dropped off my thighs or stomach or testicles, leaving a couple of dozen spots almost sealed with drying blood where they had been sucking for hours.

'Thanks, Mac,' I said. 'Hate to say it, but I don't feel too good. I'll have a snooze before we get down to business.'

Siloma brought me a bowl of Chinese soup, shreds of

chicken in steaming liquid, but as I took my first sip I started to retch. 'Maybe I'll feel better later,' I said, but when I woke I didn't feel better. And I knew the symptoms of fever only too well: the racking headache as I shivered, teeth chattering, yet sweating like a pig. Every joint in my body felt as though it were being twisted and wrenched.

Since it couldn't be malaria – though it felt like it – I knew there was only one alternative: blood poisoning. One of the sores had become infected even before we burned off the leeches – or perhaps a thorn had brushed one leech off my body, scratching the open sore.

Only now there was no Sick Bay to go to! How often we had been warned as kids that the slightest scratch could prove fatal in the tropics, how often Mama had whisked us off to a comfy bed in the Sick Bay. Now all I had was a straw mattress on wooden planks.

Not that I knew what was happening. That night and the next day were part of a phantom existence. In the dark shadows of the long house, with slits of light peeping through gaps in the attap roof, I hardly knew night from day, unless I heard the dawn wail of a wa-wa gibbon. I woke occasionally, saw the concern on the fat, worried face of one of the older wives. The young wife, Siloma, vaguely appeared from time to time and bathed my head with a cold wet cloth. Macmillan told me later that I shouted in my sleep, but he never told me what I said. Once when I woke he was there with some soup, for he knew how weakening fevers can be. But the moment I swallowed the first mouthful I vomited all over the bed, adding to the stench and, later, to the flies, the hallmark of tropical illness. Everything I wore was drenched in sweat. I could smell myself. Yet at times I felt as though someone had packed me in ice cubes. After that another night vanished without coherent memory. And another day and night after that.

I had no idea of the time I spent between awareness and unconsciousness, but I woke one morning and dimly saw Macmillan and Siloma standing over me. Yeop was there too. I heard a woman's voice say in Malay, '*Mati hidupnya belum pasti.*' Did my life really hang in the balance? I tried to get up, and heard another voice — it must have been Yeop's — say to the girl-wife, '*Ia masih belum sedar, tetapi ia akan siuman segera.*' I, too, wondered, how long had I been unconscious. I tried to speak, found it difficult. I could only see them through a haze, for the pain was clawing at me — my bowels, my testicles, my belly.

'We've got to cut ye up a bit, sorr,' I heard Macmillan speaking. 'We've nae got a choice. You're covered with boils.'

The word boils terrified me — they had always been one of Grandpa Jack's pet aversions — and I managed to sit up for a couple of seconds before I slid back. Siloma was grasping a pan of hot water. Macmillan was holding some strips of white cloth, Yeop my razor-sharp killing knife.

'Can ye see the boils, sorr?' Macmillan pulled back the blankets. Half a dozen huge, fiery blobs stood out on my left thigh — inflamed scarlet, with yellow centres of pus.

'We've got to lance them, Major,' he said. 'And ye'll have to grit your teeth, sorr, because there's three nasty ones on your private parts.'

They started first with the thighs — to get me used to keeping still, not to jerk with a sudden pain when the knife slid in — a knife that had just been plunged into boiling water — after which Yeop grabbed the boil and with a piece of cloth squeezed the poison out.

'Ye're doing fine, sorr.' Macmillan wiped the sweat from my eyes while the girl fetched another pan of water. Curiously, I was for a few moments suddenly more awake, a little more alert. The pain, I think — specially when the knife slipped in.

'Now's the worst bit, Major,' grunted Macmillan. As he spoke Yeop returned. Out of the corner of my eye I saw him fill a bamboo pipe with opium he had been heating on a small lamp, turning the quid of opium on a skewer until it blistered with heat, a sign it was cooked.

'It will help,' said Yeop as he held the pipe to my lips. 'It always does.' I nearly vomited after the first few draws, but then the sickly-sweet drug took some sort of effect. It was not a complete anaesthetic — far from it. It made me more resigned, that's all. I couldn't see the boils on what Macmillan politely called my private parts. But I did feel the knife go into my scrotum, which was burning with agonising pain anyway. I screamed.

I woke vaguely for a few seconds; Siloma the young wife knelt beside me holding a bamboo stick and a piece of white cloth. She had split the bamboo a quarter of the way down the middle, so that it retained the tension of a clothes peg or an outsized paper clip.

She looked at me with genuine concern, and said, 'I try no hurt my husband's war colleague. The Chinese have a saying, *Cha boh heng!*'

'That means,' Yeop explained, 'We have eyes in our finger tips.'

I looked at the bamboo with fear. Yeop gave me a few more whiffs of opium, then Macmillan cut into my scrotum again. The young wife waited on her knees holding open the bamboo clip, and clapped it on the filthy deflated boil, squeezing it between the two prongs, squeezing away as much of the poison as she could. That hurt even more and – aided perhaps by the opium – I passed out; and woke up imagining I was still dreaming – for there, standing over me, was Tony Scott.

'No, it's not a nightmare.' He bent down. 'We thought you'd bought it – you and Mac – so I came along in case you were wounded.'

'Ye dinna have to worry any more,' said Macmillan. 'Ye've passed the crisis, sorr. A few days' rest and ye'll be as right as rain.'

'Is the camp all right?' I asked Tony feebly.

'Sure. Kai-shek is in charge. I only left last night. I'm going right back.'

'My first visitor in hospital.' I made a poor attempt at humour. 'Did you bring me any grapes?'

'Bananas.' Tony handed me one – and to my surprise I ate it and enjoyed it – though I had to ask Tony to peel it for me, I was so weak.

'You'd better get back,' I said to Tony. 'You know what Standing Orders say – one European in camp at all times.'

'I regarded this as an urgent dispensation.'

'What date is it?' I had lost all count of time, but we had arrived around the middle of June, and I had a feeling the month would soon be over.

'July the fourth.'

'Christ!' I cried and tried to sit up, only to fall over. 'The fourth!' I had been out for over two weeks. 'The day after tomorrow is the meeting at Ara. For God's sake get back — both of you. That bloody man Soong is trigger-happy.'

I broke out into another sweat, knowing that for the time Tony was away from camp Soong was technically in charge — and he had been furious when I vetoed the attack on the Japanese at Ara. Kai-shek was a pathological killer; if he thought Macmillan and I had been killed, and with Tony out of the way for a few hours, he would have every right to make his own decisions. Even if we all showed up later and accused him of disobeying the spirit of my orders, we would never be able to nail the bastard down. Even if we lived to see the defeat of Japan, even if I started a postwar enquiry, he could never be pinned down. All this flashed through my brain as I almost panicked.

I found it difficult to talk, to formulate long sentences — not only because I was weak but because my balls were on fire and searing with excruciating pain. Finally I gasped, 'If we can get some sticks — make some crutches — I think I could make it back.'

'Go away with ye, sorr,' cried Macmillan. 'Ye've nae got the strength of a bairn.'

Of course he was right. 'Then both of you must get back and take command. Both of you. You too Mac. And take Wung — he'll cut the time of the journey by hours.'

'I canna leave you. It's nae our custom to leave our friends behind. I dinna care for mysel', but I dinna want aught to happen to ye.'

'Don't be a bloody fool, Mac. You remember what you told me the day we killed Satoh — and four innocent Chinese? Nothing must interfere with the objective. *You* made me do it that day. I'll make *you* do it now. Only this time, if you go now — really now — and reach base in time you'll be *saving* innocent lives. Probably this village, for a start.'

'I'll stay with you,' Tony suggested.

'Don't be stupid. Christ! If that bugger Kai-shek goes on the rampage the Japs'll be here, there and everywhere. You've got to stop him. You too, Sergeant-major. As they say in the films, "That's an order."' I tried to smile. 'I'll lie up here and as soon as the crisis is over one of you come back with Wung and collect me.'

'There be some things a man canna be asked to do,' Macmillan muttered, but he was a good soldier – and he knew I was right. They left ten minutes later, promising to return.

Yeop, his four wives and a dozen assorted children seemed to think it perfectly natural for me to remain as one of the family. The wives took it in turns to feed me and change the rough dressings on my thigh and scrotum. On the second day I tried to get up. I balanced for a few seconds until, without warning, I keeled over, head swimming, legs buckling. I was as weak as a dishrag, and when I saw myself in the small decorated mirror nailed to the wall – a dirty face with a straggling blond beard – I didn't at first realise I was looking at my own reflection.

That was the day the high-ranking Japanese officers were supposed to be meeting at Ara. For once, much though I loathed the Japs, I prayed they would come to no harm.

37

Dusk. Three days later – three days in which the vomiting had stopped, though I was still very weak. As the others ate their evening meal in the main living room, Yeop suddenly banged on the floor with a wooden pole: a prearranged alarm. The chatter of the family, the squeals of kids, ceased as though a soundproof curtain had been drawn across the room. In the light from an opening I could see Yeop's fleshy, handsome face cocked to one side, listening.

The sound came again and this time I heard it, the faintest agitated jabber of machine-gun fire.

'They are coming,' said Yeop quietly. 'Go, all of you. Quickly!'

That was the moment I knew — in my aching bones if not as a fact — that Tony and Macmillan must have failed to reach base camp in time to stop Kai-shek.

'They are shooting up the next kampong.' Yeop drew me aside as everyone made a dash for the narrow steps. 'They will not be here for some time, it is over a mile away, but they will come along the farm road by the paddy fields in their armoured trucks.'

'Can you get away — hide?'

'I will lead the villagers into the jungle, if we are lucky.' And then Yeop added, with a very Malayan old-fashioned courtesy, 'I hope I of value to your cause, *tuan* blond. May I ask for favour in return?'

'Anything — but you *must* rush. With the rest of the villagers. Where are you going? Where can you make for?'

Weak and still hardly able to run, I was exasperated when he said, 'We have time, *tuan*.'

'We haven't!' I cried.

What the hell had happened to Tony and Macmillan? Macmillan was the best sergeant-major in the business. How was it possible they had not reached the base camp? Kai-shek must have gone on the rampage, shooting up the Japs; and now they were exacting reprisals. But Macmillan had had three days to reach camp and stop any nonsense on my orders. He had failed to get there. So had Tony. They might be dead now. Christ! I *would* be as weak as a kitten at a crisis like this.

I was thinking not only of this village, where they had nursed me through an illness close to death, but of the workers on the Ara estate, many of them willingly risking their lives to spy for us against the Japanese. They would be slaughtered to the last man, woman and child – and only the lucky ones would die quickly.

Yeop's thoughts were running on different, more practical lines.

'My wives bless me with only two sons.' He might have been addressing a meeting of village elders. 'I take one son into jungle. You too weak for such a journey. So please, you take the other – the newborn child – across river to safety?'

'But I don't know anything about babies!' I managed to stand up. 'And' – looking at the slow-moving yellow water behind the long house – 'that's a quarter of a mile wide. I couldn't paddle across it for a million dollars.'

'Not alone.' Patiently he explained that he and the villagers would make for the jungle on this side of the river with his three older wives and his eldest son. I would take his fourth wife – the mother of the baby – to the other bank of the river, thus increasing the chances that one son would survive. It didn't need much imagination to realise that if I *could* cross the river I should be fairly safe – if, that is, I didn't starve to death. Yeop seemed to read my thoughts, said, 'She is strong and she will help you. There is an old camp two miles into the jungle. There you will never be discovered until it is over and I come to fetch you. And the Japs cannot follow because we have only one boat. The others are away.'

'But you should go –'

'My place is with my people. I am their leader and we cannot all cross. There is one boat – a pirogue – below the rice drop at the back of the house. Take it, *tuan* blond, and protect my second-born and his mother Siloma.'

The garrulous chatter of machine-gun fire sounded vaguely closer, more ominous. 'I can't take the only boat,' I protested. 'It's your boat – your kampong – and we have done enough harm to you already.'

'You are not taking my boat,' said Yeop. 'Siloma is taking it and she is my favourite wife. She give me a son. I ask you to help *her*.'

I knew I hadn't the strength to help anyone anywhere – and he knew it too. But there was no time to argue.

'God be with you, Yeop.' I gripped his hand and made for the trap door in the L-shaped annexe. Siloma, suckling the baby — I had hardly ever seen her without the baby glued to her breast — somehow caught me as I stumbled. The others were filing down the village street, a ragged procession lumbered with pots and pans and tattered cases, all gathered up in the haste of instant flight, a small-scale reproduction of the pictures I had seen of the exodus in France when the Germans attacked.

'I don't think I can make it,' I gasped in Malay, knowing that unless I was very careful I would never be able to lower myself from the floor of the house on stilts into the narrow dugout canoe in the water below.

'You hold baby, *tuan*?' the girl asked.

I nodded. She tugged it away from her breast, whereupon it started yelling its head off — not that noise mattered. I gripped it close to my chest and then, keeping it to one side so that it didn't get squeezed, I lay half across the open trap, legs dangling. It was no good; I almost squashed the baby. She took it out of my arms, laid it on the floor, grabbed both my wrists and gently helped to guide me down until my feet touched the long, narrow, pointed boat, made from a single tree trunk, and already half full of water.

'Be seated,' she whispered, then leant over the hole and passed the baby down to me, and after that my pack — which contained not only spare magazines but fieldglasses, groundsheet and compass, matches and water tablets — and my Sten. I already had my killer knife in my belt. I squatted at the far end of the boat, clutching the child as Siloma twisted round and lowered herself, legs first. It was a knack, the way Malays balanced themselves in their narrow canoes. I had never in my life seen a Malay capsize a pirogue, and now Siloma landed feet-first without causing a ripple on the water. As she untied the boat and pushed off from the stilt, she handed me an old tin pan.

'I paddle,' she explained. 'You hold baby and take out water.'

Even the simple act of baling — of lifting up the pan of water over and over again — sapped what little energy I had left, and I almost dreaded the prospect of reaching the far bank, for I knew I could not walk far. It was nearly dark now and under a faint moon the river glistened in places like pale yellow silk as we inched our way across, the girl paddling with a steady rhythm, the child squalling.

We reached the opposite bank long before the Japanese arrived in the village. The shallow water was lined with mangrove swamp - downward-thrusting roots, hanging from branches above, many taking root again under water so that in places they were as solid as the bars of a cage. It was very hot, but there was no rain.

Eventually we tumbled out of the canoe. I was still clutching the baby, while Siloma tied up the boat, then handed me my Sten and my pack. Only then did she take the baby to her breast to quieten it.

I had to rest. We didn't dare to show a light, for one flicker of a match would be seen when the Japs arrived. They reached the kampong about two hours later. Crouching behind some areca trees, I heard the sound of cars and people shouting; almost at the same moment the kampong was lit by what looked at first like swivelling horizontal search-lights – twisting, probing beams of light, ferreting out dark empty corners. They were the headlights of the small armoured trucks which the Japanese had used so success-fully to carry troops through rubber estates, the same estates that the British had boasted were impassable to vehicles.

We waited for the sound of shooting, but none came. 'Thank God for that,' I whispered. 'They must have all got away.'

The Japanese seemed to have the same thought. Of course we could make out no details, only blurred glares and shadowy figures, but I could imagine them making house-to-house searches – and finding nothing, for there was an outburst of noise, vehicles being started, revving up, gears jarring, orders shouted. The headlights swivelled again until suddenly – as though an entirely different set of lights had been switched on – there was a stream of red rear lamps and the Japanese swept out, vehicles rattling along jungle paths. Then silence and darkness.

I had learned enough about Japanese tactics – about Japanese brutality – to know that we could not paddle back across the river, not for several days. The Malays have an almost obsessive desire to return to their small villages and the Japanese knew that if they thought the danger over they would do just this. Time after time when the Japanese were engaged in ruthless reprisals they waited patiently to stage them in the villagers' own kampongs, sometimes to bury the victims alive, as though to warn any who had escaped of the fate that awaited anyone rash enough to raise a hand against the masters of the Co-prosperity Sphere.

There was no thought of sleep that night. I had started to shiver again – and that meant another dose of fever. I knew I could expect another bout before I had sweated out the last of the poison, and now my teeth started chattering unmanageably. They felt loose in my mouth.

We had no food, but I was not hungry, though I had a raging thirst. The opium Yeop had given me while they lanced my scrotum had given me a dry mouth, but even worse was the dehydration after days of dysentery. But the water near the river bank was undrinkable unless boiled, and I still didn't dare light a fire, not for a day or two.

Siloma went off to cut some brushwood and ferns with her parang. On her return I spread out my groundsheet and offered it to her and the baby, but she refused it.

'You weak, you sleep.' She searched for an English word to show off her husband's teaching. 'Or you soon deceased.'

It was the first smile I had managed for a long time. 'You know I speak Malay,' I said, 'Why do you use English words – and such long ones? Deceased!'

'I practise the *tuan*'s language.' She had a very pretty, shy smile. 'My husband promise me on the birth of son that he take me to Singapore where only speak English. My husband teach me three words a day, so you permit me to practise? But now you must sleep.'

I agreed. 'I don't want to be deceased,' I smiled again and lay down. She leaned back against the tree, fitting into the available curves with the ease of a healthy young animal. Soon she was gently snoring, the baby asleep in its usual position at her breast. I had no sleep. First the dysentery still plagued me. I nodded off, only to wake with the feeling of searing hot knives tearing at me, warning me that in less than a minute I would empty my bowels in a stream of stinking water next to her.

I staggered to a place I had picked out by the edge of the river, where I could support myself on a mangrove branch. Then I returned to sleep – until the next fiery warning, perhaps only minutes later. On top of that misery – and when I thought there could be no more liquid inside my body to evacuate – the red ants came. With their unerring instinct for blood, they discovered that one of the lanced boils on my scrotum was still bleeding slightly, and I woke with a scream as the first one bit me, the sting as agonising as if someone had burned me with a red hot knitting needle.

For three days we had nothing to eat and I became weaker and weaker. I can remember only episodic moments, but I did realise that the baby was worse. If it is possible for a brown skin to turn blue, his had done. He was too weak now even to suck his mother's milk. She tried but his mouth kept slipping off. It was not even crying now. On the second day I held it while Siloma went foraging for any food she could find. She returned with a few berries. 'You can eat them,' she assured me. 'They are not poisonous.' We shared them between us.

She found some more on the third day, and we also caught some rainwater in my groundsheet during a down-pour. That was the day the Japanese returned to the village, this time in daylight.

We heard the familiar roar and grating of army vehicles and, by lying flat on my belly, hidden by mangrove, I saw much of what happened through my field glasses – though at times I was too weak to hold them to my eyes. Several small scout cars arrived first, with an officer in the inevitable white helmet directing operations. After the soldiers had spilled out of their vehicles two ancient country buses lumbered into view – the kind so popular in rural Malaya, wheezing with age but gaily painted in bright colours with slogans. I could hear faint orders rapped out, but not until the bus doors opened and the shouts were magnified did I realise what had happened.

They had been caught — the villagers, almost all of them, it seemed. 'They didn't make it,' I muttered to Siloma.

A hundred or so were pushed out of the buses. Through the glasses I tried to recognise faces. I saw Yeop's older wives, countless children, but there was no sign of Yeop himself. And I knew I would recognise him. 'I think he must have escaped,' I whispered.

The villagers were herded from the buses by Japanese wielding rifle butts as they forced everyone to enter the chief's long house. They clambered up the steps, oblivious to the blows. When the last had been pushed inside the officer shouted an order. Two soldiers ran with bundles of dry grass and wood and made piles under the house, between the stilts. Others lit torches of rags doused in petrol. A third group stood outside the house with fixed bayonets.

The fires were lit, the torches hurled on to the dry attap roof. In seconds the wooden building was an inferno.

In the smoke I could see some children jump out of the wall openings — or perhaps they were thrown out. The soldiers were on to their falling bodies like men chasing insects, stabbing them, sometimes two or three lunging at the same tiny body. Escape was impossible. I felt Siloma grip my arm so hard that her nails bit into my flesh, but she didn't say a word.

Before long half the village was in flames. The Japanese waited an hour or so, looking for stragglers. Then, as though a routine exercise had been performed, as though they were anxious to be off to barracks, perhaps for an early lunch, the officer in the white helmet barked an order then jumped into the leading armoured car, and the Japanese left. Only the brightly-coloured buses remained in the village street.

The next day the baby died. I was too weak to help Siloma bury it. She took the body away and did not say what she had done.

I must have been delirious that night, and for the first time since I landed behind the Japanese lines – for the very first time in all these years – I realised I was close to death. If I didn't eat I would die.

Semi-conscious, I heard Siloma say, as though discussing something with herself, '*Ia kurus sekali*.' Yes, I *was* nothing but skin and bones, so thin I could feel the muscles quivering in my matchstick legs each time I tottered to the river toilet.

We had collected some more rainwater during another downpour, and I said to her, 'You had better go back across the river, Siloma. Try to find your husband. No point in staying here.'

'I stay with you,' she said, 'and I make you live. I think only one way.'

I owe my life to Siloma – Siloma and the dead baby. I was too far gone, hovering between fantasy and reality, slowly losing even the will to live – though not quite – balanced between dreams and a kind of cloudy wakefulness to know even the days that passed.

I do remember vaguely that she sat down beside me, pulled me into a sitting position near the tree against which she slept, and placed an arm behind my back to hold me up. Then, as she sat there, and with an almost biblical simplicity of motion, as though it were the most natural thing in the world, she undid her baju and cupped one of her big breasts in her right hand and pushed it towards my mouth.

That was the turning point. For three days she fed me, and though I was still wandering I could feel some of her strength oozing into me. She lit a fire for the first time, as there was no more danger of the Japanese returning, and found some bamboo shoots out of which she made a stew. A day or so later she killed a mouse deer, one of the fawn-like creatures that roam many parts of Malaya. She cleaned and roasted it, and the meat lasted for two more days.

'We must cross the river,' I told her then, when the food was running out. 'The village is empty, but your husband may be close. And anyway, there's food. Chickens or something – and fruit. And I must try to find my camp.'

'You no travel, *tuan* blond. You never reach your friends.'

'I could rest up in your kampong – get my strength back – now that you have saved my life. What you did was wonderful.'

'You take place of my child, but you right, we go. I also need food for' – she searched for the right English words – 'my tits are dry!'

'Tits!' It hurt terribly to laugh, for the inside of my stomach felt as though it was lined with broken glass, but I couldn't help it. 'Siloma, where do you get these crazy words?'

'Is not right? It is one of my husband's favourites.'

'I'll bet it is!' I thought, though aloud all I said was, 'Well – "breasts" would perhaps be more ladylike.'

'I like tits – is shorter.'

'Will it be safe to cross – tomorrow perhaps?'

'By dusk, yes. You are weak, but I take you. You must remain many days in kampong before you travel.'

She certainly knew how to give the orders – for a seventeen-year-old. 'I know that,' I said meekly. 'After the way you saved my life I'm not going to throw it away.'

We left the following evening, though I was still feeling groggy. As a last thought before sitting down in the pirogue – I think I was scared it would overturn in mid-river and I would be a gonner – I said to Siloma, 'In case we don't make it – if we get shot out of the water or anything – please will you look after my identity disc, and after the war tell the British what happened. Once we're over the river you can give it back to me.'

She didn't understand what I was saying. 'You know – this.' I felt for the small circular metal disc which we all wore in the jungle, not only for identification but to prove if caught by the Japanese that we were regular soldiers. It wasn't there! All I could mutter stupidly was, 'The bloody thing's gone. I've lost it!' To me it seemed a heinous crime, the quintessence of stupidity to lose the one tiny metal chip that would tell the world – and that meant Julie – if anything happened to me. I was lost, I had almost died in the jungle, and the only person who knew me was Siloma. And she called me 'tuan blond'. I felt as though I had been robbed of my identity.

The agony of our return to that once peaceful village started the second I stumbled out of the dugout canoe, by the edge of the marshy bank. My boots slithered ankle deep into mud and I felt something hard. I looked down. I had trodden on a dead man's face. I had pushed it under the ooze, but as I took my foot away it returned to the surface like a rubber doll.

The village stank of despair, of blood, of guts. Though most villagers had been burned in the long house – now a pile of ashes – corpses of those trying to escape had been piled up at one end of the village; a few were stinking and covered by a restless agitated swarm of bloated green flies, though most of the bones were clean, picked by vultures. Here and there one had escaped the attention of the scavengers, still circling overhead. On harder ground a head and half a body lay awaiting them, but the arms and legs had been hacked off, the eyes gouged out and the ants were ravaging in their sockets. A few yellow pi–dogs howled or cringed in the dust or chased the occasional chicken foraging for worms in the untended plots by the jungle fringe.

Even the huts that still stood – most of them at the far end of the village by the river – had an air of desolation, as though ashamed of what had taken place there that terrible morning. What had Julie said in her poem? 'An air that kills.' That is what the village smelt of, heavy with the smell of guilty men killing the innocents. The hate was boiling up inside me – how could anyone *ever* look a Jap in the face without spitting on him, I thought. And yet my real hate was reserved for Soong Kai–shek. It was he who had indirectly caused this village to die. His blood lust for killing was maniacal, and he had known perfectly well that when he went ahead with his attack on the Japanese headquarters the Japanese would automatically reply with reprisals. He simply didn't care.

I managed to prevent Siloma from seeing most of the worst that first day. I sent her off to get some fruit, then to make a fire. We ate our best meal for a long, long time, washed down with a drink I had never tasted before.

'It is *jaggery*, *tuan* blond,' she explained, 'and it give strength.' *Jaggery* was a kind of coarse, sugary gruel which the Malays make from the sap of palm trees, boiling it until it is drinkable. I could feel its strength with every sweet mouthful.

We spent the night in one of the huts that had escaped the fire. It was at the perimeter of the kampong, not far from the river. The next morning I went to see what remained of the long house, her home. It was a pile of ashes — ashes and bones. Hardly a recognisable object remained. I did not need to persuade Siloma to keep away from the centre of the village. With the same detachment she had displayed in the jungle when her baby died she nodded gravely and said, 'I understand, *tuan* blond. When you are recover, I search for my husband. I know he is alive.'

The way she spoke made me wonder once or twice if she really cared for Yeop. She spoke of him with affection, but she was only seventeen, probably pressed into marriage by her family. But love? That was different — though she obviously enjoyed learning the erotic English words he had chosen to teach her from his study of Frank Harris. But only rarely did she really laugh. What did she think? I could never find out.

My health was returning swiftly, and during the days that followed she did everything to help me. Rummaging in old houses still standing she found some pairs of khaki shorts for me, washed them and cleaned my two shirts. She cooked, and soon I was able to start doing exercises twice a day to tune up what remained of my muscles. I had to get back to camp.

I still had no idea of the date or where the Japanese were stationed, and ten days after we had set up camp in the village I told her I must start to return. I felt certain I could find Ara. This was my territory, I had been brought up here for part of my youth, and though the jungle did change its shape from day to day Ara was only a few hours' march; I had my compass, though I had lost my maps. Still, if I struck northeast I would have to find a landmark I knew. Even this river might join up with the river on the edge of the Ara estate. Food would have presented a problem, but no longer – Siloma would provide me with more than enough.

It was early morning, before the heat of the day pressed down, when I said, 'Two days more, then we must pack up some food and you will come back with me to safety.'

'No, *tuan* blond. I search for Yeop. I want tell him how you give me help.'

'It's you who've helped me,' I protested.

'I gave what I had, but I unhappy, and you gave me' – she searched for the English word to impress me, 'spirited help. For this Yeop Hamid and I must repay you.'

'We'll have a wonderful reunion when the war's over.' Or did she mean something else? Instant repayment? I had wondered more than once as I grew stronger, while we lived together almost like man and wife – or to put it a better way perhaps, like castaways on a desert island – was she offering me herself as repayment of a fanciful debt? It couldn't be, for I had done nothing – indeed, I had been a burden. But Malays think tortuously – and it was true that if I hadn't been in the long house she would probably have not crossed the river but gone with her husband. And would have been killed.

'Not after war,' she said gravely, 'but now. My husband say you very brave, you kill many Japanese, and he very displeased if I fail to provide his friend with' – another English word – 'contentment. Is right word, *tuan*?'

'It's a very beautiful word, Siloma, and I am very honoured.'

'Shall we lie together then? It will bring you happiness.'

'You saw me naked, when they were cutting open my' – I hesitated at the word – 'my balls. You saw what a mess the leeches made of me. Do you think I *could*?'

'The Europeans have many strange ways.' She sat up on the mattress of rushes. 'They always think lying together mean' – and out came a word of which she was obviously very proud – 'ejaculation.'

'Honestly, Siloma,' I laughed. For a man who had only one book in his library Yeop had certainly made the best use of it.

'You do not like? You laugh at me.'

'Never, Siloma. That I promise.'

'Is not lying together without performance a wonderful comfort to tired body?'

'I'm sure it is. But with a beautiful girl – you must realise that lying together usually does lead to something else.'

'With us, hopefully.'

'There is only one thing.' I was thinking of Julie's poem to me, 'I have been faithful to you in my fashion'. 'I have a lover who is like you, Siloma. War tore us apart, but I love her.'

'She loves you?'

'I hope so.'

'Then is all right, we lie together. If she love you, she feel sad you not lying with a woman all these months. Is bad for you.'

'You are wonderful Siloma, and I am very honoured. But this girl of mine, she might not like it at all.'

'I think you wrong. When my husband sad, I go out, find girl. It make him happy. It is good medicine, a change.'

Temptation hit me right where you feel it most. I knew I *wouldn't* be hurting Julie, but even as I felt myself throbbing and growing in my tattered khaki shorts I hesitated. But I suddenly remembered brother Tim asking me if I would mind if Irene had an affair behind my back; and I had told him that I would hope she enjoyed it. But Irene was my wife. Would I say the same if Julie, alone in Ceylon, waiting for me all these years, felt the need to take a lover? Would it matter to me? I knew it would, that I would never feel the same about her again. And if I expected that much from Julie, shouldn't I repay her by behaving to her as I wanted her to behave to me?

Even so – I might have given in, because reason told me that it didn't mean a damn thing. I was tempted. And then a sudden icy stab of fear shot through me and all the size of my urge left me. I had heard the sound of someone or something moving.

'Stay here,' I whispered. '*Whatever happens, don't leave the hut.* Keep the Sten. I'm going to recce – to see.'

It was probably only an animal, an early morning gibbon, but even in convalescence I had never never forgotten my security. Sliding my killer knife into my belt I slithered out of the hut on my belly. Down by the river I heard splashing, shouts of 'Hai!' Japs!

By now I knew every tree, every possible ambush point between the hut and the river, and it was obvious they hadn't any idea someone was living in the village. Ahead of me, four yards away perhaps, was a wild banana tree, its thick glossy leaves flourishing almost from the base of the trunk. They always grew this way when no one cut them back. Three years in the jungle had given me a kind of enhanced vision, something far more acute than noting sudden movements of birds or the snap of twigs. A puzzled Macmillan had once said, 'You seem to see *through* things, sorr.' It wasn't true, but I could instinctively see when even the tiniest element of a familiar scene was wrong; and I could see that now. Behind the edge of one long, flat shining leaf a tiny speck of grey gleamed in the early morning sun.

It was the tip of a tommy gun – it had to be – the muzzle, the gun held crooked in the arm of someone behind the tree. And it had to be a Jap.

I stopped, crouching, pulled the knife out of my belt. I heard more sounds from the river, laughs, cries, splashing. I had a few seconds while the Japs concentrated on their bathing. This man must be a sentry.

To live – to escape torture or death and not to see Siloma killed – we had to flee. Instantly. And for that I had to do two things. First, kill the sentry – silently, before he could give an alarm. Second, get my Sten from the hut and kill the men in the river. Then bolt before any more Japs arrived, attracted by the sound of firing.

The killer knife was razor sharp, its long, thin blade

running into the short metal hilt, designed so that a man's fingers could grip it when silently cutting across the flesh as distinct from stabbing, for that was not only clumsy and amateurish but noisy.

My mind racing back to the YMCA lessons, I waited, knife in my right hand, the sharp edge of the blade pointing downwards, so that I could see my knuckles, white. For a hundred years, it seemed, I had practised the right way to hold that knife before cutting a man's throat from behind before he could cry out. I knew every movement by heart. It was not strength that was needed, but skill.

He moved slightly. A clicking noise. A new different smell. Petrol. Another smell. Tobacco. He had lit a cigarette. Now was the moment – before he put his lighter back in his pocket, for during that half second he would have one hand less. I had no need to remember Chalfont crying, back in the YMCA, 'Half a second can cost you your life!' In this split second, when his concentration lapsed, when he was thinking of his pockets, taking the first puff, I struck.

He never heard me sidle round to the right hand of the banana tree. It had to be the right hand, for I had to slice his throat from left to right. As I clapped my left hand over his mouth, jerking his head back, I plunged the knife straight into his neck just below the left ear, near the point where the pulsing artery pumps blood to the brain. As I struck he squirmed, but he had no time – and luckily his gun was looped over his arm so it did not fall.

Blood spurted over my right hand. I twisted the blade – sharp edge always downwards – into the deep hole, and pulled it across in one savage slice. His throat seemed to open, and as the blood gushed out his head fell back and he slumped in a curious, disjointed sort of way, like a pile of kid's bricks tumbling over. For the first time I saw what was left of his face, eyes staring. He looked about sixteen.

I crept back to the hut where Siloma was waiting, immobile with fear. I clapped a wet, bloodstained hand over her mouth to stifle any noise and whispered, 'Japs! Wait here. *Don't leave the hut on any account*. I'll be back.'

There were six of them in the river, washing in the yellow water, washing with the Japanese passion for cleanliness, so fervent it sometimes outweighed caution.

Then I spotted the vehicle: one small personnel carrier. That meant an isolated patrol, lost perhaps, which had decided to enjoy an early-morning bathe before trying to find its way back to its unit. The men had left the young sentry on guard, and he had been confident there was nothing to guard. But soon they would find him — with his throat cut. Or perhaps not if I acted first.

I had no idea if there were any other Japanese in the area, but I had no option. I had to gamble — or die. I could not use the knife — one against six, I would never have a chance. But they were all grouped laughing and splashing in the river, and if I crept up I could kill the whole damn lot with one burst of the Sten. And then run like hell — perhaps cross the river in the only canoe left — before other Japs arrived.

Sliding back the safety catch I doubled up across the few yards between the trees and the river. I had almost reached the bank before they spotted me. There were shouts of 'Hai!' They were all in one tidy group. They couldn't have done better if they had been arranging a target grouping at a Bisley competition. I let them have the entire magazine, the stutter shaking my arm, plumes of water shooting out of the river like jets balancing ping pong balls in a fair ground their bodies quivering with the impact of bullets.

I slid in a new magazine. The hot barrel burned my fingers. I ran to the water's edge — a bloody lake. One man was only wounded. I shot his face off at point blank range then, just to be sure, sprayed the floating, drooping corpses, half naked, to be certain there were no survivors.

Then I ran back to the hut. No need for silence now.

'Come on, Siloma,' I cried. 'Get as much food as you can, then let's go, quick.'

She didn't reply — but then she never was a talker. I bent to enter the hut, caught a glimpse of her in the corner, cowering terrified like a heap of old rags, saw the raised arm of a Japanese uniform swinging down, never giving me a chance to twist, to defend myself. My heart was thumping,

I was thinking, 'This is death!' Then the arm, with something hard and rough at the end of it, sliced viciously at the back of my head.

38

At first, as I struggled towards consciousness, it was like a dream; over and over again I saw a monstrous, grinning Japanese savagely swing something above his head before the moment he prepared to split my skull. And as the swing took movement, as the arc started, he apologised with a hiss, 'Sorry, Johnnie.'

The impossibility of it all, the madness of the nightmare, made it all the more terrifying. At the moment of regaining consciousness the nightmare lingered on, the words drumming into my ears, that hissed, 'Sorry, Johnnie.' They were the last words of the dream, the first words of reality as I struggled against darkness.

My eyes refused to see anything. I blinked, trying to focus, as though clicking from one camera lens to another to get a better picture. Through the blur I felt a hand – a woman's hand – grasp mine and I cried out 'Siloma, Siloma!' She squeezed it, and said, 'Everything all right, *tuan* blond.'

I could barely see her in the corner of the attap hut as she helped me to struggle to a sitting position.

'Where is he?' I whispered, terrified, for somewhere a Japanese was waiting, playing cat-and-mouse, waiting to kill me. But why wait? And why was Siloma – mortal enemy of the Japanese – why was she still alive? Why was she not afraid?

Again I tried to blink my eyes into focus as a disembodied voice, from a vague outline above me, hissed softly, 'Sorry to hurt you, Johnnie. I come to save you. But if I don't hit first you would kill me before I can explain.'

The voice was dim, marked as Japanese by its sibilance, and it was vaguely familiar – enough to enable me to add a personality, an image to the voice, an unseen but known face.

Miki! It couldn't be! I rubbed my sore head, searched out the dark corner of the hut with pain-filled eyes and cried, 'Siloma! You all right, Siloma? Did the bastard hurt you?'

'No hurt me, *tuan* blond. This man your friend.'

Miki! Couldn't be! Couldn't be!

'He's a Jap,' I said savagely and to the man, 'What the hell do you want? Kill us? Get it over with, for Chrissake. What are you waiting for?'

'I want to help.' A hiss of friendship. It *was* Miki.

'By hitting me like you did?'

'By letting you kill all my men,' he whispered softly. 'I watch you, I do nothing, I could have killed you. But when you return here I had to hit you hard before you kill me. I see you in action – very professional, a change from old Johnnie.'

'Thanks to you lot,' I said bitterly, still not trusting. 'I can see you now. Find it hard to believe it is you. But what's the game? And whatever it is, this girl, Siloma, she's not the enemy of the Japanese, so let her go. Kill me if you like – I'm your enemy. But the girl. That's a favour I ask you.'

'You can go too.'

'Tell that to the marines! What are we waiting for? The Kempetei?'

'Wait for no one. Here,' he took the revolver he had been holding in his right hand and put it on the floor between us. 'Take it. It's loaded. I no use it against you. If you hate all Japanese, you kill me. Very welcome.'

I left the gun on the rush-strewn floor. 'Then what?'

'I explain,' said Miki. 'I am sent to kill you, but I cannot do this.'

'Why the generosity?' I gave a short laugh.

'You old friend.' My eyes were getting clearer now, the pain receding. I could see him more clearly, very different in

590

uniform from the white-clad figure chasing tennis balls at Queens.

'Siloma,' I asked her, 'Any hope of a drink? Maybe limes?'

'*Bodohkah dia?*' To Miki her question might have sounded innocent, but she was asking, 'Is he stupid?'

'No, *sekali-kali tidak*,' I replied, '*Sebaliknya dia pintar*.' When she realised that he was in fact rather clever she got up and added, 'I will also bring more water to bathe your head again.' She rose, uncoiling herself with ease and grace. I turned to Miki; a million questions bubbled in my brain, but one was predominant, thrusting the others into the background; how was it possible for this one man, this Miki I had known for years, this man who had introduced me to Irene, how was it possible for this man out of millions of Japs to be here? 'It's an impossible coincidence,' I said.

'No coincidence. You known to Japanese as heroic guerilla, all very frightened of you. You Number One on death list.'

'I'm flattered,' I said dryly. 'But that doesn't explain a damned thing. Why you? You don't look like the head of a killer squad sent to eliminate a British officer. It's not so simple as a coincidence. What the hell's happening?'

'I volunteer —'

As he started to explain a horrifying thought struck me. 'Did you burn this village? Because if you did —' I reached for the gun.

'No, no, no. I no live this area. I head of civil reconstruction admin in Ipoh. I no fight. I build. Intelligence and admin. Very important.'

'Then what the hell are you *doing* here? Why aren't you in Ipoh?' There was something fishy. I was focusing better now, though shaking my head from time to time like a dog recovering from an unexpected kick.

Siloma returned with mugs of lime, the water warm but refreshing. She bathed the superficial wound on my head again. As I watched Miki drinking slowly I was thinking, he hasn't killed us so far, so perhaps he really is going to let us live. Even the loaded revolver was safely between us.

'What are you planning? What are you thinking about?' I drained the last of the lime juice and handed the mug back to Siloma.

'Tennis at Queens.' His face wore a sour, bitter smile. 'The world is mad! How can Japan conquer whole world? How beat America?'

'You shouldn't start these things,' I couldn't help saying.

'I know. We start. But still – Japanese people very proud, like British. Americans drive us into corner, must fight. You would fight if Americans say to your king, no oil for you.'

'No sense in arguing,' I said. 'I'm still waiting for you to tell me why this meeting isn't a coincidence. What did you mean, you volunteered?'

'I never kill a man in all my life. All the same' – a polite hiss – 'I volunteer to kill you.'

'I was always told never to volunteer for anything in the army,' I said. 'What happened? And by the way, what's the date?'

'Today is August the sixth,' said Miki.

'It's not possible,' I said slowly, turning to Siloma. 'Altogether it's nearly seven weeks since I arrived here first.'

'You very ill, *tuan* blond, everyone think you die.'

Nearly two months! What, oh what had happened to Ara, to Tony, to Sergeant-major Macmillan? Where were they all, why had they not tried to find me? I tried to push the fears and doubts into the back of my mind, to concentrate on the present, on the best way of getting away, of finding for myself what had been going on during my absence. 'Missing, presumed dead.' Had a 'missing' message gone to Colombo? To Julie? No, of course not. If the Ara squad was in disarray no one would send any messages likely to give information to the Japs if they intercepted.

'Go on,' I said to Miki. 'Tell me what happened.'

It was quite simple really – and it was no coincidence. Miki had been summoned to the conference of high-ranking officers at Ara – the conference of which Colombo had given us advance warning. But it had *not*, as Colombo thought, been called to organise resistance or massacre if the Japanese faced defeat. Hardly any of the officers attending it were from fighting units. The Mikis of the Japanese army were meeting to discuss coordination in civil administration.

'Everyone know about you – Japanese even know you by name since Satoh killing and we all warned, be careful. And then when you attack us –'

'Hey! Wait a minute,' I protested. 'I didn't attack you. I had nothing to do with it. I've been stuck in the jungle, almost dead for weeks. Remember?'

'Know now. But did not know then. Now glad, now conscience clear at letting you go free. But anyway, we were attacked, and seventeen high-ranking officers of Emperor tortured, most burned alive.'

So now I knew. That bugger Kai-shek had beaten Tony to the punch and gone on the rampage against a bunch of pen-scraping officers – and after that, just what I feared. The Japs had gone mad with rage. And among other things had wiped out Siloma's village.

Miki confirmed my thoughts. 'Japanese very angry. I escape with many others, but Kempetei take over and order big purge, kill hundreds to teach lesson. Mad, mad, everyone mad.'

'But you – why are you of all people here?'

Miki explained. He was an intelligence officer. He had an unrivalled knowledge of prewar Singapore. And when my modest exploits started worrying the Japs someone riffling through his files realised that Miki was the man who had cleverly manipulated the Dexters into building barracks for Japanese troops. It had even earned him a promotion, he said.

Even so, Miki was not involved in any operations around KL – in fact he was preparing to return to Ipoh – until the Japanese patrol which had set fire to Siloma's village reported back to camp. One man carried an unusual souvenir – my identity disc, which he had found, wrenched from its string, *before* the village had been burned. Apparently it was lying in the village street. The officer picked it up and realised immediately from the torn string that I had lost it by accident. There was an immediate outcry for a killer squad to hunt me down.

The Japanese had had a hunch that I was ill – for several reasons. The guerilla assault on Ara, led by Kai-shek, bore all the marks of a Chinese-led attack without British supervision. We killed all the men we could, but we did *kill* the enemy. The officers at Ara had suffered no such merciful end. To a man they had been tortured, dropped into their own Jap traps and doused with petrol. Others had been staked out and left to the ants. The manner in which the raid was carried out, the torture (well deserved for most Japs, but strictly against Standing Orders) indicated the work of Chinese with a lust for cruelty. It was a strange fact but each guerilla unit had over the years established its own hallmark. Trained observers could tell almost immediately which unit had been employed on a raid, who had led it. The Japanese were quick to grasp that this was not the work of Major Dexter, or of any British officer.

'So everyone know you not in camp at that time,' explained Miki, but one fact worried the Japanese Intelligence. If I was really such a 'great heroic' figure I must be cool and efficient too, and therefore I couldn't have just lost such a damning piece of evidence as my ID tag and left it in the street for anyone to find. It didn't fit in with the character they had built up about me. Therefore, as Miki explained, 'They know you not stupid, therefore you very ill, too ill to travel far, too ill to know you lose your disc. So maybe you hide near this kampong. I volunteer to kill you because then perhaps I can save my friend in mad stupid war. Everyone pleased as I am only man in camp who know your face by sight.'

He had arrived in the dead of night, had watched all that had happened the following dawn – the killing of the sentry, the bloodbath as I sprayed the men bathing.

'I feel most guilty at sacrifice of men, an offence against dignity of Japanese army. I plan to commit *hari kiri*, but then as I watch, I suddenly think – if you kill *all* Japanese soldiers, maybe both of us can live.'

To save my life, and his own, Miki realised that he had to make certain that I did not kill *him*. So he had crept into the hut while I was by the river, threatened Siloma into silence, and waited to cosh me before I killed him.

'Thanks, Miki,' I said a little awkwardly, for though he had justified everything, even sacrificed his own men, I still wanted to kill every Jap I could – except perhaps Miki. And there was Siloma's life to thank him for too. He was unaware that she had saved my life, but he hadn't killed her. 'And thank you for the life of Siloma too,' I said. 'Now what? What about us – and you? How are you going to explain –' I waved vaguely in the direction of the blood-stained river.

'You go with lady,' said Miki. 'Find your brother officers. For me, I don't know. On reflection, not possible for me to live.'

'You can't stay here. They'll come looking for the squad.'

'Then I die. Different kind of honour! Maybe' – with a toothy grin – 'maybe not much difference between British officer code and Japanese *bushido* code. Honour very important.'

'Isn't life worth more than honour – sometimes?' I was thinking of Paul urging me to escape from Singapore with Julie, asking me, wasn't Julie worth more than my word of honour to Shenton Thomas and his government as they led us headlong to disaster?

Miki shook his head. 'Honour important. Death not important. Death only terrible if you aware in advance. You go now, find your friends. Future uncertain, so you happy. Maybe shot later, chance of war, but you don't know, so you happy. I die here, for if I go back to camp for me terrible shame. So death can be happy occasion.'

I was silent for a moment, thinking. 'I can't take you with me, Miki. But I can't send you away to be tortured. Are you sure you don't want to kill me?'

'Never, I your friend. Good times had by all at Queens, eh?'

'Yes indeed. Long time ago, Miki.'

'You my friend too.'

'You know I am.'

'Then' – he pointed eagerly to the gun – 'you do me honour of killing me.'

'Don't be so bloody daft!' As the Yorkshire word jumped out of my throat I almost laughed. 'I'm not an executioner.'

It was Siloma who suggested a solution. Why shouldn't Miki do what we had done – hide in the jungle? With the difference that he could take food, he was fit, he would be able to make it to the camp Yeop had told me about but which I had been too ill to reach. Both of us felt that enormous developments were imminent in the war, and though Japan could fight on for years Malaya might soon be liberated, at which time Miki could become a POW. Meanwhile some of the bodies in the river would probably have sunk or been washed downriver by the time the Japs came looking for them, so Miki would be presumed killed in an ambush.

I pointed to the far bank of the river, then to the shallow dugout canoe.

'You have your gun and food. You just wait over there in the jungle. Everyone will think you are dead, and when Malaya is liberated – and I have a feeling that won't be too long now the Japanese have lost the Philippines – well, come out. Give yourself up. Become a POW.'

We argued for a little while, but the idea obviously appealed to him. He certainly seemed to think it preferable to death – after seeing how I felt about life, perhaps. Finally he decided to go.

'Maybe war over soon,' he said. 'Hitler dead. Germans beaten. Soon Japanese must say "Sorry."'

'I think it will take the Americans a little time to accept your apologies for Pearl Harbor,' I said.

As he got up, looking rather ridiculous in his badly-cut breeches, he gave Siloma a solemn bow and said, 'Before I go I apologise on behalf of Emperor of Japan for bad conduct of Japanese troops in this beautiful village. Please to remember not all Japanese bad men. Some good. Some feel sense of disgrace.'

I found it hard to believe his words, though I didn't doubt

that he meant them honestly. But then, if all Japs revelled in brutality what about Kai-shek? And who knows how many happily married, law-abiding British citizens, suddenly given a gun and a bayonet and a brutal enemy – who knows how many had taken their revenge in ways that would never bear scrutiny?

'I accept apology,' said Siloma gravely. '*Tuan* blond tells me one day my country free – and we may meet again.'

'It is my earnest hope,' said Miki. 'But how many generations must we wait?'

Siloma looked at me and said, 'Do not ask *me*! All I know is *whatever* happens Singapore and Malaya never the same again.'

'Maybe some good for Asia come out of Japan?' Miki sounded hopeful.

'Well – I wouldn't tell that to Mountbatten,' I retorted as he got into the boat and pushed off. 'War soon over,' were his last words as he paddled away.

'I hate all Japanese,' said Siloma watching him grow smaller, 'but he not like others.'

'They never are,' I sighed. 'The trouble with the Japanese is that the only nice ones are the ones you know.' I thought for a moment. 'I don't suppose we'll ever see him again. Sitting it out there! We haven't even got plans yet to invade Japan.'

I knew before I tried to persuade her that nothing would stop Siloma from going now to search for her husband. But we had to hurry, to get away before any nearby Japanese patrols started worrying about their missing men.

After Miki had left, she said simply, 'He my husband, and you no like me if I no go to him.'

'No, I wouldn't,' wondering as I looked at her, young and desirable – though sex was far from my mind at that moment – whether with a twist of irony one of our enemies had prevented me from 'lying with her', as Siloma had so elegantly put it.

A few minutes later she prepared some food – cold rice,

cold curried chicken, fruit, water – and made her grave goodbyes.

'We will meet again, *tuan* blond,' she said by the hut. I could not fathom in those dark, wide eyes whether she was happy, relieved, sorry, that we had been interrupted.

'*Kau harus percaya kepada, Tuhan,*' she said.

'And you trust in God too.' I kissed her lightly before she strode off one way, and I, pack on back, compass in hand, set off to find Ara.

I didn't know then, of course, on that warm, tropical, bloodstained morning, so filled with incident, that on this date which Miki had told me was 6 August 1945 an American plane, loaded with a single bomb, was already returning from a raid. Its target, at eight-fifteen local time, had been a Japanese city called Hiroshima.

Eight days later the war was over, and before the end of the month I was back in Singapore, where a sergeant cut my orders to fly to the UK – with a stopover in Colombo.

PART SIX

Singapore and Malaya, 1945–1948

News of the victory came to me from the cheering passengers of a rattling country bus painted in nursery colours, as I stood, wondering what to do, near the path entrance to our base camp at Ara. For our sentry had been murdered – and no one could reach the camp without a jungle guide. The man had been shot in the back of the head: I could tell by the way the bones were smashed in the skull. And some weeks previously, judging by the way the flesh had been eaten away by ants.

I didn't know what to do, specially as there was an uncanny quietness in the countryside, a complete absence of any Jap patrols. After all, this *was* a main road. Something had happened. It should have been busy with traffic. Instead, the empty roads, the lack of noise, had an inexplicable, ominous quality.

Then I heard the sound of a vehicle approaching. I scurried behind some ferns in the beluka. The bus came nearer. The passengers were singing and cheering, without a care in the world, almost as though the Japanese had gone.

Then it dawned on me. The Japanese *had* gone!

Concealment was ridiculous. I jumped out into the roadway waving my arms – a scarecrow with straggling blond beard, hair over my shoulders, clothes falling off my back.

Anxious hands helped me, clapped me on the back. A Chinese offered me a cigarette, a Malay a sip of rice wine from an old medicine bottle.

'Jump in!' someone cried.

'What's happened? Where are you going?' I asked.

'Jalan ini menuku ke Kuala Lumpur!'

'I know it goes to KL,' I said. 'But is it safe?'

And that is how I learned the war had ended.

The bus dropped me at the Spotted Dog which had been taken over by a handful of British officers. The padang was jammed with Japanese prisoners. There, for the first time, I learned of the atom bombs which the Americans had dropped on Hiroshima and Nagasaki.

The club secretary's office had been transformed into a reception centre. And since almost the only officers were members of Force 136, together with an advance guard of Mountbatten's regular forces who had been parachuted in, the sergeant-major behind the desk knew all our names, even had two messages waiting for me, and a warm welcome. 'We were getting worried about you, Major. Sergeant-major Macmillan asked me to let him know when you turned up. And here's a message I think will please you, sir.'

It was an open SG signal from Chalfont in Colombo, telling me in spare, official terms that I had been awarded the DSO. I *was* pleased. The second message was from Tony Scott, a scribbled, 'Hope you turn up, Johnnie. I've got a special dispensation to take a squad to Ara and see how the estate is. Want to get back to work!'

I had a shave, a haircut, a shower, and was fitted out with clean jungle greens – the only uniform available – and even a strip of ribbon. Then, Macmillan turned up, also spruce and shaved.

'It's a wee bit better here,' he said.

'Are you all right?' I was anxious to hear his news, still not quite able to grasp the fact that the fighting was now over.

I managed to get a signal through to Chalfont requesting permission for Macmillan and me to report as soon as possible at Colombo and received an almost immediate reply, telling me where to check in at Singapore for movement orders. Macmillan had already 'borrowed' a Japanese scout car.

We had a last look round the kampong, crowded with thousands upon thousands of Japanese, like yellow penguins on the edge of a sundrenched Antarctica.

'Rather changed their tune now,' I observed to Macmillan as we watched the abject prisoners who had discovered that dishonour was preferable to standing up and being counted – by machine guns.

Then we set off for Singapore, a heady drive of nearly two hundred and fifty miles, during which Macmillan explained why he and Tony had never arrived back at camp. They had found the body of the 'tapper' when they reached the entrance to the jungle – the same body that was still there when I arrived, left there almost as a warning.

'I wouldn'a be surprised if that heathen Chinese commander didn'a murder him to make sure we couldn't return and stop him.' I was inclined to agree.

On the way down we bypassed Seramban, stopped for a meal of sorts at Segamat and finally drank a warm beer at a small shop in Kulai, only a few miles from Johore Bahru. I had a sudden need to stop and think, almost frightened of what I might see in Singapore; afraid I might be disappointed, that the image I had carried in my mind all these years might no longer exist. How could anything remain the same after over three years of enemy occupation? Surely the Japanese must have changed the skyline, torn down buildings, erected new ones, left their own horrible imprint on the city?

Astonishingly, all my fears were groundless. Everything was almost as it had been on the last day when Macmillan took me to Tanamera – on the surface anyway. Perhaps the never-changing weather helped to foster an illusion of sameness – the sun, the pelting rains. Or perhaps it was because Singapore was a port and so its contours were not easy to redraw in a few years – Keppel Harbour, the hot shimmering outlying islands, the waving palms, the pewter-coloured gas tanks, the unchanging apparatus of dockland. Such a terrain could no more be changed than the smell of the Singapore River, still cluttered with sampans, with agile boat owners still hopping from one floating family to a neighbour, with skinny old ladies still cooking rice and fish over charcoal stoves on deck. It gave me a comfortable feeling of welcome home; a feeling duplicated particularly among the thousands of internees stumbling out of Changi, their prison for over three years.

Among the first men I met in Singapore was Tim. The way to the East Coast Road – the quickest way into Singapore city – passed the ugly entrance gates to Changi. Macmillan was driving when, in an orderly queue waiting for transport, I saw Tim. He looked a rag-bag, eyes sunk into hollow cheeks, hair grey and thin. I told Macmillan to stop.

'Want a lift?' I jumped out.

The figure stared at me almost vacantly. 'Thanks, waiting for transport,' he mumbled, screwing up his eyes as he watched me. He didn't even recognise me.

For a second I thought he might fall, but rather to my surprise no one among the group of officers next to him made any move to help him. Indeed, they hardly seemed to notice he was there. Instinctively Macmillan held out a helping arm. Angrily – angry for what reason? – my brother tore his arm away with a frosty, 'Thank you, Sergeant-major, I'll let you know when I require assistance.'

Still the same old bad-tempered sod!

'Tim!'

He peered round shortsightedly. I realised that years of malnutrition must have affected his eyesight. He couldn't recognise me – but then of course I *was* in uniform, and he had never seen me in uniform in his life. Association of ideas made him think this was a stranger.

He looked closer. 'Did you call me Tim?'

That was Macmillan's greatest moment – after being snubbed.

'May I present Major John Dexter, DSO.'

Tim's eyes narrowed still further. He put his face closer to mine and muttered, bemused. 'Good God! You! Johnnie – DSO – *Major?*'

'Come on, jump in.' This time he accepted my arm. 'I'll drop you wherever you have to report.'

He clambered in. 'You in the army – you of all people!'

'Well,' I said cheerfully, 'you're the one who told me to join up.'

He looked terrible, though he had kept his hair short and had obviously shaved regularly. But, watching him surreptitiously as we bowled along in the direction of the Swimming Club, I suddenly felt fat and sleek next to this bag of bones. Of course I wasn't, I had lost more than a stone since I joined up, but in comparison –

'Want to stop for something to eat?' We passed the occasional food hawker's barrow.

'No thanks.' He shook his head. 'I was fine until a few months ago. Then I was shoved into solitary. But – how did you get here?'

'Arrived an hour ago. I'm here for a couple of days then hope to leave for Colombo – my HQ.'

'Colombo.' I could sense the change in his attitude immediately. 'Oh, I see,' as though that explained the kind of armchair soldier I was; until, suspicious, he asked, 'But the gong – you don't get the DSO for duties at HQ?'

'No, Tim. I never left Malaya.'

'What the hell do you mean? It's been three years!'

'Well – I've been here all the time – fighting.'

He looked sceptical. 'After Singapore fell?'

I nodded. 'Sergeant-major Macmillan and I have been teasing the Japs behind their lines. In the jungle. Sort of guerilla stuff.'

'All these years,' he repeated slowly. 'But the training?'

'It was very hush-hush. In fact I joined up in 1941 – before you returned to Singapore. Only I couldn't tell you.'

'So all the time you were pretending to be a civilian – you were lying to me?'

'I wouldn't put it that way. Security is the name of the game. I *had* to look a mug in front of everyone – I wasn't even allowed to wear uniform – and I *was* under secret orders.'

Poor Tim was absolutely deflated. He must have had a terrible time in Changi, his eyesight only one symptom of the sickness that swept the camp. But even so I wouldn't have been human if I hadn't enjoyed a brief moment of revenge for all the times he had forced me to race against him at Tanamera when he knew I could never win against an older boy.

We dropped Tim at his depot from where he and his colleagues would go for a hospital checkup before sailing on a trooper to England. Then I presented myself at the Adelphi – the Force rendezvous point – and was told to report with Macmillan at Seleter airport in two days. I got a message through to Chalfont, asking him to let Julie know. Then I went to see how our old friends had fared.

First we drove up to the Cadet House. I felt sure that Li – if he were still alive – would go there once it was safe. As we turned left at the top of Orchard Road towards Nassim Hill, sweating in the hot morning sun, Macmillan said, 'It's a wee while since we last drove along this wee lane, sorr.'

'Nothing *seems* to have changed.' My heart was beating – anticipation mingled with memories of Julie – as we swung right and into the slight incline. Nothing *had* changed – except that I had been robbed of more than three years of my life with Julie.

The lallang was neatly trimmed, the beds of cannas clean and tended, the gravel drive weeded. As we crunched to a stop out came Li, a little older, a few more wrinkles, but still upstanding and with the same beatific smile turning his face into a full moon of pleasure.

'Everything ready, *tuan*,' he smiled. 'I come as soon as I can to clean up.'

I wanted to hug this faithful friend. Indeed I did grab his shoulders, and I think only the presence of Macmillan stopped Li from showing more emotion.

We went inside. Everything was in immaculate condition, but then Li explained that we had been lucky. The Cadet House had been requisitioned as the personal home for a high-ranking Japanese officer. He had stolen nothing, looked after the furniture, even repainted the old dining room with its ugly heavy chairs – as though he planned to remain in residence for a long time.

I walked upstairs into the bedroom where Julie and I had spent so many wonderful nights, the verandah where we sat each evening. This was the moment when I decided that as soon as Julie and Pela arrived we would start our life again in the Cadet House. It had been our first home, and how happy we had been. Why not make it our second home?

But if the Cadet House had been well looked after the same was not true of the office in Robinson Road, which had been used as a barracks. Most of the old furniture had been thrown out – those beautiful Dickensian desks, with their brass rails! – and the place was filthy. Two or three Eurasians from the old staff had arrived and were wondering what to do. There was no sign yet of Ball whom I presumed had been interned in Changi. The place was a pigsty, and when Macmillan saw me almost grinning he looked at me enquiringly.

'I was wondering what my father would say if he saw this mess. He'd blow his top.' Papa Jack always kept the offices spick and span, but in their haste to surrender the Japanese had left behind everything – eight cot beds in my father's office, four in mine, their lockers, doors swinging half open, meals half eaten as though they had run for their lives without time to finish them, bolting from a landlocked *Marie Celeste*. The shower which I had last seen when we washed Julie after the Alexandra massacre was no longer working. The loo next door was filthy and stopped up. Desks, chairs, typewriters – all had vanished.

I fell to wondering where we would get new office equipment. According to the BBC England might be victorious, but she had bankrupted herself in the process. There was no machinery, enormous bomb damage, and rations were now tighter than during the war. (If you wanted a good meal, said the radio, you had to go to France where abject defeat and sullen occupation had hardly affected the size of black market meals.)

The journey to Robinson Road made me realise that I would have to cut my trip to London short if I wanted to get the business back on its feet again. The visit to Tanamera – a desolate shell, only the front walls standing – made me see that rebuilding the old family home would have to wait. One thing I *did* want to see: the dog's cemetery near the jungle fringe, to make sure the wooden cross bearing the name Vicki was still in position. It was, and the thick untended lallang over the cache of dollars had obviously not been disturbed for years. If Macmillan found my interest in a dead dog a little strange I did not enlighten him. I am sure he found my conduct much more natural when I paid my respects to Grandpa Jack at the mass grave where we had buried him after the bombing of Tanamera.

So far I had been able to take pretty well everything in my stride. The very feeling of sameness – Raffles Place and Battery Road in the centre of the city, and in the outskirts the same orchids waiting to be picked on Bukit Timah Road – all had helped to cushion me against change.

Then I went to visit the Soongs.

Paul got up to greet me when I entered the big circular grey room – and for one awful moment I thought it was his father. Paul was my age – a mere thirty-two – but he looked fifty. His face was old, the skin hanging round the top of his neck in pouches. He moved with such difficulty he looked brittle enough to snap. The slightly olive skin which had given him an Italian look had turned into the kind of grey that invariably clothes sickness. Above the wrinkled face the once shining black hair was the colour of ashes.

For a moment I stood there not knowing what to say. I prayed that my face didn't betray my feeling of horror; that and the realisation how easily we accept catch phrases without a second thought. When Tony parachuted into Ara and told me that Paul had been beaten up I imagined the kind of beating you get from thugs on a dark night; a split lip, a tooth knocked out, a few bruises. But this! The sight of this old man of thirty-two hinted at sinister torture and brutality on a scale I had never envisaged happening to someone I knew.

'Slowly recovering.' Paul had managed to retain a little of his old lazy smile.

'I'm so sorry, Paul. For Chrissake don't get up.' I tried a little feeble humour. 'I heard that you'd been writing love letters to the girls in Changi. But – God, Paul! – I'd no *idea* – you and Coulson, the PWD man, wasn't it?'

'That's right. But I'm the lucky one, I survived. Poor old Coulson – he copped it. After torture. Bit of a happy release really. He'd never have been fit again.'

I didn't know what to say except, 'Was it the radio they found?'

Paul nodded. 'The first time. You warned me about the direction-finders, remember? Damned right. Found the radio after seven months. Wasn't too bad that time: I got out after a month. But when they found out about my meetings with Coulson – not so good, Johnnie. Trouble is, I underestimated the enemy. We have an old Chinese proverb about reprisals, "Before you beat the dog, be sure to learn the master's name." I didn't – and the master's name was Kempetei. Rough buggers. Operated in Sime Road. Known better hotels. But Johnnie – tell me about Julie.'

There wasn't much to tell – except that she was safe in Ceylon; to which I added that I was going to see her, that we had a daughter, that we were going to marry when my divorce came through.

'Great,' said Paul. 'I could do with a brother-in-law. And I can tell you, Johnnie – getting her away was the finest thing you ever did for the Soong family. This place was requisitioned as a sergeants' club. God, it was more like a brothel. They not only brought the girls in from the town bordellos, they took our amahs. Raped them, every one. Julie would never have escaped.'

I had a sudden thought of Julie – her fate had she stayed on. And the terrors that must have been inflicted on the amahs, the girls, to say nothing of poor Paul – and his father.

'How *is* your father?' I was not only worried about his health, but a little apprehensive at meeting him. He must have found out about us, and Chinese have long memories. On the other hand I was no longer a child, I could stand up for myself – or walk out if he got nasty.

'I know he wants to see you. Heard a great deal of *your* exploits – local hero up at KL, I'm told. Don't worry about the old man. We're older now – and not only sadder, but wiser.'

That was how it turned out. P.P. looked very much the same, still grey and impassive, finding it hard to unbend, even to smile. But – somewhat to my surprise – I suddenly realised that he was thanking me for saving Julie with (for him) an almost effusive double handshake.

'And congratulations on your DSO,' he said.

'You got a gong?' Paul asked from the sofa.

'A very important one,' said P.P.

'Nothing really –'

'I don't consider Captain Satoh "nothing".'

'How on earth do you know that name?'

'The Chinese grapevine takes no account of foreign oc-cupation. I know a great deal. One day I will tell you how I learned. You might be surprised.'

The Soongs had obviously had a terrible time. When the house was taken over by the Japanese, P.P. and Paul were given three rooms over the back part. Much of the time Paul was under house arrest after the Kempetei released what was left of his body. Medical help for Paul was minimal, drugs virtually nonexistent, and it was only because P.P. Soong somehow managed to acquire a supply of drugs that Paul didn't die. They lived in squalor. Then suddenly, without warning, an order came from some high-ranking Japanese, the entire house was vacated, and the Soongs were able for the last few months of the war to try to lead some sort of normal life.

Rather awkwardly I said to Soong, 'I just want to say how sorry I am if Julie and I hurt you. I'm *not* sorry we fell in love, but telling lies, hurting you – for that I apologise.'

'The past has gone. We have to decide on the future. We must all try to live together. I was very angry, but then I thought how you saved my daughter from a terrible fate. This you did. Now tell me your plans.'

I explained that I was flying to Colombo the following day, to see Julie and the baby. I showed him a picture of Pela. After that – London, divorce and then we would marry.

What I didn't think it necessary to tell Soong was that in the meantime, during the divorce proceedings which could drag on for some time in the English courts, Julie and I would live at the Cadet House. I *said* nothing. But P.P. was Chinese and he said it for me. Silkily but firmly. And Paul backed him up.

'I forgive you for the past' – he still spoke in his rather precise English – 'but what happens in war is one thing. Now we are at peace and I cannot forgive the future if you tread the wrong path.'

'We *are* going to get married, you must believe that.'

'I do. But before marriage – I cannot have a daughter of the Soong family living openly with a married man. You must understand that. And I don't think your father would approve either.'

'But what about Pela? Surely that makes a difference? And if Julie agrees, as I'm sure she will?'

'She won't.' This time it was Paul who spoke.

'Think over carefully what you do,' said P.P., 'for you will see that I am right. There may be a way round the problem. But it does not consist of sharing the same house, even the same city. Not until the time is ready.'

As Paul explained after his father had gone, it was really a question of face, and however reluctantly I could see his point of view. She was the daughter of a famous family. If she lived with a married man – whatever the extenuating circumstances – she would be a concubine. Nothing more or less. 'And that's a hell of a drop in social status.' Paul sounded for a moment like his old humorous self. 'Julie *is* a Soong, you know – she'd never swallow it. Go to America, even England – that's okay, but here . . .' He left the sentence unfinished.

It was pointless for me to argue that really the damage was done, we had had an affair, we had produced an illegitimate daughter.

'That's not the same to the Chinese,' said Paul. 'It's the living together bit. Having a love affair and a child – that's wiped out by her self-sacrifice – in quotes! – and her devotion to her family. But she cannot become a kept woman.

And she'd never agree. I can tell you that, Johnnie.'

'We'll see,' I said. 'I'll be seeing her tomorrow. All I do know is that we've already been parted too bloody long. I'm not going through *that* again.'

As I was leaving Kai-shek came running down the stairs two at a time. It was the first time I had seen him since I left the Ara base camp for Yeop's compound, and though I would never forget the misery he had inflicted on scores of loyal friends by his bloodthirsty attack during my absence this was no time to bring it up. I said 'Hullo!' as civilly as I could.

'Good day, Major.' He looked as sinister as ever, all skin and bone, with repressed hate burned into his creased face. The 'major' was ironic, for he added, 'Only a few more days of uniform and then you'll be a civilian again.'

'And you too.'

'Perhaps not. Your part in the struggle may be over. But now the Chinese led by Loi Tek have got rid of the Japs, we must start kicking out the British. My struggle is not yet over.'

'Honestly, Kai-shek.' I couldn't help laughing. 'You do talk the most awful crap. Do you really think the British will let a bunch of Chinese Commies kick them out?'

'They let the Japs.'

'That was different. You may as well settle down and enjoy life.'

'Thank you, no. The days of our comradeship are over,' he said sharply. 'If we can't drive the British out then we'll kill them. Specially one.'

'Meaning me?'

'It would give me great pleasure.' He almost bared his teeth at the prospect. 'I said before the war that I would kill the man who dishonoured the Soong name — and I will.'

'You'll have to catch me first,' I grinned.

'I will — I promise you.'

I had little time to see many other friends, but at the Cricket Club, which I visited for old times' sake (only to find no drinks available) I ran into Bill Jackson.

'I saw Tim outside Changi,' I told him. 'My brother. In bad shape.'

'I heard about him.' He hesitated. 'The army chaps were kept in a separate camp from the civilian internees, but some of us did meet from time to time. I saw your brother in the distance – about six months ago. He looked quite fit then.'

'Beriberi is a tough disease.'

He looked at me oddly, then said slowly, 'It is.'

There was a note of scepticism in his voice, yet Jackson was the most straightforward man in Singapore. 'Are you trying to tell me something?' I asked.

'It's none of my business. Unless it's better to hear from me than – well, rumours later.'

'Go on.'

'He had a bad time, but only at the end. Short rations, beatings – the usual stuff. Solitary.'

'Why did they single him out?'

Jackson shrugged his shoulders. 'The entire camp knows – there were about fifty of them. Your brother was found out – just unlucky –'

Of course I knew what he was trying to tell me. 'With another man?'

Jackson nodded. ''Fraid so. In circumstances – well, no one could deny it.'

Poor Tim. The past was catching up with him quickly.

40

Julie had been living near her hospital in the mountains at Kandy, Mountbatten's headquarters, but for the ten days of my visit someone had lent her a small bungalow behind Mount Lavinia, a few miles outside Colombo. It was like a picture postcard cottage, the walls trailing with bougain-villaea and the tiny garden crawling with bright blue morning glory before the sun's heat closed up the petals for the day. No one – not even a millionaire, not even Julie's favourite poet – could have found a more idyllic retreat for two lovers meeting after years apart.

The wonder of seeing Julie again, of lying in her arms, touching her, kissing her, waiting in an ecstasy of anticipation before loving her, did not need to be decked out with such poetic trimmings. From the moment I saw her waving, as I climbed down the rickety airport steps, I could tell – by the gesture of waving with abandon instead of waiting decorously – that she was unchanged.

So many times I had mentally rehearsed this moment of meeting, anticipated it, savoured it, lived it down to the final detail, wondering if there would be any shyness born of years apart. Would she have altered, even by the simple process of becoming more mature, a mother, so that she would no longer have the carefree laugh and happy smile that in themselves could make me desire her physically? It was that first wave – an intense gesture, as though shouting with her hands, 'I'm *here*! You've *got* to see me!' – it was that wave which told me louder than any words that Julie was the same.

Sometimes in the jungle I had woken in a cold sweat during a nightmare in which she had left me – always for Kai-shek. But now, with one gesture, all doubts fled. The gentle love letters which had fortified me with each air drop – letters to which I could never reply – had not lied.

In one sense it was as though we had never parted. She looked the same – no older, no lines, no wrinkles – 'Even though I'm an old lady of thirty' – she laughed – the same dancing eyes, the generous mouth, the pale, beautiful skin, the long, jet-black hair falling over her shoulders – I felt a pang of jealousy at the thought of the years other friends had been able to feast their eyes on Julie's beauty. How had they been able to keep their hands off her? And how had she, with that generous giving mouth, how had she been able to hold them off?

The moment passed. As I strode across the tarmac, returning her wave, it was almost more than I could do to stop running, to behave with the restraint of a major in uniform. I went through the customs, a mere formality, then I was in her arms, hugging her, kissing her, forgetting the people around me, even Macmillan waiting not far away. Then I looked for the first time at Pela – eyes exactly the same as Julie's, dark pools, only these were not yet dancing. They watched me gravely, forcing a kind of politeness out of her.

Strangely, I did have a different feeling to that which I had expected. I was the one who had changed rather than Julie, and at first I could not pin down what the change was. Desire was undimmed; indeed it had increased. But I could wait for that, happy in the knowledge that it was worth waiting for, but that in the meantime I could behave quite normally; I did not realise the wonderful thing that *had* changed me; this was no longer a reunion between two furtive lovers, but between a happily married couple. At least that is what it seemed like to me.

Pela's tall straight-backed Singhalese amah walked behind us with the elegance of one to whom balancing a load on the head was something done without thinking. Now she took the hand of Pela as I introduced Macmillan and Julie told him, 'I've a message for you, Sergeant-major, from Colonel Chalfont, who has told me so much about you. He's sent transport to take you to Kandy.' And to me she added, 'Robin says you've got to report, of course, but you can wait until the day after tomorrow.'

We had so much to talk about, so many years to relive, so much loving to do. That first night we had an early meal, and once the baby had said goodnight to me – a touch of suspicion in those big black eyes – and was tucked in, we went to bed.

Because of the long, different lives we had led since our last meeting – each one unable to comprehend even remotely how the other had been living – our coming together was like the night we had been reunited at Tasek Layang, when we had driven off to the small house outside Changi and fallen into each other's arms in the garden – the night the war came to Singapore.

No, it was not *quite* the same. Then we had fought from

the first — fought to please each other. Now it was quieter. I suppose it was because we were a father and a mother now, the baby asleep in the next room, an 'old married couple', as Julie said smilingly, in truth if not in fact. All these circumstances made us at first lie in each other's arms with gentleness before the tender moments dissolved into an almost savage joining until finally, I was panting with the struggle to make our enjoyment equal, to hold back until she was aroused. Then after I lay beside her, head in the crook of her neck, one breast as a cushion for me, her hands travelled over my body as though exploring it all over again to make sure I was the same man.

'You're so thin,' she whispered, 'and your body is so hard. No,' she laughed softly, a wife to her husband, 'I'm not talking about our friend down there. Your muscles, all the roundness has gone. While having Pela made my tummy flabby.'

It hadn't, of course. Watching her lying there naked, pale gold body already stirring me again, I had forgotten how beautiful she was. Over the years my imaginings of her had been focused and funnelled by photographs which she had sent me. They were beautiful, but they lacked the depth, the changes of expression. I had forgotten the devil in her eyes, the warmth in her mouth. I stroked her soft tummy, pushing my fingers through her black secret hair, scratching her softly, then moving down to her thighs, damp now until, almost with a groan, I moved across her and, with the ease of an animal that has no need to guide itself when mating, slid inside her almost before I knew what was happening.

The next morning when the baby woke, and I could hear the amah shuffling around in the small bedroom behind the connecting door, Julie got out of bed while I was still half asleep and returned with Pela.

In bed, next to me, Julie's legs just touching mine, she bounced the grave-eyed little girl on the thin blanket that covered us, and as the baby looked at me, apparently with the interest of something new, never seen before in her mummy's bed, Julie explained softly, 'This is the moment

for Pela to realise how important you are — that you're her
father, in bed with her mummy, as though it's the most
natural thing in this world.'

She was adorable. Once the shyness had evaporated, once
she realised that I was not a monster come to break up the
happy relationship with her mother, Pela responded with
the same outgoing warmth as Julie.

'She's going to be a handful when she's older,' I said, and
suddenly for no reason thought of the day I had overheard
Grandpa Jack say just the same about Julie. 'Just like her
mama.'

'I'm no handful,' said Julie almost wistfully. 'I'm a natural
one-man girl, always have been. But *you*! Maybe she'll take
after you — and you *are* a handful.' Then, the baby playing
with my stainless steel issue wristwatch, she asked, 'Were
you faithful to me? I did tell you I didn't expect you to be,
but still —'

'Beloved, I was. Not only in my fashion — wasn't that
one of the poems you sent me? — but completely. I love
you, Julie — so much I can't begin to tell you. You're everything. You and now — little Miss Pela.'

During the day we went into Colombo, strolled across
the magic strip of green by the sea, leading to the Galle Face
Hotel where we had drinks to a palm court orchestra and a
background of red tabs. I had already told her about the
bombing of Tanamera, Paul, the rape of the amahs at her
home. And after the second Scotch (the headwaiter, a grave
Singhalese wearing a comb as a mark of status, had never
heard the word stengah) I outlined what I hoped would be
our plans for the future. After two weeks in London, during
which I would arrange divorce proceedings, I would fly
straight to Singapore to restart the business. I felt certain
Irene would put no obstacles in my way, that in her heart
she would never want to return to Singapore.

'Then,' I said hopefully, 'I think we should settle down in
the Cadet House. It's large enough, it's lovely, and we'll see
about rebuilding Tanamera later.'

I could see she was thinking, and I felt I must add, 'I do
have to tell you, darling, that though your father has for-

given us, he doesn't like the idea of you living with me until the divorce comes through. Personally, I think that's silly. We have a baby now – and this is no longer an affair, a joke – it's permanent.'

It was a cool evening and we wandered out into the garden by the side of the Galle Face's beautiful pool. I could see that she was worried.

'I wish I could say my father is wrong,' she said finally.

'But he's right, darling Johnnie.'

'But we can't just live apart! What the hell do I care what people say – if that's what you're afraid of.'

'It's one thing to live together here in Ceylon, where we're unknown – a kind of beautiful lost land of escape – but in Singapore, darling, where you're the *tuan*! Apart from me, what would they say about you?'

'They?'

'Yes. The great "they"! The "they" wives who if they had stayed in England would have been the wives of clerks commuting on the train every night. *You* know, darling. Once they reach Singapore, once their husbands get a label, they're the biggest snobs –'

'But darling' – I couldn't help laughing, she was so serious – 'I don't know any of these people. They don't exist.'

'They do. Everywhere.'

'But you'd dazzle them, Julie. If they really do exist they'd collapse at the sight of you.'

'How sweet. Still a romantic. The gallant major with a DSO! A super picture, I know.' She held my hand and added, 'But doesn't the picture become tarnished in the British mind when the gallant major takes a Chinese girlfriend and has a Eurasian child? Yes, yes, darling. That's what they'd say about us and our –' she let the rest of the sentence hang in the still tropical air.

I pointed out that life was changing. The Americans in the Pacific had introduced a new free and easy atmosphere.

'It *will* change,' she agreed. 'But the war's over – that means proving yourself all over again, as a civilian. Don't give yourself an extra handicap. It's going to be tough enough for the British to put our poor little island back on the map – especially if they want to keep it painted red.'

'But we can't live in different countries. It's absurd.'

'I've been thinking. If you agree, Pela and I could live at Ara.'

It was a wonderful idea. Since we couldn't tell how long the divorce would take – after all, proceedings hadn't even begun – we would compromise. If Natflat agreed Julie and Pela would live with them at Ara once it was reopened, and I could commute from Singapore each weekend.

'You're a genius.' I stooped down and kissed her.

Because I had volunteered, because Force 136 was a law unto itself, and because America was clamouring for rubber and tin, Chalfont had arranged for my immediate discharge.

'You'll have to go to London for the final papers,' he said, 'but then you'll be given a demob suit – free, gratis and for nothing by a grateful government. I'm told they only fit round the ankles, but you can't expect everything. After all' – with a sly look – 'we did look after your girl.'

'I won't forget, Robin. It's not that she needed money – her family's got plenty of that – it's knowing that while I was in the jungle she had friends – you know, having the baby, a job to do, keep her mind off things. Even off other men.'

'I don't think you need ever have worried about other men.'

'Hope not. Sounds bloody conceited. Tell me, what are your plans?'

We were lunching on the verandah at the Officers' Club at Kandy, cool and beautiful amid the mountains, with the dark shining green tea gardens like waves in the surrounding hills, the bushes curling round every bend in every road as though to garner the precious harvest from the last square inch of soil. We promised that our friendship, started so strangely in the Adelphi, would be undying. He was, he said, going back to London's Special Branch.

I wondered – and I dare say the same thoughts flickered through Chalfont's mind too – if the friendship *would* last, if I *would* telephone him for lunch if or when I visited London. Army friendships tend to be fragile, not only because you are afraid to become emotionally involved with someone who might die the next day, but because when friendships are carried forward the circumstances are so different it is not always possible to adjust easily. It was one thing to sweat out a war together in the jungle, but I suddenly realised that I had never seen Chalfont in civvies. And he had only seen me in white ducks or khaki. What would our reactions be when we met at Scotts in Piccadilly, both dressed in sober suits on a cold and foggy London night?

'Don't forget one thing when you leave for London' – he was always pragmatic – 'I've got you VIP treatment – and that means plenty of baggage. So load yourself up with grub for your wife and family. No uncooked meat, but get Julie to half-cook some for you. They're starving over there. And cloth! Clothes are still rationed. You can take a couple of suit lengths and some silk for the ladies. After all' – with his sardonic laugh – 'even though British officers don't get a millionaire's wages, you do have three years' pay due to you.'

We were just finishing our second coffee when a sergeant steward coughed an apologetic, 'Colonel, sir, there's a cable for Major Dexter.'

I took it and tore it open.

'Not bad news?'

'Not bad personally. It's from my father.'

I had given Papa Jack the address of Force 136 headquarters just in case of bad news. It was not personal bad news, but it was bad all right.

Poor Ball, who had never turned up at the office after I returned to Singapore, was dead. His widow, who had been evacuated before the Japanese attack, had never heard a word from Ball all the time he had been interned in Changi. Almost at the same time I reached Singapore she had received a cable telling her he had died in prison two years

620

previously. No one had been allowed to inform next of kin until after the liberation.

I had wondered about Ball, but so many had died, so many had suffered, that the impact of death was diminished except for close relatives. And bad news made one automatically think forward – to the consequences of that man's death. In other words, with Dexter and Company facing a bleak future before reorganisation, how would we replace Ball?

Papa Jack might come out, but he was too old to undertake day-to-day running. I would be too busy. Rawlings would presumably stay in England to run the London office.

Obviously I would have to cut short my stay in London, but that would be a relief. And since America was already crying out for rubber and tin I was sure that Chalfont would be able to arrange air transport from London to Singapore.

'The biggest problem will be finding a replacement.' I showed the cable to Julie when I returned. 'The technical side doesn't matter – anyone can pick up the drill in a few weeks – it's finding someone you can trust, depend on. Someone who won't fiddle or cook the books. Poor Ball.'

'As the future Mrs Dexter,' Julie loved to roll those two words round her tongue, 'I suppose I shouldn't start behaving like an interfering wife, but surely you've got the right man here in Ceylon. That nice man – Sergeant-major Macmillan?'

I grinned at her. He was just the man – unattached, and however much he might cherish the dream of returning to his beloved Scotland he was surely pragmatic enough to realise that the immediate future in Britain was bleak beyond words. A trip to see relations and friends was one thing; but it would be a very different matter for a man like Mac Macmillan to find a job that not only satisfied his urge for individuality but would be rewarded on a scale beyond any that could be offered in Britain.

He was easily persuaded. I telephoned Chalfont who sent Macmillan down to Colombo, and there I explained what had happened. He was a little apprehensive about his qualifications, but I told him not to worry. He could of course go to Scotland first for a few months' leave, but I think that what finally decided him (apart from the pay, which obviously delighted him) was the dreary picture of the conditions in Britain that we read about in the newspapers reaching Colombo. It wasn't the picture of bomb damage that upset us both, but the warning of shortages that politicians said would remain in a bankrupted Britain for years to come.

'I canna say I'm not a wee bit afeared,' he admitted. 'But I must gae to see.'

No man could fail to respond to the fact that he would quickly assume the title of Number Two – answerable to me only – with a couple of youngsters whom Papa Jack would choose, and send out to do the donkey work.

'It's a deal, sorr!'

'Not "sorr", Mac, never again. The army's dead and buried. You'll be a *tuan* when you come back. And if I know anything about the Dexters with their passion for nicknames I'll soon be known as Papa John.'

Macmillan was leaving for Britain on a troopship, and I had been allotted a seat on a Liberator. This time when I said goodbye to Julie it was almost with a light heart, for – after another six blissful days and nights in the bungalow – I knew I was leaving on a mission that would eventually bring us together forever.

Past partings had been burdened with sorrow. Now that emotion had been replaced with a kind of joy – joy in just being alive, no more killing, a time for gladness, for gratitude. Julie had been tender and loving, and even Pela, after watching her mother kiss me, suddenly screamed 'Me too!' and insisted on a kiss every time she toddled towards me.

True, there were still a few outstanding problems to be solved. Julie would have to wait until after my return to Singapore before I could discover the situation at Ara. I could not be sure whether Tony would be demobbed quickly. I did manage to send a cable to Natasha in New York, and received a reply that she planned to return to Ara as soon as possible. I hadn't asked her yet whether Julie could stay there, but I knew she would be delighted to have the company.

During those perfect days and nights, often as I lay in bed, she gently sleeping next to me, smiling quietly in her sleep, I tried to analyse my sense of happiness, that elusive fragile emotion. It had everything to do with rushing back into the arms of someone I loved, but very little to do really with the act of making love. No, that wasn't quite right; that was the ultimate expression of love, but not everything.

When you are young, I thought – how long ago since I felt young! – lovemaking, the passion and the pain, the delirious ecstasy, was more than an urgent physical need, it was the only way in which both of us, immature adolescents, could show our love to each other. But there was nothing to prove now. Time and separation, love's most sinister enemies, had proved everything for us. Lovemaking was now a wonderful bonus.

Perhaps this was why those few days in Colombo produced a feeling I had never known before, that of being *necessary*. The old passions still bubbled beneath the surface, ready to erupt the moment I touched Julie, but there was something else. I could never pretend that in my youth I had been overlooked by other people, parents, girlfriends, wife. In many ways Irene had always behaved very well to me, but only now did I realise, after this magical honeymoon in Colombo, that I was not *necessary* to Irene, I never *had* been once the wedding bells had saved the Bradshaw reputation. She liked me; but that was all.

And even in Tanamera, though I was loved, I had never been *necessary*. My parents loved me, they would have grieved had I died, and I loved them, but they had not *needed* me. I had an uncomfortable feeling that I was to blame. I had never needed *them* – or Irene – as I needed Julie, and one need fostered another. Perhaps this was why for the first time in my life I realised that two people looked to me as the one person in the world whom they trusted to bring them happiness.

41

The Liberator droned on high above the fields of Europe, edging through grey skys to England. Every bucket seat in the spartan aircraft, stripped of all nonessentials, was filled with troops of every size, shape and rank, all sitting upright, yet almost all sharing one common denominator: fatigue, furrowed on every grey, lined face. Heads nodded on chests, mouths fell open in snores. It was very uncomfortable – except to me. For me it was a magic carpet.

As we approached Northolt I pondered for the umpteenth time on the kind of reception I could expect. I hoped my uniform would at least make them realise I was an adult now – and not a kid who could be ordered around. Parents sometimes find it hard to notice the added years which the young acquire so painfully. And mine had been acquired more painfully than most. I wasn't thinking of the illness in the jungle when I had nearly died. Those things are soon forgotten. Experience of brutality – and inflicting brutality – is a disease which has more lingering after effects.

When I met Papa Jack, Mama, Irene, the kids, I would be nothing like the man who had said goodbye to them on the *Pacific Rover*. I had changed 'beyond recognition', as they say – except, I thought wryly, that I looked the same.

But would they know of that inner change, the family? Would they ever be able to realise what had caused that change? I wasn't thinking of the dangers – mine were no worse, no better, than millions of dangers shared by a mad world – but they *had* been different. I had always thought of war either as an assault or a defence in which you had to act quickly, a body of men for whom it really was do or die; or if not that then a battle at long range, like the impersonal bombing of a city or shelling of a ship five miles distant.

My war, though, had been different, more cold-blooded, a kind of murder to order. No one could live for several years in the jungle, hunting his prey like an animal, cutting throats, or making home-made bombs, and remain untouched by the experience, however normally one behaved on the surface.

And what of the family? Had they changed? Was my father too old to return to Singapore and restart a family business, or had the long spell in London changed him too, made him take the rain and fog and damp of the city for granted? Or would the pull of Singapore prove too much? And, above all, would he understand *my* pull – the pull that bound me to Julie? Surely in the war he must have seen coloured troops hobnobbing with whites? Or had he? I suddenly realised, as the plane droned on through a leaden sky, that perhaps he hadn't. Perhaps I had changed, but he and Mama hadn't. Not that it mattered, really; except that it would be more pleasant to return home without a row.

The children would be different. I couldn't visualise them, not even remotely. Ben must be seven, probably going to school and unable to recognise me. As for Catherine – I had never even seen a picture of her – she would be three-plus by now!

I landed in a miserable autumn drizzle. There were no taxis. An army bus took us from Northolt to a barracks on the Chelsea Bridge opposite the Royal Hospital. Chalfont had advised me to wear uniform, in his words, 'until the very last moment before they set you free'; and a Colombo tailor had run me up a couple of winter versions of the by now universal battledress. It helped.

Papa Jack and Mama had moved after VE-day from the Hyde Park Hotel to a flat in a small block in a tiny street called Sloane Terrace, off the bottom end of Sloane Street near the square, and noted mainly for a very busy Christian Scientist church. It was not far from Chelsea Bridge but there was no way I could walk the distance simply because of the food which weighed down my kitbag. It contained not only two ten-pound joints of beef – one for Mama, one for Irene – but tins of Australian butter, meat, sweets for

625

the children and bales of cloth. However, the major's pips –
perhaps the ribbon? – persuaded a corporal to run me
home, specially after I told him I lived only five minutes
away.

Two things shocked me when I reached home. I was appalled at the lines of age which war had inscribed on my
parents' faces. Papa Jack must have been sixty-five by now,
Mama ten years younger, but it wasn't only advancing
years that had mapped their faces with new wrinkles. The
blight and dreariness of war had only made me grow up.
But I of course had not been tormented with the worries of
parenthood; my children had been in America, Julie safe in
Colombo. To Papa Jack and Mama the lack of news about
their two sons must have done much to make them what
they were now – old and slightly crotchety, Mama
wandering vaguely round the flat.

After a life of luxury she now had only a daily who came
in each morning to do the rough cleaning of the three
bedrooms, the combined living and dining room, transformed into one long room by taking out the double frosted
glass doors. There was a large kitchen – where we ate most
of the time. Mama did most of the cooking – what there
was to cook, for rationing was indeed severe, and more
often than not they walked out, a sedate elderly couple, to
one of the small restaurants in the King's Road, saving their
food coupons for a minuscule weekend joint.

When over the days they outlined their life style to me,
my first reaction had been, 'Well, thank God you'll soon be
able to get back to Singapore. No shortages there!' I was
met with blank stares.

The second thing was wonderful: understanding both by
my parents and the next day by Irene. I had been dreading
rows, but from the start they at least understood that to me
Julie had always been, from the earliest days, more than a
passing infatuation. No one of course would admit that they
had behaved wrongly – we skirted delicately over the past;
but they did understand that there was no point in trying to
fight me. It was too late now for dire warnings about the

children of mixed marriages, that dreaded word Eurasians. I was the father of one.

Perhaps my parents' acceptance of a situation which I knew embarrassed them was helped because they both seemed genuinely proud of me. The way in which I had secretly enlisted, the cloak of secrecy which had made it impossible for them to know my sinister operations; even a visit from a red-tabbed Whitehall officer telling them that I was on 'a highly dangerous mission' all helped to invest me with an aura which embarrassed *me*. They hadn't the faintest idea how I had earned my gong, and no comprehension of the life I had led. When they asked, and I started to give them a few elementary explanations, Mama actually asked me, 'Were you able to go into KL, darling?'

'But Mama,' I almost laughed, 'Kuala Lumpur was under the Japs. They'd have slit the throat of any white man they saw.'

She seemed very worried at that; puzzling over how I got my supplies in order to live, which she probably thought of in terms of my favourite cigarettes or loo paper. Even Papa Jack was unable to absorb the fact that at times in the jungle we had lived on berries and boiled bamboo shoots.

'Must have been tough' – he was genuinely sympathetic – 'we had a lot of problems here. U-boats sank thousands of tons of shipping carrying food. I must say' – he turned to Mama for confirmation – 'The Hyde Park coped very well considering, didn't they?'

For a moment I toyed with the idea of telling them – with precise details – how Siloma had saved my life, but I resisted the temptation. Mama would probably think I had become a pervert.

I phoned Irene, apologising because I had been unable to let her know the exact time of my arrival. 'Military orders,' I laughed.

'I'm so glad you're back, Johnnie – and we're all so excited about your DSO. Ben wants to know if he can have a copy to show his friends at school. He's been given the day off tomorrow. We're all coming to Sloane Terrace to see you

I offered to fetch them, to go out to meet them, but it seemed they had already arranged to come in on the tube. There was a direct line between Wimbledon and Sloane Square. 'And that helps to save the petrol ration,' explained Irene.

Her voice on the phone – distorted as voices often are – seemed so soft and inviting that my heart started pumping violently – not with thoughts of the past, not with desire, but at the prospect that she might want to kiss and make up. That *would* be hell!

I needn't have worried. 'It's a great pity about you and Irene splitting up' – my father was cutting the roast beef as though he was scraping off gold leaf – 'but maybe it's for the best. She told me she much prefers England.'

'Has she – er – fallen for someone else?'

'What a disgusting thought!' said Mama. 'With you fighting for her. How could you think such a thing?'

'Well, it happens.' I was tempted – once again – to ask how Mama had reconciled her little extramarital fling in New York so many years ago, but didn't. 'Girls as well as men do need physical love,' I said mildly.

'It's very good of you to bring this beef, it's really delicious.' Thus she closed the subject of physical needs.

After dinner – which we ate at the unearthly hour of six-thirty, apparently a habit that had grown during the blitz – I suggested again that they should return to Singapore as soon as I could pull enough strings to get them a comfortable berth. As gently as possible I implied that nothing could be so awful as this miserable bourgeois existence, with Mama working like a drudge while a dozen servants would welcome her arrival in Singapore.

'We've rather grown to like London,' said Mama with a glance at my father, as though they had discussed the possibility of my urging them to return. 'We've made a lot of friends here. And we've had a cable from Tim. He'll be back by October. We must see him.'

'I didn't mean next week, Mama, but all this – no food, no servants. I don't believe people should run away from tough times. I'd despise anyone rich enough to go and live

628

in, say, California until the shortages stop. But you're different. Singapore is your home. It's the source of the money we're all spending now, this very moment. And for the rest of your lives. You came *here*, Papa, to help the war effort. You've done your bit – just as important as Tim's bit or mine. But now it's time to go home.'

'Tanamera's gone.'

'We'll rebuild it. The front walls are standing, I've got the ready cash to start building right away. It could be ready in a few months.' I told him about the dollars I had hidden – though not how I had acquired them. 'And there's a fortune waiting to be picked up in Asia. I'm sure of it.'

'We'll see.' Both temporised, and I realised that they didn't really *want* to go back to the city I loved with all my heart. They had become set in their London ways. They took the shoddiness of life – all of it new to me, shocking to me – in their stride, hardly noticed a kind of life which I suppose had being growing imperceptibly over the years. I didn't blame anyone for the misery around. Britain had played a magnificent role in the war. But they had played their part too. Now they should want to go home . . . Only now London was their home. They had changed, they had learned to accept the kind of life thrust upon them by war – a factor which all Britain had accepted ungrudgingly and which had been a major factor in standing fast all those years. It was second nature to them now, the life they lived. I thought of my father in the old days examining the heels of his shoes to see if they were as polished as the toecaps. Now I came across him shining his shoes himself, an old copy of *The Times* spread out on the kitchen table. I thought of the breakfast times when the old Swift, then the Buick, came round to the front of Tanamera. 'Don't need a car in London,' he said. 'Public transport is fine here, and if we go away we've got enough to hire a car.'

Got enough! He was very, very rich.

'But don't you miss Singapore – and the sun?' I asked Mama. 'Both of you? All the things we loved so much. Li – remember Li? – he's waiting for you. P.P. Soong too. And your friends all miss you so much.'

'There're the grandchildren, Johnnie. Ben – he needs a grandfather if you're not going to be here. And Catherine. She'll need a grannie.'

'But the Bradshaws will make good grandparents!' What horrified me was the way in which Mama used the word grannie. In the past she would never have permitted such a word. I remember her once saying to Natasha, 'When you have your first baby, don't start calling me "granma". I'm old enough as it is.' Now she was revelling in the word. I had a sudden thought. 'You're not staying away because of Julie?'

'Oh no!' Mama meant it, I could tell that, for she added, 'It's a little unfortunate. And the baby – such a funny name, Pela – is it – er?'

'White as snow,' I laughed. 'And believe me, Mama, by the time she's a teenager this sort of racial difference will all be forgotten. Malaya is bound to become independent in a few years. Both India and the Dutch East Indies had virtually been promised independence in 1947. You ought to be in Asia then. We're facing a time of great change – but peaceful change. The fighting's over. Now we're going to live again.'

'There could be fighting,' said Papa Jack. 'What about the Communists?'

'Political hot air! I've actually been with them in the jungle. They'll never fight. Nothing to fight for if we agree to independence for Malaya.'

'This chap Loi Tek – won't he be troublesome? Dangerous?'

'I wouldn't go into mourning if someone bumped him off,' I admitted. 'But nobody wants to start another war.'

'I read an article recently,' my father persisted, 'which suggested that the Communists fighting behind the Japanese lines had been hiding their weapons – machine guns and so on – threatening to start a wave of strikes, labour disruption and even fighting.'

'There could be strikes, but fighting? Why, Chin Peng, the guerilla leader, and Kai-shek – Soong's so-called son –

they've both been invited to the Victory Parade in London. Me too, though I won't be going.'

'You won't?' asked Mama. 'That does seem a pity.'

'Why not?' asked my father.

'Too busy. And I miss Julie, and' – with a grin that drew a disapproving frown from Mama – 'my Chinese daughter.'

'Don't mind if we turn in early?' asked Papa Jack. 'Nothing much else to do in the war years – rather got into the habit.'

'I'm sure Johnnie's very tired,' said Mama, and I was. We had a sip of Scotch from a carefully hoarded bottle. 'Scotch isn't actually rationed,' my father explained. 'But if you know someone you can get the occasional bottle.' I felt almost sad at the thought of the mighty Papa Jack settling for *one* bottle. Why, Papa Jack and his father before him were so powerful that they could get anything they wanted. London was different, war made a difference, of course I realised that. But my father had built up his business by the astute process of making the right friends. He helped them, they helped him. Hadn't this business instinct worked during the war – not for black market deals, but for un-rationed goods in short supply? Surely he knew someone who could let him have a *case*. The thought of my father scrabbling around for a bottle of Scotch saddened me im-measurably.

'Shall we go down to the office tomorrow?' he suggested. 'Morning? We can be back before Irene and the children arrive for lunch.'

'Fine.' I kissed Mama goodnight. It was nine-thirty p.m., and I had seen just about three quarters of a mile of London on this, my first visit to London since the day I was married.

The building next door to the Wren church in Piccadilly opposite Swallow Street was nothing more than a mound of bricks and mortar with wild yellow flowers miraculously sprouting out of the dust. The office had escaped and looked much the same as when I had worked there. Like everything in London, it bore the marks of war – shabbier furniture, dirtier windows, unpolished floors. But these were not to be despised, for they were the badges of courage worn by a people who had never contemplated defeat, who had stood fast after the French bolted.

Rawlings occupied the office in which I had once sat; Rawlings who I had last seen the day a machine-gun bullet tore apart the face of his wife, the day I had waved farewell to Julie as they both boarded the *Ban Hong Liong*. Poor devil – how could a man ever overcome a tragedy as wounding as that, the picture anchored in the brain for life, the picture of a wife and mother killed before your eyes. Too many years had passed for me to commiserate, to ask how he had coped with such terrible tragedy.

The first difference I noticed was that he had put on a lot of weight. 'Potatoes,' he said with a laugh. I felt that with his pebble glasses he would be in danger, if he added another stone, of becoming a caricature of Billy Bunter. Until this moment I had forgotten that Rawlings had also been on the *Rooseboome* with Julie and Tony when it was sunk almost within sight of Ceylon, and that his baby had died after they took to the open boat. He asked after Mr Scott and Miss Soong and I told him all the latest news.

'Very sad about poor Ball,' he said. 'Have you heard what's happened to his wife?' I hadn't and said so, and was talking to him about Singapore when a secretary came into his office and said a little shyly that coffee was waiting for me in my father's office where he had been dealing with the morning mail. She gave Rawlings a smile, not the kind of look the pert secretary had given the late Mr Cowley, but still what novelists call 'a meaningful glance'.

Then I got a shock.

'I'd like you to meet my wife, Mr John,' said Rawlings. 'Isobel was working here when I landed in London, and we were married two years ago. Papa Jack asked her to stay on, there's such a shortage of secretaries.'

'Delighted to meet you,' said Isobel.

So much for tragedy! Would Irene have forgotten as easily as Rawlings?

In fact she had. She couldn't have been more friendly. She

kissed me, presented Ben, a sturdy, blond-haired, fine-looking boy, and without any sign of restraint. 'He's outgoing,' Irene laughed. 'Takes after you. No inhibitions.'

It really was extraordinary. He just treated me as an old friend, and though Irene had prepared him for the fact that I would be returning to Singapore she had obviously not made a single comment to encourage any antagonism. It is so easy for the scorned wife to instil hatred of a father who runs off with another woman, especially at an age when children absorb details that remain forever. Obviously Ben didn't know about Julie — but he seemed to accept that I was a here-today-gone-tomorrow parent as though it was the most natural thing in the world. It was easier for him to accept, of course, as an extension of the separations of war. After all, we had hardly known each other until this morning.

He pestered me with questions. How many Japs had I shot? Did I use a knife? Uncle Bob had shot down eleven German planes. (*Uncle Bob?*) Had I ever met a cannibal? How big was the jungle? The questions only stopped when I produced the large tin of Australian boiled sweets I had bought in Colombo, but I felt a pang of misery at his ready smile and trust, and *acceptance*, as though I was necessary. Odd, I had been thinking only a few days ago in Colombo how unnecessary I had been most of my life. How would this energetic, quick and likeable boy cope with life with no father around? It did not enter my head that he had coped very well so far; I was only aware of the sense of wrong in abandoning a boy who innocently accepted me for what I was, an absentee landlord, so to speak.

Catherine was different, six months older than Pela, and once her eyes had focused on the tin of sweets — drastically rationed in England — and some bananas I had brought — fruit never seen by children of their ages — she was blissfully ignorant of my presence.

We lunched alone at Wilton's in Bury Street because it was an old favourite of the Dexters and I knew we would eat well if Mr Marks, who had run the restaurant since 1906, knew a Dexter was coming. By the very nature of things our visits to Wilton's were few and far between, but that made no difference. We were among the accepted clients to whom all courtesies were extended not only by Mr Marks but by the elderly ladies who always served there. After we had finished our Stilton and lit up our cigarettes – I had started smoking again since the day a man gave me a cigarette on the bus to KL – I started to apologise.

'Don't worry, Johnnie.' She looked very pretty, dressed in a grey flannel two-piece suit with a white silk blouse that shouted 'Made in Singapore'. It was open at the throat and she had a good neck. 'We should never have got married in the first place. But when I missed the curse I was such a mug – I knew nothing – and you were a mug too!'

'You talk just like you used to talk in Studio Z, before we were married.'

'Perhaps it's because we're not really married any more. I know I was more fun before – there must be something odd about me. An allergy to marriage?'

'Not you. But I suppose we shouldn't have married. Still, we did. And really and truthfully, I did try to get Julie out of my system.'

'You never would have done.'

'I would – if the Japs hadn't come along.'

One of the waitresses approached with a second cup of coffee, a rare treat, for favoured customers only.

'I've heard the Japs blamed for lots of things,' she said, 'but never for *that*!'

'But I do feel terrible – especially about Ben. He's wonderful – and you –'

'Don't be so worried. Ben's the world's friend. He regards you as a hero –'

'Thanks to you. You could have painted an ugly picture. Though I know you never would.'

'I only told the truth. And whatever our troubles we have always been friends. The real trouble is that *friendship* isn't enough to hold a marriage together. But Ben is just as fond of Uncle Bob – you heard him talk about him?' She hesitated, asked for another cigarette, lit it, blew out a long slow stream of smoke and said very deliberately, 'You'll like

Uncle Bob — and if it makes it any easier for you, Johnnie, we're getting married as soon as you and I are divorced — amicably, I hope.'

An enormous sense of excitement tingled its way through my body. I'm going to be free! No hassle, no in-fighting, no bitterness! How wonderful, how lucky I am that someone fell for her! I had hoped she would understand, but I had never allowed myself to believe in the impossible — that another man would resolve our fate. One of the curiosities of marriage is that husbands so rarely realise that the wives they discard with such guilt complexes can still be desirable to other men. I only hope my excitement hadn't lit up my face as it had lit up my feelings.

'Surprised?' Irene almost laughed. 'You shouldn't be. I could never have gone back to Singapore. That was another tragedy — and that was all my fault. And then on top of everything — the war — Julie — and then Bill being killed.' She sighed, 'Even if I had loved Singapore I could never move far from Mummy and Daddy now. They're shells, Johnnie. It's pitiful. Remember our lovely old house facing Wimbledon Common? It's empty, half the rooms closed. Vegetables growing on the tennis courts. No servants. I'm just watching my father and mother die.'

Later she told me that Bob was in his late thirties, divorced, an underwriter in Bradshaw's syndicate at Lloyd's, and had recently become a Member of Parliament.

'As a matter of fact,' she hesitated, 'I don't know whether I should tell you this, but — you remember before we first spent the night together in your Fulham studio I told you I was getting over a miserable affair with a married man?' I nodded. 'Well — that was Bob. He didn't realise what a catch I was until I ran off with you! And then when I came back to London — and I admit I did tell him you had a floosie — he got his divorce.'

'You old slyboots!' I was filled with admiration. 'It's a great talent in life — never to discard anything that's made you happy.'

'That's how I feel about you. We must never discard each

other. Not only for the sake of the children – for the good of our souls.'

She brought up another point. The man in her life was not only a newly-elected MP, he was hoping for a ministerial appointment – and any connection with a divorce action could ruin his prospects.

'So,' Irene looked at me brightly, 'I'm going to ask you a favour. Since you behaved like a gentleman once before – when you married me – will you behave like one again?'

'It never entered my head to do otherwise.' We both burst out laughing, and when Mr Marks made his rounds to see if his customers were satisfied and cocked an enquiring eyebrow I told him, 'It's nothing serious Mr Marks. We're just discussing our divorce.'

That is how simple I *thought* the procedure would be – until I went to see our solicitor. I blithely imagined that evidence of adultery (the classic weekend in Brighton) would suffice. I had not reckoned with the sinister letters 'DS'. I had to tell my solicitor the truth – just as Irene would tell hers – that she had a lover she was hoping to marry after our divorce came through. And that he was a Member of Parliament with political ambitions.

'You realise, I hope,' the solicitor peered over the tops of gold-rimmed half-moon glasses, 'that under the Matrimonial Causes Act of 1937 anyone who files for divorce on the grounds of adultery must inform the judge if she has also committed adultery. This is done in a discretionary statement – we call it DS.'

'But if nobody knows –'

'Someone *always* knows. The police are circularised. She *must* make a DS. Her own solicitor would never act for her if she didn't. And by law she has to tell the judge her lover's name.'

If she didn't one anonymous letter would wreck everyone's career. It was true that Bob's name would not appear in print, but when news of the divorce appeared in the newspapers her name would be followed by the letters 'DS' in brackets. 'And when she marries her lover,' said the solicitor, 'everyone in public life will know what's been happening.' In 1945 extramarital affairs were still frowned upon in public life, and Bob apparently was terrified when he learned of the risks involved.

The alternative was divorce after three years of separation – and as we had been living apart for the duration of the war that seemed possible. But war, it seemed, didn't count. It had to be *wilful* separation. And after Bob had begged Irene not to divorce me on grounds of adultery, there was only one thing to do – wait three years. God, I thought, that'll take up to 1948, and Pela will be six years old.

But it was the only way.

42

Old familiar faces started to reappear in Singapore, often men and women who had gone to England to recuperate or to be reunited with their families after the years of Changi. Bill and Marjorie Jackson returned from England, Wilf Broadbent and his wife Joanna from a trip halfway round the world. Ian Scott had gone to Australia after being interned in Changi because Vicki had landed up there when the ship evacuating her was rerouted. Of course she had been invaluable as a top secretary in Sydney and she looked like a poster for Bondi Beach, brown, slim, blonde and ready for action.

When I dined with them in their bungalow in Keok Road I thought back to the last time I had been there – fixing the rubber deal. And, looking at Vicki – for a moment remembering her without any clothes on – I imagined briefly the fun she must have had – and given generously to others – during those four years in Australia. Still, she looked settled down now; four years older, perhaps ready for a steady, humdrum existence. I wondered if the enforced separations of a war tended to give married women a chance to have a fling and thus make them better, quieter wives, more immune to temptation, after the fighting ended. It might be a very useful by-product of war – a marriage stabiliser!

Ian looked fitter than I would have expected. The last vestige of a tummy had gone, so had the unhealthy pallor of camp life. Like everyone else I talked to he was concerned about restarting his business, and was already spluttering with indignation at the nincompoops (his word) of the military government telling us how to run our affairs.

George Hammonds had been given special priority to fly in from India to restart the presses of the *Tribune*. He looked unchanged, still the same slightly hesitant voice, still knowing far more about everything than anyone else. There was one difference: he no longer clutched his round tin of fifty Players. Universal air conditioning had meant the virtual end of cigarettes in tins. There was no need for vacuum packing to keep them fresh. 'Fags come in packets now,' he said. 'I find it very hard to get used to them.'

Most welcome of all in those first weeks was the daily improvement in Paul Soong's health. Such is the power of the human body that I could almost see the progress. His hair would always be white, but that gave him a certain air of distinction, especially after he had fleshed out the bony wreck which had so horrified me when I first saw him again. He was soon walking without a limp and allowed to drink normally, so that we could phone each other and meet for gin pahits or stengahs at Raffles. He had been advised by his doctor not to drive for several months in case his legs gave out suddenly – I hadn't realised at first that the Japs had tortured him with the bastinado – but his slow, sardonic smile, the half wink of an eyelid, were soon nearly back to usual.

Then came Natflat, within three months of liberation. She arrived with Victoria, now eight years old, and spent a couple of nights in Singapore before going to KL to join Tony who was breaking his back getting Ara into production again. Darling Natflat! She had sailed from New York to England, seen the family, then flown out on the newly organised BOAC service.

After years in America she looked stunning – a word that always sprang to mind when I thought about my sister. She had matured, and looked more like I remembered Mama when I was young, though the cornflower blue of her eyes was brighter. And she was far, far more beautiful than Vicki would ever be, simply because she didn't look as brassy, as eager.

'Poor Johnnie!' she hugged me like a returning lover. 'You must have had a terrible time while I was whooping it up in New York. I felt awful – I thought of you so often. For months I thought you were either dead or in Changi – and then one day I got a letter from Julie in Colombo. She didn't know our address so she posted it to Aunt Sonia in San Francisco who sent it on to us at Brewster. She just said she knew you were a very brave officer – those were her words – and alive. After that we kept in touch. I was so proud of you, darling brother.'

As we drank our gimlets and stengahs, sitting on the verandah where Julie and I had spent so many happy evenings, I took in the differences in Natasha. There *was* a different look about her, and at first I couldn't make out what it was. I wondered what had happened in New York. Had the naughty look gone? Been erased by experiences? Hard to tell. Her face – uncreased, no crows' feet at thirty-six – seemed to indicate that she had come to terms with herself – and perhaps at last with life.

On this first night we had a scratch dinner alone in the Cadet House, served by a beaming Li. I had thrown out the heavy old furniture from the dining room, replacing it with lighter cane tables and chairs, which gave the room a feeling of more space, making it less lugubrious.

'And after almost four years apart from Tony?' I approached the question of her marriage as delicately as I could.

'No problem. Yummy! It's good to taste *ikan meru* again, Li. Best fish in the world. Specially after that frozen stuff in America.' And with a mischievous twinkle, she asked innocently, 'You were saying?'

'Come off it, Natflat. You know bloody well what I mean. You were on the point of splitting up when I last saw you. Now you're going back. What happened?'

She put down her fork and looked at me across the neutral-coloured cane table. 'I don't really know,' she said frankly. 'Johnnie, I don't know. Even before our ship docked in America I knew I couldn't go through with the baby. I'm not *that* much of a shit. Then I heard that Bertrand had been killed, and I did go off the rails a bit. Tried out one or two fellers in New York.' I must have looked a little surprised because she added, 'Now *you* come off it. A woman has just as much right as a man to feel sexy.'

'Unchanged,' I murmured.

'They were terrible! Handsome and dashing – I guess you could call them that – but terrible.' I burst out laughing when she added, 'One even kept his socks on.'

After the sweet had been served and she was pouring syrup on the gula Malacca she added, but this time more seriously, 'I did feel desperate for a time, but then I began to think things out – that old stuff about absence making the heart grow fonder – I couldn't let Tony down, not really, specially after Julie hinted in a letter that he was with you. It suddenly dawned on me that I was approaching middle age, that I'd have a better life of it with Tony than just – messing around. What was it that some actress said? – God, I seem to be talking in quotations this evening – you know. I decided to change the hurly burly of the *chaise longue* for the comfort of the double bed. Now – I know how old I am! – I'm going to see if I can give Tony another baby.'

'It'll be fun trying.' I said. 'High time you settled down. Like your younger brother!'

'I'm so happy for you, even though Mama told me about the boring wait for the divorce. But you'll have a home with us at Ara. I'm longing to see Julie – and to see you two together.' There were actually tears in her eyes. 'You see, Johnnie, Julie has a mixture in her character that I haven't got. She can be a wild animal one day and as sedate as a mother of six the next. I can't. I have to be one or the other. That's why you two are so bloody lucky! You've got both the *chaise longue* and the double bed – on alternate nights.'

We talked of many things that night – Papa Jack who, it seemed, was still not anxious to return to Singapore. Natasha had found them cheerful and happy when she spent a few days in Sloane Terrace Mansions. 'Really happy,' she said. 'But that made *me* feel sad – that they seemed content just to stay and grow old instead of coming out here with all of us. It was awful.'

Tim was not in London when Natflat passed through, so I said nothing about him, and we touched only briefly on the death of Grandpa Jack, though she did ask what I was going to do about Tanamera.

'I've got to make all the decisions, it's no use writing to Papa Jack. I want to keep the grounds as they are. In ten or fifteen years when Singapore's independent – I'm not sure how or when, but it's bound to come. The British are talking about independence for Malaya and making Singapore a crown colony. The Chinese here – they'll never stand for that, Commies or capitalists. The Malays are lazy. It's the Chinese here who do the real work.'

'I'm not sure you're right – I don't know enough about what's happening – but how does that affect Tanamera?'

'One day this island is going to be filled with skyscrapers – you laugh, but Papa Jack used to say that there'd be a huge building boom. When that time comes – maybe with independence – the land round Tanamera will be worth a fortune. I want to rebuild Tanamera on a smaller scale, keep the land for the time being, and sell parcels of it later if I ever need to. But Tanamera itself – that's going to be smaller.'

Architects had already been to see the site with me and found, as I expected, that the great white front walls were as solid as the day they were built by Grandpa Jack. I had decided – by spending the buried treasure, which was now in the bank – to build a much smaller house, but using the walls as a facade. So the original front of the house would remain; the appearance as anyone came down the drive would be exactly as it always had been. But behind I planned smaller rooms, suitable for air conditioning. The double staircase would be torn down, a more modest one replacing it. There would still be half a dozen bedrooms, bathrooms, all the necessary equipment of a *tuan bezar*'s Singapore home. But it would just be more practical, that's all.

I had of course been in touch with Julie, who planned to fly with Pela as soon as Natasha had had time to settle in at Ara, and one man was very pleased.

'The old man's delighted the way you've handled the Julie problem,' said Paul. 'I'm glad you agreed she could live in KL.'

Soong certainly was very depressed. Several people had recently remarked that P.P. looked positively ill at dinner parties. I know it wasn't because of Julie, otherwise he wouldn't have gone out of his way to make himself so pleasant to me. Ian Scott thought he was depressed by the virtual disappearance of Soong Kai-shek – a vanishing act of which I thoroughly approved, specially after his threat to kill me. I had wondered where he had gone to, but it was not Kai-shek's disappearance that worried Soong. I heard the truth from George Hammonds. Paul, I realised, obviously knew, but had not thought it necessary to tell me. Soong was being bitterly attacked in the Chinese vernacular press, the kind of newspapers we never saw, let alone could read.

'Many of them are bitterly anti-Communist,' explained George over lunch. 'But while we talk in general terms the Chinese get down to the nitty gritty. They name names. In print. And including poor P.P.'

'But George, Soong *can't* be a Communist. You know that. I know that. It's too absurd for words.'

Hammonds speared the last of his kumquats and pushed the plate away before lighting a cigarette. 'I don't know how anyone found out, but someone has been accusing him of holding secret meetings with Loi Tek during the occupation. That'd be bad enough – branded as a Commie – but not long ago someone attacked Loi Tek in a Penang newspaper; said he had collaborated with the Japs. The article was discredited, the man who wrote it was known to be a Japanese collaborator in the war. But you know how things are – I'm told that Loi Tek *was* sometimes seen driving in a Jap car – and things rub off. Now someone has not only accused Soong of being a Communist but a collaborator.'

The one question to which I knew there could never be an answer – or so I believed then – sprang to mind. 'Why the hell *did* a rich, respectable Chinese capitalist pay regular visits to a Communist leader? It just doesn't make sense.'

'Search me. Something more to it than meets the eye. But it's certainly landed Soong in deep trouble, because he *was* in contact with Loi Tek. No doubt about it. And the day before yesterday one Chinese newspaper said he should be expelled from the Chinese Chamber of Commerce.'

Three weeks later Julie and Pela arrived at Ara, the start of a new, warm and happy life for them – and for me as well. For now I really *was* married, if not yet legally. True, I lived in Singapore during the week, but millions of men travelled five days a week in order to earn a living, returning home gratefully each Friday evening.

The only difference was that I commuted weekly in comfort. Since I was not a commercial traveller but a *tuan* I flew up to KL every Friday, with a car and syce at each airport.

Pela was now three years old – old enough to cry 'Papa!' which she did all the time, and she could already twist an adoring father round her little finger as easily as her mother could. And she had not forgotten the habit learned in Colombo of kissing me.

My commuting was made easier because Macmillan had started work – the one-time efficient sergeant-major transformed into an equally brilliant general manager. There was nothing he could not – would not – do for Dexters, for he had become integrated into the firm from his first week in Singapore.

At the same time Papa Jack had sent out two carefully chosen cadets. Both were twenty-one, ambitious and had just escaped war service – which meant they had benefited from an up-to-date education. Ralph Johnson had been articled to a chartered accountant after leaving school, but the lure of the East proved too much for him. Papa Jack had to buy him out of his articles but it was worth it, for he knew enough about figures to keep the books. Barry Stride had left Rugby with the firm intention of becoming a tea or rubber planter and had actually applied to Dexters for a job after seeing the plate outside our London office. Papa Jack had convinced him that he would have more fun, more prospects if he worked in Singapore. Both men would be trained to become the Ball and the Rawlings of the future!

They had to be housed. So had Jock Macmillan. And with the army requisitioning every building there was only one obvious place to put them: the Cadet House. I knew that Tanamera would be rebuilt before Julie and I were married, and in the meantime I only needed the two rooms with their verandah in the Cadet House. So we started a mess. The others had a large bedroom and shower each and a private balcony. When I was not attending business dinners I enjoyed the camaraderie of a communal dining room. It gave me a feeling of satisfaction to see the others there, echoes of my own youth, but more than that – a sense of the continuity of Dexter and Company, young men eager and excited, sitting in the same room where Ball and Rawlings had once eaten, sleeping perhaps in the same room where poor Cowley had been caught with his Indian girlfriend. And if I ever felt the need for change I could always go round to Paul or eat at the Cricket Club.

Li remained strictly my personal servant. I had my own syce now and – in the way that old habits are repeated – I drove to the office each morning, giving Mac a lift in just the same way as Papa Jack used to take me to Robinson Road.

Li had engaged a staff to look after everyone; Mac was appointed mess officer, though cookie chose the meals which were all free. The only item that had to be paid for personally in the Cadet House was liquor, and this everyone did monthly as in an army mess. We had always worked that way in the Cadet House.

Macmillan gave me the same feeling of security in Singapore as he had in the jungle: the knowledge, so essential in a many-sided business like ours, that I could leave details to him knowing they would not be forgotten. And his understanding of officer mentality was invaluable when dealing with occupation army officers who insisted on poking their noses into everyone's business. Who better to size up an officer than a sergeant-major?

For after the first flush of victory – after the illusion of unaltered permanence in a way of life – no one could pretend that Singapore was not changed, especially if you looked at the new white faces in its streets or lolling against the bars of its clubs. I realised the phase would pass, but for the moment, under the military government, the old trading habits had changed for the worse.

The officers who handed out the contracts were different from those we had come to know before the fall of Singapore. The high-ranking officers then had often been irritating, pompous, but they had been professional soldiers. The officers in the occupation forces, preparing the country for civilian government to take over, were often nothing more than businessmen in uniform.

The city had changed too. Old Chinese friends – the doorman at the Goodwood Park, the Sikh jagger at Raffles, Chan the barman at the Cricket Club – all were skinnier, tired, morose, not so much fed up with the British, but fed up with the effort of having to change masters once again.

In the first few months of exhilaration it was all too easy to forget that victory in Malaya was not the same as victory in England, where it signalled freedom from the threat of a tyrant's rule. In England the war was over, people were again their own masters. In Malaya and Singapore victory had little to do with freedom, it merely signalled a change of masters who had used their country as a battleground – more benevolent than the Japanese, no doubt, but still – masters.

The Chinese in Singapore felt this more keenly than others, for the Japanese had deliberately fostered racial tension by torturing the Chinese while encouraging the Malays to regard Singapore as 'their' country.

There were changes in the streets too. The rickshaws had vanished, to be replaced with trishaws which the Japanese said (with truth) were more humane and less degrading. Paul was convinced there was another reason: the rickshaw had been invented by the Chinese, the trishaw by the Japanese. Certainly the Japs were not noted for their humane considerations.

Worst of all, though, was the disorganisation. The rubber and tin industries were in a hopeless mess, especially the estates. Many prewar planters had died or just given up the job, but though there were plenty of youngsters eager to start a new life in Malaya many faced absurd difficulties in getting demobilised from an army that had no further use for them. Red tape strangled everything.

Because Tony Scott had been in Force 136 he had been able to get out quickly, and he had immediately started putting Ara on its feet again. The Japanese had let the estate run to seed, and it took several months to clear away the beluka before the first tappers could start slicing into the bark.

When this moment did arrive we had a pleasant surprise. Tony telephoned me that the latex yield from almost every tree (except the few which had died of disease) was better than it had ever been. The rich creamy flow would not always drop so abundantly into the tappers' cups tied round the trees with thin wire, but the fact that the Japanese had given the trees a three-year rest from their regular surgical operations improved the yield enormously.

Even though we were lucky with the production at Ara we still faced problems due to interference by Whitehall wallahs, who blithely fixed a price for rubber without even finding out what it cost to feed estate coolies.

'The bloody price was fixed by chartered accountants,' I said to Tony Scott during one weekend at Ara.

'Yeah,' he replied. 'Their only knowledge of rubber is from the end of a pencil – or a condom!'

All this muddle was coupled with an Asia-wide food shortage Before the war we had *given* every worker at Ara a pound of rice a day. Now this had been reduced to a ration of four ounces a day for a man, half that for a child. Yet, while food stocks were low, the poor could see how the privileged men in the army were fed.

It was impossible to explain that the army was eating tinned food from distant countries, that the Malays in the kampongs were still supplied with abundant food by a bountiful nature, that fish was there for the asking. There was a drift to the towns, and no work meant no food.

All these anomalies started a crime wave by anti-British factions exploiting the widespread humiliation of the white man all over Asia. Most of all it provided a heaven-sent opportunity for our old 'comrades' in Force 136, all of whom boasted openly that they were the real victors of the war. Chin Peng claimed that his men had killed or wounded two thousand Japanese while they fought behind the enemy lines 'after the British had run away'. At first the MPAJA had even taken over effective control of some areas in Malaya, setting up illegal drumhead courts and executing dozens of villagers suspected of collaboration.

When the British occupation forces arrived they had persuaded most units to come under the control of local commanders, giving them army rations and a gratuity of about forty-five pounds. The situation was ironic. Whatever our misgivings about men like Chin Peng and Kaishek – and we knew that almost all guerillas were diehard Communists – they had fought bravely. The British government could hardly ignore their contribution. So not only did a contingent of the MPAJA go to London to take part in the victory parade, but their leader, Chin Peng – dedicated to the overthrow of British rule in Malaya – was awarded the OBE.

We knew that large caches of arms had been hidden by Chin Peng's men in the jungle. It crossed my mind in those early days that if Loi Tek had displayed the qualities of dynamic leadership that shot him to very top of the local Communist tree he might have staged a coup at that time. The Communists had the arms, the panache, and that necessary ingredient for success, *hatred*. I did not learn for another twelve months why they chose not to use that dynamism.

What made matters worse in those postwar years was the lack of positive action by Britain, the dithering, as though they could not see the need to *reassure* people in Asia after the British debacle.

Like Papa Jack I had always felt, long before the fall of Singapore, that if Britain wanted to keep a foothold in Singapore and Malaya it must be as partners with those whose country this was. The word freedom – *Merdeka* – was in the air, for a war had ended, and a new world was being born. Across the face of Asia a thousand million people, weary of starvation, of brutality and above all of corruption, were crying the new word. Before the war their voices had been silenced by the lash, they had been impotent and ignored. But the war had changed that, had proved above all else that the power of the West would never again be strong enough to halt the tide of the East.

In all this great postwar clamour sweeping Asia Malaya was but a speck – and a country that could hardly complain of harsh treatment under the British. Still, in this speck the Japanese had washed away the old order – and in blood. What we needed now was boldness, a clarion cry, a promise that could be understood easily by every Siloma in every village kampong. Instead they got a dreary recital of ifs and buts in the vague Malayan Union proposals published in January 1946; sentences like, 'political adjustment which will offer, through broad based institutions in which the whole community can participate, the means and prospect of developing Malaya's capacity in the direction of re-sponsible self-government.'

'You must admit,' said Paul Soong when I showed it to him, 'that as far as crap's concerned this is pretty far down the shit scale.'

'It's made in Britain,' I cried with mock indignation, 'so there can't be anything wrong with it!'

That was about a week before I picked up the *Tribune* and read a short paragraph on page one announcing baldly that

P.P. Soong had resigned from the Chinese Club and also from the Chinese Chamber of Commerce. It gave no details.

I rang up Paul and we met for a drink. I went straight to Raffles from the Cricket Club after an exhausting game of singles and gratefully accepted an ice-cold Tiger.

'Father *is* very low,' Paul admitted. 'Never seen him like this. The trouble is, he won't talk about it, just mopes. I wrote to Mom the other day, even asked her to come to Singapore on a visit, hoping – you know! – but I don't think she'll come. In her last letter she wrote that she's a "part of the San Francisco scene", whatever that means.'

'Can I do anything? Would he like Julie to come down for a few days?'

Paul shook his head. 'No thanks. He's got to see this thing through himself. It's the old question of face – so bloody stupid in this day and age. What the hell does it matter if he isn't a member of the Chamber of bloody Commerce? Who gives a damn?'

'They do.' I was thinking back to the time Shenton Thomas prevented Papa Jack from serving his term as president of our Chamber. I often wondered if that was the moment in my father's life that decided him to leave Singapore. I explained what had happened to Paul.

'Your father was brighter,' he exclaimed. 'Quite right to get out if you're fed up. If I had my father's money and staying power with women, I'd bugger off tomorrow – go and live in Paris or London or the Riviera, pick up a brood of girls! Or should it be a covey of girls? Or a gaggle?' He gave me his slow wink.

The next afternoon, after I had flown up as usual to Ara, I told Julie the latest news about her father.

'I do worry about Daddy,' she admitted. 'I don't like to feel that he's down and being kicked.'

'Why don't you go to see him in Singapore?'

She shook her head. That, she felt, wouldn't solve anything. Soong had come up to KL twice and taken her out, he had even been to Ara for lunch (in midweek) and gravely played with Pela. 'But even if I can't do anything,' she sighed again, 'I can feel sorry.'

'We must be wonderful children, you and I,' I laughed. 'Here are you worried about your father, here am I feeling sorry for Papa Jack – and when I think how they treated us, kicked us out, banished us.'

'That was different,' said Julie. 'That was for our good.'

On the Monday morning I kissed the family goodbye and prepared to catch the usual six a.m. plane to Singapore. 'See you on Friday,' I promised them.

'Kiss, Papa!' cried Pela.

'Me too!' cried Julie.

'God! You Lovebirds!' Natflat pretended a groan of disgust, and then threw a duster at Tony when he grinned and cried, 'Me too!'

'Till Friday,' I repeated to Julie. 'It's going to be a long time.'

The weather was beautiful – not too warm – when I flew up the following Friday evening, exchanging the spartan bachelor existence of the Cadet House for my joyous weekend of married bliss. I sometimes felt guilty at the way I had forced Julie into the provincial backwater of a planter's life, though really it was her father's fault, not mine; and she didn't seem to mind. Perhaps she was sustained by the happiness of Pela and by the prospect that every month that passed was a month nearer marriage.

One is always discovering new aspects of love – the increasing serenity that replaces earlier anxieties and doubts; the ability to adjust to circumstances once you know there are no alternatives. When, deliriously happy, I watched Julie playing with the children in the paddling pool, or swimming in the new pool Tony had built in the garden, it was hard to realise not only what she had to endure during the war but the different sophisticated life she had lived so far away – a student at one of California's best universities, a trainee nurse, even months speaking French at Tours.

By early 1947 we had been away together several times: once up to Hong Kong, another time on a slow boat to

Cheribon in Java, where they grow the best and cheapest mangos in the world, and then on to Bali. While Julie was away from Ara, Natflat looked after both children. When Natflat took a break with Tony, Julie was mother and if possible I went up to relieve Tony.

What I loved more than anything was the relaxed atmosphere of happy families, the daughters playing together like sisters, the adults firm friends, loyalties long tested. Our occasional differences of opinion – you could hardly call them quarrels – came and went with the speed of sheet lightning and were about as important. It was inconceivable that Tony and I, who had passed through so much together in the jungle barely three miles behind the estate – it was unthinkable we could ever fight. Nor could Julie, who had never forgotten Natasha's visit to the 'Chinese butcher', ever fight with my sister.

Sometimes on a Sunday we went to the Spotted Dog in KL for a curry tiffin – my partner of course being a very decorous spinster called Miss Soong. But once home, she became Miss Soong and Mrs Dexter rolled into one, still as exciting in bed as on the first night we made love; though when we lay spent and satisfied afterwards she was subtly different, possibly because almost half of the waiting period for the divorce had passed.

'Won't it be awful if you refuse to come down to Singapore, if you want to stay here.' I tickled her tummy. We were stretched out on the bed, naked and satisfied, the door locked against chubby inquisitive fingers. 'Then I'll have to start going to Macpherson Road!'

She leaned over and grabbed hold of the tiny remains of my manhood. 'You try it!' she giggled. 'And I'll cut this trifling thing off – no, even worse, I'll bite it off.'

'Trifling? You watch!'

'I'll never get over it.' She did watch, holding it, stroking gently, fingers of the other hand caressing me between the legs as I grew in size and strength until finally, with mock despair masking the love of two people whose every intimacy is known to the other, she said, 'All right, lord and master. I suppose you insist on having it again!'

'If you don't mind.'

'It's positively indecent,' she laughed afterwards. 'Twice on a Sunday afternoon – an old married couple like us!' And then anxiously, 'How long will it last, darling, the physical side?'

'With you on top doing all the work, I'd say until I'm about eighty-five – providing you keep fit.'

What heavenly days they were in Ara, days in which the war was only a memory, in which we blindly and blithely ignored the warning signs of danger to come. Natasha had really settled down, the wild oats well and truly sown. She was thirty-seven and still she hadn't had the baby she said after the war she was determined to give to Tony.

'Aren't you leaving it a bit late?' I asked her.

'We're not leaving anything!' she retorted. 'We're trying like mad – and I don't object.'

They did seem to be making a go of it, and not for the first time I realised that Julie had been responsible in great measure for the happiness that had come late in life to Natasha. Julie had the quality of giving; like a doctor with a needle, she injected happiness into other people, providing their misery was not terminal. But it was all done so gently that no one felt the prick of the needle.

Those were the uneventful weekends we all spend together. Julie sometimes went shopping into KL with Natasha, sometimes I went on the estate rounds with Tony. The happiness reminded me of those early never-to-be-forgotten days at Tanamera, the parties, Papa Jack in a white suit, Mama in billowy pinks and blues, days in which, looking back, the weather always seemed to be perfect, the friends warm and kind, with nothing to spoil perfection.

It was that kind of weekend – the last Saturday in February 1947 – and we had all been talking about the rebuilding of Tanamera which was shortly to start. Julie and I had spent the early evening swimming, teaching the children – fortified with inflated wings – the rudiments of the breast stroke, and after a shower I was drinking my first stengah of the day when the phone rang. It was Paul, calling from Singapore.

'Hi!' I cried, 'it's a bloody awful line.'

'Can you hear me?' he shouted above the crackle, as though someone was standing on the wires outside the room, and perhaps this hid from me the desperation in his voice. 'Johnnie, you'll have to help me, you'll have to break this to Julie, I can't.'

'What is it, Paul, what's the matter?'

'It's Father – he's dead.'

I almost dropped the phone as Tony, who was pouring out a drink, said, 'What's up?'

I waved him back. 'But Paul, I saw him last week – he looked fit and –'

Of course I knew from childhood that you can be fit one day in the tropics and dead the next, but that kind of sudden fatality happened to other people, not to us or our friends. 'What happened, Paul? Was he taken ill – was it an accident?'

'I'm afraid' – he choked on the words – 'that's why I want you to tell Julie. You're her husband. I can't tell her. I can't, Johnnie. It was suicide.'

43

'It's terrible,' said Paul after Julie and I had driven down to Singapore through the night. 'He just crept away into a corner with a bottle of sleeping pills and decided to end it.'

'Poor Father.' It seemed incongruous to see Julie once again sitting in that huge, forbidding grey circular room of the Soong mansion. 'Despite all his money he didn't seem to get much fun out of life.'

Slowly we pieced together what had happened. Soong, as we all suspected, had kept a flat in Stevens Road beyond the Tanglin Club – a perfectly normal arrangement for any Chinese rich enough to enjoy concubines. The previous evening an agitated female voice phoned Paul with the address of the flat, ringing off before he could ask her name. All she said was, 'Your father! Go quickly.'

Soong was lying in bed with an empty bottle labelled Sodium Amytal. Next to it was a half-empty bottle of brandy, Soong's favourite brand, Hennessey XO. He had been dead for some time.

There was nothing I could do except quietly console Julie; and I had a feeling that neither Julie nor Paul needed *much* sympathy. Julie had hardly seen her father since before the war, and the parent–child relationship was different among Chinese. To them he had always been an austere, unbending figure, and I had sometimes wondered if that represented a true reflection of his character, or whether he felt that was the way a Chinese father should conduct himself. Surely he must have behaved very differently when he swept Aunt Sonia off her feet in San Francisco!

What did upset Paul and Julie was the manner in which he had been driven to his death. They knew it was absurd to lump Soong with the ragbag of Communists or fellow travellers. It was so out of character that only an idiot could believe in the accusations hurled against him – though no one could deny he had made those indiscreet visits to Loi Tek.

There was one gesture I could make for Paul and Julie. I decided to arrange a non-religious memorial service for Soong; after a discussion with Paul we agreed to hold it in the splendid Soong grounds, with their magnificent peacocks strutting on the lawns amidst the sculpted bushes and the most famous lotus pond in Singapore. It was my way of showing Julie and Paul that all Soong's old friends respected him. It gave Paul face.

I was astounded at the result. Papa Jack and Mama agreed to fly out, I was able to telephone Aunt Sonia in San Francisco who seemed delighted to come – if only for the sake of Julie. Business leaders from the various communities each agreed to give a short address. Papa Jack would speak for the British. And after that there would be champagne and curry puffs in the big grey room. I knew that to Paul particularly this display of friendship would mean a lot – a gesture that would show how everyone respected his father, admired his business integrity, and was not ashamed to be known as his friend. And as George Hammonds promised, 'I'll make damned sure that every name goes into the *Tribune*.'

A curious incident had happened when I first told George about my scheme. I met him in the *Tribune* office and had tried to explain why I planned the get-together. I remember it was the second week in March which had started off with perfect weather in that heady year of 1947 when independence was the main topic of conversation – with Mountbatten appointed Viceroy of India the previous month with orders from Attlee to speed up the British withdrawal, with Ceylon a dominion, with the Dutch East Indies only two weeks from independence.

'It occurred to me,' I told George, 'that I might go and see this man Loi Tek – after all, I met him once in the jungle – just to see if he *could* explain the mystery of Soong's visits. I don't even know whether he'd see me –'

I thought George gave me an odd look before he said, 'You're too late.'

I must have looked puzzled. 'Remember the date – this week might go down in the annals of Communist history. The day before yesterday – 6 March – Loi Tek vanished.'

'He *can't* vanish! He's the most famous Communist in South East Asia.'

'He has.' George shrugged his shoulders. 'That's what I've been told. No' – in answer to my unspoken question – 'I don't know what's happened to him. Bumped off, I suppose, but I do know the MCP is in a hell of a flap. Probably they just had a row – one side wanted action, the other wanted to play it safe. I don't read anything sinister in it. I imagine they just wanted a new secretary-general so perhaps Loi Tek is out in the cold somewhere – or he might be a stiff. Don't suppose we'll ever know.'

That was my last slim chance to clear Soong's name – or so I thought at the time. I suppose I had never really expected it to succeed. Dedicated Communists don't usually give explanations to dedicated capitalists.

Paul told me that his father's solicitors held a letter inscribed 'To be opened only in the event of my death'. Written by Soong, it was addressed to Julie, Paul and – me! It had to be opened if possible by the solicitor before the three of us.

It was no sentimental letter of last farewells, nor was it a will, for that had already been read, leaving the estate divided equally between Mrs Soong, Paul and Julie, apart from a few personal bequests including one to me – the lacquered table he had always promised me.

This was a letter of suggestion which concluded: 'If we wish to prevent the spread of Communism I believe the answer lies in partnership, and since I now have a grand-daughter resulting from a union between the Dexter and Soong families, I suggest to my son and daughter that the union between our two families could be further cemented by agreement on their part to merge their shares in the Soong Agency with those of Dexter and Company and form Dexter and Soong. Such action would not only benefit both families but be an important contribution to our country's stability.'

Soong might write letters so stiff that they echoed his unbending manner in life, but my God he had some damned good ideas! This was a winner. The different aspects of our two businesses screamed for integration, for Soongs now serviced several international shipping companies with every single thing they needed, from matches to accommo-dation for officers and men ashore, while Dexters filled their holds. Both would benefit enormously from a merger, for each would make a profit from the goods the other didn't handle. Together we could become one of the most power-ful agency houses in Asia – and the timing couldn't have been better, for all around us nations were being granted their independence, and all were eager to spend the lavish aid money which always went with freedom. Who better to patronise than an Anglo-Chinese firm?

We dined that evening with Ian and Vicki Scott, together

with Natasha and Tony who had come down for the weekend, and we showed Scott the letter – and everyone was
laughing after Paul suddenly exclaimed, 'My God! I hope
this doesn't mean I'll have to work.'

'Don't worry,' I laughed with him. 'I would hate to
destroy the habits of a lifetime.'

It was Julie who asked a question that had crossed my
mind. 'I wonder why father didn't include Mummy in the
suggestion?'

After a pause Ian Scott, fingering his knife as we waited
for his boy to serve the main course, said, 'P.P. was a wily
old bird. He knew there can always be only one *tuan bezar*. If
only two-thirds of the Soong shares go into the merger it
won't be enough to match the Dexter shares. And – no
offence, Paul – my guess is that he wanted two things: to
have Johnnie in control, yet to keep the Soong name going,
to make sure Paul and Julie didn't sell off the business, or
even lose control to some unscrupulous rival. After all, the
business was P.P.'s life work. Don't you agree, Johnnie?'

'A bit flattering, but it does sound feasible. But there
might be another reason. P.P. knew I would never agree to
a fifty-fifty merger. That sort of setup never works. You're
right, Ian – someone has to be the boss.'

'You mean – you!' said Vicki brightly. 'I always said you
would be one day, Johnnie.'

'Anyone else can have the job,' I smiled.

'If they knife you in the back,' Paul grinned. 'You're just
right for it. I'm sure you'll make us all a lot of money.'

'Well – as soon as Johnnie and I get married, I hope he'll
ease up a bit,' said Julie.

'What's the latest news on the divorce – when do you
hope to get married?' asked Ian.

'November next year at the latest – maybe a few weeks
earlier,' I said.

I had been keeping in touch not only with my London
solicitors but with Irene, who wrote occasional letters
giving me news of the children. The letters were always

pleasant, she always added, 'My best wishes to Julie' and I think she meant the words sincerely.

Certainly, our lives were made easier by the knowledge that while we were so happy in Ara Irene made no secret of the pleasure she got from living in London – with 'Uncle Bob' presumably on the sidelines. Not 'presumably': when Ben, now nine, wrote to me, his letters were full of 'Uncle Bob'.

Now, suddenly. I became involved in another big business deal – an astonishing proposal from a source I had never imagined. It came from Miki, of all people. I had often wondered whether he had survived in the jungle. Somehow I had never been able to picture him pitting his wits against the leeches and snakes of the rain forest. I had *not* been surprised when out of the blue I received a brief note that Yeop and Siloma had survived, for this was their home ground. But Miki! I would never have believed he could live in the jungle. But I had underestimated him – just as many of us underestimated the Japanese nation.

Not only had Miki survived but during the war his father's construction company had boomed. As the Japanese losses mounted Miki senior had turned to ship-building – knowing that every vessel he built would be sold to the government before it left the slipway. Because of the A-bomb Tokyo, where Miki had his headquarters, and Yokahama, where the firm built their ships, escaped heavy bombing, so they ended the war in a country relatively untouched by aerial bombardment, and with a new over-lord – MacArthur – who encouraged them to rise again by offering them one of history's most generous peace treaties. Added to this was an insatiable desire by an army of drone-like men and women to work; and above all there was no more hate for the white man. The Japanese, though beaten, could meet the white men on equal terms now; they had proved they were capable of humiliating them, and could, with some justification, say they had only surrendered be-cause a new and terrifying bomb would have meant an-nihilation.

Much of this I knew. Some Miki outlined in the first of several long and friendly letters. But it was the crux of the matter that excited me. Miki Construction, by now one of the major shipbuilders in Japan, wanted to build us a fleet of ten vessels to replace the *Anlaby*, the *Beverley*, the *Brough* and other Dexter ships. which had been sunk or requisitioned and never seen again.

However, without a firm export order they could not qualify for a raw materials grant. And Miki knew that though we needed ships desperately we could not expect to receive a penny of our war damage reparations claim before 1948. Miki did have cash – some of it salted away abroad, not to be disclosed to the Japanese Treasury, and therefore unusable. So he proposed an ingenious solution. He would lend us the money in Switzerland to pay for ships which would be owned by a new company, with Dexters holding fifty-one per cent of the equity, Miki Construction forty-nine per cent. This wasn't an offer born only out of generosity. The firm had to be controlled by foreign capital to qualify for raw material grants. You could have all the money in the world in Japan in those days, but without a grant for raw materials you might as well burn it.

What Miki really wanted, I could see, was a long-term investment in a shipping line which would bring in revenue for years to come; that and a way of using his money. We would pay our share of the building costs out of our fifty-one per cent of the profits only when the ships started operating.

There couldn't be a snag. We would suffer no cash flow shortage. We would be paying construction costs out of money we would have had to pay other vessels to carry our cargos. Eventually, when we received our war damage compensation, we could use the cash for other projects.

The only worry that crossed my mind concerned Paul. He was very anti-Japanese – with reason – and if he knew what I was contemplating he might refuse to put his third of the Soong fortune into Dexter and Soong. And though Dexters didn't *need* to amalgamate with Soongs it would be a pity not to. So for the time being I kept the idea to myself.

Apart from any other considerations this *would* be a separate company, though controlled by Dexters. Anyway, if we believed in a multiracial future as the only hope for Asia we would have to include the Japanese despite what had happened – or, I thought, because of them, for they were the ones who had lanced the festering boil of colonialism. And I could trust Miki. He had saved my life, almost at the cost of his own.

I had to tell Julie. That was different. After all these years I told her everything that involved any qualms of conscience. But not for the first time I was surprised by her reaction – and the way the Chinese part of her mind ticked.

'If the Americans can forgive the Japs after Pearl Harbor,' she said wryly, 'I guess we can. I've nothing against Miki. How could I have? If it hadn't been for Miki I wouldn't have a husband-to-be and Pela wouldn't have a wonderful father.' She smiled and added, 'and in a couple of years they'll be welcoming Japanese trade delegations all over the world, you'll see.'

'I'm glad you feel that way. It'll make Dexter and Soongs one of the biggest firms in Asia.'

'With you the *tuan bezar*! That's the only thing that frightens me.'

'Frightens you?'

'A bit.' She was standing up and suddenly she put her arms round my chest, and gave me a wifely kiss, just touching my lips. 'We all change,' she said. 'But remember, I fell in love when I was a girl with a tall handsome blond – that's you, darling Johnnie. But what I also fell in love with was a man with a touch of the devil to match mine – someone ready to risk everything for me. You were my story-book hero. I was innocent, and I gave myself to you, suffered a lot in the years that followed, and never regretted it for an instant.'

'I suppose we do have to grow up.'

'Of course. I'm sure we've both settled down. I'm sure I don't give you the same thrill in bed –'

'Balls, Julie! You're fishing.'

'I'm not. What I'm trying to say is that relationships *do* change – they become mellower, warmer. I love that – I love the tenderness of our so-called married life, I love the way you have transferred some of your love to Pela. The only thing that sometimes does worry me is your – for want of a better word – ambition. I want you to enjoy running the business. I'm going to be so proud to be the *tuan*'s wife. But be careful, Johnnie – don't turn the word *tuan* into tycoon. You're too nice for that.' With a giggle she added, 'Just make enough money to keep us all in super affluence with the best of everything, but don't start making money you can't see except by sitting and gloating over bank statements. Much better to gloat over me before I get so old you start looking at someone else.'

I had no intention of becoming a tycoon – at least I hoped not, though I was aware by now that tycoonery is a disease that creeps up on its subject like an insidious cancer, unnoticed until it is too late. But I did want to keep Dexters going in the family tradition. I loved the firm, and working for it, and Dexters *needed* new ships to deal with the boom. The outer roads of Singapore Harbour were congested with vessels waiting up to three weeks to unload. Every godown bulged with imports or exports, despite our share of labour troubles, echoes of the strike by six thousand dockers that had paralysed the port for sixteen days in the autumn of 1946.

Nothing could stop the boom which had been triggered by several unconnected factors. The swift transaction of the Dutch East Indies to independent Indonesia had caused panic among rich firms worried about the dangers of Communism, so a lot of the Indies trade was switched to Singapore. But the biggest boost came after the first leak that war damage compensation had been assessed in Whitehall at fifty-five million pounds. Britain would contribute an initial ten million with 'maximum additional liability to Malayan governments' of another thirty-five million. The final ten million pounds would be paid by the Japanese in the form of reparations.

Everyone would have to wait for their money – but that didn't matter. Singapore had always lived on credit.

I had already started rebuilding Tanamera, for I wanted the house to be ready for Julie and Pela to move into on the day of our wedding.

At Ara Julie and I had spent hours poring over architects' plans, looking at the delicately tinted elevations. We both wanted 'the perfect house for a *tuan bezar*'. It didn't have to be ostentatious – those days had gone forever – though it still had to be imposing enough to impress business visitors, yet comfortable enough for us to live in as a family. The new Tanamera would have no shallow lily pools in the dining room or precious Chinese tiles round the skirting boards. There would be a large living room behind the white walls that still stood, and above six smallish bedrooms, each equipped with individually-controlled air conditioning.

The main living room – a narrower version of the old ballroom – would not be air conditioned, for it was long – the shape dictated by the existing front walls which still stood – with new east and west verandahs. So in the tradition of the East India Company's architects, the breezes that sometimes ruffled the still hot air of Singapore would pass from one end of the room to the other.

Behind this main living room – and I was determined that it *would* be a living room, not a 'best room' for entertaining – I was building two smaller rooms, a sitting room for Julie, and for me a study. Julie brought up like me in the era of 'Fifty for dinner', had vowed that we would never invite more than ten guests for a formal meal, so the dining room was built with that in mind.

We both felt that a pool or tennis court disfigured a well-kept garden. So they would be hidden. Behind the wall the pool, with showers and a couple of changing rooms, had its own patio, and behind that was the tennis court – unseen unless used.

*

The memorial service was not held until the autumn of 1947, in order to allow some old friends who were abroad time to return. People like Aunt Sonia had to make the trip by sea, for Pan-Am had not yet resumed their prewar Pacific flights from the west coast to Singapore via Honolulu and the Philippines. Papa Jack and Mama flew out by flying boat, taking five days for the journey, with overnight stops in comfortable hotels at Rome and Karachi – a wonderful way to beat time lag; though soon the flying boats would be scrapped, for BOAC had already announced the start in 1948 of a faster service using Constellations.

I wish I could say the visit was a success. The service itself went off quite well, but that was about the only part that did, and I realised almost as soon as my father arrived that the visit had been a disastrous mistake. We didn't openly quarrel at first, but the change I had noticed in my parents in London had accelerated. Papa Jack was querulous, complaining, nosey about aspects of the business which he could not understand or which I had not bothered to tell him about. I needed to exercise a great deal of patience.

He seemed to have forgotten that I was not only thirty-four, but that he had appointed me *tuan bezar* of the business, after suitable arrangements had been made to safeguard his and Mama's future. But I was *boss* – the only one. Dexters had always worked on the premise that two bosses were one too many. That is why, when Grandpa Jack handed over the reins to *his* son – my father – my grandfather never again set foot in Dexters. My father was picking up letters which he found on my desk – including one discussing the plans with Miki.

'With the Japanese!' he spluttered. 'Dexter dealing with the Japanese!'

'Like it or not, they're our friends now – in theory anyway. The war's over.'

'They'll never be our friends. That contract must never be signed.'

'Don't worry, Papa.' I tried patience, but it was a mistake. He thought I was patronising him – and this is

663

what sparked off the really big row of his visit, leading to a rift that neither of us would ever be able to heal.

'*Japanese!* After what they did to Tim. Crushed his spirit so much that he had to be invalided out of the army.'

He had written to me earlier that Tim had left the army and was looking around, which meant living off Dexter money; but that was all right, for I realised he could never return to Singapore. But I knew well enough why Tim had been invalided out – it was a polite term for dismissal, used to save embarrassment. He had been kicked out after the scandal of Changi. I said nothing until Father said again defiantly, 'The Japs nearly killed poor Tim.'

'Come off it, Papa, you know that's not true. The Japs *did* torture millions of people. But Tim was only being punished, and you know it. Tell me one thing: why do members of the same family have to kid each other? You know Tim wasn't invalided out of the army. He was kicked out.'

'Meaning what?' he asked frostily.

'Meaning, as you damn well know, that the Japs found him in bed screwing another soldier. All right, Papa. Keep the skeleton in the family. But at least within the family tell the *truth*.'

He covered his face with his hands, an old, old man of sixty-seven. The ache inside him was not because of what Tim had done, but because I knew. I realised that when he looked up and asked, 'How did you find out? You haven't told anyone, have you?'

'Of course not,' I said. 'Tim's life is his own. It's nothing to do with me – or you! I only feel sorry that Tim had to face more problems in life than we do. But what *does* disgust me is that you blame *me*.'

For a moment I thought he would choke, then the grey face sagged, despair replaced anger, the illusions that come with old age took over the brain and he muttered, 'You're an evil man, Johnnie, to talk about this sort of thing. You are the one who ruined the good name of Dexter. Taking a Chinese mistress. Producing a half-caste daughter.'

'Let's leave Julie out of this.' I tried to control my anger.

'If you had really loved me when I was young Julie and I would have been married years ago.'

'Thank God I did stop you!'

'Forget it.' I didn't want a scene, I just wanted my father to get out of the office, to leave Singapore, to return to London. The world — the war — me — Tim — had been too much for him to absorb. Inconsequentially I suddenly thought, 'Thank God he prefers London to Singapore.' It would be impossible when Julie and I married to share a house with my father and mother. Was that, I wondered, one significant reason why Irene never liked Singapore? The overwhelming burden of three generations, then four, living on top of each other in the same house?

I thought — hoped — my father would leave then, go and see his cronies at the Tanglin Club. But instead, with the persistence of the old, like a dog worrying a bone for the last trace of marrow, he roughly pushed away the arm I had put on his shoulder and muttered, 'I blame the Soong girl more than I blame you. She was the one who led you on.'

'Shut up, father.' My anger was mounting, but I still tried to control it. 'Don't let's spoil your trip to Singapore. Just keep Julie out of this, that's all.'

I didn't want a row, but he insisted on going on and on.

'I remember when Soong came to tell me he had found out. By God, I should have kicked you out of the house. But you've forgotten that, of course.'

'No, I haven't. I remember everything. I remember how I longed for a little loving kindness from my father. Instead I got a dressing down from an old fool. Like a bloody clot I listened to you; I did as you asked. If I'd been half the man you pretend that fairy Tim is I'd have walked out on you. You ruined our lives, Father, *ruined* them. I got them back, and I can tell you one thing here and now — I'm not going to give you the chance to fuck up our lives again. You or Mother.'

'Keep your mother out of this!'

'Sounds like an echo of "Keep Julie out of this".'

Even then I was ready to help him to understand — if he had given me half a chance, even if he had said nothing, just

665

walked quietly out, so that the next time we met it would never have been mentioned. Instead he jutted out his jaw and muttered, 'She wanted you – the Soong girl. And she made certain she got you.'

That was the moment my temper snapped – the more so as it was such a lie, so stupid. That was the moment I could not keep from shouting, 'Like Mother was certain she would get Tim's father when she left you and went to New York?'

'You bastard,' he choked with rage. 'How dare you say a thing like that – a monstrous lie – about your own mother?'

'No, Father, Tim's the bastard, not me. Grandpa Jack told me everything. But what I can't understand is why you have to stand up for a bugger boy who isn't even your own son against me. I'll never know. I used to *want* to please you because I loved you. No more, Father. I just don't like you any more, and the sooner you get back to London the better.' I banged my way out of the office.

I didn't say anything to Julie, and it was obvious that my father said nothing to Mama who was her usual vague self, not unpleasant, just not understanding – about anything. I knew after that morning in the office that we would all be glad when the visit ended, and in fact it was cut short sooner than I expected when my parents met some old friends who persuaded them to spend the last two weeks of their vacation at the Repulse Bay Hotel in Hong Kong.

They left with kisses, embraces, manly handshakes, promises, promises all round. And I do not doubt with secret sighs of relief all round too.

Before the end of the year another visitor arrived, the last man in the world I ever expected to see again in Singapore, even though he was only passing through on his way to Kuala Lumpur.

'I think I'll be staying in Malaya a long time, so let's have a reunion dinner, old boy,' said Detective-Inspector Robin Chalfont of Special Branch.

44

I hadn't seen Chalfont since my visit to Colombo to meet Julie before reporting back to London. But why was he in Singapore? He must be a policeman again, now the war was well and truly over. Special Branch – I never really understood what Special Branch did; I vaguely imagined them as strong-arm boys working in secret – and that of course would be right up Chalfont's street.

Propping up the long bar at Raffles, he looked unchanged, a few more tiny wrinkles, but still with a sardonic grin – very unlike a policeman, I thought.

'What the hell are you doing here?' I could hardly contain my excitement.

'Working.' Chalfont studied the end of an opulent-looking cigar, and added in his old flippant style, 'On expenses. God! giving up smoking was the toughest part of jungle life. But first – before anything else – how's that beautiful wife of yours?'

'Julie? She's not my wife *yet*. But won't she be excited to see you! She's living just outside KL on our old battlefield – the Ara estate. With Tony Scott and his wife. I go up every weekend – until the divorce comes through next year.'

'Seems hard work for a father,' he drawled. 'All that commuting.'

'Something to do with her not wanting to be a concubine,' I grinned. 'Fact is, Robin, I quite enjoy it. I miss her like hell during the week, but the break – changing an office for a rubber estate – is so dramatic I feel I'm living two lives. And it's pretty simple by plane.'

Chalfont! It had never entered my head that I would see him again in Singapore. I thought of the man with the

667

airy-fairy ways whom I had first met in the Adelphi – and who had accepted me as a volunteer for a stint of nearly four years – terrible years, yet years I would never have missed: what I called the growing-up years.

This was the first time I had ever seen Mr Robin Chalfont, civilian. He didn't look the same in his civilian clothes. They seemed to hang oddly on him. He had adopted the latest vogue, introduced into the Pacific war theatre by the Americans: open-necked shirts. The old boys in Singapore had been horrified at first, but they had been forced to capitulate, and by now – albeit reluctantly – club secretaries and restaurant managers were allowing members to lunch without ties, though they still insisted on formal dress after eight p.m.

'Don't worry, I've got a tie in my pocket,' Chalfont reassured me. 'I'll put it on before we go in to dinner.' He wore a sand-coloured lightweight suit.

'Does it fit?' He pulled the jacket straight, half turned on his bar stool. 'Had to get it off the peg, old boy. Only given twenty-four hours' notice to fly here.'

'Why the rush?'

'All in good time. Let's have another round. Look! Magic.' He took his tie out of his pocket and knotted it round his neck without the aid of a mirror, much to the amusement of the barman. 'How are your parents, by the way?'

I had the feeling he was bursting to impart some exciting news but was determined to wait. 'Fine!' The lie came easily. 'They were here not long ago. Came for a sort of farewell service for Julie's father, the famous P.P. Soong. I don't suppose you know what happened.'

'I do. Suicide is a fearful business. It must have been a terrible shock to Julie. I hope after your – well, elopement, she and her father –?'

'We all made it up if that's what you mean. Soong even visited Julie at Ara. Wanted to meet his granddaughter. But he was a sad man towards the end, fighting off the rumours that he was a Communist, even some suggestions that he worked for the Japs during the war.'

'So bloody unnecessary, the whole business,' Chalfont sighed. 'Such a *good* man. And all these people accusing him.'

'Well, I suppose he *did* hobnob with Loi Tek – not only before the war, we know that, but, according to some, during the war too.'

'Loi Tek? How that name keeps on cropping up. In fact that's why I'm here – because of Loi Tek.'

'But he's vanished – or so I was told. Typical of the government to let him off the hook. It's just like the war all over again – bloody incompetence.'

'Not this time.' Chalfont actually chuckled. 'Remember the day Loi Tek visited our camp?'

Of course I did. The Chinese had talked about the great leader – and the honour he'd done them – for weeks. 'It was the Commie equivalent of a royal visit.'

'That's what it looked like – what it was *meant* to look like. In fact, dear boy, Loi Tek came to have a confidential chat with me.'

'In the middle of a war? What the hell for?' I looked at Chalfont.

'I told you, remember. I was – still am – Special Branch.'

'Okay,' I laughed, 'but the jungle wasn't the time or place to make an arrest.'

'Now, Johnnie, sit down and make yourself comfortable. Prepare yourself for a shock. Come over here.' He waved to a boy to carry our drinks from the bar to a circular glass-topped bamboo table with low armchairs round it. 'And bring two more, please.' Chalfont waited until the drinks arrived, signed for them with his room number and then said, 'Take a deep breath. This is going to shake you. Loi Tek and I worked in harness all through the Japanese occupation.'

I must have looked like an idiot, mouth gaping at the preposterous suggestion. Chalfont laughed, ran a finger round the rim of his glass until it made a singing noise, and then, very seriously, added, 'Loi Tek was no more a Communist than you are, or poor old Soong.'

'But he was *Secretary-General* of the Party in Malaya. Christ! That's the top man.'

'We put him there.' Chalfont tried to appear modest. 'Actually rather proud of the way we fixed it. He was one of our top agents – right through the war.'

Puzzled, I said, 'I can understand that people manage to infiltrate into political parties – you can, I suppose, put someone into a Communist party – but you can't just elect your man to be the *boss*. What about the others? You mean to say he was a British spy?'

'We prefer the term agent. I'll explain. Loi Tek was an Annamite working in Indo-China. You knew that. Built up a terrific reputation as a dedicated Communist. But what you didn't know was that all the time he was working for the French. Only when his cover was blown in Saigon did the French send him down to Singapore. Loi Tek was an agent out of work. We gave him a job.'

'But getting him into the committee or whatever they call it – all right, I suppose it's possible to do that. But to become the *leader*?'

'That's the part we're rather proud of. Once he was on the committee – and, remember, before the war the Communist Party was proscribed in Singapore – he tipped us off when a secret meeting of the full Central Committee was being held. We nabbed the bloody lot – and banished them. All except Loi Tek. We arranged to arrest him on a traffic offence while he was on his way to the meeting. After that – it was easy, dear boy. He was the only committee member left, and so took over automatically.'

So that was why Loi Tek had become such a shadowy figure, why so few people ever saw him! Had he been afraid of recognition by someone he had known in Saigon? And of course, as Chalfont pointed out, his elusiveness, his secrecy, helped to increase the legend among the rank and file. Secrecy *was* the only way to escape jail or banishment. The more he was unknown, the greater the legend he built up around himself.

'And old Soong – how did he fit in?'

'That's the tragedy. Soong was the link man. There were

only two men in Singapore who knew about Loi Tek – not even the governor knew – thank God! Soong was one, I was the other. And of course I could never tell you. Then your brother started to get suspicious of old Soong. That's why I had to pull rank and get your brother off Soong's back. That's why we had to watch Julie. Not because there was anything on *her* files – but in case she found out something. And of course I knew – though I didn't think much about it at the time – that Soong Kai-shek was a Communist. We damned nearly chucked him into jail. Would have done – except that he volunteered for Force 136.'

Then Singapore fell. And that, according to Chalfont, was when Loi Tek really came into his own – because, while he was a British agent posing as a Communist leader, he actually started working for the Japanese as well, with British knowledge. It was easy for him to arrange for the Japanese to massacre party members as they did in the Batu Caves outside KL. Loi-Tek tipped the Japs off – and then, as usual, was conveniently delayed on the way to the meeting.

'It's quite incredible, really,' Chalfont said. 'During the entire Japanese occupation he was Secretary-General of the Malayan Communist Party, he was a Japanese agent, sometimes being driven in a Japanese car, and all the time he was telling Force 136 everything that was happening, almost every move the Japs were making, the traps they were setting for us.'

'But even if he worked for them, why should the Japs tell him details like that?'

'Don't you see – they *had* to. If they killed too many Chinese guerillas, Loi Tek would be discredited – or even refuse to supply them with information. And you're going to find this hard to believe – but the Japanese actually asked Loi Tek to arrange the assassination of Satoh. Remember that bastard?'

'But Robin' – I ordered two more drinks – 'I killed the bugger.'

'I know. Tough assignment. But the Japs wanted it. Loi Tek was behind it.'

I still couldn't see why the Japanese should ask the Chinese to kill one of their own officers.

'Quite natural. The Japs were trying to build up good will to win over the peasants. For a time reprisals almost stopped among the Chinese and Malays. But every now and again some bugger like Satoh behaved so monstrously that he almost wrecked their good will plans. He was well connected, the Japs didn't want a scandal, so the easiest thing was to arrange for him to be bumped off. You did a nice job on that one, Johnnie.' His blue eyes were twinkling with laughter.

'I'm not sure I find it that funny,' I grunted.

'You killed a swine. That's enough.'

'Well, the good will plan didn't seem to work for long, did it? I mean, the reprisals after Kai-shek attacked the Ara conference were not exactly neighbourly.'

'They certainly weren't. And nothing could excuse them. Nothing. But there was a reason for that too. If you hadn't been ill there would never have been any trouble. When you vetoed the attack, we told Loi Tek – and he was then able to guarantee that the conference wouldn't be harmed. But the unexpected happened. It *was* attacked. Kai-shek went on the rampage, a whole squad of top brass was massacred – just as every one could see the Japs were being driven back. The local commanders jumped to the obvious – but wrong – conclusion: that Loi Tek had betrayed them – had decided the Japs were going to lose the war. So the reprisals weren't on the villagers; they were a warning to Loi Tek.'

As Chalfont sat there, talking calmly, it was almost impossible to believe – all those years in the jungle, imagining ourselves cut off, working and killing by instinct – and behind the scenes so many of the actions we took motivated by a strange unknown man working for three masters.

'He saved dozens of Force 136 lives,' said Chalfont. 'It might well include yours, though we'll never know. You know, like never knowing what would have happened to you if you took one turning instead of the other. He is a very brave man.'

'Is?'

'He's not dead – but he has ceased to exist.'

As Chalfont started to explain, my mind went back to rumblings of discontent in the Party that had reached my ears – the article in a Penang Communist newspaper all but calling Loi Tek a traitor, though when it was rumoured that the author had worked as a Japanese agent, most people thought he was trying to settle an old grudge, and the article was quickly forgotten. According to Chalfont, the growing suspicions gradually crystallised until Chin Peng decided to act. Not only because of his suspicions, but because he was heir apparent to the coveted 'throne'. He demanded a show-down.

'When we realised the game was up – that Loi Tek was on the point of being blown – we got him out,' said Chalfont. 'And damn quickly, I can tell you. When the Central Committee assembled five miles outside KL last March to have a showdown with Loi Tek he never showed up. We gave him a new passport, new identity, lots of money and' – with a typical Chalfont grin – 'we suggested that as he was doing a bunk he might as well pinch all the Party funds as well. That *really* made the Commies hopping mad.'

'Where is he?'

'That'd be telling. But historians who write about this – and one day it will no longer be top secret, I suppose – will never find out. At least I hope not.'*

'Now of course I see the part poor Soong played.'

'That's why he forgave you Johnnie, you and Julie. He *knew* what you were doing. Loi Tek told him. *And* how you got Julie away.'

'I wonder if he knew about Soong Kai-shek?'

'Hard to say, but probably not.'

---

* It is still not certain whether Loi Tek is alive or dead. Professor Anthony Short in his masterly *The Communist Insurrection in Malaya* (Muller) says that he went to Hong Kong and then Siam, where one message reaching the Malayan Communist Party said that he had been killed by a Chinese killer squad, but 'from time to time reports reached Malayan intelligence of Loi Tek manifestations: that he was again active in Siamese Communist circles'.

'Any sign of him?' I added with a grin, 'I have a slight interest, you know. He's sworn to kill me.'

'Don't know where he is, but probably gone into the jungle. Waiting – he's a bastard all right.'

'Seems crazy. Living in the jungle when he could be having a whale of a time in Singapore on the Soong millions.'

'You lived in the jungle.'

'That was different. I was fighting for Britain.'

'He's fighting for a cause.' Chalfont added cryptically, 'Men don't change; only habits.'

'I can't believe Paul had any idea what his father was doing.'

'Not a clue. I'm sure Paul doesn't know that after he had been beaten almost to death old Soong went to Loi Tek for help. Loi Tek got the drugs – from the Japs of course. It's damned ironic when you think of it, one lot of Japs beating the hell out of a chap, another lot doling out precious drugs to save his life.'

'What a tragedy about poor Soong,' I said. 'As you say, his suicide was all so unnecessary.'

'The sad thing is,' Chalfont sighed again, 'that all the accusations came before Loi Tek was blown. Everyone thought he was a double-dyed Communist. And Soong couldn't deny the accusations without giving away one of our finest agents. And of course we couldn't help Soong – that's the first rule if you're an agent. Get into trouble, and it's up to you to get out of it. Unaided. If only he'd waited a couple of months. Today there'd be no secret to betray.'

What did puzzle me all through dinner was: why had Chalfont returned to Singapore? 'Not that I'm not delighted to see you,' I grinned.

'Because there's trouble ahead. The defection of Loi Tek is going to force the hands of the Communists. They've lost out politically – they're in disarray. But they're damned strong when it comes to guns. We reckon there's a nucleus of five thousand dedicated fighters – trained by us – with all the guns they've kept hidden since V-J Day. If you're driven into a corner there comes a time when the only way out is to fight. After all, the Commies can still pose as heroes. They drove the Japs out – so they say. Now it's time for them to drive the imperialists out.'

'Couldn't a strong government cope?'

'You haven't got a strong government. Sir Edward Gent, the High Commissioner – well, it's not up to me to say things, but you know how to keep your mouth shut. There have already been discussions in Whitehall about recalling him.'

During the spring and early summer of 1948 we saw a great deal of Robin, especially at weekends. Almost every Sunday he drove the ten miles from Kuala Lumpur to Ara for a swim in the pool and then a huge curry tiffin. Occasionally I would go to see him if Julie had to visit the hairdresser or shop in KL, and then I would watch the progress he was making in what he sardonically described as 'our dirty tricks department'.

It was hidden behind a rubber plantation not far from KL and covered an astonishing ten acres, surrounded by an electrified ten-foot barbed wire fence.

'But what for?' I asked. 'Don't you think you're being alarmist? There's no sign of any Communist uprising.'

'Only because you don't choose to see the signs,' said Robin. 'It's bound to come. And then you'll be bloody grateful for all this.'

He led me through a bewildering assortment of bugged cells, two-way mirrors, a lab for processing documents, a machine shop working on secret devices. In one large room radio experts were working patiently on scores of ancient battery sets which had been quietly bought in small shops. Each one was being taken to pieces and remade – using only old wire and solder that had been deliberately dirtied.

'They'll be leaked into shops known to be Communist sympathisers, and we've put a bleep-bleep homing signal in every one. A Communist won't hear that bleep in a jungle camp but we can monitor it here, and it will give us a pinpoint location of his camp, whenever he switches the radio on.'

On another visit he said to me, 'Come and take a look at this, old boy.' An earnest Chinese was opening the bottom of a tube of toothpaste, millimetre by millimetre, after which he extracted a tiny piece of rice paper with a message on it. This was rushed away to be photographed, then reinserted and the tube closed so that it was impossible to detect that anyone had tampered with it.

'The Communists have already established a courier network covering all Malaya,' said Chalfont. 'Luckily we've got a few agents planted as "postmen", but it's not enough for them to give us the message. Sometimes they're hidden in fruit, inside a cigarette, a tube of toothpaste like the one you've just seen – and every message has to be returned looking as though it's not been touched. The only way we can use information of this sort is if the Communist doesn't realise we know what he's up to.'

Though I was fascinated I could not pretend at first that I was at all apprehensive. It all seemed like playing war games in peacetime, for there was no war. Even the old club on the Bentong Road had just reopened – shades of Satoh! – though now we ate steaks and chips instead of bangers and mash at the monthly dances.

Still, even if I was not unduly worried at the prospect of violence I was, like all businessmen, deeply concerned at the increasing industrial strife. In 1947 more than three hundred Communist-inspired strikes had paralysed rubber estates or tin mines. In the last month nine labourers had been shot, while police in one town had been forced to open fire on rioters armed with spears, stones, bottles and lead piping, killing seven after they refused to disperse. On rubber estates posters appeared tacked to trees, screaming, 'Death to the Running Dogs!' And outside Malaya, as though part of an orchestrated attempt to kill and destroy, Communists were harrying the new independent Burmese government, while others were fighting in the streets of Indonesia. In Singapore we had faced increased violence at the Harbour Board ever since the dock strike paralysed the city; and when the offices of the Harbour Board Union were raided by the police in April they found details of plans 'to exterminate all worker-traitors who were detrimental to the interests of the working class'.

'Isn't it really the same old Communist waffle?' I asked Chalfont, cooling off in the Ara pool as I tried to teach Pela, a born swimmer, the crawl.

'I don't think so.' He shook a wet head.

'But damn it – we've promised Malaya independence!'

'That's *capitalist* waffle,' Chalfont laughed. 'Promises without dates. Like a hostess who gushes, "You *must* come to dine with us," but never says when.'

It was in early May that I first began to be alarmed, after the Central Committee of the MCP met in Singapore and I read a copy of the manifesto they issued after the meeting. It was nothing more or less than a clarion call to all Communists to prepare for direct violent action. It admitted that subversive labour tactics such as strikes and arson had failed, and this was dangerously significant, for it left only one alternative, which the manifesto spelled out with chilling simplicity: 'The masses cannot tolerate British Imperialist suppression any longer and want to use action to smash their reactionary legal restrictions.'

'That means a change in the basic struggle,' I warned Julie the following weekend at Ara. 'If they can't beat us legally they're going to try force. I don't like it. Honestly, darling, I think you and Pela should come to Singapore for a bit until this hoo-ha blows over.'

'Run away!' Julie was indignant. 'First the Japs, now my own countrymen. And leave Natasha and Victoria? Never!'

It was the last week in May and Chalfont was lunching with us. 'Johnnie's right,' he said. 'I'll tell you something off the record. In the middle of April – only a few weeks ago – our old chums from the jungle, members of the ex-service Comrades Association of the MPAJA, were all warned to get ready.'

'For what?' asked Tony.

'For war. Every one received a circular. There's been a complete re-registration of members. Old ones who lapsed have been tracked down, and now I'll tell you something hard to believe: they've started actual mobilisation in Perak and Johore. Top Communist officials have been told to sell any property while they've got the chance and prepare to take to the jungle. I tell you, it's no joke.'

'But they can't get away with it,' cried Julie. 'It's the factory workers, not the tappers, who are Communists. And if we all leave our estates as Johnnie wants me to we're playing into their hands.'

That was true. Yet anti-British demonstrations were increasing in rural areas. Labour disputes which would normally be forgotten after they were resolved now flared into murder or arson before anyone had a chance to settle them, almost as though the workers didn't *want* disputes to end.

Early in June the Communist party paper *Min Sheng Pao* told its readers bluntly, 'When Imperialism orders its running dogs to oppress us we will take the same methods against them. For the sake of our lives we cannot give in any further but must fight our way through struggle.'

'Them's fighting words,' agreed Tony.

'The trouble is' – Chalfont was more serious than I had seen him for a long time – 'they mean it. And they mean it because they're backed up by five thousand highly trained, armed jungle fighters with itchy fingers, dying to squeeze the trigger on the Stens they stole from us. They're killers, Julie. I know. I helped train them.'

'But even if there are a few riots the masses won't support Communism. Malaya has been promised independence,' argued Tony. 'The peasants don't want any more fighting, surely.'

'They don't have to fight, only support,' said Chalfont. 'Passive assistance. And remember, "Independence" is a heady word, and to the average Malay it's got nothing to do with Communism. They think that's just a means to speed up the process, though we know better.'

It was only natural that every Malay and every Singaporean should dream of unlocking their colonial handcuffs, for though Malaya was an earthly paradise, with almost every want supplied by nature, even paradise has its cramping sophistries, and the Communist argument was dangerous because of its half truths as well as its omissions.

Malaya, they cried, had been a simple, happy, self-sufficient country until the white man came along. From him the Malays had inherited the evils of so-called civilisation as the white man robbed the country of its riches – until driven out by the Japanese. Why should they be allowed back into a country they had been unable to hold?

'What they never say,' added Chalfont, 'is what Malaya will be like under Mao Tse-tung. For that – not independence – is the objective.'

'Well, I'm not going,' declared Julie.

'Nor me,' said Natflat, adding with a touch of humour, 'and leave Tony here with all these planters' wives! My God, the next thing you know he'd be appearing in a story by Somerset Maugham.'

Before Chalfont set off for KL, I asked him a question that had been puzzling me. If Chalfont was so sure of his facts could he not take some preventive action?

''Fraid not, old man,' he explained. 'We're only here to advise, not keep law and order. I was sent out *in case* things blow up. Taking action in peacetime is the job of the police force. And that –' He shrugged his shoulders, almost a gesture of despair.

He explained what he meant. The Commissioner of Police by this time was H. B. Langworthy, the same man who had helped to quell the rioting Indians before the war. But he was a sick man now, trying to reorganise a shattered police force which was split down the middle by hatred. On the one side were those who, at the fall of Singapore, had obeyed the stupid orders of Shenton Thomas to 'stay at your posts until the flag has been hauled down'. Ranged against them were those who had escaped to carry on the fight when defeat became inevitable. (Langworthy was in England on leave so faced no such choice.) Those who remained – and spent the war years in Changi – never forgave those who got away, even those who joined Force 136.

'It's a full-time job for Langworthy to try to boost police morale,' said Chalfont. 'But the trouble is, Gent, the High

Commissioner, listens to him, but Langworthy doesn't really take the right advice. One of the most brilliant police executives here is Hugh Barnard. He sent in detailed reports of secret Communist arms dumps and jungle training grounds, but they were virtually ignored.'*

'Sounds bad,' I admitted.

'It is,' agreed Chalfont. 'Get the girls out if you can. I hope I'm wrong, but I've got a feeling the balloon's going up soon.'

'I'll talk to Julie – if not this weekend, next Friday. Try to knock some sense into her.'

'Not so easy.' Tony poured out a final Scotch. 'You've got to be married to a woman before you can give her orders.'

I was waiting at the Cricket Club to meet George Hammonds for lunch when the pips on the radio behind the bar announced that it was exactly one p.m., and time for the Malayan Broadcasting Company's news bulletin.

It was terse and frightening. At around half past eight on that warm morning of 16 June 1948 three Chinese had murdered Arthur Walker, the planter of the Elphil Estate twenty miles east of Sungei Siput in north Malaya. Half an hour later and ten miles away, at the main office of the Sungei Siput Estate, John Allison, the fifty-five-year-old manager, and his assistant, Ian Christian, who was twenty-one, were tied to their chairs and shot dead in cold blood. That was all I knew – until George arrived.

'Bad business about those planters,' I said after ordering a couple of gimlets.

'Don't tell me,' he almost groaned. 'Let's go out on the verandah, can't get used to the freezing air in here.' We walked outside, and the warm tropical air hit us like a curtain, beautiful; I too liked to feel the heat writhing round

* W. F. N. Churchill, Adviser to the Sultan of Kelantan, noted in his diaries, 'The Special Branch had a good idea of what was brewing but Gent did not heed the warnings; he remained obstinately of the opinion that no danger really existed. Langworthy also preferred not to listen to his Special Branch.'

my body rather than have to rush for a jacket whenever I went inside a room. Our modest air conditioning before the war had just cooled the room down. American expertise had now developed air conditioning to the point where it almost froze you.

'Did they get away with much cash – the robbers?'

'They weren't robbers,' said Hammonds. 'They left two thousand dollars in notes in the safe. They were armed killer squads – Communists.'

I knew Sungei Siput, with its main street of shophouses, coffee shops and one cinema. It was typical of a dozen mining towns north of Kuala Lumpur, surrounded by strange moonscapes – a hangover from worked-out mines, with pale ochre dredging pools, often sprouting tall lilies against a background of sliced earth and spidery, derelict dredges.

To the east, away from these environmental eyesores, unmetalled roads led towards the foothills – and the rubber estates. Rubber, too, was booming, as we knew from the prices and production at Ara. Three million acres in Malaya were now under rubber.

'You don't really mean it?' I must have looked sceptical, though I did remember Chalfont's warnings. 'Not yet – anyway.'

'I know the Elphil Estate where Arthur Walker was shot,' said George. I knew of it too, for at times we had shipped rubber for the estate, but I had never been there.

'What happened?' I signalled to Chan for another round.

Hammonds's answer was frightening. Elphil was a lonely estate, the red laterite road ending at the main estate office, with its corrugated iron roof. Arthur Walker's wife had gone shopping early to escape the heat, and she and her husband were looking forward to their leave in England, due in a couple of weeks. Like all good planters, Walker had made the rounds of the estate early in the day and returned to the office about eight o'clock.

'As far as I can make out,' said George. 'He had just finished giving orders to the estate clerk, an Indian, and was clearing up a few papers when three young Chinese rode up to the office on bicycles. They apparently greeted him, "*Tabek, tuan*" – the usual form, "Salutations, sir" – and seconds later they shot him. From the next office the Indian saw them walk quietly out to their bicycles. He dashed into the room – found Walker's body slumped by the office safe, but then the most frightening moment occurred. The leader of the murderers stared at him unblinkingly, to show that he was not afraid of being identified.

Allison and Christian were murdered by a gang of twelve Chinese and, as at Elphil, the most haunting memories of the estate clerks were, as one told the police, 'They seemed like soldiers obeying orders, who weren't even very interested.'

We went into the dining room and ordered *ikan kuru* – they always did deep-fried fish well at the club – washed down with Tiger.

'It's bloody terrifying,' I said. 'If what you say is true. I know the Communists have been hiding Sten guns and ammo, but can they get really organised? And anyway, George – *why*? The Federation of Malaya has been a fact since the beginning of the year. We've promised independence. They've seen what's happened in India. Christ! Even Ceylon became a self-governing dominion early this year. There's nothing to fight for. So why fight?'

'Self-preservation of the Communist party. Its morale needs boosting. History never changes. When morale is low you improve it by fighting. They *have* to fight.'

'But surely we can nip it in the bud – now, right away?'

'Not so easy. Look how *you* kept hidden for nearly four years. And your pink face stands out for miles. It's a damned sight easier for them. They can come out of the jungle, terrorise villagers for food.'

I couldn't quite believe the situation was as serious as George had painted it, but I phoned through to Ara that evening and told Julie flatly that if she was worried she must come to Singapore right away. She and the others all laughed at me.

'Tony came home at lunchtime with a revolver,' she said,

'and he says he's going to build an armoured car.' She thought it was a great joke.

'But I get panicky, darling – and for Pela.'

'Apart from anything else,' said Julie, 'You'll be up in two days. Let's talk then. And drive carefully – I love you.'

The next day there was a terrifying outburst of violence, this time directed against the Chinese. On the Senal Estate near Johore Bahru – within easy driving distance of the Sultan's palace – ten men ambushed a Chinese head labourer and pumped fifteen bullets into him. In Pahang an anti-Communist family was burned alive in a house. A Chinese contractor was murdered at Taiping not far from Sungei Siput.

'There seems to be no pattern to it all,' I said to Hammonds.

'There's a pattern, all right,' said George. 'This is the preliminary stage – they're instilling terror all over the country. They're warning the Chinese: help us with food, money, shelter – or you'll be killed. The worst case so far came in early this morning.'

According to George, five terrorists dressed in British jungle greens with red stars on their caps and holding Sten guns walked into a kampong near Voules Estate in Johore, dragged out the headman, a Chinese tapper called Ah Fung, and told him, 'We need subscriptions. You will gather fifty cents a week from every tapper on the estate.' Ah Fung pleaded that it was impossible, that he had a police record.

The terrorist looked at him without emotion, nodded to one of his men, 'Tie him up!'

A terrified Ah Fung shrieked that he would try to get the subscriptions, but the terrorist brusquely said it was too late. Ah Fung's wife and children were rounded up, the father was tied to a tree. The family was forced to watch as the leader sliced each one of Ah Fung's arms off above the elbow with a parang. Then he turned to the wife and children and said, 'I am in a benevolent mood today. I will spare his life.'

'Christ!' I said to George, 'I'm going to get Julie out even if I have to drag her by the hair. It's one thing for men –

Tony Scott can look after himself, I'm sure – but women – that's different.'

'Knowing Julie, will she leave?'

'She bloody well will!' With a grin I showed him the leader in the *Straits Times*. 'I know I shouldn't flaunt the opposition, but I like this!'

The leading article was a violent attack on Gent, the High Commissioner, headed 'Govern or Get Out'. It was the culmination of frustrated pleas by planters and miners for protection. Many had begged him to declare a state of emergency. But all demands for arms and protection by planters in lonely estates were ignored by Gent who openly said they were 'alarmist'.

The *Malaya Tribune* printed an even more detailed account of the meeting, and quoted 'Mr Anthony Scott, the planter at Ara Estate near Kuala Lumpur, was heard to shout in a loud voice, "Why don't we all recommend Gent for a bar to his OBE".' At the same meeting Gent told W. F. N. Churchill, the adviser, 'Planters make me sick. Do they want me to put a bloody guard on every estate bungalow?' That was just what planters *did* want.

Now I was becoming really frightened – haunted by the same fear common to all men when they are not certain their loved ones are safe. How could I go about my daily business when Communist terrorists were chopping off people's arms and some bloody nitwit of a high commissioner sat back and talked of panic? What I wanted – as every man had wanted during the war – was to know that Julie and Pela were safe, sleeping in beds where no one could molest them. And now I wasn't going to take no for an answer. I telephoned Julie again and told her, in a voice harsh with fear, 'No bullshit, darling. I'm coming up tomorrow to get you and Pela and Natflat. You're coming to Singapore. You can live with Paul in your house and I'll sneak in.'

I could sense the hesitation – fighting her sense of loyalty to Natasha if she refused to come.

'Don't worry about Natasha,' I said. 'I'm going to tell Tony a few grisly details. She's *got* to leave.'

'I hate it, but I know you're right.' Julie said. 'We've been given a policeman as a guard, but Tony says we're heading for a full-scale war — well, a sort of war. And though half of me feels I should stay the other half says I shouldn't risk Pela, and that my man wants me. Do you?'

'I adore every single thing about you. And I'm coming up to collect you tomorrow.'

The next morning I told Li, 'I'm going to fetch Miss Soong and our daughter. They will be living with Mr Paul at the big house, but we'll have them over for lunch on Sunday. Then you can see Miss Pela.'

Li of course knew that Julie and I were to be married after the divorce, but he had never seen Pela before.

I left at five in the morning to get a good start before the heat of the day. I decided to drive, for by now I had a much bigger, faster car, as befitted a *tuan*, a Buick which I had been able to buy directly from America, and I loved it, though Paul had said jokingly, 'Sign you're getting old when you give up small cars.'

Well, I thought as I raced over the causeway and set off along the main Segamat Road, maybe he's right. And why not? We were all growing older.

I had passed Segamat by the time I switched on the car radio to listen to the eight o'clock news.

The lead item caused me to give a whoop of joy, for it was an official announcement that a State of Emergency had been declared by Sir Edward Gent over the whole of Malaya. 'Good old Tony!' I thought. 'That'll teach these dithering politicians what's what!' What the announcer (and I) didn't know was that this was the date, 18 June 1948, which marked the start of a vicious war on terrorism that would last for twelve blood-stained years.

I reached over to turn off the radio. Local news never excited me very much, but then I thought that maybe Gent would be issuing a statement.

Instead the cold impersonal voice of the announcer droned on, 'There were far fewer incidents in Malaya, though two women, including the daughter of a prominent Chinese family, have been abducted, apparently by Communists.'

A fearful premonition gave me a sudden, blinding pain over my heart. My chest seemed to constrict, I found it hard to breathe. I knew, *I knew*! As I panted for breath, clutching the wheel, eyes unfocused, I found myself whispering as the road tore past me, as the looping lines of phone wires dipped and rose between each ancient telegraph post, 'Please, O Lord, I have never asked for anything – but please, O Lord, not Julie.'

'More news is just coming in of the abduction,' said the announcer. 'The missing women have been identified. One is Mrs Tony Scott, wife of the well-known planter of the Ara Estate, and the other is Miss Julie Soong, who was staying with the Scotts.' I heard the rustle of paper. 'It is not yet known whether or not they are alive. Mr Scott was on his rounds when the terrorists launched their attack, but two children were rescued by a planter who happened to be visiting the Ara bungalow just as a terrorist was taking them away.'

45

Two thoughts hammered at my brain as I tore the last few miles towards Kuala Lumpur and Ara, killing a couple of squawking chickens in the main street of Kendong, a village at the foot of the Rambau mountains, nearly three thousand feet of glowering black jungle. Further on near Rahang I grazed a parked car when swerving to avoid two villagers daydreaming in the crowded street. Again I didn't stop.

As always the twin thoughts. *I must tell Chalfont.* (It never entered my tortured brain that as a policeman he would already know.) And *I must contact Macmillan* – for in this most desperate crisis of my life I needed one more man by my side. At Serdan, a few miles south of KL, I jammed the car to a halt at the local post office, thrust aside a queue of patient Malays and Indians and got through on the phone to Mac. He promised to catch the next plane.

When I braked in a flurry of red dust at Ara the first man I saw was Chalfont.

'Thank God you're here!' I cried. 'Where are they, Robin? *Where are they?* What can we do?' Brokenly I told him I had sent for Macmillan. And for the first time I realised that a second man was standing silently by Chalfont. I was so distraught I hadn't really accepted his presence. His face was vaguely familiar. He was dressed in blue shorts, a flowered shirt. He came forward, hand outstretched and introduced himself, 'I'm Sando. I plant one of the estates round here. If there's anything I can do? . . .'

Then I remembered. He was the planter whose stupidity before the war had so inflamed the Indian work force that they set fire to his bungalow and then chased him all the way to Ara. 'Christ,' I muttered, 'you're a bad omen at this time.'

Chalfont laid an arm gently on my shoulder. 'Mr Sando saved the children, Johnnie.' I must have looked at them both stupidly for he added, 'He arrived purely by chance as they were being taken by a Chinese to a waiting car. Tony was still on his rounds. Sando sensed something was wrong and started questioning the man. The man drew a gun. Our friend here was unarmed, but he brought the man down with a rugger tackle and shouted for help. He and Tony's head boy tied the man up, got Pela and Victoria into the bungalow, and Mr Sando phoned me.'

'Sorry, under a bit of a strain,' I muttered. 'Most grateful. Bloody good show.'

'The children are upstairs and we've got a police guard on the estate,' Chalfont explained.

Poor Tony looked done in, face haggard, bags under his eyes. But he realised that I felt as bad as he did, and tried to tell me what had happened. Not that he knew much, but his servants had filled him in. He had left around six o'clock to take early muster in the lines and make a brief tour to allot work before breakfast. Julie and Natasha apparently both rose early, partly because the children did, so they were all downstairs by seven o'clock when there was a knock on the door.

Two men in jungle greens, their hats adorned with red stars, burst in waving Sten guns. They beckoned the women and children to leave. The head boy remembers Julie crying, 'What do you want? Is it money? Please don't harm the children.' When the boy tried to gather up the children to protect them he was coshed with a gun barrel. There was some evidence of a brief struggle. Julie and Natasha must have been taken to a car; the children told Tony they had been ordered out, but there was no room in the tiny van for everyone. One of the men remembered there was a sentry outside and he, too, had a small car. So he was told to take the children and follow.

During this time Tony's boy had recovered consciousness – but not his courage. Even so, what he decided to do was in fact intelligent. Knowing that if he tried to stop the men he would be coshed or shot he lay still, trying to see or hear as much as he could. Then he heard the sound of a car he knew well – not in fact a car, but Mr Sando's Jeep, a new acquisition (from war surplus) of which he was very proud. The rest we knew. As soon as Sando floored the man and cried for help the boy regained his courage and helped Sando to tie the man up.

'Where *are* they, Robin? For God's sake, we've got to *do* something. We can't just stand here nattering.'

'Calm down, Johnnie.' Chalfont's voice had a new, sharp bite to it, the old nonchalant drawl of his army days replaced by an urgency I had never known before. Perhaps, I thought, that's what happens when your own friends are involved. Or perhaps it masked a worry he didn't want to reveal?

Finally, almost with a sigh, and speaking slowly, he said, 'This is no ordinary Communist attack, no ordinary kidnap, despite what the radio says. It doesn't bear the stamp of the Sungei Siput murders. Revolutions *always* follow a pattern. The first murders were a public demonstration of formal executions, in full view of Malays or Indians. Partly to terrorise them, I'm sure. This one smacks of – revenge. It isn't too impossible a word. Otherwise, why no killing? Abduction? It's ridiculous, really. All our information says the jungle Communists must be short of food. Why waste food on two white women? Unless they're being kept alive for a reason.'

At first, even when I was driving north, hearing only the bare bones of the story, plunged into a state of near shock, the announcer's words had indicated that this was an extension of the violence which was spreading with the speed of a bush fire. But then, as I drove on, I began to wonder if Soong Kai-shek was behind it. Not likely perhaps, but he *had* taken to the jungle, he *had* sworn to kill me. The thought had joggled loosely round my brain, but now I spoke just one word, 'Soong?'

'It's possible. At first I dismissed the idea. Despite what they say in detective stories it can be very dangerous to act on a hunch. Might lead you in the wrong direction for days, weeks. But then something happened – and that *did* shock me.'

When they took the Chinese who had tried to kidnap the children to jail they were able to identify him from a mugshot file of Communists which Special Branch was building up. He was a well-known Party member.

'And there was a bonus,' said Chalfont. 'I didn't even see the man when he was bundled into the police van. But back at the cells, after I was shown his picture, I realised I knew him. What's more, Johnnie, you know him too. Does the name Ah Tin mean anything to you?'

No brain-racking was necessary to remember the man whose twin brother, an innocent anti-Communist, I had deliberately killed. I should never forget the look of horror and hate as Ah Tin backed away after I blew up the bomb which killed Satoh – and Ah Tin's brother – and the moment when Ah Tin started to run and Macmillan begged me to shoot him because he knew the way to our camp. I had held my fire – and now this had happened.

'We know that towards the end of the war, when you were

689

ill, Ah Tin joined Kai-shek's guerilla force,' said Chalfont.

At this moment Macmillan arrived by taxi from KL.

'This has nothing to do with their so-called glorious revolution,' I said. 'Kai-shek's using it as a blind. Don't you agree?'

'Ninety per cent,' admitted Chalfont.

'Well, then, we've got to find him, for Chrissake! My bet is that he's in our old camp. Ah Tin knows the way. We'll force the bugger to take us.'

The inaction would drive me crazy if I didn't take a hold of myself. And Tony too. I could see that he was near breaking point. But what could I do? She had been taken – but where? And instead of action there was the torture of *inaction* – thinking the worst because there was nothing to do but imagine what a psychopathic killer who had hated me for years planned to do with them.

I could even imagine the place where they were being held captive – if, that is, they were alive – the hot, wet jungle camp, the parade ground ringed by tall trees, where we had all spent so many dreadful years. In between snatches of conversation, rambling thoughts on what to do, I relived those days – the monstrous food, the insects, the makeshift washing facilities in the small river, the worse-than-makeshift toilets – the lowest section of the river, no screens, no seats, just a pool of water over which we squatted by the river. Was it a 'mixed' lavatory now? Poor girls, victims in a campaign of hatred to make me suffer.

'I know how you and Tony feel, but' – Chalfont turned to Macmillan – 'Don't you agree, Mac, that we must play a waiting game – until we get a message? This is kidnap and blackmail. And we've got to wait for the blackmailer to state his terms. My bet is that they'll come this afternoon.'

Chalfont was right. Shortly after two o'clock a small, dark-haired Tamil boy with shiny white teeth approached the bungalow along the red road, each footstep sending up a tiny puff of dust. As he arrived at the back entrance, I saw Tony's amah point us out and the boy came round, polite, smiling, and enquired, 'May I be speaking please to *tuan* Dexter?'

Before I could speak Chalfont said sharply, 'This is Mr Scott's estate. Who is Mr Dexter?'

'Not knowing, *tuan*. I am offered fifty cents to deliver this letter to *tuan* Dexter at Ara. Is all I know.'

He had an obviously honest face, and most people in the area knew I spent my weekends at Ara. But now, in a crisis, a message could mean anything. As I started forward Chalfont held up his hand and said, 'I'm Mr Dexter. Where's the letter?'

The boy handed it over. 'May I?' Chalfont looked at me before ripping open the soiled envelope. To the boy Chalfont said simply, 'Wait.' Then in dead silence, as though all of us were afraid of impending drama, he took out the contents.

'I imagine you recognise this, Johnnie.' Chalfont's voice was flat, masking suppressed fears.

With a sick feeling I held out my hand. I didn't need to look twice at the brilliant circle of emeralds, diamonds, rubies, at the eternity ring I had given to Julie that wartime Christmas.

'Any message?' My voice was a croak.

Chalfont peered into the envelope while I looked stupidly at the ring I had given to her when we were so happy together. I was miles away in thought when Chalfont's voice interrupted me.

'Yes, there is,' he said. 'Brace yourself, Johnnie. You're going to need all your guts now.'

He handed me a slip of paper on which was a long message printed in capital letters. My fingers were trembling so much I had to grip the paper as though I was holding a pan of boiling fat. It was very simple:

DEXTER'S MISTRESS AND SISTER ARE SAFE BUT ONE MUST DIE BY WEEKEND. DEXTER WILL CHOOSE WHICH ONE TO EXECUTE AND PLACE INNOCUOUS ADVERTISEMENT WHICH WE CAN UNDERSTAND IN FRIDAY'S MALAY MAIL. IF NO ADVERT APPEARS BOTH DIE.

For a moment I thought I would faint dead away. I had to grab the back of a chair for support. My head was swimming as I cried, 'What the hell have I done to deserve this?' Blind rage, tears of despair, were fighting as I thought, God! Friday is the day after tomorrow.

Through my mind jumbled pictures flashed – Natflat and I listening to Grandpa Jack, Julie and I in the tennis pavilion, Natflat after the abortion, Julie vanishing into the *Ban Hong Liong*. As Tony looked at me his normally ruddy, tanned face grey and drawn, a pang of guilt twisted my guts with an actual stab of vicious pain as I tried – failed – to stifle the question, Which one? I had to save Julie, I thought wildly, a wife must come before a sister, surely? Then I saw Tony's glazed eyes, tears starting to burst out – Tony who had shared so much with me, and now at last happy with Natflat.

'Take it easy,' Chalfont's voice was like drops of ice. Fear? Determination? Anger?

I appealed to no one when I cried, 'I can't. *I can't!* That sonofabitch Kai-shek is doing this to torture me.'

'You won't have to make that choice.' I had never heard Chalfont's voice so harsh.

'I couldn't, Robin, I couldn't.'

If only there had been an offer for me to take her place! It sounds dramatic, pseudo-heroic now, but I would have gone like a shot.

The Indian boy could tell us nothing, despite Chalfont's expert questioning. He was obviously an innocent lad, he worked after school in a coffee shop in a nearby village, and a stranger had offered him fifty cents to deliver the letter.

'I feel so bloody helpless,' I cried.

'Calm down.' Chalfont tried to soothe my jangling nerves. 'At least now I'm convinced the girls are alive. Now we've got to find them – in time. The first thing is to grill that bloody Chinese Ah Tin. That's my job. He's locked up at the Dirty Tricks centre, and he's not going to feel very well when I've finished with him.'

'Ye should ha' shot the heathen when I asked ye to,' said Macmillan.

'Perhaps we'll be glad you didn't,' said Chalfont. 'All our information points to the fact that whenever possible the Communists are using our old jungle camps – the ones we used in Force 136. After all, it's obvious: they were the only ones who could guide us through the routes.'

'You mean Soong might be in our old camp?' Tony interrupted. 'If he's in the area, that is.'

'Exactly,' Chalfont agreed. 'Though I've no proof, I'm sure Soong *is* in our old camp, and now we have to find our way there – without being ambushed. And we need complete surprise.'

'And Ah Tin knows the way – if he will tell us,' I said.

'That's the object of my visit to him,' said Chalfont dryly, 'to persuade him to take up a new profession – as guide.'

'But we've got to *move*!' cried a distracted Tony. 'And quickly. Before it's too late.'

I was as scared as Tony. All too often during the war I had seen the horrors of torture on the bodies of women who had fallen into the hands of men reduced to savages. Kai-shek had been a sadistic monster all his life. The message in itself might be a trick. He needed no war to stir him to cruelty.

'Couldn't we use Yeop?' Macmillan asked suddenly. The name meant nothing to Chalfont, but of course! – Yeop's knowledge of the area was unsurpassed and he had a talent for survival. I had heard from him once, a quaint letter thanking me for saving Siloma's life – a compliment I hardly deserved, but the Malays have a passion for politeness – and since then not a word.

'Ah Tin may know the route,' Macmillan continued. 'But even if he agrees to lead us it could be up the garden path – the wrong garden, ye ken.'

'You mean, Yeop could shadow Ah Tin?' asked Chalfont.

'Good idea, Mac,' I said. 'If we go in alone with Ah Tin we'll *never* be sure he's not tricking us. But with Yeop behind him – with a sharp knife, perhaps.'

'Can you find him?' Chalfont turned to me.

'I think so.'

'Right. You and Mac go and get hold of him, see if you

can persuade him to report here this evening – for the night and all tomorrow. After you've met him, Johnnie, can you come to KL where I'll be working on Ah Tin? Tony, I know it's tough doing nothing, but one of us *must* stay here. Apart from needing someone to look after the kids, there's always the possibility we might hear again from Kai-shek. I'll leave a couple of policemen to help guard the estate, and let's all meet here at seven this evening.'

'Seven! All that time wasted!' I cried. 'What about the girls? We can't waste half a day.'

'It won't be wasted, Johnnie, I promise you that. We can't go into the jungle unprepared. I know it's tough for you and Tony, but please – trust me. This has got to be planned like a military operation. For one thing I've got to lay on chopper support with the RAF. And knowing the Chinese, it's going to take a few hours to break Ah Tin.'

And then, with an almost fatherly look, he added gently, 'This double-dyed bastard is probably enjoying himself at this moment. He thinks he's damned clever torturing you, Johnnie. He's mad – but he's a brainless bloody fool. He's trying to crucify you. He always swore he would. He probably thinks you and Tony are here alone, dying of fear. He's so stupid he doesn't realise that you've got friends who can help – that he's signed his own death warrant with this message. We're going in tomorrow – and we're going to kill him.'

I wasn't even certain I could find Yeop's kampong. I knew the general location, but during the war we had always approached it through the jungle, shunning roads or pathways. Even so, I knew many kampongs were linked by dusty roads – for want of a better word – and after all, Miki and his men had driven there.

Thank God Macmillan was with me. I had a renewal of the sense of security which had wrapped my fears with relief when he first told me he was coming into the jungle with me. I had been scared then, but only for myself: now my terror was for others. I couldn't bear the thought of being alone, and had the terrible manic feeling that every second counted, that we were wasting precious minutes driving round the countryside, that our only hope of rescuing the girls – if, if they were still alive – lay in speed.

The kampong proved to be surprisingly easy to find, though at first I hardly recognised it, for the village had been rebuilt. All that filthy pile of rubble, the ash, the corpses, all the terrible agony, had given way to a new long house, new village dwellings. Only the huge banyan by the side of the street was unchanged.

Our approach had obviously been noticed. Every Malayan kampong seemed to be crowded with children ready to give the 'alarm' when any stranger approached. As Mac and I walked down the village street two brown girls came skipping down the steps of the long house, smiling shyly as they held out small sago and coconut cakes on plates of banana leaves.

'That takes you back,' I said to Mac before shouting, 'Yeop! Siloma! Anyone home?'

Siloma appeared almost instantly at the top of the steps, face alight with astonishment, and cried, 'My husband! *Tuan* blond is here!' She almost ran down the steps and I was astonished too, for she not only looked exactly as she had done when I first saw her, but she even had a baby glued to her breast. 'He is a son,' she said proudly. 'My husband calls him a replacement child.' She looked at me and Mac, gave an incline of the head that was almost a grave bow and said, 'Our house is honoured by your presence, and my husband will surely arrange a great feast to greet you.'

'Siloma' – torn with fear though I was I couldn't help realising how beautiful she was, this girl who had saved my life in the jungle, who had offered herself to me when I was returning to a life I thought was ended. But the quick spurt of memories was engulfed immediately by the desperation of the present. 'Siloma,' I repeated, 'we need help urgently. My wife faces great danger of death. My sister too. Yeop can help.'

Without a word she ran upstairs and fetched Yeop. At the foot of the steps he needed no pleas to sense my fear. He too

695

was unchanged; a warm, brown face, a man who lived well. We all climbed the stairs and sat down in the dark main room, strewn with mats. The other people inside – wives, aunts, mothers, cousins – completely ignoring us. Only the children, the whites of their eyes like pools in their dark faces, watched our every movement.

'You have been blessed with another son, Yeop.' However urgent the need for help I had to respect the courtesies.

No doubt after continued study of Frank Harris Yeop replied gravely, 'It is a fine boy, and it was pleasant in the making.' Then, perceptive as ever, he said, while pouring out some kind of arak or toddy, 'Your eyes looked troubled, *tuan* blond.'

As simply as I could I poured out the whole terrible story, the dilemma which faced me, the awful choice I had been ordered to make. 'So Yeop, my old friend,' I concluded, 'we have to find them before Friday. We believe Kai-shek is in our old guerilla camp, or near there, and we are going to force Ah Tin to lead us to it. But even if he agrees to, how can we trust him? I could never be sure, but you – you know the jungle, Yeop, you would be able to tell right away if he was leading us into a trap.'

I knew the answer before he spoke, before he grabbed my hand, then Macmillan's.

'Not only will I help but I have staying in the kampong a man who is more skilled in the jungle than I am. He shall help too. Come, I take you to him.'

I must have glanced at my watch for I was desperately worried the way time was flying by. Yeop saw me, added, 'It will be time well spent, *tuan* blond.'

Round the corner from the long house he presented, almost with a flourish of pride, like a ringmaster in a circus tent, an incredible man. He was young, lithe, and very, very dark. He was nearly six feet tall, with long black hair worn in a pigtail down his back. He wore only a short sarong round his waist and the rest of his body – chest, back, arms, legs – was covered with intricate tattooed designs. But even that was not the feature which intrigued me most. As he smiled a welcome, I saw that he had a set of false teeth –

in gold, every single tooth. And that of course stamped him as a Dyak, for I knew that these one-time headhunters, masters of the blowpipe, often had their own teeth extracted once they could afford a gold set.

'This Sardin,' said Yeop. 'He from Borneo. Many are being brought to Malaya to help the authorities if there is trouble. He will help. He best tracker in Asia, and expert headhunter with blowpipe – you watch.' The long straight blowpipe was standing against the wall of the hut.

Sardin plucked an arrow from his quiver which he wore in front of him, inserted it, raised the blowpipe to his mouth – and the next thing I saw was a pi-dog roll over in the dusty kampong street fifty yards away.

'He very old dog, kind to kill. But he not dead yet,' explained Yeop 'Only unable move.'

It was horrible. The dog lay on its back, feet stuck up in the air, unable to move a muscle, only the open eyes begging piteously for help.

'It's nae possible, nae human,' muttered Macmillan.

'How long does it last?' I turned away. The cruelty was too horrible.

'If pure drug, all time,' replied Yeop cheerfully. 'Dog stay alive until ants eat him.'

'Shoot the poor bugger,' said Macmillan hoarsely to Yeop.

Paralysing drugs were not new, though I had never seen the actual results. I knew that an English botanist who had parachuted into wartime Borneo had described how he came upon eight Japanese in the jungle, apparently dead, but all lying in grotesque positions. But then, as he described it, he noticed that there were no flies buzzing around and he realised the men were not dead. Paralysed and left for dead, they could not stop the ants from devouring them.

Old Sampson, the Dexter family doctor, had once told me that one poison came from curare, the bark of a tree, and that it blocks the transmission of the pulse from the nerves to the muscles, so they can't contract. Sampson had mentioned it only when explaining how surgeons found curare an aid in major operations for, despite anaesthetic, a patient's muscles often contract involuntarily under the surgeon's knife. I wondered how diluted the drug would have to be if the patient didn't end up like the Japs in Borneo, for as I watched the Dyak calmly standing there I visualised that terrible scene in the jungle; but instead of the Japs I saw Kai-shek being eaten by ants. The Dyak smiled at me as I gestured to examine his blowpipe. It was at least seven feet long, hollowed out (according to Yeop with a sharp iron rod) leaving a hole the length of the pipe and barely a third of an inch in diameter.

'No touch darts!' cried Yeop as I went to inspect them. The Dyak had a quiver full, splinters of palm wood presumably dipped in poison, fitted to the end of a soft, pithy wood which slid exactly into the blowpipe.

All the darts, I noticed, had notches on them so that even if a victim tried to tear it out and broke off the pithy wood he wouldn't have time to tear out the jagged dart itself before the poison took effect. All I said to Yeop was, 'That's the man for me.'

'When shall we work together?' asked Yeop.

'It's terribly urgent. Could you both come to the Ara Estate this evening – say seven o'clock? I'll send a car for you. And stay the night and tomorrow?'

'I have a truck, never mind. I come with Sardin.'

After I had briefed Yeop and paid my respects to Siloma, I drove into Kuala Lumpur and once there sent Mac back in my car. Apart from the fact that Chalfont had asked me to go to KL, I wanted to take a look at Ah Tin. I could still remember his moonlike face with its small, frightened staring eyes – the face I saw when he first offered to guide me to Satoh's headquarters, and then his second face – the look of horror, when I pulled the wire that killed his twin brother – 'a military necessity', as Force 136 would have called it. And I could hear, too, above the engine of the car as I drove along the Bentong Road, the sinister noise as Macmillan had slid back the breech of his tommy gun and cried, 'I'll have to kill him!' And my cry of 'No!'. . . What a sentimental fool I had been to spare the life of a man who had shown his hatred for me so openly – and who had now tried to steal my child.

I didn't see him, however. Almost curtly Chalfont said, 'Be your age, Johnnie. This is a top secret hideout. You're not even supposed to be here at all.'

'Then why did you send for me?' My nerves were so raw, the edges of fear gripping me with a pain that tore into my stomach, that I couldn't help the note of sarcasm.

'I know, Johnnie – sorry, I know. But I wanted you to see the special radio we're building for you take into the jungle. But first – what about your man – what was his name?'

'Yeop. He's okay. Even better, he's bringing along a Dyak headhunter who gave me a terrifying demo this morning.'

'Fine. Now here's what *we're* doing.' In the large ware-house-type room, where a dozen or so mechanics with thin pliers or soldering irons tinkered with clapped-out radios, one man was working on a shining new battery set.

'For you,' explained Chalfont. 'We've fixed it so that once you switch it on you'll give us a bleep. We'll be able to keep within fifty yards of you – on the ordnance map.'

'Looks good. What's next?'

'We're waiting for a courier who is due to take a message to Kai-shek – I'm sure it's for him, even though it has a code word. There's been a hell of a lot of traffic through the jungle post office. Kai-shek has asked for an expert mech-anic. God knows what for. We intercepted his message two weeks ago, let it go on, and the postman between these two drops is one of ours. We have to wait for the reply.'

A Chinese came up to Chalfont and whispered. Chalfont nodded and led me towards his car. 'This may be it, but we've run into a snag,' he said.

'What snag?'

'Hop in and you'll see for yourself.' Chalfont banged the door of his car and turned the nose in the direction of downtown KL.

'Our problem is urgency,' he explained. 'We've got to meet the postman, collect the message, undo it, photograph it, and let the man get back on his rounds, so to speak. We can't allow more than an hour in case we arouse any suspicions.'

'Where's the postman?'

'In a small down-beat Chinese hotel round the corner from the Coliseum bar. From the bar – it's highly popular with planters – we can watch the Chinese hotel. What worries me is that the courier hasn't come out to hand over the message. I only hope nothing has gone wrong.'

The Coliseum was crowded, planters in shorts, rowdy, cheerful, many of them with revolvers, some with shotguns which they left by the revolving door. Despite the whirring fans it was hot – perhaps fear made me hotter than the others. I could feel the sweat pouring down the back of my neck.

'Don't look obviously,' said Chalfont over his beer, 'but out of the window you can see the entrance to the hotel. The old Chinese outside – he's our contact man. The postman should have come out for a walk by now.' He looked at his watch. But the postman didn't come out – even after another fifteen minutes.

'Something's wrong,' muttered Chalfont. 'Probably something simple we can't predict. Maybe a Commie guest gone to his room and our man can't get rid of him.'

After another five minutes Chalfont went to the phone in the corner, asked for a number, spoke, returned and said, 'Watch carefully!'

Within minutes a Chinese carrying a small parcel walked into the hotel.

'Know what's in the parcel?' I shook my head.

'Opium,' Chalfont grinned. 'Our man is planting it in the front hall. Now watch.'

Three minutes later two patrol vans, sirens screaming, roared up to block the entrance to the shabby hotel. Chinese policemen spilled out, running round the back, boots clattering on pavements. A knot of curious sightseers gathered quickly. An officer shooed them away. Others, arms indicating positions, shouted orders as the police formed a cordon round the building.

Some of the planters walked over to the window to see what the fuss was about. 'A raid!' one said. 'Probably dope,' said another.

Ten minutes later a dozen bemused or angry hotel guests, together with the staff, were shepherded out of the hotel and bundled into the Malayan equivalent of black marias. 'He'll be in the cells in five minutes.'

'All stage-managed?'

'Sure. We had to get him out – time was running short. This way is foolproof. Sorry about the poor bloody hotel-keeper, he probably had a clean record, but not now – not with all that opium on his premises.'

The message was in a mango. Chalfont let me watch the technicians working. The mango was one in a basket of fruit. It had been opened so skilfully that it was impossible to see the cut in the thick pinky-golden skin without a magnifying glass.

Within half an hour the original slit in the fruit had been delicately reopened enough to extract a slip of rice paper. Chalfont examined it, ordered it to be photographed and then replaced, after which the slit was sealed perfectly. No one could ever know the slit had been opened and resealed. As the postman went on his way experts started decoding the two-line message.

'Just the break we need,' said Chalfont. 'Headquarters is sending the qualified engineer Kai-shek asked for. Now we can move in.'

We sent Pela and Victoria to stay in a hotel in Kuala Lumpur under the protection of Mrs Briggs, the wife of a neighbouring planter, and accompanied by their amah. At first they asked for their mamas, but we said they had gone for a holiday, and then promised both children that they would see a cinema show each evening.

Around dusk on the verandah at Ara, with Sardin squatting on his hunkers outside, hardly able to understand a

701

word, but with Yeop next to me, we held a full-dress conference as Chalfont produced his operations plan.

'I realise now what engineer means,' Chalfont was referring to Kai-shek's request in the jungle post. 'He must want someone to repair some of the Stens that suffered after years hidden in the jungle. By midnight Kai-shek will have received the jungle letter – he'll know an engineer is on the way. So he will alert the sentry at the roadside entrance to expect him. Yeop will impersonate the engineer, right? We don't know the password but that doesn't matter because no sentry would allow Johnnie and Macmillan to enter the jungle.'

The plan was simple. First, Ah Tin had been 'persuaded' to help. Second, as he could not be trusted, Sardin would stand close to him, with a blowpipe at the ready in case of betrayal. And it had been made clear to Ah Tin that if he did betray us he would *not* be killed. He would be left paralysed in the jungle to be eaten alive.

During the coming night, Chalfont explained, Yeop and Sardin had volunteered to go into the jungle and lay diversions. Yeop would hide an old sponge which had been slightly perfumed with eau de cologne. If any guerillas even faintly smelt it reinforcements would go to check that trail, far from ours. Sadin took a tube of toothpaste to squeeze a small amount under the bark of a tree on a different trail a mile away. A good jungle guerilla would pick up the faint odour of white man's clean teeth without any difficulty.

First man to go into action the next morning would be Sardin, who would make his way along the south side of the Bentong Road – on the opposite side to the camp entrance – until he could see the tapper sentry. Meanwhile Yeop, posing as the engineer, would arrive with Ah Tin and confront the sentry who would be expecting Ah Tin. During the preliminary greeting Sardin would shoot a dart from across the road. Macmillan and I would be waiting some distance away, behind the bend in the road that hid the old club, ready to advance as soon as we were summoned.

This plan would be repeated as we reached the two sentry posts on the way to camp. I not only remembered there were two, but Ah Tin sullenly confirmed this. Each time we approached a sentry post inside the jungle Mac and I would fall back, leaving Ah Tin to advance with Yeop. Sardin would also keep out of sight – killing each sentry in turn, but also ready to wound Ah Tin instantly if necessary. We expected the journey to take four hours, and the radio would be kept switched on, though without any voice, so that our track could be followed in the radio ops room.

'You'll start at six a.m.,' suggested Chalfont. 'Meanwhile, "back at the ranch", as they say, we'll start warming up two helicopters which the RAF are laying on. Now here's the vital point. You don't have a transmitting set, yet you must keep us informed of your progress. Here's how, but for God's sake remember the drill. When you actually *see* the camp – and not a second before – switch off the radio. That will alert us to several possibilities – either that the radio has gone on the blink, or that you've been rumbled and killed or – as we devoutly hope – that you're there. You have to let us know which.'

The method was simple. Macmillan would switch the radio on again for thirty seconds, giving HQ a bleep, then switch it off for thirty seconds, on for another half minute, then off – right off. The bleep would of course be on a military wavelength; you wouldn't hear it on an ordinary set.

'When we hear the interrupted bleeps followed by silence we'll know you're okay,' said Chalfont. 'Then – *with the radio switched off, remember* – you'll prepare for surprise attack. According to Ah Tin there's about a dozen men in camp. The only way you can achieve surprise is by waiting until Sardin can blow a poisoned dart at Kai-shek. *No other man will do*. You'll have to wait until he comes into view.'

Chalfont's point was that since the dart didn't kill but only paralysed, any of the Communists seeing Kai-shek stumble or fall would jump to the natural conclusion that he had suddenly been taken ill. There would be a general pandemonium for perhaps fifteen to thirty seconds until someone saw the dart.

'Kai-shek's the boss,' said Chalfont. 'When one man sees

703

him fall he'll yell for help. The others are bound to come rushing out, every man jack of em. Then you go in. I've indented for three sub-machine guns. They're back in the house, stacked up in the hallway. So long as the girls aren't in the line of fire – and they obviously won't be allowed to wander around the camp – you should be able to spray the whole lot. Then – but not until you've found the girls – *switch the radio on*. That will be our signal that all's well – or that you're in deep trouble. In any case, the choppers will have been warmed up, and I reckon it will take only three or four minutes for them to fly from the RAF pad outside KL to your bleep spot. They should know the target to within fifty yards. Tony will fly in with the first chopper because he knows the camp in case we need a visual sighting, and in case you need reinforcements. I'll stay here' – with a grin – 'safe and sound, to mastermind the operation.'

He asked Yeop to tell Sardin, and to explain what was at stake, then turned to me and added, 'It's our only chance. If all goes well Kai-shek will be dead by this time tomorrow and the girls will be back here. And you, Johnnie, will never have to give the bastard the satisfaction of making the choice. Because if we're not here tomorrow night – well, I hope you kill him with the first shot before . . .' We all knew the rest of the sentence, the alternative.

'He's a loner – and they're the most dangerous.' I was thinking of the Ara attack he had made.

'But also the most vulnerable,' Chalfont said. 'That kind of man has nothing behind him except hate, no substance. When the right moment comes you can push him over as easily as a dead tree.'

'Hope so. What about the guns?' I asked.

'I'm going to show you how they work. Dead simple, once you know how.' Chalfont went to fetch one of the three murderous-looking automatic weapons I had seen in the hall.

'They're the best in the world' – Chalfont was showing one off – 'New Stens Mark Five. In theory they'll fire over five hundred rounds a minute, though each magazine only holds twenty-two rounds. But they're nine millimetre calibre high velocity bullets. You've got five magazines for each Sten, and you can fire single shots or automatic.'

The gun handled beautifully.

'One for you, Johnnie, one for Mac, one for Yeop. I'm going into KL. To fetch Ah Tin – myself. Without him we'd never get through the jungle in time, even if we eventually found the right tracks. He's more precious to us than the crown jewels, and I wouldn't trust even the SAS to guard him. And he's no good to us dead either. Ah Tin is going to spend the night chained to the bottom of my bed.'

Jugs of coffee and tea were waiting for us in the dining room at five-thirty. It was still dark, with a touch of pre-dawn rawness, though perhaps apprehension chilled the bones more than cold. No one spoke much, no one drank much, no one asked for eggs. You could feel the tension splitting the air. Most of us had hardly slept. Yeop and Sardin went to the kitchen and returned with bowls of Chinese soup. Chalfont sipped his coffee black and said, 'As soon as you set off I'll drive Tony to the RAF helicopter pad and then go on to the Dirty Tricks department to watch the radio signals. We've got a private line to the RAF so the second I get the final go-ahead from you Tony can set off.'

Chalfont had given me a pair of field glasses, a pack of emergency rations and water, and – most precious of all – a small medical kit which included several do-it-yourself morphia injection needles, already loaded, the kind the RAF issued to aircrew during the war. Then we checked our Sten Mark Vs – vastly better than those we had used in the jungle. We had to sign for them in a book which Chalfont left on the hall table next to our old gun case.

The Dyak was very quiet, partly because he could understand only a little English. But he was examining his darts with a professional air, like a footballer making sure his pads and boots are in order before a crucial match. I prayed he wouldn't touch one of the tips of palm-wood splinters bundled in the home-made pouch of skin slung round his neck. His long blowpipe was standing up against a wall, but I was intrigued to see him handling a shorter blowpipe, no more than two feet long.

'Long one for making sure he kill victim when far away,' explained Yeop. 'Smaller one for men like this dog,' he gestured at Ah Tin who *had* spent the night chained like a dog to Chalfont's bed. I had forgotten the haunted, frightened face I had first remembered. Now he looked ready to die of terror – or exhaustion.

Despite the apprehension, my own fears that we might fail, the prospect of action, danger, risk, pumped the adrenaline straight to the heart. I could see that Tony, despite any qualms he harboured for Natasha, was, like me, tingling with the excitement that comes with action.

The awful inaction, the listless waiting with time to think, time to imagine, had ended. Though the stakes were far more desperate – far more personal – than in any war, I imagined this was the kind of excitement infantrymen must have as they wait for the whistle that will summon them to go over the top, to start hand-to-hand fighting with cold steel. There was just no time to be afraid.

My only worry was the wretched Ah Tin, on whose cooperation everything depended..

'I hope he'll last out,' I whispered to Chalfont. 'He looks as though he's going to keel over.'

'I warned you he wouldn't be feeling very well after our little talk.'

'What happens behind the barbed wire fence?' I couldn't restrain my curiosity.

'I'm not much for rough stuff, but when you're dealing with men like this – well, murderers can't be choosers. After the normal interrogation failed I left him to the Chinese detectives. They're more' – he coughed suggestively – 'more understanding of what we want.'

'His hands?' I noticed he wore a bandage, with a few spots of blood seeping through.

'He took a lot of persuading. Must hate your guts, Johnnie! He didn't give up until they'd cut one finger off – with heavy-duty steel cutters. But he'll be all right. His real fear is not that we'll *kill* him if he betrays us. It's that we *won't* kill him.

Chalfont raised his voice so that all could hear him.

'Let's go through the drill again.' I had never seen him so grim, so serious. 'Remember all your lives depend on keeping the proper radio contact. I'll be powerless if I don't get clear instructions from you — even though you can't talk to me. If we send the choppers in too early Kai-shek might panic, and kill the girls out of spite. So for God's sake remember the drill — *precisely*!'

In the old days Macmillan had always handled the radio in camp, and now Chalfont went through the sequence with him just once more.

'You go the first hour into the jungle without the radio on — to save the battery. Then you switch it on to give you the bleep signal, but of course you keep the sound right down. This will give us an accurate picture of our route as you approach the camp. When you actually reach camp — when you have visual contact — you switch the radio off. Then on for thirty seconds, to give us a bleep, off for half a minute, on for half a minute, then radio silence. And then?'

'We move in, Johnnie and I behind the others. Once we've done our job — taken prisoners, or whatever —'

'No prisoners!' said Chalfont harshly.

'Noted. Then we switch on the radio again — and that will tell the choppers to fly in.'

'Right. Well done,' said Chalfont. 'As soon as I hear the first off-on-off routine the choppers will start to warm up. When we get the final go-ahead — which might mean success or that you're in trouble, need help urgently — I reckon the flight shouldn't take more than four minutes. That is if the camp is where I'm sure it is.'

Chalfont turned to Yeop. 'And tell Ah Tin there's one thing more which might encourage him not to play any tricks. We've roped in his wife. Here — we took a photo of her so Ah Tin can see we're not bluffing.' He handed over a mug shot of a woman. 'You can tell him she's unharmed, and she'll be released the minute we return — if Ah Tin behaves.'

I looked at my watch. Ten to six.

'Time to get going,' I suggested. The dawn was coming up over the jungle, the night noises were stilled, only the occasional cry of a monkey broke the silence, the sky grey still but faintly tinged with pink giving a strange brown and pink striped effect to the river beyond the lines, with their first spirals of blue smoke.

Somewhere behind, in the tall dark trees of the rain forest, my beloved Julie and Natasha were lost in the darkness that blotted out all sun. Soon we too would be lost in that darkness, our lives, theirs too, depending on the forced cooperation of a man who had tried to kidnap our children. I felt a shiver of fear up my spine. I knew that either I or Kai-shek would be dead by noon.

46

Sardin was the first to leave. He wore only a strip of sarong and a quiver. No shoes, nothing to cover his tattooed chest. A few minutes later Chalfont drove all of us along the laterite road to the point where the ara tree near the Bentong Road marked our estate boundary.

Here he dropped Ah Tin and Yeop who set off the mile or so to find the sentry guarding the jungle path leading to the camp behind the estate. Mac and I walked along until we reached a point some way behind the corner before the rendezvous where we expected the sentry to be. Chalfont and Tony then drove off towards KL. To anyone – even the suspicious sentry they would have to pass – they were just a couple of planters, early risers as usual, off to Kuala Lumpur to buy stores before a good tiffin at the club.

For fifty minutes we waited – no smoking, no talking – until Sardin appeared at the distant corner and waved. Round the bend Yeop stood, one of Sardin's darts touching

Ah Tin's shirt, guarding him during the Dyak's absence. The tapper–cum–sentry was dead.

Yeop flashed white teeth and set off into the jungle walking two feet behind Sardin and Ah Tin. If our information was true two more sentries would have to be killed before they could alert the camp by pulling one of the rattan ropes leading to the parade ground. Kai–shek, it seemed, had not changed the system which worked so well when we both shared the camp, though the 'alert ropes' would only be laid nearer the camp.

There was just one way we could achieve surprise. Ah Tin had to lead the way along the trail, for if he were spotted his presence would not surprise a sentry, since he was expected. The sentry had been *told* to expect Ah Tin and 'an engineer'.

Sardin had other duties before he finally shot the all-important dart at Kai–shek. He was the most accomplished tracker among us, and he watched for any signs – flattened leaves, broken twigs, crushed undergrowth – which might indicate that Ah Tin was betraying us. We all knew that a dedicated Communist could be capable of sacrificing his life for the cause. And though we hoped that our promise of a slow death – coupled now with the knowledge that his wife was in jail – would deter him we couldn't take anything for granted. Yeop followed next. Mac and I brought up the rear, at least ten yards behind, for at each crisis point we would have to be invisible.

It was a strange feeling being back in real jungle, carrying a gun, field glasses, a compass, entering a world in which no one – no one at all – could ever dare to make the slightest error of judgment, where the trees could close in on you and imprison you for life if you lost your way. 'Like old times,' I whispered to Mac who nodded and whispered back, 'Aye, that it is. I only wish we'd had this laddie with his wee blowpipe against the Japs.'

At first, before the jungle thickened, the filtered sunlight glimmered through the web of branches, and the track opened up on occasional patches of clearing, the darkness of tall trees giving way to a glimpse of a less sombre world –

one of light-filled, heat-hazed air, with hundreds of butter-flies hanging like iridescent curtains, with vividly coloured birds darting like jewels between clumps of wild hibiscus, the wax-like blossoms of frangipani or the occasional tulip trees, with their clusters of perfectly formed tulips growing at the ends of straight stems on the high branches.

But these were the early moments and soon the jungle thickened. Apprehension increased. Now our world was bounded only by one future – the camp. Apart from that we were dangling in an uncertain present, the horizon of our existence limited to the few yards we could see ahead, the span of our lives at the mercy of a desperate Chinese mercenary whose doubtful loyalty to us had been purchased at the cost of a finger.

For perhaps two miles we travelled, sweat-soaked, scratched by thorns, watching out for leeches. I wondered how the girls had fared on this awful track, so narrow in places that the fat juicy leaves slapped our faces with clammy hands. The track seemed to have been beaten recently. Even I, no jungle tracker, could see fresh cutting marks where parangs had cleared the way. But there was hardly a whisper of air in the dense near-light of the forest and no European could have even noticed the warning signs that Sardin saw at the same moment as Ah Tin held up a hand.

This was the signal for Mac and me to remain just where we stood – frozen as statues.

I could not see what the warning was, though Yeop confirmed later that nothing had changed since the days when I ran the camp. I *could* see a kind of *rentis* – the Malay word for a strip of cleared jungle or beluka that marks a boundary. All the undergrowth had been cut down to the roots. To an untrained man stumbling on it the *rentis* could be nothing more than a welcome sun-dappled clearing, a chance for a breath of hot air, a resting place formed by nature and devoid of suspicion.

It was nothing of the sort – that I knew from the past. The clearing made space for a sentry, hidden now in the trees behind, to provide a signal of dry sticks scattered as naturally along the trail as our lethal bamboo bombs had been strewn in the path of Satoh.

When Ah Tin trod on them – deliberately – with Sardin inches behind him, the sentry was alerted. He took no action. Only if the visitor proved to be an enemy would he pull the alarm rope. But that was a last resort. The sentry would receive no thanks if the camp was abandoned and everyone took to the jungle, all because of a false alarm.

Since Yeop, Mac and I remained hidden, Ah Tin and Sardin advanced full of confidence. Sardin might prove a surprise to the sentry, but he would see Ah Tin's familiar face first and in the early moments of greeting and explaining Sardin struck. He blew, as Yeop explained later, with the short pipe in his right hand, holding another dart in his left hand which touched the cotton shirt sticking to the back of a terrified Ah Tin.

The sentry's knees buckled, he toppled over without a sound. Yeop waved us to stay where we were, then joined Sardin as he guarded Ah Tin. One of them soundlessly – but mercifully – killed the sentry, then waved us on, fingers to lips for silence.

'Next sentry post last one, two hundred yards away,' whispered Yeop. 'Camp hundred yards after. Noise very bad.'

Julie and Natasha were only three hundred yards away! If, I thought with a sick feeling, they were still alive. But they had to be. Kai-shek's demand for me to choose which one he should execute *must* mean that? And yet, as I wiped the sweat from my eyes, I thought it might all be a cruel bluff, an extra torture for me; or they could be sick, dying of disease, leech bites, dysentery. Worse still, *we* could cause their deaths if we made even the smallest error of judgment.

Two hundred yards doesn't seem very long, but they were the longest, most terrifying two hundred yards I ever walked. There had been no heavy rain for several days, and the dryness underfoot increased the noise hazard. Ah Tin might be expected, but that would not prevent a diligent sentry from investigating a suspicious noise – and that could mean death for the girls.

Rivulets of sweat poured down the small of my back. Out of condition, I thought. But I knew it wasn't my physical condition alone. I was frightened. The jungle thickened again after we left the *rentis*, and Yeop, barely five yards ahead, was at times invisible until I had gently brushed away the green curtain that blotted him out. Every movement had to be taken with care. There could be no waving of the parang which Yeop had used in the early stages. Each single step forward had to be made with the intense care of a man picking his way barefoot through a bed of charcoal, half of which he could see was burning, half of which he knew was cool to the feet.

The first fat black leeches appeared in great numbers, waiting patiently for human beings to brush against the leaves on which they lay. When they did stick to us we could not burn them off. We could not even try to knock them off with a stick. We could only pray they were on our clothes – not our flesh. As a background to our silence was the noise of the jungle: the flying foxes, the chatter of unseen monkeys, the screech of parrots, all hidden in a sombre evergreen world that never knew the stripped black branches of winter. The jungle noises created another hazard, for they were *natural* noises. But they would only remain natural if we gave them no cause for alarm. If we disturbed their morning, if they sensed our presence, their noises would change – nothing changes more quickly than the screams of monkeys suddenly scared – and even the dumbest guerilla fighter would ask what had caused the change.

We despatched the second sentry as efficiently as the first. I looked at my watch – eleven-thirty-eight a.m. Already we were behind schedule, and now we faced the last hundred yards. It was not only sweat now that tormented me, running into my eyes. My stomach squirmed. My heart thumped like a piston. Each time I felt it bang against my chest it seemed as though it would burst out. My legs no longer belonged to me; two self-propelled automatic legs, hired for the occasion, had taken their place.

I wanted to move on – I had an urge to 'do or die', to

replace the agony of suspense with action, for suddenly, inconsequentially, I had a premonition that the girls were dead, and that we must rush the camp, kill Kai-shek – No, no! Paralyse him, let the jungle eat his life away – or die in the attempt. I knew it was nonsense, a kind of delirium. Prudence above all else.

The first leeches had reached our skin and were starting to suck blood, though we could not feel them. I saw three on the back of Mac's neck, and though I couldn't see my own I knew the neck was a favourite leech path to the warm hidden crevices of the body.

Yeop nudged Sardin, pointed to us, to his own neck, explaining without words. The Dyak walked towards Mac, bare feet so quiet he might have been treading on air. As he drew a dart from his sack no one needed to warn Mac that a sudden jerk meant death. With the expertise of an eye surgeon removing a cornea from an anaesthetised patient – in our case anaesthetised by fear – he touched each leech with the poisoned tip. They didn't fall off, but no matter, we could burn them off later. In the meantime they were at least too paralysed to suck. He must have touched me eight or nine times after which he smiled, proudly displaying his personal fortune in the vast expanse of his gold false teeth.

We moved forward cautiously. Vaguely I remembered the approach from the past. Not the actual path, the trees, but I could visualise the camp ahead. We were approaching from the south, so there would be a hill behind the camp parade ground, dense jungle, the river to the left, and the huts straight ahead and to the right, so that anyone could be lost in the jungle in thirty seconds. New huts may have been built by now, but they would have to be erected in roughly the same position. They could never be erected on the south side of the parade ground – which we were approaching – for the only route to the camp led from the Bentong Road. In any other direction the jungle stretched across mountainous country with no exit.

The jungle circling the parade ground (apart from the river) reached almost to the clearing – it had to, in order to give guerillas (Communist or Force 136) quick cover in the event of attack. We had to surprise the enemy – but with strings attached. We could not start the killing until we knew the girls were safe. Now I moved up front, the safety catch of my Mark V off, but the gun crooked in an arm: none of us could open fire until Sardin had blown the dart at Kai-shek and so divert attention for a few precious seconds.

When at last we reached the jungle edge and the camp was spread out in front of us it was for me, in a macabre way, almost like coming home. Nothing seemed to have changed. I caught myself thinking not of Julie in danger but of the irony that at last she would be able to picture something of the life I had lived apart from her.

As my field glasses scanned the clearing I had an uneasy feeling that something was wrong. At first I couldn't place it. We knew there were only ten or a dozen Communists in the camp, and most of them were in front of us, in the open. Some were laughing, giggling even. It didn't make sense. Chinese guerillas had been trained to perfection. Their discipline had been as much a factor in our success as their dedication to killing the enemy. But here they were behaving like shop assistants on an outing.

It was out of character. Kai-shek had the reputation of being a really tough disciplinarian. And yet, watching the camp – no sign of the girls or Kai-shek – the men milling around, I suddenly caught my breath. Perhaps Kai-shek *wasn't* a man of iron discipline once the killer instinct took over. He had shown no discipline when attacking the Japs against my known wishes. He had run amok. He really had been thirsty for blood, even though then the hate had not been as violent as now. For he had never hated the Japs as much as he hated me.

Suddenly I realised what was wrong. It was inconceivable, but the tones in their voices, their laughter, the way they moved, spelled out one five-letter word as plainly as the label on a bottle of gin: drink. It couldn't be, but it was. Not drunk, far from it, but warm with arak or palm toddy or even stronger stuff. It was not the rowdiness of a drunken evening after pay day, more the happy flush of drink at a wedding.

A *wedding*! A kind of wedding, perhaps. They were celebrating, that was it, *but what*? It must have to do with the girls. For a terrible moment I was convinced they were celebrating an event which had already taken place, but then I could sense the anticipation in the air. They were waiting. *But where was Kai-shek?* Where were Julie and Natasha? The celebration had to do with them – their execution? some form of torture? Whatever it was, this was a day off, a party to celebrate, safe in the knowledge that no one could ever find their jungle hideout.

I lowered the glasses, letting them rest on my chest, the strap round my neck. Yeop made one movement only. He raised his hand, drinking fashion, to his lips. I nodded. I knew the celebration *must* concern the girls. But how? When? I made a twisting motion with my right hand to Mac. He too nodded, turned the radio off, carefully timed it with his watch, turned it on again, then off.

No field glasses were needed to see Kai-shek and another Chinese emerge from a hut on the right of the parade ground. There was a thin but spirited cheer from his followers. To my astonishment he was wearing a Malay sarong and his chest was bare.

As Kai-shek shouted I touched Sardin. I wanted to identify to him the man he had to paralyse. He nodded. Two Chinese ran back to the hut where Kai-shek was standing shouting. He went in with them and the four men emerged carrying a low trestle bed – the sort which jaggers place across the entrance of the building they guard (and sleep by) at night. It was light, made of rattan.

A naked figure lay on it, tied to it, on her back. The face was hidden by the men carrying the front end of the bed. I caught a glimpse of legs and, as I put my glasses to my eyes, blonde pubic hairs. Instinctively I thanked God for two things in that first moment of horror. That Tony wasn't there to see Natasha, for nothing could have stopped him charging in, automatic blazing, killing everyone, including Natasha. The second thanks was a selfish one: an unspoken prayer of gratitude that it wasn't Julie, followed immediately by a spasm of shame.

For now I could sense what was going to happen, so clearly that I almost vomited, standing there, helpless, just watching – *watching* the faces of men feasting on my own sister's naked beauty, strapped to the bed, being shown off, prepared like some ancient sacrifice, but not for death – that was too easy – but for what the Chinese, in their search for exquisite refinements of torture, quaintly called 'friend rape'.

I had heard about it, and knew it existed as a sickening way to punish a man, his pride, by allowing all the members of a gang their turn to penetrate the wife or daughter of the man they were teaching a lesson. Usually they tied up the father or husband and forced him to watch. This time, with supreme irony, I was forced to watch without restraining bonds.

The bile came up again. I glanced at Macmillan. It was not *his* sister, not *his* wife, yet he looked white with a rage he could barely contain. The guerillas had started almost to dance round the trestle bed. One man bent down, fondled Natasha's breast, then sucked a nipple, laughed and moved on. The next man started to push his fingers into her pubic hair, and I could see her wriggling, and realised she must be gagged. But I couldn't scream, I couldn't do a thing. Instead, my stomach heaved. I turned aside. At one and the same moment a retch of filthy green bile oozed down my khaki shirt front and I felt salt tears on my cheek. Poor Natasha – and next, without doubt, poor Julie. I forced myself to turn back, a stony determination – or was it hate? – forcing me to watch and wait; to wait for revenge, however difficult, rather than kill and be killed.

The naked figure was loosely pinioned. Then Kai-shek appeared, as though waiting for the crucial moment. He looked at her, then stroked her mound of venus, probed inside the join of her legs, savouring the anticipation of rape. He muttered an obscenity – it must have been, because of the roar of laughter – then beckoned the nearest man to examine her more closely.

The shock was total, so that without thinking I brought up the barrel of my automatic weapon into a firing position. Gently Macmillan pushed the barrel downwards, lips hardly moving as he whispered, 'Leave it to Sardin.' But Sardin too was powerless to do anything, because the trestle bed with her lying on it was between Kai-shek and us.

Now I realised why he wore a sarong. Pulling the front open, he stood within a few inches of Natasha's face, laughed and exhibited a huge penis, stiff with anticipation. There was a strangled scream from Natasha, a kind of animal chuckle from the men looking on as he held it up in front of her nostrils then, as she tried to twist away he pulled her head back by the hair and leant his penis on her face. I was waiting for him to come forward into the line of Sardin's fire. I knew one thing: he would *have* to part her legs before he could rape her. He would have to untie the loose bonds of rattan thongs. And he would have to lean over back to us.

And then Sardin would shoot.

But something else was happening. Amid a great deal of excitement the others had found a bag and were putting into it several short lengths of bamboo. One man shook the bag. Yeop whispered, 'The one who picks the shortest stick gets the second turn, then they draw lots for the next time.'

At last Kai-shek turned towards the others. Soon he would be standing in front of the low trestle, hiding for a few vital seconds Natasha's body. The others crowding around continued to stare, fascinated, at Natasha's naked body, touching it. Then Kai-shek said something I could not hear, but everyone laughed, as though they were about to take part in a victory celebration – and what sweeter victory in the jungle than for each one in turn to possess a beautiful blonde white woman?

As I stared at the horrible scene an extraordinary thing happened. For perhaps two or three seconds I forgot where I was, what was happening, what was *about* to happen. As an ugly yellow-brown hand stroked my sister's pubic hairs, outrage was replaced by memory – of the day we had shown ourselves to each other to prove that I could change my size. I had never seen Natflat naked since that day when we were children. And now, fascinated by the sight of her, I had become a peeping tom – until suddenly Kai-shek held up his hand and horror wiped out memory.

This time Kai-shek spoke in Cantonese – the only dialect common to all – and I could just catch a few words. 'I will take the blonde first . . . after . . . the splinters . . . decide who goes next . . . and after, the Chinese whore . . . each . . . in turn.'

There was a cheer, babbled talk, laughter, while one man pointed to his chest, as though to indicate that he had drawn the shortest stick, that he was the man after Kai-shek to violate my sister.

The bile rose in my mouth as at last Kai-shek slipped off his sarong and stood there naked. The others cheered at his size. He called for a knife, then undid the bonds that tied Natasha's legs to the bottom of the bed. She kicked out the second they were freed. It made no difference. Two men sprang forward, forced her legs apart, held them down and spread out like a star by the ankles. Kai-shek turned his back to us and prepared to climb on her.

I pressed Sardin's arm. A sigh of wind passed my ear, and I heard Kai-shek scream as he stumbled, half fell, clutching the home-made bed, turning it on its side, with Natasha still fastened by her arms to the far end.

None of the group realised what had happened, no one *could* even imagine. The centre of the parade ground erupted in shouts, orders – no panic, but consternation – as everyone rushed to Kai-shek's side. To every one of them, in those first few seconds, it looked as though he had had a sudden heart attack or some illness that made him stumble. They rushed to help without fear. Several men tried to lift him back to his feet. During these seconds Natasha was lying, struggling to free herself, ignored in the chaos. Suddenly one man gave a scream – fear, anger, a warning, a compound of emotions. He had seen the dart stuck in Kai-shek's back.

'Now!' I screamed. 'But the girl – be careful!'

The three of us fired together. The deafening noise filled

the compound, sent hundreds of angry birds swirling round the treetops. Unable to realise they had been shot in a hideout they felt sure no man could find, for a few precious seconds the guerillas refused to accept what was happening. As they fell, some killed, some wounded, the one common factor was shock and outrage. As we rushed in, as they tumbled on the dusty ground, they seemed stupefied by surprise. The impossible had happened, and even in their dying moments they refused to believe it.

One wounded man, at last realising the truth, pulled out a long stiletto-type knife, tried to rise to one leg, couldn't, and crawled round the bed to stab Natasha as a last gesture of revenge. I heard no sound, only a whispering hiss and the man toppled over trying desperately – but in vain – to tear out a barbed dart. The harder he struggled the deeper the dart sank into the flesh. Suddenly he rolled over, fingers still clutching at the shaft in his last gesture.

By now I was on my feet by the edge of the clearing. Running up, I grabbed his knife and cut Natasha's bonds. Her eyes were glazed, dumb – she had no idea who I was, for she screamed and struggled and kicked out at me. I shouted to Mac to help. He picked her up like a child, and I heard her sob as she went limp.

'Switch on the radio,' I shouted, 'and I'll see if Julie is in one of the huts,' hardly daring to go in case she was dead. But she couldn't be dead, I thought, for Kai-shek had promised her as the next victim. I started to run but at that moment I saw the wild eyes of Ah Tin as he charged me. At the same instant I caught the flash of a murderous-looking sliver of steel. He had been searched, but must have picked up a knife somewhere. As he leapt for me the sound of a gun exploded in my ear and Ah Tin bowled over like a ninepin, one shoulder ripped to shreds. Yet he didn't die, and as I tried to run past him he twisted deliberately, with his last ounce of strength, determined to kill me before he died, using his body as a trip.

I fell over him, started to fight free, suddenly felt a screaming pain in my leg. The unexpected agony clawed its way up my body. He had tried to sink the knife into my leg, but his damaged shoulder had robbed him of any power and he hadn't the strength to strike deep. It hurt more than it wounded, but he didn't know that and with a bloodless laugh of satisfaction he rolled over. As I shot him another man who had only been nicked also fumbled for a knife. I dived on the ground next to him, butting him in the chest, ramming his neck against the jagged corner of the bed. The sharp point of a rattan pole pierced his throat, and the blood erupted all over my face as I brought my gun down on his head. Even that was not enough. He spun round on top of me, still struggling, until the crack of a shot blanketed out every jungle sound. In the haze of fear that follows a fight you have nearly lost, I saw the figure of Macmillan. He had shot him in the head at point blank range, spewing his brains over the dusty ground.

'Where's Julie?' I gasped.

Yeop had beaten me to the hut. As I clambered up, the pain in my leg forgotten, I saw him come out of the hut, supporting her like a sack of flour, dragging her feet in the dust. He shouted, 'She okay, *tuan* blond! She tied up, but okay.'

Then she fainted too. As I reached her I smothered the drawn, taut face in kisses. But she hadn't the faintest idea who I was.

'I've switched on the radio,' cried Macmillan. 'They'll be here in three minutes. I'll finish off this bugger Kai-shek.'

Jock told me later that I screamed like a man demented. 'Don't kill him! Don't touch him! He's mine!' My face was covered with the blood of the man who had nearly killed me, and I must have *looked* demented. Macmillan and Yeop fell back aghast as I peered into the staring eyes of Kai-shek, unable to move a muscle, curled up like a child dying of starvation, unable even to squeak. Only the eyes moved and already the first red ant, attracted by the smell of blood, was making its way across his chest and face. I could see no fear in his eyes, for he was Chinese, a fatalist, and he knew that he was about to die, to join his ancestors, and that gave him in these awful last immobile moments of his life a hidden strength, the knowledge that life would soon be mercifully ended.

No. He didn't *know* he was going to die. He *assumed* it. Knowing the ways of the white man, he *assumed* I would never stoop to the delights of Chinese torture. I would shoot him. *That* was the message I read in his eyes. In them I saw almost a look of triumph. He was Chinese and strong enough to face death. I was British and too weak to torture him. No word was spoken, none could be, but in those eyes I saw the sneer of a superior race, the unspoken words, 'Fuck you. white monkey, you haven't the guts *not* to kill me.'

Hadn't I? Hadn't I? As I heard the noise of the chopper approaching, as the others went to carry the girls to safety, I too sneered and whispered, 'No, you yellow bastard, you're wrong. I'm *not* going to kill you. The ants will do that!'

Then – only then – I saw the eyes change, the hatred slide away, the terror move in, the mute pleading of two small orbs staring out of an almost dead body, crying without speech, 'Mercy! Mercy! Kill me! Shoot me!'

I actually smiled as I shook my head.

'There's only one chopper,' I heard Macmillan shout as the whirlybird landed, spraying dust and muck all over us, waiting impatiently on the parade ground I had known so well for more than three years. The chopper wasn't very big. Tony jumped out.

'They're near that hut – unharmed.' That was the first thing he must want to know. With a sob he ran towards where they were waiting. 'Go get 'em, Tony. You help, Mac.'

'Where's the second chopper?'

'Something wrong with it,' shouted Tony. 'Couldn't get her airborne.'

For those few seconds, as the RAF pilot beckoned us to hurry, I stood and watched Kai-shek. 'No, you shit,' I whispered, 'I'll never kill you.'

The blades of the chopper made a noise matching the swirl of dust. The pilot beckoned me, cupped his hands round his mouth and shouted, 'We'll have to make two trips. I can't get you all in. Too much payload.'

'Take the others,' I shouted back. 'This chap and I' – with a gesture to Yeop – 'we'll hang on till you get back. The essential thing is to get the women to hospital. They must be suffering from a hell of a shock. Okay?'

The girls came out, half-carried by Tony and Macmillan.

'All over, darling Julie, all over now. Pela is waiting to see you.' She looked at me, recognising me I was sure, but too shocked to be able to tell me she did.

A moment later the chopper whirled off like an ungainly prehistoric bird of prey.

The dust settled. We were alone, Yeop and I, old comrades in arms. The parade ground looked like a toy soldier scene in a shop window, too ridiculous to believe, its posturing figures like dummies, caught in the moment they died, and in the centre the paralysed figures of Kai-shek and the man who had tried to kill me. Suddenly reality replaced imagination as a swarm of buzzing flies, attracted by the smell of the blood-drenched open space, filled the air. Where on earth had they come from, these foul blue and green monsters? What had they been eating or drinking until we killed each other, providing them with an unexpected feast on which to gorge? The stench was already overpowering. I saw a hundred – perhaps double that number? – settle on the face of Kai-shek, together with one lone red ant, scurrying about but smelling blood.

'You want the honour of killing him, *tuan* blond?' asked Yeop.

'No, old friend. This is the man who was responsible for burning your village, he much more than the Japs.' I turned to the foetus-like ball of flesh, curled up, more ants busy now. 'This is the man who really killed Siloma's son, your son.' I looked into Kai-shek's pleading eyes, begging for the ultimate mercy of a quick death, and asked Yeop, 'Isn't death too good for him?'

'You mean leave here?' Even Yeop looked startled. 'He going to be eaten alive by ants and leeches will leave no blood?'

'Just that. He's a monster. He swore to kill me. He was ready to violate my sister. You saw that, Yeop. Why should I have any pity on him? No, we have four or five minutes before the chopper picks us up. I'm going to drag the bastard into the jungle.'

Forgetting my throbbing leg, I grabbed the thick black hair of Kai–shek and lugged the paralysed figure to the edge of the trees, just out of sight. I saw his eyes look up with new fear. I followed them. On the green leaves above him, just above his head, a dozen blind, fat black leeches were waiting. They would smell him even before we reached KL.

I ran back across the parade ground to the river and started to wash the blood off my hands and face in the tinkling water. I had finished just as the chopper returned, smothering us again in dust. I picked up my gun and prepared to clamber into the tiny cabin after Yeop.

'All set?' The pilot checked that our seat belts were fastened.

'Yep!' I cried and then added, 'Damn! Forgot something.'

'Christ almighty!' shouted the furious pilot. 'This is a military operation, not a bloody picnic.'

'Sorry, chum. Won't be a sec.'

I had to do it. I ran, crouching under the blades of the helicopter, to the edge of the jungle. Already two leeches were creeping towards the corners of his eyes.

As I looked at him, the leeches on his face, the ants scurrying round, I knew I had to kill him. Your crimes are beyond the tolerance of humanity, I thought, but I mustn't sink to your level. Yet I hated myself for doing it, for giving him the final satisfaction: a proof of my weakness, letting him die with the pleasure of knowing that I who hated him didn't have enough courage to let a mortal enemy die in misery.

As I looked in his face I could see that he knew. He *knew*! Goddam the bastard, he was actually gloating at the prospect of death, at the sight of an executioner. Well, that was understandable. Instant death was infinitely preferable to being eaten alive. But there was more in his eyes than satisfaction at the thought of death. Racked with pain though he must have been, his eyes reflected a kind of triumph. I had come back. And he knew why. He was going to win – for though he hadn't killed me, to him a quick execution by a man who hadn't the guts to make him suffer *was* victory. His eyes glistened with triumph. He would have spat at me had he been able to open his lips. I looked at the rolled-up ball of flesh, the ants scurrying into an open scratch on his arm.

'You don't deserve it, you shit,' I shouted as I raised my gun and prepared to shoot.

Yeop said nothing until we landed, perhaps because speech was difficult above the noise of the chopper.

'I am glad you did that, *tuan* blond,' said my old wartime ally. 'We have a saying in Malaya, "He who shows mercy to an enemy escapes from a prison." You will sleep better tonight.'

AFTER

It was four months later.

As I took Julie in my arms, standing in the bedroom at Ara where we had spent so much of our life, I thought she had never looked more beautiful, more tender. She always did have that supreme quality of giving, of radiating a kind of happiness, of making other people share it.

And on this particular day there was a special reason for our eyes to shine. That morning we had been quietly married at the KL registrar's office, exactly four months after the nightmare in the jungle. Both girls had spent a week in hospital – not only to recover physically from a terrible ordeal but to give them a kind of privacy that can only be enforced there.

For above all Julie and Natasha had to heal the scars of the mind. Luckily they were both resilient, but they needed time to forget what had happened, or at least consign a terrifying experience to a compartment of their brains which they would rarely have occasion to open.

Physically they had come through the nightmare better than any of us expected. But physical torture is in many ways easier to overcome than mental anguish. If you break a leg skiing you can soon forget the pain; but if you break that leg in a car crash that causes the death of your passengers there is a picture forever etched in your brain.

The cable from Irene, telling me I was free to marry, was the finest medicine any doctor could have prescribed for Julie, an elixir sent across five continents at the speed of sound.

That evening, after the marriage ceremony, the three of us left for Tanamera, now rebuilt, on the night sleeper.

Everything was ready except Pela's nursery and Julie's own sitting room. I had left those white so Julie could decide how to decorate them.

All that was eleven years ago.

During those years much had happened. The Communist uprising – by 1959 in the mopping-up stage – had torn Malaya apart; nearly two thousand security forces had been killed, more than two thousand five hundred civilians murdered, another eight hundred were still missing. And yet, despite the fact that over the years a hundred thousand British troops were involved, the bitter struggle was never dignified with the title of war, only an 'emergency' – ironically because the London insurance market covered losses of stocks and equipment through riot and civil commotion in an emergency, but not in a civil war.

Though the war of the running dogs, as many called it, tested the planters and miners to the limit, most refused to submit to terrorist threats. However, Tony and Natasha were not among them. Natasha had suffered more than we realised and she did stick it out for another six months, but when Ian Scott decided to retire and let Tony take over Consolidated Latex Natasha welcomed the opportunity with open arms. Luckily we had an eager replacement in Barry Stride, the cadet who had originally applied in Swallow Street to become a planter.

Vicki and Ian had talked about buying a villa in the South of France when Ian retired, but as the years passed, and as it became more evident that independence was just around the corner, they decided to remain in Singapore. They had two children, and Tony and Natasha were neighbours. They had the money to travel several months of the year but, as Vicki put it, 'All the money in the world can't buy us as many friends abroad as we have here.' They were not the first or last Singaporeans to find themselves lonely when they decided to go 'home', wherever that was.

Papa Jack died in Sloane Terrace Mansions soon after his seventy-third birthday, and a cable from Mama was not really a surprise, for he had been in bad health for several years, a shadow of his old self, and on the last leave in London when we said goodbye we both felt we might never see him again. He had mellowed with age – he fell in love with Pela – but a mental block made it difficult for him to appreciate that I was no longer married to Irene. Perhaps the fact that he saw a great deal of Ben and Catherine made his reasoning a little fuzzy.

And in Ben there lay for us a wonderful bonus to our bliss. For on that visit – it must have been in 1953 – Irene, now Mrs Robert Graham (whose husband was already being tipped for junior cabinet rank) insisted that the Dexters and the Grahams and their grown-up children should have a celebration lunch.

Pela was our only child, but 'Uncle Bob' and Irene had had another son, too young for a party of this sort. However, Pela, Ben and Catherine, who was eleven, all came to l'Ecu de France in Jermyn Street, after which the three kids planned to go to a movie matinee.

Irene was obviously very happily married and no doubt that helped to wipe any bitterness from the slate, while 'Uncle Bob', the suitor who had missed out before I arrived on the scene, turned out to be pleasant, and intelligent enough to handle two stepchildren as though they were his own. But it was Ben who fascinated me.

'He looks just like you did when you were sixteen – exactly the same!' said Julie.

'And he thinks like his father,' added Irene as the kids, in high spirits, left for the cinema in the Haymarket just round the corner.

'Meaning what?' I asked as we ordered more coffee.

'Meaning that he keeps on asking if he can spend the next holiday in Singapore,' said Irene.

'Chip off the old block,' said Uncle Bob. 'I think he ought to be allowed to go,' adding hastily, 'Don't misunderstand me – I'm not coming the heavy stepfather stuff, wanting to get rid of him for a bit – but I do think he's old enough to – well, try out his father.'

'But that's wonderful,' I cried, adding a thought, 'Is it me or Singapore he wants to see?'

'A bit of both,' said Irene. 'He's got a lot of you in him. He keeps on saying he never wants to work in England when he leaves school –'

'Can't blame him. No hope here,' chipped in Bob.

'And if he does insist on working abroad, well – at least he should see Singapore first.'

And that is how it started. Ben came to Singapore for three consecutive summers, and fell in love with the country, with Tanamera, with the people – even with the business, and – I like to think – Julie too.

I had to be very careful not to face a charge of stealing his affections, so all the running had to come from him and his stepfather. Yet after the first visit I had naturally wondered: who in the years ahead would take over the business from me? Tim, according to the latest news, had set up house in Tangier – and not alone, for Tangier was a postwar haven for men who liked to live openly with their male friends. Paul would never work, so there was only one real heir to the Dexter and Soong empire. And if Ben loved Singapore like his father, why should he not carry on the line?

And that is what happened. There was a sprinkling of tears in Wimbledon, but Irene did understand. After Ben finished at Westminster, where he was a weekly boarder, what real chance was there for a youngster in postwar England? And as Uncle Bob put it when I flew over, it was the most natural thing in the world for a boy to be trained to take over his father's thriving business.

Anyway, the earth was shrinking, the old days of home leave every three years had gone forever. Ben would be able to fly home to see his mother every holiday, Irene and her husband could fly out to see him whenever they wished.

So Ben moved in to Tanamera. So did one other friend – Paul Soong. The forbidding grey Soong mansion had never really been a home – not for anyone, father, mother, or children. But Tanamera *was* a home, not merely a house in which to live, and so, soon after Julie and I were married, Paul sold the Soong house and came to live with us, a brother – a real brother, as apart from a brother-in-law – for me.

All is changed now. The great city has grown outwards and upwards since the war; outwards on the fingers of reclaimed land, upwards in towering buildings that put the old Cathay Building – once Singapore's highest skyscraper – to shame. Many of the new buildings are grouped round Raffles Place where the first Japanese bomb fell – the rectangular piece of ground where every urgent request to build an underground shelter against Japanese raids was vetoed by the British government on the grounds that the marshy ground was too unsafe to support such a building. It is an ironic reflection on that government that now there is a busy underground car park in Raffles Place.

Over the Anderson Bridge the white government buildings are unchanged and so – in appearance anyway – is the Cricket Club, with its angled verandahs facing the padang, the tennis courts, the silk-like bowling green. But though it may look just the same, Miki, who visits Singapore regularly, was recently elected a foreign member; and Julie plays her mixed doubles there instead of at the YMCA.

In the magic moments before dusk, when a tiny Sumatra breeze rustles the lacy casuarina trees, as I sit watching a lizard on the ceiling pounce on an insect, I sometimes find it almost impossible to believe that all the misery through which we lived was not just a bad dream.

Was it really here, in this club, that I heard the radio announce the loss of *Repulse* and *Prince of Wales*? Was it here that Chan the barman apologised because I could no longer sign for my drink, that the tennis courts below once sprouted with steel pylons to thwart any Japanese paratroopers, where British internees were finally paraded after the surrender of Singapore to a foe so tyrannical that millions trembled at its might?

Probably no one thinks about all that now. No one has time in a city so bustling that its traffic jams are as irritating as they were (in a different way) when they forced Grandpa Jack to help found Raffles to save him the drive home for tiffin.

Ah! Raffles. It is still an oasis of the past, the ballroom unchanged since the afternoons when Julie and I danced there and where later we dined with Paul the night the bombs came raining down.

Tanamera is another place that had not changed. True, it has been rebuilt and is now less ostentatious than before the war, but it was still a magnificent home, and it is a family home, it exudes warmth; the beauty of its grounds, with the jungle fringe, is unchanged; it still has the traditional 'Dexter' east and west verandahs, one for the mornings, the other for the evenings. The great white walls still stand, but above all the *spirit* of Tanamera has not changed, so that when Singapore and Malaya became independent states this year the decision to hold a celebration ball was almost automatic. After all, nearly every historic event had been suitably celebrated at Tanamera.

The ballroom – the big front room behind the white walls is still affectionately known by the name which Grandpa Jack bestowed on it – is lighter now, gayer, more cheerful, for the old pseudo-French and Italian furniture has gone, so that today it looks as it should look – a large party room in a tropical city.

But the champagne is still the best, and it is still served in copious quantities. The buffet suppers at Tanamera are still as renowned as they were when Papa Jack announced the engagement of Natasha and Tony. There are still enough tables for every one of the hundred and fifty guests to sit down, either on the lawns or in a huge striped marquee erected in case it rains, and the supper and party are organised by Li, still Julie's devoted slave.

'Just like the old days,' Paul grinned. His health was much better, though he was never going to be the Paul I knew of old. But the grey hair in a way suited him and though Tanamera was his home he spent more and more time travelling. 'It's bloody amazing when you come to think of it,' he added, 'to think that you and Julie actually beat the system! Fathers, mothers, the unwritten laws of Singapore, even if it *did* take a war to help you! Just shows what you can do given a bit of patience.'

As I stood there, mind locked in the past, sipping a glass of champagne, I felt a hand seek mine, and I knew it was

Julie, as beautiful as ever, and she didn't have to ask me to dance; I could tell she wanted to. We slid into a foxtrot, I at forty-five with the same warm feeling of love as on the night we danced in Tanamera when Grandpa Jack had his stroke; the night we ran in the warm air to the moonlit tennis pavilion. I could see by the look on her face, by her own special secret smile, that Julie was also thinking of that wonderful and terrible night when she became mine.

'I know, Johnnie,' she whispered. 'Sometimes I think that none of the past ever happened.'

The band stopped, the couples drifted to their tables, some stopping to wish us well, others to congratulate Julie. In a way, now, my greatest pride lay not in the mighty success of Dexter and Soong, its tentacles spreading over all Asia, nor the equal success of Dexter and Miki Enterprises, flourishing since the day we founded it after the war.

No, my pride lay in something altogether simpler, the way in which everybody adored Julie – *everybody*. I never met anyone who disliked her – and of course it wasn't difficult to understand why. People loved Julie because she radiated love – and it bounced back.

And too, as I looked at her, serene and smiling, I realised once again that she always carried with her a sense of *presence*. She was a Soong, and though she was aware what that meant she didn't parade it, the easy grace came naturally. She was a lady – and everybody knew it, from the governor to the bathboy.

Looking round, thinking back, I asked, 'Where's Pela?'

'She went out with Ben. They were going to see if the fireworks were all right. Oh! There they are.'

At that moment the double doors from the portico opened, as they had done in almost exactly the same way on the night of the great engagement ball, and as I watched I could actually feel the constriction of my heart as I felt it on that night in the past when I had watched the scene that now faced me again and made me catch my breath with joy. Then I had been talking to Paul, the young and dashing Paul, asking where Julie was, and he had pointed to the doors as they opened and said 'There!'

I had looked towards the entrance, and I remembered now my exact thoughts on that night: 'The most beautiful girl in the world looked at me and smiled.'

And like the second showing of an old movie, it was happening again, for there, smiling at me with love, as though conjured up by magic, was the Julie of that ball so many years ago – the same white dress, the same black hair, the same warm smile. Only there was a difference tonight, one I could not at first understand, as though my senses were playing tricks with me.

For I was not only looking at my wonderful Julie as she had been on that night, I was looking at myself too, for Pela stood by the double doors with Ben – tall, blond, mad on tennis. Looking at my son and daughter I suddenly felt – no, dammit! They're *not* my son and daughter, they are Julie and me, on the night everything started, just a few moments before we went to the summer house, both of us young, eager, in love, oblivious to the dangers ahead, laughing in our hearts, knowing only the beauty of first love, unaware of the agonies of separation, the bitterness of banished years.

Had we really looked like that, had we really suffered so much in order finally to stand where now we stood? And would they, our children, that handsome couple, ghosts of our past, suffer, too, when each found love?

I hoped not – and yet, surely the ecstasy of our secret passion in the tiny mirrored room of the Love Club outweighed the terrible day when Kai-shek threatened me with the Alsatian and Julie shot it, or the row with Papa Jack, even the hell of London after Julie stopped writing. How long ago all that was – and here, now, in front of me stood the living reason for my marriage to Irene – the lanky, blond portrait of myself as a young man.

Ian Scott and Vicki waved towards me from the other side of the room and I waved back and smiled – as I had smiled the night I made love to Vicki pretending it was Julie, as I had smiled the day when Natflat lay gasping with pain in Vicki's bungalow after her abortion, with Julie saying, 'I must go or I'll be late.'

Idly I wondered, looking at them, if Julie and I would be standing here in Tanamera if the Japanese had not attacked Singapore. Or for that matter if Miki, who I could see in a corner talking, had not saved my life in the jungle. If there had been no war, if life had continued its undisturbed, unhurried colonial way in Singapore, would I have ever been able to escape? Would I have ever spent that wonderful night at Tasek Layang, lying naked on the lallang, Julie on her back reciting a fragment of Russian doggerel, 'You will be counting the daisies, and I will be counting the stars.'

Pela walked over to greet some friends and for a moment Ben stood there, his hand idly resting on a collection of walking sticks and Malacca canes. Normally the hollowed-out elephant's foot which held them stood in the portico, but someone must have pushed it inside. I saw Ben's puzzled face as he picked one out. It wasn't a stick at all, it was a heavy, brass-knobbed poker.

Grandpa Jack! I could almost hear the swelling throats of the choir as he conducted with that old poker. What a man among men! *He* knew I was right to love Julie, knew that some forces are too strong to be denied. In this very house – or at least behind these very walls – he had died, after our long drinking session together on that last night, and I liked to think that he had died with his boots on, in the house he had built himself, happy at the end, a death of high drama that matched perfectly the drama of his life.

My thoughts of that night when the bomb dropped on Tanamera were disturbed by a faint explosion, the boom of a distant gun – but not this time a cannon aiming to kill, instead a salute to independence, and for all of us a signal to make for the grounds where, as on the night so long ago when Julie and I became lovers, and Grandpa Jack set off on the long and painful road to death, the fireworks had blazed.

There they were again, the rockets tearing into the sky, but this time without the sense of despair that had marked the great engagement ball. If only Grandpa Jack and Papa had been alive to see the people in the garden now – not just Europeans, but Chinese, Indians, Japanese, all mingling on equal terms, all part of the new world they had fought for, the world of partnership, to use Papa Jack's favourite phrase.

It had never entered my head to make any speeches at this private dance to celebrate a public event. But as the last of the rockets faded into the black air, restoring to the stars their right of way, and as we all crowded back into the ballroom for more champagne, Paul Soong, he of the many shared confidences of youth, whispered to the band, there was a roll of drums, and then Paul held up a glass.

'It won't take long,' he said, 'but I think we'd all like to wish Johnnie and my sister Julie, his wife, well in the new age of Singapore that dawned today – a dream in which I know my brother-in-law passionately believes. I'm the first to admit' – with a trace of that old, slow, sardonic smile – 'that I sometimes wondered if I wouldn't wake up, and find that it *was* only a dream, especially after the nightmares of the war – the night when Johnnie and I stood on this very spot after Grandpa Jack was killed and Tanamera had been bombed into a heap of smoking rubble.'

Paul paused for a moment, and somehow as I watched the years, like greyness, seemed to drop away, and he was the Paul of old – to me, anyway.

'And there was the night before that – the terrible black Friday when Johnnie got my sister away. I wondered if I should ever see *her* again. I wondered, I had doubts. But Johnnie had no doubts – he refused to leave the Malaya he loved, he stayed and fought – with the gun and the dagger – to make sure we could all meet here. It all seems a long, long time ago. But here we all are, and here *they* are, a couple of genuine, home-made Singaporeans – and so ladies and gentlemen, I give you a toast – to John and Julie Dexter, to Tanamera, and to *all* who live in her.'

THE PEOPLE
ALEX
CROSS

JAMES PATTERSON is one of the best-known and biggest-selling writers of all time. His books have sold in excess of 375 million copies worldwide. He is the author of some of the most popular series of the past two decades – the Alex Cross, Women's Murder Club, Detective Michael Bennett and Private novels – and he has written many other number one bestsellers including romance novels and stand-alone thrillers.

James is passionate about encouraging children to read. Inspired by his own son who was a reluctant reader, he also writes a range of books for young readers including the Middle School, I Funny, Treasure Hunters, House of Robots, Confessions and Maximum Ride series. James has donated millions in grants to independent bookshops and he has been the most borrowed author of adult fiction in UK libraries for the past eleven years in a row. He lives in Florida with his wife and son.

Why everyone loves
James Patterson and Alex Cross

'It's no mystery why James Patterson is the world's most popular thriller writer. Simply put: **nobody does it better**.'
Jeffery Deaver

'No one gets this big without **amazing natural storytelling** talent – which is what Jim has, in spades. The Alex Cross series proves it.'
Lee Child

'James Patterson is the **gold standard** by which all others are judged.'
Steve Berry

'Alex Cross is one of the **best-written heroes** in American fiction.'
Lisa Scottoline

'Twenty years after the first Alex Cross story, he has become one of the **greatest fictional detectives** of all time, a character for the ages.'
Douglas Preston & Lincoln Child

'Alex Cross is a **legend**.'
Harlan Coben

'Patterson boils a scene down to the single, telling detail, the element that **defines a character** or moves a plot along. It's what fires off the movie projector in the reader's mind.'
Michael Connelly

'James Patterson is **The Boss**. End of.'
Ian Rankin

Have you read them all?

ALONG CAME A SPIDER

Alex Cross is working on the high-profile disappearance of two rich kids. But is he facing someone much more dangerous than a callous kidnapper?

KISS THE GIRLS

Cross comes home to discover his niece Naomi is missing. And she's not the only one. Finding the kidnapper won't be easy, especially if he's not working alone . . .

JACK AND JILL

A pair of ice-cold killers are picking off Washington's rich and famous. And they have the ultimate target in their sights.

CAT AND MOUSE

An old enemy is back and wants revenge. Will Alex Cross escape unharmed, or will this be the final showdown?

POP GOES THE WEASEL

Alex Cross faces his most fearsome opponent yet. He calls himself Death. And there are three other 'Horsemen' who compete in his twisted game.

ROSES ARE RED

After a series of fatal bank robberies, Cross must take the ultimate risk when faced with a criminal known as the Mastermind.

HOPE TO DIE

Cross's family are missing, presumed dead. But Alex Cross will not give up hope. In a race against time, he must find his wife, children and grandmother – no matter what it takes.

CROSS JUSTICE

Returning to his North Carolina hometown for the first time in over three decades, Cross unearths a family secret that forces him to question everything he's ever known.

CROSS THE LINE

Cross steps in to investigate a wave of murders erupting across Washington, DC. The victims have one thing in common – they are all criminals.

A list of more titles by James Patterson
is printed at the back of this book

JAMES PATTERSON
THE PEOPLE VS.
ALEX CROSS

arrow books

1 3 5 7 9 10 8 6 4 2

Arrow Books
20 Vauxhall Bridge Road
London SW1V 2SA

Arrow Books is part of the Penguin Random House group of companies
whose addresses can be found at global.penguinrandomhouse.com.

Penguin
Random House
UK

First published by Century in 2017
This edition published in paperback by Arrow Books in 2018

www.penguin.co.uk

A CIP catalogue record for this book is available from the British Library.

Printed and bound in Great Britain by Clays Ltd, Elcograf S.p.A.

Penguin Random House is committed to a
sustainable future for our business, our readers
and our planet. This book is made from Forest
Stewardship Council® certified paper.

For Carole—my baby sister, absolutely one of my three favorites, definitely the smartest Patterson

Prologue

A HOT SUMMER'S EVE

ONE

FROM INSIDE A RAMBLING WHITE Colonial home on a shaded street that smelled of blooming wildflowers, a woman called in a pleasant Southern accent: "TW-Two? Where are you? Mama needs you to go to the store now."

There was a pause before she called again. "TW-Two? Deuce?"

Timmy Walker Jr., TW-Two, also known as Deuce, was twelve and standing just inside the woods that adjoined his backyard.

Go to the store? Deuce thought. He had better things to do than ride his bike all the way there and back for his mom. As a matter of fact, he had much better things to do.

The back porch door opened with a creak.

"Deuce," his mother called. "C'mon, now. I'll take you out for an ice cream sundae later?"

That was tempting, but Deuce stuck to his plan and eased off on a familiar path that led downhill to an old logging road and a creek that meandered through the woods. It was late in the day. The light was slanted, coppery, and the air was still sticky and hot.

Holding a beat-up old pair of binoculars his granddad had given him, Deuce thought: *Hot and sticky. That's good. Seems there's way more activity when it's all hot and sticky this time of day, getting on into night.*

Deuce looked down at his camouflage T-shirt and shorts and thought, *I'm dressed perfect. Should be able to get real close, and I've got the right gear.*

Mosquitoes whined. He slapped at one that bit his ear, hearing the building thrum of cicadas in the trees and smelling smoke from a distant fire. He dug in his pocket and got out a cigarette he'd taken from his mom's secret pack.

He lit it, took a drag, and blew smoke at the mosquitoes. That helped.

Still smoking, Deuce crossed the creek and kept on the logging trail, which paralleled the waterway for almost a mile before splitting off. He went left, then started uphill, pausing every few moments to listen. Nothing.

Even so, the boy remained certain he'd see something good tonight. It was late Friday afternoon. Prime time. Late summer. Primer time. And you didn't always have to hear them first. He'd learned that, hadn't he?

When Deuce neared the top of the rise, he put on a camouflage head net that almost matched the T-shirt and shorts. He eased slowly up onto the crest of the hill, peering through the tangle of vines and leaves in the last golden rays of day. Nothing.

He took a step. Nothing. Another step.

There!

Deuce smiled, hunched over, and snuck forward and down-hill toward a clearing at the end of a rutted dirt road. There were beer cans and wrappers strewn about, a brush pile, and, on the far side of the clearing, a lone blue Toyota Camry.

The engine was off. The windows were down. No music was on. Deuce was sure he knew why the car was there. He lifted the binoculars and peered across the clearing into the Camry's backseat, where a couple was writhing.

Deuce saw the naked back of one of them. The girl!

Perfect.

And blond! More perfect.

She sat up suddenly; she was seventeen, eighteen—beautiful! Then another topless blonde, younger, very pretty, rose up beside the first one. They began to kiss and caress.

TWO

THE TWELVE-YEAR-OLD THOUGHT he was going to have a heart attack, the scene made him so breathless. Shakily, Deuce lowered the binoculars, dug in his pocket, and came up with an iPhone 4 he'd bought used online. He found the camera icon and pressed it.

This is going to be epic, Deuce thought. *No one will ever forget this one.*

He took a soft step, and then another, which brought him right up to the clearing. He focused a moment on the passionate girls in the backseat of the car but did not raise his binoculars for a closer look.

He was on a mission now. Deuce thumbed the camera mode to video and pressed Record.

He stayed just inside the trees, in the shadows, and circled the clearing, going past the brush pile toward the Camry and coming up on it from behind and to its right. He imagined himself a panther and moved slow and careful until the car and

6

the girls were down a bank and slightly below him, not twenty yards away.

From that angle, he could see the girls were both completely naked. He was flustered, fascinated; part of him wanted to go even closer, right in the backseat if he could. But that wouldn't get him anywhere, now would it?

He had them framed perfectly. And the light wasn't bad at all. He was sure this would be his best effort yet. *Two blondes? I'll be a hero!*

Deuce almost laughed out loud but became transfixed when one girl's hand left the other one's breasts and slid south toward—

The boy heard the grumble of an engine and looked around. It sounded like a vehicle was coming fast and heading toward the clearing. The girls heard it too and scrambled for their clothes.

Are you kidding me? Deuce groaned.

He heard a shriek. He looked back at their car. One of the girls was staring out the window at him.

"There's some pervo kid in camo out there!" she yelled. "He's filming us!"

Deuce freaked and ran. He bolted deeper into the woods and then arced back the way he'd come, jumping logs, dodging trees, and smiling like he'd just escaped some tower with a king's jewel in his pocket.

And in a way, he had, hadn't he? He glanced at the phone gripped tightly in his hand as he continued to sprint back toward the trail. It wasn't the epic video he'd hoped for, but it was still—

Deuce heard a vehicle roar into the clearing and skid to a halt. One of the girls screamed.

7

Deuce stopped and looked back. Sweat dripped down his face, and he strained to see the clearing through the thick foliage.

The boy told himself to go, get home fast, upload the video to his computer, and spend the night reliving his victory before trying to figure out which website to sell it to. But his natural curiosity overwhelmed him, propelled him back toward the clearing's edge.

The sun was setting. Shadows were taking the opening in the woods. A white Ford utility van with a souped-up motor was idling next to the Camry, blocking Deuce's view of the girls.

He lifted his binoculars, saw the van's windows were darkly tinted. A magnetic sign on the near side said DISH NETWORK.

Dish? Out here? Wasn't that like a—

"No!" one of the girls shouted from the other side of the van. "Please! Don't do this! Help! Kid! Help us, kid!"

Deuce realized she was screaming for him and didn't know what to do.

Another scream followed, louder, terror-stricken. One of the girls was sobbing, blubbering, begging for mercy.

Deuce began to tremble with fear. A voice in his head yelled, *Run!*

A car door slammed. The van door slid shut, muffling the girls' cries.

I'm probably wrong for taking the video, Deuce thought, *but this is seriously messed up. I've got to do something.*

He dug furiously in his pocket, came up with a little magnetic doubling lens that he fitted to his phone's camera lens. He slid the mode to photo for better resolution and zoomed in on the van's rear license plate, lit by its parking lights, some sixty yards away.

The van's headlights went on. The engine revved. They were leaving.

Deuce squeezed the upper volume button of the iPhone to shoot without flash or autofocus. *Click, click, click.* He got five shots in all before the van rolled forward, picked up speed, and left the clearing.

The boy watched the van go, then raised his binoculars to look at the Camry. It was empty in the last fading light. No movement. Both girls were gone.

The boy began to tremble; he felt sick. Those girls had been screaming.

Deuce decided he had to do something. He needed to erase the porn part, make up some story about why he'd seen all this, and then tell it to the police. They'd go find the Camry, figure out who the girls were, and find whoever was driving that Dish van.

And he had to do it sooner rather than later.

He looked at his phone. He punched 911 but got no connection. *No Service,* the screen read. He'd have to go back to the other side of the creek before reception turned solid.

Deuce looked around, got his bearings, and set off toward the logging trail. It would be dark before he knew it, but he'd been walking around in these woods since he was four.

When the boy hit the logging road, a three-quarter moon was rising behind him. He broke into a jog and went up and over the rise.

Right where the trail got steep again, Deuce caught a glimpse of something dark, heavy, and long coming right at him.

He tried to duck, but it was too late.

A forearm smashed into the boy's neck and clotheslined him. Deuce's feet went out from beneath him, and his upper body, arms, and head whipsawed violently before crashing onto the logging road.

The boy felt bones break on impact, and he took a nasty crack to the head. He saw stars, and his limp fingers and arms flung wide. His iPhone sailed off into the woods, along with all the wind in his lungs.

For a second, maybe two, Deuce was dazed and saw only shadows and darkness. He heard nothing but the sound of his own choking and felt nothing but pain that seemed everywhere.

Then the boy heard a man's voice right beside him. "There, now," he said. "Where did you think you were going, young man?"

Part One

PLATINUM DAMAGES THE BRAIN

I LOOKED IN MY BEDROOM mirror and tried to tie the perfect necktie knot.

It was such a simple thing, a ritual I performed every day before work, and yet I couldn't get it right.

"Here, Alex, let me help," Bree said, sliding in beside me.

I let the tie hang and said, "Nerves."

"Understandable," Bree said, coming around in front of me and adjusting the lengths of the tie.

I have a good six inches on my wife, and I gazed down in wonder at how easily she tied the knot.

"Men can't do that," I said. "We have to stand behind a guy to do it."

"Just a difference in perspective," Bree said, snugging the knot up against my Adam's apple and tugging down the starched collar. She hesitated, then looked up at me with wide, fearful eyes and said, "You're ready now."

I felt queasy. "You think?"

"I believe in you," Bree said, getting up on her tiptoes and tilting her head back. "We all believe in you."

I kissed her then, and hugged her tight.

"Love you," I said.

"Forever and ever," Bree said.

When we separated, she had shiny eyes.

"Game face, now," I said, touching her chin. "Remember what Marley and Naomi told us."

She got out a Kleenex and dabbed at her tears while I put on my jacket.

"Better?" Bree asked.

"Perfect," I said, and opened our bedroom door.

The three other bedrooms off the second-floor landing were open and dark. We went downstairs. My family was gathered in the kitchen. Nana Mama, my ninety-something-year-old grandmother. Damon, my oldest child, down from Johns Hopkins. Jannie, my high-school junior and running star. And Ali, my precocious nine-year-old. They were all dressed as if for a funeral.

Ali saw me and broke into tears. He ran over and hugged my legs.

"Hey, hey," I said, stroking his head.

"It's not fair." Ali sobbed. "It's not true, what they're saying."

"Course it's not," Nana Mama said. "We've just got to ignore them. Sticks and stones."

"Words can hurt, Nana," Jannie said. "I know what he's feeling. You should see the stuff on social media."

"Ignore it," Bree said. "We're standing by your father. Family first."

She squeezed my hand.

"Let's do it, then," I said. "Heads high. Don't engage."

Nana Mama picked up her pocketbook, said, "I'd like to en-gage. I'd like to put a frying pan in my purse here and then clobber one of them with it."

Ali stopped sniffling and started to laugh. "Want me to get you one, Nana?"

"Next time. And I'd only use it if I was provoked."

"God help them if you are, Nana," Damon said, and we all laughed.

Feeling a little better, I checked my watch. Quarter to eight.

"Here we go," I said, and I went through the house to the front door.

I stopped there, listening to my family lining up behind me.

I took a deep breath, rolled my shoulders back like a Marine at attention, then twisted the knob, swung open the door, and stepped out onto my porch.

"It's him!" a woman cried.

Klieg lights blazed to life as a roar of shouts erupted from the small mob of media vultures and haters packing the side-walk in front of our house on Fifth Street in Southeast Wash-ington, DC.

There were fifteen, twenty of them, some carrying cameras and mikes, others carrying signs condemning me, all hurling questions or curses my way. It was such a madhouse I couldn't hear any of them clearly. Then one guy with a baritone voice bellowed loudly enough to be heard over the din:

"Are you guilty, Dr. Cross?" he shouted. "Did you shoot those people down in cold blood?"

CHAPTER

2

A BLACK SUBURBAN WITH TINTED windows rolled up in front of my house.

"Stay close," I said, ignoring the shouted questions. I pointed to Damon. "Help Nana Mama, please."

My oldest came to my grandmother's side and we all moved as one tight unit down the stairs and onto the sidewalk.

A reporter shoved a microphone in my face, shouted, "Dr. Cross, how many times have you drawn your weapon in the course of duty?"

I had no idea, so I ignored him, but Nana Mama snapped, "How many times have you asked a stupid question in the pursuit of idiocy?"

After that, it took everything in me to tune it all out as we crossed the sidewalk to the Suburban. I saw the rest of my family inside the SUV, climbed up front, and shut the door.

Nana Mama let out a long breath.

"I hate them," Jannie said as we pulled away.

"It's like they're feeding on Dad," Ali said.

"Bloodsuckers," the driver said.

All too soon we arrived in front of the District of Columbia Courthouse at 500 Indiana Avenue. The building is a two-wing, smooth limestone structure with a steel-and-glass atrium over the lobby and a large plaza flanked by raised gardens out front. There'd been twenty vultures at my house, but there were sixty jackals there for my rendezvous with cold justice.

Anita Marley, my attorney, was also there, waiting at the curb.

Tall and athletically built, with auburn hair, freckled skin, and sharp emerald eyes, Marley had once played volleyball for and studied acting at the University of Texas; she later graduated near the top of her law-school class at Rice. She was classy, brassy, and hilarious, as well as certifiably badass in the courtroom, which was why we'd hired her.

Marley opened my door.

"I do the talking from here on out, Alex," she said in a commanding drawl just as the roar of accusation and ridicule hit me, far worse than what I'd been subjected to at home.

I'd seen this kind of thing in the past, a big-time trial mob with local and national reporters preparing to feed raw meat to the twenty-four-hour cable-news monster. I'd just never been the raw meat before.

"Talk to us, Cross!" they shouted. "Are *you* the problem? Are *you* and your cowboy ways what the police have become in America? Above the law?"

I couldn't take it and responded, "No one is above the law."

"Don't say anything," Marley hissed, and she took me by the elbow and moved me across the plaza toward the front doors of the courthouse.

The swarm went with us, still buzzing, still stinging.

From the crowd beyond the reporters, a man shouted in a terrified voice, "Don't shoot me, Cross! Don't shoot!"

Others started to chant with him in that same tone. "Don't shoot me, Cross! Don't shoot!"

Despite my best efforts, I could not help turning my head to look at them. Some carried placards that featured a red X over my face with a caption below it, one reading END POLICE VIOLENCE and another GUILTY AS CHARGED!

In front of the bulletproof courthouse doors, Marley stopped to turn me toward the lights, microphones, and cameras. I threw my shoulders back and lifted my chin.

My attorney held up her hand and said in a loud, firm voice, "Dr. Cross is an innocent man and an innocent police officer. We are very happy that at long last he'll have the opportunity to clear his good name."

CHAPTER

3

THE POLICE OFFICERS MANNING THE security checkpoint watched me as I entered the courthouse, the media still boiling behind me.

Sergeant Doug Kenny, chief of court security and an old friend, said, "We're with you, Alex. Good shoot, from what I hear. Damn good shoot."

The other three all nodded and smiled at me as I went through the metal detectors. Outside, the horde descended on my family as they fought their way toward the court entrance.

Nana Mama, Damon, and Jannie made it inside first, looking shaken. Ali and Bree entered a few moments later. As the door swung shut, Ali faced the reporters peering in. Then he raised his middle finger in a universally understood gesture.

"Ali!" Nana Mama cried, grabbing him by the collar. "That is unacceptable behavior!"

But with the security team chuckling at him and me smiling, Ali didn't show a bit of remorse.

"Tough kid," Anita said, steering me to the elevators.

"Smart kid," said the young African American woman who'd just appeared beside me. "Always has been."

I put my arm around her shoulders, hugged her, and kissed her head.

"Thank you for being here, Naomi," I said.

"You've always had my back, Uncle Alex," she said.

Naomi Cross, my late brother Aaron's daughter, is a respected criminal defense attorney in her own right, and she'd jumped at the chance to help me and work with the renowned Anita Marley on my case.

"What are my odds, Anita?" I said as the elevator doors shut.

"I don't play that game," she said crisply, adjusting the cuffs of her white blouse. "We'll inform the jury of the facts and then let them decide."

"But you've seen the prosecution's evidence."

"And I have a rough idea of their theory. I think our story's more compelling, and I intend to tell it well."

I believed her. In just the past six years, Marley had won eight high-profile murder cases. After I was charged with double homicide, I reached out to her, expecting to get a refusal or a "too busy." Instead, she flew from Dallas to DC the next day, and she'd been standing by me in legal proceedings ever since.

I liked Anita. There was no BS about her. She had a lightning-fast mind, and she was not above using her charm, good looks, or acting skills to help a client. I'd seen her use all of them on the judge who oversaw pretrial motions, motions that, with a few disturbing exceptions, she'd won handily.

But mine was as complex a trial case as she'd ever seen, she said, with threads that extended deep into my past.

About fifteen years ago, a psychopath named Gary Soneji went on a kidnapping and murder spree. I'd put him in prison, but he escaped several years later and turned to bomb-building.

Soneji had detonated several, killing multiple people before we cornered him in a vast abandoned tunnel system below Manhattan. He'd almost killed me, but I was able to shoot him first. He staggered away and was swallowed by the darkness before the bomb he wore exploded.

Flash-forward ten years. My partner at the DC Metro Police, John Sampson, and I were helping out in a church kitchen. A dead ringer for Soneji broke in and shot the cook and a nun, and then he shot Sampson in the head.

Miraculously, all three survived, but the Soneji look-alike wasn't found.

It turned out there was a cult dedicated to Soneji that thrived on the dark web. The investigation into that cult led me, in a roundabout way, to an abandoned factory in Southeast DC, where three armed people wearing Soneji masks confronted me. I shot three, killing two.

But when police responded to my call for backup, they found no weapons on any of the victims, and I was charged with two counts of murder and one count of attempted murder.

The elevator doors opened on the third floor of the courthouse. We headed straight to courtroom 9B, cut in front of the line of people trying to get seats, and, ignoring the furious whispers behind us, went in.

The public gallery was almost full. The media occupied four rows on the far left of the gallery. The front row behind the prosecution desk, which was reserved for victims and victims' families, was empty. So was the row reserved for my family, on the right.

"Stay standing," Marley murmured after we'd passed through the bar and reached the defense table. "I want everyone watching you. Show your confidence and your pride at being a cop."

"I'm trying," I whispered back.

"Here comes the prosecution," Naomi said.

"Don't look at them," Marley said. "They're mine."

I didn't look their way, but in my peripheral vision I picked up the two assistant U.S. attorneys stowing their briefcases under the prosecution table. Nathan Wills, the lead prosecutor, looked like he'd never met a doughnut he didn't eat. In his mid-thirties, pasty-faced, and ninety pounds overweight, Wills had a tendency to sweat. A lot.

But Anita and Naomi had cautioned me not to underestimate the man. He'd graduated first in his class from Boalt Hall at UC Berkeley and clerked at the Ninth Circuit Court of Appeals before joining the Justice Department.

His assistant, Athena Carlisle, had a no less formidable background. A descendant of sharecroppers, Carlisle came from abject poverty in Mississippi and was the first person in her family to graduate from high school. She'd won a full scholarship to Morehouse College, graduated at the top of her class, and then attended law school at Georgetown, where she'd edited the *Law Review*.

According to profiles of the prosecutors that had appeared the week before in the *Washington Post*, both Wills and Carlisle were ambitious in the extreme and eager to prosecute the federal government's case against me.

Why the U.S. government? Why the high-powered U.S. Attorney's Office? That's how it's worked in Washington, DC, since the 1970s. If you're charged with a homicide in the nation's capital, the nation is going to see you punished.

I heard shuffling and voices behind me, turned, and saw my family taking their seats. Bree smiled at me bravely, mouthed, *I love you.*

I started to say it back to her but then stopped when I saw a sullen teenage boy in khakis and a blue dress shirt with too-short sleeves enter the courtroom. His name was Dylan Winslow. His father was Gary Soneji. His mother had been one of the shooting victims. Dylan came up to the bar, not ten feet away from where I stood, pushed back his oily dark hair, and glared at me.

"Frickin' hell's in session for you, Cross," Winslow said, his smile smug and malicious. "Honestly, I can't wait to see you go down in flames."

Ali jumped up and said, "Like your dad did?"

I thought Winslow was going to go ballistic and attack my younger son. Damon did too, and he stood up behind Ali.

Instead of taking a swing at Ali, the teen smiled even more malevolently.

"That's right, kid," he said coldly. "Exactly like my dad did."

"All rise!" the bailiff cried. "Superior Court of the District of Columbia is in session. Judge Priscilla Larch presiding."

A woman in her mid-fifties, with thick glasses and dyed-black hair pulled back in a severe hairdo, Judge Larch stood four foot ten. She was so short she looked almost comical climbing up behind the bench.

But I was not laughing. Larch had a richly deserved reputation for being a hanging judge.

After striking her gavel twice, Judge Larch peered out through those glasses and in a smoker's voice growled, "The People versus Alex Cross. This court will come to order."

CHAPTER

4

Six weeks earlier...

JOHN SAMPSON TRIED TO REMAIN calm, tried to tell himself that he would be okay with whatever decision awaited him on the other side of wooden double doors on the fifth floor of the Daly Building in downtown DC.

But Sampson couldn't remain calm. He smelled his own sweat and was almost consumed by anxiety.

His stomach did a flip-flop when the secretary at last nodded to him around five p.m. and said, "He'll see you now, Mr. Sampson."

"Thank you," Sampson said. He got to his feet and, like the therapists had taught him, widened his stance to counter the occasional bouts of vertigo he'd suffered since the gunshot wound to his head.

Sampson walked to the door, trying to exude confidence. He opened it, stepped in, and spotted Bryan Michaels sitting behind his desk, signing documents. Silver-haired and in amazing physical condition for a man in his mid-fifties, DC's chief of police looked up, smiled perfunctorily, and waved Sampson to a seat.

"If it's okay, sir, I'd rather stand," Sampson said.

Chief Michaels's smile disappeared, and he set his pen down as Sampson approached and stood at ease. The chief leaned back in his chair and studied the big man for several long, disquieting moments, glancing more than once at the scar on the left side of the detective's forehead.

"You shot well in qualifying, I see," the chief said at last.

"Not a stellar performance, but I passed, sir."

"You did," Michaels said. "And you almost matched your personal best in the physical tests."

"I've worked very hard to be here, Chief."

Sampson caught Michaels glancing again at the scar on his forehead.

"You *have* worked hard, John," Michaels said in a tone that instantly troubled Sampson, made him feel lost and, well, about to be discarded.

The chief went on. "But I also have to use my best judgment in deciding whether or not to return an officer to the field after the kind of trauma you sustained. And I have to ask myself if you will be a liability to other officers in times of crisis."

Sampson had wondered the same thing, but he said nothing, just gazed at the chief without expression. A beat went by, then two.

Chief Michaels broke into a smile, stood, and offered his hand. "Welcome back, Detective Sampson. You've been greatly missed."

Sampson grinned, grabbed the chief's hand, and pumped it wildly. "Thank you, Chief. You won't regret this."

"I know I won't," Michaels said. "You're an inspiration to many of your fellow officers. I want you to know that."

"Yes, sir. Thank you, sir."

"You'll be needing a new partner," the chief said, his face falling a bit.

There was an awkward moment before Sampson said, "I'm ready for that."

Chief Michaels studied him a moment and then said, "I hate that there's a gorilla in the room."

"Yes, sir. But I believe the gorilla will win out eventually."

Michaels softened. "I hope so. How is he?"

"Hung out his shingle to pass time until the trial," Sampson said.

"Give Alex my best. I mean that."

There was a sharp knock at the door, and in stepped an angular and highly agitated redheaded woman with a detective's badge on a chain around her neck.

"Fox?" Michaels said, irritated. "I hadn't asked you in here yet."

Fox glanced at Sampson, then back at the chief. "I apologize, sir, but Detective Sampson and I, we just pulled a bad one. Kidnapping and shooting at Washington Latin."

"Latin?" Sampson said. "Ali Cross goes to that school."

CHAPTER

5

ALI WAS BADLY SHAKEN BUT physically okay when Sampson found him on the steps of the Washington Latin Public Charter School, his backpack between his knees, wiping away his tears. A patrolman said Ali had seen the entire brutal incident. So had five other students involved in an after-school debate program.

"You okay, buddy?" Sampson said, folding his huge frame down beside Ali and putting an arm around the boy's shoulders. It was mid-October, chilly with night falling, and he was shaking.

"My dad's coming," Ali said in a flat tone. "So is Bree."

"Tell me what happened."

Before he could, Detective Ainsley Fox said, "Detective Sampson? Could I have a word?"

She was standing at the bottom of the steps, frowning at him.

"Hang tight," Sampson said. He patted Ali on the back, got up, and climbed down the steps to her.

In a low, scolding voice, Fox said, "You may have forgotten during your leave that we have rules against physical contact with minors."

Sampson squinted at her. "The kid's like my own, Fox."

"But he's not your own, and the rules are the rules. Shot in the head or not, you've got to play by them or suffer the same kind of consequences your old partner now faces."

Sampson gritted his teeth, said, "Fox, there are five other kids to interview *by the rules*. They're right over there."

Fox hesitated, put off, but then lifted her chin and strode toward the cluster of other upset children. Sampson returned to Ali in time to see Alex Cross and Bree Stone running past the crime scene tape. Alex grabbed up Ali and hugged him fiercely. Ali hugged his dad back just as intensely and started to cry.

When they'd both calmed down, Sampson again asked Ali to describe what he'd seen.

Ali said it was dark out when he exited the charter school behind a group of his friends on the debate team. He was the youngest and shortest by far, so his view was blocked when the screaming started. Then they all started running in different directions. Ali didn't follow them. He stood his ground and got out his cell phone.

"You called 911?" Bree asked.

"No, I videoed them."

"You videoed them?" Sampson said, impressed.

"I wasn't going to fight them," Ali said, pulling out his phone and starting the video.

The footage was shaky at first, but then steadied, showing three men in dark coveralls and masks dragging a screaming blond teenage girl across the terrace in front of the charter school toward Second Street.

"That's Gretchen Lindel, Dad," Ali said. "She's, like, a junior."

On the screen, the kidnappers almost had Gretchen Lindel to the sidewalk. A woman came barreling into view from the left. She was spitting mad and went straight at the masked men.

"Ms. Petracek," Ali said softly. "Our debate coach."

On-screen, one of the men let Gretchen Lindel go, pivoted, and, with zero pause, shot Ms. Petracek in the face at point-blank range. Sampson pulled back at the coldness of it.

The courageous teacher of English and public speaking at Washington Latin died in a heartbeat. Her body fell hard. The gunman turned to Gretchen, who was being forcibly held between two parked cars.

Ali said, "Here's the worst of it."

Siren wailing, blue lights flashing, a Metro DC patrol car came screeching up in front of the kidnappers. The men yanked open the cruiser's doors, threw Gretchen in the back, and jumped in themselves, and then the patrol car, tires squealing and siren still wailing, sped out of sight.

CHAPTER

6

SHORTLY AFTER SHE TOOK ME in following the death of my mother down south, Nana Mama caught me sad and lazing around on her front porch, doing just about nothing.

I was ten. Nana asked me what I was doing, and I told her the truth.

"Breathing," I said.

"Not hard enough," Nana Mama said. "I know you don't like it here, Alex, but give it time. You will. Between now and then, I want you busy. You up to nothing but breathing? You come see me. I'll give you something to do."

"What if I don't feel like doing anything?"

My grandmother, eyebrows raised and hands on hips, said, "In my house, you don't get that option. And you know what? When you're all grown up and gone from here, you won't get that option either, 'less you marry some rich girl or win the lottery."

Ironically, almost four decades later, my grandmother, in her nineties, did win the lottery—the Powerball, in fact. She took the single-payout option, paid a whopping tax bill, and imme-diately formed a foundation to promote literacy, aid the poor, and provide hot-breakfast programs at local churches.

She also made sure my kids could have whatever education they aspired to. Even then, Nana Mama had enough money left over that the entire Cross family could have sat on the front porch doing just about nothing until we were all pushing up daisies.

But that wouldn't fly with my grandmother. She was all about having a purpose in life that bettered and benefited others. After months on suspension pending my murder trial, and even though I'd been helping Anita and Naomi with my defense, Nana Mama felt I needed to do more than figure out ways to keep myself out of jail. She was right. I'd caught myself "just breathing" too often for my own comfort.

I'd decided that if I couldn't be a cop for the time being, I had to have a reason to get out of bed, a way to be useful to someone besides myself. So I returned to my first profession, psychological counseling.

I fixed up an office in the basement that had its own separate entrance, put up my framed master's and doctorate diplomas from Johns Hopkins, and hung out my shingle after nearly two decades in law enforcement.

I called every social services agency in the metro area, of-fering my skills and asking for referrals. Luckily I'd gotten a handful, and then a few more, and my practice slowly built.

Two days after Ali witnessed a kidnapping and a murder at Washington Latin, I was down in my office and heard a soft knock at the outer door.

I glanced at my scheduling book: *Paul Fiore. First visit.* Right on time.

I went to the door and opened it, saying, "Welcome, Mr. Fio—"

The stocky man who stood before me was five ten, maybe two hundred pounds, with curly dark hair, brown eyes, olive skin, and a baby face. I couldn't have guessed his age. But by his clothes, I certainly knew his calling.

"I'm sorry, *Father* Fiore," I said. "Please, come in."

7

THE CATHOLIC PRIEST LOOKED CHAGRINED as he came into my office. "I should have told you on the phone, Dr. Cross. I just didn't know what you'd think."

"I'd think I'd be glad to meet you," I said, shutting the door behind him. "And how can I help?"

Father Fiore smiled, but it was strained.

"Please, Father," I said, gesturing toward an overstuffed chair in my office.

"This *is* odd," the priest said, sitting down and looking around.

"How so?"

"I'm usually the one hearing confessions."

I smiled and took my chair. "If you don't mind my asking, doesn't the church provide counselors?"

"It does." Father Fiore sighed. "But I'm afraid this is a delicate subject, Dr. Cross, one they frankly might not understand even in the enlightened age of His Eminence Pope Francis."

"Fair enough," I said, picking up a yellow legal pad. "Why don't you start at the beginning?"

Fiore told me he got the calling to the priesthood when he was fourteen. He was ordained at twenty-two and worked in some of Chicago's poorest neighborhoods. He made such an impression there that the church transferred him to Washington, DC, where he split his time between the parish of St. Anthony of Padua and the cardinal's office, working to fund programs for the poor.

"My grandmother's foundation makes grants to similar programs," I said.

Fiore's smile was genuine. "How do you think I got your name?"

I had to laugh. Leave it to Nana Mama to get me a priest for a client.

"She's quite a lady, your grandmother," Fiore said. "Won't take no for an answer, and yet extraordinarily generous in spirit."

"That describes her to a tee. But let's get back to why you're here."

The priest's face fell a bit as he continued his story. He explained that earlier in the year, he'd attended a fund-raiser with the cardinal at a hotel in Georgetown. He'd found a young woman named Penny Maxwell alone and weeping in a back hallway. He stopped to console her.

Mrs. Maxwell was a widow. It was the second anniversary of her husband's death in Afghanistan, and try as she might, she couldn't keep her emotions bottled up.

"She was suffering, grieving," Fiore said. "So I did what a priest does. I listened and talked and prayed with her."

After the party, he walked with her along the Georgetown

35

Canal and spent three hours listening to her describe the challenges of her life as the widow of a gifted army surgeon and the mother of two wonderful boys.

Fiore was amazed and inspired by how courageous Penny was, by how determined she was to raise her sons right, and by how much she wanted to honor her late husband's memory in their lives. To his surprise, Fiore learned Penny went to St. Anthony's for services from time to time.

"Penny started bringing the boys to Mass, and I got to know them," he said. "We did things together, hikes, a trip to the beach, and it was like I experienced a dimension of life that I'd thought I understood, but didn't."

"And what dimension was that?" I asked.

"Love," Fiore said, sitting forward, hanging his head, and rubbing his hands. "I didn't just fall for her, Dr. Cross. Penny became my best friend, and I became hers. And those boys are just…every time I leave them, Dr. Cross, I feel as if my heart has a new hole in it."

"Does Penny know how you feel?" I asked.

He nodded. "We both feel this way."

"Have you slept together?"

"No," he said firmly. "We both believe in the sanctity of marriage."

"But the church does not believe in married priests," I said.

He nodded miserably, said, "So what do I do, Dr. Cross? Leave the only calling I've ever had or leave the only woman I've ever loved?"

8

AN ASHEN-FACED AND DISTRAUGHT woman walked to a bank of microphones.

"Please," Eliza Lindel said in a tremulous voice. "I beg you, from a mother's broken heart, if you know anything about my daughter's kidnapping, come forward, call the police or the FBI, and give me hope. Gretchen is a sweet, innocent young woman. Please help us find her before it's too late."

The feed cut away to a local station's news desk and an anchor who began prattling on about the kidnapping.

In her office downtown, Bree hit the mute button on her remote. She didn't want to hear the talking heads sum up the case. She knew the situation cold.

The critical first forty-eight hours of the investigation had elapsed with little progress. Part of that was due to the fact that the FBI had stepped in to take over the case because it was a kidnapping and Gretchen had likely been taken across state lines. Bree and DC Metro had been largely cut out at that point, especially after the FBI reviewed the tape of the snatching and saw the police car. As far as she knew, there'd been no ransom note, no attempts by the kidnappers to contact anyone.

"Chief?" Sampson said, knocking at her door. "We've got something."

Before Bree could reply, Detective Fox barged in front of Sampson and said, "I think we should be reporting this to the FBI. They're the higher authority now."

Bree's expression hardened. Ainsley Fox had never met a regulation or rule she didn't worship as gospel.

"Detective Fox," Bree said. "Last time I looked, your badge said DCMP, and you report to me. Anything you have, I want to hear."

"For Christ's sake, Fox," Sampson said when the detective hesitated. "I'll tell her if you won't."

Sampson took a seat, opened a file, and began by noting that all DC Metro patrol cars carried GPS trackers that transmitted their locations to databanks. A check of those banks showed no Metro cruisers in the vicinity of Washington Latin at the time of the kidnapping and murder.

"But Ali Cross's video clearly shows a patrol car with all the right markings and decals of a Metro rig," Sampson said. "Someone detailed that car to perfection, even configured the sirens and blues exactly the way we do."

"Where does that take us?" Bree asked. "To body shops? Places that rent stunt vehicles to the movies?"

Sampson glanced at his new partner and said in a grudging tone, "At some point, maybe, but Detective Fox *has* turned up a more promising lead."

Fox almost smiled. She pushed back her lank hair, got out her laptop, typed something, then spun the screen around.

Bree saw a picture of a blond woman, late twenties or early thirties, earth-mama sort, no makeup but very attractive in a wholesome way. She was vaguely familiar.

"Cathy Dupris," Fox said. "She disappeared from her home in small-town southern Pennsylvania ten weeks ago."

Bree remembered, then said, "The neighbors claimed an ambulance came, and men dressed in EMT uniforms rushed into her house and took her out on a stretcher. But there was no record of a 911 call or a private ambulance request."

"And no ransom note," Fox said, nodding.

"What's the connection?" Bree asked.

Fox called up another photograph of another pretty blonde, Delilah Franks, a bank teller in Richmond, Virginia, who'd vanished six months before.

Bree said, "Don't they think the boyfriend's responsible?"

"She was having an affair behind his back," Fox said. "But maybe that's just a coincidence. Maybe Delilah was taken for some other reason."

"You think you know that reason?" Bree said.

"Show her the pair first," Sampson said.

Fox typed a third time and showed Bree a split screen featuring school portraits of two teenage girls, both blond, both very cute.

"That's seventeen-year-old Ginny Krauss on the left," Fox said. "Alison Dane, sixteen, is on the right. Both girls disappeared nearly seven months ago from rural Hillsgrove, Pennsylvania."

Bree frowned. "I haven't heard anything about this."

"Because the families and police up there have kept it mostly quiet," Fox said. "The parents of both girls are devout Christians. They and the sheriff's investigators believe the girls ran away because of their parents' extreme views about the evils of lesbianism."

"The girls are gay?" Bree said.

"And in love, evidently," Fox said, and she typed again.

She pulled up a photograph of a blue Toyota Camry in a muddy clearing in the woods. The rear and front windows were blown out, and the driver's door was ajar, revealing shattered glass on the seats.

"The day after the girls failed to come home, sheriff's investigators found Alison's car at a popular party and make-out spot in a clearing way out in the state forest," Fox said, typing some more. "Now here's the change in pattern."

Bree sat forward when she saw a handsome little boy.

"Timmy 'Deuce' Walker," Fox said. "Twelve years old. The same day the girls go missing, Deuce vanishes from his neighborhood, which is less than a mile from where the car was found. A month later, a hiker discovers Deuce's remains in the woods roughly six miles from where the girls' car was."

"You think they're all related?"

"I don't believe in coincidences," Fox said, typing.

The screen jumped to a web page that displayed the photos of the missing women against a backdrop of chalk outlines of bodies on a pavement. Across the top of the page there was a platinum wig that looked like Marilyn Monroe's hairdo the night she sang "Happy Birthday" to President Kennedy.

Below the wig, letters that looked like melting red wax spelled out the site's name: www.Killingblondechicks4fun.org.co.

9

I STUDIED FATHER FIORE AND saw the priest's anguish. I took a deep breath, let it out, and said, in sincere sympathy, "That is a doozy of a dilemma, Father."

"It's torn me apart," Fiore said, tears welling. "I want what I can't have."

I didn't know what to say; not at first, anyway.

But then I asked, "Do you think God lays out a path for all of us?"

"I do," he said without hesitation.

"So you think you were meant to meet Penny and her sons?"

"I believe that's true. But why? As a test of my faith?"

"I don't think anyone could ever question your faith, Father. And I don't think this is a lesser-of-two-evils situation. More like the greater of two goods."

"I don't follow," Fiore said.

I set my notepad aside. "If you stay a priest, you'll sacrifice personal happiness to continue to help the poor and the members of your congregation. But if you leave, you could find similar, rewarding work, marry Penny, and raise her sons with as much love as possible, which is a noble thing too."

He thought about that. A sharp knock came at my outer door.

"I should go," Fiore said, looking at the time.

"They can wait."

"No," the priest said, standing. "You've given me much to pray about, Dr. Cross. I appreciate it. I really do."

I shook his hand. "You'll let me know what you decide, Father?"

"I will," he said. "And say hello to your grandmother for me."

I followed him into the hallway and to the door. When I opened it, John Sampson was standing there. The two men nodded to each other, then Father Fiore climbed the stairs and left, and John came in.

"You here for counseling?" I asked Sampson, shutting the door behind him.

"Got that covered," he said, going into the office and taking my chair. "I'm here off the record—*way* off the record. Not supposed to be talking to you about cases at all, per order of your wife and Chief Michaels. But my new, uh, temporary partner is driving me up the wall, and I needed your perspective."

"Honored to give it," I said, glancing at the scar on Sampson's forehead, remembering how he'd looked in the moments after he was shot by a follower of the late Gary Soneji. It was a miracle I was even talking to him.

John brought me up to speed on the crimes that appeared related to the disappearance of Gretchen Lindel. Then he logged on to my Wi-Fi and said, "My partner, Ainsley Fox, was

42

in a chat room where people were discussing the kidnappings and murders, and she found this hyperlink."

He showed me the screen and a link that read XRAYBLOND.BIZ.

He clicked it, and it took him to a site called Killingblonde-chicks4fun.org.co. I studied it several moments before asking, "Is this for real? I read that fake sites often use a double thing like that, dot org and then dot co."

"Hold that thought," Sampson said.

He showed me several pages on the website dedicated to kidnappings and killings. The writing was atrocious and, according to John, had many of the facts wrong. But each page did contain links to legitimate news articles about the cases, as well as clips from local TV broadcasts.

"Why does the original link not match the name of the website?" I asked.

Sampson smiled. "You noticed. There's more. When you Google either site, or use any other search engine, you get nothing. No results."

I thought about that. "So it's part of, what, the dark web?"

The dark web was a secret part of the Internet accessible only via encrypted software.

"Hold that thought too," Sampson said, clicking on Reenactments. The screen jumped to a page of MPEG thumbnails.

He clicked on one titled "Delilah Goes Down." A picture of Delilah Franks, the Richmond bank teller, came up, a photo I'd seen on the web page dedicated to her disappearance.

The image dissolved into a poorly lit, shakily shot video of a blonde being chased through the woods; it was taken from a camera mounted on her pursuer's chest or head. You could hear footsteps that matched the jerking motion of the camera, which quickly got close enough to the woman to show the back of her filthy, tattered dress and reveal that she was barefoot and bleeding.

She seemed to sense how close her pursuer was; she looked over her shoulder and screamed hysterically before jumping down the side of a steep embankment. She slipped, tumbled, and sprawled in the mud at the bottom.

"Don't," she wept, pushing herself up on all fours in the muck, shaking her head back and forth. "Please, not that. Haven't I been through enough?"

The camera focused down on her, and a computer-altered voice said, "It's never enough, Delilah. Once is never enough."

10

A KNIFE BLADE APPEARED IN the camera frame, obsidian black and curved tightly back toward an ornate knuckle guard and the fingers of the cameraman's gloved right hand. The wicked-looking blade began a slow, sinewy dance in the air. The chest-mounted camera jiggled as it moved even closer to the shaking woman.

The woman looked up, saw the knife, shrieked in terror, and tried to scramble away. The camera swung crazily after her and blurred the action for several moments.

When it stilled, a gloved left hand had the hysterical woman by her blond hair, and the right hand held the knife so the curve of the blade's cutting edge was poised just above the crown of her head.

"Do blondes have more fun, Delilah?" the computer-altered voice said.

Before she could respond, the screen froze on the image of the two hands, the knife, and the back of her blond head. Superimposed over the image, an icon of a lock appeared.

"Dark web," Sampson said. "Encrypted. Completely out of our league."

"Are all the videos like this?" I asked. "Blocked at the moment of crisis?"

"Yup," Sampson said.

"Think he killed her?"

"That's the point. You've got someone with a high-def GoPro camera mounted on a chest harness, wearing gloves, and carrying that knife. He turns loose the screaming woman, chases her down, and takes her right to the point of complete terror before the screen locks. You're left hanging, wanting to see the ending."

"And how do you do that?"

"I don't know. There's no promo offer anywhere on the site that I can see, but Fox found references to the site and comments about it on an open bulletin board for hackers and coders. They're extensive, and disturbing."

Sampson called up the hackers' website, and it was quickly apparent there was a significant cheering section for Killingblondechicks4fun.

I want in to that site, read one comment from Lone Star Blondes Must Die. *I can contribute. Help. Break some skulls, even.*

Death to all blondes, read a post by Brunette Lover. *Platinum damages the brain.*

Scalp every one of them bitches, read another by 1889B1.

There were, according to Sampson, more than two hundred posts on the hackers' board in that vein from ninety unique posters, all callous, merciless, and hateful. Why? Because of a woman's hair color? What the hell was that all about?

I said, "Any idea who built it? Owns it?"

"None," Sampson said. "But don't you know a cyberwizard at the FBI?"

"I know a cyber*witch* at the FBI," I said. "I can call her if you—"

I heard the door at the top of the basement stairs open.

"Alex?" Bree called. "Are you down there?"

Sampson shut his laptop. I got up fast and called out, "Still with a client, hon. I'll be up soon."

"Oh God, I'm sorry," she said. "I thought you'd be done by now."

The door shut and clicked. I didn't like deceiving Bree, but I didn't want to get John in trouble on his third day back on the job, and it felt so good to be on a case with him again.

"I'm sliding out of here," Sampson whispered, getting up.

"It's dark out, and I'll turn off the outside light over the stairwell."

"It'll be like I was never here," he said. He stopped at the door to gaze at me. "That felt good in there—you know, natural, me and you."

I smiled. "It did feel good. It does."

"You're gonna beat this, Alex. We'll get back to the routine again."

"Natural you and natural me," I said, and we bumped fists. Then I opened the door and the best friend I've ever had slipped off into the night.

Part Two

A KILLER'S SON

11

THE NEXT AFTERNOON, I STOOD in the stands inside the field house at the University of Maryland, watching Jannie, my sixteen-year-old, jog and loosen up on the track. I clapped as she came by. She gave me the thumbs-up and smiled, but I could see something troubled in her expression, as well as something that I'd never seen on her face before a race: the fear of the unknown.

That wasn't good. I supposed it was understandable for the first race back after a long layoff due to an injury, but it wasn't good. In the past Jannie had always gone to the starting line confident, loose, and ready for battle.

But she'd broken one of the two sesamoid bones in the ball of her right foot during a race, and it had healed excruciatingly slowly. The sesamoids act like the kneecap of the foot, only much smaller; they protect the major tendons and ligaments coming off the big toe. Without the sesamoids, the only way you can run is in burning pain.

Jannie's coaches and doctors had cautioned her not to run

until it healed. That was like asking a cheetah to sit still, and it had depressed and frustrated her no end. But she'd endured and built her strength, and now the X-rays showed the sesamoid had solidly fused.

That was ten weeks ago. Since then her coaches had been taking her workouts up slowly, trying to get her in shape before—

"Alex?"

I turned to my right and saw a fit man in his fifties with graying hair coming at me in silver warm-up pants, a blue hoodie, and white Asics running shoes. A small pair of binoculars and a stopwatch dangled around his neck.

"Nice of you to come, Coach," I said, shaking Ted McDonald's hand.

"Couldn't miss wonder girl's return," McDonald said. "How's she looking?"

"A little stiff and a little scared, frankly," I said.

The coach's face fell. "That's not good."

"I know," I said. "But let's see how it plays out."

"Only thing we can do. In the end, it's up to her."

McDonald was a private coach from Texas who'd started working with Jannie the year before the injury. At the time, he'd been talking about her track-and-field potential in Olympic-level terms. I wondered if that would be the case an hour from now, or ever again.

"This is a good test for her," McDonald said, as if he could read my mind. "Good surface. Short track. And tight curves. No matter how Jannie runs, her sesamoid will be stressed."

"How's that a good thing?"

McDonald had always been straight with me, so I expected candor, and I got it.

"We'll know quick if we're beyond this setback," the coach said. "And if we are, we can turn our attention to something other than the bottom of her foot."

No wonder Jannie was feeling uncertain, I thought. No wonder she was afraid. This was like a verdict coming down.

I tried not to let my mind wander to my own upcoming trial, and I kept up an easy conversation with McDonald before the four-hundred-meter competitors were called to the line. Jannie stepped up in lane three of the stagger, as ready as she'd ever be for two laps around the indoor track.

She'd gained ten pounds of muscle since she'd last raced, but she was still built like a gazelle, with long springy legs and arms, and still fairly thin compared to the other, older competitors moving to their starting blocks.

McDonald pointed at the young lady in lane five. "That's Claire Mason, Maryland high-school indoor record holder in this event. She just signed a national letter of intent to run at Stanford."

"Our girl know that?"

"Nope," McDonald said. "She's just down there to work her plan."

The starter called the runners to their marks. My stomach was doing flip-flops. In her last race, Jannie fell coming out of the blocks, which may have contributed to the fracture.

"Set," the starter said, his pistol raised in the air.

Jannie coiled.

At the crack, she broke clean and I heaved a sigh of relief at the way she came out attacking, her legs churning, her torso fighting to get upright, and her arms pumping toward the first curve and the first real test of the injured bone.

She blazed through the tight turn with relative ease in no

evident pain and accelerated down the backstretch. The staggering of the runners began to evaporate as they came through the second turn, Jannie in fourth.

"Be disciplined, now," McDonald said, glancing at his stopwatch.

Jannie raced down the front stretch, picked off the girl in third, then passed the one in second. That left only Claire Mason in the lead with one lap to go.

"Damn it, Jannie," McDonald said. "That's not what we—"

My daughter thundered after the Maryland high-school champion, but Mason held her off through the third turn. From my daughter's past performances, I figured that the second time down the backstretch would be Jannie's surge, that she'd find some reserve no one had predicted and blow past the girl in the lead.

Instead, Mason pulled away from Jannie. The girl in third overtook Jannie in the fourth turn. Jannie was gritting her teeth, giving it everything she had. But forty meters from the finish, the girl in fourth passed her. The girl in fifth got by her two feet before the wire.

Jannie slowed to a stop, glanced around in bewilderment, then looked up at Coach McDonald and me.

She threw up her hands in despair and exploded into tears.

CHAPTER

12

I JOGGED ALONG THE REFLECTING pool between the Washington and Lincoln Memorials. The dawn was cool, almost crisp, and it felt good to be moving and breathing fresh air.

During my morning runs, I usually tried not to think about anything besides putting one foot in front of the other. But that day I couldn't get my mind off Jannie.

Coach McDonald had told her before the race that she wasn't there to attack the leaders and win; he wanted her to get a clean start, stay close to the leaders, and kick at the end. A training session and a test of her foot.

Instead, Jannie got full of herself and went after what she wanted instead of staying with McDonald's program. It had caused a rift between them. The coach told me he was rethinking how much time he had to dedicate to her.

Nonetheless, her foot had held up. No pain. No discomfort.

I checked my watch and picked up the pace until I was nearly sprinting up the marble stairs toward the imposing statue of the sixteenth and greatest president our country has ever known. I'd been inside the rotunda where the figure of Lincoln presided and read his quotes dozens of times, but they always gave me a chill.

I didn't have a chance to glance at them today because a petite, intense, Indian American woman in a blue business suit and a trench coat stepped out from behind one of the columns. She carried a briefcase and a large Starbucks coffee cup, and she tilted her head, indicating we should leave.

"I should not even be here," FBI special agent Henna Batra said in a low voice. "I should be talking to Sampson or your wife."

"But you're here," I said as we climbed down the memorial steps. "Did you look at the website link I sent you?"

Batra did not reply, just cocked her head in a way that said I was a fool to have even asked.

Men and women far smarter than me will tell you that we are on the verge of the singularity, a moment in time beyond which all human brains will be able to access all possible information through the power of the Internet. As far as I was concerned, Batra was *already* at one with the Internet. Plugged in, she could reach across vast digital landscapes, unlock almost any door, and peek into some of the web's dimmest hiding places.

She was also one of the smartest people I'd ever known. Before Batra had even graduated from the Massachusetts Institute of Technology, she had eight high-paying job offers with the search-engine-and-social-networking crowd. Instead of accepting any of them, she'd joined the FBI and its growing cybercrimes unit. I'd met her during the course of the investigation that led to the murder charges pending against me.

That alone explained Batra's reluctance to meet me in a public place. She was proud of being FBI, and she was a woman of great personal integrity who cared deeply about her reputation. But she'd come, which meant she thought it was worth the risk, which meant she had looked at Killingblondechicks4-fun.org.co.

"C'mon, Batra," I said. "Any luck unlocking those videos?"

"Can a pickpocket pick?" Batra said, heading toward the Vietnam Memorial.

"What did you find?"

"Nothing," she said. "The videos all end a second or two past the locking point. I suspect if a user has the correct passcode, the two extra seconds are revealed and a secret onion router message is sent to the webmaster. At that point, the webmaster would send back an onion router message with the complete encrypted film attached."

"Hold up," I said. "Most of that went right over my head. Start with onion."

The cybercrimes specialist took a sip of her coffee and said an onion was a digital message or order that left a computer surrounded by layers and layers of encryption and code, almost like an onion. "When you send out an e-mail or look at a website," she said, "you're leaving digital tracks all over the so-called clear web. But when an onion message or order is sent, the surrounding codes direct it through dozens of routers on the deep, or unorganized, web. Each router peels away layers of encryption and metadata that would identify the original sender.

"Onions guarantee anonymity," Batra said. "We can't look at them. The NSA can't even look at them. Why? Because we won't even know they exist. Done right, they leave virtually zero trace."

"You're kidding," I said, disappointed.

"I'm not kidding," Batra said, her face clouding as we entered the Vietnam Memorial. "This is serious black-net stuff you've gotten yourself into, Cross. Almost everything having to do with that website was done through onions, so I have no idea who built it or who maintains it."

"Can't you hack it?"

"What's to hack?" Batra said. "The website is anonymously built and self-sustaining. I can shut down whatever the hosting URL is, but I'd imagine there are dozens of mirroring sites with the content on them already."

I thought about that. "You said *almost* everything having to do with the website was done through onion routers."

Batra arched an eyebrow and said, "You're smarter than you look, Cross."

"One of my redeeming qualities. What was *not* done through an onion?"

"Those posts on the hackers' bulletin board. *Those* I could track. And I did."

"All of the posters?" I said, impressed.

"Just the high-volume ones so far," Batra said.

"What do we know about them?"

"Creeps," the FBI agent said, taking another sip of coffee.

I was getting chilled, so I untied the hoodie around my waist and put it on as she continued.

"On the clear net, they troll porn," Batra said. "In the dark-net areas where I can track them, they're into lots of the sicker stuff. I wrote it all down."

"Where are they?"

"You mean physical location? All over the world, though one of the regular creeps posting is definitely local."

"How local?" I said, stopping.

"Right here," she said, waving her coffee cup. "DC."

"You have a name? Address?"

Batra studied me several beats, calculating what to tell me, no doubt, and then said, "Close enough."

CHAPTER

13

LEAVING THE BROOKLAND-CUA METRO stop later in the day, I knew damn well I shouldn't have been walking up John McCormack Drive. I could hear Bree in my head saying I had no authority here and that my time would be better spent working on my defense for trial.

But I was back in the game, and who was going to tell Bree or anyone?

The creep?

Not a chance. The creep would want to avoid any contact with legitimate law enforcement. And I just might learn something useful about Gretchen Lindel and the other missing blondes, which would more than justify my actions as a concerned citizen.

With that firmly in mind, I went to the security guard at the main entrance to the Catholic University of America and asked how to find the alumni office. The guard gave me a map. I thanked him and started in that direction until I was around a corner and out of sight.

Then I made my way to Flather Hall, a brick-faced dormitory for male freshmen. Classes were over that Friday. Rap and heavy-metal music pulsed and dueled from inside open dorm rooms. I spotted a few underage drinkers and smelled hemp burning as I made my way to the second floor and down a long hallway that reeked of too many young men living on their own for the first time.

The door I sought, number 278, was ajar. I stood there, listening, hearing nothing, and then knocked. No response.

I pushed open the door, saw bunk beds to my right and a single twin bed across the room. Two white males in their late teens sat on a love seat between the single bed and me, wearing Beats headphones and holding video-game controllers. They were absorbed in a violent game playing on a screen on the wall, oblivious to my presence.

Beyond them, at a desk tucked in the corner, there was a third white male, small, scrawny, oily brown hair, lots of acne. Three computer screens dominated the small desk where he sat, and he had headphones on as well, engrossed in the screens.

I reached over and flicked the dorm room light off and on twice.

As if a hypnotist had snapped his fingers, all three of them came up out of their virtual trances and looked around groggily. The closest kid, a chubby towhead named Fred Vertze, spotted me first. His double chin retreated, and he tugged off his headphones.

"Who are you?" he said. "What are you doing in here?"

I waited until the other two removed their headphones before making a show of shutting the door behind me and locking it. They were alarmed when my cold attention swept over them.

"Who are you?" Vertze demanded again.

"Who I am is irrelevant," I said.

"Hell it is," said Juan Cyr, the other young man who'd been playing the video game. Cyr was built like a fullback and stood up to show me he was no one to be trifled with.

Brian Stetson, the kid with the acne and the three computer screens, said, "Don't do anything *el stupid-o,* Juan. I'm calling campus security."

"Do that and I'll have to tell campus security what I know about what goes on in this dorm room," I said.

They glanced at one another uncertainly.

Vertze, who could have used a shower or two, said, "We don't know what you're talking about, man."

"Okay, let's cut right to it, then, before I alert the NSA, the FBI, and six other law enforcement agencies. Gentlemen, which one of you is Lone Star Blondes Must Die?"

CHAPTER

14

VERTZE'S EYELIDS DRIFTED ALMOST SHUT. Stetson frowned, as if he'd heard a foreign phrase spoken at a distance. Cyr acted like I'd punched him in the gut.

Then the burly teen's expression shifted from shock to anger. He twisted his shoulders and hissed at Stetson, "I told you messing around with that kind of crap was mind poison."

"Shut up, Juan," Stetson said, studying me calmly. "Who *are* you?"

"The worst kind of poison, unless you come clean," I said, feeling like I'd identified the leader of this crew. "How old are you, Brian?"

"Eighteen," he said. "How do you know my name?"

"I know all your names. I know you get your kicks exploring the dark web. Pushing the boundaries. Looking into nasty places."

"Free world," Stetson said.

"Dogfights?" I said. "Explicit war clips? Hardcore S-and-M fantasy sites?"

"There some law against watching I don't know about?" Stetson said.

"No, but there are several against abetting the kidnap and advocating the murder of five women."

That seemed to rock the kid, who looked less certain as he said, "I know what that means, *abetting*, and no one in this room abetted anything."

"Didn't you post a comment on a bulletin board about the Killingblondechicks website? Quote: 'I want in to that site. I can contribute. Help. Break some skulls, even.'"

He looked at me dumbly, then at his computer. "You hacked me?"

"FBI hacked you, Stetson. You screwed up. Forgot to use onion routers. Which means that I should go to the dean's office and tell him what you've been up to, which means you most certainly will be expelled, which means your parents will be called, which means you'll be escorted out of here in complete disgrace and humiliation."

I let that sink in before saying, "Or you can talk to me."

After several tense beats, Vertze said, "I'll talk."

"Fred," Stetson said. "Don't."

"Brian, my old man will skin me alive if I get expelled," Vertze said sharply.

"I'll talk too," Cyr said.

Stetson's face flushed. He glared at me, caught in a fierce internal argument, and then finally said sullenly, "What do you want to know?"

Over the next twenty minutes or so, the story came out.

Stetson was a math and computer genius who should have gone to Caltech, but his father was a trustee and fervent supporter of Catholic University. His first night at the school,

Stetson had introduced Cyr and Vertze to the dark web. They'd found the Killingblondechicks website and started posting about it for fun.

"Fun?" I said.

"C'mon," Stetson said. "No one thinks those videos are real."

"Have you unlocked the videos?"

"You can't. I tried. The locked world, the unknown, it's just part of the fantasy of virtual reality, man, a place to safely experience and vent frustrations without consequences."

I reappraised the eighteen-year-old, thinking that he was entirely too smart for his own good. "You boys experience frustration with blondes?"

"Hasn't every guy on the face of the earth?" Vertze said.

Cyr and Stetson both started laughing. I had to admit it was a funny line, and I fought not to smile.

Finally, I said, "If I look around in your pasts, am I going to find a blonde one of you disliked so much that she ended up kidnapped? Or dead?"

Cyr said, "My first girlfriend was a blonde. Caught her messing around with my best friend's older brother. They're married now. Not kidnapped. Not dead. Just miserable."

Vertze said, "My anti-blondeness stems from a severe German teacher junior year who had zero sense of humor. I thought about sticking a pin in her ass but refrained—at least, long enough to get an A."

Stetson and Cyr laughed again. I couldn't help it and smiled.

"What about you, Brian?" I said, looking at Stetson.

Stetson sobered and said, "My blonde story is like all blonde stories. They're all about the princess complex that's sold to them each and every day."

CHAPTER

15

AFTER DINNER, ONCE JANNIE HAD gone upstairs to do homework and Ali had settled in to watch *Meru,* an excellent documentary about extreme mountain climbers, I told Bree and Nana Mama about Brian Stetson, disguising him as a client and not revealing his name.

"The princess complex?" Bree said. "And how exactly did he define that?"

"He said it starts at birth with blond girls," I said. "They're dressed as princesses in the crib. Then they're sold the princess story in movies, in advertising, all around them, until they believe that if they can just be beautiful enough, they'll attract Prince Charming and live happily ever after."

Nana Mama said, "An eighteen-year-old told you all that?"

"A sharp one. He had the root theory of blonde stories figured out."

Bree said, "I knew a blonde who was just like that, treated

like a princess her whole childhood. Leanne Long. She was an honest-to-God nice person, and she became a nurse and married a really nice guy, so it doesn't always work according to that kid's theory."

"This old lady needs her sleep," my grandmother said, taking her cane and getting up.

"We're right behind you," I promised. "We'll make sure the place is spotless for you in the morning."

"Bless you, dear," she said, and she kissed my forehead.

When Nana Mama was out of earshot, Bree turned serious and said, "Alex, how long did you think you could be involved in the Gretchen Lindel investigation without me knowing?"

"The client story didn't work?"

"Uh, no."

I told her the truth, the whole truth, and nothing but the truth.

When I was done, Bree was spitting mad.

"What were you thinking, going onto campus like that?" she demanded. "Entering a dorm room without a warrant? Threatening possible witnesses without authority and while on suspension due to pending homicide charges?"

I'd known most of that was coming, but it still hurt. I'd let her down.

"I wanted to be useful, Bree," I said. "It felt like I was back in the game."

"Your clients and practice are your game now. Have nothing to do? Work on your defense. Help Anita and Naomi make your case ironclad. And the next time you feel the need to lie or hide things from me, Alex? Please don't."

I had a hollow feeling in my stomach and said, "You're right. I just...you're right. It will never happen again."

I hoped she'd forgive me. I hated going to sleep when one of us was mad at the other.

After several moments, Bree sighed and said, "So you don't think those college boys are involved?"

My shoulders relaxed. I felt like we were getting back to level ground.

"Beyond the posts, no, not as far as I could tell."

"You don't think we should get a warrant for their computers?"

"And get them all expelled for being smart, nosy, teenage male nerds with blonde chips on their shoulders?"

"Well, when you put it like that," Bree said, getting up and extending her hand to me.

I took it, kissed the back of her hand, and said, "Princess?"

She started laughing, said, "Charming?"

I got up, grinning. "That's me."

16

JOHN SAMPSON HAD NEVER HEARD a collective grief quite like this. The crying, wailing, and whimpering seemed to come from every room he passed.

Innocence destroyed, Sampson thought. *Up until now, their lives have been one shooting star after another, and that's gone.*

Looking shell-shocked, Wally Christian, Georgetown University's security chief, walked beside Sampson and Detective Ainsley Fox down a hall on the first floor of Village C West, a residential building for freshmen. A DCMP patrol officer stood aside so they could go through the double doors into the common area.

Sampson paused just beyond the doors and took in the carnage with one long, sweeping glance.

A young brunette in a Hoyas sweatshirt was sprawled on a couch, dead, a gunshot to her neck. A second young woman with short brown hair lay facedown and dead on the carpet. EMTs rushed out of the room with a gurney carrying a very large Samoan American male with two chest wounds.

"How many saw it?" Sampson asked.

"Seven," Wally Christian said. "We've moved them to the common room upstairs. The chaplains are with them."

"Who's the missing girl?" Fox asked. "The blonde?"

"Patsy Mansfield," Christian said. "A sophomore. Real star."

"As in, people knew who she was?" Sampson said.

"On campus, you bet. She plays lacrosse, all-American as a freshman, and, well, you've seen the picture of her I put out with the Amber Alert. She's quite the looker."

As all of them took the stairs to the second floor of the dorm, Sampson thought of what Alex had told him over the phone about the three freshmen at Catholic University with bad attitudes about blondes. He wondered if they were involved here and made a note to check on their whereabouts at the time of the incident.

The seven witnesses to the homicides of the brunettes and the kidnapping of Patsy Mansfield all told much the same story. Eleven students were hanging out in the lounge around seven that Saturday evening when two men came in from outside. They wore black balaclavas and olive-green workman's coveralls with *Georgetown University* written on the back. They drew pistols with silencers and ordered everyone to the floor except Patsy Mansfield.

"Wait," Detective Fox said. "They used her name?"

"Definitely," said Tina Hall, a freshman. "They knew who she was."

Hall and the others said the two men told Mansfield that things would go easier if she just went with them. But then Keoni Latupa, a linebacker on the football team and a good friend of Patsy's, grabbed one of the men and threw him to the ground so hard that his gun clattered away. Latupa scrambled for it, but the other man shot and wounded him before he could get to it.

The loose gun came to a stop at the feet of Macy Jones, the brunette in the Hoyas sweatshirt. She went for it and was shot too. At that point, Denise O'Toole, Jones's roommate, went to help her friend. She was shot in the leg.

"Then the first guy got up and retrieved his pistol," said Tina Hall. "He went over to Keoni and shot him again. Then he went to Denise, who pleaded with him not to shoot her, just to take her but not shoot her."

Hall paused, tears welling in her eyes and then dripping down her cheeks. She went on, "Know what he said before he killed Denise? He said, 'Why would we take you? Nobody pays for brunettes anymore.'"

17

THE DC POLICE UNION HAD referred my latest client to me. She knocked on my basement door shortly after nine Monday morning.

I opened the door and found a dark-haired woman in her mid-thirties standing there, her shoulders slumped. I knew her, but she was so haggard I almost didn't recognize her.

"Tess?" I said, holding out my hand. "It's good to see you."

Detective Tess Aaliyah lifted her head, tears streaming down her cheeks. "I'm embarrassed and uncomfortable to be here, Dr. Cross, but my union rep said you were the only counselor available on short notice."

"Come inside, and please don't be embarrassed or uncomfortable. I'm not a detective now and not here to judge you in any way. You need to talk. I'm available to listen. And, of course, nothing said ever leaves the room."

The detective hesitated and then came inside. I followed her into my office, remembering the confident, smart, and attractive woman who'd helped save my family after they were taken by a madman named Marcus Sunday.

Aaliyah was from a police family. Her father, Bernie, had been a top detective in Baltimore, and she'd lived and breathed the job when we'd worked together. I knew some of the trauma she'd been through lately, and as I shut the office door, I prayed that I was up to the task of counseling her.

I got coffee for her and gestured to a chair. She sat down, her head tilted low and her upper torso and shoulders rolled forward, as if in surrender.

"How are you feeling?" I asked.

"You've seen the news? How should I feel?"

"Forget the news," I said. "Lift your chin, straighten your shoulders, and give me your side of it."

Conflicting emotions flickered on the detective's face as she made a slight alteration in her slouch before telling me the story.

She and her partner, Chris Cox, had gone to a high-rent apartment complex off Judiciary Square to serve a warrant on and arrest one Drago Kovac. Kovac had immigrated to the U.S. from Serbia when he was nine, become an American citizen at fifteen, and become a car thief shortly thereafter. He wasn't very good at his chosen field at first. Kovac was caught and convicted of grand theft auto twice before his eighteenth birthday. After that, he wised up and got sophisticated. He formed an auto-theft ring that worked the Miami-to-Boston corridor, boosting in-demand cars, chopping them up for parts, and then selling the parts over the Internet.

Kovac was now twenty-seven and operating his illegal enterprise from his luxury flat on Third Street in DC. Aaliyah, looking for spare parts for her Ford Explorer, had happened on one of his websites, which offered "gently used" parts for a third of what other sites and stores were asking. When she learned the company and Kovac were based in DC, one thing led to another, and then to a year of additional investigative work.

"We had him," Aaliyah said. "I mean, this was a major criminal operation. Millions of dollars, and we had him dead to rights."

"So you go to Kovac's apartment building to serve the warrant," I said, pushing her toward the awful truth.

"Yes." Aaliyah sighed. "We went in at the exact same time arrests in this case were supposed to go down all over the East Coast. Synchronized, you know?"

But unbeknownst to Aaliyah and her partner, several warrants had been served early. When police in New Jersey went through the front door of a Kovac chop shop, one of his men got off a text warning of the raid.

"Seconds before we reached the tenth floor of his apartment building, Kovac and his men left his flat," Aaliyah said. "Cox saw them at the far end of the hallway and ordered them to the ground. They ran, and when we pursued, they shot."

"They definitely shot first?"

"No question," Aaliyah said, a smolder of the old fire in her eyes. "Surveillance cameras back us up."

"Okay. Kovac and his men shoot first. Then what?"

That glowing ember died in Aaliyah's eyes. Her neck muscles went taut as piano wires before she said, "Then it all became a nightmare."

Provoked into a gun battle, Aaliyah and her partner followed protocol and returned fire. Her first shot hit the meat of Kovac's thigh. Her second and third shots missed the car thief, who, howling in pain, lunged into the stairwell.

"I was in pursuit when the wailing started behind the door at the end of the hall," Aaliyah said, and she broke down sobbing.

I knew the rest. She and Cox caught and arrested Kovac and two accomplices, but at an unfathomable cost. The bullets that went wide of the car thief had gone through the door of the apartment belonging to the Phelps family—Oliver, a young, successful attorney; Patricia, a young, successful physician; and their twins, four-year-old Meagan and Alice.

Alice had been playing in the front hallway. The nanny had rushed to get her at the first shot.

"What are the odds, Dr. Cross?" Aaliyah asked, still weeping bitterly. "What are the odds of wounding the nanny and killing the girl?"

18

AFTER AALIYAH POURED OUT HER anguish, her grief, her guilt and despair, she pulled her feet up under her on the chair, wrapped her arms around her knees, and stared off into the distance.

"In the end, I'll always be the cop who killed a child," she said hollowly. "No matter who I was before or who I become after, that's who I will be."

"To who? You?"

"I pulled the trigger, Alex. That's what they'll write after I die."

"I empathize with the pain and regret you must be feeling, but you don't know what the future holds for you. None of us do."

She blinked slowly, said, "There is a way to know your future for certain."

That got my attention and concern. "Have you thought about that, Tess?"

Aaliyah took a big breath and then shook her head. "No. Not really."

"Not really?"

"Not at all. I'm just trying to find a way to process this, you know?"

There was little conviction in the detective's voice, and she appeared preoccupied.

"Are you sleeping?" I asked.

"Some days it's all I do."

"Self-medicating? Alcohol? Drugs?"

"Honestly, I wish they'd work, but they don't, so I don't."

"When does the civil suit go to trial?"

Aaliyah continued to avoid eye contact. "I don't know what they expect to get from me. This has already cost me everything."

I continued to watch her, thinking about the flat affect in her voice and expression, the defeated way the detective was holding herself, and some of the statements she'd made, especially talking about herself in the past tense.

"Tess, I think I'd feel more comfortable if, for your own safety, we take you somewhere to get a proper, in-depth evaluation of your current condition."

Aaliyah raised her head for the first time in many minutes, gazed dully at me, and said, "I'm nowhere near the padded room."

"Given what you've been through, suicidal ideations are cause for serious concern, Tess. This could be a medical issue that—"

"No one's putting me in a psych ward," Aaliyah said, getting to her feet angrily. "Least of all me."

"Tess—"

"Sorry," she said, heading for the door. "I thought I could trust you and I was wrong. Good-bye, Dr. Cross."

After a long look at the situation I came to a decision, grabbed my jacket, went outside, and hailed a cab.

CHAPTER

19

WE PULLED UP IN FRONT of the DC Police Union building twenty minutes later. I paid the cabbie, went inside, and asked to see William Roth.

Did I have a meeting set up with Mr. Roth? the receptionist asked. No. Had I tried to call him? I'd thought it was a dire enough situation to come down to talk with Mr. Roth in person. It wasn't until I told him it might be a matter of life and death that he called upstairs.

Mr. Roth was in an important meeting, the receptionist told me after hanging up the phone.

"You didn't explain the gravity of the situation. Call back."

The receptionist rolled his eyes, snatched up the phone again, and dialed. "He says break into the meeting. It's that important," he told someone.

The receptionist waited, waited, and then hung up and said, "Go on up, third floor, second door on the right. Roth's not happy."

"I don't care," I said, and I took the stairs up.

I knocked on the door and then entered an anteroom with a very irritated secretary at her desk. "Mr. Roth has been working for this meeting for six months," she said.

"Would it matter if someone you cared about was in danger?"

"Well," she said, flustered. "I suppose so."

"Where's Roth?"

"Roth's right here," said a flushed, bald man who appeared in the open doorway behind the secretary. "This better be good. I've got people at the table I never expected to—"

"It's Tess Aaliyah," I said, walking past the secretary into Roth's office. "You're her rep, correct?"

"Aaliyah?" Roth said with mild disdain. "Dear God, what's she done now?"

"You sent her to me this morning for an evaluation. I believe she's depressed and possibly suicidal."

"No," Roth said, taking a seat at his desk. "I saw her last week. She was bummed but knew it wasn't her fault that the little girl was playing in the front hall before the shooting started."

"I don't think Aaliyah cares. About anything. Which can be chemical, and which is why I need your help getting her into a psych ward for three days so she can be evaluated by medical professionals."

"You want me to commit Aaliyah?" Roth said incredulously. "No, absolutely not. Even if I had that authority, and I don't, absolutely not."

"Aren't you supposed to look after her, represent her?"

"In the shooting, yes, but this? No."

"The depression and suicidal thoughts followed from the

shooting," I said firmly. "She needs help. More than I can give her."

"You tell her that?"

"I did."

"What did she say?"

"That she was upset but fine and nowhere near the padded room."

"There you go, then," Roth said, getting up. "I have a meeting to run."

I blocked the door and said, "You don't care about Aaliyah's well-being?"

"I care," Roth said. "But if you want her in a psych ward, convince her doctor or someone in her family to recommend it. Or get the department to make it a stipulation of her suspension revocation. Any way you try to do it, though?"

"Yes?"

"Expect her to fight."

CHAPTER

20

AFTER SEVERAL UNSUCCESSFUL ATTEMPTS TO reach her, I spoke with Esther Dodd, an attorney for the police department. It was obvious by her curtness that Ms. Dodd was none too happy to take my call, probably due to the murder charges pending against me. She listened impatiently and dismissed out of hand my request to have Aaliyah undergo psychiatric evaluation as soon as possible as a stipulation of her rejoining the force.

"She's on suspension with a lawsuit pending," the attorney said. "That puts Detective Aaliyah in limbo and gives us very few options, especially since your evaluation was done on behalf of the police union. With all due respect, it holds no weight from a legal perspective. Good-bye, Dr. Cross."

I tried to find Aaliyah's doctor next and lucked out when a friend in the human resources department checked some old records and gave me a name, Dr. Timothy Cantrell. I looked Cantrell up and found he was not only an internist but affiliated with GW Medical Center and its famous tropical medicine division. I called Cantrell's office but found that the physician, a member of Doctors Without Borders, was currently out of the country, working in Brazil to stem a yellow fever outbreak.

I was frustrated but refused to give up without making every effort.

At 2:12 p.m., after making the long drive, I turned down Francis Street in the small town of Arbutus, a suburb of Baltimore, and soon found a small blue-and-white bungalow with a neatly tended yard.

A raw northeast wind had picked up and caused me to shiver as I ran up the walk and knocked at the door. A tall and very put-together redheaded woman in her late fifties answered the door.

I introduced myself, and her features softened.

"I've seen you on the news," she said. "Tess and Bernie say you're innocent, wrongfully charged."

Her name was Christine Prince. She was Aaliyah's father's girlfriend and was happy to tell me that Bernie had gone off surf-fishing, his passion in retirement. I asked when he'd return, and she said that he'd gone to one of his favorite spots out on Assateague Island, so he probably wouldn't be back until around midnight.

After a few moments' hesitation, I asked if she knew where on Assateague he went to fish.

"You're going all the way out there?" she said after showing me on a map.

"I need his advice, and I think he'd want to give it to me sooner rather than later."

"Tess?" she said softly.

"You're a mind reader, Christine," I said. "Thank you for the help."

Two hours later, I pulled into Assateague Island State Park. The ranger station was closed, and I found Bernie Aaliyah's Jeep Wagoneer parked right where his girlfriend said it would be.

When I got out, the wind clipped me, and the sky spat rain. I dug in the trunk of my car and came up with an old rain jacket and a pair of calf-high rubber boots I kept around for crime scene work. I put them on, and with my hood up to block the wind, I walked up the trail, through the dunes, and onto the beach.

The Atlantic was gray and roiling. But to my left, there were surfers out on the swells, clad head to toe in black neoprene, and to my right, there were six or seven anglers. I stood there, looking at the anglers one at a time, until I saw an older man limp fast toward the crashing surf and then use his powerful shoulders to whip out a heavy fishing rod with a big pink lure.

I thought the lure's arc would die quickly in the wind, but it had just the right angle, and it punched through, landing in the water far offshore. As I started toward him, he pumped the rod tip up and down several times, paused, then did it again. When I passed his chair, his cooler, his tackle box, and two Coleman lanterns yet to be lit, he twitched it a third time.

"Bernie Aaliyah?" I said.

The old man startled and looked over his shoulder at me, huddled in my rain jacket and hood. "I know you?" he said.

I pushed back the hood. "Alex Cross, sir."

Tess's father's face broke into a toothy smile. "So you are. Been a long time, Dr. Cross. I've been following your career from way back."

"I followed yours when I was at Johns Hopkins, sir," I said.

"Hold on, let's do this proper," Bernie said, sticking the butt end of his fishing rod into a piece of white PVC pipe buried in the sand. "There, now."

He turned awkwardly, due to a gunshot wound to his pelvis that had ended his remarkable career in Baltimore Homicide, but he shook my hand with the vigor of a man half his age.

"To what do I owe the honor of you driving all the way to hell and gone to see me?" Bernie asked.

"It's about Tess," I said. "It's serious."

CHAPTER

21

AFTER I DESCRIBED MY CONCERNS and the evidence to support them, Bernie Aaliyah was quiet for several moments, standing there, looking off toward the waves crashing in the falling light.

"I saw my daughter three days ago," he said at last. "Tess was still grief-stricken, still remorseful, but I didn't see suicidal, Dr. Cross. And I certainly will not go to court over her wishes."

"I don't discount your observations, Mr. Aaliyah," I said. "And maybe you don't want to legally compel Tess to undergo a full psych evaluation. But you could convince her to commit herself. If I'm wrong, I'm wrong, but I'd rather stand here with my tail between my legs than stand next to you at a grave."

Before Aaliyah's father could reply to that, there was a sharp popping noise. We both turned to see his surfcasting rod bending hard, the line straight and quivering.

"That's a good one!" he cried, scrambling over to the fishing rod and grabbing it before it could come free of the PVC pipe.

Bernie held the rod tight about two feet from the bottom,

the butt still in the pipe. He leaned back, testing the weight of the fish and its strength.

"Oh, Jaysus," Bernie said. "He's gonna go forty minimum, maybe fifty!"

The reel started to whine. Aaliyah's father reached down and adjusted the drag to let the unseen fish run. He let it tear out a hundred yards and saw the line slacken before he snatched up the pole from the PVC pipe and reset the drag.

"Bernie," I began.

He barked, "I've been waiting on this quality of fish for two years running, Cross. So you can either leave or wait until I'm done here."

I held up my hands. "Don't let me get in your way."

So I stood back and watched the retired homicide detective engage in an epic battle on the beach. Every time Bernie was able to pull and crank the fish closer to shore, it would make another run that left him gasping.

"He could go sixty," Aaliyah's father said with a grunt twenty minutes into the struggle. "Big, big striper."

Thirty-five minutes into the fight, he said, "Maybe seventy pounds. My God, what a pig of a fish!"

Fifty-two minutes into the battle, Bernie had the striper in the surf thirty yards right in front of him. We saw the leader and a flash of a big fin before the pig of a fish rolled over and started to shake its head against the pressure of the line and the hook.

Then the fish ran, leaped up out of the water, head still shaking, and crashed sideways into the surf. I was shocked at the size of it. So was Bernie.

"Jaysus H," he said in awe. "He has to be pushing the world rec—"

The striper thrashed once more. There was a twanging noise as the line snapped in two. Bernie staggered and fell back into the sand.

I felt bad and expected him to be mad, curse his luck, or at least cry out in dismay. But Aaliyah's father just sat there in the sand, holding his fishing rod, staring at the surf and what could have been.

After several minutes, he said, "You get a chance at some things only once in this life, and sometimes they slip right through your hands. I'll support you, Dr. Cross. One way or the other, I'll see to it that Tess gets the help you say she needs."

CHAPTER

22

JOHN SAMPSON KNOCKED ON THE door frame of Bree Stone's office.

"Chief, we've got her in interrogation," he said.

Bree looked up from a stack of papers, put her pen down, and got up.

She and Sampson went to a booth with a one-way mirror overlooking an interrogation room. A young woman with elaborate parrot tattoos on both arms, multiple face piercings, and half her jet-black hair shaved off sat at the table, staring at the mirror.

In an accent that sounded straight out of Appalachia, she said, "Sally Sweet doesn't have all day. You either want to know or you don't."

Detective Ainsley Fox was also in the observation booth. She said, "Let me talk to her alone, Chief. Get her to relate to me."

Sampson wondered whether that was possible, given that Fox was one of the most abrasive, obnoxious people he'd ever worked with.

Bree was skeptical too, and shook her head. "Detective Sampson will take the lead. He has years of experience at this kind of thing."

Fox scowled but offered no argument as she trailed Sampson out into the hallway. Sampson stopped and said, "You listen. You study. You learn."

His partner did not like that, but she nodded. She and Sampson entered the interrogation room and sat down in front of the woman.

"Sally Sweet?" he said after introducing himself.

"It's what my driver's license says," she said, smiling. "For real. Approved by the court, even."

"Taken in on charges of soliciting prostitution," Fox said. "And possession of a controlled narcotic."

Sampson had to fight not to ask Fox to leave right then.

Sweet shrugged. "Like I told the vice cop, the Oxy I got legit, cause of a herniated disk in my lumbar, and anyway, I got a get-out-of-jail-free card, and I want to use it."

"Describe the card," Sampson said.

"It's a big one."

Fox leaned across the table as if to speak. Sampson put his hand on his partner's thigh and squeezed it hard. Fox sat back and looked at his hand and then at him in outrage.

Sampson squeezed harder, and then let go. He looked at Fox, then turned his head to Sweet, who couldn't figure out what was going on.

"I can't promise you a thing until I hear what you have," Sampson said, ignoring the fact that Fox's normally pale skin had gone beet red. "If it's strong evidence, we'll inform the prosecutor who draws your case. In return for testimony, you'll get some kind of deal."

Sweet's lips curled as if she'd sniffed something foul. "I didn't say nothing 'bout testifying. This is a tip. I give the tip to you. You let me go."

Fox was about to open her mouth, but Sampson pushed back from the table, stood up, and said, "I guess we're done, then. You'll be taken back to central holding. Detective Fox?"

Fox didn't move for a beat but then stood up stiffly.

"Wait, what?" the hooker said. "Shit, okay, then. I'll talk, but Sweet Sal's got to get some good out of this."

Still ignoring Fox, Sampson sat back down and said, "So talk."

Sweet told him to check with the Kansas State Police for a missing-persons report on a seventeen-year-old blonde, Emily McCabe of Wichita, who'd run away and came east after her uncle allegedly abused her.

McCabe lived on the streets until she met a man named Neal Parks; he introduced her to coke, meth, and heroin and turned her into a call girl. Sally Sweet also worked for Parks, who set up meets with his girls and johns via smartphone, like a cyberpimp.

"Emily was good people," Sweet said. "I liked her, even when she became Neal's favorite for a while."

Parks evidently lavished attention on the new girls so they'd do anything he asked. Sweet had once been favored like that. In fact, she still had a key to the pimp's apartment.

"Neal was holding cash back on me, and I knew where he kept it," Sweet said. "Lemme back up a second. Right around then? I hadn't been seeing Emily regular like I used to, and Neal said she'd gone up to New York to work for a friend of his for a few weeks. I waited until Neal went out to eat one night with another of the girls, and I got into his place."

Sweet said she retrieved a lockbox hidden in the ductwork above Parks's computer desk, got the key for it from his dresser, opened it, and took out fifteen hundred in cash.

"Just what he owed me," she said. "I put the rest back."

"What does this have to do with Emily?" Fox said impatiently.

Smug, the hooker said, "When I climbed up there to put the box back, I accidentally kicked Neal's computer mouse. The screen lit up on his desktop. There was a picture of Emily on the monitor."

Sweet realized the image was part of a video, so she played the clip.

"It looked like Neal shot it with his GoPro," she said. "From his—what do you call it—point of view?"

Sampson remembered the GoPro videos on the Killing-blondechicks4fun website, and he nodded, thinking that Sweet's story might have legs after all.

"What did you see?" Fox said.

"Neal in full dominance mode," Sweet said, sounding shaken. "He was hitting Emily, saying and doing nasty things to her. And she's all submissive. And then, like, he's got a rope in his hand, and he flips it around Emily's neck."

She stopped, her lip quivering at the memory.

"Neal started to strangle her," Sweet said at last. "He put the camera in her face. You could see how terrified she was before the screen went black."

23

AT HOME AROUND TEN THIRTY that evening, Bree said she was exhausted and going to bed.

"You coming?"

I said, "I'm going to type up some notes downstairs, catch the eleven o'clock news, and then I'll be up."

"Don't fall asleep in front of the TV again," she said, and she kissed me.

"I'll try not to," I said, and I kissed her back.

"You promised Jannie and Ali you'd go for an early run with them."

"I remember. Love you."

"Love you too," she said and waved her hand wearily as she left the room.

I waited until Bree had climbed the stairs and shut our bedroom door before going to my basement office and putting on a dark jacket and baseball cap. Then I hit Send on a text I'd written an hour before.

I opened the outside door as quietly as I could, slipped out into the night, and went along the side of my house, creeping under our bedroom window. The light went out up there, and I trotted down the sidewalk to a waiting car.

I climbed into the passenger seat. John Sampson was at the wheel.

"Glad you could make it," he said, and then he smiled and put the car in gear.

"You going to explain why we have to sneak around?" I said.

"I am," Sampson said, and he told me about Emily McCabe, Sally Sweet, the video Sweet saw on Neal Parks's computer, and how the clip had ended before the strangulation was complete.

"You believe her?" I said.

"We're here, aren't we?"

"Warrant?"

"We got blowback on the ask," Sampson said. "Can't get a search authorization based solely on the hearsay of a prostitute eager to avoid jail time. But I figure blonde lives matter, and think we should have a chat with old Neal Parks sooner rather than later."

"Why me?" I asked. "What about Fox?"

Sampson shook his head wearily. "She's threatening to file a complaint against me for squeezing her leg hard when she refused to follow my lead during my interrogation. She has total disregard for rank. Even dissed Bree on the deal."

"So things are going well between you?"

"Oh, yeah, just peachy," he said. "Which is why you're here."

"For a talk?"

"I figure we rattle Parks's cage a little. See if we can shake anything loose."

I knew I should ask him to pull over and get a taxi home. Bree would have a fit if she found out I was out with one of her detectives and both of us were defying her direct orders. But still, it felt so good and achingly familiar to be rolling with Sampson late at night that I blocked out my promise to Bree.

We cruised through the city, heading for a saloon Neal Parks liked to frequent after eleven o'clock at night. The Parrot was a serious dive bar by DC standards; it occupied the first floor of a shabby six-story building near the Maryland state line. Parks lived on the fourth floor.

"Convenient if you're an alcoholic," Sampson said.

"Is he?" I said.

"No idea," he said, parking down the street. "Sally says he sits in a booth and handles business there until the Parrot shuts down. Runs the whole thing off his phone. Cyberpimp."

"How are we going to see the video clip of Emily McCabe?"

"I thought about just going up there to watch it for ourselves," Sampson admitted, climbing out of the squad car. "But we risk fruit of the poisonous tree. If we can get a warrant, we don't want that clip excluded at trial."

Trial, I thought, getting out the other side. My own day in court was fast approaching, and yet I seemed to be doing everything I could to avoid facing the issue head-on. What was that about?

"There's an alley exit, and the front door," Sampson said, gesturing down the block at the neon-blue macaw flickering above the bar's entrance.

"I'd take the back," I said, "but I'm unarmed."

John stopped, stooped into the car, and retrieved a small Ruger nine-millimeter, which he handed to me. "I'm coming in the back," he said. "You go in, make him, and wait."

I looked down at the pistol a moment, knowing this was the worst idea I'd had in weeks, but I stuck it in my waistband at the small of the back and pulled my shirt down over it.

We split up. I strolled up the street and entered the Parrot. The place was a pleasant dive doing a healthy business, considering the hour. On the jukebox beyond the two pool tables, Lenny Kravitz was singing "Are You Gonna Go My Way?" The bar itself was to my left; a row of booths lined the opposite wall.

Photos, paintings, and posters featuring parrots were everywhere, and two live African gray parrots croaked and fluttered in a large wire cage near the center of the saloon. One of the parrots climbed the cage wall using its talons and beak. As I passed it on the way to the bar, the parrot cocked its head and goggle-eyed me a moment before squawking, "Five-O! Five-O!"

How the bird knew baffles me to this day, but it just kept squawking, "Five-O!" Many eyes were on me as I stepped up to the bar. The bartender ignored me, so I looked over my shoulder. On the other side of the parrot cage, a lanky guy with short orange hair was slipping out of the third booth from the front door.

Neal Parks glanced my way.

Our eyes met.

Parks bolted.

CHAPTER

24

FOR A SPLIT SECOND I thought he was headed straight for the back door, the alley, and Sampson. Instead, the pimp dodged right in front of me and vaulted over the bar before I could grab him.

John stormed into the room with his gun drawn and his badge up.

"Parks!" he yelled. "Stop! Police!"

Parks disappeared through the curtains to the back. Patrons began to scream and yell, and pool players dived for safety. I jumped onto and over the bar, then barreled at the bartender who'd ignored me. He looked like he was thinking of blocking my way, but I yelled, "Five-O!" and he stood aside.

Sampson came around the bar and reached the curtains first. Remembering the day he was shot, I said, "Be cool now, brother."

He hesitated and then tore back the curtains, revealing a room with empty kegs, a walk-in freezer, and a staircase that climbed up into darkness. We went to the stairs and heard Parks running above us.

Sampson charged after him, and I charged after Sampson. We ran up a utility stairwell with cleated steel treads and steel fire doors on every floor. As we passed the third floor, a door above us opened and then slammed shut.

"Stop," Sampson whispered.

We did. Nothing.

"He's going for his apartment, for the computer and that video clip," Sampson said softly, and he started to climb again.

We reached the fourth floor and opened the stairwell door. Several quick looks revealed no one in the hallway. I grabbed the sleeve of Sampson's coat and said loudly, "His place."

Then I let the door shut and held my finger to my lips. Sampson nodded. We stood there in the stairwell, listening. Ten seconds went by. Then twenty. I was about to concede that Parks had indeed gone to his apartment when I heard a squeak above me, and then another.

"Neal Parks?" Sampson yelled. "This is DC Metro. We've got you surrounded."

We could hear him pounding up the stairs again, and we chased him and saw him climb up a ladder bolted into the wall. It gave access to a hatch, which was open. John went first, climbing up and onto the gravel roof. The bluish light cast by the Parrot's neon sign made the shadows strange.

Sampson gestured to me to take the left flank while he went right. We flipped on Maglites and cast the beams about. There were air-conditioner compressors on the roof, eight of them. Parks was either hiding behind one of them or going for a fire escape.

We crept forward, staying parallel to each other, about

eighty feet apart, using the flashlights to pierce the shadows and the darkness. We'd gone by the fifth and sixth compressors when Sampson flushed him out.

Parks exploded from behind one of the two remaining compressors and ran at a diagonal across the roof. I flipped off my light and tried to cut him off.

He was running out of roof and I was running out of time when I realized he meant to jump to the roof of the next building.

The pimp was three steps from doing just that when I managed to snag him by the collar of his jacket and shirt. I meant to haul him back and down. Instead, his momentum yanked me forward two steps.

My lower legs hit the raised roof edge hard, so hard I started to topple over, along with Parks, into the seventy feet of air that separated us from the pavement in the alleyway below.

25

MY HEAD WHIPPED FORWARD AND smashed into Parks's head as my body jerked backward. Sampson had somehow gotten two handfuls of my shirt, and he pulled both me and Parks to safety.

My heart was racing, my stomach had turned sour, and I gasped for air. I'd almost fallen six stories to certain death. The pimp was equally shaken and offered no resistance when Sampson cuffed and searched him.

Parks was unarmed and without his cell phone, which was suspicious, given that Sally Sweet told Sampson that Parks operated his entire cyber-prostitution ring with it.

"Where's your phone?" I asked, shining my flashlight in his face.

"Lost it the other day," Parks said, blinking and lowering his head. "I was going to get a new one tomorrow."

"Uh-huh," Sampson said. "Why'd you run?"

"I like to run," Parks said.

"You mean you like to run prostitutes," I said.

"No, like, for fitness," he said, calm and collected now.

"No, like, for hookers," Sampson said. "You've got a whole stable of them."

"Not true," Parks said, and he laughed. "Now, who says that?"

"Vice."

He looked up then, squinting, and said, "You're not vice?"

"We're homicide," Sampson said. "You know Emily McCabe?"

Parks acted puzzled. "No, I don't know an Emily McCabe."

"Don't be cute," I said. "We can prove you know her."

The pimp said nothing.

"We're investigating her murder," Sampson said.

"Her murder?" he said, seeming genuinely surprised. "She's dead?"

"She's dead, and you killed her," I said. "Strangled her on-camera."

Parks seemed thrown. His mouth hung slightly open, and he stared down at the ground, his mind whirling with questions, no doubt. How had we gotten hold of the video? How should he respond?

Sampson said, "We know you made a snuff film, Neal. We're gonna see you fry for it."

"No way," he said. "I didn't kill no one."

"You put a rope around Emily's neck while you were having S-and-M sex with her," I said. "And then you strangled her to death."

"No," he said. "I—"

"Killed her," Sampson said.

"No," Parks said, struggling, and then he apparently resigned himself to the situation. "Look, okay, I know Emily, but I did not kill her, because she is not dead. That video was just a fantasy. She made it for me as a kind of going-away present."

"Give us a break," I said.

"It's true," Parks said. He went on to claim that Emily McCabe had told him she'd saved enough money to quit the business and was going to school in Florida somewhere.

"Florida somewhere?" Sampson said. "That's the best you can do?"

Parks lost his cool then and snapped, "It's the only thing I have. Look, I liked Emily. A lot. I would never kill her."

"So tell us how to reach her," I said.

"I don't know how to reach her," he said. "She didn't want me to know. She wanted a clean break and an entirely new life. I respected that."

"No phone number?" I asked.

"Lost my phone, remember?"

"I'm not buying it," Sampson said, marching him back toward the roof hatch. "We're taking you in, and we'll be searching your apartment. That snuff film you made is going to send you to prison for the rest of your life."

"No, wait," Parks said. "I'm not lying. Emily's alive. Somewhere."

"Hell of a defense," I said.

He said nothing this time. After I'd climbed down through the hatch, Sampson removed Parks's handcuffs and ordered him at gunpoint onto the ladder. The pimp dropped down and offered no resistance when Sampson put the cuffs back on.

When we led him down the staircase, Parks said, "How about I help you and you help me here?"

Sampson grunted. "How can you help us, Neal?"

Parks licked his lips and said, "I want you to know that I could be killed for saying this, but I can tell you about real snuff films and the crazy, sick bastards that make them."

"Uh-huh, and what good does that do us?" I asked.

Parks hesitated again but then said, "Maybe you'll figure out what happened to those blondes that have been disappearing."

"Like Emily McCabe?" Sampson said.

"No," Parks said. "Like two blond lesbian bitches from Pennsylvania."

CHAPTER

26

TWO GIRLS CRYING.

Those were the last clear sounds Gretchen Lindel had heard, and that had been hours ago.

Two girls crying, Gretchen thought, and she strained to hear more.

But through the plywood walls, the seventeen-year-old heard nothing. No voices. No floorboards creaking. Not even a jangle of chain. Or a desperate sob.

The silence made Gretchen mad beyond reason. She kicked and shook the chain that ran from her left ankle to the wall, and she glared at the little camera mounted high in the far corner, where she couldn't reach.

"Who are you?" she screamed. "Why am I here? What do you want?"

Gretchen collapsed into sobs as she had too many times since she'd woken up in a plywood box about the size of a prison cell dressed in a cheap white flannel nightgown, lying on a new mattress still in its wrapper, and covered with thick wool army blankets.

There'd been food. A big tub of Kentucky Fried Chicken and bottles of Gatorade. A metal bucket to relieve herself in the corner where her chain would reach. And the single LED light overhead that never went off.

The constant light had made Gretchen lose track of time. As her crying subsided and she pulled the blankets up around her, she realized she had no idea how long she'd been in the box. Three days? Five? A week? Longer?

The kidnapping itself had felt like a nightmare, like something that she'd wake up from. But no matter how many times she slept in the box or how hard she tried to forget, she kept seeing the men grabbing her, kept seeing Ms. Petracek murdered.

They shot her like she was nothing.

What will they do to me?

Gretchen felt panic surge and tried to turn her thoughts to something else. She'd heard her father talk about doing that many times as a way out of pain.

She breathed deep into her stomach, held it, then exhaled slowly, seeing her father and mother in her mind, so in love and yet so apart now.

What is this doing to Dad? To Mom?

Gretchen felt sick at these questions and wanted to cry again.

He doesn't deserve this. Neither does she. Haven't they suffered enough, God? Haven't they suffered enough?

She thought of her best friend forever, Susan, and her sometime boyfriend Nick. *What are they thinking? Are they trying to find me? Is anyone?*

Curling up into a fetal position, Gretchen tried to find strength in prayer and in her belief in the good. But the questions kept circling and elbowing their way back into her thoughts.

Why am I here? Why is this being done to me? What did I do, God, to deserve this? What if I never see Dad or Mom again?

The soft squeal of metal on metal stopped her thoughts, made her sit up and stare in fear at the crude door with the two dead bolts. It had never opened before.

The door swung inward.

The teenager's hand flew to her mouth, and she stifled a scream.

He was football-player big and dressed in black, from his motorcycle boots to his wool cap and tinted paintball visor. There was a blinking GoPro camera mounted in a harness on his chest. But she was focused in terror on his right gloved hand, which held an ornate knife with a curved and wicked-looking blade.

"Hello, Gretchen," he said in a strange electronic voice. "Are you ready to play a game for us?"

CHAPTER

27

I SLIPPED INTO BED SHORTLY after one thirty in the morning, unsure of how much of Neal Parks's story I believed and too tired to think about it anymore.

It felt like only minutes passed between my head hitting the pillow and someone shaking my shoulder.

I came to consciousness thickly and cracked open a groggy eye to see Jannie and Ali standing by my bed, dressed for the morning jog I'd promised them. I could feel the heat of Bree's body behind me, and not wanting to wake her, I held a finger to my lips.

They nodded and crept out of the room. I got up, feeling a little dizzy and wanting three, maybe four more hours of sleep. But these days a promise to my kids was a promise I tried to keep.

I got dressed in the closet and eased out of the room, smelling coffee brewing downstairs. I went to the kitchen, where Nana Mama, in her navy-blue nightgown and robe, was already pouring me a small cup of coffee. Jannie and Ali were tying their shoelaces.

"Bless you," I said when she handed the cup to me.

"You fall asleep in front of the TV again?" Nana Mama asked.

I nodded and took several reviving sips of the coffee.

"I think that TV should have an automatic shutoff," my grandmother said.

"It does," Ali said. "Or the cable box does."

"Let's go," I said, wanting to end the conversation. I set the empty cup down. "I have a new client coming this morning, and I don't want to be late."

We went outside. The first light of day showed in the sky, and the air was cool when we started to run. We took a route that led to Lincoln Park and back, about four miles round trip.

When I ran alone, I rarely thought, and yet I often got home to find I'd figured out one problem or another. The subconscious at work and all that. But a mindless run was impossible with Ali, especially once Jannie picked up her pace after a mile and left us in the dust.

"Dad?" Ali said, jogging beside me. "Did you know that running for more than thirty minutes promotes brain-cell regeneration?"

I glanced down at him, in wonder again that a nine-year-old, my nine-year-old, could know about brain-cell regeneration.

"Can't say that I did," I said, puffing along. "I mean, I know it's good for your heart."

"And good for your brain," he said. "I saw a thing about it online. That's why I told Jannie I wanted to start running with her."

"So you could regenerate your brain cells?" I said. "C'mon,

bud, you're nine. You're still growing brain cells and will be for a long time."

Ali looked at me with mild indignation. "I'll grow more by running."

I raised my hands in surrender. "I'll trust you on this."

He smiled and said, "But not too much running, otherwise my brain will get too big, and my head will explode, won't it, Dad?"

There was my nine-year-old boy.

"Dad?"

"No, your brain won't explode from running too much."

"You're sure?"

"You think Jannie's head's going to explode?"

I glanced over and saw he was alarmed by that idea.

"No one's head is exploding from being fit," I said as we neared the arboretum. "Next subject."

Ali didn't say anything until we'd reached the park, reversed direction toward home, and were jogging down South Carolina Avenue.

Then he said, "Dad, do some police in our country hate some people so much they'll just shoot them for no reason?"

28

THAT ONE SHOCKED ME, AND I slowed to a stop, hands on my hips and sweat dripping down my nose. "Why would you say that, son?"

Ali heard the tone of my voice, looked uncertain, and said, "I saw some people on TV say that black kids get shot just 'cause they're black and that you shot those Soneji people just because you hated that dead guy they worship."

My stomach felt hollow. A caustic taste came up my throat and made the back of my tongue burn.

At last, I said, "Let's start with the first part. Are *you* scared a police officer might shoot *you* because of the color of *your* skin?"

"Should I be scared?" Ali asked, crossing his arms. "They said it happens all the time."

"First off, being a police officer is a very difficult job. You understand that, right?"

"I guess. Yes."

"Second, too many black men *are* getting shot," I said. "And some of them by racists. But, on the whole, I think it's more a question of police officers who aren't trained correctly, who don't follow the rules and the most up-to-date methods of law enforcement."

Rather than getting calmer, Ali became more upset and started to run away. I ran after him, stopped him, and saw he was in tears.

Before I could ask him what the matter was, he blubbered, "You don't follow the rules, Dad. That's what the people on TV said. They said you were out of control and represented everything wrong with the police in America today."

That felt like a kick to the head. "Do you think that?"

Wiping at his tears, Ali sniffled. "But that's what people are saying, Dad. Even at school."

I put one knee down on the sidewalk and looked up at my son, who was searching my face for answers.

"I wasn't out of control that night, Ali," I said. "I shot those people because they were trying to shoot me."

"But they said—"

"I know what they've said," I said, trying to keep my voice from breaking. "All I can say is it's not true, son. Your dad is not a cold-blooded killer. It was self-defense. You have to believe me. You do believe me, don't you?"

Ali studied my face for so long I thought I'd lost him, but then he nodded and hugged me so tight that tears welled up in my eyes and love choked my throat.

"Thank you, little buddy," I said hoarsely. "I don't think I can do this without you watching my back."

CHAPTER

29

TWO HOURS LATER AND SITTING in my basement office, I was feeling depressed by my conversation with Ali. I suppose it's always a blue day when your nine-year-old questions your personal and professional integrity.

I tried to get my mind off it by thinking about the things Neal Parks had told us the night before. The pimp said he'd seen a fully downloaded video from—

There was a sharp knock at the outer door to the basement. I glanced at my watch. My new client was five minutes early.

When I opened the outer door, I found a wrung-out, sandy-haired man with sad, sunken blue eyes and weathered looks that made it hard to judge his age. He was dressed in pressed jeans, a starched white shirt, and polished boat moccasins with no socks, and he wore a hammered-gold wedding ring, a Rolex watch, and a tiny gold crucifix on a chain around his neck.

"Mr. Lindel?" I said, holding out my hand.

"Alden Lindel," he said, shaking my hand and training those

sunken eyes on me. "So glad you could make time to see me, Dr. Cross."

"Glad I could find an opening," I said, even though he was my only appointment for the day.

I steered him toward my office. "Lindel. That's an unusual name."

"Not in Norway," Lindel said.

"No, it's just that I've heard it twice recently and—"

"Gretchen is my daughter, Dr. Cross," Lindel choked out. "She goes to the same school as your son, yes?"

"Yes," I said, seeing him new all over again. "Yes, of course she does. Ali and I and my entire family, we've all been praying for her safe return."

"Thank you, Dr. Cross," he said as his eyes reddened and he gazed toward the ground. "We need…I need…"

I've always found that if you ask a direct question, you get a direct answer, so I said, "How can I help, Mr. Lindel? Why are you here?"

Lindel hesitated and then looked at me while turning his palms upward. "To be honest, I'm here to see Dr. Cross the shrink because of my guilt and anxiety, and Dr. Cross the detective because of my dwindling faith in my daughter's survival."

I took a seat. "You do know that I'm suspended pending trial?"

"I read that," Lindel said. "I also read that before your recent troubles, you were one of the best detectives in the country."

"Whoever wrote that was being too kind," I said. "And I know the FBI agents in charge of your daughter's case. They're top-notch."

"When my mom bakes a cake, she says you can always use

more frosting," Lindel said. "Please say you'll help me find Gretchen before it's too late and…"

Tears dripped down his cheeks. "She, our daughter, our Gretchen, she's everything to us, and now they're torturing us with these unspeakable images."

"I'm confused," I said. "Who's torturing you?"

Lindel took a tissue and wiped away his tears before reaching into his jeans pocket and coming up with a small blue flash drive in a plastic baggie.

"This was in the mailbox when I checked this morning before breakfast," he said. "Go on, plug it in."

CHAPTER

30

I TOOK THE BAGGIE AND looked at the flash drive, a Toshiba with 128 GB printed on the face.

"You didn't give this to the FBI?" I asked, putting the baggie down and finding latex gloves.

"I was on my way here and wanted you to see it first. I…I don't think the FBI can get to the bottom of this without you. Can you make a copy and give the original to them for me? I have to catch a plane to New York right after I leave here. On top of everything else, my mother's in the hospital."

Reluctantly, but curious to see what was on the drive, I nodded. With latex gloves on, I took out the drive and plugged it into my laptop. The screen flashed brightly before a video came up that I found sickeningly familiar.

A blond girl in a white nightgown ran through a dim, leafless forest with the camera operator in full pursuit. It was dusk, and when he caught her and knocked her down, you could not make out the girl's features for the graininess.

"Please don't," she begged when the gloved cameraman pulled her up to her knees by her hair.

"No?" the computer-altered voice said. "Then you want it to be the last time? No more cat-and-mouse? No more fun?"

"I just want this to be over," she whimpered, a vague shadow now in the gathering darkness on my screen.

"Okay, then," the voice said. "You'll get your wish."

I saw a dark slashing motion across her neck. I heard a slick, slicing sound and a disturbing *pah* noise before the screen froze and that icon of the lock appeared above a link that read www.Itsoverblondie.org.co. "Tell me if it's a fake or not," Lindel said, crying again. "That's all I want you to do. Stop this torture before it drives my wife and me mad."

I didn't have a private investigator's license. I was suspended pending trial. I should have expressed my sympathy and turned him down flat.

But I was a father too, and I could see the turmoil the kidnapping and now this possible snuff film were churning up in him.

"You're sure that's Gretchen?" I asked.

"I'd know her voice anywhere," he said, looking at me like I was his last best chance.

"I'll do what I can," I said.

His fists clenched, Lindel smiled through his tears and said, "Bless you, Dr. Cross. From the bottom of my heart, bless you."

CHAPTER

31

FBI AGENT HENNA BATRA CROSSED her arms and stared furiously at me from behind the main security station at Quantico.

When I cleared security, I said, "I'm sorry, but you weren't picking up your phone, and I needed to talk to you."

Agent Batra didn't answer, just pivoted on her black high-heeled pumps and marched down the hallway. I hurried to keep up. When I was abreast of her, she hissed, "Coming here like this? Are you trying to get me fired, Cross?"

"I said it was critical. And I'm obviously not on a watch list. Sidney let me right through the front gate."

"Sidney's known you eighteen years."

"Well, exactly. We're on the same team."

"You don't get it, Cross. You're being tried for murder in DC. That puts your case within the Bureau's purview."

"Believe me, I get it. But what if analyzing this video can save Gretchen Lindel's life? Or at least put her parents' fears to rest?"

She squinted at me. "I'm confused. Why didn't Lindel give this drive to the agents investigating his daughter's disappearance?"

"He was in rough shape, hadn't slept in days when I saw him, and he was on his way to New York. His mother's been hospitalized."

Batra walked a few more steps without comment and then stopped. She bit her lip, looked at the ceiling for a moment.

"Video analysis isn't exactly my thing," she said at last. "For that we have to go to the basement. And Dr. Cross?"

"Agent Batra?"

She studied me with cold eyes and said, "Before we go downstairs, you need to swear, in writing and in the presence of two witnesses, that you'll never tell a soul what you see down there."

Ten minutes later, I got in a secure elevator outside the cybercrimes unit feeling like I'd just signed a little bit of my life away. Agent Batra stepped in beside me, put a digital keycard in the lock, and hit SB2.

"That made me feel quite the criminal," I said as the doors closed.

"Close enough these days," Batra said.

"Want to clue me in to the reason for all the secrecy?"

"You're a bright guy, you'll figure it out," Batra said as the elevator passed the first subbasement and began to slow.

I noticed a throbbing and thumping sound that got louder and more distinct when we reached the second subbasement. The elevator doors opened and we were blasted with electronic techno-pop music. It was loud. It was pulsating. It oddly made me want to dance.

The music obviously had the same effect on the guy with

the flaming-red Mohawk twerking and gyrating inside the glass-walled lab directly in front of us. He wore denim shorts, a denim vest over a sleeveless black tee, and nothing else. Barefoot, and in time with the beat, he was shaking his booty, pumping both fists, and slashing the air with his Mohawk.

I broke into a smile. Batra didn't.

She exited the elevator and crossed the hall to the lab door. I followed her, saying, "Okay, who the hell is that?"

"Keith Karl Rawlins," she said, sounding pained. "He calls himself KK or Krazy Kat, depending on the occasion."

CHAPTER

32

SPECIAL AGENT BATRA STOPPED AT the lab door and looked back at me in real discomfort.

I said, "He works for the Bureau? That's why the no-disclosure?"

Batra glared at me. "Rawlins is as brilliant as they come if you want to analyze anything digital. Far better than me, as a matter of fact."

That surprised me. I'd always thought Batra was one with the Internet. Then I realized the reason for Rawlins's banishment to subbasement two.

"He doesn't fit the conservative J. Edgar G-man image, does he?"

"No," Batra said, twisting the doorknob. "KK definitely does not."

The music was even louder inside the lab. Past benches clogged with electronic test equipment, on the far side of the room, Rawlins danced before an arced array of eight large computer screens. The screens all showed the same video: people dancing in urban streets, shaking their rear ends to the addictive beat of the music.

Batra got around in front of Rawlins and waved wildly at him.

Rawlins made his hands into pretend guns that he pointed at Batra, and then he punched a key on a control board that looked like it belonged in a recording studio. The lab went quiet. Rawlins stopped dancing.

He waved his fingers playfully at Batra and in a soft voice that reeked of New Orleans, he said, "I'll forgive you this time for interrupting my daily Diplo fix. I was just about done re-generating my brain cells anyway."

"My son told me about that," I said before Batra could reply. "Exercising for brain regeneration."

Rawlins saw me, studied me, and then smiled. He picked up a hand towel from the chair and came over to us, still smiling and patting his sweating skull on either side of the Mohawk. He had a gold hoop through his left nostril, and his earlobes featured stretched piercings. In shiny sequins across the chest of his T-shirt were the words GODDESS DANCES.

"You're bigger in person, I must say," Rawlins said coyly. "And your son must have read the same article. What are the odds of that, Dr. Cross?"

"I don't know."

"I do," Rawlins said. "Two in one-point-six-four billion, unless you look at it from a string-theory perspective, in which case the chance of brain waves vibrating out and crossing others rises exponentially with every person who reads that article."

"I have no idea what you're talking about," I said.

"That's a pity," Rawlins said with a pout. "I so enjoy fiery brains and rippling brawn in a single package."

CHAPTER

33

I CHUCKLED. "YOU'RE OUT OF luck on both counts, Special Agent Rawlins, which is why I came to see you."

Rawlins glanced at Batra and laughed. "No *special* this or *agent* that, Dr. Cross. It's just KK or Krazy Kat. I'm a contractor. The Federal Bureau of Investigation could never make me a sworn agent. Am I right, Big Baby B.?"

Batra rolled her eyes, said, "We're here to work, Kat, not wallow."

"I think I'd be quite a badass crime fighter." Rawlins sniffed. "Despite appearances, I'm honest to a fault and expect the same from those with whom I work. Tell me, Dr. Cross, did you murder those Soneji followers for sport?"

"No."

"Or to right some wrong?"

"It was self-defense."

He studied me for tics and tells but saw none. "How can I help you?"

"First, a little context."

I gave him a synopsis of the story the cyberpimp Neal Parks had told Sampson and me. Parks claimed he had been in Newport News, Virginia, several weeks before, scoping out the military town for an expansion of his business. Partying in a strip club there, the pimp met two men in their early thirties who went by Billy Ray and Carver.

The three men hit it off and drank and snorted too much late into the night. Billy Ray, who was more a talker than Carver, told Neal Parks they were trolling for blondes to use in movies they produced for several profitable sites on the dark web. One of the most recent, and most successful, Billy Ray said, featured two young blond lesbians from Pennsylvania. He gave Parks the URL of one of the websites: www.Itsoverblondie.org.co. I dug in my pocket and came up with the Ziploc containing the Toshiba flash drive. "The same URL is featured on the video on this drive. I want to know if the video's real or not."

Rawlins became all business at that point. He took the bag and asked where I'd gotten the drive, and I told him about Gretchen Lindel's father.

"He should have brought this directly to the agents on his daughter's case," Rawlins said, moving toward one of his workbenches.

"It's complicated," I said.

"You've watched what's on the drive?"

"If it's real, it's the first actual snuff film I've ever seen."

"You just want to know if it's fake?"

"He wants to know everything and anything," Batra said. "So do I."

Rawlins said, "You make a copy?"

"On my laptop at home," I said.

"No crashes?"

"Worked fine."

"I'll check it anyway," he said, sitting down at a computer. He donned latex gloves, got out the drive, and inserted it into a USB port.

A few moments later, I watched a scanning icon count down the minute and forty-five seconds it took to do a full inspection of the flash drive. At the end of the scan, a message appeared: *No known anomaly detected.*

"Well, all righty, then," Rawlins said.

He disconnected the flash, took it to the larger control board below the eight big screens, and plugged it into a server linked to the internal FBI network.

A digital index of the drive popped up on the large center screen; it showed the icon of the single MPEG movie file. Rawlins clicked on it. There was a brilliant flash, and then the clip played—the grainy video of the hysterical blonde running through the forest with the cameraman in hot pursuit.

"What was that?" Batra asked. "That flash at the beginning there?"

"I don't know," Rawlins said, freezing the video.

I said, "You know, come to think of it, when I hit the icon on my laptop, it did the same thing, only my screen's much smaller and older, so it wasn't as bright as that."

Rawlins grunted and gave his computer orders to list all running processes and applications. The directory opened and showed them in a stack sorted by the time each was launched, beginning with the most recent app.

"That's what just flashed there?" Batra said with an arched eyebrow. "Porngrinder?"

34

RAWLINS LAUGHED AND SAID BLITHELY, "Oh, no, Porngrinder is on me. What can I say? It's a lonely life in the basement at times."

"My God," Batra said, disgusted. "The Bureau frowns on that kind of thing."

"Have them sue me, won't you?" Rawlins said.

"What was the flash?" Batra said.

"I don't know. A blip, a screen hiccup. They happen, you know."

"Or a bug in the plug-in that drives the video player?" Batra said.

Rawlins held up a finger. "A momentous occasion. Special Agent Henna B. and I might agree."

Batra rolled her eyes. "Tell us about the video."

I won't bore anyone with the details of Rawlins's technological savvy and instincts, but they were shrewd and his results conclusive. At first, he used ordinary software to try to access the video file's so-called dark data. No luck. The video had been run through an onion system similar to the one used to create the Killingblondechicks4fun website. The dark data had been stripped away.

"Not surprising." Rawlins sniffed. "But I've still got the dust rag."

The "dust rag" was software Rawlins had designed and coded himself to raise the faintest trace of old dark and meta-data. He compared the software to the Hubble Space Tele-scope looking for cosmic debris a thousand miles behind a comet's long tail.

Sure enough, his screen was soon filled with fragments of code that played out in sync with the video. By focusing on the moments where the lighting was dimmest and the noise of the alleged killing most pronounced, Rawlins found evidence in the data dust that suggested an audio splice in the sound track roughly six seconds long. Those six seconds included the knife-across-the-throat slitting noise and the *pah* that sounded like air bursting out of a frightened and dying chest.

"She's alive," Rawlins said barely fifteen minutes after start-ing his examination. "Or at least, those weren't the sounds of *her* murder."

I sighed with relief. I wouldn't have to give Alden Lindel or his wife more heartbreaking news. "Explain how you know. The parents will ask."

Rawlins said, "The sound patch itself is fairly sophisticated CGA. Computer-generated audio. So someone's had advanced training in sound effects. You're looking for a film-school grad or someone who worked in a special-effects company out in Hollywood, not a coder."

"Why's that?" Batra asked.

Rawlins gave his computer a command, and the video on

the center screen rewound to the beginning of the six-second splice. A second screen showed the remnants of the dark data. He pointed out a jagged line of data that almost connected top to bottom.

"That's your digital splice," Rawlins said. "A more adept coder would have hidden it better, sewn it up as clean as a plastic surgeon. There wouldn't have been even a hint of a scar."

"So this is basic sound-editing work?" I said.

Rawlins touched his Mohawk as if it were a high-fashion hairdo and said, "Three steps above butchery. And that's all I can manage now. I have a lot to do before Goddess opens."

I was puzzled.

"His favorite dance club," Batra explained.

"Do you dance, Dr. Cross?" Rawlins said.

Before I could reply, my cell phone buzzed in my pocket. I pulled it out, saw the number.

"My son's school," I said. "I have to take this."

CHAPTER

35

ALI CROSS BELIEVED HE WAS smarter than the average kid at Washington Latin but not brilliant, not a genius. The kids he considered supersmart were also the shyest and the most awkward. He decided within a month of starting at the charter school that brilliance was overrated. He'd take very bright, very hardworking, and very curious any day of the week.

Ali was the youngest kid in fifth grade at Latin by at least a year. With his attitude and sense of humor, he fit in with most of his older classmates. But, as his father always said, there were jerks in every crowd.

Ali met two of them shortly after the school bell rang to announce the end of classes. He had fifteen minutes before debate practice and decided to go sit outside. It was a nice sunny afternoon, not too cold.

Ali stopped on the front steps and looked toward the plaza, remembering the hooded men who'd grabbed Gretchen Lindel and shot Ms. Petracek. Rather than dwell on those violent events, he sat up on the wall at the top of the stairs and started playing a game on his phone.

He was aware of knots of kids walking past him, and he caught snatches of their conversation. Suddenly, someone grabbed him by the collar, right below his chin, and pushed as if to shove him backward off the wall. Then whoever it was yanked him forward again.

Shocked, surprised, Ali felt his stomach go sick with adrenaline and fear before he'd fully realized what had happened. George Putnam, a burly sixth-grader, still held Ali so tight by the collar, he was having trouble getting his breath. The older boy laughed at his reaction.

"Saved your life," Putnam said. "You little turd, Cross."

"Let go!" Ali said. "You're choking me!"

Putnam's buddy Coulter Tate was taller and already fighting acne. Tate leaned over, got right in Ali's face, and gave him a crazed, zitty look.

"How's it feel to be a killer's son, Cross?" Tate said. "How's it feel to have murder in the genes?"

Putnam tightened his hold, making Ali's eyes feel like they were swelling. There was no thought, no consideration on Ali's part after that. He just pulled back his head and then slammed it forward. His forehead connected with Tate's nose, and he heard a distinct crunching noise.

Tate screamed and stumbled back, holding his hand to his nose, which was gushing blood.

"He broke it!" He sobbed in disbelief. "He broke my nose!"

Putnam was still holding on, looking shocked as he stared at his bleeding buddy, and Ali punched him in the throat. Putnam let go of Ali's collar and went down on the stairs, bug-eyed and coughing, his hands to his neck.

Ali was still in a fighting stance and trembling head to toe when Mrs. Dalton, the headmistress at Washington Latin, came running out of the school.

"My God, what's happening?" she cried.

Ali didn't reply or move. He kept his attention on the two sixth-graders, as if daring them to get up.

"He broke my nose, Mrs. D.!" Tate said, the blood dripping between his fingers. "And the little frickin' insane-o hit George in the throat!"

"Ali?" Mrs. Dalton said. "Why did you—"

"I'm not talking until my dad's here," Ali said, trying to stay calm.

"You will tell me now, young man," she said, sounding angry and full of authority. "Right now."

"Sorry, Mrs. Dalton," Ali said, feeling weak as he dropped his fists and turned to face her. "Please get my dad here, or a lawyer, and then I'll tell you exactly what happened."

CHAPTER

36

TRAFFIC WAS SNARLED AS I crossed back into the district, and I wondered what Ali had gotten himself into that was so bad it deserved an immediate meeting. The headmistress wouldn't tell me a thing.

Inching over the Theodore Roosevelt Bridge, I decided to call Alden Lindel. He answered on the third ring.

"This is Alex Cross, Mr. Lindel. I'm happy to tell you that Gretchen did *not* die in that video. It was a fake."

Her father made a noise partway between a cough and a cry.

"Oh, good!" He gasped. "Oh, thank God! Are you sure? How do you know?"

"Because a very talented FBI computer wizard said that the video's audio was altered. The sounds weren't real."

"But it was Gretchen's voice," he said. "I'd swear it."

"I believe you, Mr. Lindel. But that wasn't the sound of her dying. I wanted you to know. Please tell your wife."

"Yes. Yes, right away."

"I'll be in touch if I hear more."

"Well, I could still use someone to talk to, Dr. Cross," he said. "Eliza, Gretchen's mother, and I...we were separated before Gretchen was taken, and this has been even more of a strain. And my mother's not well, and we're thinking about endings."

"I'm sorry to hear all that, Mr. Lindel. Give my office a call tomorrow. We'll make an appointment."

"Thank you, Dr. Cross."

"You're welcome," I said, and I clicked the phone off.

Traffic was moving, finally. Fifteen minutes later I parked close to Washington Latin and hurried inside toward the waiting area outside the offices of the headmistress and the other school administrators.

From well down the hallway I could see Coulter Tate sitting on the right side of the waiting room. He held an ice pack to his face. A woman I took to be his mother had her arm around his shoulders and was whispering in his ear.

Two or three chairs away, George Putnam pressed a bag of ice to his throat. Sitting beside him was a man I figured was his father, a big dude with a wrestler's build stuffed into a five-thousand-dollar suit. He was staring bullets across the room at Ali, who sat with his eyes closed.

"Dr. Cross?"

I looked behind me and spotted Mrs. Dalton hurrying over.

"Dr. Cross," the headmistress said with an exasperated sigh. "Before we get to the fight, I must speak to you first about your son's insubordinate behavior. A school like Latin—"

"Please, I'd like to speak to my son in private, right now."

"Dr. Cross," she said, raising her chin. "I don't think you—"

"As far as I'm concerned, and with all due respect, I think Ali did the right thing by not talking, Mrs. Dalton. He's a minor, but he has certain rights. Among those is his right to have a parent present during questioning."

"That's with the police," she said. "I run a school, and I wish to be present when he first tells his side of things."

"You really want to fight me on parental rights? Because you'll waste a bunch of money on lawyers and you'll lose."

Mrs. Dalton was a smart woman used to getting her way, a woman who hated losing. I could see it in her eyes.

But she said, "Very well, Dr. Cross. You can use my office. Ten minutes. There are other parents and students to consider."

"Thank you, Mrs. Dalton. I know you're in a difficult situation, and I appreciate your handling it with such grace."

She hesitated, but then tilted her head and gestured toward the waiting room. I walked in. When I did, Coulter Tate, the kid with the broken nose, shrank away, curled up, and whined fearfully.

"What's gotten into you, honey?" his mother said, craning her head over her shoulder to look at me.

"He kills people, Mom," Tate said. "He teaches his kid to kill too."

"Shut up, Coulter," Ali said, opening his eyes. "You are such an ass."

"Language," I said.

Ali looked relieved, got up, and hugged me. I looked at Mrs. Dalton and ignored the others. She led us down a hall to her office and closed the door after we went inside.

"You okay, bud?"

"My forehead hurts," he said, and he hugged me again.

"Mrs. Dalton's not happy," I said. "So give me the truth, everything."

37

I OPENED THE DOOR TEN minutes later and found Mrs. Dalton standing there looking flustered.

"I was about to knock," she said.

Or you were trying to listen in, I thought, but I said, "Call in the others. They'll want to hear Ali's side of things."

"Why?"

"Because those boys are lying to you. And Ali can prove it."

Five minutes later, three kids and three parents were crammed into Mrs. Dalton's office. None of us looked happy.

"Expect a suit for damages, bucko," George Putnam's father said, shaking a big finger at me. "I'm a lawyer."

"You're kidding," I said. "I never would have guessed."

"Let's be respectful, shall we?" Mrs. Dalton said. "Hear Ali's version?"

"He's a liar," George Putnam said in a hoarse voice.

Ali shook his head. "You dolt, Putnam, I haven't said anything yet."

I put my hand on Ali's shoulder and squeezed.

"Stick to the facts," I said. "No name-calling. Address Mrs. Dalton."

Ali wasn't happy, but he nodded and told Mrs. Dalton that Putnam had grabbed him while he sat on the wall and pushed him back, hard. If he'd let go, Ali would have dropped close to six feet to the concrete and probably would have been gravely injured.

"But I didn't let go," Putnam said. "I pulled you back. It was a joke. Saved your life. Jeez."

Ali said, "He did pull me back, and he did say, 'Saved your life.' But then Coulter stuck his face in mine and started talking trash about my dad."

"So you head-butted him?" Tate's mom said bitterly. "You can't do that. They were fooling around, but you took it as a chance to really hurt someone."

"Like father, like son," Tate said.

"It's true," Putnam's father said. "Ali didn't have to punch George in the throat. The game was over, and he suckered my boy."

"George was still choking me after I head-butted Coulter," Ali said, looking Mrs. Dalton right in the eye. "I feared for my life. I swung for his face, but I hit him in the throat."

"Feared for your life?" Putnam rasped. "Are you kidding?"

"Did you have hold of my collar when I hit you, George?" Ali said. "All the other kids have gone home, but I know someone must have seen it. They'll back me up eventually, so tell the truth now."

Putnam opened his mouth angrily, painfully. He hesitated, swallowed hard, and said, "I might have been holding your collar, but I never choked you."

"Never?"

"No."

Ali unbuttoned several buttons on his shirt and then spread the lapels. There were raised welts around his neck.

"Clear sign of attempted strangulation," I said.

"What?" Putnam's father cried. "That's BS. You could have done that when you were in talking to him!"

Ali held out his phone, said, "I may be nine, but I'm not stupid. I took pictures in the bathroom an hour ago. A bunch, all time-stamped. So case closed. This was self-defense, or should we take you all to court and sue for batteries?"

I hid my smile and said, "That's multiple counts of battery."

"Oh," Ali said, grinning. "Right."

There was a long silence in the room. Finally Mrs. Dalton said, "George? Coulter? A five-day suspension."

"Are you serious?" Coulter's mother whined.

"No," Putnam's father said.

"Yes," Mrs. Dalton said. "And if they're ever involved with something like this again, they will be expelled from Washington Latin."

"I'm writing the board of overseers about this," Putnam's father said. "Five days for them and nothing for the kid who did the damage? I don't think so."

"I didn't say that," Mrs. Dalton said, and she looked at me and then my son. "Ali, a three-day suspension."

"What?" he cried. "It was self-defense."

The headmistress was unmoved. "You signed a code of conduct when you enrolled in Washington Latin. That code says, among other things, 'No fighting will be tolerated under any circumstances. None.' Remember?"

"Yes, but—"

"No buts," she said, looking at me. "He signed the contract. So did you, Dr. Cross, and your wife."

"Yes, we did," I said. "And we will abide by it."

"Dad?"

"Case closed," I said.

38

THE NEXT MORNING, AFTER A long jog with Jannie and an excellent shower, I went down to the kitchen with Nana Mama and poured a mug of coffee for Bree. She shuffled to the table, yawning and running on fumes. There'd been a gang fight the evening before, three dead on top of a homicide caseload that was already bulging with backlog. She hadn't gotten home until two and now she had to turn around and go back in for a meeting with the chief at nine.

I put the coffee in front of her.

"Bless you, baby," Bree said, smiling weakly. She sipped the coffee.

"I'll be your barista anytime," I said.

"So tell me about Ali."

"Humph," Nana Mama said, and she went back to stirring eggs for a scramble.

I took a seat across from my wife. "Well, he was like a little pro arguing his defense in there. Very logical. And it was his idea to lay a trap for them by not mentioning the neck welts to Mrs. Dalton before then."

"A regular Perry Mason," Nana Mama said, and she didn't mean it in a good way. "Fighting on the school steps. That would not have happened back when I was a vice principal. Never."

My grandmother, dressed in her quilted blue robe, still had her back to us and was whipping the eggs furiously. Bree shaped an O with her lips and tried not to smile.

"Nana," I said, "what was Ali supposed to do? Let himself be choked to death?"

"I didn't say that," she said sharply, and she turned to face me. "I'm just concerned for your son's reputation, which takes a long time to build."

Hearing echoes of similar things she'd said to me over the years, I said, "Yes, ma'am. That's a fact."

"Long as it takes to build, a reputation can die in two seconds, Alex," she said, and she made a *shh* sound of disgust.

"I know that, and honestly, Nana, I think Ali did the right thing, considering the circumstances, and he's getting punished for it, so he's learning the world can be unfair sometimes."

"I agree," Bree said. "In a lot of ways, Ali's reputation will only be stronger after this. I mean, he's nine years old, and he stood up to bullies who were twelve. Be proud of him, Nana. He did good even if it meant getting suspended."

My grandmother looked perplexed. I got up and hugged her. "Sometimes you have to break the rules. Sometimes you have to protect yourself."

Nana Mama held herself rigid at first, but then she melted and hugged me back. "You know I don't like fighting."

"I do."

"Where'd he learn to fight like that?"

"He says from YouTube videos on Krav Maga, the Israeli fighting system."

"Maybe his time on the Internet should be limited?"

"I agree," I said and kissed her sweet old head.

My cell phone rang. I let go of my grandmother and answered. "Alex Cross."

"Bernie Aaliyah, Dr. Cross," he said gruffly. "It's Tess. She's barricaded herself in her bedroom. She's got a gun, and I'm afraid she's going to kill herself if you don't come talk to her."

CHAPTER

39

SUSPENDED DC METRO DETECTIVE TESS AALIYAH lived in a duplex row-house walk-up near downtown on a street heading from renovation toward gentrification. Dumpsters squatted in front of three or four other row houses on the block; hammers and saws popped and whined inside them.

A circular saw squealed nearby, masking the sound of me climbing up to Tess's front porch. Her father opened the door before I could ring the bell, and he limped out to shake my hand. Bernie Aaliyah was pale, and his face was scratched and bruised. I could see everything from fright to anger in his eyes.

"I told you I'd get Tess the help she needed, Dr. Cross," Bernie said in a low, agitated voice. "And I tried in the best way I knew how. But she got real defensive when I suggested the evaluation. When I told her it was for her own good, just to know what's what, she went out of her mind. She attacked me, scratched me, and hit me with something that knocked me on my ass."

He shook his head in disbelief and sorrow. "Tess was always like her mother, always levelheaded, even as a little girl."

"She's still your little girl," I said. "But she's been wounded."

"Talk to her. Make her see it wasn't her fault."

Feeling his desperation, I took a deep breath and said, "I can try. Where's her bedroom?"

"Top of the stairs, to the right."

"The gun?"

"Her backup. She surrendered her service pistol."

"You know what prescriptions she's taking?"

"What isn't she taking? The kitchen counter's covered with them."

"Then I want to take a look there first."

He led me inside, past a steep staircase and into a small modern kitchen. The counter held a blooming array of prescription drugs.

I picked up the canisters one by one and studied them. Some names I recognized. I got out my smartphone and typed names of the medicines I didn't know into Drugs.com. I scanned all the drugs' therapeutic effects, scribbled a few notes, and then used the site to look for possible interactions.

When I finished, I was upset, and I whispered, "Bernie? Is Tess taking all of these? Or just some?"

"She won't tell me, and I can't get her damn doctors on the phone."

I grabbed the bottles and looked for the prescribers' names. In all, five physicians had prescribed twelve different meds for Tess Aaliyah in the past six weeks.

Her father said, "What do you think?"

"If she's taking half these drugs at the same time, it's a wonder she hasn't been committed for psychotic behavior already."

"Jesus H. Christ." Bernie moaned. "I knew it. I told my girlfriend something was wrong. But, Jesus, I…I just didn't push it."

"Tess is a grown woman," I said, and I patted him on the arm. "You coming? She'll want you at some point, but please don't say anything unless I give you the nod. Okay?"

He didn't like that. "I've done my share of talking people off ledges."

"I bet you have, Bernie. But it's like a surgeon operating on a close relative or a man acting as his own lawyer in court. Never a good move."

Tess's dad gave me a sour expression but said, "I won't speak unless you give me the green light."

"Let's go upstairs, then."

CHAPTER

40

THE CARPETED STAIRS MADE NO noise as I climbed to a narrow landing. I turned right and went around the banister to Tess Aaliyah's bedroom door. Before I could knock, I heard her in there talking.

"Rats," Tess said in a soft voice that sounded bewildered. "I saw rats. Here? Believe it. I saw…I heard…them scratching in the walls…and her screaming. Mom screaming. Mom's always screaming." Tess cried quietly. "Always screaming."

She sounded so close, I squatted down and saw a shadow that suggested she was sitting on the floor with her back to the door.

I got up, took a deep breath, knocked, and said softly, "Tess?"

"Go 'way," she said in a whisper that I had to strain to hear.

"It's Alex Cross," I said, a little louder. "I wanted to see if we could talk."

"Quiet!" she snarled. "I know my…my rights. I'm not seeing another shrink. No more rats chattering in my closets, no way."

Before I could reply, Tess said, "Alex, you're the big rat. One chitchat, and you start all this drama...put nasty thoughts in my dad's head. 'Poor Tess. She's crazy enough now. Stick her in a hole.'"

"I'm not here to stick you in a hole."

Tess sniggered. "Course you are."

"I'm not. I just want to talk things over."

For several seconds, there was no reply. The door creaked as she leaned against it. I heard her shift position on the floor.

I glanced over at her father, who stood at the head of the stairs looking like he was listening to someone drown.

"Tess?" I said. "Can I just talk, then? Would that be okay?"

"Whatever you want," she said, returning to that bewildered voice. "Just do it nice and quiet. I hear you fine."

I paused, trying to think ahead, trying to figure out the best way to get her to come out and turn over the—

Saa-chunk.

CHAPTER

41

THE SOUND FROZE MY THOUGHTS. I'd heard it a thousand times in my life, maybe more, the particular noise a double-action revolver makes when a thumb cocks the hammer into firing position.

"Tess," I said, stepping quietly to the side of the door and out of the potential line of fire. "Do you have a gun in there?"

In that off voice, she said, "Hate rats in my closets."

I glanced at her father, motioned for him to be patient, and said, "A lot of people care about you, Tess. They'd like to help you. I'd like to come in and help you. Your dad would too."

"No need," Tess said wearily, sounding as if she might be falling asleep. "Ask my dad. Tessie's an impatient girl, can't wait for pest control to do its thing."

"Will you do me a favor? Will you put the gun down beside you, at least?"

"No, Alex," she whispered. "What would be the point of that?"

I decided to shake her a bit. "I asked you before if you were self-medicating. You said no. But your dad just showed me twelve different meds in your kitchen."

After a pause, she said, "Legitimate prescriptions from licensed docs."

"Except I don't think the other doctors knew everything you'd been prescribed, Tess," I said. "There are several drugs down there—antidepressants and antipsychotics—that pose a significant risk when combined. You could have a very serious drug interaction, one that could stop your heart, trigger a stroke, potentially damage your brain, wipe out your long-term memory."

In a slow, modulated whisper, Tess said, "Hasn't. Worked. Yet."

The gun barked.

It startled me so badly I jumped back before feeling the horror and disbelief well in me. Tess had shot herself. She was dead, right there on the other side of that door. My knees went to rubber and I grabbed at the banister, feeling like I was going to be sick. Bernie Aaliyah roared in panic and despair, "No!"

He limped fast to her door and pounded on it. "Tess! Answer me! Tess, you answer me right now!"

In the short silence that followed, I said, "Bernie?"

Tess's father twisted his head to look at me, enraged. "Shut up, you. I never should have called you, Cross. You've killed her, that's what you've done!"

Part Three

THE PROSECUTION OF ALEX CROSS

CHAPTER

42

Four weeks later...

STRIKING HER GAVEL TWICE, Judge Priscilla Larch peered out through thick-lensed glasses and in a gravelly voice said, "The People versus Alex Cross. This court will come to order. Sergeant Holm, you may seat the jury."

"Yes, Your Honor," the bailiff said, and he went out.

"I'm praying we chose right," my niece Naomi said.

Anita Marley nodded stiffly and looked to her opening arguments, not bothering to watch the five men and seven women who held my fate in their hands now filing into the courtroom and taking their places in the jury box. I understood why. Anita was still upset with me about jury selection.

During voir dire—the questioning of potential jurors by the prosecution and defense prior to jury selection—we'd disagreed over two picks: juror five and juror eleven. Five was a man in his seventies who had something wrong with his spine. His upper back was twisted and hunched. He walked slowly with a cane and had to turn his shoulders and rib cage to look up at you.

Juror five had also been sharp in his answers, especially when it came to describing his general skepticism about nearly everything in life. An electrical engineer before retiring, he said he took his time making decisions, tried to get to the truth before he acted, and was firm in his convictions.

Anita had wanted to dismiss juror five because he had a friend whose son had been shot by the Baltimore police. But he also said that he had "nothing against cops. They have a tough job. I can apply the law fairly, given that."

I overruled Anita's objection to juror five, telling her we wanted people skeptical enough to hear the facts and honest enough to deal with them fairly.

Juror eleven was a big, stylish, and beautiful woman in a gray Chanel suit. A brassy redhead, she had a beaming smile, an infectious laugh, and an accent as smooth as West Texas honey. She worked for a big PR firm in DC and was friends with several U.S. Capitol Police officers. Anita wanted her off the jury because a police officer had hit her brother with a baton during a riot at a music festival in Austin.

But juror eleven had also said that her brother "deserved to be hit because he was drunk, crazy, and took a swing at two cops." I reminded Anita of that and overruled her.

The others we agreed on. On the whole, my jury seemed a cross-section of the capital. In addition to jurors five and eleven, there was a thin, hyper woman who worked as a U.S. Senate aide and was furious she hadn't been excused from serving, a beefy guy who wrote a tax newsletter, a lobbyist for agribusiness, and a young mother from Adams Morgan who seemed delighted to serve, apparently seeing it as an extended break from her kids. There was also a male nurse who worked at GW Medical Center, a retired teacher, and a bartender at the Four Seasons Hotel. Two grandmothers and an ex–merchant mariner completed the dozen people who would decide whether I would go on with my life or take a very long detour into a federal penitentiary.

When they were seated, Judge Larch said, "The floor is yours, Mr. Wills."

43

"THANK YOU, JUDGE," the assistant U.S. attorney said, and he got up. Wills tucked his shirt in over his big old belly, smiled sheepishly, ambled midway to the bench, and stopped.

The federal prosecutor took a breath, played the silence a moment, and then said, "Some police officers in America believe the judicial system is in ruins. They get so frustrated, they begin to see themselves as judge and jury, and then executioner. They do. I am with the U.S. Justice Department, and I'm telling you that in every major police force in this country, there is one or a pair or even a handful of cops who believe they are above the law."

Wills paused and then directed his attention at me. "The defendant, Alex Cross, is a prime example of a police officer who thinks he is above the law, a cop who believes that he alone can identify evil and that he alone has the ability to stop it, even if it means his killing someone in the process."

The prosecutor nodded to Athena Carlisle, his co-counsel,

and she hit a button on her computer, bringing up two pictures, a man and a woman, on a screen opposite the jury.

Wells said, "Virginia Winslow was a mom, a welder, and a survivor of terrible abuse during her years married to Gary Soneji—"

"Virginia's a martyr!" someone in the courtroom yelled.

I pivoted in my chair to see a bearded man with wild eyes standing in the aisle and pumping his fist. He shouted, "So's Lenny Diggs!"

Judge Larch banged her gavel. "Bailiff, have this man removed from my court. I said I would not tolerate any outbursts and I meant it."

"Both were persecuted!" the man shouted. "Both were killed by the chief persecutor, Alex Cross!"

Two U.S. marshals grabbed the guy, who offered no resistance and said nothing more as he was taken out. I guess he figured he'd made his point.

"The jury will ignore the outburst," Judge Larch said. "Mr. Wills, make it snappy. We've got a lot of ground to cover."

"Yes, Judge," the prosecutor said, and he walked to the jury box. "Ladies and gentlemen, it is critical for you to know one thing about Virginia Winslow. She was sick and tired of being targeted by law enforcement simply because she'd unknowingly been married to a vicious criminal.

"Virginia changed her last name after divorcing Gary Soneji. The cops still came for her. She moved. They found her. She tried to hide her teenage son, Dylan, from his father's legacy. But in this case, the defendant, Cross, acted to cruelly change that, seeking out and telling the boy in lurid detail what his father had done and making the young man feel as if he were also to blame."

Wills turned to look at me. "Alex Cross made him feel that way because Alex Cross did indeed hold Gary Soneji's son, his ex-wife, and everyone else who had ever been associated with the deceased killer partially responsible for the man's crimes. Alex Cross was obsessed with Gary Soneji. He hated all things Soneji with such a passion that he decided he had to go above the law. He decided these Soneji people had to die, be wiped off the face of the earth. He'd kill every one of them."

Wills paused and looked around. I heard Ali whisper, "He's lying, isn't he, Damon? That man is standing there and lying 'bout Dad. How come no one's saying a thing?"

"Shh," Damon said. "We'll get our chance."

The assistant U.S. attorney went on. "The evidence will show that Detective Cross used intimidation tactics to get an admirer of the late Gary Soneji to take him to meet the leader of a group of people interested in the dead killer. Alex Cross defied well-established police protocol. He went alone, without backup. He marched into what turned out to be a trap, a trap that featured people wearing masks and clothes that made them look like Gary Soneji, all part of a performance designed to evoke a reaction from Detective Cross.

"They got more of a reaction than they expected," Wills said somberly. "Alex Cross shot three of them down in cold blood. Virginia Winslow died first. Cross shot and killed a cameraman, Leonard Diggs, next. Then he tried to kill Claude Watkins. Watkins lived, but he's paralyzed and confined to a wheelchair. Now, you will hear the defense assert that all three victims were armed and threatening the detective when he shot them. That is a false statement, and the evidence will prove it."

The prosecutor put both his hands on the jury-box rail and looked at each of the jurors in turn.

"Dr. Cross and other rogue cops across the country have gone above the law and gotten away with murder over and over again. Isn't it time that we, as a nation, as a people, say, 'Stop. That's enough. No more killings by cop'?"

Wills paused for dramatic effect, and then with anger laced through his voice he said, "I'm asking you, ladies and gentlemen of the jury, to look at the evidence. And I'm asking you to say, 'No more.' I am asking you to say, 'That's enough, Alex Cross. You might be a great detective. You might have solved many cases. But you will not kill with callous disregard for our judicial system ever again. You will be judged on the facts in a court of law. And you *will* be found guilty and you will be punished for your cold-blooded actions.'"

44

WHEN WILLS SAT DOWN, JUDGE LARCH rapped her gavel, called for a ten-minute recess, and hurried off the bench.

I glanced at the jury and saw jurors five and eleven looking at me as if I were some lower order of species.

"That went well," Anita Marley said.

"If that went well, I'd like to see your version of getting crucified," I said.

"Take a breath, Uncle Alex," Naomi said. "It's not that bad."

"Pretty damning."

"No, Naomi's right," Anita said. "Did you notice there weren't a whole lot of bombproof facts mentioned? They've got a few, but not enough. If they had enough, they'd have said so. That's why prosecutors try to tie in some national trend to their cases. All spin aside, it means they haven't got enough to try the case on the merits."

Before I could reply, I heard, "Alex?"

I looked over and saw Bree at the bar. She waved her cell phone at me. "I've got to go."

I walked over and hugged her. "Thanks for being here."

"I want to be here every minute," she said, and she kissed my cheek.

"I know. But go to work. I've got good people fighting for me."

Bree wiped at a tear when we broke apart, nodded, and left with a little wiggle of her fingers at Nana Mama, Damon, and Ali. I winked at my sons and my grandmother. Ali winked back. Damon smiled weakly. Nana nodded without conviction and worried the small string of rosary beads she'd brought along.

"All rise," the bailiff called.

Judge Larch strode back into the court.

I was too far away to smell it, but I knew she'd have the odor of Marlboro cigarettes about her. Larch was forever trying to quit and never succeeding, which contributed to her general surliness on the bench. At least, that's what her clerk had told me once.

"Ms. Marley, you may proceed," Judge Larch said, and she popped a mint in her mouth.

My defense attorney looked at me and smiled. Then she put her hand on my shoulder. She stood up and kept her hand there, gazing at the jury, sweeping her eyes over each one of them.

"*Not* this man," Anita said, and she paused for several moments.

"This man is not the creature that Mr. Wills just described. This good man is Alex Cross, and let me tell you a few hard facts about Dr. Cross, facts that cannot be denied or molded like mud into something other than the truth."

She left my side. "Alex Cross won a scholarship to Johns Hopkins University, where he graduated with high honors. He took a PhD there in criminal psychology as well. He worked seven years as a member of the FBI's Behavioral Science Unit, the people who hunt serial killers by profiling them. Cumulatively, he has been a homicide detective with the Washington DC Metropolitan Police Department for more than fifteen years.

"During all that time with the FBI and DC Metro, Dr. Cross has been repeatedly cited for, among other things, bravery in defense of fellow police officers, arresting bombers, rescuing kidnap victims, capturing mass murderers, and defeating a terrorist plot to blow up Union Station. Did I mention that the last citation was signed by the president of the United States? It was."

CHAPTER

45

JUROR FIVE WAS CRANING HIS neck and shoulders to look at me, and juror eleven seemed impressed enough to jot something down on her notepad.

"Sadly, that is why the U.S. Attorney's Office is pressing this case," Anita Marley said, returning to my side. "You see, with the rash of police shootings across the country, the Justice Department needs a prominent individual to prosecute as a way of demonstrating to the outraged masses that the government is actually doing something about police violence."

She put her hand back on my shoulder and said, "But, ladies and gentlemen of the jury, I ask you not to be swayed by the government's tactics because the facts of this case are on this good man's side, and they demonstrate far, far beyond a reasonable doubt that he is innocent. Let me lay them out for you."

Anita took the jurors through a straightforward summary of the events that led me to shoot three followers of Gary Soneji in self-defense, starting with telling them about the Soneji, a violent cult that had risen up around the myth of the late kidnapper and bomber.

"The cult targeted the investigators who had hunted Gary Soneji," Anita said. "They targeted Detective John Sampson, and they targeted Alex Cross. They made death threats to Dr. Cross and to his family."

Then she explained how the FBI Cyber Division identified a woman named Kimiko Binx as the secretive builder of a website dedicated to the cult. Records showed that Binx had a partner in the website named Claude Watkins. When he was sixteen, Watkins was tried as an adult and convicted of carving the skin off a little girl's fingers.

"Ms. Binx told Dr. Cross she could take him to see Watkins, who had served his time and was now a successful artist," Anita said. "Ms. Binx led Dr. Cross to an abandoned factory where Watkins and a group of his followers were waiting, all dressed up as Soneji, using Hollywood-quality masks."

She nodded to Naomi, who hit a button on her laptop. An old mug shot of Gary Soneji popped up on the courtroom screen along with a crime scene photograph of one of the masks.

"Three of the cult members wearing masks like this one were armed," Anita said. "They carried nickel-plated pistols that they used to threaten Detective Cross, an officer in the course of his duties. Dr. Cross gave them fair warning, and then he defended himself.

"When he left the crime scene to meet police and ambulances he'd called to the factory, someone took the three pistols. The defense believes a member of the cult did this in order to frame Dr. Cross, to portray him as yet another policeman gone over the edge."

Anita paused, and then showed outrage. "The U.S. Attorney's Office should be ashamed for buying into what is obviously a fabricated story. The Justice Department and the attorney general should be ashamed as well. They don't care about Alex Cross's exemplary record with the FBI. They don't care about the great good he's done repeatedly in the course of his career. They just want a high-profile scapegoat, and Dr. Cross fits the bill."

She crossed back to me, put her hand on my shoulder, and said in an even, forceful tone, "But, ladies and gentlemen of the jury, I say to you: Not Alex Cross. Not this good man. This good man will not be made a scapegoat. This good man's reputation as one of the country's finest detectives will not be dragged through the mud. Dr. Cross's remarkable career will not be ruined, and he will never see the inside of a prison cell, because this good man is completely innocent of these charges."

46

PRISCILLA LARCH CALLED FOR A lunch recess at the end of Anita Marley's opening argument, and judging from the body language of jurors five and eleven as they left for the jury room, it seemed that my lawyer's remarks had evened the score.

Nana Mama thought Anita's speech was strong as well. But my grandmother was tired after the stressful morning and said she was going home for a nap.

I encouraged the kids to go with her. Both boys refused. Jannie decided to accompany Nana, do some studying, then go to practice.

Damon and Ali went out for lunch. Anita, Naomi, and I ate takeout Chinese in a conference room down the hall from the courtroom as we went over the testimony of several witnesses who might be particularly hostile to my case.

Assistant U.S. Attorney Wills had a reputation for not holding back at trial. He liked to attack with his strongest evidence right off the bat to make a deep impression on the jury. We were preparing for a rough afternoon.

We had no idea how rough it would be.

The prosecution started the after-lunch proceedings by calling DC Metro detective Harry Chan, the first investigator to arrive at the factory after the shootings. Two patrolmen had driven into the lot five minutes before Chan, but I'd kept them outside pending arrival of detectives and criminologists.

"He wanted to keep the scene as uncontaminated as possible," Chan said.

"Can you describe the defendant when you first encountered him that day?" Wills asked.

"He was excited, talking fast," the detective said. "He was sweating and pacing. He complained of being dizzy and having a headache."

"What happened then?"

"The ambulances and Chief Stone arrived," he said. "She wanted him—Dr. Cross, her husband—kept away from the scene, and she took him home without giving me much time to interview him. I entered the factory with the EMTs and my partner, Detective Lorraine Magee. When we got to victim one, Virginia Winslow, she was dead of a gunshot wound. Victim two, Leonard Diggs, was barely clinging to life. Victim three, Claude Watkins, was more alert but badly wounded. Diggs died en route to hospital."

The prosecutor paused as if to think about that and then said, "Did you see a nickel-plated pistol in the hands of or around any of the three victims?"

"We did not."

"And did crime scene techs find pistols hidden in the factory?"

"No," Chan said.

"Any footprints near the victims?"

"Lots of them," he said. "Watkins and some of his followers had been living there for some time."

"Nothing conclusive?"

"Not in my book."

"Any gunpowder residue on the hands of any of the victims?"

"No."

"Your witness," the prosecutor said to Anita Marley.

Anita smiled and stood. "Tell me, Detective Chan, have you ever been in a gunfight with three assailants?"

"No."

"But, given your years of experience, would it be reasonable to say that having survived such an ordeal, Dr. Cross would be excited, sweating, talking fast, pacing out of nervous energy, and even dizzy or suffering a headache from the gunshots?"

Chan said, "I suppose it's as reasonable as saying Dr. Cross had just shot three people for his own ends and was acting that way because he was trying to figure out if he'd done it well enough to fool me."

Anita looked annoyed. "Objection, Judge. Will the Court instruct the witness to answer my question?"

"Asked and answered, Counselor," Larch said. "Motion denied."

"Defense reserves the right to recall Detective Chan at a later time," my attorney said, and she sat down.

"The United States calls Norman Nixon to the stand," Wills said.

"Jesus, they're not fooling around," Naomi muttered under her breath.

47

NORMAN NIXON WAS A HEARTY-LOOKING man in his fifties, neatly groomed with scrubbed skin, slick iron-gray hair, and a competent, earnest expression. He wore a khaki suit and a blue-striped tie, and he carried a file folder to the witness stand.

After Nixon was sworn in, Wills quickly established the witness's bona fides as an expert on police shootings. Nixon had been a decorated cop in Chicago before joining the FBI, where he had worked as an investigator in the civil rights division. He was involved in the U.S. government's investigation into police killings. After his retirement from the Bureau, Nixon continued to study the forces that contributed to citizens' death by cop.

"Sometimes the officer's a racist," Nixon said. "Sometimes the officer's just burned out from the day-to-day pressure of the job and is feeling inordinately threatened. And sometimes, more often than you'd think, the police officer shoots because he believes he's above the law."

Wills looked at the jury. "In your opinion, Mr. Nixon, does Alex Cross fit the profile of a police officer who believes he's above the law?"

"Objection—argumentative," Anita said.

"Overruled," Judge Larch said. "Answer the question, Mr. Nixon."

"He does fit the profile," Nixon said. "In fact, he's a prime example of the phenomenon."

"A prime example," Wills said. "What does that mean?"

"It means I've studied him at length," Nixon said, looking earnestly in my direction. "It means I've researched every shooting Dr. Cross has ever been involved in."

"Wait," the prosecutor said. "Dr. Cross has been involved in shootings other than the three in question today?"

Anita sprang to her feet. "Objection! Relevance?"

Wills said, "We're trying to give the jury the context in which these three shootings took place."

"Overruled," Larch said.

"Judge!"

"Overruled!"

Wills said, "Was Alex Cross involved in other shootings before the three in question?"

"Yes," Nixon said.

"How many times does the average police officer in America discharge his weapon in the course of a career?"

"Zero," Nixon said. "The vast majority of police officers never fire their weapon in the line of duty."

"Zero," Wills said. "And how many times has Dr. Cross discharged a weapon in the course of his careers at the FBI and DC Metro Police?"

The witness shifted in his chair, said, "I don't have *all* the records. Some are sealed. But just from the public documents I've looked at, Alex Cross has fired his weapon at least thirty-one times."

I blinked and felt my stomach go sour. There was a louder reaction in the audience, which caused Judge Larch to pound her gavel. "Order."

By their expressions, jurors five and eleven had turned against me again. And no wonder. I was as shocked as they were to hear the number.

Thirty-one times. Is that true? And have I shot more than that? He said at least, didn't he?

Wills said, "Can you break down the shots for us in a meaningful way?"

Nixon nodded. "The records I've seen indicate that Dr. Cross missed fourteen times and wounded someone eight times."

"And the other nine times Dr. Cross pulled his trigger in the line of duty?"

"His shots were perfect," Nixon said. "All of his victims died."

48

BY THE END OF THE first day of the trial, I felt like that side of beef Rocky Balboa used as a punching bag.

For three solid hours, Wills and Nixon had kept up a relentless barrage of facts about the nine deadly shooting incidents that they said collectively cast me as a cop who believed he was above the law.

"They've almost got me believing it," I said after court was adjourned for the evening. We'd gone to a conference room to reassess before heading home.

Anita said, "You must absolutely not believe it."

Naomi nodded. "She's right. Your belief in your innocence has to shine through your body language. The jury will pick up on the slightest doubt you feel."

My lead attorney put her hand on my forearm. "This is classic Nathan Wills, from what I understand, and we still have more than a few cards up our sleeves. Go home, Alex. Be with your family. Don't watch the news. We'll see you in the morning."

I nodded. "Sampson's picking me up in the garage."

"Perfect," Naomi said. "And have you thought about that interview request from Gayle King?"

"I don't see an upside."

My niece said, "The upside is you get to tell your story to a national audience and counter all the horrible things people have been saying about you."

"I'll think about it," I said, and left.

Sampson was waiting for me in the garage in his Jeep Grand Cherokee.

"How'd it go?" he asked after I'd shut the door.

"Slightly better than the Spanish Inquisition."

"Shit. And here I was, hoping the iron maiden and the rack were making a comeback in our legal system."

I glanced at him, saw him grinning, and laughed. "Yeah, I get it. I suppose it could have been worse. I just don't know how."

We left the courthouse garage, skirted around the media mob waiting for me to exit the building, and headed home.

"Anything I can do?" Sampson said.

"Not unless you can speed up lab work faster than Bree can."

He looked over at me, puzzled.

"Some saliva tests Anita wanted done. They might help."

"With what?"

"I can't talk about it."

"I understand," he said, but his tone said he didn't, and there was a strained silence between us the rest of the ride.

Sampson pulled over well down the street from the small

171

crowd of journalists camped outside my house. "You best take the alley home."

"It'd be easier," I said. "Thanks for being a standup guy, John."

He paused, and then nodded and said, "I have a great role model."

He drove away. Knowing Sampson still had my back, I felt okay as I walked down the alley that ran behind my block. Even better, the air smelled like garlic and basil when I went through the back gate and stole through the side door.

Ali and Jannie were on the couch in the great room, watching the NBC evening news with Lester Holt, when I came in.

"Dad!" Ali said, running over and hugging me.

Jannie's eyes avoided mine. She was barefoot but still in her warm-ups, watching the screen. Holt wrapped up a piece on the latest budget impasse in Congress and then turned grim and said, "Thirty-one times."

Behind him, a dark silhouette of a man appeared. He held a pistol. Beneath the image, a caption read POLICE GONE BAD?

Holt said, "The trial of noted detective Alex Cross opened today in Washington, DC, amid what prosecutors are saying is a long-needed discussion in America about police gone bad and gone violent, above the law."

The screen jumped to footage of me and Anita entering the courthouse that morning, with Holt talking in a voice-over. "After opening statements, the prosecution brought in star witness Norman Nixon and almost immediately there were fireworks and harsh accusations, including the stunning news that Detective Cross has fired his weapon at least thirty-one times in the course of duty when the average police officer never fires his gun at all. Before the two killings he's on trial for, Cross's shots have proven fatal nine times."

The screen jumped to a frizzy-haired woman identified as a sociology professor sitting in front of a wall of books. "Thirty-one times?" she said. "He kills nine before these two? I'm sorry, but this is a cop who shoots first and asks questions later."

CHAPTER

49

"TURN IT OFF," I SAID.

Jannie didn't move.

"Jannie," Ali said, going over and grabbing the remote.

"Don't," she said. "I want to know how bad it really is."

Ali hit the power button and the screen went dark. Jannie glared at him and then at me before jumping up and leaving the room.

"What's with her?" Ali said.

I gazed after Jannie as she stormed through the kitchen. My grandmother popped up from behind the counter.

"I'll ask later," I said, and then I went into the kitchen, where Nana Mama was finishing dinner preparations.

She patted me on the back. "Hang in there. The truth will out, son. It always does."

"I know," I said, but there was little conviction in it.

Nana Mama motioned me into her arms. It was still a miracle to me how such a tiny old woman could radiate so much positive energy.

"Don't let them get you down," she said, rubbing my back. "When they hear your side of what happened, old Lester Dolt and Chuck Fraud will be singing a different song."

I laughed and looked down at her. "Lester Dolt and Chuck Fraud?"

"That's what I call him and the political reporter guy."

"But Lester Holt is not a dolt."

"And Chuck Todd's not a fraud," Nana Mama said. "But calling them that when all the news is depressing gives me a reason to smile."

I gazed into my grandmother's eyes and saw both confidence and fear.

"You are one complicated old lady," I said, touching her cheek.

"I should hope so," she said, pulling away. "Dinner in fifteen minutes?"

"What's cooking?"

"Chicken roasted in Nana's special herb rub. Go on, wash up. Bree texted she'll be home any minute."

I was about to head up the stairs when Bree came through the front door. There was strain everywhere about her, and she dropped her gaze and hesitated before coming into my arms.

"I'm sorry I wasn't there," Bree said. "It must have been awful."

"Sobering," I said. "Thirty-one times. I had no idea."

Bree lifted her head to look me in the eyes with cold curiosity. "And the nine dead and the eight wounded?"

"I remember each and every one of them," I said. "You can't

forget things like that. Ever. Even when they were righteous shoots."

She studied me, her eyes welling with tears, then hugged me tight.

"Jesus," she said hoarsely. "They want to tear you apart."

"They better pull hard," I said, and I kissed her head.

CHAPTER

50

GRETCHEN LINDEL LAY CURLED UP on her filthy mattress, scratching her head, staring at the plywood walls that imprisoned her, and wondering if her torture would ever end.

Coated in grime, her nightgown in tatters, Gretchen reeked, and her feet were cut and swollen. Her hair was tangled with burrs, leaves, and twigs. She couldn't pick them out, no matter how hard she tried, and she hadn't tried in days, at least since the last time they'd come for her.

How long had that been? Five days ago? Six?

She couldn't tell, and in the end it didn't matter.

I'm here until I'm not, Gretchen thought. *It's like I'm not even me already.*

How bad can the last step be?

The big man in black, the one wearing the tinted paintball visor and carrying the knife, had come for her four times since her kidnapping. Each time it had been dusk when he'd untied her blindfold and she'd found herself in the woods.

There were two or three others there, all dressed similarly, all laughing at her when the big one said, "Run, now. Give yourself a chance, and give the boys a show."

Gretchen played competitive volleyball, and she ran hard the first time, took off, not caring about the stones and sticks that jabbed her bare feet. She'd gotten ahead of them and thought she'd lost them.

Before it turned dark.

Then they were all suddenly around her, yelling in the woods, taunting and calling, "Where are you, blondie? Where are you, uptown girl?"

They had to have been wearing night-vision goggles or something like that, because they'd caught her every time, and every time they'd taken her right to the point where she believed with every cell that they were going to kill her, slit her throat and watch her bleed out, all on-camera, all to their delight.

The first three times they'd hunted her, Gretchen had survived by focusing on her friends and her parents and on how desperately she wanted to see them all again, especially her dad. She shared a special relationship with him, a real friendship as well as respect and love.

It would kill him, she'd thought when she'd wanted to give up and ask them to end it. *It would kill him, and I can't do that to him. To either of them.*

The fourth time they'd hunted Gretchen, the last time they'd hunted her, had been different. They'd barely let her run before catching her. They'd dragged her to a building in the woods. The big one had torn off her panties while the others held her down. They'd—

She'd gone to a far-off place in her mind then, where there

was no hurt, no feelings at all, as if she'd already found death. That feeling of passing, of being already gone from her body, had stayed with her even after they were done, even after they'd thrown her back in her plywood box, even after days without eating.

Someone threw the door's dead bolts.

Gretchen cringed and tried to keep staring at the plywood wall.

"You don't eat, you don't deserve to play the game," the strange electronic voice said. "You don't eat, drink, keep your strength up, you don't deserve to live."

"I don't want to live like this."

"We kind of thought that."

She looked at the big guy in black wearing the GoPro camera and the paintball visor and saw something that cut through her feelings of nothingness, made her retreat.

He wasn't carrying that knife he'd brought the first four times they'd played the game.

This time he carried a coil of rope tied at one end into a hangman's noose.

CHAPTER

51

JUDGE LARCH GAVELED THE COURT to order at precisely eight a.m. She took care of several administrative issues before reminding Norman Nixon he was still under oath when he returned to the witness stand.

"Ms. Marley," Larch said. "Your cross-examination, please."

Anita patted me on the thigh, got up, and said, "Mr. Nixon, of the nine fatal shooting incidents you looked at involving my client, how many were judged wrongful police conduct?"

He shifted uncomfortably. "None. It's a—"

"So you're saying that in each of these cases, Alex Cross was investigated and found to have taken prudent action in accord with police and FBI protocol?"

"I don't know about prudent when you end up with a dead suspect."

"Objection," Anita said.

"Sustained," Judge Larch said. "But rephrase, Ms. Marley."

Anita seemed taken aback for a moment. Then she said,

"Was Dr. Cross found to be in compliance with police and FBI protocols in each of those nine shootings?"

Nixon acted like he had something stuck in his teeth but eventually said, "He was."

"All nine?"

"All nine."

"And in the cases of wounding?"

"Yes, but—"

"A simple yes will do, Mr. Nixon. Since you have had a chance to look at Dr. Cross's record in such detail, would it be fair to say that the criminals involved were dangerous people? Violent people?"

"Doesn't mean they had to die by a police bullet," Nixon said.

"It's a yes-or-no question."

"Yes, they were dangerous."

"Killers?"

"Often."

"Bombers?"

"Their crimes are not the issue here."

"They most certainly are the issue," Anita said. "Dr. Cross has a reputation for going after the worst criminals, taking on the biggest cases, isn't that so?"

"He's well regarded as an investigator."

"Did Dr. Cross put himself in personal danger to solve the cases you looked at?"

"Every cop in America is in danger every day."

"Point taken," Anita said. "But in light of the *kinds* of cases Dr. Cross worked for the FBI and DC Metro, wasn't he bound to come into contact with more violent suspects than the average cop?"

Nixon paused and then said, "Probably a higher incidence of contact with that sort of criminal, but I can't tell you what that is statistically."

"A higher incidence of contact will do," Anita said, and she smiled at the jury as she went back to the defense table. She put on reading glasses and scanned her notes for a moment.

When she was done, she pivoted and looked at the witness. "Just to summarize, Mr. Nixon, in each of the nine fatal cases you looked at, Dr. Cross, because of his job, came into close contact with a hardened criminal, correct?"

He thought about that and then said, "Correct."

"And violence ensued," she said.

"Violence ensued and someone died by Cross's hand."

Anita removed her glasses and cocked her head at him. "In those nine fatal incidents, Mr. Nixon, how many times did Alex Cross shoot first?"

He cleared his throat. "It's more telling to look at escalation, Ms. Marley."

"How many times did Dr. Cross shoot first?"

Nixon looked ready to argue but then said, "Zero."

"Zero?" she said, looking at the jury. "And how many times did Alex Cross shoot first in any of the wounding incidents?"

"Zero."

"Zero," Anita said, looking right at jurors five and eleven. "Not once in Dr. Cross's career has he fired his weapon in anything but self-defense. He deals with the worst of the worst. He tries to avoid conflict, but these people are violent, and he has the right to defend himself, isn't that right, Mr. Nixon?"

"No," Nixon said. "That's not right. Cross seeks conflict. He charges in."

"Sounds to me like a brave cop doing his job."

"Objection," Wills said.

"Sustained," Judge Larch said. "The jury will ignore that."

But of course they couldn't. I could see in jurors five and eleven that Anita's line of questioning had been effective and revealing. To those two, at least, maybe I wasn't the out-of-control cop the prosecution described earlier.

"I have nothing further for this witness, Your Honor," Anita said.

Wills stood and said, "The prosecution calls Kimiko Binx."

CHAPTER

52

KIMIKO BINX RAISED HER RIGHT arm and took the oath. A fit Asian American woman in her late twenties, Binx wore a chic gray pantsuit. Since I'd seen her last, she had grown out her hair and gotten it cut in a geometric style.

She perched in the witness chair and slowly swept her gaze around the courtroom, looking at everyone, it seemed, but me.

"You may proceed, Mr. Wills," Judge Larch said, and she coughed.

The assistant U.S. attorney adjusted his pants, grinned sheepishly at the jury again, and then said, "Ms. Binx, what is it you do exactly?"

"Web design and coding," she said.

"Good at it?"

"Very."

"Well," Wills said, and he smiled at the jury once more. "Do you remember the afternoon and early evening of March the twenty-ninth?"

"Like it was yesterday."

The prosecutor led Binx through her version of events. She reported that she'd found me waiting for her outside her apartment door when she came in from a run, that I'd tracked her through a website dedicated to Gary Soneji that she'd designed, and that I asked her to take me to see her partner in the website, Claude Watkins.

"What's your big interest in Gary Soneji?" Wills asked.

Binx shrugged. "It was a phase, like that woman who wrote the book where she visits all the graves of assassinated presidents? Kind of ghoulish, but interesting at the moment, you know?"

"So you're not obsessed with Gary Soneji?"

"Not anymore. Seeing friends of mine killed for their intellectual interests soured me on it."

"Objection!" Anita said.

"Sustained," Judge Larch said. "The jury will ignore the last statement."

Wills bowed his head, crossed to the jury box. "So you led Dr. Cross to an abandoned factory to see Mr. Watkins, isn't that correct?"

Binx nodded and said that Claude Watkins and some of his friends had been using the old factory as an art studio and living space.

"Did you coerce Dr. Cross in any way to go find Watkins?"

She leaned forward to the mike. "I didn't have to. He wanted to go."

"But you wanted him there as well, correct?"

"Well, Claude did, that's right."

"Why's that?"

"Claude's an artist—visual and performance. He thought it

185

would be interesting and telling to see what Cross would do if he were confronted with one Soneji after another."

Under further questioning, Binx continued her tale in mostly accurate fashion until she had us moving deeper into the factory and reaching a large rectangular room. At that point, she began to lie through her teeth.

Wills said, "When you went inside, was Claude Watkins at the far end of that long room wearing the Soneji disguise?"

"Yes," Binx said.

"Was Mr. Watkins armed?"

"No."

"No nickel-plated revolver in his hand?"

"No. Claude had his hands open, and he turned his palms to show Cross."

53

I LEANED OVER TO NAOMI, whispered, "That is categorically false."

My niece patted me on the arm. "Don't worry. We'll get our chance."

Wills said, "What happened next?"

"Cross aimed his gun at Claude and told him to drop the gun and get down on the floor."

"Did he?"

"He didn't have a gun, but Cross didn't seem to care. I knew he was going to shoot Claude, so I hit Cross's gun hand. Claude took off and tried to hide."

"What was Dr. Cross's state before you hit him?"

"He was acting weird, creepy."

"In what way?"

"Sweating, looking like he was loving the fact he was aiming down on Claude, you know, like he dug it."

Wills crossed to a blown-up diagram of the factory floor and pointed at the far left end of the rectangle. "Watkins was here before he ran?"

"Yes, in front of that alcove."

"What happened then?"

For the first time, Binx looked over at me. "Cross went crazy."

"Objection!" Anita cried.

"Overruled," Judge Larch said. "Continue."

Binx testified that Virginia Winslow stepped out of the shadows of an alcove in the middle of the far long side of the factory room and that I then shot Soneji's widow without provocation.

"Was Mrs. Winslow armed?" Wills asked.

"No way," Binx said. "She hated guns."

"Tell us why she was part of this performance in the first place."

"Virginia told me that she couldn't get away from Soneji's legacy, so she'd decided to try to make art out of it, a bitter commentary, you know?"

"And Dr. Cross shot her?"

"Right in the chest. I couldn't believe it. I started screaming, but he didn't care. He just kept shooting, Claude, and then Lenny Diggs."

"All of them unarmed?"

"Yes. And after he shot Lenny, he was swinging his pistol around and yelling for more."

"What exactly was Dr. Cross yelling?"

"Like 'Who's next? C'mon, you bastards! I'll kill every single Soneji before I'm done.'"

Wills looked at the jury. "'I'll kill every single Soneji before I'm done.'"

Juror five was shaking his head. Juror eleven was shaking hers.

Wills rubbed his hands together as if he were washing them and said, "Thank you, Ms. Binx, that must have been difficult. Your witness, Ms. Marley."

CHAPTER

54

ANITA HAD BEEN SCRIBBLING NOTES on her legal pad. She looked up and said, "Your Honor, the defense asks the Court's leave to delay our cross-examination of Ms. Binx pending an ongoing line of inquiry we are following."

"An ongoing line of inquiry?" Wills asked.

"Right," Anita said.

Judge Larch didn't like that. "How much of a delay are you asking for?"

"I would think tomorrow afternoon would work, Your Honor."

Larch got a sour look on her face, but then seemed to think of something that brightened her mood. She said, "Ms. Binx, you are excused for the day. Ten minutes' recess before Mr. Wills calls his next witness."

The judge banged her gavel, got up fast, and hurried for the door, no doubt dreaming of that first puff.

Larch came back in a much better mood exactly ten minutes

later. She returned to the bench, popped a mint, and said, "Mr. Wills?"

"The prosecution calls Claude Watkins to the stand."

I heard a creak as the double doors to the courtroom swung open. I turned to see a man in a wheelchair being pushed by Gary Soneji's son, Dylan. Claude Watkins was in his late forties with salt-and-pepper hair, a stubble beard, and a buff upper body. A blanket hid his withered legs.

Dylan left him at the bar, and Claude Watkins rolled the chair over in front of the witness stand.

The prosecutor looked at Judge Larch and said, "I'd like to treat the witness as hostile. He has been highly uncooperative."

Larch glanced at the man in the wheelchair, who looked fuming mad.

"You going to answer questions under oath?" she asked.

"Depends on what's asked," Watkins said, not looking at her.

She ordered the bailiff to administer the oath, which he did without enthusiasm.

"How are you, Mr. Watkins?" Wills asked.

Watkins sneered at him. "About as good as you can be when you're confined to a wheelchair and have to use a catheter to take a piss."

"How did you wind up in that chair?"

Watkins's face bunched up in loathing before he pointed at me and said, "He put me in it. Cross. Shot me for no good reason."

"Objection," Anita said.

"Overruled," Judge Larch said. She popped another mint into her mouth.

Wills said, "Can you take us through the events of March twenty-ninth?"

Watkins grudgingly said he'd gotten interested in Soneji and then me by accident. But the more he read about me, the more he was convinced I was "borderline out of control" when it came to the mass murderer.

He testified that he decided to entice me into a situation that could result in an "interesting and revealing piece of performance art." He would lure me to an abandoned factory where he'd confront me with one Soneji after another.

"So *you* could see his reaction?" Wills asked.

"Oh, hell no. I wanted *everyone* in the world to see Cross's reaction."

Beside me, Anita cocked her head to one side.

Wills squinted as if he'd heard something new from the witness and said, "How were you going to do that?"

"By filming it, of course," Watkins said.

"What?" Wills said.

"What?" Naomi whispered.

Anita said, "What the hell is—"

"You had to have found them," Watkins said. "I mean, you had to have searched the factory and found the smartphones with the add-on lenses, right?"

Anita and the prosecutor's assistant both shot to their feet.

Anita said, "Judge, there has been no mention of any such cameras or phones in discovery."

"Because we found no cameras or phones," Wills said.

Watkins looked like he wanted to spit in disgust. "I put them there myself. What is this? A cover-up? I was wondering why you weren't badgering me about them from the get-go. I'm telling you, we got the whole thing from three different angles!"

CHAPTER

55

THE COURTROOM ERUPTED. JUDGE LARCH banged her gavel, demanding order. She told the jury to ignore Mr. Watkins's testimony for the time being and ordered both prosecution and defense into chambers along with the U.S. marshals who worked in her courtroom.

"Judge, the government asks that it be given time to find the phones Mr. Watkins claims are in that factory," Wills said when they were all in chambers.

"Judge, there is no way to know if these phones, if there are any, have been put there after the fact as a ploy by Mr. Watkins," Anita said. "Whatever is on them should be excluded."

"That factory has been sealed for months," Wills said.

"But not guarded."

"We don't even know if the phones exist, Ms. Marley," Judge Larch said. She looked at one of her marshals. "Collins, you and Avery, please go talk to Mr. Watkins. Find out where he says he hid these phones, call a forensics team, and go look. If you find them, establish a perfect chain of custody and bring them here."

"Judge, that's the rightful role of the government," Wills said.

"We're seeking swift truth and justice here, Mr. Wills," Larch said. "If the cameras are there and they do show what happened that day, we'll all see it together. At the same time. Here. In my chambers."

The marshals left. The judge ordered that the jury be sequestered and given lunch. We ate down the hall, all of us wondering how the cameras could have been missed, and me worrying about the confidence with which Watkins had revealed them. What would they show?

An hour later, word came that three smartphones with extender lenses had been discovered where Watkins said they'd be: in recesses cut into the factory's support beams, hidden with thin pieces of sheet metal.

An hour after that, Larch's marshal entered her chambers with three evidence bags, each holding an iPhone 6s. They were dusty and their batteries were dead. Between the group of us, we had enough cords to recharge the devices.

One by one, they blinked on. Claude Watkins was asked to provide the security codes for the phones, which he did. They all used his birthday.

U.S. Marshal Avery, a thin woman with an intense bearing, wore gloves to enter the codes. Then she attached the first phone to a laptop computer, and the laptop to a screen on the wall of Judge Larch's chambers.

Fifteen minutes later, as the last of the three videos played, there was dead silence in Judge Larch's chambers. I felt steamrolled and had no doubt I was heading to a federal pen for a long, long time.

"Compelling, Judge," Wills said, triumphantly. "The government wishes to introduce these into evidence immediately."

Anita said, "Your Honor, you cannot allow these videos to be introduced until we've had time to analyze them."

"I'd say the videos speak for themselves," Wills said. "The important parts, anyway. To ignore them would be a travesty of justice, Your Honor."

"Allowing them into evidence without giving us the chance to examine them would be a gross miscarriage of justice, Your Honor," Naomi said.

Judge Larch sat back in her chair, closed her eyes, and puffed on an electronic cigarette.

"Your Honor?" Wills said.

"I'm thinking," Larch said. "You've heard of that, right, Counselor?"

The prosecutor was taken aback but said, "Of course, Your Honor. I've been known to think myself every once in a while."

The judge opened one eye and fixed it on Wills. "I'll allow the videos to be introduced."

"What?" Anita cried. "Judge—"

"Ms. Marley," Larch said curtly. "The prosecution wants the videos introduced. If you can impeach their value and credibility, you'll be free to do so at the appropriate time."

"With all due respect, Your Honor," Anita began, "these will bias the—"

"For a few days, perhaps," Larch said, putting her e-cig on her desk. "If they're fake, you'll know soon enough, won't you? And maybe you'll make Mr. Wills look like a fool for being so impetuous."

"Your Honor?" the prosecutor said, looking as if he'd sniffed something unpleasant.

"I've given you lots of rope, Mr. Wills," she said. "Try not to hang yourself with it."

Wills blinked and said, "Yes, Your Honor."

56

NANA MAMA SAW THE DEVASTATED look on my face when we returned to the courtroom. She came to the rail.

"You okay, son?"

"It's bad, Nana."

"The truth will out. Just stay fixed on that."

I nodded but felt like the weight of the world was on me when Judge Larch gaveled the court back into session and announced to the jury that she was admitting the videos. She also cautioned them that the government had decided not to analyze the videos before they were shown to the jury.

"In that light, keep an open and skeptical mind," she said. "The defense will have its say about these videos, I'm sure."

As Marshal Avery called up the videos on a screen facing the jury, Nathan Wills was so pleased he jigged a little as he crossed to the witness box. Claude Watkins was again sitting there in his wheelchair.

"Mr. Watkins," Wills said. "Have you seen this footage?"

"No."

"They're all black-and-white, three or four minutes long. We'll watch them simultaneously. You'll see the scene from three angles at once."

The deputy marshal hit a key on her computer. The screen, divided into three frozen feeds, lit up.

On the left, there was an elevated, look-down perspective on the dimly lit rear of the factory where the shooting had occurred. It was a long and largely empty assembly-line space with dark storage alcoves off it on all four sides.

From the perspective, I figured the smartphone had been placed atop an alcove in the middle of the long south wall of the room. On the opposite wall, a mural was lit by soft spotlights.

The middle of the screen showed the feed from a smartphone camera that had been hidden almost directly across the room, above the opposite northern alcove, and aimed back at the floor area, though you could see the bottoms of the three spotlights.

On the far right of the screen, we were afforded a view from above the west alcoves. That angle showed the full length of the factory floor and the spotlight beams bisecting it right to left.

The deputy hit Play and all three feeds started. The people in the courtroom saw me enter the space at the east end of the factory floor, carrying my service weapon and leading Binx along by her handcuffs. Exactly the way I remembered it.

At the west end of the room, Claude Watkins stepped out. He was dressed as Gary Soneji, and in a cracking, hoarse voice he said, "Dr. Cross. I thought you'd never catch up."

"Freeze them," Wills said. "Show feed three only."

A moment later, the screen was filled with Watkins in disguise standing there, palms turned out.

"No gun," Wills said. "Absolutely no gun."

It was the second time I'd seen the image and the second time I got furious thinking that, if I wasn't guilty, I was being railroaded by pros.

"That's fake," I whispered to Naomi. "I don't know how they did it, but that is wrong."

Before my niece could answer, the screen unfroze. The three videos showed me raising my service pistol, aiming at Soneji, and moving toward him, shouting, "Drop your weapon now or I'll shoot!"

Watkins's right hand moved, but there was nothing there, and nothing like the clatter of a gun dropping that I remembered.

"Facedown on the floor!" I shouted. "Hands behind your back!"

Soneji started to follow my orders but then Binx came up from behind and hit my gun hand with both her fists. The blow knocked me off balance, and my gun discharged before a fourth spotlight went on, blinding me.

Then the lights died. I threw myself to the factory floor. I stayed there several moments, peering around, before I lurched to my feet. Gun up, I ran hard to the nearest alcove on the north wall.

I shouted, "I've got backup, Gary. They're surrounding the place!"

Leaving the alcove, I moved west along the north wall of the factory to the next anteroom, the one directly beneath the mural. The camera on the opposite roof caught me from behind and gave the viewer a decent look inside the north alcove, where large rolls of canvas were stacked on tables made of ply-wood and sawhorses.

From deep in that alcove, Virginia Winslow, disguised as her late husband, stumbled out of the darkness. Stooped and far forward on the balls of her feet, she took two sharp, halting steps before straightening up. The camera zoomed in on us. Her right hand started to rise.

"Stop," Wills said.

The screen froze on Gary Soneji's widow with her palms almost turned up.

"No gun," Wills said.

The videos started again.

Mrs. Winslow opened her mouth and raised her hand. I shot her. She fell and Binx screamed.

It went on like that for several more minutes, with Wills stopping the videos to show Watkins dressed as Soneji and me shooting him, then taking cover behind two old oil drums. The prosecutor froze the video one last time to show Leonard Diggs unarmed and up on the roof above the north alcove just before I shot him. Before the videos mercifully ended, you could hear Binx sobbing.

I blew out some air and looked over at the jury. Juror five had recoiled in his chair and was studying me like I was a war criminal. Juror eleven covered her mouth with a well-mani-cured hand and shook her head in horror.

57

THE NEXT AFTERNOON, I COULD see outright suspicion on the normally guarded face of Gayle King, co-anchor of the CBS morning news.

As a sound tech hitched me up to a microphone in our house, King came over and said, "Five minutes, Dr. Cross?"

"I look forward to it, Ms. King."

"Call me Gayle. And we're agreed? No ground rules?"

"Ask away," I said. "I've got nothing to hide."

"Your grandmother?" King said. "She's something."

"She is that."

She smiled, but I saw some pity in it. She walked away.

Bree came over and handed me water. "You're sure about this?"

"Anita and Naomi seem to think it will humanize me. And there's nothing else we can do until Anita's experts have a go at those videos."

At the close of court proceedings, Judge Larch had granted

Anita's motion to adjourn through the following Monday morning to do just that.

"Your FBI friends?" Bree asked, adjusting my tie.

"Mum," I said. "Not surprising. I would think the U.S. Attorney's Office got Rawlins analyzing the videos for the prosecution."

"Well, that would be good, right? He'll find the flaws."

Before I could answer, King said, "Dr. Cross?"

"Good luck," Bree said and kissed me on the cheek.

The journalist gestured to a chair across from her. I mirrored her posture, sitting on the first third of the chair, back straight, chin up, and facing her with my hands relaxed, open, and resting on my thighs. Two small spotlights lit us. King put on reading glasses.

"You're on," one of the camera operators said.

The morning news anchor got right to it and pulled no punches, noting that the introduction of the video in court the day before had to have been a devastating blow.

"Understandably, we weren't happy about it, Gayle," I said. "But we're confident the video's been doctored and we intend to prove it."

"How many times have you drawn and fired your service pistol in the course of your career, Dr. Cross?"

"Norman Nixon says at least thirty-four times, counting this case," I said.

"And killed eleven now in the line of duty?"

"In all those cases, I acted in accord with proper police protocol. Until the shootings I'm on trial for, I had never pulled the trigger first. But I was at close quarters in that situation. When I saw the guns, I gave them one chance to drop them and then fired to save my own life."

"You still maintain the three victims were armed?"

"I do."

King said, "The prosecution paints you as an 'out-of-control' cop."

I controlled my temper, said, "Every time an officer fires his weapon in the course of duty, there's a diligent investigation. I've gone through the process more than most officers, but in every instance I have been cleared."

"What do you say to those who characterize those earlier cleared cases as having been whitewashed?"

CHAPTER

58

I LOOKED DIRECTLY IN THE camera with the red light glowing and said, "Read the investigative documents yourself, Gayle. I'll give them to you, and you can post them on the CBS website where anyone can read them. I'm confident that you'll agree with the shooting boards' assessments."

"I like that," King said, and she paused. "Are you above the law, Dr. Cross?"

I had to fight not to let my hands curl into fists and said, "No, Gayle, I am not above the law, and I'm frankly insulted at the characterization. I have spent my life in service to the law as a homicide cop and an FBI agent. I have more than twenty meritorious citations for my actions with both agencies and not one reprimand for excessive violence or any other disciplinary action. Not one."

King's eyes locked on mine. She said, "Did Gary Soneji deserve to die ten years ago?"

I thought about that and said, "Personal opinion?"

"Is there any other kind?"

"Then my opinion is yes."

King's eyes went wide. "Yes?"

"Soneji bombed people with impunity. He kidnapped and tortured others. He used a baby as a human shield while trying to bomb Times Square. I chased him into the New York subway system when he was wearing an explosives vest. He tried to kill me. I did everything I could to make sure the vest did not go off, including killing him. So, yes, if I've ever met someone who deserved to die, it was Gary Soneji."

"Are you obsessed with him?"

"No more than you'll be obsessed with me when you move on to your next story. Look, being a detective is my job, not a crusade or a vendetta. I do my best. I move on."

"'I do my best. I move on.' I like that," she said, and she smiled and took off her glasses. "Virginia Winslow and Leonard Diggs. Did they deserve to die?"

"No," I said. "But they made decisions that led me to make decisions as a police officer that ended their lives. I still don't have a crystal-clear rationale for their actions other than their wanting to frame me."

"In the video, none of your victims are seen carrying guns."

"In person, they were all holding nickel-plated revolvers," I said.

She chewed on one arm of her reading glasses. "And you, what, believe that Claude Watkins's followers somehow erased the images of them?"

"Something like that, yes."

"If you watch that video, you look like the coldest of killers, Dr. Cross."

"Or the biggest of patsies."

King put her glasses back on, referred to her notes. "With all the shootings across the country involving white cops killing black kids, isn't it ironic that there was no real federal involvement in this issue until the U.S. Justice Department put a black cop on trial?"

I felt my expression harden as I said, "I've never really wanted to play that card, but it sure makes you think, doesn't it?"

It went on for another twenty minutes before King finished. When the cameras were off, I stood and let the tech remove the microphone while King spoke with her producer.

She came over afterward, shook my hand a second time, and said, "I apologize for some of the tougher questions. Like you said, it's the job."

"I don't mind tough questions as long as they're unbiased."

"How'd I do?"

"I thought you were fair. How'd I do?"

King held my gaze before saying, "You're either a pathological liar and a killer or you're being framed by real smart folks."

"That how you're going to spin it?"

"No spin, Dr. Cross," King said. "We'll lay out both sides as we go and let the viewers decide."

CHAPTER

59

BREE, ANITA, AND NAOMI WERE convinced I'd done myself a great deal of good with the interview. And Nana Mama was still buzzing with the excitement of meeting Oprah's best friend forever, which I thought was kind of sweet and funny.

But as the hours ticked by I grew more anxious. What if Anita's analysts weren't good enough? What if we couldn't prove the video had been doctored?

Around nine that evening, I was feeling claustrophobic. Ali found me pacing around in the kitchen.

"Dad?" he asked. "Can I see those videos everyone's talking about?"

"Why would you want to see things like that?"

He shrugged. "Your attorney Ms. Marley thinks something's wrong with them. I wanted to see if I could see it."

I thought about that for several moments and then said, "I don't think I'd be the best father if I let a nine-year-old see a recording of people dying needlessly."

"Oh," my son said, sounding taken aback. "I just wanted to help."

"I know you did, bud," I said, and I hugged him.

Ali left me looking disappointed, which made me feel even more claustrophobic. I went upstairs and got changed into sweatpants, an old FBI hoodie, and running shoes. I found Bree in the front room watching *The Voice* and said I was going out for a jog.

"You want company?"

"Not this time," I said. "I need to get some things straight or I won't sleep."

Bree gave me an even gaze. "Just for the record, Alex, I think it sucks you're going through this. It guts me."

"It does suck," I said. "But like Nana Mama said, the truth will out."

"I don't want you spending a day in prison before that happens."

"Me neither," I said.

"Don't forget Jannie's racing in the morning."

"I won't be longer than I have to be," I said, then kissed her and went out the door. I ran down the block well out of sight before slowing and hailing a cab.

I got in the back and gave the driver an address. Twenty minutes later I was climbing out into a crowded parking lot in a light industrial area off I-95 not far from Dumfries, Virginia. I'd probably driven by the steel building there several thousand times while I was based at Quantico and never noticed it.

Then again, ten years before there had been no big glittering sign on the side facing the road that said GODDESS!

Throbbing electronic music pulsed from the building. For a moment I thought the two shaved-head bouncers weren't going to let me in because of what I was wearing, but the manager happened by and said, "The FBI is always welcome. More and more of you brave ones every day."

I paid the twenty-five-dollar cover fee and went inside the club, an homage to 1970s disco, with black walls, lots of mirrors, and flashing balls spinning and flickering above the dance floor, which was packed with gyrating gay men in all manner of dress, from tuxes to leather bondage outfits.

As I moved around, I turned down two offers to dance myself before spotting the man I'd come to see. Krazy Kat Rawlins was right in the middle of the mob of sweating dancers, shaking his booty, tossing his red Mohawk around, and waving his tattooed arms overhead as if he were at a revival for some of that old-time religion.

When the song changed, Rawlins came off the dance floor sweating, gasping, grinning, and flirting with several pals before he spotted me. Suddenly, the FBI's top digital analyst wasn't so exhilarated anymore.

"Unless you drive on my side of the highway, what are you doing here?"

"You haven't been returning my calls."

Rawlins patted his Mohawk, gauging its stiffness, before saying, "I don't believe you deserve to talk to me or to Batra anymore."

"Excuse me?"

He squared off, crossing his arms. "I've looked at the videos, Dr. Cross. Metadata's all there and I don't see any evidence that the sections that show the victims' hands have been altered in any way."

The words took a moment to sink in, and then I felt detached from my body. I looked around the dance club as if it were part of some weird dream.

"I saw guns, pistols," I said.

"The data doesn't lie," Rawlins said.

"No, that's not right. I'm telling you, Krazy Kat, that—"

"I can't help you."

I put my hands to my head. "I feel like I'm in some alternate universe, like I'm losing my mind."

He knit his brow. "Then you should go talk to someone, like a therapist, someone who can help you understand what you've done."

"But I didn't—"

"The videos say you did," Rawlins said. "The videos say Winslow and Diggs were unarmed. You killed them in cold blood, not self-defense."

"I saw guns!"

"Then your brain invented the guns so you could deal with what you'd done. You'd gotten off before. You'd do it again."

The FBI tech guru walked away and disappeared into the mass of writhing bodies on the dance floor with me staring dumbly after him.

CHAPTER

60

I HAVE NEVER BEEN A quitter in my entire life, never tried to do anything but face my responsibilities and duties head-on. But sitting in another cab twenty minutes after Rawlins vanished back onto the dance floor at the club, I felt like telling the driver to take me to National Airport or Union Station instead of home.

I wanted to flee, get a new identity, and hide out on a South Sea island, do anything except go home to tell Bree, Nana Mama, and the kids what Rawlins had said. There'd been no guns. I'd been deluded at best, downright evil at worst. In either case, I was going to federal prison, probably for life.

I shut my eyes, trying to remember the entire incident, clearly seeing the gun in Watkins's hand, and in Virginia Winslow's, and Leonard Diggs's. It made me sick to my stomach when I thought of the videos, clearly showing no guns before I shot.

How in God's name was that possible?

I thought back again, trying to remember every instant, and recalled that I'd felt odd, light-headed when Kimiko Binx and I arrived at the factory. Inside the factory, I'd felt…giddy? Why would I have been giddy? There were people with guns trying to kill me and I'd been…elated?

Maybe Rawlins was right. Maybe I did need to see a shrink, or at least someone who might understand what I was going through, someone like…

"Driver," I said. "Change of plans. Take me downtown."

He dropped me on a corner not far from the courthouse. I walked north several blocks to a familiar street with lights blazing in some of the town houses and big dumpsters out in front of the ones that were dark.

There were a few lights on in one of the duplexes, which did and didn't surprise me. Bernie Aaliyah had been fixing up the place.

As I climbed the stairs to the porch and the front door, my mind fled back to the last time I'd been here. I remembered being outside Tess Aaliyah's bedroom door, hearing the gunshot, and jumping back in shock and despair. And poor Bernie Aaliyah pounding on the door, begging the silence for an answer, some hope.

I shook off the memory, hesitated, and then knocked. A few moments later, the dead bolts were thrown and the door opened.

"Dr. Cross?"

"I wonder if I could talk to you."

"I'm doing good since we last spoke," Tess said, and she smiled. "We have another meeting set, don't we?"

"This time it's not about you," I said.

"Oh," she said, and frowned. "Well, then, of course, please come in."

61

I FOLLOWED HER INSIDE, REMARKING to myself how good she looked after only a month off the various interacting drugs that had helped put her behind a locked door with her backup pistol talking about rats, and her father and I outside thinking suicide.

It turned out that the construction projects up and down the street had disturbed the neighborhood's urban rat population and caused a migration. Tess had seen rats twice in her closet upstairs earlier that day. After her fight with her dad, and in a semidelusional state due to the drugs, she decided she'd clean out the closet, put crackers and birdseed in a pile, and then sit back and wait for a shot. It was why she'd insisted on talking quietly. She'd been hunting.

After Tess shot the rat, the ringing in her ears was so loud that for several long, agonizing moments, she didn't hear her father pounding on the door. Then she'd opened the door and looked at us with bloodshot, drug-puzzled eyes, as if she couldn't imagine what we were so upset about.

It had taken several hours to convince Tess to enter a psychiatric facility in Virginia so she could be properly evaluated. But she eventually agreed and spent a week there getting clean and undergoing tests. She'd gone into the psych ward taking a multi-pill cocktail and left on a single drug for depression. The doctors said that in her effort to forget, she was lucky she hadn't done permanent brain damage.

"You want a beer?" Tess said. "Dad left some."

"Water if you've got it," I said.

"Coming up," she said and got me some chilled from the fridge.

I sat in Bernie Aaliyah's favorite chair. Tess gave me my water, curled her feet under her on the couch, and said, "Thank you again for helping me, Alex. You were the only one who saw I was a danger to myself."

"I'm glad you agreed to get help," I said. "Which is why I came to see you."

"Okay?"

"Have you been following my trial?"

She shook her head. "My therapist advised me to go on a no-media diet for a few months."

"That's not a bad idea," I said, but then I brought her up to speed on the latest trial developments, including the video and Rawlins's contention that it had not been doctored.

"But you saw those pistols?"

"Every time I close my eyes, I see them," I said.

"Any chance you imagined them?"

I started to tell her absolutely not but then said, "Part of me doesn't know anymore, Tess, and it's got me scared that I did something heinous and that my mind has somehow erased it and put something else in its place to justify my actions. Does that make sense? Has that ever happened to you?"

Pain flickered on her cheeks before she shook her head. "I remember every detail, the first shots, me returning fire, and then hearing the Phelps's nanny wailing beyond that apartment door. I can't forget a second of it."

"That's how the other part of me feels."

"Then those pistols were there and removed from the videos. You just have to prove it."

My cell phone dinged, alerting me to a text. I pulled it out, saw it was from Bree: Where are you, Alex? I'm worried.

I texted back, Talking to an old friend. On my way.

I looked at Tess and said, "I have to go. Thanks for talking."

"One good deed deserves another."

We both stood and headed toward the door. I opened it and looked back at her before leaving.

"I forgot to ask. How are you keeping busy?"

Tess smiled wistfully and said, "Running twice a day, reading, and trying to learn how to forgive myself without a bunch of drugs in my brain."

CHAPTER

62

AT TEN THE FOLLOWING MORNING, I was in the stands inside the Johns Hopkins University field house with Damon, a sophomore now. We were watching Jannie take her last warm-ups. She'd been quiet on the ride up for the meet, so quiet that I had finally asked her what was going on.

Jannie didn't want to talk at first, but she eventually admitted that she was upset because someone had uploaded the shooting videos to YouTube. Social media was incensed. Terrible comments had been directed at her and at the boys.

That only made the day worse. When I'd told Bree the night before that Rawlins said the videos had not been doctored, I'd seen something in her eyes that I swore I'd never see there. Doubt. Not open suspicion, not a lack of faith, but doubt about the facts of the shootings as I'd described them.

"How are *you* doing, Dad?" Damon asked.

"Let's focus on Jannie," I said. "I'm sick of thinking about everything else."

"How's our girl looking?" Ted McDonald asked, breaking into my thoughts.

I was surprised to see him. "Thought you couldn't make it, Coach."

"My plans changed last night."

"Does Jannie know?" Damon asked.

"She will after the race."

"You mean after you see if she executes your race plan," I said.

"That too," McDonald said. "The field's pretty much the same as last time, including Claire Mason, so we can kind of hit reset today."

"Same tactics you recommended before?"

"A few tweaks based on her recent practice times," he said, and he dug in his pocket for a stopwatch.

Jannie had pulled the inside third lane. Claire Mason, the Maryland state champion and future Stanford athlete, was two wide in the fifth slot.

Whatever frustration and hurt Jannie might have been feeling on the ride to Baltimore appeared to be bottled and corked when the race starter called the young women to their marks. Our girl went to the blocks bouncing, shaking her arms, and rolling her head, all the while staring into the middle distance.

McDonald lowered his binoculars, said, "She's good."

I thought so too. She looked like the old Jannie out there, especially when she smiled after the starter said, "Set."

At the pistol crack, my daughter came out of the blocks well, more smooth power than explosive. Her stride lengthened, her legs found a relaxed cadence, and her arms were driving fluidly by the end of the first straight. She ran the curve cleanly and confidently, no sign of foot pain.

Exiting onto the backstretch, Jannie was exactly where she'd been in the previous race, in fourth, just off the shoulder of the girl in third, with Claire Mason leading by two body widths. But there was no move for the front. Jannie stayed right in her groove through the second curve and back up the near straightaway.

"Nice," her coach said, clicking his stopwatch as she flashed by. "I like that number a whole lot."

Claire Mason tried to run away with it coming out of the third turn, but the three athletes chasing her, including Jannie, reeled the state champion in down the backstretch. They were running in a tight bunch entering the final, far turn.

"Well done," McDonald said, watching through his binoculars. "Now gallop for home, girlie-girl."

Jannie seemed to hear her coach's words in her head because he'd no sooner said them than she found another gear. She passed the girl in third and was right off the shoulder of the athlete in second coming out of the last curve.

I couldn't help it; I started yelling, "C'mon, Jannie!"

Damon shouted, "Show them who's boss, sis!"

My daughter did something then that I hadn't seen since the foot injury. Her gait became more like bounding, and she blew by the girl in second place and bore down on Claire Mason with thirty yards to go. Mason gave a backward glance, saw Jannie coming, and ran in fear. But even sheer terror wouldn't have helped the state champ's cause that day.

With fifteen yards remaining, Jannie caught Mason. She was a full body width ahead at the wire.

CHAPTER

63

JANNIE SLOWED, LAUGHED, AND THREW her arms up to the sky. Damon cheered. I whooped and hollered and felt better than I had in days. Poor Claire Mason looked shell-shocked; she was a senior heading to a top track program, and she'd been bested by a junior just back from a long time off for a foot injury.

McDonald clapped when Jannie came up a few moments later.

"That is *exactly* how you do it," he said, giving her a high five. "The win's nice. So is beating Mason. But I'm prouder of you for being a disciplined and smart athlete."

Beaming, Jannie said, "It worked staying just off them. I felt like I had a lot in the tank when it counted."

"Sometimes I do know what I'm talking about," McDonald said, and he winked at her. "Enjoy the moment. I'll talk to you Monday."

"Leaving already?" Damon asked.

"Noon flight to Dallas," he said, and he looked to Jannie. "Ice bath ASAP."

Jannie groaned. "I hate ice baths."

"But she'll do it," I said.

After we'd left Damon to his studies, Jannie was bubbling with excitement as she got into the car and for half the way home. Then she checked her cell phone and got quiet again.

"They giving you a hard time?"

For several moments Jannie did not reply, but then she said, "They're idiots, Dad. They don't know you like I know you, so I think it's time I do some serious de-friending and maybe take a week or two vacation from all social media, even Snapchat and Instagram."

"Two weeks? I read somewhere that it's virtually impossible for teenage girls to get off their smartphones."

"Alert Mark Zuckerberg. I'm going to be the first."

I laughed. "Good for you."

"I'm sorry for the way I've been acting. I guess I could only see what the trial was doing to *my* life."

"And I'm sorry you've had to suffer for my actions. It's not fair to you or to your brothers."

We drove on in silence for a while. "Dad?"

I looked over and saw tears dripping down her cheeks.

"What's the matter, sweetie?"

"I love you, Dad, and I believe in you, but I'm also really scared for you."

A big ball of emotion surged in my throat. "I love you too, Jannie, and don't be scared for me. We're going to be all right."

But the closer we got to DC and home, the less I believed it.

CHAPTER

64

ALI CROSS HEARD JANNIE COME through the front door, and the excitement in her voice and then in Nana Mama's, but it wasn't enough to get him up from the desk in his father's attic office or make him take his eyes off the computer screen showing a YouTube video of his father shooting three people.

Ali had heard about the videos on Facebook and had watched them nearly twenty times by then. The first playing had been the most difficult. He'd jerked back and shut them off when his dad pulled the trigger, killing Virginia Winslow. It reminded him so much of seeing his debate teacher shot during the kidnapping of Gretchen Lindel that he almost got sick.

Deciding not to finish the tape, he almost shut down the browser. But then he remembered Ms. Marley, his dad's attorney, quoted in the *Washington Post* the day before, saying that there was something wrong with the videos, that they had been altered somehow. And he saw the comments people had posted on YouTube, most of them saying that Alex Cross was guilty as hell and deserved to spend life in prison or worse.

Ali had fought off the urge to cry reading the posts and forced himself to play the videos to the end, and then again and again, freezing the screen whenever one of the victims' hands was visible.

No gun. No gun. No gun.

But his dad said they'd all had guns, so he'd watched the videos over and over and over again. It wasn't until the fifteenth or sixteenth time that Ali noticed that the lighting seemed to change in the moments before each of the victims appeared, going dimmer but not dark enough that you couldn't see them and then brightening so you could see their empty hands just before the shot.

Ali had looked at those parts of the videos in detail at least three times and could not figure out what the change in lighting meant. He reached for the computer mouse and was about to play the videos yet again when he heard someone climbing the stairs.

Heart pounding, Ali clicked off the browser, revealing a Microsoft Word file that he pretended to be scanning when his dad came in.

"Nana Mama says you've been up here all morning," he said.

"I have a paper due on Monday," Ali said, still not looking up.

"Really? What's your topic?"

"Magic," he said, lifting his head. "Like Harry Houdini magic."

"The best there ever was," his dad said. "How's it going?"

The truth was Ali had finished writing the paper two days before, but he said, "Pretty good. I should be done on time if I work hard."

"Good for you," his dad said, looking around at the stacks of boxes that crowded the little office. "I've got to do something about this. I can't move in here half the time."

"Bree said it's evidence stuff and not to touch it."

"Too much evidence stuff," his dad said, distracted. "Don't stay up here all day. Go ride your bike at some point, or maybe we can go shoot a few hoops."

"That'd be good," Ali said, and he smiled. "Why was Jannie so happy?"

"She won her race, beat the strongest girl in Maryland."

"Wow," Ali said. "And no foot pain?"

"None," his dad said and turned to leave.

"Dad?" Ali called after him. "Do you think real magic exists? That there are people who can make things appear and disappear for real?"

"No," he said. "It's all deception, sleight of hand, smoke, light, and mirrors."

Ali nodded. "I think so too."

"You want lunch?"

"I'll come down in a bit," Ali promised. He watched his dad duck his head going out the door and listened to him drop to the second floor, then the first.

Ali felt a moment of guilt before launching the Internet browser again. He didn't like lying to his father or directly disobeying him, but someone had to figure out what was wrong with the videos.

He hit Play again and decided not to fast-forward, to watch them all from the beginning. He focused on the middle camera, the north one, looking back across the width of the factory floor with the bottoms of the three spotlights on the roof of the southern alcoves visible. Ali froze the screen and zoomed in.

He'd hoped to see some shadow there behind the spotlights, the suggestion of a silhouette, but he saw none. He hit Play again and noticed a tiny blue pinpoint light flash. And then it was gone.

It took Ali three attempts to freeze the middle video feed on that tiny blue light. He zoomed in on it but couldn't tell what the light was attached to. Frustrated, he hit Play again. He focused on the third feed, the one showing the length of the factory room, with the spotlights aimed toward the mural.

He zoomed in on the spotlights, but saw no one behind them.

Who was running the lights? And where was that blue pinpoint? Try as he might, he couldn't spot it.

"Ali!" Nana Mama yelled up the stairs. "I've got your bacon, lettuce, and tomato down here waiting."

"Coming, Nana," he cried. He cleared the browser's history to cover his tracks, then shut down the web page.

Ali got up and headed toward the stairs, only vaguely aware of the stacks of evidence boxes he passed. Indeed, he was thinking so intently about that pinpoint blue light that he barely noticed that the box on the filing cabinet closest to the door was labeled AUTOPSIES.

65

WE WERE FINISHING UP LUNCH when I heard a knock at our side door.

"Who's that now?" Nana Mama grumbled. "A damn reporter again?"

"If it is, I'm calling a real cop," I said, grinning and tousling Ali's hair because he seemed lost in thought.

I put my dishes on the counter, crossed to the side door, and opened it. A distressed Alden Lindel stood there.

"Mr. Lindel?" I said, stepping out and closing the door.

"I'm sorry, Dr. Cross," the father of the kidnapped girl from Ali's school said. "I know you've got your own issues, but I didn't know where else to turn."

I took a deep breath and then gestured to the basement door.

In my office, Lindel reached into his jacket pocket and came out with another flash drive in a baggie. "This time they hanged Gretchen."

He dropped into the chair, hid his face in his hands, and sobbed. "God damn it, they hung my daughter, or made it look that way, and they're selling tickets to the show on the Internet."

I flashed on Jannie and felt sick to my stomach. I walked over, put my hand on Lindel's shoulder, and said, "I can't imagine what you're going through."

He looked up at me with bloodshot eyes. "My wife and I barely talk. I can't work. My boss has threatened to fire me. Some days Gretchen's all I think about. And then, just for a while, she slips my mind. I get a little rest, and then something like this shows up in the mailbox. What do they want, Dr. Cross? Why are they doing this?"

"I don't know," I said. "But you need to take the drive straight to the FBI. I've been cut out of the loop because of my trial."

He continued to look at me, his face wretched. "You can't help me?"

"I want to," I said, sitting down across from him and leaning forward, my elbows on my knees, hands clasped. "Mr. Lindel, I want to help find your daughter and the other missing women in the worst way. I really do. But the ugly truth is, given my situation, I'm afraid I'd be more of a hindrance than a help to you. I hope you understand, sir. I'm not much good to you at the moment."

He didn't understand, not really. He got up, looking abandoned.

"You were our last chance," Lindel said, defeated. "But I wish you luck in your trial."

Feeling helpless, I shook his hand. "Don't give up. They're keeping Gretchen alive, which means there is hope you'll see her again. But the FBI can't find her if you're not turning over things like this flash drive."

He nodded. "I'll take it straight to their office."

When Lindel left, I went back into my office and collapsed on the couch. I felt bad, but what choice did I have? I couldn't have gotten Rawlins or Batra to expedite an analysis of the flash. They thought I was a killer.

My cell phone rang. It was Anita Marley.

"Alex," she said. "I've got bad news. Judge Larch is in the hospital. Possible stroke."

"What?" I said, shocked. "When?"

"She was taken to GW last night," Marley said. "They got drugs into her fast, so they're hopeful, and they're running more tests."

I shook my head, seeing little Judge Larch striding up onto the bench in a way that made her seem ten feet tall, larger than life. A stroke?

I said, "What if she can't go on?"

Anita sighed. "It will be a mistrial."

I shut my eyes. "And months before any kind of verdict."

"Let's wait to hear the diagnosis."

"I've got some bad news too," I said. "The videos weren't monkeyed with. At least, according to the metadata."

There was a pause. "And how do you know that?"

"A well-placed source in the FBI told me last night."

When Anita spoke again, she was irritated. "And you didn't think it smart to alert me or Naomi? We've lost twelve, maybe fifteen hours of—"

"The news was pretty devastating. I guess I wasn't thinking straight."

She sighed and said, "Well, I'm trying. My people are still working on those videos despite what the FBI tells you. And I do have a bit of good news. The saliva tests are done. I've put in a call to an old chemist friend in San Francisco just to make sure I'm interpreting the results correctly, but let's just say they're interesting."

"Can they clear me?"

"Given our inability to impeach the videos, no, it's not enough. But if I'm right, with luck, we'll be able to muddy the prosecution's waters a bit, show there were mitigating circumstances."

I started kneading my forehead and said, "Mitigating circumstances? Sounds to me as if I should be getting my affairs in order."

There was a long pause before Anita said, "Always better to be prepared."

CHAPTER

66

THE FOLLOWING TWENTY-FOUR HOURS were some of the lowest of my life. When Bree came home, I took her for a walk and told her what Anita had said. We held each other for the longest time.

"I can't believe this is happening," Bree said.

"Makes me wonder what I did to deserve this."

"No self-pity. What do we do?"

"No self-pity, and we move to protect you, Nana, and the kids," I said. "I can't have you all being punished for something you didn't do."

The next morning, after church, we went down to my basement office, shut the door, and made a list of things that would have to be done if I was convicted. Transfer my personal bank account to Bree. Find a trustee to step in to oversee my grandmother's philanthropic foundation. Transfer sole medical authority for Jannie and Ali to Bree. Transfer authority on the kids' college funds to her. Ask Nana Mama if she still wanted me as the executor of her living will. Make Bree my executor should I die in prison.

"I feel like we're getting ready for a funeral," Bree said.

There was a knock on my office door.

"Dad?" Jannie said.

"We're busy, sweetheart," I said.

"There's someone here to see you."

I closed my eyes. *When did people stop believing in Sundays?*

"Tell them to come back tomorrow."

Nana Mama said, "I think you'll want to come out."

Throwing up my hands in surrender, I went over, opened the door, and found Sampson and my father, Peter Drummond, a big, robust black man in his late sixties, standing there in the hall. Drummond had a face almost devoid of expression due to nerve damage associated with a large burn scar that began beneath his right eye and spread down much of his cheek to his jaw.

"Dad?" I said.

"I came to provide some moral support," Drummond said and he gave me a hug and a clap on the back. "John picked me up at National."

"It was supposed to be a surprise," Nana Mama said.

"It is a surprise," I said. "It's…good. Is Alicia here too?"

"Indisposed, but sends her prayers," Drummond said.

"Let's go upstairs," Nana Mama said. "I'll make a big breakfast."

Afterward, my dad, Bree, Sampson, and I took a walk. My father asked a lot of questions. Drummond knew as much about murder as we did and more about enduring tough times than we could imagine. He'd worked sheriff's homicide in Palm Beach County, Florida, for thirty-two years. Before that he'd served in the first Gulf War, where he was caught in an oil-well explosion that burned his face.

After we'd walked several miles and I'd brought him up to speed on everything, he said, "I know your case looks bleak, son, but you can't lose hope. I'm living proof of that. I lost hope of ever seeing you or Nana or your children, and then there you were down in my neck of the woods, looking for Reverend Maya. Miracles happen every day."

"From your lips to God's ears," Sampson said, and he checked the time. "I've got to go. Promised Billie I'd watch the Redskins game with her."

"Any progress with the blondes?" I asked. "Anything from that latest video of Gretchen Lindel? The one showing her hanged?"

Sampson glanced at Bree and then shook his head. "I haven't heard about that one. But on my end, it feels like I'm banging my head against a brick wall."

"And the new partner?"

"She's the brick wall."

"John," Bree said, but she couldn't hide a smile. "It's not that bad."

"If you say so, Chief," he said. Then he gave us a salute and walked away.

CHAPTER

67

AT FOUR THIRTY THE NEXT afternoon, a Monday, there was a knock at the basement door. Closing my laptop, I got up, happy for the new client and grateful to have something beyond my own fate to think about.

I opened the door to find a tall and very attractive woman in her early thirties. Her hair was long, luxurious, and black, her skin mocha and flawless, and her exotic chocolate eyes were wide and turned up at the outer corners. She wore a tight black skirt, stiletto heels, a chic white blouse, and a simple strand of pearls beneath a black leather jacket. Lots of other jewelry. No wedding ring.

"Ms. Cassidy?"

Annie Cassidy smiled weakly, adjusted the cuff of her jacket, and said, "It's so good of you to see me on such short notice, Dr. Cross."

"Any friend of Father Fiore is always welcome," I said. "Please come in."

I stood aside, and she looked at me uncertainly before coming down the stairs. As she passed, she glanced up shyly before continuing on into my office, leaving the faintest smell of her perfume.

After I closed the door, I found her on my couch, fiddling with her iPhone.

"Just making sure no bells," Cassidy said.

"I appreciate it," I said, taking a seat across from her.

She set the phone facedown on the table beside her and then took a big breath and blew it out. "I'm sorry. I've never done anything like this before."

"Just so you know: There are no judgments here. Ever. And nothing you say will ever leave this room."

"Okay. Don't I have to fill out forms or whatever?"

"You'll do it electronically. I'll give you the information after we decide if we can work together."

Cassidy thought about that, said, "Fair enough."

"So," I said, picking up a notepad and a pen. "How can I help?"

She hesitated, squinted, said, "Are you a sleepwalker, Dr. Cross?"

"Is that what you're having trouble with? If so, I can refer you to an excellent sleep specialist."

Cassidy made a show of crossing her legs. "I'm not a sleepwalker myself, but I'm wondering if you are so I can understand you before I try to explain."

It seemed like an odd and convoluted reason for the request, but I said, "I don't think I have sleepwalked since I was a child."

"Or since you were married," she said, her head tilted in deference.

"I'm afraid I'm not following."

"Of course not," Cassidy said, and she smiled. "Sleepwalker."

As I readjusted my position in my chair, I was thinking that I might have someone mentally unstable on my hands.

She straightened her legs and then crossed them the other way. "To be plain: I'm an addict, Dr. Cross, and I need your help."

"Opioids?" I said with a sigh. "If so, there are better—"

"No, not opioids."

"What then?"

"How does that old Robert Palmer song go?" Cassidy asked, smiled, and then sang quietly, "'Might as well face it, you're addicted to love.'"

Her happiness vanished. "That's the long and short of what's wrong with me, Dr. Cross. I'm a straight-up, strung-out, love junkie if ever there was one."

68

I'D HEARD AND ENCOUNTERED PATHOLOGICAL love stories before, especially when unrequited desire and obsession were motives for murder. But in the hour that followed, Annie Cassidy gave me a crash course in the little-studied, rarely discussed world of love junkies and so-called sleepwalkers like me.

Cassidy told me she was like most of the love junkies she knew in that, as a little girl, she'd bought hook, line, and tiara into the myth of the fairy-tale princess. Cassidy's mother dressed her up as a princess when she was young. She entered Cassidy in beauty pageants. And every night before bed, she read her daughter fairy tales where Prince Charming always appeared to scoop the princess out of her poor Cinderella life and ride her into the happily ever after on the back of his valiant white steed.

As I listened, I realized this story was a variation of the princess story the computer geek at Catholic University had told me as a way of explaining the minds of blond women, but I kept my mouth shut and kept an open mind.

"All my life, I dreamed of happily ever after," Cassidy said wistfully as she sat back on the couch. "When Kevin appeared in my life, senior year at NYU, I was sure he was my Prince Charming. I'd never felt like that with anyone before. Breathless. Sick when we were apart. And when we were together, I could hold his hand, feel his love coursing through me, and tell him every dark secret in my heart. Is that what falling in love was like for you, Dr. Cross?"

I thought of Bree and me in our early days, how smitten I'd been by her, breathless and tongue-tied after our first kiss, and how euphoric we were to be together after we'd been apart.

"Yes," I said. "We couldn't get enough of each other."

"Roughly two years of that, right? Like there's no one else in the world who matters?"

I smiled. "Yes."

"That's because when you fall in love, there's a chemical cocktail mixing in your brain. First it's norepinephrine, and then the serotonins kick in, give you wild energy. It's like bathing your brain in cocaine."

"I think that's right," I said.

"You would do almost anything for that feeling once you have it. You might do crazy things that no sane person would do. Like abdicate a throne. Or walk away from your family, your life, just to be with your new love."

Cassidy said she and Kevin fell into that kind of passionate love. They married after college and were still living the romance two years later.

Their third year together, however, Kevin began working longer hours, and when he was home, he was too tired to do much beyond sit in front of the television with his computer in his lap. He gained weight. He lost interest in her.

She grew more frustrated, in part because, while the chemicals of falling in love carry with them the rush of amphetamines, the chemicals of long-term love are more like a gentle opioid calming the brain, sedating it, in a sense.

"In retrospect, there was that, for sure," Cassidy said. "I felt groggy all the time, like a sleepwalker. Even through the haze, I could see that I'd screwed up. I realized I hadn't married the Prince Charming in my fairy tale. I'd married the frog."

That crushed Cassidy. She felt like she'd settled for less than the perfect love and the beautiful life she'd been promised. Shortly afterward, she met Chet, a man who came to work at her real estate firm. Chet was handsome and funny. They flirted. He listened to her. The chemicals of new love trickled in her brain.

"I came awake, alive again," Cassidy said. "But I did the right thing."

She said that many women raised in the traditions of the princess myth will ask for a separation from the frog, hinting that they might be willing to recommit at a later date. They string the frog out for years, punishing him with hopes of reconciliation dashed, unwarranted restraining orders, and false charges of abuse and neglect.

"It's all done out of spite," she said. "They feel cheated. The fairy tale is not true, so they take their rage out on the husband while getting some love chemicals on the side.

"But I absolutely did not do that. I did not play torture-the-frog just because Kevin was not Prince C. He could have easily turned out to be an ogre, am I right? The point is that as soon as I had a commitment from Chet, I told Kevin to his face that I had to be free to love and that I wanted a divorce."

Cassidy moved in with Chet until the chemical attraction

wore off, about two years later. Chet's place in her heart was soon occupied by Steven. Twenty-six months later, she met Carlos, a deep sleepwalker, who was ten years into his marriage.

"I woke Carlos up," Cassidy said, and she chuckled. "In a big way."

I glanced at the clock. "Our hour's almost up, but I have a quick question."

Cassidy said, "Okay."

"What do you want out of our sessions? If we go on, I mean."

She sighed, studied the ceiling, and said, "I've been eighteen months with Carlos. He's a stand-up guy. He divorced his wife for me, and I really do love him. Not only that, I genuinely like him. He's my best friend ever. But I know what's coming in six months, a year at the outside, and I...I guess I want to learn how to be a sleepwalker and stay with someone forever."

I smiled. "That's a good goal."

"Something we can talk about next time?"

"Sounds like a plan."

Cassidy took her iPhone off the table and got up. "Thank you, Dr. Cross."

"You're more than welcome. I'll need an e-mail address to send my forms."

"Oh," she said, her brow knitting. "I had a computer virus over the weekend and I'm between e-mails at the moment. I'm opening a new account on Gmail tonight. Can I ping you with it?"

"That works."

"Thank you for understanding all this."

"It's what I do."

"And you do it well," she said. She smiled uncertainly and left.

I stood there a few moments, wondering if Bree and I were sleepwalkers, then deciding that if we were, I was more than happy in my semiconscious state of marital bliss.

Remembering I had to take some leaves I'd raked and bagged out front for pickup, I went outside. The light was fading. Drizzle fell. I got the leaf bags, carried them around the house, and put them on the sidewalk.

I happened to look down the block and saw Cassidy getting into a black Nissan Pathfinder. Wondering if her Carlos might be driving, I walked a few yards that way and was in deep shadow near a retaining wall when the Pathfinder came closer, headlights off.

I could see the silhouette of Cassidy sitting sideways, facing the driver, who was just a dark shape until the Pathfinder crossed beneath a street lamp. For a second his face was clearly visible through the windshield.

Recognition stopped me cold. I was confused.

What was Annie Cassidy doing with Alden Lindel?

CHAPTER

69

GRETCHEN LINDEL'S FATHER USED TO tell her that the brain could be the strongest part of the body, or the most fragile.

"It's your choice, Gretch," he'd said not long before she'd been taken captive in the twisted world of sickos.

Lying on her filthy mattress in her plywood cell, holding her left leg so it wouldn't be irritated any further by the manacle around her ankle, the seventeen-year-old was doing everything she could to keep her mind strong.

I am going to get out of here, Gretchen kept telling herself. *I just have to survive long enough to get the chance. I'm going to be like Dad. Nothing they've done hurts me in any way. It makes me stronger. This only makes me stronger.*

But it had been several days since they'd come for her. Hour upon hour of silence created all sorts of dark voices in her mind.

Doubt crept up on Gretchen and whispered that she'd die there in the box. Fear wormed its way into her stomach and said they'd take her again before that happened. Self-pity wrapped her head and heart, told her she was defeated.

But time and time again, whenever Gretchen realized the voices of despair were taking control of her thoughts, she'd think of her father and everything he'd endured, and she'd take heart.

I will survive. They can't hurt me. This will only make me—

The dead bolts turned. She closed her eyes, not knowing if this was a meal or another of their twisted games. If it was a game, she was done crying. She was done being scared. They seemed to feed on her fright, and as the door swung open she vowed to give them none.

The big one in black came in carrying a semiautomatic AR rifle. Her father had one just like it.

"It's time, Gretchen," he said from behind the paintball mask. "We're all but done here. Cleanup time now."

Gretchen said nothing, just stared through him as if he didn't matter anymore, as if nothing mattered anymore.

Be like Dad, she thought as he went to work on her ankle manacle.

For God's sake, be like Dad.

CHAPTER

70

HAD THAT BEEN GRETCHEN LINDEL'S father driving the Pathfinder?

I kept trying to convince myself I was wrong, but each time I closed my eyes, I saw Alden Lindel clearly. But why? And how?

When Annie Cassidy called to set up the appointment, she'd said that Father Fiore had referred her, hadn't she? Well, now that I thought about it, she hadn't actually used his name. She'd said she'd gotten my number from "a mutual friend, a priest with challenging problems."

And Lindel? He'd contacted me directly. No reference that I remembered.

What were the odds of two people who knew each other coming to my office and never mentioning it to me?

I thought about Gretchen Lindel's mother, Eliza, and how distraught she'd been in the days after her daughter's kidnapping. Was Annie Cassidy the reason she and her husband separated? Had she used fake names for her lovers? Was Alden Lindel actually Carlos?

I went inside, told my grandmother I was going out, and got the car keys.

By the time I drove into a residential neighborhood west of the Cabin John Parkway, it was pitch-dark and the rain had stopped. I found the address I was looking for and parked the car across the street from a brick-faced Colonial with a big flower bed gone dormant, a crushed-gravel driveway, and a bronze Volvo station wagon. Lights gleamed in the narrow windows that flanked the front door.

I climbed out, smelled wet leaves, and started toward the house, wondering about the reception I'd get, a lone man at night unannounced. My cell phone buzzed. I ignored it, climbed the stoop, and rang the bell.

A dog started barking. A small Jack Russell terrier was soon bouncing and barking an alarm on the other side of the lower right window.

"Tinker!" a woman said. "Get back, girl!"

The dog kept barking and then yelped in protest when the woman grabbed her and held her in her arms. She peered blearily out the window at me. Despite the exhaustion and despair that seemed to hang off her like rags, I recognized her.

"Mrs. Lindel?" I said. "Eliza?"

The terrier in her arms showed her teeth.

She said, "If you're a reporter, please go away, you're not helping the situation. No one's helping the situation here."

"I'm not a reporter," I said. "My name is Alex Cross. I'm a...my son Ali goes to school at Latin with Gretchen."

Eliza studied me a long moment before opening the door. The dog growled like a little demon.

"Hush, now," Eliza said, and the dog stilled but kept a close eye on me.

The missing girl's mother was in her mid-thirties but looked older in baggy sweatpants, Birkenstock sandals, and a George Mason University tee. Her hair was in disarray and graying at the roots. Her eyes were bloodshot, rheumy.

"Alex Cross," she said. "You're that cop on trial for murder."

"Innocent as charged."

"I read you've killed eleven people."

"In the course of duty I have, that's true."

"I also read you've found kidnapped girls before."

"That's also true. Including my niece, who today is part of my defense team. Life *can* go on after an abduction, Mrs. Lindel."

"That why you're here?"

"In part. Can I come in?"

She hesitated, then stuck her face in her dog's face. "You be good now, Tinker, hear?"

Tinker licked her cheek. Eliza set the dog down. The Jack Russell eyed me when Eliza stood aside and I entered. I smelled gin and cigarettes as I walked past her into a center hall lined with hooks where pictures had once hung.

"Is there somewhere we can sit and talk?" I asked.

"The kitchen. Straight ahead."

She followed me down the hallway through an open doorway into a dingy white kitchen where dirty dishes were piled high in the sink, newspapers and unopened mail covered the table, and prescription bottles took up two entire shelves of a bookcase. I caught a whiff of something antiseptic and thought I heard muffled voices.

"How are you holding up?" I said.

Eliza pushed back a strand of hair. "How does it look like I'm holding up?"

"I can't help asking—the pictures in the hall?"

She stared at me. Her lower lip quivered. "I couldn't take looking at Gretchen anymore. She was ripping me up every time I walked through there."

"The stress must feel unbearable."

"You don't know the half of it."

"Your husband?"

She stiffened. "Alden? Alden's Alden. A trouper. Never gives up hope. Never says die."

"I'm a clinical psychologist by training. I don't know if he's told you, but he's been seeing me for therapy."

She crossed her arms and studied me skeptically. "No, he didn't say anything."

"Two sessions."

"Really? You'd think he would have told me. Why don't we go ask him why he didn't?"

My pulse quickened. "He's here? I just saw him heading toward Capitol Hill. He looked like he was out for a night on the town. With another woman."

"Another woman?" She laughed sarcastically. "I bet he smelled of cheap perfume, didn't he?"

"I didn't get close enough."

"Well, you can now," she said, gesturing at a door at the far end of the kitchen. "Alden's right through there, watching *Game of Thrones*. Let's go talk to him. Get things out in the open."

"Let's do that," I said. I crossed the kitchen and went through the door.

CHAPTER

71

A WAVE OF ANTISEPTIC SMELLS hit me as I stepped down into a space set up as a hospital room.

To my right, shelves bulged with medical equipment, supplies, and clean linens. To my immediate left there was a tall green oxygen tank with a hose that ran over to a hospital bed with its back raised.

Beyond the tank, an array of electronic monitors cheeped and beeped over the sounds coming from a speaker system linked to the big screen mounted on the opposite wall. According to a tag in the lower right corner of the screen, season 3, episode 4, of *Game of Thrones* was showing.

I took a few more steps into the room and saw a man in the bed. He reminded me of the physicist Stephen Hawking, gaunt, bent, and curled up by disease. Breathing oxygen through a nasal cannula, he lay on his right side, wore glasses, and watched the screen intently, seeming to have no idea we were there.

"That's not the Alden Lindel who came to see me," I said.

"I didn't think so," Eliza said.

"I don't know why I didn't check."

"Why would you? We're private about Al's challenges because that's the way he wants it. How could you have known he has end-stage ALS?"

"I suppose," I said, and I felt baffled until I realized that the man who'd posed as Alden Lindel brought me the flash drives that showed the mock executions of Gretchen Lindel.

No one had sent those drives to him. He was part of Killingblondechicks4fun. And so was the love junkie.

Tinker darted by us and jumped up on the bed, wagging her tail.

"E-liza," an electronic voice said.

She smiled at me before going to his side. "Right here, Al."

"N-ext?"

"You're not even through that one yet, and the next is in the queue," she said with a glance at me. "He loves this show."

"S-mart dwarf," he said. "B-oobs."

"Yes, Tyrion and lots of boobs," she said matter-of-factly. "I'd like you to meet someone, Al. He's trying to find Gretchen for us."

I came over to her husband's bedside. Laboring for breath, the real father of the missing blond girl rolled his eyes up to me.

"I'm Alex Cross, sir," I said.

He had a digital tablet next to him on the mattress. He rolled his eyes down and blinked eleven or twelve times, maybe more.

"I know you," the tablet said a few seconds later.

"Wow," I said. "How does that work?"

Eliza said, "The tablet's built with three camera lenses that triangulate to pick up where he's looking on the screen, which shows a keyboard layout. He looks at a letter on the keyboard and blinks. When he blinks twice, he's done with the word. Blinks three times and the voice comes on."

"That's amazing."

"I think so."

The tablet voice said, "B-lows, you ask me."

Lindel was peering at me again, and I nodded in sympathy.

He looked at the tablet. A few seconds later, the voice said, "Where's my Gretch?"

Thinking about the fake Alden Lindel and Annie Cassidy coming to my office, I said, "She could be closer than we think. Within driving distance."

The missing girl's father looked down at the tablet. His synthesized voice said, "Can't even cry for her."

Eliza's hand shot to her lips. "It's true. His tear ducts are shutting down. We have to put drops in every two hours."

Her husband rolled his attention to the tablet for the longest time yet before the voice said, "My time is near, Cross. My last wish is to see my Gretch again. One last time."

He peered up at me. Even though his body and face were virtually frozen, I could see the desperate hope in his eyes.

"I'll do my best, Al," I said. "Just hang on."

I gave Eliza Lindel my cell phone number, said good-bye to her and her husband, and left the house feeling humbled.

The day before, with the weight of the evidence in my murder trial so stacked against me, I'd been thinking that life was treating me pretty damn unfairly. But here the real Alden Lindel's life was being squeezed from him by a disease that was killing him one paralyzed muscle at a time. And there was his courageous wife, caring for him and worried sick about their missing daughter.

All in all, I had nothing to bitch about.

I got in the car thanking God and the universe for the blessings in my life: my wife, my family, my home, my health, my friends, my—

My cell phone rang. It was Anita Marley.

"Judge Larch had a transient ischemic attack," she said. "No stroke."

"Hey, that's good news."

"It is," she said. "I like Judge Larch. A lot. Her clerk's saying we're back in session the day after tomorrow."

"Even better."

"You still sticking with your story about the guns?"

"Yes. I'm telling you I saw them."

"My analysts agree with the FBI. There's no evidence of doctoring. But we'll try to raise some reasonable doubt based on the fact that the phones were supposedly in the factory for months."

I wasn't convinced it would do any good. Later, as I was turning onto Fifth, my phone rang again.

Sampson said, "Are you busy tomorrow?"

"No trial until Wednesday."

"Tell Bree I'm taking you fishing in Pennsylvania to get your mind off things. I'll pick you up at five."

CHAPTER

72

IN THE CHILL GRAY LIGHT of an autumn dawn, I watched fog swirling around the trunks and through the branches of leafless oak trees. Clusters of acorns still clung to some, but many more littered the forest floor. It was quiet but for the distant sound of a creek and the irregular patter of oak mast falling.

"Alex?" Sampson said behind me. "I got it to work finally."

I turned to find him looking at an iPad on the hood of his Grand Cherokee. Still clutching my second big cup of fast-food coffee, I walked over and looked at the iPad, which had a satellite connection.

Sampson had the Google Earth app launched. It gave us a bird's-eye view of a rural area forty miles northwest of Williamsport, Pennsylvania, where several creeks met and formed a trout stream roughly three miles from where we were standing. The stream ran by a fifty-acre property adjoining an unpaved country road. A long two-track driveway wound from the road past meadows to a line of mature pines that shielded a large hollow between two ridges.

A modest ranch house sat in a clearing in the bottom of the hollow. There was a barn larger than the house and five other sheds and smaller structures. A substantial garden flanked the back of the barn. Beside the garden stood a big satellite dish.

I tapped on the dish. "That what they're keying on?"

Sampson nodded. "Big bandwidth coming and going. Lots of electricity being used on the property. And many of the recent uploads to Killingblondechicks have evidently come through that satellite dish. We've got the IP address."

"Seems strange," I said. "When Krazy Kat Rawlins looked at that website, he couldn't tell where most of the videos of blondes were coming from because they used onion routers. And our guys were able to track them?"

"Maybe the guys making them got lazy," Sampson said. "It happens."

"The woods around here do look like the woods in the videos of Gretchen Lindel and Delilah Franks," I said. "The blondes running in the trees?"

"I remember," Sampson said. "And the lesbian girls disappeared less than sixty miles east of here. They could all be in that house or in any of those outbuildings."

"Wish you'd gotten the search warrant."

"Not enough evidence yet, the judge said. Which is why you're here and Fox isn't. Like I said, we're going fishing."

We got back in the car. It felt good to be riding shotgun with Sampson again. My world seemed even better than it had leaving the Lindels the evening before.

I switched the iPad app to Google Maps and used it to navigate the labyrinth of dirt roads around the property. Somewhere on it, there was a computer belonging to a twenty-seven-year-old named Carter Flint. In the satellite image, there were six or seven vehicles in Flint's yard.

But driving past that line of pines into the hollow, we spotted only two: a faded red Ford Ranger pickup and an old Toyota Corolla that looked in need of springs, both with their noses toward an embankment below the ranch house.

Sampson parked sideways behind them, blocking anyone trying for a quick exit. We got out. The fog was lifting from the ridges above the hollow. A dog barked in the distance beyond the pole barn. Closer, I heard the blatting of a sheep and the squeal of a pig or two.

We went up a crumbling brick walkway and knocked on the front door. No answer. No sounds inside. Sampson knocked again, and I thought I caught a flutter of movement in a window to my right. But again there was no answer.

"Let's take a look around," I said. "Maybe he's in the barn."

As we crossed the yard and got closer to the barn, the animal sounds got louder, more frantic, the dog barking, the sheep blatting, and the pig squealing. I knocked at a side door, then tried the knob. It turned. I pushed the door open. Bells hanging on the inner knob jangled.

The pig started squealing in an even higher pitch. The sheep blatted in terror. So did the dog; it sounded desperate, crying and yelping.

We stepped inside and took in the cavernous space in one long, sweeping, and horrified glance.

"Jesus Christ," Sampson said. "This isn't right."

CHAPTER

73

THE PIG WAS FORTY POUNDS or so. It was in a low wire pen and was missing a two-inch-wide strip of skin along the length of its spine; it was clearly in terrible pain.

A lamb was in a pen beside the pig. Three of its legs were broken and it was struggling piteously.

The dog, a beagle, had been beaten with a blunt object. It tried over and over to get to its feet, but it kept falling and yelping for help.

Three GoPro cameras on tripods were aimed at the cages. Beyond the pens, a long workbench stretched the length of the side wall. On it were dozens of pieces of grotesque taxidermy, animals stuffed in their tortured state.

Behind the bench, the rear sliding door of the pole barn was open to the big garden. Thirty, maybe forty more creatures— small dogs and cats, wild things like skunks and opossums, even an owl—were stuffed in positions that preserved their agony and set in the garden in neat little rows. A few were dressed in doll clothes, which only made the situation more disturbing.

"We need to call in the locals," Sampson said.

Before I could reply, a man wearing headphones appeared in the open doorway to the garden. Bone thin and dressed in painter's pants and a green wife-beater, he had skin as pale as a fish belly, pinkish eyes, and wispy hair the color of snow.

Two steps into the barn, as he was smiling at the wounded animals in their pens, he spotted us over by the door. He ripped off his headphones.

"Who the hell are you?" he demanded.

"Police," Sampson said, holding up his badge. "You Carter Flint?"

Shock locked Flint in his tracks for a second as he looked from John's badge to the suffering animals. Then he whirled and flew out the barn door.

I tore after him. I had no jurisdiction. I wasn't even a cop, technically, but after what I'd seen, I wasn't letting the sadist who'd done it get away.

Neither was Sampson; he was off my left shoulder, exiting the barn into the garden. Flint was surprisingly fast and nimble. He was already beyond the garden's borders and racing behind two other outbuildings toward the north tree line at the base of a ridge a hundred and fifty yards away.

"If he makes those woods, we'll lose him," Sampson growled.

I gritted my teeth and danced through the stuffed animals until I hit the grass, then I told myself to be like Jannie—relax and run. For thirty yards I was convinced I'd catch him, but Flint was younger and, judging from the way he was gaining ground, much fitter than me.

But not fitter than Sampson, who blew by me.

When Flint was forty yards from the woods, he hit tall, tangled grass. It slowed him. But it didn't slow John, whose long legs had him leaping after the sadist. Flint looked back in desperation and then lunged for the woods.

Sampson ran up a hummock in the weeds and dived after him.

CHAPTER

74

SAMPSON'S SHOULDER AND HIS two hundred and twenty pounds drove into the back of Flint's legs, flattening him in the deep wet grass. I ran up, gasping, as John straddled the sadist and kept his shoulders pinned.

"My knee." Flint moaned. "Something snapped. And I got broken ribs."

Sampson dug out zip cuffs and wrenched Flint's arms up behind him, which provoked another round of howling.

"My ribs!"

"Screw your ribs," Sampson said. "And screw your knee. You're lucky I don't kick out your front teeth."

I helped Sampson up and then pulled Flint to his feet. His left leg buckled, and he began to whimper.

"I can't help it, man. I got a mental sickness. I tried to stop. I did, but—"

"Save it for a judge," Sampson said.

"Where are the blond women?" I said. "Which building?"

He didn't react at first. Then he looked confused. "What blond women?"

"The ones you made those movies of," Sampson said. "Fake executions. Uploaded them to the Killingblondechicks site."

"No," he said. "I watched some free videos on that site, but that's not me."

"All the recent uploads have been coming from your IP," Sampson said.

Flint shook his head. "I've never submitted to that site. Never. I do animals for animal sites. Not humans. I'd never do humans."

"Try telling that to a jury after they've seen your barn," I said.

"I'm telling the truth," he said. "Maybe I deserve punishment for what I've done, who I am. But if those blonde videos came through my IP, man, someone frickin' hacked and hijacked my computer! I'm being framed!"

Part Four

IN DEFENSE OF ALEX CROSS

CHAPTER

75

SHORTLY BEFORE DARK, SAMPSON DROPPED me off at the entrance to the alley that runs behind my house. With my trial starting up again in the morning, there were bound to be more journalists in front of my house.

There'd been other journalists gathered at the bottom of Carter Flint's road when we left. After Sampson called the local sheriff to tell them we'd made a citizen's arrest, we'd waited until Flint was in custody and the three animals mercifully euthanized before we helped in the search for the girls. We'd found enough disturbing evidence to put Flint behind bars or in a psychiatric institution for years but no trace of Gretchen Lindel or Delilah Franks or the four other missing women.

I used the back gate to our yard, happy for the darkness, and went in the side door. My dad and Jannie were watching a tape of her race at Hopkins. Bree was in the kitchen with Nana Mama.

"How was fishing?" my dad said.

Before I could answer, Bree called archly, "Yes, how *was* fishing?"

I gave my dad a chagrined look and walked to the kitchen. "You know?"

She crossed her arms. "I know everything. What were you thinking, going up there and just barging in like that?"

"That was John's call on his own time. I just tagged along."

She really wasn't happy. "You said you'd be straight with me."

I lowered my voice, said, "Straight with you? Okay, it was bad. The worst animal cruelty I've ever seen. I feel like I've been dipped in a jar of creepiness, but we stopped more animals from being tortured by that piece of shit."

Bree struggled, her eyes searching mine, and then threw up her hands. "Go take a shower."

Turning from the stove, Nana Mama said, "Dinner in half an hour."

"Smells good. What is it?"

"It's a secret."

"I'll be right back down," I said. I leaned over Bree's cold shoulder and kissed her on the cheek.

"There's something on the table in the hall for you, Alex," my grandmother called after me as I left the room.

In the front hall I spotted a small U.S. Postal Service mailer addressed to Dr. Cross. No return address. I opened it to find the same kind of flash drive that the fake Alden Lindel had shown me. It was inside a plastic sleeve.

"You might want to see this," I said, waving the envelope at Bree.

We went down to my basement office. Bree put on latex gloves and plugged the drive in. A few moments later, a

QuickTime App launched and showed a low-light video of a handcuffed, barefoot woman in a tattered white nightgown. She had a white hood over her head and was being led to a mossy stone wall by two guys dressed in black from shoes to hoods.

When they reached the wall, one of the men spun her around. The other yanked off the hood, revealing a gagged blond teen.

I felt sick, said, "Gretchen Lindel."

They took off the gag. The camera pulled back to show three men about fifty feet from Gretchen. They were all hooded, all dressed in black, and all carrying AR rifles.

"Ready," the cameraman said.

The three men shouldered their rifles.

I expected Gretchen to go to her knees and beg for mercy.

But instead, she stood tall against the stone wall and stuck her chin out at the firing squad.

"Go ahead!" she yelled at them. "I'm not afraid. You can do anything you want and I am not afraid of any of you!"

"Aim," the cameraman said.

"You won't do it!" Gretchen screamed. "You kill me, you don't get to play your games anymore. You kill me—"

"Fire!"

The guns went off. In the low light, orange flames shot out of their muzzles. By the sparks the ricochets threw, the bullets hit stone inches around her head.

It broke Gretchen, who went to her knees, shaking in terror.

"Don't," she wept. "Don't."

Then the screen froze, and I heard the voice of the fake Alden Lindel say, "Next time, it's for real, Dr. Cross. Next time every blond bitch, including little Gretchen, dies. And forget about finding me before then. I exist in the digital void, invisible, ten steps ahead of you and the FBI."

The video ended with that same brilliant flash I'd seen the first time I'd plugged in one of his thumb drives.

"He's definitely part of the Killingblondechicks conspiracy," I said, thinking about Flint's insistence that someone had hijacked his computer.

Then I thought about the fact that the fake Alden Lindel had mailed the flash drive to me rather than bringing it in person.

"He knew I'd figured him out," I said.

How? That flash at the end of the videos kept playing in my mind until I formed a very strong suspicion.

"I think there's a good chance he's bugged my computer somehow," I told Bree. "And maybe the FBI's. That would keep him ten steps ahead of us, wouldn't it?"

76

WHEN I FINALLY GOT IN the shower, I was no longer merely suspicious but convinced my computer had been compromised by the fake Alden Lindel. I'd called Rawlins and Batra at the FBI to alert them, but neither of them picked up the phone. I left them messages saying that I believed their system was at risk as well, and I hoped they'd call sooner rather than later.

Under the hot water, I felt sickened again at what Flint had done to those animals and at the fact that he claimed there were tens of thousands of subscribers to the websites he sold his footage to. Was that true? What possible pleasure could someone find in innocent animals suffering?

It was so beyond me that I got angry. That anger only deepened when I considered my inability to make headway in the hunt for the missing blondes, especially Gretchen Lindel. What a brave thing she'd done, standing up to those men like that, defying them.

When at last I turned my thoughts to the trial, I got angrier still, and then depressed.

Two eyewitnesses had testified that I'd shot three people without just cause. There were videos of the shootings and no sign of computer-generated imaging or anything to suggest I was being framed.

The weight of those cold, hard facts kept growing as I showered myself into a darker mood. A conspiracy had been hatched and directed at me. The conspiracy was working. The gears of justice were grinding, and I could see no path out.

I got dressed and went downstairs in a black cloud.

"Doesn't it's-a-secret smell incredible?" Bree said when I came back into the kitchen.

Distracted, I nodded.

Out in the great room, my dad chuckled. "I think I love it's-a-secret."

"You will," Nana Mama said. "Where's that Ali?"

"Where he's been the past four days," Jannie said with a roll of her eyes. "Up in Dad's old office in the attic with the door shut."

"He's still working on his Houdini paper?" I said. "I'll go get him."

"Let me," my dad said, coming into the kitchen. "Give me some time to bond with my grandkiddo."

Drummond disappeared. I helped Bree set the table, wondering how many more times we'd get to do this simple chore together. I opened a bottle of white wine and poured myself a generous glass.

Bree was watching me.

"One healthy one," I said.

"You deserve two healthy ones."

"Dinner's on," Nana Mama said, bringing a big iron skillet with a lid to the table. She set it on a lazy Susan. "Rice is coming. Where's that Ali, now?"

Before I could reply, she left the kitchen and went to the bottom of the stairs. "Dinner, Ali! You don't want dinner cold, you better come on down."

"Two minutes," my dad called. "He's showing me something."

My grandmother came back, muttering under her breath. She'd always been a stickler for us being at the table when she was ready to serve, and she had a sour expression on her face when she brought a big bowl of steaming jasmine rice in and sat down.

"Let's say grace," she said. "We don't have to wait."

When we were done thanking God for the meal, Nana Mama lifted the lid on the skillet. The smells that wafted up made me close my eyes and smile.

My grandmother said, "Tiger shrimp in fresh tomatoes, onions, garlic, and it's-a-secret."

"Mmm, Nana," Jannie said after taking her first bite. "What is that?"

"That's the secret," she said, smiling. "Good, isn't it, Alex?"

"Amazing," I said, but my mind was elsewhere.

"You don't sound very amazed," Nana Mama said.

I set my fork down. "It's delicious, Nana, really, but I think we all need to talk about what life will look like if I'm sent to prison."

Nana Mama's face fell. Bree grew distant. Jannie's eyes welled with tears, and she said, "I don't want to think about that, Dad. I—"

Ali came running into the kitchen. "Dad, you won't believe it!"

My grandmother said, "Now is not a good time, Ali."

My son stopped short. "But I—"

"Not now, Ali!" Jannie shouted, and she broke down in tears.

My father came in behind Ali and said to me, "You better listen to him, son."

CHAPTER

77

LOOKING WEAK BUT DETERMINED, JUDGE LARCH rapped her gavel and called the court to order at nine the next morning. Bree and my dad sat behind me. I'd been up until three a.m., had slept fitfully, and was feeling fuzzy and on edge from two cups of high-test Brazilian coffee.

Larch stared down through her thick lenses and said in a restrained voice, "Ms. Marley, have your analysts examined the videos?"

Looking chagrined, Anita said, "They agreed that they have not been tampered with digitally. The defense has no further objection to the videos."

The judge seemed disappointed. Assistant U.S. attorney Nathan Wills was stone-faced but nodding his head and jiggling his knee, probably already working on his closing arguments in his mind.

"Mr. Wills?" Larch said.

"A moment, Your Honor," the prosecutor said, then he

leaned over to his assistant, Athena Carlisle, and whispered something in her ear.

Carlisle drew back with a startled expression and shook her head emphatically. Their conversation got heated, and then Wills stood up.

He glanced at his scowling assistant and threw back his shoulders, which thrust his belly forward against his starched white shirt.

"The People rest, Your Honor."

That surprised me and it didn't. According to the witness list Wills and Carlisle had provided, there were six or seven more people slated to appear, mostly to testify about ballistics and other basic crime scene evidence. But why bother when the videos were legitimate?

"Ms. Marley," the judge said. "You're up."

Anita had evidently been half expecting the prosecution to rest as well, because without hesitation, she said, "Defense calls Kimiko Binx for cross."

Binx came forward wearing black slacks, black pumps, a black blouse with a high collar, and costume pearls. I got the distinct feeling she was more concerned about her appearance than about facing the formidable Anita Marley.

"You're still under oath, Ms. Binx," Judge Larch said.

The web designer nodded and sat down with composure and poise.

Anita said, "Ms. Binx, did you alert Claude Watkins that you were on your way the day of the shootings? Call to tell him you were coming to the factory with my client?"

"No," she said. "I don't think so."

Naomi handed Anita a plastic evidence bag. Anita took it over to Binx.

"Recognize this?" Anita said.

Binx frowned and took the bag, saw what it was. "It's a SPOT."

Anita looked to the jury. "A SPOT is a satellite personal tracker, a GPS device that tracks the wearer. Runners like Ms. Binx use them to plot their workout routes, isn't that correct?"

Binx nodded. "And in cases of emergency, you can send an SOS signal."

"There's also a button that allows you to send a prepared text to people you list on the SPOT website, correct?"

"Um, I guess."

"Actually, we looked at your account with SPOT, Ms. Binx," Anita said. "On the day of the shootings, from your apartment and twenty minutes before you arrived at the factory, you pressed that button and sent a text to Claude Watkins that read 'Game on.'"

"I don't remember that," Binx said, pushing back her hair. "And what does it matter?"

Anita smiled and said, "It shows premeditation, Ms. Binx."

CHAPTER

78

BINX'S FACE FELL, BUT SHE said, "Premeditation of what? Performance art?"

Anita did not answer. Instead, she said, "As I understand it, you were taken into custody after the shootings. Is that correct?"

"They let me go after they figured out the truth."

"But you were booked, yes? Fingerprints. Cheek swabs. Photographed for your mug shot."

"It was humiliating," the witness said coldly. "I'd done nothing wrong."

Anita returned to the defense table. Naomi handed her several thin files and a large sealed plastic bag. Anita handed one of the files to Wills and then went to the bench.

"The defense would like to introduce exhibits A, B, C, and D," she said, handing Judge Larch a file. "Exhibit A includes chain-of-evidence documentation for cheek swabs taken from Ms. Binx by DC Metro Police shortly after the shootings. Exhibit B documents the FBI's chain of evidence following cheek swabs taken two days later from my client upon his arrest. Exhibits C and D include the results of tests of those swab samples that the defense requested from the FBI lab."

"Genetic analysis?" Judge Larch said.

"Your Honor," Wills said, rising. "This is the first we've heard of any swabs or lab analysis."

"Not true," Anita said. "My assistant found reference to the swabs in the materials you sent us during discovery, Mr. Wills. And no, Your Honor, we did not do genetic analysis. We had tests done on the saliva, not the cheek cells used for DNA testing."

"I'll admit the files," Larch said.

"Your Honor," Wills said.

The judge fixed the prosecutor with a withering stare, and I realized it was well past her usual time to recess for a puff or two. Wills was swimming in very dangerous waters.

"The reports are in, Mr. Wills," Larch said. "Ms. Marley?"

Anita brought a copy over to Binx, handed it to the witness. "Can you look at page four of Dr. Cross's saliva-test results, third line of the summary?"

Carlisle and Wills were frantically turning the pages of the report. Judge Larch was already studying her copy. Binx glanced up sharply at Anita.

"Can you read it out loud, please?" my attorney said.

Binx twisted uncomfortably, looking as if a lasso had been looped over her head and cinched snug beneath her rib cage.

In a dull monotone, she read, "'Saliva tests detected the presence of methylenedioxymethamphetamine, MDMA, a hallucinatory drug also known as molly or ecstasy.'"

CHAPTER

79

ECSTASY. MOLLY.

I flashed back to that weird giddy state I was in when I entered the factory and how I'd screamed in an uncontrollable rage that I was going to kill every Soneji in sight. No wonder my emotions had been on a roller-coaster ride that entire day. No wonder I'd felt like hell for days afterward.

Anita pivoted from Binx to the jury and said, "MDMA. A euphoric, mind-altering drug. A drug that doctors say leaves the body at a fairly predictable rate based on dosage. Ms. Binx, what does line four of the summary say?"

Binx was clearly uncomfortable now but read, "'Further tests indicate dosage of one hundred and forty milligrams or more of MDMA introduced to subject forty-two to forty-eight hours prior to the gathering of samples.'"

Anita said, "One hundred and forty milligrams of ecstasy taken forty-two to forty-eight hours before the saliva samples were taken. That is a six-hour time span that, if I'm not mistaken, includes the two hours prior to the shootings when you were with Dr. Cross, Ms. Binx."

I expected Wills to object. His assistant, Athena Carlisle, obviously expected the same thing because she glanced at her boss. When she saw he wasn't moving, she stood up.

Carlisle said, "Your Honor, is Ms. Marley honestly laying the foundation for an insanity plea? Saying Dr. Cross was out of his mind at the time of the shooting because of ecstasy?"

"We are not, Your Honor," Anita said hotly. "Dr. Cross is one of the sanest people I've ever known. I'm just setting the context for what Dr. Cross did or did not see that day."

"Objection," Wills said, standing beside his assistant. "Who's testifying here, Ms. Marley or Ms. Binx?"

"Ms. Binx," Anita said, and she returned to the witness box. "Can you look to page five of the report, the results of tests done on saliva samples taken from *you* several hours after the shootings? Lines three and four?"

Binx lowered her head and then shook it. "That's not true."

"The FBI says it is indeed true," Anita said, and she looked to her own copy of the files. "Line four, quote, 'Further tests indicate a dosage of a hundred and nineteen milligrams introduced to bloodstream four to six hours prior to the gathering of sample.'"

Binx said nothing.

"Did you ingest ecstasy earlier on the day of the shootings?" Anita asked.

Binx looked around warily. "That would be illegal, wouldn't it?"

"Answer the question."

Binx hesitated for several moments before straightening up in her chair and saying, "I refuse to answer on the grounds that it may incriminate me."

That set off a hubbub in the courtroom. Larch gaveled for quiet.

Amused, Anita said, "You're invoking the Fifth Amendment for taking ecstasy?"

"I didn't say that," Binx said.

"You kind of did."

"Objection!" Carlisle cried.

"Sustained," Larch said. "The jury will ignore that."

Anita showed no reaction. "Ms. Binx, the morning of the shootings, after you came back from your run, do you remember tripping in your apartment and Dr. Cross catching you before you could fall?"

She hesitated, frowned. "No."

"Yes, you tripped over an electrical cord. When Dr. Cross caught you, you put a piece of clear adhesive tape on the underside of his forearm, didn't you?"

"Objection," Wills said wearily. "Where is the foundation for this?"

Anita said, "Your Honor, Dr. Cross and his wife, DC chief of detectives Bree Stone, will testify that they found a piece of tape on the underside of Dr. Cross's right forearm in the hours after the shootings. We believe that the ecstasy was on that tape in a gel or powdered form and that it was absorbed into Dr. Cross's bloodstream transdermally, through the skin."

"Where is this tainted tape?" the prosecutor said. "Render the body, Counselor."

Anita ignored him, said to the judge, "Neither Dr. Cross nor Chief Stone thought much of it at the time, and they threw the tape out at GW Medical Center."

Wills shook his head even more wearily. "Move to strike

everything Ms. Marley has said about this phantom piece of tape, Your Honor."

"So moved," Larch said.

"Your Honor—" Anita started.

"No tape, no talk about tape," the judge said sharply.

Anita sighed, said, "Ms. Binx, did you dose Dr. Cross with ecstasy?"

Binx blinked, chewed on her lip, glanced at Wills, and then said again, "I refuse to answer on the grounds that it may incriminate me."

WHEN JUDGE LARCH CALLED FOR lunch recess and left the courtroom slowly, the prosecutors weren't looking quite as confident as they had earlier.

Anita had asked Binx several more questions about the ecstasy, including how it was that she had been given the perfect dose of MDMA for her weight and how it was that I was given the perfect dose for mine.

Binx had replied to every question about the drug by taking the Fifth.

"Tripping on ecstasy doesn't get your client off," Wills said to Anita as she packed away some files.

"No?" she said. "Fortunately, a jury gets to make that decision."

"No tainted tape, no causality. Even you can see that."

Anita gave him a blank expression. "Save it for your close."

Athena Carlisle said, "Given the videos, are you open to talking plea bargain? Dr. Cross might get out in time to meet his great-grandkids."

Anita glanced at me. I shook my head.

Carlisle puffed her cheeks, then blew out air. "We tried."

"Suit yourself," Wills said, and he chuckled as he left. "But I hear it's hell for an ex-cop in prison."

Naomi, Bree, my dad, and I ate takeout pulled-pork sandwiches in a conference room. Even though Anita had scored big points with her cross-examination, we were a somber, focused bunch.

For the first time in a week I felt jurors five and eleven leaning a bit my way, or at least developing some skepticism regarding the prosecution's case. But Wills had been right. The ecstasy might be a mitigating factor, but it wouldn't be enough to acquit me of two murders and an attempted murder.

We were back in court with two minutes to spare. Anita was already there.

"We good?" I asked.

She leaned over to me, murmured, "Pray for a knockout."

"And David slew Goliath," I said before the bailiff called, "All rise."

Judge Larch looked considerably less agitated when she retook the bench and called the court to order.

"Ms. Marley," Larch said, "do you wish to cross-examine Mr. Watkins now, or does the defense have its own witnesses in mind?"

"Defense witness, Your Honor," Anita said. "We call Ali Cross to the stand."

I twisted in my seat in time to see Ali enter the courtroom holding my dad's hand with Jannie and Nana Mama behind them. My boy was in his Sunday best: gray pants, an ironed white shirt, and a paisley bow tie. Juror eleven smiled seeing him.

At the bar, Nana Mama whispered something in her great-grandson's ear, and he nodded. Ali did not look at me or Anita before pushing open the gate and walking confidently to the witness stand.

Wills said, "Your Honor, the defense gave us no notice of this witness."

"Ali is Dr. Cross's son, Your Honor," Anita said.

Judge Larch looked skeptical. "And he has business before this court?"

"Yes, Your Honor, he has a few things to say."

The judge peered over at Ali, who was standing in the witness box now.

"How old are you, Ali?"

"Nine, but I'm in fifth grade already."

"Where do you go to school?"

"Washington Latin."

Larch smiled. "Good for you. Swear him in."

Afterward, the bailiff had to get pads for the witness chair so Ali could sit higher and be seen easier by the jury.

Once he'd settled in, Anita said, "Ali, do you normally do what your father tells you to do? By that I mean, when he gives you a direct order, do you obey it?"

"Yes, ma'am. I try."

"But you defied one of his direct orders recently, didn't you?"

"Yes, ma'am, I did."

"Objection," Wills said. "Your Honor, where is the relevance of this?"

Anita looked at him, said, "The Court is about to find out."

"Get to it, Ms. Marley," Larch said.

"What did you do that your father didn't want you to do?" Anita said.

Ali said, "My dad told me not to look at the videos of the shootings in that factory, but I secretly looked at them on YouTube."

"Once?"

"No, like a hundred and seventy times."

That provoked some nervous laughter, and I could tell juror five, the retired engineer with the hunched back, did not like the idea of a nine-year-old boy looking at those videos even once, let alone one hundred and seventy times.

"Why did you watch it so many times?" Anita said.

"To figure out where the guns went so Dad wouldn't go to prison."

Anita glanced over at Wills and then at the jury. "Did you figure out where the guns went?"

"I think so."

"Objection," Athena Carlisle said. "Your Honor, we've been through this. Real experts have looked at the videos and found nothing wrong with them. We're expected to believe a nine-year-old discovered something that they didn't?"

"Ms. Marley?" Judge Larch said.

"Let the boy speak, Your Honor," Anita said in a reasonable tone. "Echoing what you said when you allowed the videos to be introduced, the prosecution is free to rebut if Ali is wrong."

The judge adjusted her glasses and then looked over at Ali. "Did you really figure it out?"

"I think so," he said.

"Let's hear it."

Naomi put the videos up on the screen and gave Ali a remote control. Stopping the three videos in strategic places in much the same way the prosecution had made its case against me, Ali was able to show the jury how the lighting changed in the videos, how it grew slightly dimmer before each victim appeared and then brightened considerably just before I shot.

"What do you think is happening there with the lighting?" Anita said.

Ali said, "Whoever was controlling the spotlights dimmed them just before Mrs. Winslow, Mr. Watkins, and Mr. Diggs stepped into view. It's hard to see them in that weaker light, but they're there, and then the spotlights are boosted and you see the empty hands just as my father shoots."

"Okay," Anita said. "So what?"

"That's what I kept thinking," Ali said. "So what?"

"Until?"

"Oh, until I read the autopsy reports."

81

JUDGE LARCH WHIRLED HER CHAIR around and glared at me through those Coke-bottle lenses.

"You let a nine-year-old read autopsy reports, Dr. Cross?"

"I wasn't supposed to, Judge," Ali said, twisting in his chair to address her. "But I did it anyway."

Larch looked away from me, squinted at my boy, and said, "You on the road to criminality, son?"

Ali smiled nervously. "No, ma'am. Uh, Your Honor."

"No, I know you're not," Larch said, softer, and her expression eased toward amused resignation. "Go ahead."

Ali testified that he'd defied Bree and me and dug out the autopsy reports on Virginia Winslow and Leonard Diggs, looking for something odd about the gun hands of the three victims.

"Did you find something odd?" Anita asked.

"Yes," Ali said.

"Gunpowder residue?"

He shook his head. "They had sticky stuff on their palms."

"Adhesive glue?"

"Yes, like from tape. And there was also, like, some silicone."

"Is there an explanation for the glue or silicone in the report?"

"No."

"Can you explain why it was there?"

My son sat up straighter. "I think I can explain why, but not exactly how. That's like physics, and I haven't studied that yet. Maybe next year."

The jury members started laughing. Anita smiled, letting the moment last, then said, "Why was the glue and silicone there?"

"Well, if you think about it, because of this," he said, running the videos back and stopping them. "See the three spotlights in the middle feed? And to the right at the bottom of the right spotlight there's a pinpoint blue light? That's where I almost had it figured out. But like I said, the rest is physics that I don't get."

Anita smiled. "Thank you, Ali. Your Honor, if it please the Court, I'd like to call a second witness who can explain more clearly than Ali can what the pinpoint blue light, the glue, the silicone, and the dimming and brightening mean. Mr. Wills can cross-examine them both afterwards."

"Any objection, Mr. Wills?"

Wills and Carlisle conferred. Wills looked irritated when he turned from his assistant and said, "Be my guest, Counselor. Take us on a wild-goose chase."

"The defense calls Keith Karl Rawlins," Anita said.

Krazy Kat came in wearing a fine blue Italian suit, black loafers buffed to a high shine, and a coral-pink shirt open at the collar. His Mohawk was down, dyed black, slicked over to the left side of his head, and tucked behind his ear.

As he walked past Ali, who was leaving the stand, Rawlins nodded and winked at him. Wills and Carlisle acted like someone had brought a jester into court, but they didn't know what to do about it yet.

After he was sworn in, Anita said, "Dr. Rawlins, can you describe your academic training and current position?"

Rawlins said, "I have dual PhDs from Stanford, one in physics, the other in electrical engineering. I'm working on my doctorate in computer science at MIT, and I am currently employed as an independent contractor by the Cyber Division of the Federal Bureau of Investigation."

Wills and Carlisle jumped to their feet.

"Objection," Wills said. "No one at the Bureau informed the prosecution this witness was testifying."

Carlisle said, "Your Honor, agents are required to notify the U.S. Attorney's Office that—"

"I am not a special agent, and I'm not even an employee," Rawlins said. "As such, I am not obligated to notify the FBI or the U.S. Attorney's Office. I came at the request of a very bright young man who sought me out at my home during my free time and presented his rather brilliant theory of the videos. I do not speak for the government, only for myself, as a citizen compelled to tell the truth."

"Your Honor, we still object to—"

"Asked and answered, Mr. Wills," Judge Larch said.

Both prosecutors looked like they'd swallowed worms, but they sat.

Anita said, "What kind of work do you do for the FBI, Dr. Rawlins?"

"It's classified, so I can't give you specifics. But you could say I help the Bureau on the techno side of things."

"Physics involved?"

"Sometimes."

"Is physics involved here—with the video, I mean?"

"Yes," he said. "Basic physics. Wave theory."

82

ANITA GLANCED AT THE JURY. A few, including juror five, were attentive. The eyes of the rest, including juror eleven's, the PR executive, appeared glazed over by this turn in the trial. Physics? Wave theory?

But Anita had foreseen this response. She looked to Naomi and nodded.

As my niece got up and left the courtroom, my attorney said, "Dr. Rawlins, let's keep it very basic, shall we?"

Rawlins shrugged and looked to the jury. "All you really need to know is that light travels in waves, just like in the ocean. When the waves from different light sources collide, they're both changed, just like waves on the ocean coming from different directions and crashing into one another."

Naomi came back into the courtroom pushing a cart loaded with several cardboard boxes and a small spotlight.

"Keep that in mind," Rawlins said, getting up from the witness stand. "Waves colliding on the ocean. With the Court's permission?"

"Granted," Larch said. "I always liked show-and-tell."

"I was a big fan too," Rawlins said.

He went to Naomi, took the spotlight, and set it up on a tri-pod.

"Judge, can I use an assistant?" Rawlins said.

Larch waved her hand, and the FBI contractor called Ali from the audience.

Rawlins got a manila envelope from the cart, drew out something he kept hidden, and put it in Ali's palm. When my son opened his hand, you had to look closely to see what seemed to be one of those protective films people put on cell phone screens. Thin, translucent, and rectangular, it was af-fixed to Ali's palm and went up to the first joints of his fingers.

"What is that, exactly?" Judge Larch asked, peering over the bench.

"A piece of medium," Rawlins said. "A polymer that includes silicone. On the medium itself, there is an encoding of a light field captured in the form of an interference pattern. Remem-ber the waves crashing? If you can imagine looking down at the sea crashing around rocks and then taking a three-dimen-sional picture of it and freezing that moment, you're on the right track."

"Okay?" Judge Larch said.

Rawlins had Ali stand with his left shoulder to the bench, facing the jury box. Then he positioned the spotlight at an an-gle to Ali.

Anita said, "Can we have the courtroom lights dimmed?"

Larch nodded, and the bailiff dimmed the lights until Raw-lins, who was holding a small light meter in his hand, said, "Stop."

You could still see Rawlins and Ali and everyone else in

the windowless courtroom, but it was like looking at them in a grainy photograph. Then Naomi hit a switch. The spotlight beam found Ali, who put on sunglasses.

Every one of the jurors was sitting forward, watching intently. Juror five rested his chin on his hands, which were folded on the curve of his cane handle.

Rawlins said, "The coding on the medium, that snapshot of light waves crashing, is done with lasers, tiny intense light beams that are of a specific high-wave frequency."

He came over in front of the jury, brushed back his strip of lank black hair, and said, "The interesting thing about this three-dimensional coding is that we can see the snapshot of the waves crashing around the rock only if it's lit by lasers tuned to the same exact wave frequency as the ones used to encode the image in the first place."

"That went right over my head," Judge Larch said.

"It's one of those things better seen anyway," Anita said.

She moved in front of the bench and faced Ali's left side. Rawlins stood over by the bailiff's desk facing Ali's left side at a forty-five-degree angle.

Naomi killed the spotlight. We were all cast back into that dim, grainy vision of the courtroom. Three hair-thin, gray-blue laser beams flipped on, one held by Anita, one by Rawlins, and the last by Naomi. The beams were easy to see at their sources, but the farther the streams got from the lasers, the harder it was to make out the beam as it passed through the gloom.

But not so the dull blue dots at the end of each laser beam. The three dots danced over Ali's side and arm before finding his outstretched palm.

"Get it bull's-eye, now," Rawlins said. "Exact spot."

The blue dots quivered and squiggled to a meeting dead center of the encoded medium affixed to Ali's empty hand.

Gasps went up in the courtroom.

"Son of a bitch!" Wills said, standing in disbelief.

Even I couldn't believe it. But there it was.

My nine-year-old son's hand looked like it was wrapped around the pale blue holographic image of a nickel-plated .357 Colt Python revolver.

83

NAOMI SWITCHED ON THE SPOTLIGHT. The gun vanished from Ali's hand. He was grinning wildly.

Rawlins said, "The gun disappeared because the waves of the spotlight came crashing down and drowned the waves of the laser beam so they could no longer reach the code in Ali's hand."

Naomi killed the spotlight. The hologram of the gun reappeared in Ali's hand, provoking another round of murmurs, and many in the jury box shook their heads in wonder. Even juror five seemed impressed.

Rawlins then showed the court what the hologram looked like through a video camera set to black-and-white and adjusted to take in a specific amount of light. In the dimmed courtroom, you could see the hologram of the pistol clearly, but through the camera lens and on the screen, there was only a gray wash in Ali's palm. The spotlight beam came on, and even the gray wash was gone from the image on the courtroom screen.

"Your Honor," Anita said.

"One second, Counselor," Judge Larch said. She stood up behind the bench and gazed down at Ali. "How did you figure this out, young man?"

Ali took off the sunglasses and said, "Um, when I couldn't see anything from just looking at the videos, I figured I had to think about it in another way."

Ali explained that he'd stopped watching the videos and started thinking how a gun could be there and yet not be there. He thought for almost a day before he remembered the holograms he'd seen on some of the rides in Disney World, and he started reading about holograms on the Internet.

"There was stuff about the photographic medium being clear and silicone-based, and the wave frequency of the lasers being the key. And I remembered the glue and silicone on the victims' hands from the autopsy report and thought maybe the glue could have been to hold the film in place. But Dr. Rawlins figured it all out for real."

"Just the details, no more," Rawlins said with a bow toward Ali. "The kid had it nailed before he rang my bell."

"Where did the film go?" Larch said.

Ali said, "I think after the shootings, after my dad went out to call for backup, someone stripped the holographic film from the victims' hands and left with the cameraman who shot the video."

"Objection," Wills said. "This entire exercise is a clever and, I must admit, very creative stunt, but there's nothing here that's concrete. No holographic film has been introduced into evidence, so no testimony about holographic film should be allowed. Move to strike this entire line of questioning."

"There's evidence," Ali said hotly. "That tiny blue light I

showed you. Someone had the laser on by mistake for four point seven seconds. And the silicone? And the glue? Were you even listening?"

Wills shot my son a contemptuous glance but didn't answer.

Anita said, "Your Honor, the defense has given a plausible explanation for the apparent absence of the guns in the videos and for the glue residue and silicone found on the victims' palms. Let the jury decide."

For several long moments, the judge showed no reaction and made no response. She studied the top of the bench so long, I figured she was having some kind of fit. At last she said, "Overruled, Mr. Wills."

"Judge Larch—"

"I said overruled, Mr. Wills. We'll let the ladies and gentlemen of the jury decide which explanation they believe. Ms. Marley?"

"Move to dismiss."

"Denied."

"Move to suppress the testimony of Kimiko Binx and Claude Watkins."

"Denied."

Anita called Watkins back to the stand for his cross-examination, and he steadfastly maintained he'd had no holographic film on his hands at any time in his entire life.

"And yet glue and silicone were found on your hands after you were shot."

Watkins snorted. "I'm a sculptor, and who knows what was on that factory floor to begin with."

"But you wanted your encounter with Dr. Cross to be recorded. Were you trying to provoke him into shooting with the holograms?"

"I repeat, no holograms," Watkins said firmly. "And, sure, I wanted to film him. I wanted to see how he'd handle himself, whether he'd revert to the mean of police behavior and go violent. But no one expected to get shot. Least of all me."

"Do you hate Dr. Cross?"

"I hate the violence he stands for."

"Enough to frame him?"

"Not enough to take a bullet in the guts and through the spine," Watkins said. "That's a fact. No one would wish this on themselves no matter how much they hated someone."

"No further questions," Anita said.

When Watkins had wheeled through the gate, Judge Larch said, "Ms. Marley?"

Anita glanced at me. I nodded.

She said, "The defense rests, Your Honor."

CHAPTER

84

ANY COURT BUFF WILL TELL you that a quick verdict favors the prosecution. So after the jury heard closing arguments, received instructions, and were sequestered for deliberations, we treated every minute without word as a minor miracle. Hours passed. Then a day.

I tried not to think about the verdict but found that impossible. My case had dominated local news and was featured on national and cable news coverage. The talking heads babbled about Ali's holographic demonstration, the presence of ecstasy in my blood the day of the shootings, and whether together they were enough to create reasonable doubt in the jurors' minds.

A few were confident it would. But more sided with the prosecution, noting as Wills had in his closing argument that for the hologram theory to be true, the three victims had to have knowingly put themselves in harm's way in order to frame me. He'd argued that it ran counter to self-preservation, pointed at Claude Watkins in his wheelchair, and asked if anyone could believe he'd risk paralysis to see me in prison. Other commentators continued to hammer the fact that I'd been at the center of nine other officer-involved shootings in the course of my career, and they championed the idea that I should go to jail to set an example for police conduct across the nation.

At noon on Friday, I couldn't take it anymore. I snuck out of the house and down the alley with my laptop. Sampson picked me up on Pennsylvania Avenue and we went to Quantico. Special Agent Batra met us at the gate, and before long we were in Rawlins's underground lab.

"I don't know if we are bugged or not," Rawlins said, taking my computer. "Based on the fact we both uploaded the contents of that flash drive from the man posing as Alden Lindel, I've been digging in our system, but I haven't come up with anything definitive yet."

"This is a smaller universe," I said.

Rawlins winked. "I see that."

He'd kept his Mohawk down and black, but he'd added dark eye shadow, which made him look somewhat demonic as he plugged my laptop into a closed network. Rawlins ran a number of tests and still didn't find anything. He decided to search uploads my computer had made recently over Wi-Fi or Bluetooth.

"There you are, you bugger," he said, highlighting a file with a nonsense name and extension.

The date stamp said the upload from my laptop had taken place from 4:33 p.m. to 5:29 p.m. the prior Monday.

I thought about that and realized the time frame coincided with my hour with Annie Cassidy. The beginning and the end of the session, when she'd been fooling around with her smartphone.

"That file was probably sent to her phone," I said. "She must have been downloading it the entire time I was in session with her."

"What's in the file?" Batra said.

Rawlins clicked on the file, and it was quickly apparent that it contained a record of everything done on my computer for the previous fourteen days.

"Spying on us, the little roaches," Rawlins said.

He analyzed the file further and discovered that it had been generated after an order from a piece of "elegant and ingeniously coded" malware Krazy Kat found buried deep inside my operating system and made to look like innocuous support code.

Once he had the malware identified, Rawlins searched for it on the FBI system and was shocked to find a copy sitting dormant on his own server.

"This is impressive," he said, rubbing his chin. "I actively monitor for intrusions, and I never saw this. A deep, deep, deep Trojan horse, created by a master coder."

"Can you figure out the coder's identity?" I asked.

"I might. Give me that flash drive you got in the mail. We'll launch it, see what happens."

Before he did, Rawlins wrote tracking code designed to attach itself to any file the malware created. Then he plugged the drive into his server and launched it.

The mock firing-squad execution of Gretchen Lindel played, followed by the warning to me that the next time all the blondes would die. There was a screen flash before the video closed, just as there'd been when I uploaded it.

Rawlins stood there, drumming his fingers on his workstation, head swiveling as he studied the array of screens around him.

"C'mon," he said. "Something happened there. Where are you?"

My cell phone buzzed. I took it out, saw Naomi was calling. I answered. "Any news?"

My niece's voice was strained. "The jury has contacted Larch."

I closed my eyes, thinking, *Hung jury,* wondering whether my family could take another trial.

But then Naomi said, "They've reached a verdict, Uncle Alex. You need to come to the courthouse."

CHAPTER

85

I TIGHTENED THE KNOT ON my tie in the car as Sampson turned the corner toward the courthouse. From two blocks away, we could see the media mob waiting, anxious, no doubt, because it was pushing four that Friday afternoon and they were right up against deadline for the East Coast evening news broadcasts.

"The offer's still there to go in through the prisoner-transfer door," Sampson said. "Chief okayed it."

"No," I said. "I want them to see me."

I glanced over and saw Sampson rubbing at the scar on his forehead.

"You okay?"

"I will be when I take my meds," he said, pulling up across the street from the courthouse and putting his hand on my forearm. "We'll all be right behind you, no matter what happens."

But instead of being encouraged by his support, I climbed from the squad car with my mind reeling through all the counterattacks the assistant U.S. attorneys had made in their closing arguments, especially at our theory of the holographic gun images.

The glue could have come from their makeup, they said. The silicone came from something they'd all touched, probably the masks they wore or, as Watkins had suggested, the grime on the old factory floor. Wills had also hammered home how absurd it was to believe that two people would willingly die and another would willingly be wounded and crippled in order to frame me.

"Alex!"

Anita and Naomi were climbing out of a cab behind us.

"Let's be as disciplined as we were on day one," Anita said. "No one talks on the way into court."

As we'd done the first day of the trial, we walked together toward the crush of cameras and klieg lights that flared and trained on us. The reporters' shouting canceled out the protesters' shouting, so all I really heard as we pushed on through the mob was a garbled roar of desperation and hatred.

Reaching the courthouse was a relief, but I felt distant going through security. I tried to focus on the officers wishing me luck, but I was thinking that my life as I knew it might be over in a matter of minutes and I'd be condemned to an eight-by-twelve, a target for every con who had it in for a cop.

My phone buzzed, alerting me to a text from Bree: ETA five minutes! Love you! Believe in you!

But on the way up the elevator and walking toward Judge Larch's courtroom, I felt hollow, separate, and alone.

Nana Mama was already there in the front row with Ali, Jannie, and my dad. I ignored everyone else gathered in the court and went to them. My grandmother took my hand and squeezed it.

There was so much fear and anxiety in my children's faces that I had to fight to smile and say, "Be strong, now."

"You too," my father said. "We've been praying."

I went to the defense table as nervous as I'd ever been in my entire life. I glanced past Anita and saw the prosecutor Nathan Wills fiddling with his phone. His assistant was looking down, studying a document.

Behind them sat Soneji's son, Dylan Winslow, who had a smirk on his face. Kimiko Binx was perched beside him, dressed in black and shooting me dark glances. Claude Watkins was rolling his wheelchair down the aisle.

Before he parked beside Binx, he looked at me with open loathing, and in a voice loud enough for the reporters and other spectators to hear, he said, "You're not getting away with this, Cross. If there's any justice left in the world, you're going down for a long time."

Anita put her hand on mine. I didn't need it. I wouldn't give Watkins the satisfaction of reacting or replying.

"All rise," the bailiff said. "Judge Priscilla Larch presiding."

The judge looked better, far less pale than she'd been at closing arguments. Larch was wearing a new pair of glasses too, ones that made her seem less, well, birdy. She banged her gavel, called the court to order, and asked the bailiff to bring in the jury.

In the course of my career, I've sat in the cheap seats watching juries come back with verdicts at least fifty times. In every case, I've searched the faces of the jury members for clues to their decision, but I have been surprised by the outcome almost as often as I've been right in my predictions.

Juror five hobbled in. He looked tired and grim, as did several other jurors who filled the seats around him. The remaining members of the panel appeared upset but resigned to the verdict.

Juror eleven, the PR executive, had been voted foreperson. She came in last, wearing a sharp blue suit with a pink blouse. She gave me a glance as she climbed into her seat in the jury box, swallowed hard, and looked away with such uncertainty that I was shaken inside.

"Madam Foreperson, have you reached a verdict?" Larch said.

Juror eleven stood. "We have, Your Honor."

The judge accepted a copy of the verdict from the bailiff, opened it, and showed no reaction before saying, "Dr. Cross, please rise."

As Anita, Naomi, and I got to our feet, I heard the courtroom doors open behind me. I glanced back and saw Bree and Damon rush to seats beside Sampson and his wife, Billie.

Everything felt surreal as I heard Larch say, "On count one, in the death of Virginia Winslow, murder in the first degree, how do you find?"

CHAPTER

86

JUROR ELEVEN WOULD NOT LOOK at me. No one in the jury would look at me.

"We find the defendant, Alex Cross," she said as she finally turned her hard gaze my way, "not guilty."

There were gasps, cheers, and a war whoop behind me. My knees went rubbery, and I almost started to cry when Nana Mama said, "I knew it!"

Naomi grabbed my left arm, Anita my right.

"What?" Dylan Winslow yelled angrily, jumping to his feet. "He shot my mom in cold blood!"

"Not guilty!" Ali shouted at him, standing up. "Not guilty!"

Judge Larch pounded her gavel and then shook it at Ali and Soneji's kid. "One more outburst out of either of you, and you'll be banned from my court. Clear?"

Dylan was fuming and red-faced, but he slammed his butt back down on the bench beside Binx. Ali grinned with satisfaction and sat more slowly.

Turning back to the jury, Judge Larch said, "On count two, in the death of Leonard Diggs, the charge is murder in the first degree. How do you find?"

"We find the defendant not guilty, Your Honor."

"This is bullshit!" Binx shouted. "I saw it with my own two eyes!"

"One more word and it'll be contempt of court, Ms. Binx," Larch said, standing and glaring at her.

Binx shook her head in a rage, but she said nothing else.

"On count three of the indictment," the judge said, "attempted murder of Claude Watkins, how do you find?"

"There was reasonable doubt. Not guilty, Your Honor."

The courtroom erupted. I let out my breath long and slow and hung my head in deep gratitude, thanking God for my deliverance, before spinning around and reaching across the bar to kiss Bree, who was grinning through tears.

"Welcome back from the edge, baby," she said.

"This is a travesty of justice!" Claude Watkins shouted. "I've got a piss bag and he's frickin' not guilty? He guns down three and he's not guilty?"

Larch banged her gavel, said, "That's enough, Mr. Watkins."

"I reject this!" Watkins roared, and he spun his wheelchair around and headed out. "I do not recognize this jury or this court!"

"Neither do I!" shouted Binx, and she stormed after him.

The judge called to the officer at the door to the hallway, "Fuller, arrest them both. I want them held on suspicion of conspiracy, murder, and perjury."

Binx whirled around and shouted, "You can't be serious! This is insanity!"

"It's government persecution, that's what it is," Watkins said.

"They cooked up that whole pack of lies to bury us. It's what the police state does! Shoots you down, then makes up a god-damn excuse for shooting you down!"

As Binx struggled against the zip cuffs around her wrists and a second officer restrained Watkins in his wheelchair, my gaze snagged on Soneji's son. Dylan Winslow was on his feet, looking back at Binx and Watkins as they were taken from the courtroom. The fingers of the troubled teen's left hand trembled as he tried to grip the bench in front of him.

He was part of it, I thought. *He's got something to hide.*

The prosecutor was on his feet and furious as well.

"Your Honor," Wills said. "The verdict is the verdict, but I echo Ms. Binx and Mr. Watkins. This *is* a travesty of justice, one you can undo by vacating this verdict and demanding a re-trial."

"What? And undo double jeopardy?" Anita cried. "On what constitutional grounds, Counselor?"

Larch held up her hand to stop further argument. Then she tugged her glasses down the bridge of her nose and gave the prosecutor a withering stare.

"Mr. Wills," she said. "As far as the Court is concerned, this entire trial has been a travesty of justice. Because of the naked ambitions of yourself and Ms. Carlisle, as well as the government's need for a scapegoat for the country's rash of police-involved shootings, the two of you and your bosses not only bought into a sophisticated framing of the defendant, but fully participated in a rush to justice. I anticipate someone in-vestigating both of you very soon."

For once, the federal prosecutors were speechless.

"Dr. Cross?" Larch said.

"Your Honor."

"I am sorry this happened to you."

"Thank you, Judge Larch. I am too."

"Go and enjoy your freedom. Take care of that son of yours." She banged her gavel. "The jury is released. Case closed."

I threw my hands up and whirled around to see Bree, Jannie, Damon, Nana Mama, and my dad cheering behind me.

Tears welled in my eyes as I kissed Anita and Naomi. Then I went around, picked up Ali, and hugged my boy like he was life itself.

CHAPTER

87

TO BE HONEST, DESPITE THE verdict, I was feeling mixed emotions sitting in a chair outside Chief Michaels's office the following Monday.

My arrest, the trial, and even the verdict had forced me to do a lot of reevaluating about my priorities and my purpose in life.

I had always seen homicide investigation as a way to represent the slain and help the friends and family of the victims find not only closure, but justice. I think of it as an honorable profession, one that, until I was arrested, gave me a great degree of fulfillment.

But turning back to clinical psychology and counseling, my first loves, had reminded me why I enjoyed that work so much. Ultimately, my job was to help people trying to understand and improve themselves and their lives. Being a psychotherapist was as noble a calling as being a homicide detective, and fulfilling in an entirely different way. And yet here I was, ready to put an end to the counselor part of me again.

"Dr. Cross?" Michaels's secretary said. "He'll see you now."

I went into the chief's office. Crossing the room to his desk, I watched Metro's leader closely, trying to read his body language. The chief had played it political during the months I'd spent on suspension pending trial. In private, he'd expressed support. In public, he'd covered his ass.

So it was a bittersweet experience when Michaels summoned his politician's smile, reached out his hand, and said, "I knew you'd be back, Alex. What would Metro do without you?"

I swallowed whatever uncomfortable feelings I'd had and thanked him for reinstating me on the Major Case Unit. In the squad room, Bree ended Sampson's suffering by reassigning Detective Ainsley Fox to another partner and putting the two of us back together. That was good, really good, maybe even better than the verdict. No bittersweet feelings at all.

I spent the rest of that first day filling out forms that sought back pay in light of the verdict and doing a pile of other administrative nonsense. But on Tuesday, Sampson and I were back on the job, with the missing blondes the first order of business. We started early, leaving DC long before dawn and driving north.

Four and a half hours later, we left Interstate 180 for State Route 220 toward Muncy Valley, Sonestown, and Laporte, Pennsylvania. It was timber country. The road was narrow, winding, and flanked on both sides by state game lands and big leafless forest tracts.

We got coffee in Laporte before stopping in at the Sullivan County Sheriff's Office to talk with Detective Everett Morse, who was working with the Pennsylvania State Police on the murder of twelve-year-old Timmy Walker Jr. and the disappearance of Ginny Krauss and Alison Dane.

Morse was collegial enough and showed us the murder book, but it had been months since Ginny and Alison had disappeared and Timmy's body had been found. The trail had gone cold. Morse told us not to bother trying to talk to the girls' parents. They'd barely spoken with Morse or the state police.

When we stopped at the Pennsylvania State Police barracks on the north side of Laporte, Investigator Nina Ford largely confirmed Morse's take on the case. She allowed us to look through her files as well, and, like Morse, discouraged us from trying to talk to the missing girls' parents.

"What about Timmy's parents?" Sampson asked.

"Big T's out of the picture," Detective Ford said. "Lenore's at the house. You could stop at Worlds End State Park, where Timmy's body was found. By the time you have a look around and get to Hillsgrove, Lenore should be up and almost coherent."

From GPS coordinates Ford gave us, we were able to pinpoint the exact location where Timmy Walker's corpse had been discovered—roughly a mile east of the parking lot at Worlds End State Park and several miles from where the missing girls' car was found.

But for an older model white Chevy pickup truck with a toolbox in the back and decals on the window from the National Wild Turkey Federation, the park's lot was deserted when we pulled in twenty minutes later.

A cold, raw wind blew while we hiked the trail and followed the GPS navigator to the rugged ground where a hiker had come across Timmy's arm sticking out from under a pile of branches and leaves.

"That's a workout, getting up here," Sampson said, chest heaving. "Trail was steep."

I nodded, my heart still hammering. "Timmy weighed ninety-two pounds, so it was someone very strong."

"And someone who knew how to get to this particular stretch of nowhere," Sampson said about two seconds before the shooting started.

CHAPTER

88

BOOM! CA-CHING. BOOM!

Sampson and I whipped around and dived for cover behind a downed log.

Boom!

"Where the hell is he?" Sampson hissed.

Hearing popping noises, clucking, and branches snapping, I peeked up over the log and saw a flock of wild turkeys racing through the woods. Up the hill, I spotted movement. I grabbed my binoculars, focused them, and saw a teenage girl in camouflage scrambling down the steep hillside, a man carrying two shotguns right behind her.

"I got him, Dad!" I heard her yell and she threw her hands up in the air. "We both did!"

We stood and waved at the hunters as they got busy with the two dead turkeys. It wasn't until we were close that they noticed us.

The father stood, glanced at the shotguns propped up

against a tree. I guess it wasn't often he saw two men wearing coats and ties in the turkey woods.

We both showed our badges. He got stiffer. "This was a clean hunt."

"I'll take your word for it," I said. "We're here looking into the death of Timmy Walker."

He softened. "That's a tragedy. My Ellie here went to school with him. I'm Howard Young, by the way."

"Nice to meet you, Mr. Young," I said. I shook his hand and then looked at his daughter. "Tell us about Timmy."

Ellie played with a camouflage scarf around her neck and her expression soured. "TW-Two was nice growing up, but then he kind of became a creep."

"More like a little pervert," her father said.

"How's that?" Sampson said.

Ellie looked around and then said, "I don't know if it's true, but he supposedly put a hole in the wall at school so he could look into the girls' locker room. The rumor was he took pictures and showed them to his friends."

Sampson grimaced.

I said, "Was that investigated?"

"The principal said so," Ellie said. "The school even had police look at Timmy's phone, but there was nothing on it."

Her father said, "Doesn't mean there wasn't another phone or a camera. I wanted that boy thrown out of school, but they didn't do a thing. And then he died, so we'll never know, will we?"

"We're hoping to help figure out why he died," Sampson said.

Young nodded uncertainly. "Well, we've got birds to clean, and Ellie's got classes this afternoon."

We thanked them for their time and hiked back down the steep hillside to the parking lot. Had Timmy been killed for taking pictures he shouldn't have? Had the killer brought Timmy up that trail in the dark? His mother had reported him missing well after sunset, so there was a good chance. That meant the killer had a headlamp or a helper. Did that matter?

I set that thinking aside and went back to the iPad, looking at an aerial view of the area with pins that marked the locations of the girls' abandoned car, Timmy's botched burial site, and his home. The car and the house looked about a mile apart, but the killer had dumped his body miles away.

Why? To try to separate the two cases in the minds of police?

I supposed that was likely, though any detective worth his or her salt would have known the two cases were related. Same day. Same general time frame. The proximity of Timmy's home to where the girls' car was found.

So what happened? Did Timmy see the kidnapping, blunder into it somehow, and get killed for it?

That was our working theory when we pulled into the driveway of Timmy Walker's house, a restored Colonial with fresh paint and a new, seamless metal roof. It was by far the nicest home in this small mountain hamlet where most of the structures looked like hunting camps. Brown leaves covered the modest front yard. A tricycle lay tipped over by the birdbath.

Sampson knocked on the door. No answer.

He knocked harder, and the door opened. A young girl, six or maybe seven, stood there in food-stained pajamas. She had a Winnie-the-Pooh blanket around her shoulders and studied us with red eyes.

"Hi there, young lady," I said. "We're police officers. We'd like to talk to your mom."

"She's sleeping," the girl said.

"Can you wake—"

"I'm up!" a woman said, pounding down the stairs.

Mom was in a blue terry-cloth robe and barefoot. Her hair was a mess. Her eyes were puffy, rheumy, and wild when she said, "You get him? Timmy's killer?"

"Mrs. Walker?" I said.

She came up behind the girl, hugged her. "I'm his mom, Lenore. This is his sister, Kate."

We identified ourselves, said we'd like to talk to her.

"So you didn't get him?" she asked, bewildered.

"Not yet, ma'am."

The dead boy's mom swallowed thickly and looked off in despair. "No one tells me what's going on. Months Deuce has been gone and no word from anyone in weeks, not the sheriff, not the state police, not the FBI...not even my coward of an ex-husband." She broke down weeping.

Her daughter scowled at us and then turned around to hug her mother.

"It's okay, Mommy," the little girl said. "It's going to be okay."

89

WHEN WE GOT LENORE WALKER calmed down enough to talk, she invited us in, and we learned that she had, by her own description, led a fairly charmed life until the night Timmy disappeared. She'd grown up in the suburbs of Philadelphia and met Tim Walker her junior year at Pennsylvania State.

Walker got a good job working as an oil engineer right out of school and made enough in the fracking industry that they bought the house, restored it, and had kids. Timmy—Deuce—was his father's favorite, and they spent many hours together early in the boy's life.

Then Walker started moving up the corporate ladder and was gone a lot. And then he discovered "playthings," as Lenore put it, and he was gone a lot more. After Deuce died, her husband, heartbroken and in love with a twenty-four-year-old, had left for good.

We asked her about the rumors, about the hole in the wall at the school. "Never happened," Lenore said.

"Your son have a computer?" Sampson asked.

"Two, or one and a half, I guess, at the end. He was always buying and selling them on eBay."

"Really?" I said. "At twelve?"

"Oh, sure. Computers, phones, iPods, anything electronic, long as it was used and cheap. It was kind of his hobby. He made pretty good money doing it."

"Police look at his computers?"

"They took them," she said. "I assume they looked at them."

"And his phone?"

"They found one."

"He had more than one?" Sampson asked.

"Sometimes three, but I only knew of two at that time. A Samsung, which they found, and a used iPhone, which they didn't."

"Anything else?"

"No. There's not much left other than pictures, videos, and my memories."

She started to cry again. Her daughter came over and hugged her until she was composed enough to tell us about the day her son disappeared.

"I wanted him to go to the store for me." She sniffed. "He'd been in for a snack and then said he was going out to play. But when I called after him, he never answered."

We asked her to point out the trail she believed Timmy had used to reach the forest clearing where the missing girls' Toyota was found. As she went to the window to show us where to find the path, Lenore expressed bitterness about the investigation, saying that state and local detectives had been more interested in the lesbians than her son.

"Then again, they're probably still alive, and my son's dead, buried, and forgotten," she said morosely as she led us to the door. "So thank you for thinking about him."

"You're welcome," I said. "We'll let you know if we make any progress."

"I believe you," she said. "Even if no one else seems willing to help."

Walking down the driveway, feeling Lenore Walker's tortured gaze on my back, I was once again grateful for my many blessings and hyperaware of how the gifts of life can disappear in the blink of an eye.

"There but for the grace of God go I," Sampson said in a soft voice.

"I hear you, brother," I said. "Loud and clear."

We found the path and went into the woods. The trail ran out across a shelf and then dropped steeply downhill to a logging road. When we came over the edge of the shelf, a black, whirling explosion went off down in the bottom.

I lurched back, ducked, and threw up my arms to protect my head.

CHAPTER

90

A BIG FLOCK OF WILD turkeys had been feeding in the logging road when we appeared above them. They erupted off the forest floor and roared right over our heads, causing us to duck and take cover until they were gone.

"You should have seen the look on your face when they came blowing out of there," I said, grinning.

"I almost had a heart attack." Sampson laughed. "You did too."

"I'm a city boy, not used to getting attacked by wild critters."

"Critters?"

"I'm trying to channel my inner country."

"Yee-haw," Sampson said and dropped down the bank onto the logging road. "Boy, those damn birds really tear up the place, don't they?"

I saw what he meant. For a good fifty yards in every direction, the leaves were all fluffed and piled up where the turkeys had scratched and overturned them looking for food.

"There had to have been forty of them," I said.

"At least," Sampson said, heading down the trail to where it met a creek.

We paralleled the creek for almost a mile to a fork in the two-track road. We went left and found the creek crossing Lenore Walker had described and continued on up a short hill.

At the top of the rise, we could see through the bare trees some ninety yards across a wide flat to the clearing where Alison Dane's Toyota Camry had been found, abandoned. The flock of turkeys had been there before us, tearing up the forest floor on both sides of the trail all the way to the clearing.

I had a picture on my phone of the Toyota Camry as it was found, and we were able to use it to figure out roughly where the car must have been. We crossed the clearing to the spot.

Looking back to where the logging road met the opening, I said, "So Timmy comes to the edge of the woods over there, and sees what?"

"The car, the girls," Sampson said. "And maybe whoever grabbed them."

"Sure, it's not far. Sixty yards? Seventy?"

"Sounds right, but then what? Someone sees Timmy?"

I nodded. "Chases him down, crushes his throat."

Sampson took a big breath and let it go. "Poor kid."

"Right?" I said, looking around and feeling upset.

I guess I'd hoped driving to this place four and a half hours away would help, and while seeing the crime scene gave us a clearer sense of where the girls and Timmy had been on the day in question, I didn't see any new light indicating the end of the tunnel.

Sampson said, "It's pushing noon. We should go back, get the car, and find somewhere to eat before we head home."

"Sounds like a plan," I said.

We crossed the clearing, bowing our heads and pulling up our coat collars against the raw wind blowing. It was calmer in the woods, but I still hustled to get back to the car and the heater.

So did Sampson, until something caught his eye. He pulled up, said, "Hold on a second. I saw something back there."

He walked back down the trail a few steps and then went right six or seven more through the leaves and loose forest duff the turkeys had scratched and turned over.

John stopped and glanced around. He took one step and then another before halting, digging a handkerchief from his pocket, and crouching in the leaves.

When he stood up, Sampson held out a dirty white iPhone.

CHAPTER

91

THE FOLLOWING EVENING AROUND SEVEN, Ali dashed into the kitchen where the rest of us were cleaning up after dinner.

"Jannie!" he cried. "A cab pulled up! He's here!"

"Oh God," Jannie said, holding her stomach. "I shouldn't have eaten so much. I think I'm going to be sick."

Nana Mama squeezed her arm gently. "You're going to do just fine. If he wasn't already impressed, he wouldn't be here, so just be yourself."

"Great advice," I said just before the doorbell rang.

"I'll get it!" Ali cried.

"No," I said. "Jannie and I will get it."

"C'mon, Ali," my dad said. "Sit down, have a piece of Nana's shoofly pie."

"With ice cream?" Ali said.

"He deserves ice cream," I said as I followed Jannie.

"You've been saying that every night since the trial ended," Nana Mama complained.

"And I'll be saying that every night for a little while longer."

Before I left the kitchen, I blew a kiss at Bree, who caught it and smiled. We'd both carved out time for each other the past few days despite our busy schedules, and all in all my personal life was starting to feel much more balanced than it had for well over a year.

Not that things couldn't be better. Lenore Walker had said that she thought the iPhone Sampson found in the woods was her son's, but she wasn't sure. And when we'd taken the device to Keith Rawlins at Quantico earlier in the day, he'd noted that the water damage was going to make it exceedingly difficult for him to access the phone's data, if he could do it at all.

Despite Rawlins's promise to work every bit of magic he knew, we'd left the FBI's cybercrimes lab feeling frustrated. In our minds, the phone *was* Timmy Walker's, but unless we could get into it, we were once again at a dead end when it came to his murder. And even though we didn't have a smoking gun connecting the boy's death to the missing blondes, it felt like, without the phone, we would never find Gretchen Lindel, Ginny Krauss, Alison Dane, Delilah Franks, Patsy Mansfield, and Cathy Dupris.

But good things had happened too. Nana had taken a phone call for Jannie at home and relayed the message to me, and that had led to near pandemonium as everyone in our family tried to rearrange things in order to be home when the doorbell rang.

In the front hall now, Jannie looked over her shoulder, and I said, "Go on."

She opened the front door, revealing a tall, lean, African American man in his early forties. He wore a blue suit with a green and gold tie, and he beamed when he saw my daughter.

"Jannie Cross," he said, smiling as he shook her hand. "I'm so glad we could work out a time to meet."

Jannie was dumbstruck but managed to say, "I am too, sir, uh, Coach."

I said, "She's thrilled you're here. We all are."

"Dr. Cross?" he said, turning his hundred-watt smile on me and reaching to shake my hand. "I'm Robert Johnson."

"Please, come in, Coach," I said. "My grandmother makes a mean pie if you're interested."

"I'm always interested in pie," he said. "What kind?"

"Shoofly pie without the sugar bomb," Jannie said. "She got the recipe from an Amish cookbook and altered it with maple syrup."

"I would love some of that," he said.

I led the way back to the kitchen, where Coach Johnson introduced himself to everyone and good-naturedly submitted to Nana Mama when she ordered him to sit down and have some pie and a cup of green tea.

"Jannie," Johnson said after finishing his dessert, "I'm not going to lie to you. The food at the University of Oregon is not as good as you're used to at home."

My grandmother loved that.

"Unless you could convince Nana to move to Eugene with you," he said. "Then the entire Ducks track team could benefit."

That pleased Nana even more. "You're scoring brownie points, Coach."

"I was hoping so," Coach Johnson said, and he winked at her. "Can I tell you all about our program?"

"Please," Bree said.

Johnson said, "Since I took over as head track coach at the University of Oregon three years ago, we have won eight national championships: men's indoor and outdoor track, women's indoor and outdoor track, and women's cross-country. Oregon has been honored as the national Men's and Women's Programs of the Year in each of the past two years. The women won it the year before that as well."

Once Coach Johnson started his recruiting pitch, his attention rarely left Jannie, who was listening raptly.

"Twenty-eight Duck athletes have won NCAA individual championships under my watch," Johnson went on. "Including Phyllis Francis."

Jannie sat up straighter. "She set the American record in the indoor four-hundred."

"She did," Johnson said, and he paused to look around at us all. "And I think you can beat that record, Jannie."

CHAPTER

92

JANNIE LOOKED AS STUNNED AS I felt. The American record?

"I really do believe that," Johnson said to me. "I've watched Jannie's films. I've reviewed her training times, her program, and her progress with Coach McDonald. We both feel that record is within the range of possibility *if* she chooses and applies herself in the right program."

"Your program," my father said.

"There's none better," the coach replied. "Oregon's track-and-field tradition is deep and wide. We have the finest facility in the country at Hayward Field. The weather is near perfect for year-round training. And we have the best coaches and trainers. Period."

"What about the academics?" Bree asked.

"Amen," Nana Mama said.

"The university offers two hundred and seventy different majors, from the sciences to engineering to education and the arts. Our program in sports marketing is ranked number one in the country. The Clark Honors College is the oldest of its kind in the country and attracts many gifted students such as yourself, Jannie.

"Academics and sports aside, the campus is stunningly beautiful. Eugene is one of the most vibrant places I've ever lived. And we offer all of our athletes tutors to make sure they stay eligible to compete and, most important, to graduate."

"Are you offering my sister a scholarship?" Ali asked.

Coach Johnson laughed. "You don't fool around, do you?"

Ali grinned and shook his head.

"Maybe *you* should go into sports marketing, young man," Johnson said. "Be your sister's agent someday."

Ali smiled and said, "You didn't answer the question."

The coach laughed again, looked at me. "He's a little tiger."

"Every day," I said.

Coach Johnson turned to Jannie. "You know how I first heard of you?"

My daughter shook her head.

"When you were on ESPN."

Imitating the ESPN announcer, Ali said, "That girl ran so fast she broke her foot!"

The coach nodded. "That's the one. How's the foot doing?"

"Really good," Jannie said.

"No pain?"

"Not for a long time."

"You're a lucky, lucky young lady," Johnson said. "That injury could have been a career ender. But it wasn't, and so, Jannie Cross, I *am* here to offer you a scholarship, a full ride—tuition, room, and board—at the University of Oregon in exchange for a signed national letter of intent to run for the Ducks."

I don't think Jannie expected that. I know I didn't. She hadn't even competed in her junior year of spring outdoor track. I'd figured if she ran well from now on, she might start getting real offers in the fall of her senior year.

"I'm thrilled, but do I have to answer right now, Coach?" she said, smiling and biting her lip.

"Of course not," he said. "It would make my life easier if you did, but my life isn't what's at stake. Yours is. So I'm going to give you some advice, because I think you're a rare talent whether or not you come to Eugene to run for me. Jannie, you are going to get multiple scholarship offers. You should visit every school that you're interested in and really explore the people and the places and the track programs before you make a decision. I know Eugene is far from Washington, DC, but would you be interested in paying us a visit?"

Jannie looked relieved that she didn't have to decide on the spot, glanced at me, and nodded. "I'd like that, Coach."

"Excellent," Johnson said. "When could you bring her out?" he asked me.

I glanced at Bree, who said, "Winter vacation?"

"Perfect," he said. "Oh, and those plane tickets will be on the Ducks."

"Can I come?" Ali asked.

"Absolutely not," Jannie said.

Coach Johnson stayed a few more minutes, answering our questions, and charming Nana Mama no end.

"I'll be back for more of that pie," he told her as he was leaving.

"You're always welcome, Coach Johnson."

When the door shut, we were all grinning like fools. Bree kissed Jannie, who said, "Did that really just happen?"

"Best track program in the country," I said, feeling my eyes water.

"Long way from home," Nana Mama said in a way that made me realize she probably wouldn't get to see Jannie run in person if she went to Oregon.

"It is a really long way," Jannie said. "I don't know about that."

"You don't have to know right now," I said. "We'll listen to everyone, and you'll make the decision when *you* are ready. Okay?"

Jannie hugged me. "Thanks, Dad. I'm so glad you were here for that. It could have been different. You know?"

I closed my eyes, kissed the top of her head, and said, "I do, baby girl. I really do."

CHAPTER

93

WHEN THE ELEVATOR DOOR OPENED onto the second subbasement below the FBI's Cyber Division, Keith Rawlins had the tunes cranked inside his lab. The thudding, infectious bass line of Flo Rida's "My House" came right through the glass window and seemed to vibrate in my chest.

It was a few minutes past seven in the morning, and Rawlins had evidently been in the lab all night. But you wouldn't have known it. The digital wizard was stripped to his denim shorts, covered in sweat, and bouncing up and down on a mini-trampoline while punching the air in time to the beat.

"I still can't believe this guy works for us," said Special Agent in Charge Mahoney, my old partner at the FBI, who had taken over the missing-blondes case for the Bureau.

"I suffer the indignity of it every day," Special Agent Batra said.

"This could have waited a few hours," Sampson said, and he yawned.

I said, "He was excited enough about it to call us at five a.m."

"This better be good," Sampson said. "All I'm saying."

Batra rolled her eyes and shouldered open the lab door. The music was blasting. Rawlins had Flo Rida's music video playing on all screens. He spotted us and high-stepped our way, slinging his limp black Mohawk back and forth while singing, "'Welcome to my house!'"

Mahoney and Batra looked like they'd spent the night sleeping on coarse sandpaper. I smiled and drew my finger across my throat.

Rawlins stopped dancing, pouted, picked up a remote, and froze the video. The lab got quiet.

"The best part was just coming," he said. "Clay Pritchard lays down the best saxophone licks since—"

"You woke us up, called us in here," Batra grumbled. "It wasn't to dance, was it? Because if it was, I'm gonna be pissed."

"Beyond pissed," Mahoney said.

Rawlins sighed, said, "Sometimes I wonder if the academy's training just squeezes the soul and celebration out of every agent who graduates Quantico."

"Let's see what you've got, Krazy Kat," I said.

Rawlins fashioned his hair into a bun like a samurai's top-knot, a style that appeared to give Mahoney and Batra indigestion. The computer scientist waved a finger at me with one hand and snatched up a towel with the other.

"Took me almost three days straight, but I was able to raise the dead."

"You calling yourself the Messiah now?" Batra said.

"Just a miracle worker," Rawlins said as he toweled his upper body dry.

He put on an FBI sweatshirt and a pair of black-and-white

330

checkered sneakers before strolling over to the keyboard for the main screen array.

"A lot of the data was corrupted," he said, typing. "But I was able to salvage a few things from the day Timmy Walker was killed."

Rawlins hit Enter, and Flo Rida and his house disappeared on the screens, replaced by shaky video showing a wooded scene. The cameraman was sneaking through thick foliage.

I had no idea where it was shot until a boy's hand came forward and pushed aside leafy vines and saplings to reveal the lip of a dirt bank. The camera tilted down the bank and out twenty feet toward a blue Toyota Camry in a familiar clearing. The windows of the car were down.

The camera trembled, and you could hear Timmy Walker breathing hard while Ginny Krauss and Alison Dane made love naked in the backseat.

"The little Peeping Tom creep," Batra said.

"It is creepy," Rawlins said. "But I think you're going to like little peeping Timmy, God rest his soul, before it's over."

The camera settled and zoomed in. Alison Dane's hand slid from her lover's breast and trailed down over her belly, and then she seemed to hear something. The cameraman did too.

The focus went haywire for a moment before settling back on the girls, who were scrambling for their clothes. Then Ginny Krauss happened to look out the window and up the bank, straight at the camera.

She screamed, "There's some pervo kid in camo out there! He's filming us!"

Timmy apparently whirled around and took off back into the forest. The next twenty-seven seconds were herky-jerky, mostly flashes of green in a dim forest.

Then, over the croaking of tree frogs and the thrumming of crickets, you could hear a vehicle roar into the clearing and skid to a stop. One of the girls screamed.

The camera turned back and began moving again, going closer to the clearing, zooming in on a white Ford utility van idling in front of the Camry.

One of the girls started screaming again. "Please! Don't do this! Help! Kid! Help us, kid!"

The screen went black.

Rawlins said, "Unfortunately, that's all the video I could recover."

"Shit," Sampson said. "Can you give us a blown-up look at that van?"

"I don't need to," Rawlins said. "Timmy did."

He gave the keyboard several more orders and the biggest screen was filled with a digital photograph showing a grainy zoomed-in view of the van. The windows were tinted, so we couldn't get a look at the interior, but the signage on the side was clearly visible.

"Dish Network?" Mahoney said.

"And those are Maryland plates," I said. "Five, seven, E, one…can't make out the—"

"It's a six," Rawlins said. "You see it better in the other photographs."

"How many other photographs?" Sampson said.

"Five. Timmy could have just kept running after the girls spotted him. But he heard them screaming and decided to take these pictures. I think he was going to go to the police with them. Otherwise, why take the risk? Why not do the natural thing for a twelve-year-old boy caught with his hand in the pervert cookie jar and just run?"

Judging from her body language, Batra seemed to have some issue with the theory, but Mahoney said, "I think you're right."

"I do too," I said. "I also think those pictures got Timmy Walker killed."

"Oh, I know they did," Rawlins said. "The phone died less than twenty-five seconds after the last picture was taken."

CHAPTER

94

JUST AFTER DARK THAT SAME day, Sampson, Mahoney, and I were watching FBI crime scene techs getting ready to tear apart a white Ford utility van with Dish Network signage on both sides. It was in the parking lot at the Dish authorized-seller store in Rockville, Maryland, and roped off with police tape.

The store manager, a small, cranelike man named Lester Potter, was rubbing his hands together and watching nervously.

"You know that van was stolen, right?" Potter said.

"When was that?" Sampson asked.

"Five, six months ago? One of my techs was out doing a residential satellite install in Gaithersburg. She's in the house not ten minutes, comes out, and the van's gone. Boosted in broad daylight. They disabled the tracking device. Six weeks go by, and the company's written it off, figured it was looted and chopped up for parts. But then we get a call. Pennsylvania state troopers found it abandoned in long-term parking at the Harrisburg airport. It's crazy, but they didn't take a thing. That van was as clean and shipshape as it was when it was stolen. Someone just took it for a joyride."

"No," Sampson said. "Someone took it to kidnap two teenage girls who are still being held captive and terrorized to satisfy the twisted fantasies of Internet trolls."

"Oh," Potter said, his face turning pale. "I had no idea."

"Who was the driver the day it was stolen?" I said.

"Lourdes Rodriguez," he said. "One of my best employees ever."

"Can we talk with Ms. Rodriguez?"

"She doesn't work here anymore," Potter said. "Lucky gal inherited a pile of money from a great-uncle and took this job and shoved it a few months ago."

Sampson said, "I guess the glamour of being a satellite installer wasn't enough to keep her on the Dish Network career path."

The store manager gave him an odd look, said, "Who could blame her?"

"No one," I said. "You have contact information for Ms. Rodriguez?"

"I'm sure I do somewhere."

"Could you do us a solid and dig it up?"

Potter's nose twitched as if he thought the task beneath him, but he went inside.

"Why take nothing?" I said.

"How many people without training know how to install satellites?" Sampson said. "And I can't imagine they're easy to sell on the black market. They say *Dish* all over—"

"Agent Mahoney?" Karen Getty, an FBI crime scene tech, called out.

Getty was standing at the rear of the van wearing disposable white coveralls, latex gloves, and blue booties over her shoes. The two rear doors of the van were open, revealing shelves, boxes of supplies, six satellite dishes, and stacked rolls of cable.

"You're going to want to see this," Getty said.

We all went to the rear of the van, which looked spotless.

"Kill the lights," she said.

The interior lights died. So did the spots brought in to illuminate the search. She picked up a bottle marked LUMINOL and started spraying it around.

Luminol is a compound that glows when it's exposed to certain substances, like the iron in hemoglobin. When someone tries to clean up blood, traces of it are left behind; spray that area with luminol, and the chemical glows blue for a brief period.

There were a few blood spatters immediately visible on the van floor close to the doors. The more Getty sprayed, the more spatters appeared, until it looked like a starry night had been superimposed on the van's floor, ceiling, and walls.

"What the hell is that?" Potter said. The manager had come up behind us.

Sampson looked at him and said, "Evidence of a slaughter."

CHAPTER

95

THE NEXT MORNING, SAMPSON AND I drove to the address of the woman who'd been driving the van the night it was stolen. Lourdes Rodriguez lived in Silver Spring, Maryland, on the eighth floor of a large, midpriced, brick-faced apartment building.

At the locked front door, we buzzed Rodriguez's apartment number, 805, and got no answer. We figured that with an apartment building that big, there might be a live-in superintendent, and we lucked out when Arnie Feiffer answered our ring and soon buzzed us in.

Sampson and I entered a foyer featuring 1970s decor that showed the dings and scratches of time and neglect.

"Not where I'd be living if I'd inherited a boatload," Sampson said.

I agreed, thinking that I'd expect a woman in her early thirties with newfound wealth to choose to live in one of the newer, more luxurious apartment buildings in downtown Silver Spring or…

A door to our right opened. A television blared the patter of an announcer for *American Ninja Warrior*. A nebbishy man in his sixties shuffled out of the apartment wearing a maroon bathrobe over his clothes, slippers, and a blue-and-white yarmulke on his head.

He squinted through round glasses. "You the cops?"

"You the super?" Sampson asked as we showed him our identifications.

"Lord of the castle," he said. "Arnie Feiffer. How can I help, Detectives?"

"We'd like to go knock on Lourdes Rodriguez's door," I said.

"Why? What's she done?"

"We just want to ask her a few questions about her prior workplace."

Feiffer hesitated, then said, "I'll go with you, if you don't mind."

"Not at all," I said.

"C'mon, then," he said, and he shuffled by us, heading to the elevators. Posted on one of the two was a handwritten sign that read *Out of Service*.

We rode the creaking, shuddering lift to the eighth floor. The doors squealed open, and we stepped out into a musty hallway with dingy rugs.

We walked down the hall to apartment 805 and rang the bell. There was no answer. We knocked, but no one came to the door. I was about to suggest we leave business cards with a note asking her to call us when from inside we heard the high-pitched mewing and cries of a cat that sounded very upset.

"A cat?" Feiffer said furiously. "No cats. No dogs. The lease is clear."

After a glance at me, Sampson said, "It's within your rights to remove the cat from your property. We'll help. It's the least we can do for you."

The superintendent studied us suspiciously. "You're not looking to get around a warrant, are you?"

Sampson said, "If we wanted to do that, we'd tell you we smelled gas."

"I run electric," Feiffer said as the cat's cries turned frantic.

"Sounds like it's hungry," I said. "We could always call in Animal Control for suspicion of neglect on Ms. Rodriguez's part. They could get us in."

The super didn't like that and grudgingly dug under his robe for a key ring. He found the master key and used it to turn the dead bolt and unlock the door.

Feiffer pushed the door open. A filthy yellow-and-orange tabby sprang out and darted between our legs before any of us could grab it. The cat sprinted down the hall, took a sharp right, and disappeared.

"I'm getting too old for this crap," Feiffer said with a moan, his palm to his forehead.

I saw he wasn't talking about the cat but about the apartment. The place was empty and swept clean.

CHAPTER

96

FEIFFER TRUDGED INTO THE MODEST one-bedroom apartment and we followed.

When he reached the living area, he gazed around in disbelief. "She never said anything about leaving."

"We heard she'd inherited a lot of money," I said.

"That right?" the super said, raising one bushy gray eyebrow. "She never mentioned it, but why would she? How long ago?"

"Few months."

"Big money and she lived *here* for months?" Feiffer said, incredulous.

What could I say? The man knew his place in the market.

"Could we see your copy of her lease?" Sampson asked.

"Why?" he said, suspicious again.

"I gather you have no forwarding address since she skipped out, but there will be bank and reference information in the lease agreement that might help us figure out where she's gone."

Feiffer considered that and then nodded.

After confirming that Rodriguez had indeed removed all her possessions, we were on our way out when I noticed some newspapers in a brown paper bag behind the door. I picked the bag up, hoping they'd give us an idea of how long she'd been gone.

I pulled out a stack of loose newspaper sections and flipped through a few.

The sections were all from the *Washington Post*, several going back a month or more, front pages mostly, with a few Metro sections thrown in. I kept looking through the newspapers as we rode down and noticed something that quickly became a troubling pattern.

I kept it to myself until Feiffer had gone into his apartment and we were alone in the lobby.

"We're keeping these papers," I said, slipping them back in the bag.

"Why's that?" Sampson asked.

"In almost every section there's a story about Gretchen Lindel or one of the other missing girls."

"So maybe Lourdes Rodriguez had reason to sneak out in the middle of the night."

"Maybe she did."

Feiffer emerged from his apartment with a file marked APARTMENT 805—L. RODRIGUEZ. I flipped the file open, took a glance at the standard rental-agreement form, and then zeroed in on a photo of the tenant stapled to the contract.

"Huh," I said, seeing Rodriguez in a whole new light. I took a picture of the rental agreement and the photo, then handed the contract back to Feiffer.

"That it? I've got to go find that cat."

We thanked the super for his time and left. The second the front door clicked behind us, Sampson said, "What did you see on that lease?"

"My poker face didn't work?"

"I have known you since we were ten."

I pulled up the shot of the picture stapled to the contract.

"Lourdes Rodriguez?" I said. "I know her by another name."

CHAPTER

97

THE ULTRA-LUXURY UNION WHARF apartment complex on Fell's Point was the most expensive place to live in Baltimore, costing five times what Lourdes Rodriguez had been paying at Feiffer's. We'd used the bank account and other information on Rodriguez's old lease to track her to her new digs.

A small moving van was snarling traffic on South Wolfe Street. The front door to one of the apartment buildings was propped open for workmen carrying furniture wrapped in blankets. We followed them inside and up the stairs to 2E.

The door was open. Reggae music was playing. The workmen went in. So did we.

I trailed Sampson past stacks of moving boxes choking the front hallway, hearing a familiar voice saying, "Be careful with that! It was my mother's!"

We stepped out into a living area with large glass windows that gave a sweeping and dramatic view of Baltimore Harbor. Wearing jeans and a loose-fitting pink jersey, Lourdes Rodriguez paced by the window, watching the workmen move a table into position.

She looked puzzled when she saw Sampson standing there holding his badge. Then she noticed me.

I stepped into the room, said, "You never sent me your new e-mail, Annie."

For a second, the love junkie was so shocked, I thought she might faint dead away.

Then she croaked, "Dr. Cross? What are you doing here?"

"I could say the same, Annie. Or is it Lourdes?"

She swallowed, looked away. "Lourdes."

"Why'd you use the fake name when you came to see me?"

Rodriguez blinked, puffed out her cheeks, and glanced at the workmen, who were leaving the room. "Isn't this privileged?"

"Not when it comes to murder, kidnapping, and torture," Sampson said.

That threw her. "What are you talking..." She looked at me. "Dr. Cross, I came to you under an alias because of the addiction I told you about. I don't know anything about any torture or murder or kidnapping."

"The van that was stolen from you when you were working for Dish," Sampson said. "We ran tests on the interior. Whole lot of blood spatter."

She looked down. "Blood spatter? I don't...it was stolen. I had nothing to do with that."

"Didn't you?" I said. "The same van was caught on film when two blond girls from Pennsylvania were taken."

Her jaw dropped, and she took a step backward.

"Seemed a big coincidence," Sampson said. "Given that you left behind all those articles about the same missing girls at your old apartment at Mr. Feiffer's."

"And given that I saw you leaving my office in a car driven by a man posing as Alden Lindel, the father of one of the missing girls," I said.

She shook her head as if trying to clear it. "Wait. What? The father of one of the missing girls?"

"A man who's been claiming to be him. You got into his Nissan Pathfinder right after our one and only session. I saw you. What is going on, Annie, Lourdes, whatever your real name is?"

She threw up her hands in exasperation. "Last time I left your office? I called Uber. They sent some Uber guy. You can check. I'm sure there's a record."

Uber? Was that possible? The fake Alden was an Uber driver. You call for an Uber car and usually the one that's closest responds. Which meant what? That the impostor, whoever he was, had been close by, watching my house?

"We will check Uber," Sampson said. "What about the news articles?"

Rodriguez rubbed her neck, didn't look at us, and didn't reply.

"It's going to come out sooner or later," I said. "Courts go easier on the first person in a conspiracy to flip."

"Conspiracy?" she said sharply. "No, it's nothing like that. Not really."

"What the hell does that mean?"

Looking flustered now, Rodriguez wrung her hands and then held them up in surrender.

"Okay, okay, I got caught up in something a long time ago, Dr. Cross, and…I'll tell you everything I know. Everything. The honest-to-God truth."

98

TWO HOURS AND FORTY-FIVE minutes later, Sampson had gotten off I-95 and was driving us north on Front Street, which parallels the freeway and the Delaware River as they pass through Philadelphia. The weather was changing. Dark clouds boiled on the western horizon.

"Chalabi sounds like a first-class creep," Sampson said.

"He won't be the first to achieve film success that way," I said. We went over the high points of Rodriguez's confession for the fourth or fifth time.

A childhood friend of Lourdes Rodriguez, Casey Chalabi, had always wanted to be a movie director.

"He ended up making porn films under the name Dirk Wallace," Rodriguez told us. "It's all S-and-M, bondage, the hard stuff."

She said Chalabi put aside money from the porn shoots to fund production of a horror film he'd written.

"Horror's cheap to film," she'd said. "Casey said you can

do them for under a million. James Wan did *Saw* for a little over five hundred thousand, and it made, like, fifty-five million. Casey's trying to model himself on Wan."

Rodriguez claimed that even with the porn money, Casey's horror flick was being shot on a shoestring. When he learned she was going to inherit her great-uncle's fortune, he was immediately after Rodriguez to help fund his film.

"I gave him some, and I didn't even have the inheritance yet," she said. "I took it from my savings. Five thousand. And then another five. Then Casey wanted the van, my van at Dish. He said even with the money I'd given him, he couldn't afford to buy or rent one, and mine was perfect. He wanted me to just lend it to him for the night."

"What'd you say?"

"I said no. No way. But Casey can be a vindictive a-hole."

Sampson raised his eyebrows. "You saying Chalabi stole your van?"

"I'd put money on it. And that blood you found inside? Was it human?"

"We don't know yet," I said.

"It's probably pig's blood. He uses lots of pig's blood in the big slasher scenes in *Blade*."

I thought about that for several moments. "So he steals your van, uses it in a killing scene in his movie. I'm still having trouble seeing how this connects to those newspaper articles we found at Feiffer's."

Rodriguez swallowed hard. "I haven't spoken with Casey since my van was stolen, but I read his script a long time ago. It's about these four sisters who inherit an abandoned factory and this old Victorian house. Then it's pretty much like every other horror flick you see. Except the sisters. They're all ethereal and blond. Every one of them. And they get killed, one by one."

Which was enough for us to drive to Philadelphia to talk to Mr. Chalabi face-to-face.

Rodriguez had given us the last address she had for Chalabi. She said she thought it was where he shot the porn movies. We found the address, a rehabbed old school called the Emerson that had been turned into lofts and work spaces down the street from the Theatre of Living Arts.

Rodriguez couldn't remember the exact name of Chalabi's company, but we found C. C. PRODUCTIONS listed on a board at the entrance to the Emerson. It was on the second floor, unit 2, the address Rodriguez had given us.

We took the staircase and walked down a long hallway past the open doors of artists' studios and the closed doors of others in the arts and entertainment fields. The place smelled nice. There was music playing.

It had a good vibe, all in all, and that bothered me as we walked up to the closed door of C. C. Productions. I couldn't see the management letting him shoot porn or slasher flicks on the premises.

Sampson knocked, turned the knob, and opened the door. I took one look inside and swore to myself.

C. C. Productions was an animation company. There were framed cartoon stills on the wall above the workstation of an Indian American woman in her twenties who looked up and smiled.

"Can I help you?" she said.

Sampson said, "We're looking for Casey Chalabi."

"I'm Cassandra Chalabi," she said.

"Of course you are," I said, furious. "Sorry to bother you."

We shut the door. Sampson said, "Con artist."

"Total pro. Pathological liar."

"How much you wanna bet she's started making a third move since we left?"

"Not a nickel. Lourdes Rodriguez, Annie Cassidy, whatever she calls herself, is in the wind."

CHAPTER

99

WHEN SAMPSON AND I RETURNED to the front door of the arts building, gloom had set in outside, and a chill rain fell on hurried pedestrians bent to the storm.

"We're gonna get soaked," Sampson said.

"Run for it," I said. I jerked open the door and hopped out. Rain driven by a strong north wind pelted my face and eyes, forcing me to duck my head and throw my forearm across my brow as I ran toward the car, virtually blind.

As I was crossing Seventh Street, I stepped in a pothole. My right foot and shoe were submerged, my ankle and lower shin hit the edge of the depression, and I stumbled and sprawled in front of a Chrysler Sebring waiting at the light.

But that probably saved my life, because as soon as I tripped, I heard a thumping noise and the Sebring's right headlight exploded.

"Shooter!" Sampson shouted; he grabbed me by the back of the jacket, hauled me behind the Sebring, and threw me to the ground just before a second bullet smacked into the grille and penetrated the radiator, which threw steam.

The Sebring's driver started screaming in a language I didn't recognize. My shin was screaming in a language I didn't recognize. But I forced myself to dig for my service weapon and badge.

"Where is he?" I said.

Sampson said, "I caught a flash of the first shot, elevated slightly, northwest corner of the intersection and back. Sounded suppressed too."

I ignored the pain in my leg and got up enough to look over the hood through the teeming rain. The traffic light on one-way South Street had gone yellow. Two cars passed. Their headlights threw glare that dazzled me until the third shot.

I saw the flare of it, and then the Sebring's windshield and passenger-side window fragmented as the bullet passed through both. I ducked down, hearing the frightened screams from the driver turn petrified.

"Pickup parked on the north side of South Street," I said.

The light turned green on Seventh. The hysterical Sebring driver stomped on the gas, but the car bucked, stalled, and belched steam and smoke before dying ten feet into the intersection. The drivers of several cars behind us spun their tires, trying to get around the Sebring.

Other cars began honking frantically.

Sampson said, "Pickup's running the red."

In one motion I stood and had my pistol in my shooting hand over the Sebring's passenger-side mirror. I was aiming at the pickup, which was trying to avoid the skidding cars in the intersection. For a moment I had nothing to shoot at.

Then I picked up a shadow, someone dressed in black standing in profile against the back of the truck cab. He shifted, exposing the sound suppressor on the muzzle of his rifle.

"Gun," I said; I fired, and missed.

The gunman returned fire, but the shot went wide. Sampson's shot went wide as well, two feet to the gunman's right, shattering the truck's driver-side window. The brakes went on. A Volvo station wagon turning the corner onto South smashed into the truck's rear corner panel, throwing the gunman off his feet. He fell behind the walls of the truck bed.

I hobbled after a charging Sampson, his gun and badge up to oncoming traffic, and my gut feeling was that something terrible was going to happen unless I kept up with my partner.

Trying to back up, the Volvo almost ran us over. We dodged around it as the pickup's brake lights went off and the truck started to roll again, passing beneath street lamps as it slowly gained speed.

We ran with it, and I caught a glimpse of the driver, a scruffy-faced guy with a tangle of dark hair and bleeding cheeks. The pickup pulled away. The gunman rose to his knees in the bed and looked at us, grinning.

The truck sped up and was gone into a mash of red taillights long before the police sirens started to wail.

"No light on the license plate," Sampson said in disgust as we walked through the still-pouring rain back to the smoking Sebring. "Probably smashed when it got rear-ended."

"There was enough light on the shooter, though," I said, limping and feeling twisted and toyed with. "He likes to call himself Alden Lindel."

Part Five

ALL BLONDES
MUST DIE

CHAPTER

100

AT HOME THE NEXT EVENING, I was on my back with my ankle elevated and iced, watching coverage of the shooting incident on a DC station.

"There Detective Cross goes again," said assistant U.S. attorney Nathan Wills, peering in disgust at the camera from under an umbrella. "He's not back on the job a week and already the bullets are flying."

"Those bullets flew my way first," I said and stabbed the remote until the screen went black.

"The brass know that," Bree said, coming out of the kitchen into our great room and setting a cup of coffee on the table beside me.

"Michaels put me on leave," I said. "Again."

"Department regulations," Bree said, sitting beside me. "Sampson's no better off than you."

"Better ankle," I said.

"Well, there's that," Bree said.

We fell into a silence that got longer. I stared at the blank screen, wondering for the hundredth time why the man impersonating Alden Lindel was fixated on me. Was he part of the crew that tried to frame me for murder? Picking up where Claude Watkins and Kimiko Binx left off?

And what about Lourdes Rodriguez? Was that even her real name?

In the wake of media uproar surrounding the shooting in Philly, Chief Michaels had been in no mood to seek a search warrant for her new apartment, even when we explained that she'd set us up to be assassinated.

"I'm beginning to wonder if this is worth it anymore," I said, looking over at Bree. "Being a cop, I mean."

Cocking her head, frowning, she set her coffee down. "You're serious?"

"I'm serious enough to know that I want to stay being a psychologist, a counselor, at least part-time," I said. "I enjoy it. It feels right and matters in a way hunting down bad guys just doesn't anymore, Bree."

She gazed at me, blinked. "You are serious."

"I guess I am. Maybe it's time. They say most people have five careers in their lives. Maybe this is how I'm supposed to be the best I can be in the future."

"A higher calling?"

I sighed. "Is that so hard to believe?"

Bree smiled at me, but there was a tinge of sadness in it. "No, I could understand it. At least of an ordinary cop, who'd seen too much. But you're no ordinary cop, Alex Cross."

"That's debatable."

"Tell that to the awards and citations you have piled in your attic office. Tell that to all the families of victims you've helped just by being you, relentless, smart, and professional with a moral compass that is unwavering."

"I'm impulsive," I said. "I get shot at. A lot."

"Because you have the God-given knack of getting close to bad guys and upsetting their plans. You actually do that on a regular basis, Alex. Very, very few detectives can say that."

Before I could reply, Ali pounded through the kitchen and out to us.

"Dad!" he said. "I think I've finally found my sport!"

Of my three children, my youngest might be the brightest, but he is, shall we say, challenged athletically. Ali had tried various sports—basketball, baseball, and even lacrosse—but nothing ever clicked, and he seemed to trip over his own feet a lot.

"I'm hoping your sport's not ice hockey," I said.

"What?" Ali said, almost indignant. "No."

"Horse jumping?"

"No. Darts."

"Darts?"

"There's a tournament coming up," he said. "I've been playing a bunch at my friend Charley's house after school, but I need my own board and a set of good darts if I'm going to have any chance of qualifying."

Feeling a twinge in my ankle, I closed my eyes. I heard Bree say, "Where's this tournament?"

"At a bar on Capitol Hill," Ali said.

"A bar?" I said, opening my eyes.

"Technically, a tavern. I walk by there all the time after the bus drops me."

"You're not going to a bar or a tavern to play darts."

"It's a ten-thousand-dollar prize, Dad!"

"You're too young to be playing darts where people are drinking alcohol."

"No, I went in and asked. As long as you're with me, they said I can play."

The doorbell rang.

"I'll get it," Bree said.

"Let Ali," I said.

"Can I get the dartboard?"

"Start by getting the door."

He hesitated, then ran out.

"Darts?" Bree said, trying to hide her smile. "In a tavern?"

"Nana Mama is going to have a cow," I said, laughing.

"She's going to have two cows. Maybe an entire dairy farm if this becomes a regular thing."

"Darts," I said, and I shook my head at how quickly Ali went from a sharp and analytical adult-like person to a young boy attracted by the next shiny object.

I heard his footsteps pound back to us, and I thought for sure he was going to ask about the darts again.

Instead, he said breathlessly, "It's Ned and Krazy Kat!"

101

KEITH RAWLINS'S MOHAWK HAD BEEN redyed flaming red and shel-lacked to jut off his head like a jaunty rooster's comb. But the normally upbeat cybercrimes expert looked subdued when he came into the room.

"Dr. Cross, Chief Stone," he said. "I need to show you some-thing. With your permission, I'd like to connect my laptop to your television screen?"

"Go ahead," Bree said.

"What's going on?" I asked Mahoney when he came into the room after speaking with Nana and my dad.

Ned said, "Rawlins says he knows why Lourdes Rodriguez was so quick and quiet about leaving her old apartment. He started to explain it on the way here, but most of it went right over my head."

"I'll try to dumb it down further, Agent Mahoney," Rawlins said, sounding annoyed as he typed on his laptop.

A moment later the television screen came on, showing

a gibberish of coded numbers, letters, and symbols. Rawlins scrolled down through the mess until he found what he wanted.

He highlighted a sequence in the sea of code. "That's a time stamp from a few days ago, immediately after Lourdes Rodriguez's name was entered into the FBI's database as part of the ongoing investigation."

Rawlins typed. The screen jumped to another coded document and highlighted a new sequence.

He said, "Two seconds after Rodriguez's name goes in, this second time stamp is triggered in a different file, a familiar file, that ingenious, eloquent piece of malware code I found in your computer and then in the FBI database."

Bree said, "You're saying Rodriguez's name triggered the malware?"

"And the malware triggered Rodriguez's swift departure from that apartment. The troubling thing is that I should have seen this sooner, but after the marathon work session I put in to resurrect Timmy Walker's iPhone, I went home and slept for twenty hours, and I woke up with a nasty stomach bug that cost me another day."

Rawlins said that he'd finally returned to his lab earlier that morning to see the alert from the code he'd attached to the malware.

"Where did the stuff about Rodriguez go?" Bree asked.

"Through onion routers, of course," Rawlins said, typing. "A dozen in all. But I intentionally overrode the malware's code so that every time it passed through the onion it would send me a ping so I could track it."

The screen jumped to a map of the world with glowing lime-green pins denoting onion routers and orange arrows showing the direction of travel after the message cleared the device. From Quantico to India to China to the Philippines to Ecuador and on and on, until Rodriguez's name reached Japan.

"That's only eleven routers," Ali said. "You said twelve."

"I did indeed," Rawlins said and he typed. The screen switched to Google Earth, a satellite view of a checkerboard of woods and farmland.

"You are looking at an unincorporated area in southwestern Pennsylvania due east of the Michaux State Forest," he said, then zoomed down on a compound of three buildings. The biggest, a mansion, really, was sprawling and sat beside a large pond surrounded by hardwoods and pine thickets.

"That's a twelve-thousand-square-foot home with carriage house, barn, and personal bass pond," Rawlins said. "But notice the satellite dishes on the roof. Even for a big place, it's overkill."

"And this is where the malware went after Japan?" I said.

"Most definitely."

"Who owns it?"

The cybercrimes expert sobered. "Nash Edward Edgars. You've probably never heard of him, but Mr. Edgars is infamous in certain circles. Circles that often disappear into the dark web."

Rawlins described Edgars as a secretive, reclusive, and extremely wealthy computer-code writer in his late thirties. At seventeen, after his freshman year at Cal Poly, Edgars left and became the behind-the-scenes coder for several edgy, successful tech businesses.

"That we know for sure," Rawlins said. "The dark-web stuff is rumor and conjecture, but some very smart people swear Edgars has been developing and operating in the unorganized, encrypted, and untraceable Internet for a decade. Maybe longer."

I squinted at the screen. "What connects him to Rodriguez?"

"I don't know exactly."

"No photo of him?"

"A poor one, seven years old," Rawlins said. "But first…" He returned to his typing. "We're lucky this sat view was shot in late winter or early spring, or I wouldn't have noticed them."

Rawlins scrolled down the Google Earth image, taking us past the compound and over the forest. The image stopped where we could look down through the branches of bare hardwood trees.

Rawlins put his cursor on a smudge and zoomed in, revealing another structure, a long building with a tin roof. He moved his cursor to a second smudge on the satellite view and magnified it to reveal the lines of a large square.

"What is that?" I asked.

"I believe it's an old foundation, with a high stone wall here, similar to the one Gretchen Lindel was put up against during the mock execution."

"Jesus," I said, sitting forward. "Can we see that photo of Edgars?"

The question seemed to irritate Rawlins, who typed and said, "Give me a second to find it. But what's critical to understand here is that Edgars didn't leave Cal Poly to follow Bill Gates and strike out on his own at seventeen. In fact, Edgars was expelled from Cal Poly at seventeen, when he was still a juvenile, so the case is sealed."

"No idea why?" Bree asked.

"I know exactly why," he said as the screen changed to a blurry photograph of two men leaving an urban restaurant.

One was scruffy, dark-haired, and wore jeans, a Metallica T-shirt, and flip-flops. The other man was slightly older with a military haircut and aviator sunglasses.

Blurred or not, the picture made my stomach lurch.

Rawlins's cursor moved to the scruffy, bearded guy. "This is Nash Edgars. The other one's name is Mike Pratt. He's Edgars's bodyguard."

I said, "Edgars was driving the pickup in Philadelphia the other night. Pratt was both the shooter and the Alden Lindel impersonator."

Rawlins looked deflated to have some of his thunder stolen from him, but then he recovered and said, "Here's the kicker from my corner. I hacked into Cal Poly's system and found Edgars's file. He was accused of sexually assaulting three coeds his freshman year. Every one of them was blond."

CLOUDS OF STEAM BILLOWED FROM our lips at 4:10 the following morning.

It was bitter cold as we huddled in puffy jackets, wool caps, and gloves around a laptop computer bolted to a steel table inside an FBI special weapons and tactics van parked in the barnyard of a dairy farmer who lived two miles from Nash Edgars and who had nothing good to say about his reclusive neighbor.

"Give us the drone feed," Mahoney said into a cell phone.

The screen changed from the sharpness of Google Earth to an opaque gray-green that revealed bare-limbed trees and then the road that led past Edgars's gate. Thermal images appeared: two men were guarding the gate, carrying weapons. Flying on, the drone found the mansion, but the screen showed no thermal images of bodies—or much of anything, for that matter.

Mahoney said, "Drone pilot says the place appears heavily

insulated so there might be people inside or not. We'll have to go on the assumption the house is manned and heavily armed."

"Smart," I said.

Mahoney said into his cell, "Fly to that structure out in the woods."

The drone found the building. A thermal sensor revealed four faint images of people inside, all lying flat or curled up, located in separate little rooms.

"Those could be some of our missing women," Special Agent Batra said.

"Easily," Bree said, and she sipped from a go-cup of steaming coffee.

"That changes things," Mahoney said. "Show me the Google Earth image again."

Rawlins switched it back to the satellite image.

Mahoney pointed to a rocky knoll on the estate's far north boundary. "This is excellent high ground. We'll put four agents there to cover the back door."

I noticed something in the trees along a creek well to the east of the knoll, but before I could say anything, Rawlins switched back to the drone's feed showing more gray-green forest but no other distinct thermal images.

"Thanks for the flyby," Mahoney said into his cell, then he ordered four agents to enter the woods at the estate's northeast corner. He also moved a six-man hostage-rescue team, or HRT, into position to get to and storm that building in the woods as soon as possible. Bree and Sampson would ride with Mahoney and follow a breach team of FBI agents onto the property to arrest Edgars and Pratt.

"Alex, you'll be with Batra and Rawlins in a follow car, where you will remain until the clear is given," Mahoney said.

Before I could protest, Bree said, "Be practical, Alex. With your ankle like that, you won't be much help if things go south."

"It's not that bad, really," I said. "I'm not even on crutches. But I hear you."

"We'll give you a radio," Mahoney said. "For once you'll have to just listen to the action."

CHAPTER

103

AS I LIMPED INTO THE backseat of Agent Batra's black Chevy Tahoe, I had to admit I was feeling guilty for wanting to be part of the raiding party and hostage-rescue attempt.

The evening before, I'd been telling Bree that I wanted to get out of police work, away from dangerous moments like these when the adrenaline starts to drip and your senses get super-sharp and super-clear.

But as I shut the door and Batra started the engine, I knew a part of me could never leave the police game. Not entirely. Being a psychologist had its own deep and fruitful rewards, but it could never replace the rush of catching bad guys, ending their dark work, and seeing them get just punishment.

"Let's roll," Mahoney said.

I heard his voice over the radio and the light headset they'd given me.

"Isn't this exciting, Dr. Cross?" Krazy Kat Rawlins said, looking over the front seat at me as Batra put on her headlights and followed Mahoney's Tahoe onto a rural route heading east.

"The trick is not to get too excited," I said. "You have to keep your head."

"Oh, of course," he said, slightly crestfallen. "I guess I'm just looking forward to seeing Nash Edgars in handcuffs and telling him that I beat him. Do you ever feel that way?"

"From time to time, sure," I said.

"Right now?"

"Right now, I look forward to seeing those women safe and sound."

Over my headset, Mahoney said, "Half a mile out. HRT, you are go. Breaching team, you are go."

The acknowledgments came back fast, and in my mind I was seeing the rescue team flipping on their thermal-imaging goggles, surging into the woods, and angling through the forest toward the shed and four of the missing women.

We came over a rise in the road and saw a huge, black, six-wheel-drive armored FBI truck roll to the gate. I expected the guards to immediately stand down, but instead there were flashes from behind the gate and reports of gunfire over the radio.

"Take it down," Mahoney said.

The big armored rig backed up and then sped at the steel gate and blew it off its hinges. Agents inside the truck fired from portholes at the guards, who'd retreated up the hill into the trees toward the compound. Mahoney followed the armored truck, driving across the downed gate, with us trailing.

"HRT?" Mahoney said.

"Two hundred yards out, SAC," came the reply. "No visuals on the shed yet, but you have lights going on up the hill."

The breaching rig sped up on that news, disappeared around a curve in the long serpentine driveway. By the time we reached the edge of the compound, spotlights were blazing on the courtyard between the main house, the carriage house, and the barn.

Ten FBI agents in full SWAT gear poured out of the armored vehicle, divided into teams of two, and fanned out toward the mansion, a modern building made of stone, redwood, and glass.

The doors of the carriage house at the far side of the yard were up. The interior wasn't lit, but there was enough light from the exterior spotlights to reveal a white Range Rover and a black pickup truck in the first two bays and several ATVs and dirt bikes in the third.

Black pickup truck, I thought. *Bet it has a window with a bullet hole or two in it.*

In front of us, Mahoney got out of the Tahoe. Caught in Batra's headlights, he blinked, held up a hand, and signaled for her to shut them off. Bree and Sampson got out. The radio chatter from the raiding team and the HRT forces started coming nonstop. I got whining feedback in my headset for a moment.

Four agents went to the front door, used a battering ram to break it open, and then vanished inside.

In the woods to our north, the HRT unit had the plywood-faced building surrounded. Thermals showed the four people were still inside, still lying flat or curled up. That didn't seem right to me; they should have been sitting or standing. But maybe they hadn't heard the gunfire? Or maybe they were restrained?

"HRT, go in and get them out," Mahoney said over my headset. "Now."

"Lower front hall clear," said an agent inside the house.

"Walkout basement clear," said another.

"Where is he?" Rawlins said from the front seat of Batra's car. "Don't tell me Edgars isn't here."

Even with the windows up, even with the heater going and the radio chatter in our ears, we all heard the first explosion.

CHAPTER

104

"HRT AGENT DOWN," THE RESCUE commander said. "Repeat, HRT agent down. The place is booby-trapped."

"Back out and contain," Mahoney said. "How bad?"

"We'll need Life Flight ASAP."

"Calling now."

On the radio, the search commander inside Edgars's mansion said, "Watch for booby traps, gentlemen."

"Kitchen clear," said another.

"Home theater clear," said a third.

"All first-floor closets and bathrooms clear," said a fourth.

"First floor cleared in full," the commander said.

Bree and Sampson left Mahoney and started toward the mansion. I got anxious, felt claustrophobic, and opened the car door.

"You're to remain in the car, Dr. Cross," Batra said.

"I'm going to stand outside." I got out and shut the door.

My wife and my partner entered Edgars's house with the FBI agents inside already moving to clear the second story.

Mahoney told the HRT commander that Life Flight was eleven minutes out and then he headed inside as well.

I caught some of the communications between the hostage-rescue commander and the incoming Life Flight medic. The agent had opened a door to the building and triggered a small explosive. He had shrapnel in his right thigh and a severed femoral artery. They'd applied direct pressure to the wound so he wouldn't bleed out and were preparing to move him from the woods to the county road for pickup.

"Roger that," the medic replied. "We are seven minutes out."

An agent in the house said, "Second-floor landing and hall-way clear."

"All bedrooms cleared," another said. "Place is empty, Cap."

A high-pitched tone screeched through the headset, so loud I thought my eardrums would burst. I tore the headset off, stuck it in my pocket.

The dark second-floor windows facing the courtyard suddenly flashed as automatic-weapon fire broke out inside the house. Two guns, three, maybe more.

I took several limping steps toward the courtyard and the mansion, wanting to see Bree, Sampson, and Mahoney retreat out the front door. But they didn't, and the shooting went on in bursts and waves, and—

"Dr. Cross!" Agent Batra yelled behind me.

I ignored her, pulled toward the violence, wanting to end it. But the gunfire stopped as I passed Mahoney's Tahoe and entered the courtyard. I caught a flicker of motion in the third bay of the carriage house just before a second bomb exploded, much closer, on the other side of the mansion.

At the blast, the spotlights flickered and died. The shooting stopped too.

Then I heard a noise I'll never forget—shrill, primitive, and terrified—coming from the carriage house.

I pulled out my weapon and flashlight and hobbled fast in that direction as something large and boxy tore out of the third bay. I got my flashlight beam on it as it was leaving the courtyard for the woods: a red-and-black side-by-side Honda Pioneer 1000 utility vehicle.

I caught only a glimpse of the driver and the front-seat passenger before it disappeared, but the blond teen in the bed, blindfolded, gagged, and hog-tied, was plain as day. Gretchen Lindel was writhing and trying to scream, and then she was gone.

"Batra!" I yelled, flashing the light around and seeing a Kawasaki ATV in the third bay. "Batra!"

The shooting started again inside, drowning my second cry.

Ignoring the pain shrieking in my ankle, I hobbled to the ATV, yanking the radio from my pocket and tearing free the headset cord, figuring to stop the feedback. But it was worse, and I had to turn the squelch almost off.

My flashlight found the ATV ignition but with no key in it. I lifted the seat, revealing a storage for helmets, and located the key. I straddled the seat, looked at the controls, turned on the headlights, and started the engine.

I roared out of the garage, praying Batra could see me, turned onto the two-track lane that went from the compound to the woods, and accelerated.

CHAPTER

105

BREE, SAMPSON, AND MAHONEY HAD gone into a large, open, and vaulted space on the main level of the mansion to wait while the upper floors were cleared. The room contained Edgars's state-of-the-art kitchen, a rustic dining area, and several leather couches set before a massive stone fireplace that was flanked by built-in wooden cabinets and shelves crammed with books.

Sampson said, "Place looks spick-and-span."

Mahoney nodded. "Ready for that *Architectural Digest* photographer."

Their radios crackled: "Second-floor landing and hallway clear." "All bedrooms cleared. Place is empty, Cap."

Empty? That felt wrong to Bree. She'd been on edge since hearing the bomb explode in the distance. Why booby-trap the outer building and not—

A piercing whine went off in her earbud, the worst feedback ever, and she tore it out. Sampson did the same.

Across the room, Mahoney threw his down too. "What the hell is—"

Automatic weapons began to bark and rattle upstairs. Bree instinctively dived behind the kitchen counter with Sampson right beside her.

The shooting stopped, leaving them shaken and going for their guns.

"Agents down!" someone shouted upstairs. "Arthur and Boggs. Bedroom five. Far east end of upper hallway."

The search commander at the bottom of the stairs bellowed back over the shooting, "How many? I thought the place was cleared!"

"It was, Cap! Shooters must have been—"

An explosion outside shook the house. The lights died.

"It's an ambush!" Mahoney yelled from over by the couches. "They're jamming our radios and cells. Bree, take Sampson and get out of here, establish communication with—"

Bree was about to turn on her flashlight when sound-suppressed automatic weapons lit up. She covered her head as slugs ripped into granite countertops, splintered cabinets, and shattered dishes.

The bullets moved left to right and then right to left, punching holes in the stainless-steel appliances, ten, maybe fifteen shots in all, raining debris down on Bree and Sampson before stopping.

Bree shook from fear and adrenaline. Smelling the burned gunpowder, she felt nauseated, but her mind whirled. Where was the shooter? Where had he hidden? Those cabinets weren't big enough to hide a grown man, were they?

She felt a tug on her leg.

"Chief?" Sampson whispered. "You okay?"

"Fine. Where's the shooter?"

"Hit," Mahoney croaked.

The fear fled her. Bree flicked on her flashlight and belly-crawled across the kitchen tiles, calling, "How bad, Ned?"

Mahoney gasped. "Gut. You tell me."

Somewhere a generator coughed and hummed. Dim light returned. Agents upstairs were shouting, but Bree ignored them.

"Where's the shooter, Ned?" she called, louder.

"Behind me. Cabinets."

Bree turned her flashlight off, inched forward, and peered around the bottom corner of the kitchen cabinets. She could see well enough to tell Mahoney was sitting upright on the floor by one of the leather couches, but there was no sign of the shooter.

"We have to get him out, Chief," Sampson said behind her. "Now!"

"Not until I know where that shooter is. I won't get us all killed."

She thumbed on her flashlight again, peeked around the corner, and let the beam play over Mahoney about forty feet away. He was hunched over and squinting. Bree focused on the large patch of dark blood showing on his white shirt, just below his armored vest.

Low liver hit, she thought, and fought to swallow down the panic creeping in the back of her throat. They did have to get him out fast. But the shooter...

Bree shifted her light toward the stone fireplace and the cabinets and shelves to either side. The beam flickered over doors far too small for a child, much less a man, and then over rows of books before stopping cold on a small open cabinet.

"Jesus Christ," she whispered.

CHAPTER

106

THE ATV WAS EQUIPPED WITH a heavy-duty muffler, so the engine barely made any noise as I drove on the two-track deeper and deeper into the estate.

Edgars's side-by-side was no more than three or four minutes in front of me. I couldn't see tracks in the frozen mud, but the leaves were broken and shiny where it had passed.

Snowflakes hit my face. With my free hand, I tugged out the radio and turned it up. There was no longer screeching coming over it, just a dense hiss.

"This is Alex Cross," I said. "Copy?"

Out of the static, I heard clicking and fragments of an unfamiliar voice. I turned it off, stuffed it back in my coat, tried my cell. No service.

The snow flurries turned to thick heavy flakes.

They're going to get away, I thought. *The sadistic bastards are going to get away.*

There was an intersection ahead, and I stopped. The snow covered the leaves, making it impossible for me to say which way Edgars had taken Gretchen Lindel.

I tried to recall the satellite view of the property. The shed and the wounded HRT agent were somewhere to my left. The knoll at the rear of the property—where Mahoney had sent four agents—was somewhere straight ahead of me. That unidentified smudge on the satellite picture was down the right fork in the trail.

I went with my instincts, twisted the ATV throttle, and went right. The snow slapped my face, got in my eyes, and forced me to drive at a crawl.

Ten minutes later, the snow squall ended as abruptly as it had started. I rolled downhill to a wide, shallow, iced-over creek, seeing where Edgars's machine had broken up the ice. My instincts were dead-on. I drove across the creek, noticing the sky brightening in the east.

How far ahead were they? Were those four people back in that booby-trapped building all dead? The HRT guys said they hadn't moved when the booby trap went off. Or was Edgars taking Gretchen to where he had the other blondes stashed?

One hundred yards beyond the creek crossing, I lost the tracks and drove on through virgin snow to a turnabout walled in by pines. A dead end.

But Edgars had come this way. I was positive. That ice had absolutely been freshly broken, and those tracks…

I drove back, shining the headlights on the crossing, seeing ice covering the creek upstream. I used my flashlight to look downstream. The ice there had been broken up to where the stream disappeared beneath a steep embankment, eight, maybe ten feet high, and covered with green and tan vegetation frosted with new snow.

Where the hell had they gone? I couldn't imagine any machine climbing straight up the side of that wall of...

I looked closer at the embankment. Green plants? That was impossible. The leaves had fallen. The ferns were dead.

I drove into the creek and rolled slowly to the embankment, headlights on and my flashlight playing around. Even through the frosting of snow, I could see I hadn't been looking at plants but at thin strips of dull green, gray, and brown cloth, thousands of pieces sewn into a huge swath of camouflage fabric that hung from a stout length of black metal bolted into the rocks above me.

I grabbed the radio again and turned it on. The static was weaker. I triggered the transmit button, said, "This is Alex Cross, come back."

Almost immediately a garbled, oddly familiar voice answered.

"Batra?" I said.

The voice replied, but I couldn't understand a word.

I said, "Repeat, this is Alex Cross. I am in pursuit of Edgars, who has Gretchen Lindel. I am somewhere in the northeast quadrant of the estate."

The voice came back even more garbled.

I almost stuffed the radio in my pocket but then had a moment of inspiration and said, "If you can hear me, track me by Find My iPhone."

I put away the radio that time, traded it for my service weapon. Staring at the camouflage curtain, I hesitated, anxious about what might be waiting on the other side. I killed the headlights, teased the throttle. The bumper touched the fabric and then ripped apart the Velcro that had been keeping it closed.

I held my pistol in my left hand, rested the barrel on the handlebar, eased off the safety, gave the throttle more gas, and went through into darkness.

CHAPTER

107

BREE GAPED AT THE SMOKING Uzi machine pistol mounted on a thin metal post inside the open cabinet. A long banana clip hung below the gun, too big for just ten or fifteen shots.

Mahoney coughed and shifted. The gun pivoted his way, and she saw the thin scarlet line of the laser sight fixed to its barrel pass six inches over the wounded agent's head. It stopped.

"What the hell's going on?" Sampson whispered, crawling up beside her.

She pulled back, said, "Remote-control Uzis. Unless…"

Bree peeked around the corner again, flashed the light at the machine pistol and the cabinet, looking for a camera.

Mahoney groaned and shifted, and the couch moved, hitting a table behind it. The lamp on the table wobbled.

The Uzi opened up again, that same left-to-right, right-to-left spray of bullets; it cut the lamp in half, and then the gunfire continued on toward the kitchen. Bree looked up after the shooting stopped, saw that the slugs had hit some of the same things they'd hit during the first barrage.

No, she took that back. They had ripped into *the exact same things* at the *exact same height*.

"No one's operating that gun, Ned!" Bree shouted. "I think there's a motion detector involved. See it?"

"No," he grunted, sounding weaker.

An agent yelled down from upstairs that he had to move his wounded men.

"The whole place is booby-trapped!" Sampson yelled. "Hold your position!"

"One's critical! He'll die if we don't move him!"

"You'll all die if you come down those stairs," Bree shouted as she wriggled back past Sampson and crawled to a low line of untouched cabinets next to the stainless-steel stove.

She looked in three cabinets before she finally found the items she wanted. She grabbed them and scooted back to Sampson.

"What's with the cookie sheets?" he asked.

"Motion," Bree said, then she called out, "Ned, if you can, get down."

She flung one of the cookie sheets over the counter that separated the kitchen from the living area.

The Uzi lit up, rattling bullets left to right, right to left again. She threw another cookie sheet and then a third before the action of the machine pistol locked open, the breech and barrel smoking hot.

She stood up cautiously, saw Ned lying on his side by the couch. His eyes were open but glassy, and his breathing looked shallow.

"We're clear!" she shouted to the FBI agents upstairs as she ran to Mahoney. "Get your men out!"

Kneeling by Alex's old FBI partner, Bree refused to cry. "You with me, Ned? Talk to me."

Mahoney nodded and blinked. "Gut shot."

"I can see that."

Sampson came up behind her. "We've got to get him to a hospital, and the jamming's still going on."

"Help me get him up," Bree said.

They lifted Ned to his feet. Mahoney passed out from the pain, becoming deadweight, and Sampson got him up on his shoulders in a fireman's carry. Bree ran in front of him to the front door and stepped out into the falling snow, shouting, "Alex? Agent Batra?"

A flashlight went on. Keith Rawlins called timidly, "Just me, Chief Stone."

Sampson came out the door with Mahoney over his shoulder.

The snow fell in big flakes and coated the pavers as they hustled across the courtyard to the Tahoe Mahoney had driven into the estate. Rawlins stood outside it, looking as bedraggled as a cat in the rain.

"Drop the rear seat backs, would you?" Sampson said.

Seeming grateful to have something to do, Rawlins sprang into action, saying, "The jamming system is remarkable."

"We know," Bree said impatiently. "Where's Batra's car?"

"When the jamming started and then all the shooting, she decided to drive out, try to call for reinforcements."

"Good," Bree said as Sampson put Mahoney in the back of the Tahoe. "Where's—"

"Don't leave yet!" an FBI agent yelled down in the courtyard.

He carried a badly wounded man. They'd gotten blood-clotting agent into a chest wound, but his breathing was ragged and harsh.

"Get him in," Bree said. "And the next one."

"I'll drive," Sampson said, going through Mahoney's coat pockets and finding the keys.

Everything was moving fast, and Bree was still in semi-shock from the ambush, so it was not until she saw Sampson throw the Tahoe in reverse and fishtail back down Edgars's long driveway that she realized the snow had stopped.

She felt confused and overwhelmingly tired. She looked up at the sky, saw the clouds parting and a shaft of moonlight shining through, making the frosted courtyard look like a movie fantasy.

"Did Alex go with Agent Batra?" she asked Rawlins.

"Uh, no."

She turned to look at him. "What? Where is—"

Thaa-wumph!

Bree felt the ground tremble. The muted explosion sounded like it had come from deep inside the mansion.

"What was that?" Rawlins said, backing away.

"I don't know," she said. "I...*where* is Alex?"

"Dr. Cross? He—"

A second, much louder explosion cut him off; it lit up one of the second-story bedrooms like aluminum in the sun, blew out the windows, and ignited a fierce blaze. Yellow, orange, and ruby flames billowed out of the mansion and licked at the shake-shingle roof.

Bree moved back fast, feeling dread grow in her stomach. "Where's Alex, Rawlins?" she shouted. "Where's my husband?"

CHAPTER

108

THE HEAVY CAMOUFLAGE CURTAINS FLAPPED shut behind me. My eyes adjusted. I was in a storm-drain culvert, a good ten feet in diameter. Either the potential existed for extreme flash-flooding in the creek or Edgars had put the culvert in place as an escape route. I was betting that the smudge I'd seen on the satellite view was dirt from an excavation.

Forty yards ahead of me, the culvert ended, and gray light was building.

If Edgars and Pratt knew I was trailing them, they could be waiting at the other end of the culvert. But by my reckoning, the culvert had to pass beneath the dirt road that ran along the estate's eastern boundary, which meant the other end would leave me somewhere inside the Michaux State Forest.

They're not waiting to ambush me, I thought. *They're getting out of here and as far away as possible.*

I gunned the throttle and shot out of the culvert, feeling exposed, a target.

But no shots rang out as I left the creek bed for a trail through hardwood trees. With dawn nearing, I could see tire tracks, obscure at first but growing more distinct the farther I followed them.

As I drove, I tried to anticipate Edgars's next move. Either he was in full flight mode, in which case I would find his UTV abandoned and the tracks of a car leaving the area, or he had something more sinister planned.

In my mind, I saw Gretchen Lindel writhing in the truck bed. I began to fear that Edgars did not intend to take her or any of the other women with him. If he was as ruthless as I thought he was, he would kill Gretchen and the other blondes. Maybe he already had.

No witnesses, I thought. *He'll want no witnesses.*

It was full daylight when I reached the rim of a bluff that looked out over a broad patchwork of farmland a good five miles from the estate. Looking down the steep trail, almost a quarter mile below me, I could see a farm, or at least the roof of a ranch-style home, most of a steel building, and definitely Edgars's side-by-side Honda Pioneer 1000 parked in the snow beside it.

I switched off the Kawasaki and left it. Carrying my pistol and my phone, I sidestepped down the hillside, staying tight to the brush, hoping no one would spot me from below. I kept checking my phone for service, but there was none.

My ankle and shin were swollen and unhappy, but I refused to stop.

Snow was starting to melt off branches when I reached the rear of the farm. I stopped behind a tree, listening, watching. Nothing moved in the yard. Nothing showed in the windows of the ramshackle ranch house.

The three overhead doors on the long side of the steel building were closed. The porthole windows in the doors looked covered. The small sash window twenty feet to the right of the back door, however, was not shaded. I could see bright, glaring light inside.

I checked my phone. Still no service. But the fact that Edgars was a master coder, a creature of the dark web, made me check to see if he had Wi-Fi. He did, a password-protected access called Pharm, and another, Pharm Guest. I tried to log in to that one, thinking I could e-mail or text Bree, but it too required a password.

Inside the steel building, someone let loose with a heart-wrenching scream.

I clenched my jaw and went over the fence, moving with a stiff, painful gait. The scream faded and died. When I reached the rear window, I ducked beneath it, got to the right side of the sash, and turned to face the back door.

"No!" a woman screamed.

"Please!" another yelled. "Just let us go!"

I snuck a peek through the window and saw a John Deere tractor and some other farm equipment parked around a large open space in the middle of the building. Running down from pulleys attached to a steel beam overhead, seven taut cables were clipped to leather restraints around the wrists of Gretchen Lindel and six other women, who dangled in a line, arms stretched overhead, their toes barely brushing the floor.

I couldn't tell exactly who was who among the other six at first or second glance. They were soaked in dark blood that dripped and pooled beneath them. Only Gretchen was clean.

Six others? I thought. *Seven all together? I thought there were only six blondes missing.*

In any case, three of the women looked unconscious, their chins sagging to their chests. Gretchen and the other three had their heads up, were focused on the two men in black clothes moving around them.

Wearing the GoPro camera on his head, Nash Edgars seemed agitated, hopped up, like he was on something chemical and a lot of it. In his left hand he held an SLR camera and in his right an AR-style assault rifle with a halo sight.

Edgars kept moving, videoing the women and the other man, who wore a black balaclava and carried a red plastic bucket and a knife with an obsidian-black blade that curved tightly back toward an ornate knuckle guard. It was the same knife I'd seen in several of the mock-execution videos.

The hooded man walked around behind Gretchen Lindel, who twisted, trying to see him, and dumped a bucket of blood over her head. She shuddered and trembled with revulsion but did not cry out.

"Last baptism before the fire," he said, and I recognized his voice. It was Pratt, Edgars's bodyguard.

Pratt dropped the empty bucket next to a second assault rifle leaned up against the tractor's tire. He came around behind another of the alert women and pressed that wicked-looking knife to her throat.

She began to shriek and shriek. "Nash! Don't let him! Please don't let him! I'm not one of them! I'm Latina! I'm not a blonde!"

Edgars, the cameraman, came in close and laughed. "You're a blonde in this scene, Lourdes."

"Please, Nash," Lourdes Rodriguez said, weeping. "You don't have to do this!"

"Of course we do," Edgars said in a reasonable tone. "It

wouldn't be a real snuff film if we didn't snuff the blondes at the end."

Pratt took the knife away from Rodriguez's throat and gestured to one side at two stout green metal tanks about five feet tall and two feet around. They were chained to a metal post.

"We're giving you a chance," Pratt said. "You can die by the knife or take your chances and pray you pass out from the gas before this whole place ignites and blows you to kingdom come."

Still videoing their reactions, Edgars moved sideways toward the gas tanks. He put the AR down, reached behind the tanks, and came up with a gas mask, which he tossed to Pratt before getting a second for himself. He put it half on his head, knelt, and retrieved the assault rifle.

Pratt said, "So what is it, ladies? Knife or fire?"

"Can't you just make it look like we died, like all the other times?" another of them whimpered, and I recognized her. Delilah Franks, the bank teller.

"Everyone's had it with special effects," Edgars said. "We're going all the way. For the first time. Show her, Pratt. Wake up the others. Let them see tough little Gretchen die first. Then they can decide how to go."

CHAPTER

109

I STIFF-LEGGED AND HOPPED to the back door. The handle turned and the door swung slowly open on well-oiled hinges. I smelled something dead.

Sliding inside, my back to the wall, I saw Pratt forty feet away. He'd kicked awake the other three women and gotten behind Gretchen Lindel. His right leg was extended to the rear, braced against the floor. His left knee was pressed into the teenager's spine, arching her back. Pratt had her by the hair too, her head wrenched back, his wicked-looking blade at her windpipe.

"Scared now, blondie?" Pratt said.

"No," Gretchen said. "You can't hurt me."

"Oh yes, I can."

He was so close to Alden Lindel's daughter, I didn't dare try a killing shot, and I didn't want to shout a warning that might cause him to slit her throat. I aimed at the meat of Pratt's extended right leg, touched the trigger, and fired.

The slug went through his right ass cheek, spun him around, and broke his pelvis. He fell down screaming, the flung knife clattering away.

I limped hard and fast to my right, seeing Edgars spin toward me with the cameras and the AR. Just as he opened up in full automatic, I dived and landed behind a steel seed spreader. Slugs clanged off the spreader and punctured the sheet-metal wall behind me.

The shooting stopped. The women were all screaming and crying. Pratt moaned in agony, then shouted, "Kill him! Shoot his ass, Nash!"

Amid the shouting and the confusion, Edgars yelled, "Come on out, Cross. Join the wrap party for the whole cast and crew!"

Saying nothing, peering all around me, I noticed a three-inch gap between the bottom of the spreader and its wheels. I rolled onto my side and extended my right arm and pistol, trying to spot Edgars's feet and lower legs.

But he was too far to my right, blocked from view by the blade of a small bulldozer. I needed the man to move.

"The FBI is surrounding this place, Edgars!" I yelled out. "Put your weapons down!"

"Bullshit," Edgars said, holding his ground. "The FBI would never let you come in here alone. I've hacked into their systems, read their protocols."

"They're right behind me. I radioed them my position!"

"Impossible. I've jammed everything within ten miles."

That idea seemed to embolden him because he burst out from behind the bulldozer blade at a steep retreating angle, so fast I had no shot. He skidded to a stop right behind the gas tanks. Definitely no shot.

Unaware of what I could and couldn't see, Edgars kept

his camera rolling, set his rifle on the ground, and stood back up.

He's filming and needs a free hand to open the gas valves, I thought, realizing in a split second that I had only one option, and I needed to take that option right now or never. I aimed at the top turret of the halo sight, right above the AR's action, and fired my .40 S&W.

The hundred-and-fifty-grain bullet hit the turret, blew through the sight, and smashed into the action with four hundred foot-pounds of energy. The gun went skidding across the concrete floor and under a combine's blades.

I pushed myself up into a crouch, saw a shocked Edgars spin away from the gas tanks, yank down his gas mask, and run toward the combine. I took off after him, gun up.

"Stop or I'll shoot!" I yelled a moment before I smelled the propane hissing full force from the tanks.

With my left arm and jacket sleeve across my nose and mouth, I hobbled past the women and Pratt, who was unconscious, and the tanks. Edgars was flat on his belly thirty feet beyond them, reaching under the combine. I feared shooting because of the gas. Before I could get close enough to jump on him, he twisted around, pointing the rifle and the camera at me. I skidded to a stop, aiming my pistol at him.

"Shoot him!" Lourdes Rodriguez screamed.

"Shoot him!" the other women cried.

Edgars bellowed from inside the mask, "He shoots, you all die!"

I stared at him. "*You* shoot, *we* all die."

"Maybe that's the point."

"Why the hell are you doing this, Edgars?"

He looked at me as if I were stupid and said, "I hate blondes. I always have. Bitches, every one of them."

"No one will see your last little film if you shoot and blow this place up."

He beamed at me through the glass eyeholes of the gas mask. "The cameras are streaming, uploading over Wi-Fi."

"We can all walk out of here."

"No, we can't," he said, and he looked over the top of his busted sight at me. "Best thing? I can't miss from here, so I get to see you die first. Just a half second before we all go up in flames."

For the first time, I felt woozy from the gas. Edgars lifted his camera higher and glanced at the screen on the back as if trying to frame me, the gas canisters, and the women behind me for one final shot.

"All blondes must die eventually," Edgars said. "And cops and geniuses."

"Don't!"

He pulled the trigger.

110

THERE WAS A CLANK AND a tremendous bang, and my heart almost stopped; I expected the gas to ignite and blow up the tanks, and me and everyone else with them.

Instead, Edgars screamed and writhed on the concrete floor, his bleeding hands clawing at the gas mask, his rifle three feet to his right, ruptured and smoking. Adrenaline poured through my veins, making me shake so bad that several moments passed before I realized what had happened.

Damaged by my earlier shot, and set to full automatic fire, the action of Edgars's gun must have backfired, jammed, and exploded, sending chunks and slivers of metal back into the coder's face and neck.

Edgars tore off the gas mask. His left eye was punctured and weeping blood. His cheeks and forehead were gashed horribly, flayed open, and gushing blood.

My head swooned from the gas. Throwing my jacket sleeve

across my mouth again, I kept my gun on him and moved forward fast, meaning to subdue and handcuff him.

But when I got close, Edgars lashed out with his steel-toed boot and connected squarely with my bad ankle. I felt something snap. A bolt of fire shot through me; my leg buckled, and I went down on my side.

My ankle felt like someone had set a torch to it. My stomach turned over from the agony and the gas, and my head swam; I thought I was going to pass out.

"The gas!" Gretchen Lindel cried weakly behind me. "The gas!"

I shook my head, saw Edgars struggling, trying to get to his feet. I aimed my gun at him but didn't shoot because he seized up before he could fully stand, looked at me puzzled, and then felt his neck.

Something had ruptured, probably the carotid, pumping out blood. He staggered, moving his lips but making no sound, and then fell for the last time.

The gas, I thought through a building daze.

Forcing myself up onto all fours, I turned my back to Edgars and crawled toward the tanks. I reached the post they were chained to and, holding my breath, used the post to pull myself to my feet.

I grabbed the knob to the hissing gas valve, tried to twist it shut. But it wouldn't budge. Neither would the other one. They were locked open somehow.

My stomach roiled. I fought the urge to puke. But then I looked to Gretchen Lindel and the other six women hanging from the cables. Heads down. Bodies slack. They were dying.

Dying.

My head spun again, and I almost went down for a second time.

You're dying, Alex.

It was Bree's voice. It was Nana Mama's voice. And my children's voices. All at once, telling me to fight.

In a haze I raised my head, looked around, saw the door where I'd entered the building. *Open it, Alex.*

Not enough air.

I saw the window I'd looked through. *Break it too,* I thought.

Not enough, the voices said.

Turning my thickening, spinning head, I looked past the dying women and spotted my only hope.

Do it, my family said.

My love for them surged up inside me. I used it to steel myself and push away from the post and the gas tanks. The pain in my ankle felt electric, and it jolted me, made me more alert and more determined.

My head started to pound. Every step was brutal. With every breath I wanted to stop, lie down, and surrender. But my family's voices kept urging me on, telling me that pain was temporary, but death was not. Death was…

I reached the long wall of the steel building and fell against it, gasping, tasting the gas, and feeling like my ankle and my head were going to burst at the seams and split apart. Dark dots danced before my eyes, gathered, and threatened to blind me.

Dad!

Alex!

On the edge of collapse, I reached up and flailed at three buttons on the front of a metal box attached to the wall. I missed, groped, stabbed at them again, and felt them click one by one.

Nothing happened, and for a single, disbelieving moment, I thought there was no hope. That I was—

Gears engaged. Electric winch motors turned. And one, two, and then three of the overhead garage doors began to rise.

I ducked under the one closest to me and felt a strong cold breeze hit me in the face as I stumbled and went to my knees outside in the melting snow and mud.

I coughed and swooned but then scooped up a handful of snow and cold mud and splashed it in my face. I had to go back. I had to get them out.

I crawled back and saw Pratt lying motionless on top of his gas mask. Taking a big breath, I scrambled to him, rolled him over, and put the mask on.

After opening the door I'd come through, and the window, and feeling the air moving, I found the ropes attached to the cables holding the women and cut them all down.

One by one, I grabbed them and, still crawling, dragged them out into the snow. They were all outside and breathing when I heard the chug of a helicopter, looked back toward the bluff, and saw a Life Flight chopper coming in for a landing.

111

SHORTLY AFTER FOUR THAT AFTERNOON, Eliza Lindel broke down sobbing in Bree's arms. I leaned over on my crutches and rubbed her back.

"Please," she cried softly to me when she drew away from Bree. "You'll have to come with me to tell Alden."

I glanced at Bree, who nodded.

"Of course," I said.

Gretchen Lindel's mother wiped at her tears, then reached up and kissed my face. "I want you to know that you're a good man, Dr. Cross."

My eyes started to water. "Thank you."

Bree held her hand. I followed them through the door at the far end of the kitchen into Alden Lindel's small world. The shriveled man in the bed took his eyes off the latest *Game of Thrones* episode.

Eliza Lindel came around me and shut it off. "Dr. Cross has news, Alden."

His eyes went to the tablet. The synthetic voice said, "Gretch?"

I smiled. "She's safe, Mr. Lindel. They're all safe. She's on her way here. We tried to convince her to stay in the hospital, but she wouldn't hear of it."

Lindel shut his eyes tight, and then he looked to his tablet. "Thank God," his mechanical voice said. "Thank God."

Tinker, the Jack Russell terrier, started barking and yipping with excitement in the kitchen.

"Mom? Dad?" Gretchen cried weakly.

An EMT was pushing her in a wheelchair. She'd been washed clean of pig's blood and wore a pair of hospital scrubs. An IV in her arm was connected to a bag mounted on a pole attached to the chair.

Her mother ran to her and hugged her, and they sobbed with joy, the little dog dancing on her hind legs and barking madly. They all went to Alden's side. The dog jumped on his bed. Gretchen got up on wobbly legs, threw her arms around her dad, and kissed him.

"I never gave up, Dad," she said, weeping. "They tried to reach inside and destroy me, but they couldn't. Because of you, and what you taught me, they couldn't."

He broke down, made choking sounds of love, which Bree and I took as our cue to slip out, our job done. Outside, we smiled like happy idiots. It was a crisp late-fall afternoon, and I felt damn lucky to be alive.

"That Find My iPhone app is something, isn't it?" I said, putting the crutches in the backseat and then hopping to the front, grimacing as I gingerly drew my splinted lower leg inside. "It can track the phone even if the phone's not signed in."

"Definitely helped find you faster," Bree said, starting the engine. "That and Batra and the Life Flight pilot hearing your radio call."

We drove toward GW Medical Center, where Ned Mahoney was in surgery. While Bree called Chief Michaels and filled him in, I prayed for Ned, and for Delilah Franks, Cathy Dupris, Ginny Krauss, Alison Dane, and Patsy Mansfield, hoping to God that they'd come to find peace with what had happened to them. Somehow, I knew Gretchen Lindel was going to be all right.

I thought about the four mannequins the HRT team had found in the shed, all lying on electric heating pads that made them look like real people on the infrared scopes. I thought about the FBI agent who'd been closest to the first *thaa-wumph!* in the basement of Edgars's house, which he'd said held computers and large editing screens.

He said a fireball had gone off in there, fueled by an accelerant, and that, together with the explosion upstairs, had burned the mansion to the ground. Edgars had thought of almost everything; it was as if he'd been certain we'd find him at some point and had planned for it.

Bree ended her call with the chief.

"Michaels says, 'Well done,' and you're on paid leave pending an investigation again."

"Is it possible to be double-suspended?"

"You're going to be cleared, Alex. Pratt was going to kill Gretchen Lindel. There are multiple witnesses. You had to shoot him. And Edgars effectively shot himself."

"I know."

"Then why the long face?"

I hesitated, wondering if I was still suffering from the effects of the gas, but then I said, "I've decided not to go back even if I am cleared."

She was quiet for a while. "What would you do? Just counseling?"

"No, I've got some big ideas. And the best part about them? They all include you."

When I glanced over at her, she was smiling. "That makes me happy."

I reached over and squeezed her hand. "Me too."

112

TEN DAYS AFTER WE REUNITED his daughter with her family, Alden Lindel passed away in his sleep, a happy man.

I heard the news from his wife on a chill, windy Saturday afternoon as I crutched after my family on the east side of Capitol Hill. Mrs. Lindel was grief-stricken, of course, but also relieved. With Gretchen at his side constantly since she'd returned home, Lindel had found grace, and he'd passed holding his daughter's hand and his wife's. I promised Eliza that I would be at the funeral, and I pocketed my phone.

Ali was dancing around. "C'mon, Dad. I'm going to be late."

"Go on in, then," Nana Mama said, shooing him toward the door of Elephants and Donkeys, a relatively new pub with a poster in the window advertising the District Open Darts Championship.

Ali yanked open the door like he owned the place and went in.

Bree started laughing.

"What's so funny, young lady?" my grandmother demanded.

Bree waved a hand. "I just never thought I'd see the day when you'd be attending a darts tournament in a bar, Nana."

"I'm not done growing yet, dear," she said good-naturedly and winked.

We followed her inside and found Sampson, Billie, and Krazy Kat Rawlins having drafts at the bar. I helped Ali sort through the release forms and got a number to pin on the back of his shirt.

"They have a practice board," he said. "I'll be there."

"You've been practicing every night for two hours."

He frowned, said, "Repetition is the mother of skill, Dad."

"Yeah, okay, I've heard that too," I said, surrendering. "Go on."

I smiled as he walked toward the knot of older darts competitors gathered at the rear of the pub, thinking that I had never been that fearless at his age.

Sampson handed me a beer, offered me his stool.

I took it and kissed Billie on the cheek. "You guys didn't have to come."

"What else were we going to do on a cold day off?"

Nana Mama sat up on a bar stool beside Jannie watching a college football game, eating buffalo wings, and drinking a Sprite.

"I know we're technically on leave pending investigation," Sampson said to Bree. "But is Lourdes Rodriguez still spilling her guts?"

Bree hesitated.

Rawlins said, "I've talked to her. The woman won't shut up."

"It's true," Bree said with a sigh.

Between the two of them, we got a thumbnail sketch of Rodriguez's involvement with Nash Edgars. They'd met at a coding conference she'd attended because she'd heard coders made better money than satellite-dish installers.

Edgars seemed to have anything he wanted whenever he wanted it. Better, he could get her anything she wanted whenever she wanted it. Rodriguez wasn't going to inherit a dime from any uncle ever, and here was this genius computer guy offering her the world.

"Through the dark web," Rawlins said. "She claimed he was worth forty to fifty million in Bitcoin alone."

"But it wasn't until he started acting on his hatred of blond women that the real money started coming in," Bree said, disgusted.

"Hundreds of thousands of subscribers," Rawlins said, shaking his Mohawk, which was a startling violet that day. "All of them paying to see those women terrified and abused."

Rodriguez told Bree that Edgars's hatred of blondes stemmed from years of dealing with a drunken blond mother and more years of fair-haired girls harassing him when he was grossly obese and growing up in Southern California. Because he was an avowed computer nerd, the abuse continued even after he'd dropped the weight.

"So, what, he decided to get his revenge and help others live out their anti-blonde fantasies?" Sampson said.

"It was more twisted and diabolical than that," Bree said. "She said he planned on putting the clips together into a horror documentary film called *All Blondes Must Die.*"

"That's something we'll never be seeing, thank God," Sampson said. "What about that kid Timmy Walker?"

"Lourdes said if anyone killed that poor kid, it was Pratt," Bree said. "She said there wasn't a good bone in his body, that Alex did the world a service."

Billie said, "How's Ned?"

"Better," I said, brightening. "I saw him this morning. Like you said the day he was shot, the liver's a remarkable thing. It's already starting to regenerate. The docs are saying he'll make a full—"

Nana Mama appeared, said, "Enough of that. C'mon, your son's about to throw or toss or whatever they do with darts."

113

I WISH I COULD SAY that Ali slayed it, threw darts with consistent, dazzling accuracy, but that didn't happen. He did toss three bull's-eyes and an almost, but he was wild otherwise and lost in the first round to a nice guy from Texas named Mel Davis who owned a barbecue joint downtown.

Ali was crushed until Davis offered him and his friends free barbecue brisket the next time he was in. My youngest was back to his old self walking home, gabbing nonstop with Jannie and Nana Mama about his plans to make a comeback in the tournament next year. We lagged behind.

After a few moments, Bree said, "What did Ned think about your big idea?"

"He likes it. A lot."

"Michaels?"

"We haven't had that talk yet."

"You're sure you'll be happy?"

"Extremely. I'll have the best of both worlds."

Ali, Nana, and Jannie went into Chung's convenience store to pick up milk and ice cream. Bree and I kept walking.

Night had fallen when we reached our steps. The house and porch were dark. We climbed onto the porch together, hand in hand, and but for a few unresolved issues, I felt as solid as I had in—

"Hands up, or I'll shoot you both right now."

We startled and looked to our right, saw the silhouette of someone crouched by the railing and aiming a revolver at us. We raised our hands.

"Hello, Dr. Cross," he said, straightening. "Chief Stone."

Dylan Winslow, Gary Soneji's son, swung the gun back and forth between us, and even in the low light I could see a demented smile on his face. It was a smile I'd seen before, months ago, when I'd caught him torturing pigeons in his mother's barn in rural Delaware.

"What do you think you're doing, Dylan?" I said.

"Giving you what you deserve for killing my mom."

"He was framed," Bree said. "Drugged. The jury agreed."

"I saw him do it with my own two eyes," he snarled.

"So you *were* in the factory that night," I said. "I've thought about that possibility quite a bit since the trial."

"Who cares? Winning and seeing you gone is what's important."

"You took the holographic film off everyone's hands, didn't you?"

He snorted. "That's bullshit. That whole excuse was cooked up by your brat of a kid and his gay buddy. Where is he, anyway? Your brat of a kid?"

"Far away," I said, my eyes flickering to the street and the sidewalk.

"I'll find him later, after I'm done here."

"No, you won't."

Dylan shook the pistol at me. "Don't tell me what I will or won't do, Cross! Who the hell do you think you are?"

"I'm the guy who notices things, Dylan. Even after seeing the film of me shooting your mother over and over in court, I couldn't figure out what about it was driving me crazy."

"Shut up. Get on your knees. Both of you."

I stood my ground. So did Bree.

I said, "Your mother stumbled when she came into view. Did you push your mother, Dylan? Did she know what you meant to have happen?"

"Lying again." He sneered. "Making shit up. It's what you do, Cross. But not this time. This time, you're gonna die. Like you should have before."

I heard the click of the revolver's hammer cocking.

"Don't do it," Bree said. "Killing cops never ends well."

"I don't care," Dylan said. "This is where I end too. Once I see you both—"

I caught a flicker of movement behind and to his right a split second before Soneji's son screamed and spun around, firing. The shot hit the porch ceiling.

Plaster dust and splinters hit me in the face as I charged, smashed my shoulder into his rib cage, and drove him hard against the railing. I heard ribs crack and saw all the wind go out of him before I dragged him to the porch floor and pinned him.

Bree kicked away his gun, backed up, and turned on the porch light.

Dylan Winslow lay under me, gasping for air, one hand

groping for the vanes and shaft of the competition dart buried deep in the left side of his neck.

"Who's the brat now, jackass?" Ali cried, leaping onto the porch, pumping his fist, and then pointing a finger triumphantly at Soneji's kid. "I smoked you with a ten-ringer from thirty-five feet!"

114

LATE THE FOLLOWING APRIL, ALI and I drove out to Assateague State Park on Maryland's Eastern Shore. It was a glorious spring day, unnaturally warm, and it felt good in my bones when I climbed from the car after parking beside a familiar Jeep Wagoneer.

"Why would Mr. Aaliyah want to teach me to fish?" Ali said, coming around the back. "He doesn't even know me."

"He's heard of you. Besides, he likes to teach kids to fish."

"Why?"

"Give a man a fish and he eats for a day. Teach a man to fish and he eats for a lifetime."

Ali gave me a funny face. "Who said that?"

"Someone smarter than me," I said as a Volvo pulled into the lot.

A woman in her thirties with ash-blond hair climbed out and looked over at us uncertainly. "The beach isn't far, is it?"

"Just over the dunes," I said and motioned to Ali to kick off his sneakers.

Barefoot, we walked the sand path through the dunes. My ankle didn't feel too bad at all, and there was a nice breeze blowing that smelled like spring.

"What's going to happen to him, Dad?" Ali said. "Dylan Winslow?"

"That's out of my hands. He'll get his day in court."

"I heard Bree say they think something's wrong with his brain."

That was sadly true and, if the doctors' suspicions proved correct, unsurprising. Dylan had been born on the wrong end of a DNA chain, one where psychopathic tendencies were passed on by a criminally insane father and first expressed through a delight in torturing defenseless animals. Abetting the murder of his mother and then attempting to murder us were natural progressions for him, in some ways as predictable as diseases.

"Doctors are looking at that possibility," I said. "If so, Dylan will go to an institution for people like that."

We emerged on the beach. The sky was ridiculously blue. The sea heaved and rolled in a deeper azure. Early-season sunbathers and a smattering of fishermen dotted the pristine sand.

"That guy's got a big fish!" Ali said, pointing to a man pulling one ashore.

"Nice one."

"I like this place, Dad. I want to learn to fish."

"Thought you might."

We walked south a hundred yards and found Bernie Aaliyah and his daughter, Tess, waiting for us.

"Heard a lot about you, kid," Bernie said, shaking Ali's hand. "Remind me not to get between you and a dartboard."

Ali grinned, and I knew they were going to be buds. Bernie started to show Ali how the tackle worked. I went to Tess, said, "Long time, no see."

She put her hands in her back pockets, said, "I'm doing better. Most days."

"Take a stroll?"

"Why not?"

We walked back the way I'd come.

"I've heard rumors of you leaving Metro," Tess said. "On to bigger and better things."

"It's true," I said, and I explained the deal I'd forged.

Similar to Rawlins, I was now an independent contractor for the FBI, working as a consultant on the most sensitive and high-profile cases. The same was true with Metro.

"I was getting restless," I said. "I needed a new challenge, and I'll get it. And because I'll be called to work only the most demanding cases, I'll have time to dedicate to my counseling practice, where I find a lot of personal fulfillment."

"Sounds perfect."

"I think so."

I saw the ash-blond woman from the parking lot walking our way. She'd put on big sunglasses and a tennis visor and held the hand of a pretty young girl in pigtails who wore pink culottes and carried a little bucket and shovel.

"Detective Aaliyah?" the woman said.

Tess pulled her head back, clearly not recognizing her.

The woman glanced at me and then took off her sunglasses. "My name is Patricia Phelps."

Tess took a sharp breath. Her shaking hands traveled to her lips in disbelief. The mother of the little girl she'd shot was standing right there.

"I'll let you two talk," I said, and I walked toward the dunes.

I climbed up on one and sat on top for the longest time, rubbing my ankle and watching life play out on the beach below me. I saw Patricia Phelps forgive Tess Aaliyah as she'd promised she would. Tess fell into the woman's arms, and later they built a sand castle with Meagan, the little girl.

It took a while, but Ali finally got the hang of casting and later hooked his first fish, a nice striper. He danced all around, throwing his hands up in the air, and I could hear his shouts of victory over the surf.

I smiled and gazed beyond the breaking waves to the sea and the far horizon, feeling that these kinds of moments, these small triumphs, were more than enough to keep me working for the good in the world despite all the dark webs I'd been thrust into over the course of my life.

Private Princess

James Patterson
& Rees Jones

Jack Morgan receives an offer he cannot refuse . . .

When the head of the world's foremost
investigation agency is invited to meet Princess
Caroline, third in line to the British throne,
he boards his Gulfstream jet and flies
straight to London.

The Princess needs Morgan's skills, and his
discretion. Sophie Edwards, a close friend of the
Princess, has gone missing. She must be found
before the media become aware of it.

Morgan knows there is more to the
case than he is being told.

But what is the Princess hiding?

CENTURY

Liar Liar

James Patterson
& Candice Fox

Revenge is coming, and her name is Harriet Blue . . .

Detective Harriet Blue is clear about two things.
Regan Banks deserves to die. And she'll be the
one to pull the trigger.

But Regan – the Georges River Killer and the man
responsible for destroying her brother's life – has
gone to ground. And now Harriet needs to
disappear too – before her colleagues stop her
carrying out an act that could end her career,
her freedom, even her life.

Suddenly, her phone rings. It's him. Regan. And
he wants to play 'catch me if you can'.

Within hours Harry is following his clues along a
path of devastation down the Australian south
coast. Town by town, Regan is taking lives, and
each one is someone she knows well.

**With both of them wanted by every newspaper
and every television screen, time is running out.**

CENTURY

Also by James Patterson

THE WOMEN'S MURDER CLUB SERIES

1st to Die • 2nd Chance (*with Andrew Gross*) • 3rd Degree
(*with Andrew Gross*) • 4th of July (*with Maxine Paetro*) •
The 5th Horseman (*with Maxine Paetro*) • The 6th Target
(*with Maxine Paetro*) • 7th Heaven (*with Maxine Paetro*) •
8th Confession (*with Maxine Paetro*) • 9th Judgement (*with
Maxine Paetro*) • 10th Anniversary (*with Maxine Paetro*) •
11th Hour (*with Maxine Paetro*) • 12th of Never (*with Maxine
Paetro*) • Unlucky 13 (*with Maxine Paetro*) • 14th Deadly Sin
(*with Maxine Paetro*) • 15th Affair (*with Maxine Paetro*) •
16th Seduction (*with Maxine Paetro*) • 17th Suspect
(*with Maxine Paetro*)

DETECTIVE MICHAEL BENNETT SERIES

Step on a Crack (*with Michael Ledwidge*) • Run for Your Life
(*with Michael Ledwidge*) • Worst Case (*with Michael Ledwidge*) •
Tick Tock (*with Michael Ledwidge*) • I, Michael Bennett
(*with Michael Ledwidge*) • Gone (*with Michael Ledwidge*) •
Burn (*with Michael Ledwidge*) • Alert (*with Michael Ledwidge*) •
Bullseye (*with Michael Ledwidge*) • Haunted (*with James O. Born*)

PRIVATE NOVELS

Private (*with Maxine Paetro*) • Private London (*with Mark
Pearson*) • Private Games (*with Mark Sullivan*) • Private: No. 1
Suspect (*with Maxine Paetro*) • Private Berlin (*with Mark
Sullivan*) • Private Down Under (*with Michael White*) • Private
L.A. (*with Mark Sullivan*) • Private India (*with Ashwin
Sanghi*) • Private Vegas (*with Maxine Paetro*) • Private Sydney
(*with Kathryn Fox*) • Private Paris (*with Mark Sullivan*) •
The Games (*with Mark Sullivan*) • Private Delhi
(*with Ashwin Sanghi*) • Private Princess (*with Rees Jones*)

ROMANCE

Sundays at Tiffany's (*with Gabrielle Charbonnet*) •
The Christmas Wedding (*with Richard DiLallo*) •
First Love (*with Emily Raymond*) •
Two from the Heart (*with Frank Costantini,*
Emily Raymond and Brian Sitts)

OTHER TITLES

Miracle at Augusta (*with Peter de Jonge*) •
Penguins of America (*with Jack Patterson*)

COLLECTIONS

Triple Threat (*with Max DiLallo and Andrew Bourelle*) •
Kill or Be Killed (*with Maxine Paetro, Rees Jones, Shan Serafin and*
Emily Raymond) • The Moores are Missing (*with Loren D. Estleman,*
Sam Hawken and Ed Chatterton) • The Family Lawyer (*with Robert*
Rotstein, Christopher Charles and Rachel Howzell Hall)

FAMILY OF PAGE-TURNERS

MIDDLE SCHOOL BOOKS

The Worst Years of My Life (*with Chris Tebbetts*) • Get Me
Out of Here! (*with Chris Tebbetts*) • My Brother Is a Big, Fat
Liar (*with Lisa Papademetriou*) • How I Survived Bullies,
Broccoli, and Snake Hill (*with Chris Tebbetts*) • Ultimate
Showdown (*with Julia Bergen*) • Save Rafe! (*with Chris*
Tebbetts) • Just My Rotten Luck (*with Chris Tebbetts*) •
Dog's Best Friend (*with Chris Tebbetts*) • Escape to Australia (*with*
Martin Chatterton) • From Hero to Zero (*with Chris Tebbetts*)

I FUNNY SERIES

I Funny (*with Chris Grabenstein*) • I Even Funnier (*with Chris Grabenstein*) • I Totally Funniest (*with Chris Grabenstein*) • I Funny TV (*with Chris Grabenstein*) • School of Laughs (*with Chris Grabenstein*) • The Nerdiest, Wimpiest, Dorkiest I Funny Ever (*with Chris Grabenstein*)

TREASURE HUNTERS SERIES

Treasure Hunters (*with Chris Grabenstein*) • Danger Down the Nile (*with Chris Grabenstein*) • Secret of the Forbidden City (*with Chris Grabenstein*) • Peril at the Top of the World (*with Chris Grabenstein*) • Quest for the City of Gold (*with Chris Grabenstein*)

HOUSE OF ROBOTS SERIES

House of Robots (*with Chris Grabenstein*) • Robots Go Wild! (*with Chris Grabenstein*) • Robot Revolution (*with Chris Grabenstein*)

JACKY HA-HA SERIES

Jacky Ha-Ha (*with Chris Grabenstein*) • My Life is a Joke (*with Chris Grabenstein*)

OTHER ILLUSTRATED NOVELS

Kenny Wright: Superhero (*with Chris Tebbetts*) • Homeroom Diaries (*with Lisa Papademetriou*) • Word of Mouse (*with Chris Grabenstein*) • Pottymouth and Stoopid (*with Chris Grabenstein*) • Laugh Out Loud (*with Chris Grabenstein*)

MAXIMUM RIDE SERIES

The Angel Experiment • School's Out Forever • Saving the World and Other Extreme Sports • The Final Warning • Max • Fang • Angel • Nevermore • Forever

CONFESSIONS SERIES

Confessions of a Murder Suspect (*with Maxine Paetro*) •
The Private School Murders (*with Maxine Paetro*) • The Paris
Mysteries (*with Maxine Paetro*) • The Murder of an Angel (*with
Maxine Paetro*)

WITCH & WIZARD SERIES

Witch & Wizard (*with Gabrielle Charbonnet*) • The Gift (*with
Ned Rust*) • The Fire (*with Jill Dembowski*) • The Kiss (*with Jill
Dembowski*) • The Lost (*with Emily Raymond*)

DANIEL X SERIES

The Dangerous Days of Daniel X (*with Michael Ledwidge*) •
Watch the Skies (*with Ned Rust*) • Demons and Druids (*with
Adam Sadler*) • Game Over (*with Ned Rust*) • Armageddon
(*with Chris Grabenstein*) • Lights Out (*with Chris Grabenstein*)

OTHER TITLES

Cradle and All • Crazy House (*with Gabrielle Charbonnet*) •
Expelled (*with Emily Raymond*)

GRAPHIC NOVELS

Daniel X: Alien Hunter (*with Leopoldo Gout*) • Maximum
Ride: Manga Vols. 1–9 (*with NaRae Lee*)

PICTURE BOOKS

Give Please a Chance (*with Bill O'Reilly*) • Big Words for
Little Geniuses (*with Susan Patterson*) • Give Thank You a Try •
The Candies Save Christmas

For more information about James Patterson's novels, visit
www.jamespatterson.co.uk

WHO IS ALEX CROSS?

PERSONAL LIFE

Alex Cross was born near Winston-Salem, North Carolina. He lost his parents at a young age and was sent to Washington, DC to live with his grandmother, Regina Cross Hope (Nana Mama), an English teacher and assistant principal. He has three brothers (two deceased) not raised by Nana Mama.

Damon and Janelle (Jannie) are Cross's children from his first marriage to Maria, a social worker, who was killed in a drive-by shooting that was never solved.

Cross has another son, Alex Jr. (Ali). His mother, Christine Johnson, was principal at the Sojourner Truth School. They never married.

Alex Cross now lives on Fifth Street in DC with wife Brianna (Bree) Stone – Chief of Detectives in the MPD – Nana Mama, Ali, Jannie and Rosie the cat. Damon is studying at Johns Hopkins University.

HOBBIES

The piano: Cross loves to play Gershwin and classical music. He is an avid reader of fiction and non-fiction. He used to box in his youth and now enjoys teaching his children.

Alex volunteers at the St. Anthony's soup kitchen, where he is known as 'Peanut Butter Man' and 'Black Samaritan'. He offers free therapy sessions.

FAVOURITE FOOD

White bean soup. Least favourite: grape jelly omelette. Enjoys fine wine and beer.

FAVORITE VACATION SPOT
Caribbean.

EDUCATION
Alex has a PhD in psychology from Johns Hopkins University, Baltimore, Maryland. His specialism was in the fields of abnormal psychology and forensic psychology.

Upon graduation Cross worked as a migrant farm worker for a year.

WORK
Alex Cross went into private practice in psychology. He struggled financially for three years before moving into law enforcement.

He joined the Metropolitan Police Department in DC as a psychologist, working in Homicide and Major Crimes as a criminal profiler. He worked with ViCAP (Violent Criminal Apprehension Program) as a liaison between the FBI and MPD. After his stint as an FBI Senior Agent, Alex returned to private psychology practice and continued to consult for the MPD and the FBI as needed. He rejoined the MPD as a special consultant to the Major Case Squad.

A *Washington Post Magazine* in-depth article labelled Cross 'The Last Southern Gentleman' and praised him for his work in Homicide.

Articles by Alex Cross on the criminal mind have appeared in Psychiatric Archives and the *American Journal of Psychiatry*. He also wrote a diagnostic profile of psychopathic killer Gary Soneji/Murphy.